LILIAN HARRY

A Girl called Thursday
A Promise to Keep

Also by Lilian Harry

LILIAN HARRY

A Girl Called Thursday
A Promise to Keep

A Girl Called Thursday
First published in Great Britain by Orion in 2002

A Promise to Keep
First published in Great Britain by Orion in 2003

This omnibus edition published in 2011
by Orion Books Ltd
Orion House, 5 Upper St Martin's Lane
London WC2H 9EA

An Hachette UK Company

A CIP catalogue record for this book is available
from the British Library.

ISBN 9781407234229

Printed and bound in Great Britain by Clays Ltd, St Ives plc

www.orionbooks.co.uk

A Girl Called Thursday

To the Royal Naval Hospital, Haslar
and to all VADs, especially Helen Long
whose book *Change into Uniform*
inspired this story.

Chapter One

11 November 1939

'Twenty-one today!
Twenty-one today!
She's got the key of the door,
Never been twenty-one before . . .'

The little house in Waterloo Street rocked to the sound of singing, and Thursday Tilford laughed, blushing at the attention. The song ended with cheers from the rest of the family, and Thursday's father gave her a smacking kiss, his moustache bristling against her cheek.

'There you are, love. There's your key.' He handed her a wooden key about a foot long, painted bright red. 'Made it myself.'

'Oh, *Dad*!' Thursday took it in her hands and almost collapsed under the weight. 'Am I supposed to carry this about in my bag?'

'Well, only if you want to.' He fished in his pocket and brought out another, an ordinary Yale this time. 'You can keep that for best if you like and use this for every day.'

Thursday grinned at him and slipped the Yale into her purse. 'And can I stay out after ten o'clock at night now?'

He rubbed his round, balding head and pursed his lips. 'Well, I don't know about that. Me and your mother will still worry about you, you know. That don't stop just because you're of age. Maybe we'll say eleven on Saturday nights to start with, eh?'

The rest of the family laughed. 'Go on, Walter, you know young Thursday's been able to twist you round her little finger since she was a baby,' Thursday's grandfather called out from the front room.

1

There wasn't space for everyone in either of the two downstairs rooms so they'd opened all the doors and spread between the two. 'Not like in my day. Girls knew what was what then. Knew they had to toe the line, or else.'

'Like our Flo, you mean,' Walter retorted, grinning. 'If I had a pound for every time I had to let her in on the quiet when she'd been out with Percy, so you wouldn't know what time it was—'

'All right, our Wal, no need to give away secrets,' his sister cut in. She touched her fair hair, newly waved for the occasion with a fashionable bang on her forehead – not that Auntie Flo needed much of an excuse to do herself up, Thursday thought with an inward giggle. That was a new jumper she had on too, pale blue in a lacy pattern, and she'd knitted one for Thursday's mum as well, only in pink, as well as Leslie's Fair Isle pullover. 'Stop your nattering and cut this birthday cake into slices. It's Thursday's day, she doesn't want to hear all about ancient history.'

The cake stood in place of honour on the sideboard, flanked by a pile of plates. It had been iced and decorated by Flo, who was clever at that sort of thing. The family had already admired it and sung 'Happy Birthday' as Thursday blew out the candles, and now they gathered round again as Walter picked up the big carving knife. Flo's two younger children, Leslie and Denise, stood by with a proprietorial air.

'I helped Mum make the icing,' Denise told Thursday. 'It took I don't know how many egg-whites. And I made two of the roses on top – those two, see?'

'The ones with wobbly petals,' Leslie said, and she gave him a push. 'Well, they are. And I helped too, it wasn't just you. I helped beat up the icing.'

'Sounds like you were in a fight with it,' Walter remarked. 'Move over now, let the dog see the rabbit.' He lifted the knife and poised it above the centre of the cake. Thursday's little mongrel dog, Patch, moved into the best position for catching crumbs and sat bright-eyed, his tail thumping the floor. 'I didn't mean *you*, you silly chump!'

'I'll have a bit with icing down the sides,' Thursday's younger sister Jenny said, her eyes fixed on the white sugar.

'You'll have what you're given, my girl,' her father told her.

'Your Auntie Flo made that for your sister, not you. And stop that shoving, young Steve, or I'll end up cutting slices of finger.'

'And the icing'll get blood all over it,' Steve told his sister ghoulishly. 'And if it does, that'll be your bit. And you know what you'll be then? You'll be a *cannibal*!'

Jenny made a face and squealed. 'Yeugh! That's a horrible thing to say! Tell him not to say things like that, Mum.'

Mary Tilford frowned at them, but it was a tolerant frown. Nothing was to be allowed to spoil this special day, Thursday thought affectionately. 'Don't start squabbling, now. Give your dad some elbow room.' She looked at her husband, cutting the cake, and at her elder daughter, tall and grown-up with her dark brown hair cut in a long wavy bob, wearing that new green frock she'd made specially for the occasion. You could catch quite a strong likeness in their expressions sometimes, even though in colouring Thursday was more like herself, and it was there now as they concentrated on the cake. She smiled, and then her face saddened.

'It's a beautiful cake, Flo, and it's been a lovely party,' Thursday heard her say quietly. 'But it's not the birthday I wanted for her, not really.'

'Nothing's the way we wanted it,' Flo said. 'Nobody wanted this war, for a start. Except for Hitler, of course, he's been wanting it all along only nobody could see it.'

Thursday handed them both a plate with a slice of cake on it. 'Bet we won't see many more cakes like this for a while,' she said cheerfully. 'It's a good job we saved up all the fruit beforehand.' She sat down beside them and bit into her own slice.

Mary nodded. 'They say there'll be a lot of shortages from now on. You know they're talking about rationing. I reckon people will start hoarding all sorts of things.'

'They already have,' Thursday said through a mouthful of cake. 'My friend at work says her gran's got a cupboard full of tins. Ham, peas, baked beans, plums – she's got enough to keep her for six months, Annie says.' She bent and slipped a scrap of cake into Patch's waiting jaw.

'Well, she shouldn't have. It's taking food away from people who might need it. And that dog doesn't need it, either.'

'She thinks *she'll* need it,' Thursday pointed out. 'And Patch deserves a treat, same as anyone else.'

3

Jenny had managed to secure a piece of cake with icing down the side, and went into the front room to sit on the floor at her grandmother's feet to eat it, curling her legs under her. She always preferred the floor, and in any case with the whole family squashed into the small room there wasn't room to sit anywhere else. Her grandmother, Walter's mother, ate a few crumbs of her cake and then slipped her the rest. 'Can't be doing with all that fruit,' she whispered, 'and the icing makes me teeth ache.'

Jenny giggled. Granny had had false teeth since she was quite young and loved sweets, but Jenny was her favourite and could always rely on being given little extras. She went round to see her grandmother every Sunday morning after church, and passed on all the gossip from Waterloo Street as well as from the grocer's shop where she worked.

Steve had sat down beside his cousin Mike, who was in army uniform. He'd been in the Territorials before the war started, and joined up straight away, as a private. So far, all he'd done was basic training but already he was behaving as if he were in the front line, and Steve was half envious, half thankful that as yet he hadn't been called up. It couldn't be long, though, if the war really did get started as they seemed to think it would.

'What sort of guns do they give you, Mike? D'you have your own special one?'

'Course you do. You've got to look after it, see – clean it and make sure it works properly. I wouldn't want to use another bloke's gun, just in case he hadn't bothered. Not that the sarge would let anyone get away with not bothering!' He made a face which conveyed to Steve exactly what the sergeant's reaction would be to 'not bothering'. 'It's Lee-Enfields we've got. Rifles. But we're learning to handle mortars as well, and then there's machine guns and howitzers and stuff like that. There's a lot to learn. It's not just about pointing it at a Jerry and pulling the trigger. You've got to think about the weather – wind can make the bullets drift, see – and you can't always see what you're shooting at. That's where the observers come in, they go forward of the line and register the targets.' He stopped abruptly. 'I don't know as I should be telling you all this. We're not supposed to talk about what we do.'

'Go on, I'll be joining up myself before long,' Steve said, hoping his mother couldn't hear him in the other room, but Mike shook his head and refused to say any more.

Thursday heard, however, and she felt a sudden chill as Mike's words brought home to her the fact that there really was a war on and that young men like her cousin and brother could get killed – boys who had never even thought of joining the Forces, having to learn about guns and fighting, having to go to war. And girls too – not fighting, but helping in different ways, doing jobs they'd never even have dreamed of, so that the men could go away.

It was something she'd been thinking about more and more just lately, and she knew that soon she was going to have to tell her family about her own decision.

Being twenty-one wasn't all fun and cake and keys of the door, she thought. You've got responsibilities as well. Responsibilities for your own life, and what you did with it.

Soberly, she collected the plates and took them out to the kitchen. There was already a large pile of crocks waiting to be washed up, and she rolled up her sleeves and turned on the tap. Her mother followed her and turned it off.

'Here, what are you doing? It's your birthday, you're supposed to be the guest of honour, not a skivvy.'

'And you did all the work getting everything ready,' Thursday told her. 'Anyway, you can't boss me about any more, not now I'm twenty-one.' She turned the tap on again and ferreted in the cupboard under the sink for the washing soda. 'You go and sit down and have another cup of tea with Auntie Flo. I bet it's the first time either of you's sat down all day.'

'Well, I won't say I'm not a bit tired,' Mary admitted. She regarded her daughter fondly. 'Mind you, I still can't believe I'm old enough to have a daughter of twenty-one.'

'Nor can I.' The enamel washing-up bowl was full now and Thursday turned off the tap again and swished the dishcloth into the water. 'You don't look much more than twenty-one yourself, Mum. Not a grey hair on your head.'

Mary looked into the scrap of mirror they kept over the sink. It was true that her hair was still the same rich brown, and even though she'd never bothered with her looks as much as her sister-in-law it suited her brushed smooth over the top and permed into neat

5

curls at the side. She sighed. 'There'll be a few before this war's finished, I'm afraid. It's going to be a bad business, Thursday.'

'D'you really think so?' She thought of Mike, learning about guns, and pushed the thought away. 'Nothing much has happened yet, and they say it'll be over by Christmas.'

'Christmas? That gives it five weeks!' Mary snorted. 'I lived through the last lot. They said that one'd be over by Christmas too, and it dragged on for four years. I can't see this one ending any quicker, and it'll be worse if we get the air raids they're talking about. They had a few of those last time, over on the east coast, but we'll all get a share this time.'

'Not here in Worcester, surely?' Thursday piled plates rapidly on the draining-board.

'Why not? Why d'you think we've been dished out with all these gas masks and air-raid shelters?'

'Yes, but we're right in the middle of the country. The Air Force will get them long before they get this far.' She wasn't sure if she really believed it or just wanted to, but it was better than looking on the black side. 'They won't let the Germans bomb us, Mum.'

'Well, let's just hope you're right.' Mary picked up a tea-towel and began to dry the plates. 'I tell you, our Thurs, the idea of air raids frightens me to death, it does really. I can't bear to think about them.'

Flo poked her head round the kitchen door. 'What are you two doing, skulking out here? *You* shouldn't be working anyway, it's your birthday. Leave that for now – we're listening to the wireless. The Queen's going to make a broadcast. Come in and hear it.'

Thursday couldn't remember ever hearing the Queen's voice before. The King had made a broadcast at Christmas, his voice stumbling a bit over the words – it was said that he had a dreadful stammer, as if he was very shy. It seemed odd to Thursday that a king should be shy, but then he'd never been meant to be one. It was supposed to be his brother David, the Duke of Windsor now, who had fallen in love with an American divorcee and had to give up the throne to marry her.

It sounded romantic, but Thursday could remember all the fuss and palaver there'd been at the time and she thought that by the time they'd got to the altar it couldn't have seemed romantic at all.

They must have just wanted it all to be over so that they would go back to normal life – whatever that might be for kings who had just abdicated.

So Prince Albert, the Duke of York, had become King George the Sixth, and his wife Elizabeth was now Queen. And they were very popular, they and their two daughters, Princess Elizabeth – who would be Queen one day, unless another baby was born and turned out to be a boy – and her sister Margaret Rose.

Walter switched on the wireless. He had built it himself, carefully cutting out a fretwork pattern in front of the speaker, just like you saw in the shops, and it stood on a high shelf in one of the fireplace alcoves. It looked a bit like something off the instrument panel of an aeroplane, and when it was turned on needles quivered across little dials and it made little burbling and whistling noises before the crackling stopped and the announcer's voice came through. Walter had also fixed up a loudspeaker in the front room, and he turned this on for his parents and the boys and Jenny, who were still in there.

The Queen's broadcast was aimed at women. '*We, no less than men, have real and vital work to do,*' she said in her precise, cut-glass accent, and Thursday felt a tiny surge of excitement, which turned to disappointment at her next words. '*It is the worries and irritations of carrying on wartime life in ordinary homes which are often so hard to bear.*' How did she know that? How did she know what life was like in an ordinary home? Had she ever queued for groceries, or peeled potatoes? But Mary and Flo were nodding in agreement, and Thursday could see that they were touched by this reference to their own problems. '*The king and I know what it means to be parted from our children.*' That was true – the little Princesses were hundreds of miles away at Balmoral, in Scotland. '*All this has meant sacrifice and I would say to those who are feeling the strain: You are taking your part in keeping the Home Front, which will have dangers of its own, stable and strong.*'

'Don't it make you feel proud,' Mary whispered, and brushed a tear from her eye.

'She's a lovely speaker,' Flo agreed. 'And she really seems to know what it's like to be ordinary, doesn't she? As if she's done all the things we've done. You feel as if you could ask her in for a cup of tea and not have to worry about a speck of dust.'

The wireless programme continued, talking this time about

women who had joined the Forces. Nearly fifty thousand had joined up so far, most in the ATS and the rest evenly divided between the WRNS, the WAAFs and the nursing services. There were so many wanting to join the WRNS that they'd actually stopped recruiting. You could still join the ATS, though, or the WAAFs.

'I can't remember what all these initials stand for,' Thursday's grandmother complained. 'ATS this and WAAF that. Which is which, for goodness' sake?'

'ATS stands for Auxiliary Territorial Service,' Jenny said importantly. 'That's the women's branch of the Army. And WAAF means Women's Auxiliary Air Force. And the Wrens are the Navy—'

'And JAT stands for Jabbers All the Time,' Steve butted in. 'That's why Mum and Dad called you Jennifer Ann. They knew what you were going to be like but the man said it had to be a proper name, so they chose Jenny because wrens chatter too.'

Jenny made a face at him. 'They wanted to call *you* Stupid. And Crackers for a middle name, but he said it had to be Charles.'

'Well, you can both thank your lucky stars you weren't called Sunday Morning and Boxing Day,' Thursday called out with a grin. 'Look what *I* got landed with – *Thursday!*'

Everyone laughed, but the older ones' faces soon sobered. 'It was meant to be a sign of hope,' Walter said. 'Born on the eleventh hour of the eleventh day of the eleventh month – they must have been signing the Armistice at the very moment you gave your first cry. We had to give you some sort of name to mark that, didn't we? That's why we called you Rosemary, for Remembrance, see – but we wanted something more as well so we had Thursday for a middle name.'

'That's right,' Mary agreed. 'And if you ever feel embarrassed about it, that's what you ought to remember. Mind you, we never really meant to call you by it. That was our Maudie. Being your godmother, she thought she had a right, see, and she always called you Thursday, right from the start, and then we all did. It seemed to suit you, somehow, and it seemed right – not much point in marking an important occasion if you hide it away, is there?' She paused and smiled. 'And *you* can thank your lucky stars, too, that you didn't get called something worse.'

'Why?' Thursday asked. 'What else did you think of?'

'November!' Mary said with a smile. 'That was what your dad wanted, to start with. I did put my foot down over that – but I was still half-scared he'd do it, the day he went off to register you. I had to look at the birth certificate the minute he got back to make sure he hadn't.'

'Now, when have I ever gone against your wishes, Mary?' her husband asked, and everyone laughed again as she gave him the sort of look that suggested that he *always* went against her wishes. He laughed too and gave her a quick kiss. 'All right, we all know who's boss in this house!'

'Well, I'm glad you called me that,' Thursday said stoutly. 'I get a bit fed up having to explain it whenever I meet someone new, but I *am* proud of it, really, and I like having an unusual name. There's hundreds of Rosemarys about. Pity Auntie Maud's on duty at the hospital, I could have thanked her for making sure I didn't get stuck with it.'

'She said she'd look in tomorrow for a bit of cake, and to bring you your present,' Mary said. 'You can thank her then.'

'Oh, that's a pity,' Thursday said. 'I shan't see her, I'm going straight from work to meet Sidney at the Scala at six o'clock. We're going to have tea and see the new Joan Crawford picture. I'll see her next Sunday, we're going over to tea with her.'

Walter switched off the wireless and sat down beside his wife. They looked fondly at their family.

'Well, there it is,' Walter said after a few moments. 'The first of the brood grown up. I don't reckon we've done too bad a job, do you, gal?'

Mary shook her head. 'I don't reckon so, love, no. Mind you, we've still got to see how the other two turn out. There's still time for them to go off the rails.'

'Not too much,' Steve said, coming in to look for another piece of cake. 'It'll be my twenty-first next year.'

'And mine in five years,' Jenny said, picking up scraps of icing. 'Gosh, I wonder where we'll all be then. All sorts of things could happen in that time.' She broke off at the look on her mother's face. 'I don't mean *bad* things, Mum. The war'll be over in a few months, everyone says so. You've only got to listen to the news. Practically nothing's happened.' She pouted a little. 'I bet it'll all be finished and done with by the time *I* get old enough to join up.'

'Well, I just hope it will,' her mother said. 'I hope it'll be over before any of you has to join up.'

But everyone knew this really was a faint hope. Flo and Percy's eldest son Mike was already in the Army and Steve, at twenty, could well be called up soon. Women didn't have to enlist – at least, not yet – but a lot of them were volunteering. Thursday knew that her parents dreaded hearing that she had decided to go. Maybe this was the moment to tell them.

'We've got to do our bit, Mum,' she said gently after a moment or two. 'We can't let other people do the fighting for us.'

'They won't let *women* fight!' Mary's voice was so sharp they all flinched. 'Even the Germans haven't come to that.'

'No, but we can do a lot of the jobs men do, so they can go. Anyway, I know what I want to do.' She looked around at them. 'I've decided to volunteer as a nurse.'

There was a surprised silence.

'A *nurse*?' Mary repeated at last. 'Like your Auntie Maud, you mean? Here in the Worcester Royal Infirmary?'

Thursday shook her head. 'No. I've been talking to the lady in charge of the First-Aid Post. She says as I'm in the Red Cross and have done the first-aid course and everything, I can volunteer as a VAD—'

'Not *more* initials!' Ada Tilford protested from the front room, and Thursday smiled and moved over to the door so that she could talk into both rooms at once.

'It means Voluntary Aid Detachment, Gran. It's part of the Red Cross, and you can be either a mobile VAD – that means you can be moved – or—'

'I know what mobile means, thank you very much,' the old lady said tartly. 'It's all these initials I can't be doing with. There won't be any proper words left, at the rate we're going on. So what do these Voluntary – what was it? – these VADs do, then?'

Thursday grinned. 'Well, they're nurses. Not registered nurses, of course, like Auntie Maudie, they're not trained as much as them, but they work in the wards and help look after people. Mostly servicemen, I think. That's what it's all about, you see, it's to work in the Forces' hospitals.'

'So you wouldn't be working in Worcester, then?' Mary tried to keep the disappointment out of her voice. 'Or would you? There's Norton Barracks, they must have nurses there.'

'She said there's non-mobile ones as well,' her husband reminded her. 'That'd mean you could live at home, wouldn't it?'

This was the moment Thursday hadn't been looking forward to. 'Well, I thought I'd volunteer to be a mobile one, actually. See a few other places while I'm at it.'

Mary stared at her. 'You mean you want to leave home?'

'It's not a question of *wanting* to, Mum. It's just – well, if I'm going to give up tailoring to do this, I might as well get some benefit out of it. Get a bit of experience, that sort of thing. See a bit more of the country, meet some different people.' She gazed appealingly at her mother. 'It's a chance, don't you see? I mean, what will I do if I stay here? Work at the tailor's until I get married, and then leave to be a housewife and have children. That's all, isn't it?'

'It's what I did, and it's always seemed all right to me,' Mary said.

Thursday sighed. 'I know, Mum, and I never meant there was anything *wrong* with it. It's just that nowadays – with this war and everything – well, it's different. I'd just like to take the chance, that's all. It's only while the war's on. It doesn't mean I'm going away for ever and you're never going to see me again.'

Mary sniffed. 'Seems to me you're just looking on the war as a chance to throw away everything you've got – your home life, your job, everything. And that's another thing. Tailoring. You've finished your apprenticeship and got a good trade at your fingertips. Why chuck all that away? You could stop where you are and help the war effort – they'll be turning over to making uniforms full time, if I know anything about it. Why waste all that training and start learning something else?'

'Well, if you want the truth,' Thursday said, beginning to feel exasperated, 'I'm getting fed up with tailoring. I was never all that keen in the first place. It was you got me into it, just because I was all right at sewing at school.'

'And what's wrong with that?' Walter demanded. 'That's what mothers and fathers do, isn't it, see that their children are set up in a decent job? Your Uncle Percy did it for Mike here, and I did it for Steve down at the porcelain factory, and we'd have got young Jenny into a hairdresser's only the premium was too much and she said she didn't mind going into the grocery shop.'

He was starting to sound really angry and Thursday wished she had never started this. The rest of the family was silent, and Jenny looked almost ready to cry. The party's spoilt now, Thursday thought miserably, and it's all my fault. I should have waited till tomorrow, only I'm going to the pictures with Sidney then, and I thought with everyone here together it would be better . . .

'So what's wrong with tailoring all of a sudden?' her mother demanded. 'I haven't heard you complain before, and you do plenty of sewing at home – made that frock you're wearing and that new blouse you had on yesterday, and—'

'*Nothing's* wrong with it, Mum, and I really do appreciate all you did, getting me the apprenticeship and everything. It's just that everything's different now. Girls have got a bit more chance to do something interesting before they settle down.'

'*Interesting!*' Walter exclaimed. 'Since when have we had a right to expect to do *interesting* jobs? Earning a living's what we've got to do, my girl, and if it's interesting as well, we can think ourselves lucky, but we don't chop and change just because we're a bit fed up. There's been a Depression, if you remember – people thought themselves lucky to have a job at all, never mind being *interested*.'

'But wouldn't you rather have a job you were really interested in?' Thursday asked. 'Wouldn't you rather be doing something you enjoyed? I mean, you never seem to think anything could be any better. You think everything's got to go on being the same as it's ever been. Like that time the union wanted you to go on strike—'

'We won't start talking politics,' Walter broke in, his face reddening with anger. 'You know what I think about strikes and unions. They might have done a good job at one time, but now it's all greed, that's all, and if you ask me it was the General Strike started the rot in this country. And if I hear any of you talking about going on strike, *ever*, well—'

'All right, Walter,' Mary said quickly.' No need to get aeriated. Nobody's talking about going on strike. I don't know how we ever got on to the subject.' She turned back to Thursday. 'And that's another thing. You talk about girls settling down. What do you think Sidney's going to say about this?'

'Sidney?' Thursday echoed. 'What's it got to do with Sidney?'

'Well, he's your chap, isn't he? I thought you'd probably be getting engaged now you've turned twenty-one. What's he got to say about you swanning off to goodness knows where? Or haven't you consulted him either?'

'No, I haven't, as a matter of fact. And I don't know what made you think we're getting engaged. I'm not thinking of marrying Sidney, and what's more I don't think he wants to marry me. He hasn't asked me, anyway.'

'Well, that's a relief,' Steve observed. 'We don't want a wet like that in the family.'

'But you've been going out together for the past eighteen months!' Mary cried. 'Surely you must have some sort of understanding.'

Thursday stared at her. It had never even occurred to her that her mother had begun to see Sidney as a future son-in-law. She glanced quickly around at the rest of the family, feeling embarrassed and annoyed. Honestly, if she'd thought all this would be dragged out she wouldn't have said a word about volunteering. How had they got around to Sidney anyway? He was nothing to do with the family. She hadn't even asked him to her party. To tell the truth, she'd only ever gone out with Sidney in the first place because she'd felt a bit sorry for him. She'd never meant it to become a regular thing, but somehow it hadn't been possible to give him the push without hurting his feelings, and he didn't deserve that. He wasn't such a bad chap, after all.

'Yes, we have got an understanding,' she said curtly. 'We like going dancing and we like going to the pictures and maybe for a walk of a Sunday afternoon, and that's it. It's just a couple of evenings a week, Mum. We're not talking about spending the next fifty years together.' She thought of Sidney in fifty years' time, balding like her father only thin and stringy instead of round and smiling – not that Dad was smiling much now! No, that wasn't what she wanted.

Mary stared at her again and shook her head. 'I don't know about you young girls, I'm sure. It was different in my day. When a young man and a girl had been going out together for six months or so, and he'd been coming round for Sunday tea once a month, it was as good as a ring on her finger. It was *understood*.'

'Well, it's not now. Not by me, anyway. And in any case, Sidney won't be around much longer, he's got his papers. He's going into the Army.'

13

'Oh, Thursday! And you never said.'

'Well, why should I? I'm saying now. And you don't need to look like that, Mum. I'm not breaking my heart. Look – Sidney and me are friends, that's all. Neither of us has found anyone we really like so we've just sort of drifted into the habit of knocking about together a bit, just to have someone to go the pictures with and that, and that's all there is to it. But we don't want to drift into anything more.'

'Sounds sensible,' Flo remarked. 'I've known a few girls drift into marriage and then wish the tide had turned a different way. You wouldn't want your Thursday to end up with the wrong chap, would you, Mary?'

'No, but I'm not so sure Sidney is the wrong chap,' Mary said. 'I've always thought he was a really nice boy. Polite and considerate. Got a good job. And they get on well together. What more could you want?'

'You got on all right with that Stan Gibson, if I remember right,' Walter remarked, 'but you never married him.'

'That was different,' his wife said, blushing. 'There was never the feeling between me and Stan Gibson that there was between us, and well you know it, and I'm sure I don't know why you have to bring his name into this—'

'But that's just what I mean, Mum,' Thursday broke in before her parents could embark on a well-worn argument. 'There isn't the feeling between me and Sidney either. We're just friends. To tell you the truth, I'll miss Patchie more than I'll miss Sid.' She ruffled the mongrel's ears and he gave a little whimper of pleasure and leant his head against her knee.

Walter grinned at her. He seemed to have recovered his temper a bit – maybe he hadn't been as keen as his wife to have Sidney in the family. 'I think she's got you there, Mary. Anyway, none of that's important now. What we've got to think about is what our Thursday's decided to do, and what we've got to remember is that she's of age to do it. So tell us a bit more about this nursing, Thurs. Where d'you think you'll get sent?'

'I don't know,' Thursday said, relieved to have got back to the subject. 'I don't know all that much about it, but I thought I'd go down to the office tomorrow and get the details. I don't suppose it'll happen all at once anyway.' She looked at her mother. 'You don't really mind, do you, Mum? I'll still be coming home whenever I can, and I'll write every week.'

Mary sighed. 'Well, you know we've never wanted to stand in your light, your father and me. It's for you to decide, 'specially now you're of age. It's just – well, I've been dreading you telling me you were joining up. I knew you'd probably do it some time, but – well, it's not what I wanted for you. I wanted to see you settled in a nice little house, not too far away, with your own man and your own family. It's the proper life for a woman.'

'It'll come, Mum,' Thursday said gently. 'It'll come for me, same as it did for you. But it's got to be the right man, hasn't it? And the war's made everything different. Nothing's the same any more.'

'No,' her mother said sadly, 'and sometimes I wonder if it'll ever be the same again.'

Chapter Two

Flo and Percy left soon after that to walk home. The streets were dark, with no lighting because of the blackout, but there was a glimmer of light from the sky and they knew their way well enough. They walked in silence, arm in arm, for a few minutes, then Flo said with a sigh, 'Mary was proper upset about Thursday coming out with all that about nursing, wasn't she? I can't say I'm surprised, either. It's all come so sudden.'

'It's throwing up the tailoring she doesn't like,' Percy said. 'All those years learning the trade and then she chucks it all away. I don't blame Mary for being upset over that.'

'Yes, but it's the idea of Thursday going away she really doesn't like. You don't know who they'll be mixing with, do you? I mean, they might think they're grown up at twenty-one but they're still girls really. And Mary really was beginning to hope she and Sidney would settle down together. He's a decent, sensible young man.'

'Well, maybe she'll have a talk with Maudie about it. She did say she's coming round tomorrow. A word with her own sister might help her to see it differently, 'specially as Maudie's a nurse herself. I dare say that's where Thursday got the idea from in the first place.'

Mike, Leslie and Denise were walking in front, as they'd done ever since they were children. 'You three run on ahead,' their mother would tell them, and off they'd scamper, hopping along the pavement trying to avoid the cracks or pretending they were cowboys and indians. They didn't play those games any more but, like their parents, were talking about Thursday and her sudden announcement.

'I thought Auntie Mary was going to hit the roof,' Denise said with a giggle. 'I've never seen her so cross.'

'It was a surprise to her, that's all,' Mike observed. 'She probably thought Thursday would stay safely at home, making army uniforms and getting married to Sid the Sprat. At least she seems to have a bit more sense than that!'

'I don't know why she goes about with him in the first place,' Denise said. 'He thinks he's God's gift to women, and really he's nothing but a twerp. I wouldn't walk down the street with him. Here, look out, Les, you nearly pushed me into that lamppost.'

'Sorry, didn't see it. I wonder where she'll get sent. Anyway, it livened up the party, it was getting a bit boring, what with the Queen on the wireless and everything.' Leslie shoved his hands deep into his pockets. 'Me, I'm going to join the Air Force as soon as I'm old enough, but you needn't tell Mum and Dad that.'

'The *Air*—' Denise began, and then squeaked as her brother pushed her again. 'You mean you want to be a pilot?'

'Yes, why not? I can drive a car, it can't be any more difficult than that.'

'They'll never let you. You've got to have qualifications.'

'Like what? Don't you think they'll be training blokes to fly? Like they're training Mike here to use a gun? I tell you what, they'll be crying out for pilots, and I'm going to be one. But you mind you don't say anything, see, our Dizzy. I'll see about it myself, same as Thursday has, and then tell 'em, otherwise it'll just mean a lot of arguments.'

Mike had been striding along beside them, not speaking. Now he glanced over his shoulder and, seeing that their parents were still deep in conversation a few yards behind, spoke quietly.

'There'll be nothing to argue about soon. Once this phoney war's over and the real one starts, everyone'll get called up one way or another. We'll all get sent somewhere, and it won't always be somewhere we like, but we're going to have to put up with it. If you'll take my advice, you'll get your oar in first, Les, and put in for the RAF as soon as you can, if that's what you want to do.'

'I wouldn't mind being in the Air Force, too,' Denise said dreamily. 'WAAFs, that's what they're called, and the uniform's ever so smart. I wonder if they'll let girls fly?'

'Well, that's something you're never likely to find out,' Mike told her brutally. 'I don't reckon the war's going to be over by Christmas, like some people think, nor by next Christmas neither. But it'll be over before *you* get old enough to do anything about it, our Denise. You're only fourteen, still a kid, so don't go getting any daft ideas in your head about helping to win the war.'

Denise scowled at him, but her scowl was wasted in the darkness. She scuffed her toe along the pavement and kicked a small stone. It rattled away ahead of them.

'You boys,' she said mutinously, 'you think it's all for your benefit. Well, I think Thursday's right. Women are going to help win this war, and you won't be able to do it without us. And I bet there'll be something I *can* do before it's all finished. You see if there isn't.'

To Thursday's surprise, she found that Sidney did mind her going away, after all.

'You never said anything about volunteering,' he grumbled when they met the next evening for their regular visit to the Scala Cinema. They were sitting in the little red plush tearoom, having a pot of tea and a round of toast before going in. 'You never said a word.'

'I didn't really make up my mind till yesterday. Then I woke up and thought, I'm twenty-one. I can do as I like! And I knew that was what I wanted to do.'

'You could still have said.' His mouth was pushed out petulantly, like a little boy's. Sometimes Thursday found this rather endearing, but today it irritated her. She looked at him in the Fair Isle pullover she'd knitted him last Christmas, under Auntie Flo's instruction, and the brown tweed jacket he seemed to wear every time they went out. His fair hair was combed smooth and he was clean and had had a shave, but he still looked more as if he'd *tried* to look right than actually succeeded.

She stirred her tea, even though she'd given up taking sugar because it was soon going to be rationed, and then frowned as a splash landed on her sleeve. 'Oh, botheration! It's the jumper Auntie Flo knitted me, too.' She found a hanky and dabbed at the stain, answered him as she did so. 'I didn't think you'd be that interested. You're going away yourself soon, after all.'

'That's different. I'm going into the Army.'

'I don't see why it's different. I'm going to be a nurse. You might be glad to find a few nurses around the place when you're at the Front.'

'Oh, so now you've decided I'm going to be wounded, have you? Well, thanks for nothing!' He was definitely sulking now and Thursday felt her irritation grow.

'Don't be stupid. I haven't decided anything. But it stands to reason some people are going to be wounded, and they'll need nurses. It *is* a war, Sidney.'

'They won't have girls like you at the Front anyway,' he said. 'They'll have proper Army nurses there. These VAD people, they're just dogsbodies. They're not properly trained, you know that, don't you?'

'I know they can do a lot to help,' she said quietly. 'They can make things easier for the trained nurses – take some of the donkey-work off their hands.' She met his eyes. 'I don't mind being a dogsbody, Sidney, I just want to help. I don't need to spend years going through a training course to do that, and I don't want to. I want to help *now*. And it's nothing to do with you.'

He stared at her. His face flushed and she wondered suddenly just how much she really did like him. After all, what did they do together? They came here to the Scala once a week or else went to the Odeon, depending what film was on, and they went dancing on Saturday nights. Sometimes he came round for tea on Sunday and sometimes she went to his house and sat at the table with his mum and dad and ate beetroot sandwiches and soggy fruit cake or a heavy sponge. Occasionally they'd get the train to Great Malvern and go for a walk on the hills, perhaps climbing the Beacon for tea in the little café at the top, or they might go to the little market town of Ledbury and visit Thursday's Aunt Maudie. But they didn't really have much in common, she thought. They didn't talk much, except about the films or the dancing. As she'd told her mother, they just went out together from habit.

I ought to have broken it off with him ages ago, she thought. I bet I could have had a dozen boyfriends in the time I've been going out with Sidney. We don't even kiss, except for a goodnight peck on the cheek. I've been wasting my time.

'What do you mean?' Sidney demanded. 'What d'you mean, it's nothing to do with me? What sort of a way's that for a girl to talk to her chap?'

'You're not my chap. Not in that way.'

'Well, what way d'you call it, then? We've been going steady long enough. I thought just lately we'd started to – well, you know – get really fond of one another.'

Thursday sighed. She'd been aware of a feeling of relief when Sidney had told her he'd got his papers. It solved the problem of how to break away from him. And then, feeling a little guilty, she'd set out to be extra nice to him for the last few weeks he was at home. Now it looked as if that had been a mistake and he'd got the wrong idea.

'I am fond of you, Sid,' she said. 'But just as a friend – the way we've always been. It's never been any more than that, you know it hasn't.'

'Oh, I know that, do I?' he said. 'And how would you know what I know or don't know? You don't seem to know that you ought to have talked it over with me before you went off and volunteered.'

'Well, I don't see why I should have,' she retorted. 'It's my life, isn't it? You don't own me, Sidney.'

'Maybe not. But I was going to suggest we got engaged, wasn't I? You'd know that, of course, seeing as you know so much about me already.'

Thursday stared at him. Her mouth felt suddenly dry. She licked her lips and then said huskily, 'Get engaged? What are you talking about?'

'Well, what do you think I'm talking about? Getting engaged, that's what. Proposing to you. What else d'you think I meant?'

Thursday took a deep, shaky breath and cast about for something to say. 'I never thought – I had no idea – you never even *hinted*—'

'Just like you never hinted you were volunteering to go off as a nurse.' Sidney hesitated, then said, 'Look, Thursday, I didn't mean it to be like this. I meant to ask you properly – go down on one knee and all that – but with you springing this on me – well, I just blurted it out. But I'll do it properly, if that's what you want. And we'll go and choose a ring together at Samuels.' He brushed his fair hair out of his eyes and gazed at her appealingly, his round face more than ever like a little boy's. 'Only I'd rather not do it here, if you don't mind.'

'I don't want you to do it anywhere,' Thursday said, her voice wobbling a little. She had a dreadful feeling she was going to either laugh or cry. 'I don't want you to do it at all. I don't want to get engaged, Sidney.'

'Don't be silly,' he said, his babyish look vanishing behind a scowl. 'Every girl wants to get engaged.'

'Yes, but to the right man.' Am I going to have this conversation every day? she wondered wildly. 'It's not like that between us, Sidney. We're just friends. You know that.'

'There you go again, telling me what I know! Shall I tell you what I *thought* I knew, Thursday? I thought I knew it meant something, us going out together all this time. I thought I knew you were fond of me, like I am of you. I thought I knew you'd miss me when I went away, that you'd want to belong to me. I thought I knew you'd want a ring on your finger. Obviously,' he concluded bitterly, 'I was wrong. I should have asked *you* what I knew in the first place. You could have told me that I didn't know what I thought I knew, and – oh, hell and damnation,' he swore, and several people glanced round from other tables. 'I don't even know what I'm saying any more, let alone what I'm *thinking*.'

Thursday bit her lip. If I laugh at him he'll hit me, she thought, and I'll end up crying anyway. And I don't really want to laugh. It's not funny. It's not funny at all.

'Oh, Sidney,' she said miserably, 'I'm really sorry. I didn't know you were feeling like that, honestly. I really thought we were just friends, going out together because – well, because we didn't have anyone else to go out with, I suppose. At least, that's what it was in the beginning. And then it turned into—' She was going to say 'a habit' but Sidney interrupted her.

'It turned into something more. That's what I felt, too, Thursday. I *knew* you felt it, too!' His scowl disappeared and he beamed at her. 'You see? It's all right – I know I sprang it on you, and I didn't mean to, but it's all right really, isn't it? We'll get engaged and you can forget this nursing thing. Forget about being mobile, or whatever you call it, anyway. I wouldn't mind you doing it here in Worcester. But—'

'*No!*' Once again, Thursday saw people glancing round at them. She lowered her voice. 'No, Sidney. I don't want to get engaged to you. And I'm definitely not going to give up the idea of being a VAD.' She looked at his stricken face and felt a stab of remorse, even though she knew she'd never given him any cause to think she was in love with him. 'I'm sorry if you got the wrong idea,' she said quietly. 'I never meant you to.'

There was a silence. Sidney fiddled with his toast and crumbled it into tiny pieces. He picked up his teaspoon and twisted it between his fingers. Then he looked up at her and shrugged.

'Well, I suppose that's it, then. Call it a day, shall we?'

'Oh, Sidney.' Thursday looked at him sorrowfully. 'We don't have to do that, do we? We can still be friends.'

'Don't see much point, do you?' He glanced at his watch. 'D'you want to see this picture, or don't you? It's nearly time for the start. Or don't you even want to sit next to me any more in case I get the wrong idea?'

'You've bought the tickets now—'

'Oh, don't worry about that,' he said bitterly. 'What's a little thing like a couple of one-and-sixpennies when your life's just been ruined? I can't say I feel much like sitting through it, anyway. It's only that soppy romantic thing you wanted to see.' He glanced at his watch again. 'In fact, if I get a move on I reckon I've just got time to get round to the Odeon and see the Roy Rogers. You can have the rest of the toast. Oh, and I brought you this for your birthday.' He dragged a small package from his pocket. 'Sorry it's not very much, but somehow I thought I might be buying you a ring. Dunno where I got a daft idea like that.'

'Sidney—' Thursday began, but he was already on his feet. She saw him go over to the waitress and pay the bill, and then he was on his way to the glass door. '*Sidney . . .*'

He turned and gave her a curt nod. 'It's OK, Thursday. I get the picture. Sorry I won't be seeing you home, but I dare say you can find your way, even in the blackout. Or you could always find some other poor sucker to take you around and pay for you.'

He vanished through the door and Thursday sank back into her seat, her face burning. He's made me feel like a common little gold-digger, she thought, half humiliated, half furious. But what could I do? He always insisted on paying. Men always do, and why shouldn't they? They get far more pay than girls. But it doesn't mean they own us. It doesn't mean we've been bought.

She wondered if Sidney had really wanted her to marry him, or even to be engaged. Or was it just because he was going away and wanted to feel he had a girl at home, tied to him? And because he didn't want some other man taking her out?

You're better off without him, she told herself. He'd no right to behave like that, ordering you about, telling you what you could and couldn't do. And just think what it would have been like to be married to him! You're well out of it.

All the same, she felt unexpectedly lost and miserable, sitting there by herself playing with a slice of cold toast. A few minutes ago, she'd been a girl with a regular boyfriend, a boyfriend who was a bit dull and stodgy, to be sure, but a boyfriend all the same. Someone to go around with, someone to share things with.

Now she was on her own, and it felt as if something was missing – yet at the same time she was conscious of a thread of relief. Not to have to listen to Sidney, going on about his job in the bank any more. Not to have to listen to his braying laugh as he told one of his tedious jokes. Time to herself. Time, perhaps, to find another boyfriend – a proper one this time.

People were getting up and leaving. Thursday glanced at the clock on the wall and saw that the film was due to start in another ten minutes. Sidney had dropped the tickets on the table as he stormed out. There didn't seem to be much point in wasting them. Not both of them, anyway.

Thursday picked one up and followed the other customers out of the little restaurant and into the main part of the cinema. It was Joan Crawford in *Ice Follies* and her pictures were always lovely – so romantic. She felt she could do with a bit of romance.

She forgot all about Sidney's present. It lay on the table beside the plate of half-finished toast and the teapot, and the waitress found it when she came to clear the table. It was kept in the office in case someone claimed it, but nobody ever did and in the end the waitress opened it and found a little brooch in the shape of a letter T.

Her name was Anne, so it wasn't any good to her. She took it home and gave it to her mother.

Once the film was over, Thursday walked home through the darkened streets alone. There was enough moonlight to show her the way and as she crossed the bridge to St John's she paused to look at its silver path on the river. The tower of the cathedral was reflected beneath her, like a shimmering fairy palace. It seemed impossible that war was being waged only a few hundred miles away, and even more impossible that it might penetrate this peaceful place.

A duck landed on the water with a clattering of wings, and the reflection shattered. Thursday shivered. It was almost like a premonition – a vision of what might happen, in reality, to the great tower that had for so long dominated the city. She stared at the broken shards of moonlit water and experienced a moment of strange clarity. A broken city, she thought. A city bombed from the sky; devastated ruins. It could happen. Here in peaceful Worcester – it really could happen. She felt suddenly chilled to the bone, and understood her mother's fear.

But I was right to volunteer, she thought, staring at the black and silver water. I was *right*. We all have to do our bit – every one of us. In whatever way we can.

She had been to the Red Cross office during her break from the tailor's workshop at lunchtime that day. There had been a queue of people – young women like Thursday, older women who wouldn't be able to join the Services but wanted to do something to help, and even a few men who were probably over forty and therefore also too old for active service, or not physically fit enough.

'We need as many young women as we can get, but at present we're only taking those over twenty-one,' the woman behind the desk told Thursday when she reached the head of the queue. 'How old are you?'

'I was twenty-one yesterday. I've brought my birth certificate.'

The Red Cross officer looked at it and her eyebrows went up a little. 'Thursday? Is that really your name?'

'It was because of the Armistice. My father was in the Army, and he and Mum got married when he was on convalescent leave with gunshot wounds. I was born at eleven o'clock in the morning on 11th November 1918, and they felt they had to commemorate it somehow. They made it my middle name, but I've always been called by it – nobody ever calls me Rosemary.'

'Well, you certainly shouldn't get mistaken for anyone else.' The Red Cross officer wrote it down and then handed Thursday a sheaf of forms. 'There are rather a lot of them, I'm afraid. D'you want to take them home or fill them in here? You can use that table in the corner where the other girls are sitting.'

Thursday squeezed on to the end of the table and began to look at the questions. They seemed to want to know an awful lot about you, she thought. She caught the eye of another girl who was obviously thinking the same, and they made a face at each other.

'I feel as if I'm writing my autobiography. Why ever do they want to know all this?'

'In case we get killed, I suppose,' the other girl said. 'Some Red Cross people go right to the Front, don't they. It's almost like being in the Army.'

'They won't send us to the front line, though. That's just the men, surely.'

'Well, they've probably only got the one set of forms.' The girl wrote for a while and Thursday began to fill in her own papers. 'Where d'you live?'

'St John's. What about you?'

'Powick. Are you going to be a mobile or stay at home?'

'Mobile, I hope. I want to see a bit of the world!'

'I'd like to do that, too,' the girl said wistfully. 'But my mother's not very strong and she doesn't want me to go away. I expect I'll stay here in Worcester.'

'You might be in Powick Hospital itself,' Thursday suggested, and the girl made another face.

'I hope not. I'm not too keen on being in a mental hospital. But they say it might be used for medical cases as well, so that wouldn't be so bad. Anyway, the main thing is to do something to help, isn't it.' The girl finished the last form and signed it with a flourish. 'There! That's done. And I'd better scram. I didn't tell my boss where I was going and she'll go mad if I'm late back.'

Thursday finished her forms, too, and handed them in. Then she hurried out into the street and walked quickly back to the tailor's shop.

It would be nice not have to do sewing for a living, she thought. Thursday didn't mind sewing, she'd always been good with her hands and she liked the feeling of satisfaction that came from seeing someone wear a garment she had made. But it was often fiddly work, and could be very frustrating. She'd seen the senior tailor throw a jacket right across the room in fury when he'd spent all afternoon trying to set a sleeve and it still hadn't come right. And men's suits were such dull things to sew, in their dreary greys and blacks and browns – not like pretty skirts and dresses.

I suppose I ought to have volunteered to make service uniforms, she thought, but the mere idea of sewing thick, rough khaki or naval serge made her shudder. No, she was ready for a change, and the idea of working with people, helping in a way to sew their bodies together, was much more interesting and attractive than toiling away in the hidden back room of a tailor's shop. And all afternoon, as she worked on yet another men's suit, she imagined what it would be like to be bustling about a ward full of wounded servicemen, cheering them up, helping them to recover to go back to war again.

The water had settled again now, the reflection of the cathedral once again still and serene. But it was getting cold, just standing here leaning over the bridge, and Thursday straightened up and strode briskly to the other side. Walking through the streets of St John's, she wondered where she was likely to be sent. Somewhere in this country, probably, although there wasn't much happening yet – but there'd be plenty to do if the raids they kept talking about really did happen.

She thought of the vision she'd had on the bridge, the ruined cities, the devastation, and knew that there might be a great many injuries to deal with. They'd need all the nurses they could get, and since there wasn't time to train enough new ones, the VAD nurses would be needed to take on many of the less skilled tasks. But we'll be able to learn to do the others, too, she thought, and felt a tremor of excitement. Why had she never thought of being a nurse before? Why had she allowed her parents to find her the apprenticeship in the tailor's shop and condemn her to the drudgery of the needle and thick grey flannel?

I wonder if I'd have enjoyed working in the porcelain factory any better? she thought. That was where both her father and brother worked, and she'd begged to be allowed to get a job there when she'd left school, imagining herself making some of the beautiful figurines or the famous decorated plates and dishes of Worcester Porcelain. But Walter had told her that only really artistic people got that kind of work, and she was more likely to find herself mixing slip or heaving china out of the kiln.

'It's hard work and it won't set you up for life like tailoring will,' he'd said, and that had been that. There was no more argument.

He was probably right. Her apprenticeship was over and she had a skill literally at her fingertips and a trade behind her. She could even set up on her own if she wanted to, making suits and dresses. That was what her parents had wanted for her, something that would stand her in good stead for the rest of her life.

I might even have married Sidney if we'd gone on much longer, she thought. Suppose all this hadn't happened and he really had proposed. I might have said yes, just because everyone expected me to, just because Mum liked him. I might have married him and lived a dull, ordinary life making clothes for the neighbours, and never known any different.

But now everything had changed. And as Thursday fitted her new Yale key into the lock and opened the front door, she knew that her life had turned in a new direction.

Patch rushed to greet her, and she didn't give another thought to Sidney.

On the following Sunday, Thursday caught the train and went to Ledbury. Auntie Maudie hadn't been able to come to the birthday party because she was a nurse at the little cottage hospital, and she'd invited Thursday and Sidney to tea to make up for it. She looked at Thursday in surprise when she turned up on the doorstep alone, and set her hands on her plump hips, regarding her with bright brown eyes.

'Where's that young man of yours, then?'

'He isn't my young man any more,' Thursday said, stepping over the threshold. 'Not that he ever was, really. We were just friends, Auntie.' She bent her head to kiss her aunt's cheek, feeling as always like a giant beside her.

'Is that so? Your mother was expecting an engagement.'

'Well, there isn't going to be one.' She followed her aunt along the narrow passage to the back room, fending off the attentions of the little white Jack Russell which bounded eagerly to meet her and pausing to stroke the ears of the stately white Persian cat which was sitting on the back of the armchair. 'All *right*, Nipper, you don't have to lick me to death. I'm pleased to see you, too. And how about you, Snowy? How many mice have you caught this week?'

The house was at Homend, one of a row on the opposite side of the road to the hospital, so it was nice and handy for Auntie Maudie to get to work. The front room, its window almost obscured by an enormous aspidistra in a pot, was kept for 'best' but the back room, with one wall taken up by Auntie Maudie's piano, was a cheerfully untidy muddle of newspapers, sheets of music and skeins of khaki wool. In her spare time, Maudie knitted balaclava helmets and socks for the Army.

Her aunt moved the latest piece of knitting from the battered armchair. 'Sit down here, love, and I'll make us a cup of tea. How did the party go? I was sorry I couldn't get over to it, but you know I was on duty.'

'I know. We were sorry you weren't there, Auntie. It was a smashing party. Dad gave me the biggest key you've ever seen, bright red it was, and made out of wood.' Thursday waited while her aunt went out to the scullery and filled the kettle. 'But there's something else I've got to tell you. I've got a bit of news.' She bent to fondle the little dog's ears as he pawed with enthusiasm at her skirt.

'News?' Maudie came back into the cluttered little room. 'What's that, then, if it's not an engagement?'

'I'm going to be a nurse.' Thursday felt a grin spread over her face. 'Like you. Well, not quite like you. I'm not doing the full training or anything like that. I'm going to be a VAD.'

'A VAD?' Maudie's round face broke into a smile. 'That's grand! I've always thought you'd make a good little nurse. Are you going to be mobile?'

Thursday nodded. It was a relief to be able to talk to someone who understood and approved of what she was doing. 'I thought it was a good chance to see a few more places.'

Maudie pursed her lips and raised her eyebrows approvingly. 'You might as well get what you can out of it. So what have you done so far? And what does your mother think about it? Oh . . .' Her eyes sharpened. 'Is this why young Sidney's not with you? Took umbrage, did he?'

Thursday grinned. 'You could say that. Acted as if he owned me, and we weren't even engaged! And then he said he wanted us to *get* engaged. Just so that I wouldn't go out with anyone else while he was away.'

'Cheek!' her aunt said warmly. 'They're all the same, these men, they just want a table to put their feet under whenever they choose to come home. Not that my Bill was like that. He was good as gold, and looked forward to the day when he'd be able to leave the Army and stop home for good. It was just a shame he never got to the end of his time. But I hope you're not too upset about Sidney, Thursday.'

'I'm not upset at all. I don't know why I went out with him for so long, to tell you the truth.' The kettle began to whistle and Maudie went out to the scullery to make the tea. 'I never realised how much he got on my nerves,' Thursday went on, raising her voice a little. 'It's like putting down a heavy bag of shopping, finishing with him. Not that Mum sees it that way,' she added ruefully. 'She thinks I've passed up the chance of a lifetime.'

'Rubbish!' Maudie called, rattling cups in their saucers as she set the old wooden tray. 'That's just my sister, always did think marriage was the only life for a woman. Well, mine was good while it lasted, I won't say it wasn't, and I miss Bill every day, but I can't say I haven't enjoyed being on my own as well. A nice, interesting job like nursing, looking after other people, and a couple of animals to come home to, and nobody to make a mess of your kitchen – well, there's a lot to be said for it! And so long as neither of you's brokenhearted over it.'

'Broken-hearted!' Thursday said with a giggle. 'He went straight off to see a Roy Rogers picture!'

'That's men for you,' Maudie said with a smile. 'Anyway, there's plenty more fish in the sea and you're young yet. So come on, tell me about this VAD business.'

Thursday settled into the armchair, reaching behind her to stroke Snowy's head again and letting Nipper climb on to her lap where he sat gazing adoringly into her face. 'Well, I've been and enrolled. I filled in a lot of forms and they're going to let me know if they'll take me. I'll have to do some training first, and that might be in Worcester. And then – well, they'll send me somewhere else. I have to be attached to one of the services as well, so I've applied for the Navy.'

'You're bound to go away, then. There's not much sea around here!' Maudie poured the tea. 'Well, anything you want to know, just ask me. I may have only been in a little cottage hospital but I've done plenty of nursing. And now I've got a present for you.'

Thursday stopped in the act of spreading a thin layer of margarine on a slice of bread. Rationing hadn't started yet but was expected soon, and meanwhile things like butter were becoming hard to obtain. Nobody liked the taste of margarine much, but there was a pot of home-made blackberry-and-apple jam on the tray as well. Auntie Maudie's blackberry-and-apple jam was famous in the family.

'But you've already given me my birthday present.' She had found it on the table when she came in from the pictures the evening after her birthday – a tiny box containing a pair of pearl earrings. She was wearing them now and she touched her ears to show Auntie Maud that she appreciated the gift. 'They're lovely, and I forgot to say thank you when I came in – I'm ever so sorry.'

'That's all right, love. I saw you had them on. But this isn't a birthday present. It's – it's more of a good-luck present, I suppose.' Maud jumped to her feet and bustled out of the room. 'You just stop there a minute, and don't give that dog too much bread and jam – he'll be fat as a pig at this rate.'

Thursday heard her footsteps running up the stairs. She spread another slice of bread and jam and bit into it, wondering what her aunt was up to now. Although she and Thursday's mother were sisters, they weren't really anything like each other. Mary was quiet and domesticated, her whole life revolving around her husband and family, whereas Maudie was as bright and lively as a wren, always on the go. She worked hard at the little hospital but she was just as busy in her off-duty times – going to church on Sundays, country dancing twice a week, and now organising the townsfolk into helping the war effort by knitting balaclavas or socks for the Forces. She also kept her little garden as neat as a pin, and everyone knew her and Nipper when she took him out for his walks.

'Here,' she said, running downstairs again. 'I want you to have this.'

She handed Thursday a small box. It was a bit like the one the earrings had been in, but it was longer, as if it contained a necklace. Thursday put down her slice of bread and wiped her fingers on her hanky. Then she opened it and gave a little gasp of surprise.

'Oh, Auntie Maudie! It's lovely.'

'My Bill gave it to me,' Maudie said quietly. 'When he went away in the Great War. I'd just started nursing then, you see, and he wanted me to have something they'd let me wear on the ward. It went all through with me and now I'd like it to go with you.'

Thursday stared at the little silver watch that lay in the box. It was on a slender chain, with a pin on the other end. She lifted it out, gazing at the clear face.

'It's upside down, see,' her aunt showed her. 'You pin it on your dress and then you can see it when you look down. You can use it when you're taking a patient's pulse, anything that needs timing. It still keeps perfect time.'

'But you can't give me this!' Thursday protested. 'Not if Uncle Bill gave it to you. You must want to keep it. Anyway, don't you use it yourself?'

'Not now. I've got another one I wear at the hospital. And I really want you to have it, Thursday.' She hesitated for a moment, then said quietly, 'If Bill had come home from the war we'd have had our own family. But it wasn't to be, and when our Mary asked me to be your godmother I thought of you as the nearest I'd ever have to my own daughter, and so I've always done. And if I'd had a little girl, she'd have had that watch, so I want you to have it. And since you're going to be a nurse, like me . . .' She stopped, and Thursday saw that her eyes were full of tears. She leant over quickly and gave her aunt a kiss on her round little cheek.

'I'll wear it all the time. It's lovely. Thank you.' She handed the watch to her aunt. 'Pin it on for me now, will you?'

Maudie did so and they both gazed at it, resting on Thursday's breast. The silver glowed faintly in the firelight and the glass gleamed. Maudie nodded a little.

'It looks very nice. And I'll be happy to think of it on a ward again – a wartime ward, I mean. Looking after soldiers and sailors. I'll be happy thinking of you wearing it.'

Thursday got up and went round the little table to her aunt. She bent to put her arms around the plump little body and give her a gentle kiss.

'I'll think of you whenever I pin it on,' she said softly. 'You and Uncle Bill.' She had never known her uncle, he had died the year before she was born. But his photograph stood on the mantelpiece, a smiling young soldier with fair hair just showing beneath his army cap, next to the photograph of the wedding with Maudie a plump and smiling young girl with bright eyes and dark curls.

Thursday looked at the pictures now and felt a lump in her throat. It was such a shame they'd never had more than a scrap of married life, such a shame that they'd never had a family. You could see in the picture how happy they would have been, and what lovely parents they would have made.

Maudie followed her eyes. 'I still feel he's with me, you know,' she said softly. 'I touch his photo every morning and I say goodnight to him when I go to bed. We've never really been parted.'

Thursday thought of Sidney and her impatience with him. It would never have been like that for us, she thought. If we had got married, we'd have been like a lot of other people I know, bickering and squabbling and just rubbing along together because there's nothing else you can do. But we wouldn't have felt like Auntie Maudie feels about Uncle Bill.

Maudie nodded at her. 'I can see what you're thinking, love, and you're right. You've got to wait for the right man before you give your own life over to him. And there will be one for you, I'm sure of that – only it was never poor young Sidney, decent young fellow that he is.'

Thursday smiled a little tearfully. 'I suppose there'll be a right girl for him, too. He's had a lucky escape, same as I have!'

'You're telling me!' her aunt laughed. 'It'll take a strong man to cope with you, our Thursday! Anyway, tell me about the family, I didn't have much time for a proper gossip when I called in the other evening, I had to catch the train home. How's your Auntie Flo? I bet she's worried about her Mike, isn't she? He must be going away soon.'

'Well, yes, except that there doesn't seem to be much happening yet, does there? People are saying it's just a phoney war and won't come to anything after all, and others are saying we're going to be bombed to bits. It's hard to know who's right.'

'It takes time to get a war going, I suppose. But I reckon these air raids are going to come all the same. Hitler's probably just waiting till the winter's over. And he wants to win the war at sea before he starts using the aeroplanes.'

Thursday nodded. 'Dad says that too. He says there's no sense in flattening the country if he's going to invade us, and he's got to get rid of the Navy first so he can bring the troops over by sea. Then he'll start bombing the military airfields, and harbours like Portsmouth, and the important cities like London.'

'Well, whatever they're going to do there's not a lot we can do about it,' Maudie said. 'Tell me a bit more about your birthday.

What presents did you have? I know your mum and dad were giving you that nice brooch, she showed it to me when they bought it. What else did you get? Oh—' she leant forward eagerly '—and what's the latest talk? What about that Mrs Hoskins up the road, has she really gone off with her fancy man or did her hubby send him packing? The last I heard, she'd been seen with a suitcase, getting on a number eight bus.'

They settled back in theirs chairs for a good gossip, while Nipper bustled round the rug clearing up all the crumbs he could find, and Snowy rose majestically from her perch and clambered down on to Thursday's lap where she curled into a white, foamy ball and purred herself to sleep.

At last it was time to go. Thursday kissed her aunt and touched the little watch still pinned to her blouse. It felt like a talisman, she thought, a lucky token to carry with her wherever she went. It had, as Maudie had said, already gone through one war. Now it would go through another.

'I'll take the greatest care of it,' she promised as she slipped into her coat.

'That's right,' her aunt agreed, and touched the watch's face with her fingertip as if bidding it goodbye. 'And when all this is over you can bring it back to me again. Just so that I know it's taken care of you, like it took care of me. You'll keep each other safe.'

Thursday slipped out of the door and walked quickly up the street towards the railway station. She could feel the watch, just touching her breast, as she stepped along. It was older than she was, she thought, and had already been through a world war. Now it was going to serve again.

Somehow, it felt like a promise.

Chapter Three

Jenny worked in a grocer's shop, one of a row of small shops not far from Waterloo Street. She'd been there since she left school at fourteen, and enjoyed weighing out the biscuits which were kept in glass-topped bins in front of the counter, and slicing ham or bacon on the big circular slicer. She liked putting sugar into thick blue paper bags and wrapping sweets into paper cones for children. And she liked chatting to the customers and getting all the gossip.

'Mrs Hoskins has definitely gone off with that bloke from Evesham,' she said at home, as the family sat round the tea-table the day after Thursday's visit to Auntie Maud. 'I heard it in the shop. Old Mrs Gabbage says Mr Hoskins is going after them with an airgun.' She giggled. 'Wonder where he'll aim it!'

Her mother gave her a reproving look. 'Jenny! That's enough of that sort of talk. And I don't think you ought to be gossiping about Mrs Hoskins anyway. She's had a lot to put up with from her hubby. He always was a bit ready with his fists.'

'All the same, he is her husband,' Walter said. 'He's got his rights.'

'It's enough to put you off marriage, hearing about men like him,' Thursday observed, helping herself to the Marmite. 'I don't blame Mrs Hoskins for running off.'

Walter stared at her. 'Don't blame her? She made her vows, didn't she? "Love, honour and obey", that's what the service says. "Till death us do part." Not just till some fancy-man comes long and takes her eye.'

'Well, I don't remember anything in the marriage service to say a man can knock his wife about,' Thursday said. 'I wouldn't stand for it, I can tell you.'

34

'Well, I can't say I agree with him doing that,' Walter allowed. 'All the same, the marriage vow's a serious promise, and who's to say *why* he hit her – if he really did, it's only talk, mind. If he'd found out she was carrying on behind his back—'

'Well, I don't think we need talk about it at the tea-table,' Mary interrupted. 'What else have you been doing today, Jenny, apart from gossip?'

'We've been getting all sorts of forms about rationing,' Jenny said gloomily. 'They say the books'll be out soon. Then you'll only be able to have a tiny bit of meat each week and about an ounce of butter and a couple of tablespoonsful of sugar. It's going to be murder weighing it all out.'

Mary stared at her. 'We'll get more than that, surely. That's starvation rations.'

'Well, I don't know the exact amounts, but it really isn't much, Mum. And people are starting to hoard. You can tell they are. They come and get as much as they can from us and then they go round all the other shops to get more. We've stopped serving people we don't know. It's not fair on the regulars.'

'Are you allowed to do that?' Thursday asked. 'Refuse to serve them?'

'We just tell them we haven't got what they want, and keep it under the counter. Some of them get a bit nasty, but what can they do? It's illegal to hoard, and it's not fair.'

'So that's what you're doing, Mum,' Steve told his mother. 'Hoarding. *I've* seen that bag of sultanas and raisins you've got at the back of the cupboard.'

'It's only a pound or so,' Mary protested, colouring a little. 'I've been saving them for the Christmas cake, that's all. And I'd have made it by now if it hadn't been for Thursday's birthday. You couldn't have called it hoarding then. Could you?' she added, a shade anxiously.

The family laughed at her. 'See, you're looking guilty already!' Steve grinned, but Thursday nudged him.

'Don't, you're upsetting her. It's all right, Mum. It's not hoarding, just a pound of dried fruit, and like you say, it would have been a cake by now. Anyway, what were you doing, our Steve, ferreting about in Mum's cupboards? I bet *you* weren't thinking of doing a bit of baking.'

It was Steve's turn to colour, remembering the days when he used to come home from school and, if the house was empty, steal raisins from his mother's store. He'd been caught one day when she'd come downstairs unexpectedly and found him with his hand in the jar, and he'd never been allowed to forget it.

Jenny finished her tea and pushed back her chair. 'I'm going to the pictures. *The Wizard of Oz* is on at the Scala. I might be a bit late in, Dad.'

'Oh, might you? It wouldn't occur to you to ask permission, I suppose?' Walter tried to inject a stern note into his voice.

She gave him a cheeky look. 'You wouldn't want me to miss the end of the picture, would you? I'll come straight home after – you needn't worry that I'm lurking in doorways with a boy!'

'You'd better not be, either. And just who are you going with?' Mary asked as Jenny pulled open the door to the scullery.

'Jean. Got to go now, we're meeting in ten minutes.' Jenny gave her face a sketchy wash at the kitchen sink and then whisked upstairs. They heard her light footsteps skittering above and then she bounced back down the stairs and through the back room on her way to the front door, keeping her face averted as she passed the table. Walter reached out to detain her but she was gone, calling a brightly casual goodbye as she went. Steve winked and Thursday looked at the table, hiding her grin.

Walter and Mary looked at each other.

'That girl's put lipstick on,' Walter said. 'She tried to hide it, but I saw. Bright red. You'll have to do something about her, Mary.'

Mary sighed. 'I've tried, but what can I do? She'd only put it on outside. She's nearly seventeen, Walter, they all wear a bit of make-up at that age.'

'Well, I don't like it. Making herself look cheap.'

'It's only a bit of lipstick,' Thursday said. 'And it's not a really bright one.'

'Yes, come on, Dad,' Steve said. 'There's no harm in it. The blokes don't like a girl who doesn't make something of herself.'

'That's just it! She's not old enough to be thinking of things like that. Boys, and make-up and all that. She's still a child.'

'She's old enough to get married,' Thursday pointed out. 'Sixteen. I was going round with that Billy Stratton when I was sixteen.'

'You never told me about that,' Walter said. 'I'd have put my foot down if I'd known. And she can't get married, not without my consent, not for another four years and more. It's this twenty-first of Thursday's,' he said to his wife. 'It's given her ideas. And it's this war, too. Girls not much older than her talking about joining up. And that's another thing,' he went on in a grumbling tone. 'You've unsettled her with this talk of being a mobile nurse. You could just stop on at the tailor's, they're making uniforms now and there's plenty for you to do there and it's useful war work. But, no, you've got to go off and volunteer to be a nurse, and not even satisfied with the local hospital. Seems to be you're all just itching to get away from home, the lot of you. I mean, why? What have we done wrong that you're so keen to leave us?'

'It's not that, Dad. You know it isn't. I just want to do something different, as well as useful. I've never really liked being at the tailor's, you know that. And I *want* to be a nurse. I was talking to Auntie Maudie about it yesterday, she was telling me lots of things, and *she* thinks it's a good idea for me to go.'

'It's not the nursing I object to so much. It's this wanting to go away. As if your home's not good enough for you any more.'

'Calm down, Dad,' Steve said. 'It's nothing to do with that. It's just a chance, isn't it? A chance to see something different.' He paused, then said, 'I'm thinking of volunteering myself, as a matter of fact.'

His parents stared at him.

'Volunteering? You?' his mother said at last. 'Oh, *Steve*.'

Walter leaned forward and put his elbows on the table. Jenny and Thursday were forgotten. His voice was serious.

'Are you sure about this, son? You don't have to do it, you know. They're not calling up your age group, and maybe they won't. You want to give it some thought. Once you're in, you won't be able to come out again, you realise that?'

'I know, Dad. But Thursday is right, what she says – we can't sit round and do nothing. We've all got to do our bit. You heard what they said on the six o'clock news – there might not be much going on at home yet, but there's plenty happening at sea, with these new magnetic mines Mr Chamberlain was talking about, and ships being sunk all over the place. They're going to need men, and I don't want to wait to be called up. I'd rather go now.'

'Not into the Navy!' Mary protested. 'I can't bear to think of you at sea, Steve. You know how I feel about boats.'

He grinned at her. 'It's all right, Mum, I won't volunteer for the Navy. That'd be pretty daft, when we live practically in the middle of the country. Anyway, we've got our own regiment in Worcester. It'll be the Army for me. Or maybe the Air Force, I wouldn't mind learning to fly a Spitfire.'

'You want to think about it, all the same,' Walter said. 'It's not pretty, war isn't. I saw the last lot, remember. I still got the scars of bullets in my shoulder. I saw men die and it's not what it's cracked up to be. Death or glory, they said, but there's not much glory about it, I can tell you that.'

'Walter . . .' Mary said in a trembling voice, and he glanced at her.

'There's things it's not right to talk about in front of your mother. But you need to think about them, all the same. Let's go down to the Red Lion a bit later on, have a bit of a talk. I won't stop you doing what you feel's right, but I don't want you to do anything in a hurry, all right?'

'All right, Dad.' Steve was startled. He'd expected argument, he'd expected tears from his mother, but he hadn't expected this reaction from his father. Taking him to the pub. Treating him like – well, like one of his mates. Especially after the way he'd gone on about Jenny and her bit of lipstick.

'I was just going to make a cup of tea,' Mary said a little plaintively, and once again Walter glanced at her.

'You put the kettle on, love. There's no hurry for me and Steve. And let's listen to the wireless for a bit. It's Arthur Askey and Richard Murdoch, isn't it? That'll give us something to take our minds off things a bit.'

Mary went out into the little kitchen, and Thursday followed her. She put her arms around her mother and held her tightly.

'I'm sorry about all that, Mum. I didn't want to start that argument again. 'Specially with Steve saying what he did.'

Mary looked at her. Her lips were trembling.

'I thought we'd have you all at home for a bit longer, or at least close by. Now it seems as if the whole family's breaking up. It's such a lot to take in, all at once.'

'I know, Mum. I know. But we've got to do what we think's right, haven't we? You and Dad have always brought us up to do that.'

Mary sighed and nodded. 'Yes, we have. I suppose we just didn't think of all this. After the last war, well, we just didn't ever think it could happen again, did we?'

'Perhaps it won't,' Thursday said, but without much hope. 'Perhaps it really will just turn out to be a phoney war, and all be over soon. And then we can all go back to being the way we were.'

But she knew they never could. Already, the world had been changed, and their lives with it. None of them would ever be able to go back to quite the way they were.

'I've never talked much about the Great War as they called it,' Walter said to Steve as they sat over a pint of beer each at the Red Lion. 'None of us what was in it wanted to talk about it once we were home again. We were too bloody glad to *be* home, and we just wanted to put it all behind us. But now . . .' He sighed and rubbed a hand across his face. 'Now it seems as if we ought to have said more. Maybe it would have stopped this new lot.'

'I don't see how it could have done,' Steve said. 'Hitler would have been Hitler no matter what you'd told us. It wouldn't have stopped him going into Czechoslovakia or Poland, and that's what we're fighting for, isn't it? And to stop him taking over the rest of us, too – France and England, and all the other countries in Europe.'

'I suppose so. Well, yes, you're right, it wouldn't have stopped him. But maybe we'd have stepped in a bit sooner. Or done something different . . .' Walter rubbed his face again. 'I dunno. And it's not what I brought you down here for neither. Talking about what we ought to have done isn't going to change things now. But I don't want you going into the Army, or anything else, without knowing what's in front of you.'

Steve lifted his tankard to his lips and waited. Coming out for a drink wasn't something he and his dad did all that much. Walter preferred to come to the Red Lion on Friday nights for a pint or two with his own mates, while Steve generally spent his time playing football or billiards. In fact, now he came to think about it, he couldn't ever remember them coming down on their own, specially.

Walter didn't seem to be in any hurry to start speaking. His brow was creased and his lower lip curled over the upper, as if he was pondering how to begin. He took a sip of his own beer and cleared his throat.

'Like I said, it wasn't pretty. It was a cruel war. Well, war's always cruel, stands to reason, but this one – well, it seemed worse than anything you'd ever heard of. Young boys, hardly trained enough to know how to hold a gun, hardly *big* enough to hold a gun, some of 'em, sent over the top when the generals knew full well they'd be mown down like grass in haymaking. It was always the same, see. The enemy were there and as soon as they saw a movement, they'd shoot. So if you sent enough soldiers, they'd just go on shooting till they ran out of ammo. Then the proper fighting could begin.' He looked at his son with eyes that seemed to see another time, another place. 'Cannon-fodder, that's what they were called afterwards, and that's just what they were. Sent to use up the enemy's ammo. Piles of bodies, And not all of 'em properly dead, neither. But you couldn't stop to do nothing. You had to climb over 'em or kick 'em out of the way.' His voice was as dry as sandpaper. 'It was sheer bloody murder.'

Steve could not speak. It was only what he'd already known, in a dim sort of way, but the picture his father's words conjured before his eyes was much more graphic, more shocking, than the vague knowledge he'd had before. He saw young men of his own age – younger – climbing the banks that had been thrown up by the digging of the trenches, facing a hail of bullets, falling back on those who were waiting behind . . . What was it like to have the body of a screaming, bleeding friend fall on top of you as you were yourself being urged to go over the same murderous bank?

'And it wasn't just the killing,' his father went on. 'It was the trenches themselves. Up to our knees in mud, we were, and the rain just bloody never stopped coming down. Came down like stair-rods, it did. And the cold – it got right through to your bones. You were never dry, never warm. Your feet rotted in your socks but you never took 'em off so you didn't see . . . And there was nowhere to bury the bodies, and no time. They just laid there, stinking, at your feet, till they was part of the mud and filth and stench of it all . . . And the *rats*.' He shuddered. 'The only ones with plenty to eat, *they* were. The only ones who could take it.'

He stopped. His voice was trembling. Steve stared at him, transfixed. He wanted to reach out, to touch his father, but he hadn't done that since he was a little boy and still kissing his dad goodnight. He could barely even remember it. He felt sick; sick and helpless.

That's what Armistice Day's all about, he thought. And the Remembrance Day service, and all those poppies. That's why they called our Thursday 'Thursday'.

'There was heroes in every trench,' Walter said. 'You had to be a bloody hero to stick it. And there was those that went mad, too, mad with terror and pain. You couldn't blame them, could you. You couldn't blame 'em – youngsters of sixteen and seventeen, some of 'em, no older'n our Jenny, lied about their age to go and serve, thinking it was all going to be glorious and they'd come back with medals – it was what they was *told*, see? And if you didn't go, if you didn't volunteer and didn't have no uniform to wear, people stared at you in the street and shouted after you, and girls give you white feathers to show you were a coward. And then, when they found out what it was really like – well, some of 'em bore up OK, but some of 'em just went to pieces. *And I don't blame 'em,*' he said, fixing Steve with an accusing stare. 'I don't blame 'em at all. They was just boys, that's all, bits of boys. They didn't deserve . . . what happened to them.'

There was a moment of silence. Then Steve asked huskily, his mouth dry, 'What was it? What did happen to them?'

'They were executed,' Walter said baldly. 'Shot at dawn, by their own mates. That's the ones who weren't shot by their own commanding officers straight away, without bothering to set up a firing squad. Cowards, they called 'em, cowards and deserters.'

The pub had been a noisy place a few moments ago. Now, it was as if everyone had stopped talking at once, as if the laughter and shouting had ceased. For a moment Steve felt as if he were there with his father, seeing what his father saw: a wavering line of dirty, dishevelled soldiers, some of them younger than himself, just boys, being marched on to a bleak patch of muddy ground in the cold and colourless dawn. There was no sound of birdsong in the lowering sky, no sign of life on the harsh landscape, only grey hopelessness and miserable fear in the blindfolded faces. He saw them stop and stand in line, turning sightlessly to face the guns, guns held by men they knew, men who had been their friends and comrades. He heard the bark of the command, the harsh crack of the rifles. And then it was over. The bodies lay fallen in their own blood, their own brains spattered around them. The bodies of boys who had volunteered, who had lied about their age to go and serve their country, but who had found the horror too much to bear.

'It don't matter whether you're a volunteer or a pressed man,' Walter said at last. 'You follow the same rules. They took children and treated 'em as men. And it'll be the same this time, Steve.' He came back from the past and looked his son in the eye. 'I don't want to stand in your light, son, I never have. Your mother and me, we've tried to bring you up to know right from wrong and we've tried to teach you to know your own minds. You've got to do whatever you think is right. But you ought to know what it can be like. What it *will* be like. It wouldn't be right for me to let you go off not knowing.'

'No, Dad.' Steve fiddled with his glass. 'But it's different this time. If Hitler invades – or if there's air raids, and there are *going* to be – we're all going to have to fight. It's not going to be a matter of going to France or Belgium or Germany. It's going to be here – in Worcester. None of us are going to be safe.' He looked up at his father. 'We've got to stop that happening, Dad. We can't let him march all over us like he's marched over those other countries. We can't have him putting us into ghettos like he has the Jews. This is *England*. We haven't been invaded since – since William the Conqueror. And I'm damned if I'm going to let it happen again – not if there's anything I can do to help prevent it.' He met Walter's eyes again. 'I'm glad you told me those things, Dad. I think it's right that you did. We *ought* to know what you and the others went through in that war. But we can't let them stop us now. We've got to go and fight. I just hope I'll be one of the ones that *can* take it. But if not, well, at least I'll have tried.'

There was a long silence. Steve looked at his father and went to fetch another two pints of beer. He brought a whisky too, and set it on the table.

'Drink that, Dad. It'll make you feel a bit better.'

Walter nodded. He drank the whisky and coughed a little, grinning weakly. 'Not used to it! I'm sorry if I was a bit – you know—' He looked embarrassed and Steve spoke quickly.

'It's all right. And thanks for telling me.'

'You won't say anything to your mother? Only I've never really said all that much – didn't want to upset her. And now – I wouldn't want her worrying any more than she's got to, see. It's bad enough for her as it is. It's bad enough for everyone.'

'Yes.' Steve looked at him. Mum won't know these things, he thought, but Dad will. Dad's going to be torturing himself day and night, thinking of the last war and imagining me and Thursday and even Jenny in this one. And so will all the other men who went through those things before.

'I won't say anything,' he said. 'And I'll think about it before I volunteer – I promise you that. But I'm going to have to go some time, Dad. You know that, don't you?'

'Yes.' Walter sighed and lifted his tankard. 'I know. And all I can do is wish you luck. Good luck, Steve – and God go with you.'

Chapter Four

Thursday's papers came through just before Christmas.

The envelope was on the mantelpiece when she came in from work that evening and she opened it standing in front of the fire, still in her coat. It was cold and foggy outside and the damp still hung around her, droplets sparkling on the brown woollen gloves Auntie Flo had knitted and on the hair that peeped out all around her beret. She dropped the gloves on the fender to dry and tore the envelope open with her thumb.

'When have you got to go, then?' Mary asked. She'd been on tenterhooks all day, seeing the envelope sticking out from behind the clock where she'd put it that morning. How she'd had the strength not to open it herself, she didn't know, and now she was hovering anxiously by the tea-table, picking up plates and putting them down again, moving the pepper-pot, fiddling with the cloth. 'It's not too soon, is it?'

'January,' Thursday said. 'Early January. They don't say where I've got to go, there'll be some more papers coming about that, but I've got the Wrens. I mean, that's what I'll be attached to, so it'll be a naval hospital.'

She stared at the paper, feeling a tremor of excitement. It was coming true, it was really happening. She was going to be a nurse, a VAD, and work somewhere near the sea with Wrens and sailors. It was a whole new world opening up before her. She felt a twinge of nervousness somewhere in the excitement and looked at her mother, biting her lip and grinning all at once.

'Well, at least you've got Christmas with the family,' Mary said, trying to hide her disappointment. She had resigned herself to the fact that her two elder children would be leaving home but had

44

clung to the hope that Thursday would be kept nearer to her home. Why the girl had to volunteer for the Navy, she had no idea, not when she could surely have done the same sort of nursing here in Worcester, or at Norton Barracks. It was as if she *wanted* to get away from them all. It's hurtful, Mary had said to her sister when Maudie had come over one afternoon last week, but Maudie had shaken her head and said girls were different nowadays, more independent, and this war had unsettled them all. They didn't seem to think they were doing anything unless they were sent away somewhere. 'And you don't need to worry about your Thursday,' she'd said. 'She's got a good head on her shoulders, and she'll be subject to hospital discipline, as well as Service rules.'

'We'd better make the most of it,' Mary said now. 'Christmas, I mean. It might be the last one we have all together. For a while, I mean,' she added hastily, turning away.

Since the night when Walter had taken Steve to the pub, Steve had said no more about volunteering, but that didn't mean he'd forgotten the idea. Mary never knew what it was Walter and Steve had talked about that night in the pub, only that Walter had come back looking grey and drawn, and had bad dreams for a week afterwards. It had brought back all the nightmares he'd been through in the Great War, things he'd never talked to her about and which she'd had to find out from hearing him cry out in the night. I don't want my Steve to go through things like that, she thought. But there didn't seem to be anything she could do to stop it. As Steve had said himself, if he didn't volunteer he'd get called up and then he might not have any choice at all in what he did.

Thursday looked at her mother. She knew Mary was upset about her going away, and now that it was really happening she felt a twinge of guilt and sympathy. She went to Mary and put her arm around her shoulders.

'Don't worry, Mum. I'll be all right. And I won't forget you and Dad, and everyone at home. I'll write to you as often as I can.'

Mary tried to smile. 'I know, love, and I know you won't do anything silly. It's just – it's just that I'm going to *miss* you so much! And Steve as well, when he goes. The house will seem so empty.'

'Well, I'd probably have gone soon anyway, if I'd got married,' Thursday said, but Mary shook her head.

'That's different. You'd have been living nearby, and you'd have had the sort of life I expected for you. The sort of life I could *understand*. This going off to a hospital somewhere hundreds of miles away, living with strangers and working with sailors – well, I can't sort of picture it. That's what's upsetting.'

'I'll tell you all about it,' Thursday promised. 'I'll write so many letters, you'll get fed up reading them. I'll tell you all about the other girls and the doctors and patients, and what it's like by the sea, and everything. I'll even draw pictures if you like!'

Mary laughed and brushed her hand across her eyes. 'They'll tell me a lot, I'm sure! You were never much good as an artist, our Thurs. I remember those pictures you used to bring home from school, we had our work cut out puzzling out what they were supposed to be.'

'Well, it isn't till after Christmas anyway,' Thursday said, folding the letter back into its envelope. She shrugged off her coat. 'So like you say, we'd better think about making it a good one. Is there a cup of tea in the pot? It's freezing outside.'

Making Christmas a good one seemed especially important this year, when things were so uncertain. The war news was grim. The Russians had bombed Helsinki and there was fighting on the Western Front. The King himself had visited the soldiers along the Maginot Line. The war at sea had already brought losses, and in the South Atlantic there had been a huge sea battle which had culminated in the capture and scuttling of the *Graf Spee*, the German pocket battleship which had caused so much trouble for the merchant navy.

Yet the British Isles remained untouched and there was still an uneasy feeling that the war hadn't properly started. Barrage balloons drifted like flying whales above the cities, although there was no sign of an air invasion; Canadian and Australian troops arrived in their thousands by sea and air, and still Hitler seemed to be keeping his distance.

'He's waiting for the spring,' Walter said as the family gathered round the supper-table that evening, listening to the six-o'clock news. 'It's going to be a bad winter, if you look at the holly. He'll sit tight till the weather's better and then all hell will be let loose.'

'It seems so dark these days,' Mary said, bringing a large pan of stew to the table and starting to ladle it on to the plates. 'I had the lights on and the blackout up by half-past three this afternoon. What with the Government stopping British summer time at the end of November, you only get a few hours' daylight these days.'

'Well, there wouldn't have been any more daylight even if they hadn't,' Steve pointed out. 'Still, it's murder on the roads. I think it's daft, not letting cars have any lights. You can't tell when they're coming, 'specially when it's foggy like tonight.'

Jenny nodded. 'There was a man nearly got run over outside the shop this afternoon. He fell on the kerb and someone brought him in for a cup of water. He looked ever so shaken up.'

'At this rate,' Steve said, 'there'll be more people killed on the roads than in the fighting. Hitler won't have to bother sending any planes! I wouldn't mind another dumpling, if there's any spare, Mum.'

'You just wait till everyone's been served,' his mother told him. 'Anyway, I made two each so there won't be any left over. I'm afraid there's not a lot of meat in it, but it's got the flavour and it's full of your father's vegetables.'

'Lots of carrots, anyway,' Steve remarked. 'They're telling us to eat plenty of them to help us to see in the dark. We should have eyes like cats' soon!'

'Good job I've got the allotment,' Walter said. 'And the carrots did well this year. Can't do much about the cod-liver oil they want us to take as well, though.'

'*I'm* not swallowing the horrible stuff,' Jenny declared. 'I had enough of it when I was a baby.'

'You had cod-liver oil and malt, and you liked it,' Mary reminded her. 'I'll get one of those big jars from Boots and we'll all have a spoonful after tea every day. What with all these shortages and rationing just about to start, it won't do any of us any harm.'

'How long does it take to work?' Thursday wondered. 'And how many carrots do you need to eat? Someone told me if you ate too many you turn orange.'

'That's how they help people see in the dark,' Steve said. 'They don't do anything to your eyes, they just make us all bright orange so we can see each other more easily. Anyway, if you're going to be a nurse you ought to know that sort of thing.'

'Well, I soon will if we get a lot of orange sailors coming into the hospital,' Thursday said with a giggle. 'Is Auntie Maudie coming for Christmas Day, Mum?'

'Yes, unless they want her to be on duty. But they do try to get everyone home for Christmas at the cottage hospital. And your Auntie Flo and Uncle Percy will be round, too, of course, and Granny and Grandad. The usual houseful.' Mary looked pleased, then sighed. 'Goodness knows how long it'll be before we get another chance to have everyone together.'

'Better start making paperchains,' Jenny said to her brother. 'The ones we made last year got all screwed up and torn when we took them down, remember? I wonder if we'll be able to get any coloured paper.'

Coloured paper was another thing that proved difficult to find in the shops, but they managed to track down enough to make a few strings of paperchains, the coloured strips glued together in neat loops, and they supplemented them with strips made from newspaper coloured with paints from Steve's old paintbox. The effect was cheery enough, and Walter got out the fairy lights that were stored carefully from year to year, and the glass baubles that hung on the little tree.

'It looks good, doesn't it?' Thursday said, surveying their work as they finished decorating on Christmas Eve. 'Really bright and pretty. And it'll look even better when Dad's underpants are taken off the fender.'

'Oh, you!' Mary exclaimed, snatching them up. 'I'm sure I never left them there. Anyway, there'll be no more washing done till after Boxing Day, so that's that. Now, breakfast will be at eight o'clock so that I can get the turkey in the oven – we were lucky to get it, Mr Huggins only had just enough for his regulars – and I want us all to go to church together for the eleven o'clock service. Your auntie and uncle will come round in time for a sherry before dinner, and they're bringing Gran and Grandad with them. We'll have dinner at two.'

'And we'll all turn to and help with the veg,' Maudie said. She had arrived at teatime and caught the bus from the railway station, staggering in laden with parcels, and would stay until the trains started to run again on Boxing Day. Nipper was with her, and had quickly started a game of chase with Patch, until both dogs were banished to the garden, but the white Persian had been left at home in Ledbury with a neighbour popping in to feed her. 'There's a huge pile of sprouts to be done, and plenty of carrots.'

'And a good big pudding,' Mary added. 'Flo and me put all our dried fruit together. Make the most of it – if this rationing's what they say it's going to be we'll not see another one like it for the duration.'

The dinner was indeed as good as any pre-war Christmas dinner had been, and the family crowded round the table, exclaiming over the crackers Flo had brought and putting on flimsy paper hats and reading out silly jokes and riddles. 'When is a door not a door?' 'When it's ajar.' 'When is a sailor not a sailor?' 'When he's aboard.' 'Why shouldn't you put a clock at the top of the stairs?' 'Because it will run down.' Each joke was greeted with groans of derision, and Leslie complained that he'd heard them all before.

'That's because you've *told* them all before,' his sister Denise said, poking him with her elbow. 'Now we know where you got them from – Christmas crackers.'

The only member of the family missing was Mike, who had now been posted to a camp in Northamptonshire and couldn't get leave, and after dinner Walter poured a small glass of port for all the adults and proposed a toast.

'To absent friends,' he said, lifting his glass. 'To Mike and all the other brave lads who can't be at home at Christmas.'

'To absent friends,' they all echoed, and there was a moment's silence as Mary and Flo bit their lips and gazed at their tablemats. Thursday glanced at her mother, knowing she was thinking of herself and Steve who would both be going away soon. Steve still hadn't volunteered, but he would soon, she knew – probably as soon as Christmas was over. And she herself would be gone in less than a fortnight.

Dinner over, they cleared the table and gathered round the wireless to hear the King's speech. He was speaking not only to his country but to his Empire, thanking them for coming to Britain's aid. '*The Mother Country can never be sufficiently grateful to you,*' he said in his mild, hesitant voice. '*We are all members of the great family of nations which is prepared to sacrifice everything that freedom of spirit may be saved.*' The women had tears in their eyes when he finished, and Walter and Percy cleared their throats.

'Say what you like,' Mary said, as if someone was likely to argue with her, 'he's making a good king. He might be a bit quiet and shy, but to my mind that's better than that brother of his. And he's got a lovely wife and two dear little girls.'

'Princess Elizabeth will be Queen one day,' Jenny remarked. 'I wonder what it feels like, knowing you'll be Queen and eating off gold plates.'

The boys made faces at each other. They weren't interested in royalty and gold plates. Walter switched off the wireless and Leslie produced the Monopoly set he'd been given for Christmas, and they settled down to a game.

'I'd love to go to London,' Jenny sighed, landing her flat-iron on Mayfair. 'See all those posh places. Oxford Street – Selfridges – Buckingham Palace. Can't we have a trip up there some time, Mum? It's easy on the train.'

Walter looked at her in exasperation. 'Don't be daft, girl. There's a war on, haven't you heard? London's one of the places they'll bomb first. There'll be no trips to London nor anywhere else until this lot's finished.'

'And you can pay me fifty pounds rent,' Steve told her. 'Mayfair's one of the poshest places of all, and *I own it!*'

The family laughed at Jenny's expression and Thursday felt a sense of relief. For a moment, her father's remark had brought the war vividly back to her mind. She looked round at her family, their faces laughing and happy, and wondered where she, Steve and Leslie would be this time next year, and what they would be doing.

Her eye caught her mother's and she knew by the expression on Mary's face that she was wondering the same thing.

On New Year's Day, there was a royal proclamation that made all men aged between twenty and twenty-seven liable for service in the armed forces.

'That's it,' Steve said. 'I'm going down the recruiting office first thing in the morning.'

'You don't have to,' his mother said, without much hope. 'They're calling up chaps twenty-three and over first.'

'And the rest of us by the end of the year. I can't sit around and wait, Mum. I don't want people calling me a coward. I ought to have done it before.'

Mary sighed and said no more. She knew he couldn't be stopped now. It was only a matter of months anyway.

Thursday was already packing. She was off next day, and her destination was a naval hospital on the South Coast, near

Portsmouth. 'Right beside the sea,' she said delightedly as she dragged her suitcase down the stairs the following morning. 'Just think, I've never even seen the sea and now I'll be living right beside it! I'll be able to go swimming.'

'You'll have to break the ice first,' Steve commented. Snow had started to fall a day or two after Christmas and it was bitterly cold. The roads were at a standstill and trains were being held up by snowdrifts. Flo and Percy had had a flood when their pipes froze, and people were running out of coal because the trains couldn't get through, and when they did it was almost impossible for the horses to haul the coal trucks through the icy streets.

'Well, I won't be swimming in this weather, dope!' Thursday told him. 'In the summer, I meant.' She looked out of the window at the whirling flakes. 'I don't know what time the train's going to come. The timetables are all over the place. I'll probably catch last Wednesday's 10.45!'

'You don't think you ought to wait a bit? Till the weather eases off a bit?'

'Mum, I've been called up! It's the same as in the Services. I've got to go. It's not a Sunday-school outing.'

They can't wait to get away, neither of them, Mary thought sadly. They think it's a big adventure. And all Thursday is going to be doing is scrubbing floors and wiping people's bottoms, whatever she might think. Wasting all that apprenticeship at the tailor's which would have stood her in such good stead. And it's not as if she couldn't have done war work there, she could have been making uniforms. And as for Steve – she tried to close her mind against what might happen to Steve.

'There'll be only you at home soon,' she told Jenny when Thursday had gone upstairs to fetch a family photograph to squeeze into her suitcase. 'Thank goodness you're too young to get any ideas about going away.'

'I wish I could,' Jenny said. 'I wish I could join the Wrens or the WAAFs. It's not fair, having to stay at home while everyone else gets all the fun.'

'There's not much fun about war,' Mary said sadly. 'Not for mothers, anyway.'

Thursday came downstairs again, with Patch at her heels. She pulled on her tweed coat and blue beret, and then bent and ruffled

51

the dog's ears and laid her face against his rough head. 'Oh, Patchie, I'm going to miss you so much. I wish I could take you with me.'

And that puts us in our place, Mary thought wryly. Never mind her mother and father, or her brother and sister. It's that blessed dog she's going to miss! But as Thursday hugged her to say goodbye, she caught the glint of tears in her eyes and knew that, now that the moment had come, it was as hard for Thursday as it was for herself. For all her brave talk, the girl was shaking with nerves.

'Are you sure you don't want me to come to the station with you?' she asked, but Thursday shook her head.

'It's best to say goodbye here, Mum. I'll only make a fool of myself otherwise.' She held her mother tightly, feeling suddenly like a little girl again, and wishing desperately that she need not go. 'Goodbye, Mum,' she whispered. 'I'll write as soon as I arrive. And – and look after yourself, won't you? Write and let me know everything that happens.'

'I will.' They held each other for a moment longer and then Mary pushed her gently away. 'And whatever I've said about all this – about not wanting you to go and all that – just remember that me and your dad are proud of you. Really proud of you.' She took a deep, shivering breath. 'Go on, now. Go on.'

Thursday went out into the frozen street. She looked up at the morning sky, grey and heavy with yet more snow. She gave her mother one last look, and then turned away, hefting her suitcase to cross the road to the corner.

I don't know why I'm doing this, she thought suddenly. I didn't have to. I could have done what she wanted, and stayed on at the tailor's.

But she knew that she could not have done that. Her eagerness to be doing something special, to see new worlds and different people, to be of real use, would never have allowed to her to take the easy path. This was something she must do, and as she turned the corner and looked back to lift her arm in a last wave, she felt again that tremor of excitement, and knew that what she was doing was the right thing, the only thing.

Squaring her shoulders, she lifted her suitcase a little higher and began to walk into her own new world.

Chapter Five

'Just our luck,' the soldier next to Thursday said gloomily, 'to get caught in a flipping blizzard.'

The train had stopped yet again, out in the middle of nowhere. Thursday, who was next to the window, rubbed the glass with her glove and peered out but there was nothing to be seen but whirling snow, a wasteland of white stretching away for miles. She wondered what time it was and thought about eating the sandwiches Mum had packed for her lunch.

'Could be in the middle of flipping Siberia,' the soldier said. 'In fact, I wouldn't be surprised if we were. The driver hasn't got a flipping clue. I bet he's lost.'

'How can you get lost, driving a train? You have to go where the tracks go.'

'There's tracks go all over the place. If the points are frozen and the signalman can't change them, the train'll just go wherever the track went last time they were changed. We could be in Scotland by now.'

'We could be nearly to London,' Thursday said tartly. She was getting a bit tired of the soldier's gloom. 'We could be nearly there.'

The silence that met this optimistic remark was heavy with doubt. The rest of the passengers who were crammed into the crowded compartment sighed and stared ruefully out of the windows or glanced at each other and muttered resignedly about the weather and delays. It was bitterly cold in the carriage and everyone was wrapped in heavy coats, with thick woollen gloves and scarves. When Thursday had first got on, she'd been going to take off her tweed coat and woollen gloves, but it was so cold she'd kept them on, and now it seemed even colder. There were several soldiers, another girl about Thursday's age, a man with a beard and a couple of middle-aged women festooned with shopping bags. Most of the soldiers were smoking.

Thursday peered out again, hoping to see a sign of habitation somewhere, but there was not so much as a church spire to be seen through the scuttering flakes, only a white blanket thrown over empty fields with a blurred huddle of ermine-coated trees in the distance. Maybe he's right, she thought, and we've somehow reached Siberia. Or Scotland. Maybe we're not even on the tracks any more.

The train, which had stopped a quarter of an hour ago with a heavy sigh that seemed to echo the soldier's gloom, gave a sudden shudder and the engine let out a shriek. Everyone looked up hopefully, but after a moment of shaking and rattling, the train subsided once more and the passengers sighed in unison.

'I'm going to see what's up,' the soldier said with sudden decision. He got up and pushed across Thursday to open the door. 'I'm not stopping here to flipping well freeze to death.'

'Don't be daft,' one of the other soldiers said. 'You'll freeze all the quicker out there, and if the blinking train starts again you'll be left behind out in the middle of nowhere.'

'It'd be more sense if we all got out,' he retorted. 'We're buried in a flipping snowdrift, that's what it is, and if we all went and give a hand clearing it, we'll be able to get moving.' He got the door open and a blast of bitter air and snowflakes swept into the compartment, blowing away the smoke. 'I can see the engine,' he reported, leaning out perilously. 'There's blokes shovelling. Come on.'

He dropped into the snow, landing waist-deep, and began floundering along the track towards the engine. The other soldiers glanced at each other and then got up, muttering that they might as well do something as sit here, and one by one they dropped out of the carriage and followed their comrade. The bearded man and the middle-aged women stayed where they were. Thursday glanced at the other girl.

'I'd go too, if I was wearing trousers.'

'So would I.' The other girl was small and wrapped in a navy overcoat, with dark curly hair peeping out from a scarlet beret. 'But I'd probably disappear completely, it's so deep.'

The snow had been falling ever since they had left Worcester, whipped into a blizzard by a howling wind. There had already been a week of snowstorms, and the roads were almost impassable everywhere. Nobody knew how long the severe weather was likely to last.

'I don't see why they can't let us have weather forecasts,' one of the middle-aged women grumbled. 'The Germans must know what it's like. They're probably getting it too, even worse.'

'Wouldn't make any difference if we did,' her friend said caustically. 'They're never right anyway.'

The bearded man said nothing. The dark-haired girl looked at Thursday and grinned.

'Where are you going? I'm going to train as a nurse. Red Cross VAD.'

'So am I!' Thursday looked at her in delight. 'Maybe we're going to the same place.'

They looked at each other with sudden caution. Everyone had seen the posters warning people not to talk about the war in public places. WALLS HAVE EARS, they declaimed, and there was even a picture of a railway carriage just like this one, showing two people talking with a spy hiding in the luggage rack above them. Thursday glanced involuntarily upwards, and then they both looked at the bearded man who was staring out of the opposite window.

'It'll be good if we are,' the dark-haired girl said, and mouthed the word 'Portsmouth' at Thursday. Thursday nodded and mouthed back 'Haslar', and the dark girl nodded too, her brown eyes sparkling.

Thursday knew nothing about Haslar, other than that it was a naval hospital and that it was not in Portsmouth itself, but in Gosport, the town on the other side of the harbour. The train journey was a long one, with three changes before she would arrive at Portsmouth, where she would be met by a pinnace – whatever that was – to take her across the harbour. She smiled at the other girl, relieved to have company. Perhaps she would know what a pinnace was.

'I suppose we might as well eat our sandwiches,' she said, getting out the greaseproof paper bag. The other girl did the same and they munched companionably for a few minutes. 'What's your name? I'm Thursday Tilford.'

'Thursday?' the other girl said, opening her brown eyes wide. 'You mean like the day?'

'Yes.' Once again, Thursday explained the reason for her name. 'I've got so used to it, it doesn't seem out of the way to me, but everybody else thinks it's queer, of course. I suppose I could tell people to call me Rosemary, since no one's going to know any different, but I'd never remember to answer to it.'

'Oh, no, don't do that! It's nice. I wish I had an unusual name. Mine's Patricia but everyone calls me Patsy. Patsy Martin. I'm from Evesham.'

Thursday nodded. They must have been on the same train from Worcester but in different compartments, coming together only after the second change in their tortuous journey across the Cotswolds. She'd seen Patsy on the platform then.

One of the middle-aged women shifted the bags on her knees and said, 'Nurses, are you? My daughter was a nurse before she got married, in one of the big London hospitals. She's talking about going back to it.'

'We're not nurses yet,' Patsy said. 'And we're not going to be real ones – just VADs.'

'What's that, then?'

'Voluntary Aid Detachment,' Thursday said proudly. 'We'll just help.' She remembered the bearded man and stopped abruptly, then got up and craned out of the window to see what the soldiers were doing by the engine.

'They must have cleared some of the track by now. They've been shovelling like mad.'

'But the snowdrift might go for miles,' Patsy said. 'We could be here all night.'

Thursday shuddered. 'I hope not. We'll freeze to death. Oh – they're coming back.' She drew back as the soldiers clambered back into the compartment, stamping snow from their boots and shaking it from their khaki greatcoats. 'Have you managed to clear it?'

'Enough to move a bit further. We're just going into a cutting, see, and it's filled up with flipping snow. There was some blokes digging through from the other end. We're just coming into Guildford.'

'Guildford!' Thursday said in relief. 'That's our last change.' She looked at Patsy and then at the bearded man, wondering if even that was giving away too much.

The soldiers crammed themselves on to the seats again and several got out cigarettes and lit up. The compartment filled once again with smoke and after a few exploratory shudders the train finally gathered itself together and began to rumble along the track. They looked out and saw the white walls of snow, shovelled aside by the soldiers and some of the other passengers. The sky was still heavy with leaden clouds and the afternoon was already beginning to grow dark

Patsy had moved up next to Thursday. 'D'you know what a pinnace is?'

'A sort of boat, I suppose. It's to take us across the harbour.' She glanced at the man again, but he was at the other end of the opposite seat and the soldiers were talking too loudly for him to hear. 'Mind you, with this cold the harbour's probably frozen and we'll be able to walk across!'

Patsy giggled. 'I've heard people are skating on the Serpentine, and there's lots of ice on the river at Evesham.'

'There is at Worcester, too.' The Severn was too deep and fast-flowing to freeze over, but there were floes coming down like miniature icebergs. Thursday sighed and rubbed her hands together. 'I'm turning into an iceberg myself. I can't feel my toes at all.'

'You will, when we start to warm up,' Patsy told her. 'That's if we ever do get warm again.'

The scene outside had changed. Houses and other buildings could be seen, and in a few moments the train arrived in the station. Everyone got up stiffly and began to haul luggage down from the racks. The bearded man handed Thursday her suitcase. They'd be supplied with all the clothing they needed in their uniforms, and she had brought only personal possessions and a photograph or two of the family.

'There you are, my dear.' He spoke in a cultured voice, like someone on the wireless, and she felt ashamed of her suspicions. Not that that stopped him from being a spy, she reminded herself. She smiled at him anyway, just to give him the benefit of the doubt, and turned to climb down to the platform. Patsy was waiting, her own bags beside her.

'Got your gas mask?'

Thursday touched the brown cardboard box slung from her

shoulder. 'I've got so used to carrying it now, I'd feel naked without it. Where do we go next?'

Patsy nodded across the station. 'That platform over there, and we'd better look nippy, the train's waiting to go. D'you think he really was a spy?'

Thursday grinned and shook her head. 'I reckon he was a vicar! He had a lovely voice. I expect it was one of those women who was a spy. We didn't give away any secrets anyway. Those soldiers talked more than we did.'

They hurried across the station and scrambled aboard the next train, which was already huffing and puffing in readiness to go. The compartments were even more crowded than on the last one, and the girls were forced to sit on their suitcases in the corridor. The train lurched into motion and began to rumble slowly through the silent landscape. The whiteness of the snow gave a glow to the empty fields.

'Just let's hope we don't get stranded again,' Thursday prayed as she tried to keep her balance on the small case. 'I feel as if I've been on trains all my life, and home is just a dream. All I want is a steaming mug of tea and a nice comfortable bed.'

'A hot bath would be nice,' Patsy said wistfully. 'And a cuddly eiderdown. What d'you reckon the chances are?'

'Just about nil, I should think!' Thursday glanced along the crowded corridor. There were two soldiers, but most of the men and women with them now wore naval uniform. She felt a sudden twinge of excitement. These might be the very sailors and Wrens she would be working with at Haslar. Never mind steaming mugs of tea and hot baths – the war work she'd been longing to do was just about to begin!

Portsmouth Harbour station, when they finally reached it in the late afternoon, was the strangest railway station Thursday and Patsy had ever seen.

'It's practically out at sea!' Patsy exclaimed, staring down through the boarded decking to where the murky harbour water surged below. 'It must be built on stilts, like a pier. D'you think it's safe, with all these trains on top?'

'Well, it's been here quite a while. I reckon it would have fallen down by now, if it hadn't been.' Thursday lifted her suitcase and looked around. 'Where do you suppose the pinnace is going to be?'

'It would help if we knew what it was! There are some boats at the end of the platform, see? Perhaps it's one of them.'

The two girls trudged along the platform. An icy wind sliced through the station, bringing a whiff of salt and seaweed. Clouds hung low and yellow over the grey water and although the snow seemed to have stopped for the time being it was obvious that there was more to come. Outlined against the darkening sky, they could see the grey silhouette of a ship's prow, and beyond that a clutter of buildings on the opposite shore, dominated by a tall tower.

'I wonder what that is? It's not a church, surely.'

Thursday shrugged. 'I dare say we'll find out.' There were a few more people, mostly in naval uniform, making their way in the same direction. She glanced at a Wren walking beside her and said timidly, 'We're looking for something called a pinnace. D'you know what it is?'

The girl looked at her in surprise, as if not accustomed to being spoken to by a girl in a tweed coat and dark blue beret, carrying a suitcase. Perhaps I ought to have saluted, Thursday thought nervously.

'A pinnace? Yes, of course. It's a small naval launch. Why are you looking for one?'

'We're supposed to be reporting to Haslar Hospital.' Thursday gestured to Patsy. 'We're VADs. Only we've had terrible trouble on the trains and we got delayed. I'm afraid we might have missed the – the pinnace, and I don't know how else to get there.'

The Wren smiled. 'It's all right. I'm going there, too. Just follow me. The pinnace will be waiting at the pontoon.' She marched towards the station exit, smart in her navy uniform, and Thursday and Patsy fell in behind her, thankful to be almost at their journey's end.

'So it's a pontoon now,' Patsy whispered. 'It must be a railway platform where the trains come in and a pontoon where the boats tie up.'

They came out through the big doorways and down the icy steps. They seemed now to be on a wide bridge, with railings on the other side. There were crowds of people tramping through the frozen slush, some heading down the long slipway, others making for the town. Across the bridge was part of the harbour, with small boats rocking on the dark water, and beyond those they could see the great gateway of the dockyard, with the grey bulk of naval ships tied up alongside and mysterious buildings and towers inside the walls. A huge crowd of workmen was pouring out through the gate.

'That tower you can see is the Semaphore Tower,' the Wren told them as they stared. 'The whole harbour's controlled from there. The harbourmaster has his office up high so that he can see all that's going on. The gateway's called the Lion Gate. The dockyardmen are knocking off work – it's always busy then.'

'There's a ship inside,' Thursday said. 'Those masts and – what's it called? – rigging? What sort of ship's that?'

The Wren gave the masts a proud look. 'That's Nelson's ship, HMS *Victory*. You used to be able to go aboard it before the war, and they'd show you round. But no one's allowed in the dockyard now unless they've got an official reason to be there.'

She turned and joined the hurrying throng to stride down the slope towards the little jetty that floated at the bottom. The girls glanced at each other and followed her, lugging their cases. They seemed to have been dragging them about all day, Thursday thought. She had almost forgotten what was inside, but whatever it was it was a lot heavier than when she'd set out that morning.

'Gosh, what a crowd!' she exclaimed to Patsy. 'Where on earth are they all going?'

A man dressed in rough workmen's clothes heard her and grinned. 'We're going home, love, to Gosport. Where else d'you think we'd be going?'

'That's the town across the harbour, where Haslar is,' Patsy said. 'Didn't you look at the map?'

Thursday nodded, annoyed with herself. Of course she'd looked at the map before she'd left home, and seen that Gosport lay on the other side of the harbour, on a little peninsula surrounded by sea and inlets. Haslar itself seemed to be right on the beach, looking out across the Solent towards the Isle of Wight, with a long creek almost cutting it off from the town. Obviously people who lived in Gosport would need a ferry to take them to Portsmouth.

There were several boats fastened to the bollards on the floating pontoon. The dockyardmen were shoving aboard the largest, many of them pushing bikes which they piled on the bow. It didn't seem big enough for such a crowd, Thursday thought, watching in fascination, and wondered what it was like to go to work by boat every day. Nearly as good as working in Venice, she thought with a small giggle.

'Our boat's this way,' the Wren explained briefly, appearing again at their side. 'Come on – no time for staring.'

They turned away and found themselves looking down into a much smaller boat, already filled with sailors and Wrens. One of the sailors, who was obviously in charge, gave them an impatient look.

'Look lively, now. We ain't got all day. Mind how you come, now – we don't all want to end up in the drink. Blimey, ain't you never bin on a boat before?'

'Only a pleasure-boat on the river,' Thursday said, scrambling down from the pontoon. The two rocked on the waves, now together, now apart, and she almost fell into the bottom of the boat in her hurry to get aboard before the gap between them widened.

'Strike me pink, you ain't going to make much of a sailor.' The seaman grabbed her arm to steady her. 'Sit down quick, for Gawd's sake. Let's hope they don't never put Wrens in charge of ships.'

'They aren't going to be Wrens,' the girl who had guided them down from the station said sharply. 'They're going to be nurses.'

'Oh, that's all right, then. They can soothe my fevered brow any time.' The sailor went forward to the bow and quickly unwrapped the painter from the bollard, then returned to the helm. The engine changed its note and the boat began to back away from the pontoon and then turned to head off across the harbour.

Bitterly cold as it was, the journey was all too short. Thursday and Patsy, huddled together, stared about them at the busy scene. The light was fading rapidly now but Thursday could see that the harbour stretched far beyond the dockyard jetty to a dim, snow-covered hill beyond. As well as the ships tied to the nearest jetty in the harbour, there were others beyond – great grey battleships with fearsome prows crowded with long-barrelled guns, smaller ones with odd-looking contraptions on their decks. There were other boats too, ferries and tugs, bustling about, each intent on its own business. And when she turned her head to look in the other direction, she gasped.

The harbour mouth, flanked on both sides by solid round bastions that looked as if they'd stood there for hundreds of years, looked far too narrow to admit ships of the size that had obviously come through it. Yet, even as they watched, another ship entered between the fortress-like walls. Huge and grey, it nosed through the gap, almost filling it, and everything else in the harbour slowed to allow it to pass.

'Whatever is it?' Patsy gasped, staring up at the broad, flat deck which overhung the ship's sides. It loomed above them, oddly lopsided yet grimly intimidating.

'Aircraft carrier,' a sailor beside her said briefly. 'That's the *Ark Royal*, that is. Biggest ship in the Navy.'

The very name seemed awesome. The girls watched as it passed, a swelling wave surging away from its bow and lifting the little pinnace on its bosom. They slid down the other side and rocked a little, but the seaman at the wheel steered it expertly to avoid the worst of the motion.

'Nearly there now.' They turned again to find that they were heading away from the main harbour, into a creek filled with boats of all kinds, from naval launches to yachts and small sailing dinghies. On their left was the tall concrete tower they had noticed when they first arrived and they stared at it curiously.

'Water tower,' their mentor told them. 'And that place there, that's HMS *Dolphin*, where the subs are based.'

'Subs? You mean submarines? Is *that* a submarine?' Thursday gazed at the long, almost tubular shape berthed alongside the quay. Now that she looked, she could see a number of dark, sinister shapes beyond it. She shuddered. 'I'd hate to go down in one of them.'

The creek twisted round another bend and they found themselves alongside a further quay, with a few other launches tied up. The skipper brought the pinnace expertly alongside and another sailor jumped ashore with the painter and wrapped it quickly round a bollard. The passengers began to disembark.

'The hospital's straight on.' The Wren was beside them again. 'Where are you supposed to report?'

'To someone called Miss Makepeace. She's the Red Cross Commandant.'

The Wren nodded. 'Well, that's the gate. Go through there and ask someone. Good luck!' She turned away and disappeared into the dusk, and the girls watched her go, feeling suddenly bereft.

'Is that really the hospital?' Patsy whispered as they stared up at the imposing gateway. 'It looks much too grand!'

Timidly, they approached the long brick wall. Through the big iron gates they could see a magnificent red-brick building with tall, very evenly spaced windows and an arched colonnade. Beside the gateway stood two sailors with rifles.

'Who goes there?'

'It's us,' Patsy said, as if they ought to know. 'I mean – we're supposed to be reporting here. We're VADs.'

'VADs? Sounds like something nasty you catch in a foreign port.' The sailors grinned at each other, then stared at them suspiciously. 'Where are your papers?'

'Here.' Thursday lifted her chin defiantly and produced her letter. 'You won't be so cheeky when we're giving you injections!'

'Injections? Yeugh – can't stand needles.' The guard glanced at the papers, then nodded. 'All right – you can go in. Straight through the main building and turn to starboard. D Block's straight ahead. If you get lost, ask a matelot, they'll tell you.' They hesitated and he added impatiently, 'Well, what's the matter now? Cat got your tongue?'

'It's just – what's starboard? And who are the matelots?' Patsy asked, and the two men roared with laughter.

'A matelot's a sailor, ducks,' the other one told her. 'Like us, see, in square rig. *Uniform*,' he added when they looked blank again. '*This* uniform, with bell-bottoms – bell-bottomed trousers – and a round cap and a square collar, see? *We're* matelots. But don't go calling anyone in a suit with a peaked cap a matelot, will you? They're *ratings* – that's if they ain't got scrambled egg on their caps, and then they're officers.'

'And starboard's on the right,' the other added. 'Port – left, starboard – right. Got it?' He grinned. 'Blimey, you ain't half got a lot to learn.'

'I thought we'd come to learn about nursing,' Thursday said, lifting her suitcase again. 'I didn't know we had to learn about the Navy as well.'

'Well, you're *in* the Navy now, or as good as,' the guard told her. 'So you got to learn the lingo, see? And one of the first things you'd better learn is not to distract the guards, or you'll be doing jankers before you even get as far as the door. 'Op it!'

The girls looked at each other and grinned. Once more, they

picked up their cases and trudged along the straight, smoothly paved way beneath the arched colonnade. It was almost, Thursday thought, like being in the crypt she had once been allowed to go down under Worcester Cathedral. She felt a strong sense of history, of all the sailors who had come here in the past to be nursed, and a vision of all the sailors who would come here in the future.

'We're here,' she murmured, swept by sudden awe. 'We're actually *here*.'

Miss Makepeace was tall and thin, with a long, narrow face and brown hair pulled tightly back beneath her cap. She looked elegant and aristocratic, her belt pulled in around her narrow waist and her skirts swishing as she walked. Her back was very straight and her uniform looked as crisp as if it were freshly washed and ironed every morning. She had very bright brown eyes that seemed to see everything.

She was in her office when the two girls knocked on the door, as directed by the sailor – *matelot*, Patsy whispered with a nervous giggle. The office was large and cluttered, with maps and charts on the walls and a big square desk behind which Miss Makepeace sat. She regarded them with her bright brown eyes.

'You must be Tilford and Martin. The other girls have all arrived.'

'Our train was delayed. We kept getting stuck in snowdrifts.'

The thin face did not alter its expression. 'Naval time is five minutes *before* time. All naval establishments are treated as if they were sea-going ships, and being late by *even one minute* would mean that you missed your ship. That's the worst crime naval personnel can commit. You must always make sure you have allowed enough time for all contingencies.' She paused to allow her words to sink in, then gave them a smile which lit her face with sudden warmth. 'However, today the ship hasn't sailed without you and I'm very pleased to welcome you aboard. I hope you'll be happy here.'

The smile became more severe, and her voice deepened. 'But the most important thing is that you should be *useful*. This is a major naval hospital, with a fine history. Haslar has cared for wounded servicemen from every major battle fought since Trafalgar and we expect to care for more during this coming conflict. You and your comrades will be in the front line, looking after men who have been injured fighting for their country. Always remember that this is a very great privilege, and always remember that from girls in such a privileged position we expect the *very highest standards*.'

There was a silence. Thursday wanted to look at Patsy but didn't dare. The bright gaze held their eyes, and then the smile broke out again and she knew that she would follow this woman to the ends of the earth.

'You will call me Madam,' Miss Makepeace continued. 'I am the Red Cross Commandant here, and I have charge of over two hundred VADs. As you know, you're assistant nurses – the hospital is staffed by the Queen Alexandra Royal Naval Nursing Service, generally known as QARNNS – but you'll be kept very busy and you'll do real nursing. You'll be given training for this and I'll give you your lectures myself, assisted by naval doctors and qualified nurses – QARNNs. I'll also organise your duties and regulate your living conditions. If you have any problems, you may come to me at any time. I will support you and look after you, and in return I expect *complete loyalty*. Do you understand?'

The girls nodded. She'll get it, too, Thursday thought, fascinated. She's like Mr Churchill, she's only got to look at you and you'd do whatever she said.

'Which of you is which?' Madam asked.

'I'm Thursday Tilford, Madam, and this is Patsy Martin.'

Miss Makepeace looked at her. 'Thursday? Is that your real name, or a nickname?'

'It's my real name, Madam. I was born on Armistice Day and my parents wanted to commemorate it. It's my middle name, though – my first name's Rosemary. For Remembrance.'

'Very nice,' Madam said, 'but you'll be called by your surname when you're on duty.' She looked at Patsy. 'And you're Patricia, presumably?'

'Yes, Madam.' Patsy's voice was subdued, her nervous giggle silenced. She sounded close to tears. Miss Makepeace gave her a sharp glance.

'How long is it since you had any food or drink?'

'I can't remember. We had some sandwiches on the train—'

'You must have tea,' the commandant said decisively. 'We can deal with the details later. I'm speaking to all the new intake this evening, after supper. I'll get someone to take you to the mess now, and then you can go to your dormitory and unpack and have a rest. Supper will be at seven, and please don't be late.'

'Or it'll sail without us,' Patsy murmured as they followed her out of the office and, cheered by the prospect of tea and a rest, she gave Thursday a large wink.

The dormitory had about thirty narrow iron beds in it, in two long rows. Tall windows ran along one side but it was now completely dark and the blackout curtains were all in place. We'll have to wait till tomorrow to see if we've got a sea view, Thursday thought. She put down her case for a moment and surveyed the scene.

Each bed was covered with a counterpane, with a large, dark blue anchor embroidered down its centre. Just in case you forget you're in the Navy, she thought with a little grin. The beds themselves had plain black iron frames and the mattresses didn't look all that thick. And there were, of course, no eiderdowns. She hadn't really expected that there would be.

It was warm enough, however, with a big iron stove in the middle of the room, and some of the girls had already settled themselves around it on straight-backed chairs taken from beside the beds, and were drinking out of mugs which stood keeping hot on top of the stove. There was a large coal-scuttle nearby, so at least the Navy wasn't mean about keeping its nurses warm.

The dormitory seemed to be full of girls, all wearing a variety of civilian clothes and all doing more or less the same things – writing letters home, sorting out their possessions or just lying on top of the counterpanes. I suppose they're all new too, Thursday thought, or they'd be in uniform. Some were quiet and apparently overwhelmed by their new surroundings, others chattering and animated. Small groups were already forming as they got to know each other. They looked up as Thursday and Patsy came in and some of them smiled. One gave them a friendly wave.

'Put the wood in the hole, you're letting all the fug out. There's some cocoa over here if you want some.'

'Oh, yes, please!' The two girls dropped their bags and went eagerly towards the stove. 'We're freezing – we had an awful journey. One of the soldiers in the carriage said it was like Siberia, and it jolly well was, too!'

'Well, you're here now.' The girl made room for them beside her.

She was on the tubby side, with fair hair and very round china-blue eyes. 'My name's Elsie Jackson. You must be the last two – there are only two beds left. They're by mine, over there.' She nodded towards a bed with its counterpane already rumpled and a heap of possessions scattered over it. The two beds next to it were still neat and tidy. 'We get a locker each and we share the cupboards. Bit like being at boarding-school!'

Thursday nodded. She was used to sharing a bedroom with Jenny, but twenty-nine strangers was something different. I hope we'll all get on well together, she thought a little nervously, and caught the eye of another girl, sitting opposite. She was thin and sallow with mousy brown hair, and she looked away quickly when Thursday looked at her. Well, there was one that might be a problem, for a start.

Gratefully, she sipped the mug of cocoa Elsie had handed her. It was hot and rich and made a warming pathway down her middle. The cold that seemed to have got right through to her bones started to ebb a little, and she looked at Patsy and grinned.

'Well, here we are! And we've learned things already. What a pinnace is – and a matelot—'

'And which direction's starboard!' Patsy added. 'And in a minute we're going to find out something else, too. We're going to find out what Naval food's like! My Uncle Sam was in the Navy and he says it's lousy.'

'Let's hope he's wrong, then,' Elsie Jackson said, patting her stomach, and Thursday laughed. If anyone looked as though she'd be interested in the food, it was Elsie Jackson!

Suppertime was announced by the ringing of a bell. Still uncertain of their way about, the girls trooped out on to the landing where, to their relief, a nurse in the uniform of a QARNN was waiting. She gave them a brisk smile and led them down to the mess where they were to eat their meals.

'It doesn't seem too bad so far,' Thursday whispered to Patsy. 'I mean, she seems quite friendly, doesn't she. I thought nurses were all dragons.'

'That's Sisters. And Matrons,' Patsy whispered back. 'In any case, this is just the first evening. You wait till tomorrow, when we get on the wards. I bet it'll be different then!'

Tomorrow. By then, I'll have been away from home for a whole day and night, Thursday thought. She pictured what they'd be doing at home now – sitting round the table in the cosy living-room, having their own supper and listening to the news. She thought of her own chair, empty for the first time, and her eyes prickled.

I'll write to Mum as soon as we get back to the dormitory, she thought. I'll write and tell her everything.

It seemed insulting to say that Miss Makepeace looked like a horse, even a friendly one. It made her sound ugly, and she wasn't. Thursday crossed out the last three lines in her letter and tried to find another way of describing their commandant.

'What on earth are you finding to write about?' Patsy enquired. She was lying on her bed in the long dormitory, having scribbled no more than a postcard to send home. 'All we've done is arrive, unpack and have supper!'

Thursday glanced at her locker, with the photo of the family standing on the top. Most of the girls had put photographs on show. Patsy had a photo of a young soldier beside her family. She'd told them it was her boyfriend.

'They'll want to know about the journey and what it's like here, and all about Portsmouth—'

'We haven't seen anything *of* Portsmouth! All we did was walk down the pontoon and come over the harbour in that boat.'

'Well, that was interesting, wasn't it? All those ships, and the submarines. My dad and brother will like reading about them.'

'I don't think you ought to write about those things.' Elsie rolled over and looked serious. 'Someone might think you're a spy.'

Thursday stared at her. 'But no one else is going to read it!'

'I wouldn't be too sure about that. I bet letters from here are censored. It's a naval establishment, isn't it. You don't want to get into trouble.'

Thursday looked down at the letter. She had covered several sheets of paper with her untidy scrawl, describing the hours they had spent stuck in the blizzard, the strangeness of Portsmouth Harbour station, the journey across the harbour and, finally, their arrival at the hospital. She'd tried to make it interesting and funny so that the family would enjoy reading it. Now it looked as if her efforts were wasted.

'Just tell 'em you've arrived, it's snowing just as much as it is at home and the food's lousy,' Patsy advised. 'That's all I've said.'

'I'm not sure I'll even get away with that,' Thursday said gloomily. 'Even the wireless isn't allowed to say what the weather's like.'

'And it's probably unpatriotic to complain about the food,' Elsie observed. She seemed tired out and ready to go to sleep. She must have had an even longer journey than they'd had, Thursday thought, but when they went to supper they'd got separated and there hadn't been a chance to ask.

'It was funny, coming over by pinnace instead of the ordinary ferryboat,' Elsie said thoughtfully. 'I felt quite important!'

'Have you been here before, then?' Patsy enquired, and Elsie laughed.

'I should think so! I'm Pompey born and bred. Portsmouth,' she added, seeing their blank faces. 'I've lived here all my life, and I've got a granny in Gosport, so we've always been back and forwards across the ferry.'

'You had the shortest journey of any of us!' Thursday said, laughing. 'I thought you must have come hundreds of miles, you seem so tired.'

'Well, of course I'm tired,' Elsie retorted with a grin. 'We had a bit of a beano last night at home, to give me a send-off. Didn't get to bed till three this morning.'

'But why do you have to live in?' Patsy asked. 'Couldn't you go home every night if you live so near?'

'Well, they want us on hand, don't they? Anyway, I wanted to live in. I'm a mobile really, it's just that this is where I've been sent. Doesn't mean to say I'll stay here.'

'Why not?'

'Well, we can get sent anywhere – abroad, even. My auntie was a VAD in the last war and she went to Malta. She said it was gorgeous, always hot and sunny, and they spent all their time off swimming and sunbathing. I'm going to volunteer if I get the chance – anything to get away from this sod-awful winter.'

Thursday glanced at her in surprise. She wasn't used to hearing women swear so casually. Mr Robertson, at the tailor's shop, discouraged even the men from swearing, at least when the girls were present.

'You were pretty late, weren't you?' Elsie went on. 'I thought we were all supposed to report at two o'clock.'

'We were, but the train kept getting stuck in the snow. The soldiers had to dig it out. We didn't think we were going to get here at all.'

Elsie shuddered. 'Did you notice those huge icicles under the platform at the harbour station? They must be about fifteen feet long – it's like Cheddar caves down there. And there's ice all along the seawall.'

Neither Thursday nor Patsy knew what the seawall was, but they were too tired to ask more questions. Thursday gave up any idea of starting her letter again and folded the sheets away. She picked up her soap and towel and slid off the narrow iron bed.

'I'm going to wash and then get into bed. We're not going to get much rest tomorrow.'

'Not if Miss Makepeace's – Madam's – "little talk" is anything to go by,' Patsy agreed. 'I didn't take in half she said. Except that if we're seen standing still we'll be given something else to do. Still, I dare say she'll go over it all again in the morning.'

'We get our kit in the morning.' Thursday looked at the long room with its narrow beds, its plain washstands and the one long cupboard which they were all to share as a wardrobe. The only sign that it was part of a naval establishment were the blue anchor emblems in the centre of each counterpane. Perhaps tomorrow, with their nurses' uniforms and capes and other bits and pieces scattered about, it would look more like the Navy. Or perhaps, with naval discipline, you weren't allowed to scatter things about.

In the washroom, queueing with other girls for a turn at one of the basins and then scrubbing her teeth with Gibbs' toothpaste from its little round tin, she listened to the chatter and felt suddenly homesick. I wonder what they're doing at home now, she thought. Just finishing supper – something on toast, and a cup of cocoa. Dad's giving Patchie a bit of toast with some fish paste on it and Steve's reading his *Hotspur*. And Jenny's just realised there's a hole in her stocking and she's just got to darn it before she goes to bed.

It all seemed very far away. She wondered if they'd be thinking of her too, noticing the empty chair at the table and missing her. Mum would, and so would Dad. Steve and Jenny would be just pleased to have some extra space. Yet at the thought of them her eyes filled with tears and she felt a sudden painful ache in her throat.

'If you've finished, there's a few more of us would like to use the basin,' a voice said in her ear, and Thursday moved out of the way with a muttered apology. She made her way back to the dormitory, feeling lost and uncertain.

The other two girls were already in bed. Elsie was asleep again, and Patsy did no more than open one eye and mutter goodnight. Within a few minutes the last girl came in and put out the light.

They lay in the darkness, listening to the muffled sound of waves on the shore. Thursday heard sobbing from a distant corner, and a long, trembling sigh from the next bed. She reached out a hand and felt about until her fingers encountered Patsy's, and they held each other tightly.

'It'll be better in the morning,' she whispered. 'We'll all feel better in the morning.'

Chapter Six

'**H**aslar Hospital,' Miss Makepeace began, 'was opened in 1750. It was one of the first proper naval hospitals and the largest hospital in Europe at the time. Before that, sick and wounded sailors weren't treated in any proper way – they either died at sea or they were sent to local lodging houses or even ale-houses to recover. There was a sort of hospital in Gosport, at the end of what is now Whitworth Road – it was called the Fortune Hospital, and the area there is still called Forton. But it was a shambles, no more than a clutter of tumbledown shacks, and I doubt if anyone actually got better through the nursing they received there. Things are very different today.'

She paused and fixed her piercing eyes on the forty or so girls who sat before her, like children in a classroom. They gazed back, already held in thrall by her personality and by the history she was giving them of the proud hospital of which they were now a part. That's nearly two hundred years old, Thursday thought. Sailors have been coming here for nearly two hundred years to be nursed and treated and made better.

'Not all of them recovered, of course,' Miss Makepeace went on, as if reading her mind. 'There are many thousands of men buried here at Haslar. For one thing, it had been used for some time already as a common burial ground, and then when it became a naval hospital a great many of its patients were already beyond help when they arrived. It's been recorded that in the years of 1779 and 1780 over seventeen hundred men died and were buried here. Then there were the six hundred men, including their Admiral, who died when the *Royal George* capsized two years later. There were thousands of soldiers who came back from the battle of Corunna with Sir John

Moore and died of typhus – doubtless, you all learnt about that in your history lessons at school – and it's also said that over three and a half thousand were buried in the paddock ten years before that. There was a Turkish colony in Gosport, who were also buried here—'

'Is that why it's called Turktown?' Elsie broke in, and then as Miss Makepeace stopped talking and everyone turned to stare at her, she added in some confusion, 'Well, that's what we call it in Pompey, and I've always wondered why.'

'Of course, you live in Portsmouth, don't you, Jackson?' Miss Makepeace observed. 'Well, I dare say that is indeed the origin of the term. And now, if I may continue . . . '

Haslar Hospital had, it seemed, a chequered history. The girls discussed it as they came out of the classroom and into the big quadrangle.

'Imagine all those bodies, buried under our feet!' Patsy shuddered. 'I tried to add them up as she went along but I lost count at five and a half thousand, and she didn't even say how many thousands there were who came back from – where was it?'

'Corunna,' Thursday said solemnly. 'We learnt about it at school. Miss Makepeace said so.'

'Well, *you* might have done! I never listened much in history lessons, all those kings and queens having their heads cut off. It was nothing but dead people and now we've got them here, under our feet.' She looked down at the ground. 'They must be crammed together like sardines.'

'It's a nice place, though, isn't it?' Thursday looked around at the long, rectangular buildings on each side of the big square. 'Smart, I mean. It doesn't really look like a hospital at all. Not like the one in Worcester, anyway.'

'A lot of places round here look like this,' Elsie remarked. 'With those rectangular windows all separated into squares. It's called Georgian.'

'I suppose because one of the Georges was on the throne then. Let's have a look at the little church.'

They strolled across the quadrangle, only to be halted by a yell from a man standing at the edge. He waved his arms at them and they hesitated, then turned back the way they had come.

'No – come *here*! I want a word with you.'

'In trouble already,' Thursday murmured. 'Is he an officer, Patsy?'

'Must be, he's got a lot of gold on his cap.' Nervously, the girls approached and stopped a few yards away from the officer. He glowered at them.

'Don't you young girls know it's an offence to walk across the quad? Who are you, anyway?'

'We're VADs,' Patsy answered. 'We only arrived yesterday. We don't really know anything yet.'

'Hasn't your commandant given you any information at all?'

'Yes, sir, she told us about Haslar being built and how many dead bodies there are, and—'

'Don't be impertinent!' The officer had a full beard and moustache, and heavy brows that came right down over his eyes. He looked, Thursday thought suddenly, like a sheepdog, and she stifled a nervous giggle. His glance shifted to her at once.

'Something to say, gel?'

'No, sir,' Thursday answered hastily. 'Only – we're sorry, sir, we didn't know. We won't do it again.'

'Hmph.' He glared at them for a moment or two, then gave a small, impatient jerk of his head. 'Very well. On your way. Just remember in future, understand? And tell that commandant of yours to keep you in better order!'

'Yes, sir,' the girls chorused, knowing that they would never dare tell Miss Makepeace any such thing, and they turned and scuttled away.

'Whew!' Thursday said when they were out of earshot. 'I wonder who he is.'

'An admiral at least, I should think,' Patsy said. 'Did you see all that gold on his cap? Enough to keep me for six months! Where are we going? I thought we were going to look at the church.'

'We'll leave that for another day,' Thursday said. 'I'm not risking the quad again! Anyway, I want to see the sea. It must be this way.'

'We haven't got much time,' Elsie warned. 'We've got to be back in fifteen minutes.'

They walked quickly towards the wall which surrounded the hospital and found a gate. And beyond the gate was the sea.

'Oh!' Thursday exclaimed in delight. 'Oh, look at that!'

They stood still, looking at the sight before them. The hospital was built right to the edge of the shore, with a protective seawall sloping down into the sea from the road that ran outside the walls. It was outside the harbour itself and looked across at the city of Portsmouth in one direction and to the Isle of Wight in the other. The clouds of the day before had cleared away and snow lay everywhere, covering the buildings with shimmering ice. There was a fringe of ice all along the seawall.

'It's like fairyland,' Thursday said in awe. 'It's so pretty!'

'Is that a cathedral?' Patsy asked, looking at the dome that could be seen in the midst of the city buildings. 'I suppose Portsmouth must have a cathedral.'

'Course it does,' Elsie answered. 'It's a city, isn't it? That's the old part of Pompey you can see from here. It's a bit slummy but it's sort of interesting, too – quaint, you know.'

'Pompey?' Patsy queried. 'What's that? Is it part of Portsmouth?'

Elsie laughed. She had a loud, rather raucous laugh, but it wasn't intended to make Patsy feel silly. It was just Elsie's laugh. 'Pompey's *Portsmouth*! Didn't you know that? I thought everyone did. It's a sort of nickname. They use it for the football team, too – we've even got the Pompey Chimes on the Guildhall clock.' She chanted the notes of a chiming clock. ' "*Play up, Pompey! Pompey, play up!*" '

'I don't know anything about football,' Thursday said, 'but my dad does the pools and my brother's football mad.' She gazed across the harbour again. 'We'll have to go over there some time. Mum'll want to know about Portsmouth and so will Dad and Steve. They're always going on about the football team.'

'Best in the country,' Elsie said. 'Well, they must be, they won the FA Cup last May, didn't they? You can get to Portsmouth two ways,' she went on. 'Either the ordinary ferry that goes to where the station is, or the floating bridge. It works on chains – they pull it from one side to the other, and it takes cars, too. It goes to Old Portsmouth, so you end up miles from Commercial Road, but it's handy for getting to Southsea. That's Southsea, where the pier is. We used to go out there on Sundays on the bus, and go swimming. It's good – there's a boating lake and rock gardens, and a fair at Clarence Pier, see?'

'Fancy being able to go swimming in the sea whenever you want to,' Thursday said enviously. She looked down at the seawall. 'D'you think we could go swimming here in summer? Is it safe?'

Elsie shrugged. 'I think so. People do, but it's deep when the tide's up. It comes right up the wall, see, so it's deep straight away.'

'What are those big things out at sea?' Patsy asked. 'They look like forts.'

'They are. This part of the Solent's called Spithead, see, and those are the Spithead Forts. They were built about a hundred years ago when people thought France was going to invade us. There are forts all around here. You can see them up on the hill.'

'What hill?'

'Portsdown Hill. It's at the top of the harbour. You can see the forts on top of it, and there's lots more in Gosport. They've got moats round them.'

'Forts and moats all over the town,' Thursday said. 'Gosh, it sounds really interesting.'

Elsie stared at her. '*Gosport's* not interesting. There's nothing here at all. You want to see Pompey.' The girls turned and began to make their way back for Miss Makepeace's second lecture. 'Pompey's *much* better!'

The next lecture introduced them to naval routine and discipline. Although the VADs, being part of the Red Cross, were not strictly in the Navy, they were attached to it and subject to the same rules and regulations that ordered the sailors' lives. Some of them were quite incomprehensible.

'No cycling along the quarter-deck?' Thursday echoed in a whisper. 'What's the quarter-deck? I thought that was part of a ship.'

'Haslar Hospital *is* a ship,' Miss Makepeace said. She seemed to have ears that would hear the slightest whisper, as well as eyes that saw everything. 'To all intents and purposes, anyway. As I've already told you, all shore establishments are treated as if they were ships and the same regulations apply. They're given names like ships – for instance, we have HMS *Hornet* and HMS *Dolphin* next to us here at Haslar, and HMS *Vernon* over the water – and sometimes you'll hear them called "stone frigates". Then, when the men go to sea, they slip naturally into the routine. There's a good reason for everything in the Navy, you'll find.'

'Like not being late because the ship might sail without you,' Patsy said boldly.

Miss Makepeace nodded. 'But the ship *will* sail without you,' she corrected. 'There's no "might" about it. And don't forget there are good reasons for that, too. A harbour's a busy place, with a great many ships all carrying on their own business. And all subject to the tide. In a place like Portsmouth Harbour, with such a narrow entrance, only one ship can go in or out at a time. There are only certain states of the tide in which some of the larger ships can go through at all. You can see why every minute begins to count, and if we had half a dozen ships all waiting for personnel who were a few minutes late, there would very soon be chaos.'

The girls nodded. Put like that, it was easy to understand. And it wasn't fair for the sailors to have to obey those rules if the nurses were allowed to be lax. In any case, Thursday thought, patients were entitled to have their nursing treatment on time.

'And while we're on the subject of the patients,' Madam said, 'please remember that there's to be *no* fraternisation. That means no little romances. You're here to treat them, not flirt with them – even though the men themselves may think differently. A little bit of humour and a few pleasantries are perfectly acceptable to ease their burdens, but there are to be no assignations. That must be understood.'

The girls nodded, some a little ruefully. They'd all read stories in which hospitals were romantic places, with lots of opportunity for finding sweethearts.

'Shame!' Patsy whispered. 'I was looking forward to a bit of – what did she call it? – fraternising.'

At last the lecture was over and they were allowed to ask questions. Thursday put up her hand.

'I still don't understand what the quarter-deck is,' she said. 'And why we're not allowed to cycle along it. We haven't even got bikes!'

Miss Makepeace smiled. 'A lot of my girls do have their bicycles here. You'll soon find how useful they are for getting into Gosport and even over to Portsmouth. The quarter-deck on a ship is traditionally that part where the officers and rather superior passengers would take the air. Sailors would only be permitted there to carry out essential tasks or wait upon the officers. It's still treated with great respect – and on a shore establishment the same respect applies. The quarter-deck at Haslar is the long avenue which leads to the chapel. You may walk along it, but that's all. No matter *how* much of a hurry you may be in,' she added, fixing Patsy with a gimlet eye.

'I don't know why she looked at *me* when she said that,' Patsy complained afterwards as they went for lunch. 'Do I *look* the sort of person who's always late for things?'

Thursday glanced at her and grinned. There *was* something about Patsy, with her curly hair already escaping from its pins and her stockings wrinkled, that looked as if she might have dressed rather hastily. 'I expect it was just coincidence,' she said solemnly. 'I don't suppose she really meant to look at you at all.'

Patsy looked at her suspiciously. 'All right. I know I'm not the tidiest person in the world. Anyway, we're getting our uniforms this afternoon, so then we'll all look the same.'

The issuing of uniforms had been intended to take place that morning, after the medical, but there had been some hold-up in the stores and it had been rescheduled for the afternoon. Thursday was quite relieved. The medical itself had been quite bad enough, she thought, what with having to strip off in front of everyone else and being examined for nits just as if you were a kid at school. Auntie Maudie used to do that, she remembered, go round the schools and examine children's hair with a fine-toothed comb. The children hated it, and Auntie Maudie hadn't been too keen either and had always had a good wash as soon as she got home, in case she'd caught any herself.

Thursday had had them once, when she was about eight, and she remembered the horrible black shampoo her mother had had to use, stinking of tar, and the way she'd combed through Thursday's hair every morning, pouncing on the tiny creatures and cracking their minute eggs. It had made Thursday feel sick to think of things living in her hair, and the thought of it made her want to scratch her head even now.

Lunch was in the mess, a big canteen where the meals were served by a long line of cooks. The whole place had been run by sailors until the war started, but now Wrens were starting to take over some of their domestic duties, to free the men to go to sea. They dolloped heaps of mashed potatoes, tinned peas and minced beef on the plates held out to them, and the girls found a table and sat down to eat. There were other new girls, too, and they introduced themselves – Vera Hapgood, a thin, sallow-faced girl with mousy brown hair,

Jeanie Brown, pretty with a round, smiling face and light brown curls, Ellen Bridges, who was tall and bony but had nice eyes, and a rather aristocratic girl called Louisa Wetherby. In all, there were about forty new VADs.

'I'll be glad when we've got our uniforms,' Jeanie Brown said, tweaking her plaid skirt. She had a soft voice with a touch of a Scottish accent. 'We stand out like sore thumbs in civvies. I feel like a visitor!'

'They say we won't be allowed to wear our civvies at all then,' Vera said discontentedly. 'Not even to go out. I must say, I think that's going too far. It's not as if we're in the proper Navy or anything.'

'It's as bad as being back at school,' Louisa agreed. 'Impossible to sneak out at night to meet the boys because we didn't have anything to wear that didn't immediately shout out that we were from the Abbey!'

The others looked at her. 'Did you go to boarding-school, then?' Patsy asked.

'Mmm. In Malvern.' Louisa reached for the salt.

'That's near where I live!' Thursday exclaimed. 'I come from Worcester, and my auntie lives in Ledbury. We used to go to the Malvern Hills for picnics.'

'Oh, it's a nice enough place,' Louisa allowed. 'It's just that we were never let out without a bodyguard. Well, they *called* her a matron but she was more like a prison warder. I suppose it was because of all those boys' schools down the road – the whole place is seething with boarding-schools, girls' and boys'.'

'Is it really like the stories say?' Patsy asked curiously. 'Being at boarding-school, I mean? Midnight feasts and all that?'

Louisa laughed. 'If only it had been! We were kept on the run so much we were always too tired to think about midnight feasts. Lessons, sports, prep – it never stopped. I tell you, nursing won't be any worse than that – nothing could be.'

'Well, at least you probably had decent facilities,' Ellen Bridges remarked. 'Bathrooms and things. Our school didn't even have proper lavs. We had to go down the yard to a privy with an earth bucket.'

'Where do you come from, then?' Thursday asked. 'You sound as if you're from Devon.'

'Dorset,' Ellen corrected her. 'A little village near Bridport. I thought I might get sent to Plymouth, there's a naval hospital there – I was quite surprised when I was told to come to Haslar.'

The other two girls both came from London. Vera Hapgood was from Wandsworth and Jeanie Brown from Chalk Farm. Her parents were Scottish, she said, which was why she had a faint accent.

'There are lots of other VADs here,' Thursday remarked, looking round. There was a table near them full of girls in the grey dresses and white aprons of the Red Cross, with the cross itself stitched prominently to the bibs. They were laughing and chatting with animation, and looked relaxed and sure of themselves. Thursday wondered if she would ever feel so confident. 'I feel a bit like I did on my first day at school!'

'Having uniforms will help,' Louisa confirmed. 'And finding our way around. It's like going to boarding-school – you think you'll never know which way to go, but you soon learn.'

The others looked at her. None of them had been to boarding-school, but Louisa was clearly a 'posh' girl who lived in a big house and whose family had money. There were a number of VADs like her – Thursday had already noticed the accents of girls who came from similar backgrounds and would probably never have even been inside a two-up, two-down back-street house, or played out in the street. They were girls who didn't need to earn their living, girls who could have been officers in the women's services, but wanted to nurse and so had volunteered as poorly paid VADs.

'Taking jobs away from them that needs them,' Vera Hapgood whispered to Patsy, who was sitting next to her, but Patsy rounded on her.

'Doing jobs that need to be done, I'd say! They didn't *have* to volunteer, they just wanted to help, and they'll skivvy the same as the rest of us. I think it's good that they're not too proud to get their hands dirty.'

Vera looked down her nose and turned away. The other girls were chattering and nobody else noticed the exchange except Thursday, who was sitting on Patsy's other side. She raised her eyebrows at Patsy, and Patsy shrugged. There was bound to be one who was a cat, but what did it matter? There were plenty of other girls who looked nice.

Issued an hour or two later with their own grey dresses and white aprons, together with black lisle stockings, a navy petersham belt and sturdy black shoes, they began to feel almost like nurses. They giggled as they tried to put on their caps, setting them on each other's curls and regarding the results in a mirror.

'It looks like a water-lily,' Ellen Bridges said, turning her head this way and that as she looked in the mirror. 'I think it's quite smart, really.'

'I think it looks more like a mating hen!' Patsy said, with a giggle. 'Look at the back – it's like a lot of feather stuck up in the air! I just hope none of those male pigeons on the quad mistake me for a female.'

'You're disgusting,' Vera Hapgood told her. 'It's what comes from living in the country, I suppose. You see it going on all the time.'

'Go on, I bet you've seen dogs at it in the street! My auntie's bitch – *lady dog*, I suppose you'd call her,' she added, seeing Vera's shocked expression, 'got out once and half the dogs in the neighbourhood had a go before they managed to catch her. The puppies were lovely,' she added reminiscently. 'All fluffy. We reckoned it was the sheepdog from the farm that caught her. We found homes for all of them.'

'These shoes are a bit clumpy,' Elsie said, disregarding Patsy's stroll down memory lane. 'I like my high heels better. But the belt's nice, the way it pulls your waist in. You're lovely and slim,' she said enviously to Thursday. 'I wish I was slim like you.'

'You could be,' Vera said, 'if you didn't have so much mashed potato.'

Elsie ignored her. 'Anyway,' she said, 'I take after my mum, and my dad says men like a nice cuddly armful.'

Thursday reached into her bag and took out the little box containing the small watch Auntie Maudie had given her. She opened it and hesitated, feeling self-conscious about pinning it on. Elsie peered over her shoulder.

'Oh, isn't that smashing! Where d'you get it?'

'It was my auntie's. She's a registered nurse. D'you think I'll be allowed to wear it?' She held it up and some of the other girls crowded round to look as well.

Vera sniffed. 'I don't expect they'll let you. You know what Madam said about no jewellery.'

'It's a proper nurse's watch, isn't it?' Patsy said. 'I don't see why you shouldn't wear it.'

'Well, then, it'll be only Sisters who are allowed to wear that sort of thing,' Vera said, but Elsie turned on her.

'You're just being nasty, getting your own back about the *bitch*.' She emphasised the word deliberately. 'We'll ask Nurse Stanway. She'll tell us.'

Helen Stanway, the senior VAD who had brought them over to the clothing store, looked at Thursday's watch and nodded. 'Not many VADs do wear them, but there's no rule against it. So long as it keeps good time – a watch that gains or loses wouldn't be allowed. They're much better than wristwatches because you'll be forever putting your hands in water.' Elsie gave Vera a triumphant look, and Stanway turned away and clapped her hands for attention. 'Now that you're all ready, we're going on a tour of the hospital. You need to know all the wards, as there's no knowing where you'll be assigned at any time, and you also need to know where to go for supplies. Tomorrow you'll be on the wards. Remember that Haslar's a big hospital and there isn't time to go searching for girls who've got lost, so please pay attention.'

Outside, the clouds had begun to gather again and there were flurries of snow whipping like white sandstorms over the bleak expanse of the quadrangle. The girls wrapped their cloaks around them and scurried behind the older VAD. They stopped just outside the main entrance and looked in awe at the gracious buildings and grand façade.

'That is the coat of arms of George the Second,' Stanway said importantly. 'The lion and the unicorn. That's because it was in his reign that the hospital was built. That's why it looks as it does, because a lot of important buildings were built that way then. It was the fashion at the time.'

'See?' Elsie whispered. 'Georgian. Told you, didn't I?'

Helen led them at a brisk pace back through the entrance and they marched down the long, tree-lined avenue of the quarter-deck towards the chapel. It was just like a proper church, Thursday thought, and when she said so Stanway nodded.

'It *is* a church. It's dedicated to St Luke, because he's the patron saint of doctors.' She waved her hand around at the pews and the gallery with its organ. 'They have services every Sunday and during the week, and funerals when a patient dies. I think officers can get married here, too. You'll all be expected to attend divine service, of course, unless you're of some other denomination.' She led them back along the quarter-deck and under the arches again. 'We'll go down to the cellars next.'

'Ugh,' Patsy said. 'Do we have to? I don't like dark underground spaces.'

Stanway smiled. 'Well, you may be seeing quite a lot of these so you'll have to get over that, I'm afraid. But wait and see – you might be in for a surprise.'

The girls trooped down the steps, stopping to stare in amazement as Stanway opened the big doors and led them into the vast space beneath the hospital.

'But it's all done out like a hospital itself!' Thursday said at last.

Helen Stanway nodded. 'That's right. It's in case of air raids. If there's a red alert we'll be able to bring the patients down here, and quite a number of stretcher cases, too. The aim is to keep everyone safe.' She turned to lead them through into a further space. 'But this is the real showpiece. Do you know what this is?'

The girls stared around them. Like the rest of the cellars, the floor was of brick and the ceiling beamed with huge slabs of wood that stretched from wall to wall. Doorways led to other cellars, and beyond those could be seen even more doorways. But in the middle of the underground room in which they stood now was a long table, and at the sides were long counters and trolleys bearing sterilisers and other medical equipment.

'It's an operating theatre!' Thurdsay said. 'It's a bit like the one at the cottage hospital where my auntie works – only a lot bigger.'

'Haslar's a big hospital – we have to be ready for anything. Most hospitals just get in a few serious patients each day, unless there's a disaster of some kind – though that'll probably change when the air raids start. But Haslar is always ready for a disaster. Even in peacetime we always have to be on standby, in case a ship sinks, for instance, and we may get a sudden influx of patients with serious injuries. That's why before the war started, the hospital sometimes seemed quite empty – the beds were there for emergencies. But when there's a war on, the emergencies will be much more frequent. In fact, they'll probably become quite normal.'

She spoke quite unemotionally, but Thursday felt a shiver run down her spine at the words. She looked at the long table, and at the instruments and bottles ranged on shelves and in cupboards around the walls, and thought of operations taking place while aircraft thundered overhead, while an air raid raged all around. Would you hear the bombs dropping, down here under the ground? She thought of stretcher after stretcher of men being unloaded from ships – injured men, men with broken limbs, burns, bleeding wounds. She thought of the QARNNs, the male sick-berth attendants, the doctors and the VADs themselves, fighting to save the men while the men fought above their heads; while yet more men were injured.

The war was suddenly very real. And when she looked around at the faces of her fellow VADs, she could see that they felt it, too.

They came back up the stairs and Stanway showed them the smoothly paved way with its metal tracks that ran down the middle of the wide corridor.

'I noticed these before,' Patsy said. 'They're like a miniature railway.'

'They were for the carts that brought patients from the boats,' their guide informed them. 'Most of the them came from ships that were coming back from war and anchored off Spithead. They had to be transferred to the hospital ships first – those were old ships, anchored in the harbour – and then brought to Haslar by another boat. Then they were loaded on to carts, like little trams, and brought straight into the hospital.'

'I bet they were glad to get here, after all that,' Thursday remarked feelingly. 'All that being carried from one ship to another, and tossed about by the sea!'

'From what Miss Makepeace – Madam – said this morning, a lot of them didn't live long anyway,' Patsy agreed. 'Seems it was more like a funeral home than a hospital!'

Helen Stanway gave her a severe look and for the first time her unemotional guide's voice began to show real feeling. 'Haslar has always had a fine reputation. It was the first and biggest hospital of its kind and it's going to be even more valuable during this war. We're in the front line here at Portsmouth Harbour, and you're very lucky to have been sent here. What we do here is going to be something to be proud of.'

They stared at her, taken aback by the sudden passion in her

84

voice, and then Thursday said quietly, 'I think it will. And I'm proud to be here, for one. And I bet everyone else is, too.'

'That's right!', 'So am I!' and 'Three cheers for Haslar!' cried the other girls. 'Hip, hip, hooray! Hooray! Hooray!'

The corridor echoed to the sound of their cheering and heads popped out of side doors and wards to see what was going on. Miss Makepeace herself came striding around a corner, her brows lifted as she looked at the gathering in their brand-new uniforms and capes.

'Whatever's going on here?' She looked at the VAD. 'Stanway, have you any explanation for this extraordinary conduct?'

The senior girl blushed. 'I was just showing them round, Madam, and explaining what a fine hospital Haslar is, and how much it's going to do to help the war effort. And then they all just started to cheer.'

'I see.' The commandant's face was stern as she looked at the now silent girls, but Thursday was sure she could detect a twinkle somewhere deep in those bright brown eyes. 'Well, I'm pleased to see that you understand the value of our work here, and the privilege we've been given to be a part of it,' she told them severely. 'But please remember that this is a *hospital*. There are sick people here, people who need rest and quiet and care. People who do *not* want their afternoon's rest disturbed by what sounds like a football crowd applauding a goal. Is that understood?'

The girls nodded, subdued by her tone. 'Yes, Madam.'

'Good.' She looked them over for a moment and then her smile broke out, transforming her entire face. 'You may continue with your tour. I'll see you again after tea for another lecture, and then you'll be free for the rest of the evening. And tomorrow . . . ' She surveyed them again. 'Tomorrow, you'll be on the wards.'

On the wards! The girls looked at each other and made faces of excitement and apprehension. Then they turned and trooped after Helen Stanway for their first glimpse of those wards and the patients they would be helping to care for.

There was so much to learn in that first week.

Like the other VADs, Thursday had done a course in first aid when she had joined the Red Cross. But knowing how to give artificial respiration to a friend who was pretending to have drowned and bandaging portions of that same long-suffering friend that

85

weren't really bleeding were very different from dealing with the real thing. It hadn't prepared her at all for what she was to encounter on the wards of Haslar.

'Your job is to make the tasks of the nurses and SBAs easier,' Miss Makepeace told them. 'At this stage, that means the more mundane tasks – but always remember that these are *just as essential* as the more skilled ones. A patient who is desperate for a bedpan *feels* just as much in need as one who is waiting to have a dressing changed. Possibly more. And the cleanliness of the ward is a priority. Hygiene is all.'

'And what that boils down to is that we're skivvies,' Elsie muttered as they collected dusters and brushes from the cupboard. 'Catch them letting *us* change dressings.'

'VADs do, though. And when the SBAs go to sea . . . '

The SBAs were sick-berth attendants, the naval term for male nurses. There were a number at Haslar, but there was always the chance that they'd be sent to sea, and the VADs were more or less on standby for that event. Until that happened, they worked together but the SBAs had varying attitudes to the young civilians.

'You're in the Navy now. Brightwork means *bright*work. It's no good just giving them taps a bit of a wipe, you need to be able to see your face in them. Use a bit of elbow grease.'

'And don't let anyone send you to the stores for it,' Elsie advised with a grin. 'I knew someone who spent half an hour waiting for a tub and then got torn off a strip when they went back to the ward, just for being daft enough to believe it. The Navy's full of jokes like that – paint for the Last Post, that sort of thing.'

'It's the language I can't keep up with,' Patsy complained. 'I've managed to remember that the floor's always called the deck, and the kitchens are galleys, but I still forget to call the lavatories the "heads". Honestly, it's just like little boys playing games. I mean, I know a lot of it is so that when they go to sea they know all the proper names, but surely they can tell the difference between a building and a real ship. It wouldn't be that hard to remember the names. I don't see why they can't call the lavs "lavs" anyway,' she added. 'The world wouldn't come to an end just because they used the same words as the rest of us.'

They set to with their brooms and dusters in the never-ending task of keeping the wards clean. Thursday thought she had never seen a place which shone like Haslar. Every corner was swept daily, every floor scrubbed and every surface polished. She rubbed industriously at the wide window-sills, chatting to the patients as she did so.

'You're not going to polish me as well, are you?' a young rating asked, pretending to cringe away from her. 'I don't think I'm well enough for that.'

'If you're well enough to get out of bed, you're well enough to be clean,' Thursday told him. 'The only difference is you've got to do it yourself. We don't have time.'

Once they were up, the patients did a lot for themselves. As sailors still officially on duty, they were expected to help keep the wards clean and polished, and they took round food and drinks to fellow patients and help them wash and shave. But for the VADs, blanket baths loomed ahead and it was difficult to know who dreaded them most, the patients or the girls.

'Who d'you think Sister Burton will pick to use as a demonstration model?' Patsy asked as they ate fried bread and sausages for breakfast. They had been at Haslar for two weeks now and it felt like years. 'Hope it's that young leading hand in bed one, the one with the fair curly hair. I rather fancy seeing him in the altogether.'

'Patsy! We're not supposed to *fancy* the patients. You know what Madam said about no fraternisation. Anyway, he's got a girlfriend – I've seen her picture on his locker.'

Patsy winked. 'I wonder if she's seen as much of him as we're going to.'

'We're giving him a wash,' Thursday told her severely. 'That's all. Not asking him to marry us.'

Elsie giggled. 'By the time we've finished with him, he might *have* to marry us!'

'I'm not listening to this,' Thursday said. 'You're just wicked, the pair of you. I don't know what my mother would say if she knew what sort of girl I'm having to mix with these days.'

The three of them collapsed in giggles, but their hopes were doomed to disappointment. When they trooped into the ward for their lesson, they were led straight past bed one with its curly-haired occupant, and along the length of the ward to the far end. They glanced at each other and made rueful faces, then gathered round the bed.

'You have six minutes for each patient,' Sister Burton, the senior QARNN in the ward, told them. 'We expect you to take a little longer at first, but by the end of the week you ought to be up to speed. Now, gather round and watch while I bath Stoker Davis.'

Stoker Davis's bed had been surrounded by screens. His pyjamas were removed, revealing him to be a large, hairy man with a beer belly, although his lower half was covered modestly by a white towel with the usual naval anchor embroidered in one corner. He lay watching them through eyes almost hidden by a foliage of shaggy brows, his malicious grin similarly shrouded by a heavy grey moustache and beard. Thursday wondered why Burton couldn't have chosen one of the younger, better-looking patients as an example. Probably it was because he was so repulsive, she thought, and unlikely to excite anyone's feelings. Even his wife wouldn't be excited by this mass of blubber, she thought, looking with distaste at his hairy belly.

'Blimey,' Elsie murmured in her ear, 'if this don't put us off nothing will. And he knows this is our first time, the old bugger.'

The QARNN fixed her with a cold look. 'Did you say something, Jackson?'

'No, Sister,' Elsie said meekly. 'Only that I think this is going to be very interesting.'

Burton gave her another suspicious look and turned to the bowl of hot water which had been placed on the locker beside the bed. She dipped an old and rather grey flannel into the water and squeezed it out, then rubbed it with a lump of carbolic soap. She began to rub it briskly over the hairy bulk on the bed, explaining what she was doing.

'You might not think a patient could get dirty, lying in bed in a clean ward, but there's always dust in the air and where there's dust there are germs. Patients are in a vulnerable condition, open to infection, and must be protected from these germs. Hot water and good carbolic soap are our best weapons in this war.'

'That's right,' the stoker agreed. His voice sounded like coal being shovelled into a furnace. 'That's what we oughter do against the Jerries, chuck hot soapy water at 'em. They wouldn't wanter invade us then!'

The Sister gave him a look as cold as the one she had bestowed upon Elsie. 'I'll do the talking here, Stoker, if you don't mind. Lift up your arm. The armpits are a particularly important area,' she went on. 'Sweat gathers here, as it does in all the crevices, and can result in soreness and raw skin, where germs can easily enter. It's especially important to make sure these areas are perfectly dry.'

'Hey, there's no need to rub as hard as all that,' the patient protested. 'I'm as tender as a baby's bottom under there.'

'Bedsores are another thing to watch out for,' Burton continued, ignoring him. 'Patients who can't move much will get sores just from lying in one position all the time. That's why they must be turned as often as possible. Look out for these sores as you carry out the wash.' She beckoned to Thursday to help her turn him over. 'No, Tilford, not like that. Hold him this way, you see? Then you won't pinch his flesh. That's right. Now, ease him up carefully – you're not flipping a pancake. Now, slowly, carefully – and over he goes. Well done, Stoker.'

What about well done, Tilford? Thursday wondered. All he did was lie there. Then she looked at the body that lay before her and gasped.

The sailor's body was tattooed from shoulder to hip – and probably well beyond, she thought, wondering what lay under the strip of towel that covered his most intimate parts. Apart from his most intimate parts, of course. She gazed, marvelling, at the intricate patterns and knew from the stifled giggles she heard behind her that the other girls were as startled and impressed.

A serpent that would have frightened Eve herself wound its way around his shoulder-blades and down his spine, while on either side, perfectly symmetrical, crouched two lions, so lifelike that you could almost see their tails lashing. In between were various smaller tattoos of other creatures – hawks, dragons, scorpions – and spread across his buttocks, the body hidden in the cleft, she could see the wings of an enormous butterfly.

Sister Burton gave them all a few moments to recover from their shock and then spoke tartly.

'I don't know what you think you're all gaping at. I presume you've seen tattoos before?' She gave them a stare that dared them to laugh. 'Well, I can tell you, you'll certainly see a lot more before you've finished at Haslar. They're a great favourite with sailors, and these are especially fine ones, aren't they, Stoker?' The man on the bed gave a grunt, muffled by the pillow, and Sister Burton continued briskly, 'Now then – you, Jackson – there are no sores, thanks to our care, so you can wash his back. A brisk rub with the flannel, please, though of course you'd be much more gentle if there were any injuries. And now we'll turn him back again – so . . . ' Elsie heaved until the stoker lay once again on his decorative back. 'And that's all. I'll leave you to finish off,' she said to the man, and ushered the girls back through the screens. They looked at her questioningly, and she said, 'There are certain parts of a man's anatomy that it isn't suitable for female nurses to handle. Unless he's too ill to manage it himself, we leave that to him. If he can't manage, an SBA will deal with it. The men themselves prefer this.'

'Bet they don't,' Patsy muttered as they made their way to the next bed. 'Bet there's nothing they'd like better than a pretty young VAD handling their—'

'Patsy! Stop it!' Thursday bit her lip hard to keep a straight face. Burton walked ahead of them, straight-backed. She was a small woman, dark-haired, thin and wiry and, as they'd already found, surprisingly strong. She had dark eyes in a thin, humorous face, but when it came to blanket baths she made it quite clear that she'd heard all the jokes before and no longer found them funny. That was supposing she'd ever found them funny in the first place.

'Mind you, she must be thirty if she's a day,' Patsy had observed when they had been discussing this at breakfast. 'Past it, poor old soul.'

Thursday didn't think she was past it. She'd seen Sister Burton last night setting out for an evening off-duty, wearing a turquoise wool dress that showed her slender figure in quite a different light from the QARNNS uniform. Her hair had been twisted into a pleat instead of its usual severe bun, and her lips had been touched with bright red. She looked excited and happy, and quite unlike the brisk figure now expertly turning an injured torpedoman on to his other side.

'Torpedoman Smith has back injuries,' she explained. 'His dressings have to be changed three times a day and he must be bathed with extra care. He must be turned every hour. His whole body feels uncomfortable and tender, and we don't want to cause him any more pain or discomfort than we absolutely have to.' Her fingers moved gently over the maimed body and Thursday could see the tension in the wasting muscles dissolve under her touch. She could make him better just by doing that, she thought, and her respect grew.

They made their way round the whole ward and by the end of the morning each girl had carried out at least one blanket bath. Their early nervous giggles disappeared as they ministered to the injured men, and their embarrassment was forgotten. Their only worry was that they didn't think they would ever be able to do it at the required speed.

'Six minutes for each one!' Patsy said later as they walked across the quad. The snow had stopped at last and lay in deep drifts around the edges of the big square, swept into piles by the groundsmen. The clouds had peeled away and a pale winter sun lit the walls of the hospital with a russet glow. 'I'll never be able to do it in that time.'

'It's no wonder VADs run everywhere,' Thursday said. 'They've forgotten how to walk.' They went out through the gate and gazed out over Spithead. The tide was out and the seawall sloped away below them, a steep descent towards the narrow strip of shingle. The sunlight sparkled on dancing waves and the Spithead Forts, capped with a layer of snow, looked like iced cakes. A warship was steaming slowly past the Isle of Wight.

'I wonder where they're going,' Thursday said. 'And what will happen to them. Everyone's expecting Hitler to invade as soon as the weather's better.'

'They say it's been even worse in Europe,' Patsy said. 'Terrible storms, and snow up to the roofs. Some of the Russian soldiers have been frozen to death, and they just had to stop fighting in Norway. I had a letter from my boyfriend this morning, he says they haven't been able to dig trenches for weeks in Belgium.'

'Should he be saying that kind of thing?' Elsie asked. 'Don't their letters get censored?'

'Well, this bit was left in. I suppose they know we must've all noticed the snow and ice. It's the same everywhere. Tell you what, when the weather's better I'm going to get my mum to send my bike down. It can come on the train. Why don't you get yours too, Thursday? We'd be able to get round better – go into Gosport when we're off duty.'

'I haven't got a bike,' Thursday said. 'I could get one though, second-hand. There was one advertised on the notice-board in the mess, ten bob they wanted for it. Or I could go to that shop in the high street, Clarence Cory's, they've got a lot on show.'

'I'll bring mine over too,' Elsie said. She was able to go home for her half-days. 'I wouldn't mind going for a ride sometimes, along Lee or up to Hillhead. I could pop round and see Gran, too, when I've got an hour to spare.'

Their short break over, they turned away from the view and walked back to the buildings. Miss Makepeace was giving them another lecture, on bleeding and bandages, and they had learnt by now that 'Madam' expected every girl to be in her place well before the lecture was due to begin.

After all, as Patsy remarked as they hurried to hang up their cloaks, it wouldn't do for the lecture room to sail without them!

Chapter Seven

Steve's papers arrived on the same day as Thursday's first letter home. Mary looked at the two envelopes and put his up on the mantelpiece, her heart sinking. It would be a long wait until he came home to open it but at least there was Thursday's letter to take her mind off things. She opened it, smiling at the close-written pages.

'Sounds as if she's enjoying it all,' she told Walter when he arrived home that evening. 'Plenty to do, lots of company, and some nice girls. And the area sounds really interesting. It must be nice to be so near the sea. Lovely in summer.'

'Well, so long as she feels she's doing some good.' He sat down in his armchair and rested a moment before taking off his boots. 'Blimey, I'm worn out! The roads are just ice, and half the streets are blocked with snow. And we've started the change-over in the shop. Putting in all sorts of new contraptions.'

For over two hundred years, Royal Worcester Porcelain had been making beautiful objects in bone china – dinner services, figurines, lovely decorated bowls or china flowers – but now they were to make something different – something to do with the war, he said, but if he knew more he wasn't telling even Mary.

'And our Steve's call-up's arrived,' Mary said, indicating the brown envelope on the mantelpiece.

Walter looked at it. 'Well, we knew it'd come. I don't suppose they'll send him off straight away.'

'Oh, Walter,' she said, 'it's all come so sudden. Our Thursday gone, and now Steve . . . And we're not going to be able to keep our Jenny here much longer, you know. She's just itching to be off.'

'Well, there we do have a bit of say. She's not seventeen till next

December, and she can't join anything till then. And maybe by that time there'll be no need.'

'I wouldn't put it past her to try anyway,' Mary said. 'I'm not at all sure they check up on ages when these girls volunteer.'

'They still need their father's signature, and she'll not get that till the proper time.' Walter pushed his boots away from him and lay back in his chair. 'There wouldn't be a cup of tea going, would there?'

'Sorry. I was thinking about these letters. I did put the kettle on, it ought to be coming to the boil any minute.' A shrill whistling from the scullery announced that it was and she hurried out. 'I had a note from our Maudie this morning, too,' she called through. 'The postman had something to say, I can tell you, with all these letters. Anyway, I thought I might ask her over to tea on Sunday if the trains are running.'

'They won't be, if this weather keeps up. It was snowing again when I come in. It'll be Easter before you see your Maudie again at this rate.' He accepted the cup of tea that Mary brought through and took a grateful sip. 'That's better.' He looked up at the mantelpiece again. 'Where *is* our Steve, anyway? Surely he ought to be in by now.'

The back door opened at that moment and Steve stamped into the scullery. He shouted out cheerfully and they heard him take off his boots and coat and then pour himself a cup of tea. He came into the back room, his hair wet with melting snow, grinning.

'You'll never guess what—'

'Your papers have come,' Mary interrupted, unable to wait any longer. 'They've been here all day.' She handed him the envelope. 'Open it, for God's sake, Steve, and tell us the worst.'

Steve put down his cup and took the envelope, staring at it. He looked up at his mother.

'I was going to tell you—'

'Tell us in a minute. I want to know when you're going. I want to know where you'll be.'

'They won't tell us that.' Slowly, he slit open the envelope and drew out the sheet of paper. He read it quickly. 'Well, that's all right, then.'

'What is? What's it say?'

'I'm going in the Royal Worcesters. I'm to report to Norton

Barracks in three weeks' time. That gives me time to give in my notice at work. Mr Rogers has already said he'll keep my place for me.'

'I still think it's a pity you couldn't finish out your apprenticeship first,' Walter said. 'It wouldn't have made all that much difference, carrying on till December, and you'd have got your indentures then. It would've stood you in good stead, having a trade behind you. Probably made a difference to where they send you.'

'I'm more or less finished now,' Steve said. 'A few months won't make that much difference. I've still got the knowledge and experience, though I don't know what use an apprenticeship in chinaware will do me in the Army. I don't suppose I'll be making posh plates for brigadiers. Anyway, never mind that, what I was going to tell you was that I met our Leslie on the way home. And he was telling me he's volunteered for the RAF! What do you think of that?'

'*Leslie?* But he's not old enough – he's not seventeen till March.'

'No, but he's put his name down and he can join up then. He wants to learn to fly – be a pilot. And they like them young, say they learn faster.'

'And what's our Flo got to say about this?' Walter demanded. 'And her Perce? They won't be best pleased, I can tell you.'

'Leslie says it doesn't make any difference what they say. He's set on it. He says he'll never get another chance like this.'

'If Perce refuses to sign—' Walter began, but Steve interrupted him.

'He won't. What's the point? You know what Leslie's like, he's just as likely to forge his father's signature. If he's made up his mind to do something, he'll do it, no matter what.'

'But that's against the law! He could go to prison.' Mary stared at them aghast, but Steve shrugged.

'And who's going to report him? The authorities won't care, and Uncle Percy isn't going to get him sent to prison. I don't reckon there's a thing he can do about it.'

Walter stared at his son. Then his shoulders sagged and he turned away and stared into the fire. Mary took his cup and poured fresh tea into it and at last he spoke again.

'I tell you what. This war's started already. And it's not just fighting. It's what's happening in people's homes. Our Steve here, going off to be a soldier. Young Leslie, going against his father's wishes, set on getting his own way, and him still only sixteen. Our Thursday, left home. Kiddies sent away to live with strangers. It's breaking up homes, that's what it's doing, breaking up homes and families, and that's the worst thing that can happen. Because the country's *built* on families, and when they go, everything else goes, too.'

'But that's what we're fighting for,' Mary said. 'So that we can go on living the way we always have. So that families *can* stay together.'

Walter lifted his head and stared at her, and she saw the hollowness of his eyes, and behind them the dread and the knowledge that he had carried ever since his own days in the Army, when he had seen and experienced all those horrors he never talked about and had tried so hard to forget.

'Well, let's just hope the families are still there when all the fighting is over,' he said in a flat, dead voice. 'Let's just hope we can pull them all back together again. Them that are left.'

'You've done *what?*' Percy demanded. His face flushed and the veins on his neck stood out. He'd been filling his pipe when Leslie made his announcement and he held it in his hand, shreds of tobacco still trailing from the bowl.

'You heard.' Leslie spoke in his cheekiest voice, knowing it would enrage his father still more, but inside he was quaking. He felt almost amazed by what he had done, and was wondering how he'd had the nerve to go into the RAF recruiting office and sign his name. 'I've signed up for the RAF.'

'And there's no call for back-answering,' Percy snapped. 'You know very well what I meant. You had no right. And they won't take you anyway. You're only sixteen.'

'I'm old enough to register. I put down my name for when I'm seventeen. You can join then, and be trained as a pilot. It's what I want to do, Dad. You know I've always wanted to fly, and this is my chance. I don't want to get called up for the Army, like our Mike.'

'And that's another thing. What's this going to do to your mother? You know she worries about Mike, and if you go off too – flying *aeroplanes* – she'll never have a minute's peace. And you don't even know there'll *be* a war by the time you get to seventeen. It could be all over by then.'

'Won't matter then, will it?' Leslie said sullenly. 'And why shouldn't I do what I want, just because of Mike? *He's* doing what he wanted. You never stopped him going in the Territorials when he was my age.'

'That was different. There was no war then.'

'No, but you knew if there was he'd have to go. And you never said he couldn't go when it did break out—'

'I couldn't, could I? Territorials had to go—'

'And if I'd been one, so would I, soon as I got to the proper age. So what's the difference in signing up for the RAF?' Leslie stared at his father. 'Anyway, I've done it now, all legal, and you can't do a thing about it. It's the law.'

'And I'm your father. I could go down the office and say you did it without my authority.'

'It's King and country now,' Leslie said. 'That's what the authority is these days.'

Percy took a deep breath. His face was almost purple. He stepped forward and Leslie saw that his fists were balled. He backed away, but at that moment the door opened and Flo came in, with Denise close behind her She stared from one to the other.

'What in the name of goodness is going on here?'

Percy stepped back and uncurled his fists. He looked at his wife and shook his head. 'It's this boy. You'll never credit what he's been and gone and done.'

'What?' Flo turned to her son, her face pale. 'What have you done, Leslie? You've not got in trouble with the police, have you?'

''Course I haven't! It's nothing like that, Mum. I've just put my name down for the RAF, that's all. I haven't joined up – not yet. But I will, soon as they'll take me,' he added in a determined tone. 'I just wanted to make sure of it, that's all. I didn't want to find myself shoved into the Army or the Navy.'

'There's nothing wrong with the Army—' Percy began, but Flo interrupted him.

'Let's get this straight. Let's sit down and talk about it.' She sank into her armchair and after a moment Percy followed suit. Leslie and Denise sat on the upright chairs and looked at each other. There was a moment's silence.

'Right,' Flo said. 'Now tell me what this is all about, Leslie. You've signed up for the RAF, is that right?'

'Yes.'

'But you aren't actually joining? You're too young. I hope you haven't lied about your age,' she added sternly.

'No, I haven't. It's just a sort of waiting list. But I'm not waiting to be called up,' he added swiftly. 'They're not taking men till they're twenty and I'm not waiting that long. I'm going in soon as I'm old enough, as a regular.'

'A regular? And how old d'you have to be for that?'

'Seventeen,' he muttered, looking at the floor.

'*Seventeen!* But that's in March – it's only a few weeks away.' Flo stared at her son. 'You say it's not now, but you could be gone in six weeks' time! Oh, *Leslie*.' She covered her face with her hands.

Percy gave his son a look. Leslie stared at the floor again. Denise, looking bright-eyed from one to the other, spoke up.

'Well, I think it's smashing. Our Leslie, a pilot! You ought to be proud of him, Mum and Dad, that's what you ought to be. Not going on at him like he's committed a crime.'

'And you needn't stick your oar in,' Percy snapped, rounding on her. 'None of this concerns you.'

'It does. Leslie's my brother.' Denise faced her father defiantly. 'Anyway, it won't be all that long before I'm old enough to help the war effort too, and it's time you faced up to it. The war's going to be won by young people, like Mike and Leslie and me, and old people like you have got to realise it. I don't know what you've got against us all, anyway. Look at the way Auntie Mary went on when Thursday said she wanted to be a VAD. And Steve, volunteering. We've *got* to do our bit. You can't keep us tied to your apron-strings and let other people go and do the dirty work.'

'We know all that,' Percy retorted. 'We've been through one war already, just in case you've forgotten. We know what it's like. And we don't like the idea of kids like you and Leslie going through what we went through. What's so wrong with *that*?'

'I didn't say there was anything wrong with it. I just said you can't keep us in our prams. Anyway, what about you? Didn't you volunteer to go in the last war?'

Percy flushed again. He seldom spoke about the Great War, but Flo had told the children time and time again how he'd gone to the recruiting office the minute they'd opened in 1914 and signed up for the Army. And it wouldn't take a brilliant mathemetician to know that, having been born in 1898, he must have lied about his age to do so.

Fortunately, he and Flo had never told their children exactly how old they were. They'd married young, in the last year of the war, and he wasn't even sure that Flo had realised he must have lied.

'Well, there's no use arguing about it all,' he said gruffly. 'What's done's done, and I'm sure we don't want to stand in your light, any of you. But you've got to realise, you two, that all this is very hard on your mother. She thought she'd have you home a few more years yet, and here you are all going off, leaving home, and goodness knows what's going to happen to any of us. The world's upside down, and it's not easy.'

Denise was silent. She moved a little closer to her mother and laid her hand on Flo's arm.

'Don't worry, Mum. I dare say they'll take one look at our Les's ugly face and send him straight back anyway. Pilots are supposed to be good-looking. And you're still stuck with me for a while.'

'And that's supposed to make her feel better?' Leslie asked, risking a joke now that his father seemed to have backed down a bit. He glanced at his mother. 'I'm sorry, Mum, but I really do want to do this. And I didn't want any arguments – that's why I went to the office without saying anything first.'

'Well, you shouldn't have. You should have talked it over with us.' But Flo stretched her hand out to him and pulled him close. 'I'm proud of you all the same, son. Proud of you all. And if all the youngsters in the country are like you and Mike and our Denise – well, we'll show Hitler what he's up against, that's all.' She gave him a quick kiss and then straightened her shoulders. 'And I'd be obliged if someone would set their hand to laying the table now. Denise, you get the kettle on and, Leslie, you can go up the street and get some fish and chips. All I could get at the butcher's was hearts, and you know they need soaking overnight and then half the day in a casserole to get them tender.'

Denise and Leslie jumped to do as she told them and Flo looked across the fireplace at her husband. Percy had started to fill his pipe again, tamping down the tobacco as if it had done him an injury, and she reached her hand out and touched his arm.

'Don't be angry with him, Perce. He's doing what he thinks is right, and if he was a year or two older you'd be patting him on the back. They're children we can be proud of, all of them.'

'I know,' he said. 'It's just that – well, I know what war's like, Flo. I've seen it in the trenches. I never thought we'd be sending our own children off to that. I never did.'

They sat together gazing into the fire, troubled by their memories and their fears. But they knew that their part now was to support their children in whatever path fate might lead them. In a country at war, nobody had any other choice.

Chapter Eight

The girls were allocated to their wards almost at once. Apart from Miss Makepeace's lectures, the best training was on the job. In any case, Haslar wasn't a teaching hospital and there wasn't time for the doctors and QARNNs to conduct classes, even if they'd been able to.

'Not that we need much training to empty bedpans,' Thursday remarked, carrying a pile of big metal ovals out of the sluice room. 'Or to scrub floors. My dad was right, we're just skivvies.'

'We'll have more interesting things to do later, though,' Patsy said. 'I mean, I've heard that VADs are actually allowed to roll bandages sometimes. If they're very, very good.'

'Well, at least it won't be so smelly.' Thursday set off along her side of the ward, distributing pans as she went. Some of the men could sit on them unaided, some had to be helped, some needed to be held in position. It didn't matter what rank they were, when it came to basic functions all were equal. It didn't matter what their attitude was either. They were all patients and deserved equal care.

'Ouch! Do you have to be so bloody clumsy?' the tattooed stoker complained bitterly as Thursday slipped her arm under his shoulders to heave him on to the pan. 'You've got my skin all caught up. It bloody *hurts*.'

'Sorry. It's just that you're heavy—'

'That's the trouble with getting sodding girls to do the job,' he grumbled. 'Ain't got the muscle for it. Bloody daft idea, if you ask me.'

'Now then, Stoker, mind your language,' said a passing SBA. He came to give her a hand and between them they heaved him on to the bedpan where he sat looking like Humpty-Dumpty on his wall, only hairier. He glowered at them both.

'You'll have to mend your manners a bit now we've got ladies on the wards,' the SBA went on cheerfully. He had dark, curly hair and didn't look much older than Thursday. 'None of that effing and blinding you're used to on board.'

'Ladies!' the stoker said contemptuously. 'These ain't ladies! What lady'd want to do the jobs they're doing, eh? Wiping a lot of blokes' bottoms for 'em. Scrubbin' floors. Cleaning jobs. They'd never get proper ladies doing that kind of work.'

'Women do all sorts of work now,' Thursday said indignantly. 'And all sorts of women do it, too. Some of our VADs are real upper-crust.'

'Well, I ain't come across none of 'em.' He scowled ferociously. 'Don't distract me now. I got to concentrate.'

Thursday and the SBA grinned at each other and left him to it. Within a few minutes, the men were all enthroned and the VADs went to collect the bowls of warm, soapy water for their washes. By the time they came back some of the men were ready, while others were still wearing their looks of anxious concentration. She started to collect the pans and take them to the sluice for emptying and washing out, until finally the stoker was the only man left.

'I just don't seem to be able to manage it this morning.'

'I'll put you down for a dose of syrup of figs tonight,' Thursday said, reaching for the pan.

The sailor clung on to it. 'No, don't take it away yet! It'll only be a few more minutes. I don't want none of that jollop, it turns me bowels to water.'

'Well, that's the idea, isn't it. They're like rock at the moment. You'll have to go soon. It's three days now.'

'It comes from being a submariner,' he said. 'They don't encourage it on the boats.'

'That's rubbish and he knows it,' Sister Burton said when Thursday reported this conversation. 'Tell him it's syrup of figs tonight or an enema tomorrow, he can take his choice.'

'Just make it an enema anyway,' one of the other SBAs suggested. 'This lot haven't seen one yet. It's time they learnt how to give them.'

Patsy and Thursday gazed at him. Thursday wasn't even sure

what an enema was, but Elsie had told them that her grandmother had to have them to help her go. 'It's horrible,' she said. 'They stuff all this rubber tube up your bum and then pour soapy water down it, see, till you're all full up, and then it washes everything out. Gran sits on the lav all day Monday in the hopes that she won't need one. It's Tuesday the nurse comes round,' she added in explanation.

Thursday and Patsy looked at each other. 'Is she having us on?'

'I hope so,' Patsy said. 'I can't see any of this lot even letting us start to shove rubber tubes up them.'

'They don't have no choice,' Elsie said, in a tone of satisfaction. 'They have to let us do it.'

It sounded more like a punishment than a treatment, and from Elsie's tone Thursday suspected that it might even be used as one. She thought of the stoker receiving an enema, and couldn't picture him exhibiting the docility that must be required.

She had her opportunity to see next morning. True to the SBA's threat, the syrup of figs had been 'forgotten' that night, and when the bedpan round had been completed next morning the stoker had still not 'managed'. Sister decreed an enema and the new VADs were summoned to watch.

'He's going to hate this,' Patsy whispered as they all trooped down the ward, Thursday pushing the trolley with all the equipment laid out on it and Elsie pushing the screens. The rest of the patients watched with a mixture of apprehension and interest, which turned to relief on the faces of all but the stoker. He stared at them in dismay, which changed rapidly to fury.

'Here! Nobody never said I 'ad to 'ave one of them! I was supposed to 'ave syrup of figs. That's what they told me yesterday.' He fixed Thursday with a glowering eye. 'You heard that bloke, you heard him say so.'

'You said you didn't want syrup of figs,' the dark-haired SBA said innocently. 'Didn't he?'

Thursday nodded. 'He said it turned his bowels to water,' she confirmed.

'Well, they're going to be water anyway now, ain't they? Give it me now, I'll take it straight away. I'm not 'avin' yards of bleedin' 'osepipe stuffed up me arse. I'll put in a complaint, that's what I'll do. Take it away.'

'Sorry,' Sister said, reading the stoker's notes. 'You haven't had a movement for four days now, and that's too long. It'll be all the worse for you if we don't do something to clear you. You'll be getting a blockage, and that'll mean another operation.'

'Well, at least they gives you knock-out drops for that.' The stoker watched in growing alarm as the screens were pushed round his bed. 'Look, I'll take a double dose. I'll sit on the bleedin' bedpan all day. I'll do anything, only don't put that bloody tube in me. I hates it. I *hates* it, I tell you.'

'Everyone hates it,' the SBA said calmly. 'But it's only uncomfortable, it doesn't really hurt. Now, come on, Stoker Davis, don't be such a coward. Worse things happen at sea, you know.'

'No, they don't,' the stoker retorted. 'Nothing worse than this happens at sea, and I been there and I know.' With utmost reluctance, he allowed himself to be pushed back on to his pillows and then rolled to one side. He turned his head and squinted at the VADs, standing just inside the screens. 'Are these bleedin' girls going to watch?'

'They've got to learn, Stoker Davis.'

'Why 'ave they? You're not going to let *them* start doin' this? Bits of girls, rammin' 'osepipe up decent men's backsides? It ain't right.'

'And what's going to happen when all the SBAs are at sea? You'll give yourselves your own enemas, will you?'

'We won't 'ave bleedin' enemas! That'll be one thing that'll be against the law.' He cringed and yelped as the cold rubber touched his anus. 'Here, couldn't you 'ave warmed it up a bit first?'

Nobody answered. The girls watched, embarrassed but transfixed as the rubber tubing was pushed further and further into the man's back passage. Then the dark-haired SBA picked up the jug of soapy water.

Sister Burton nodded. 'All right, West. Ready to go. You can time this, Tilford,' she added to Thursday.

The SBA's dark eyes caught Thursday's and he gave her a solemn wink. She felt her lips twitch and folded them firmly together. She lifted her watch with one finger and watched its hands intently. The stoker moaned in anticipation.

The girls watched, fascinated, as half a gallon of water disappeared into the stoker's nether regions. There was a deep groan from the bed and then a howl of misery. The SBA took no notice, but picked up a second jug. Davis began to swear.

'That's enough of that!' Sister said sharply.

'And I've 'ad enough of that!' Davis shouted. 'Gorblimey, it'll be coming out me ears if you puts in any more. Stop it, for Gawd's sake.'

Sister nodded. The younger man stopped pouring and they waited for a moment. Then the stoker was heaved back into a sitting position and placed hastily over the bedpan.

'You'll need a bloody sight more than one,' he groaned, and Thursday couldn't help feeling sorry for him. He looked the picture of misery, crumpled over his full and aching belly. 'Oh, my Gawd, 'ere it comes . . .'

'Well,' SBA West said a little later, when he and Thursday were in the sluice with the bedpans and the draught from the open windows had blown away most of the stench, 'he won't refuse his syrup of figs next time.'

'Did you really have to pour all that water into him? *Two* jugs?'

He grinned. 'Well, we wanted to make sure of it, didn't we? Don't want to waste the surgeon's time with an operation. Sorry about his language, but you'll hear worse before you've finished here.'

'But what a baby he is,' Thursday said. 'What a coward. I mean, I know it's not very pleasant – well, I've never had one, thank goodness, but it does look horrible – but what's he going to be like in action if he's going to kick up a fuss like that about an enema?'

'Oh, he'll be all right in action. He's used to that.' West glanced at her. 'He was on the *Grenville*. They reckon he's been put in for a medal.'

'The *Grenville*? Wasn't that sunk a few weeks ago? Patsy Martin had a cousin on board her. They think he went down with the ship – she said the whole family were really cut up when they heard.'

He nodded. 'Eighty-odd blokes went down with her. In the North Sea. Davis managed to get out from the engine-room and into a lifeboat. He brought two other blokes with him. They reckon he nearly drowned getting them in the lifeboat.'

Thursday looked at him in silence for a moment. 'You mean he's a hero.'

'Pretty near. But there's a lot of heroes about in wartime. They'd run out of medals if they gave them to everyone who deserved them.' He finished sluicing out and turned away. 'Come on. Back to the ward. There's work to be done.'

Thursday followed him thoughtfully. She glanced down the ward to where Stoker Davis was now lying against his pillows, his colour returning as he sipped cocoa from a large mug. It was hard sometimes, when you were scurrying about with urine bottles or mugs of cocoa, to remember that most of these men had been injured through the war, that many of them – perhaps all of them – might be heroes. It was hard, when you looked at a man in pyjamas perched on a bedpan, to remember that he lived a tough and dangerous life outside.

Anyone who thought there was nothing happening in this war ought to come here, to Haslar, she thought, and see what had happened to these sailors. The burns, the broken bones, the injuries from explosion when some German missile had hit and perhaps sunk their ship. The man whose back had been almost stripped of flesh; the boy of no more than seventeen who had lost his right arm. The thirty-year-old who had been blinded and could only walk in a shuffle, and whose young wife couldn't bear to visit him.

'I don't mind if they swear,' she said to Patsy. 'They can say what they like. What's the use of fighting for freedom if you can't at least say what you like?'

The best way out of Haslar was across the narrow bridge, which led across Haslar Lake and into the town of Gosport. One afternoon, about a fortnight after they had arrived at Haslar, the three girls set off to explore. Most of the snow had now been swept away from the pavements, but there were still patches where it had hardened into ice. The piles at the side of the road were dirty and unattractive, and there was grey slush in the gutters.

'It's like being in a flipping fort itself,' Patsy remarked as they walked under the huge archway that led out through the ramparts. 'Look at this great high wall all round the hospital. It's like a prison. Is everything round here built like this? There's those Spithead Forts, too, and the ones you can see on top of the hill, and there's others all over Gosport – what were they all for?'

'They're queer, these forts,' Thursday agreed. 'I've never seen anything like them before.'

'They told us at school that they were built by Lord Palmerston when he was prime minister in Queen Victoria's reign,' Elsie said. 'They were supposed to defend us against the French, but they never invaded so they got called Palmerston's Follies and everyone laughed at him for wasting all that money on something that would never be needed. I don't reckon he was so far wrong, though – they're all being used now. It's just that this time it's the Germans who're going to invade us instead of the French.'

'Not *going* to,' Thursday corrected her. *'Trying* to. They're not going to succeed. They'd have to get past our lads first, over in France.'

Her cousin Mike was in France now. He'd had a few days' leave at Christmas, and now he'd gone back as part of the BEF. *More* initials, Thursday's grandmother had said disgustedly, and refused to call it anything else than the British Expeditionary Force, even though her false teeth were in danger of falling out when she struggled with the words.

Thursday's mother had written to tell her how upset Auntie Flo had been when Mike departed. There would be real fighting over there, as soon as the weather got a bit better, and meanwhile he must be living in a tent amidst all the snow and ice. Flo had always gone on about Mike's chest and never even liked him going camping with the Scouts as a boy, and on top of that she now had Leslie to worry about as well. She was sure he'd be called up to the RAF the minute he turned seventeen, and nobody had been able to persuade her that even if he had volunteered they would probably take the older boys first.

They walked down the road to the bridge and stared at it. There were actually two bridges – an older one which could have taken cars, and a narrower one which stretched steeply above it. The lower bridge was unusable, since the middle span had been removed.

'Blimey,' Elsie said, staring at it. 'No wonder it's called Pneumonia Bridge. You're halfway to heaven at the top of that.'

'Why have they taken away part of the lower bridge?' Thursday wondered. 'It looks perfectly all right. Did it get damaged somehow?'

'Must have done,' Patsy said. 'So now we've either got to climb up there like mountaineers or go miles round, unless we get the boat to Portsmouth. And there's a toll to pay, too!'

'Not for us,' Thursday reminded her. 'Hospital staff don't have to pay. I tell you what, we'd better get those bikes. Otherwise we're going to be stuck out here. It's like being on a desert island!'

They began the climb up the steep span of the bridge. It swayed with the bitter wind that scoured across the harbour and they wrapped their capes round them, forgetting that they had complained about not being allowed to wear civvy clothes outside. At the top, they paused and stared at the long creek that twisted from the harbour and inland to the village of Alverstoke, cutting Haslar off from the town.

'Why did they build the hospital in such a queer place?' Patsy asked. 'It seems daft, when it's so hard to get to. It must have been even worse when it was first built and there was no bridge at all.'

'Probably they didn't want the sailors to escape,' Thursday said. 'I expect that's why they built the wall so high, too. They were all pressed men in those days, weren't they?' She looked at Elsie for corroboration. 'And didn't Madam say most of the patients came by boat from ships out in the Solent? It was easy enough for them to get to.'

'That must be why it was built in Gosport,' Elsie remarked. 'Pompey would have wanted it on their side really, but Haslar was just as easy for them and meant they didn't have to use anywhere in the harbour.'

'You talk as if Gosport wasn't really entitled to have anything so important as a hospital,' Thursday teased her, and Elsie shrugged.

'Well, it's just a dead-end, isn't it. Nobody goes to Gosport, not unless they've got to. There's nothing much here, apart from all these forts and a few naval bases. Pompey's where everything is – the shops and the dance-halls, that sort of thing.'

'*You* come to Gosport. You know it quite well.' They started the descent down the other side of the bridge and waved at the toll-house keeper in his little house at the bottom.

'I come to see my gran. I wouldn't bother otherwise. Most of the people I know at home have never been to Gosport at all, or only come over on the ferry for the ride and just walked up the high street. That's enough to show there's nothing here!'

They left the bridge behind them and walked along the causeway and past the tall red tower of Trinity Church and down to the Hard. From here, they could see the city of Portsmouth across the harbour, the ships at the jetties and the stubby little ferry-boats bustling to and fro from the wooden floating pontoon.

'Shall we go over?' Elsie suggested, with longing in her voice, but the other two shook their heads.

'There isn't time. It'll be dark by half past four. Let's walk up the high street and see what's there.'

'I can tell you that,' Elsie said disparagingly. 'Nothing.'

They turned and walked past the pub at the end of the high street. 'The Isle of Wight Hoy,' Thursday remarked. 'Funny name. It's like being in a different country – sea and forts and queer names. And look, there's a Woolworths. And a Littlewoods. We can get most of what we need there. It's not that bad, Elsie.'

'It's just not Pompey,' Patsy said teasingly. 'I tell you what, there's only one thing wrong with this place and that's not enough men! I thought there'd be plenty of sailors in a place like Haslar Hospital, but they're either doctors that won't look twice at common little VADs, or else they're patients and too sick to bother.'

'There's plenty of sailors around Pompey, and Gosport too,' Elsie said, 'but I don't know as I'd go out with one. They've got a reputation, you know – girl in every port, that sort of thing. You couldn't ever depend on one staying faithful.'

'I'm not bothered about them being faithful,' Patsy said. 'I've got a boyfriend anyway – my Jeff. But we're not serious. I don't want to be serious about anyone yet. I just want someone to have some fun with. Go to dances and the pictures and things like that. But with the ones we've got, the minute they're fit to take a girl out they're sent away again. And we're not supposed to get friendly with them anyway.' She shivered. 'I tell you what, I wouldn't mind a cup of tea. Is there anywhere we can get something that's not hospital food?'

'There's the Swiss Café,' Elsie admitted. 'I've been in there once or twice with Gran. It's not bad. Or there's the Dive – that's a sort of cellar under the Market House, over the road from the Isle of Wight Hoy. It looks all right but I've never been in it – not the sort of place Gran would go!'

They walked a little further, past an assortment of small shops – a grocer's, a bookshop, a sweetshop – and then came to the Swiss Café. It looked warm and friendly and they went inside and looked around with interest.

There were only half a dozen tables inside, and one was already occupied by three naval ratings. The girls sat down at another, pulling off their gloves and rubbing their cold fingers together. A middle-aged waitress came to serve them and when they had ordered tea and toast Thursday looked around and caught the eye of one of the young men at the table in the window. It was the dark-haired SBA.

'Hullo,' he said, staring at her. 'You're from the hospital.'

'That's right,' Thursday said, remembering that his name was West but feeling awkward about using it. She couldn't just call him by his surname but she didn't really feel that using the initials SBA sounded right, outside the hospital.

'We did that enema on Stoker Davis together.'

'Well, I didn't, I just watched. You gave it to him.'

He grinned. 'And he didn't like it much, did he?' He indicated his two companions. 'Doug Brighton and Roy Greenaway, and my name's Tony. The Three Musketeers, we are. Doug and Roy are from different wards but you'll see 'em loafing about. These are some of our new slaves,' he told the other two sailors.

The girls looked at them assessingly. Patsy's complaint about the lack of men had been heartfelt, but here were chaps they'd been actually working with yet had never seen as possible boyfriends. Maybe we just haven't been looking properly, Thursday thought. And it wasn't as if they were bad-looking. The one called Tony had nice dark brown eyes – she'd already noticed those, while they were giving Stoker Davis his enema – and curly brown hair, while Roy Greenaway had auburn hair and blue eyes and Doug Brighton reminded her of the film star Gregory Peck. He looked as if he knew it too, as his eyes moved slowly over each girl as if deciding which – if any of them – would be suitable as a girlfriend.

'So what are your names, then?' he asked, and his voice sounded smooth and silky, but more as if he'd practised sounding like that than as if it came naturally.

'I'm Elsie Jackson,' Elsie told him, preening a little. 'I come from Pompey, but I'm living in at Haslar because I'm mobile.' She grinned at Doug Brighton. 'I nearly went mad when I found I was coming all the way to Gosport! Hope they'll send me somewhere a bit more exciting when my training's finished.' She didn't seem to think there was anything wrong with his manner, Thursday thought. Perhaps it's just me.

'And I'm Patsy Martin. I'm from Evesham, in Worcestershire.'

They all looked at Thursday. 'And how about you?' Doug asked after a moment. 'Haven't you got a name?'

'Of course I have,' she answered, irritated. 'It's Thursday – Thursday Tilford.' She met his eyes, knowing he would comment. Nobody ever heard her name without at least looking surprised.

'*Thursday?*' he repeated, as she'd known he would. 'You're kidding!'

'I told you, it's Thursday.' She heard the edge in her voice and saw the other girls glance at her in surprise. 'Not Monday, Tuesday, Wednesday or Friday – *Thursday*. What's so odd about that?'

He raised one eyebrow. Again, it looked as if he'd practised it and Thursday felt even more irritated. He's nothing but a show-off, she thought, thinks he's God's gift to women.

'Well, you've got to admit it's unusual.'

'Oh, yes,' she agreed, 'I admit that. But there's nothing wrong with being unusual, is there? Or perhaps you think everyone should be just ordinary – like you.' She turned her eyes away from him and spoke to Tony. 'I suppose you'll all be sent to sea soon. Once the VADs are trained.'

'That's the general idea. That's where we're needed.' Tony West flexed his muscles. 'Can't wait to see some action!'

'Even after you've seen what happens?' Thursday asked, thinking of the burns, the injuries, the missing limbs and blindness. So far, Haslar's patients had come mostly from ships like the *Grenville*, damaged at sea, and the new VADs hadn't seen the worst cases, but she knew that some of the patients they had seen were recovering from serious injuries.

'All the more. That's what we're for, isn't it – to see the enemy off. Don't want 'em marching up Gosport high street and taking over the Swiss Café, do we!' He grinned and the others laughed.

'They couldn't,' Patsy said with a grin. 'The Swiss are neutral.'

'You mean they could take over everything else but this place'd have a sort of special dispensation to stay the same? We could all come in here and have tea and toast just as if we weren't under Hitler's jackboot?' The three young men laughed. 'And the Jerries'd have to stand outside with their noses pressed against the glass, wishing they could come in, too.'

'No, they'd be allowed in as well. That's what neutral means, you're friends with everyone.'

'I don't think the Swiss are friends with everyone,' West said. 'They might be neutral but they're all trained, and they've all got guns. They're not going to fight in someone else's war, but they won't let anyone take them over.'

'That's just being cowards,' Roy Greenaway said. 'They're not true friends at all. *We* are – we joined in to defend little countries like Czechoslovakia and Poland, not ourselves. Switzerland'd come in quick enough if they were being threatened, and then they'd expect everyone else to fight for them as well.'

'Like the Yanks,' Doug Brighton nodded. 'They're keeping well out of it, but I bet if they got attacked they'd jump in all right. Be different then.'

Thursday said nothing. She half agreed with the boys, but felt dimly that there must be more to it than that, and she didn't really take to Doug Brighton. He was just too good-looking, and knew it. As she studied him, he turned his eyes on her and she blushed and looked away quickly, but not before she'd seen a faint grin on the chiselled lips.

The tea and toast arrived and the girls sorted out the cups and saucers and poured their tea. The toast was hot and although the 'butter' was really margarine, it warmed them after their cold walk. They went on talking to the three SBAs and learnt a bit more about the town.

'The quickest way back's through Bemister's Lane. It takes you more or less straight to Pneumonia Bridge.'

'How did the other bridge get damaged?' Thursday asked. 'It must have been much more useful to be able to get cars and trucks and things across to Haslar that way. Why didn't they repair it instead of building that little footbridge over the top?'

'They knocked it down deliberately,' Tony West told her. 'So that they could get bigger vessels in and out of Gun Boat Yard. It's a big creek, Haslar Lake, there's all kinds of stuff up there. And then there's *Dolphin*, of course – you've seen the submarines?'

Thursday nodded. She felt that she could spend hours just wandering the waterfronts and hards of the little town, staring at the unfamiliar sight of ships and boats. There was so much going on – ferries and tugs bustling about, the white paddle-steamers churning their way to the Island, the grey bulk of the naval ships looming through the narrow harbour entrance. And across the water, in

Portsmouth, the jetties and buildings of the dockyard and the black-rigged masts of HMS *Victory* as a symbol of Britain's greatness at sea.

And the everlasting fascination of the sea itself. It was always different – grey and ominous, as it had been when they arrived, blue and sparkling as on the first morning when they'd looked over from the seawall at the Solent and the gleaming dome of Portsmouth Cathedral, with the tree-covered Island like a fairyland across the channel. The tides, washing in and out, so that when you looked out in the morning it was high and deep against the slope of the seawall, and a few hours later barely reaching the beach at its feet. The creeks, winding mysteriously through the town so that you could walk down a narrow street a mile inland and find yourself on yet another shingly beach, with the tide washing the end of people's back gardens.

Thursday thought she had never been in such an interesting place, a place that could change with the weather, even with the time of day. She wanted to explore it, to get to know it, and she made up her mind that this was what she'd spend her off-duty time doing.

'I tell you what,' she said, unconsciously copying Patsy, 'I'm going to see about buying that bike the minute we get back to the hospital.'

They walked back together through the lane that led from the high street to Walpole Park. It was so narrow that they could only walk in pairs, and Thursday, walking behind the others, found Doug Brighton beside her.

'I'm glad we met you in the café,' he told her. 'I've seen you around the hospital. You're pretty.'

'Thanks,' Thursday said a little shortly. She glanced up at him and saw that he was smiling down at her. Perhaps he was waiting for her to say how good-looking he was. Well, he can wait on, she thought irritably. He doesn't need telling anyway, he knows it already.

'Maybe we could slip away from the others,' he murmured, sliding his hand round her waist. 'Get to know each other a bit better, hmm?'

'No, thank you,' Thursday said, even more tersely, and shrugged his arm off. 'I think you may have got the wrong idea about me.'

'Hoity-toity!' he said, and moved away. 'Well, you won't get another chance. I don't ask a girl twice.'

'Good,' she said, and watched him step forward to walk beside Elsie. Tony, who had been beside her, glanced over his shoulder and dropped back. He gave her a wink.

'Doug hasn't been bothering you, has he? You don't want to take any notice of him. He's all right really.'

'I'll take your word for it. He's just not my type.'

Tony looked as if he were about to ask what her type was, but at the look on her face he seemed to think better of it. A few moments later, they emerged from the lane and crossed South Street to find themselves by the boating pool. There were a few small rowing-boats and canoes tied up at the far end and Tony told Thursday that you could hire one for sixpence an hour.

'The other part's for model yacht racing. It's quite famous – supposed to be one of the best in the country. They have regattas here. And just over there's the swimming baths – salt water, of course, they get it from the moat.'

'*Another* moat? Right in the middle of the town?'

'Oh, yes,' he said, grinning, 'there are moats all over Gosport. All the forts have got one. People here don't think they're anything unusual.'

They passed the tall red church tower and climbed the steep span of Pneumonia Bridge. Once again, as they reached the top, Thursday huddled her cape more closely around her. The wind whipped her skirt around her legs and threw tiny spikes of ice against her face. She hurried along, her head down, and skittered after Tony down the narrow, slippery slope, looking forward now to being back in the warm hospital. The other two couples scurried along beside her and the six of them dashed along the road, past the high wall and through the gate, past the sentry. Once inside the sheltering walls, they slowed down, laughing, and the three ratings walked to the door of D Block with the girls.

'Let's do that again,' Tony said to Thursday. 'Not the last bit, I don't mean – but let's go out and have a cuppa some time when we're off duty. And maybe we could go for a walk, or a bike ride. Didn't I hear you say you were getting one?'

Thursday nodded. 'We're all going to. Perhaps when the

weather's better we could go on rides and picnics and things. I want to see more of the seashore.'

'We could go swimming in the summer,' he said, and she nodded again.

They stood for a moment looking at each other. Then Patsy called from the doorway and Thursday turned away, feeling her heart skip a little.

Since she'd parted from Sidney, she'd hardly been out with a boy again. There hadn't really been time, and she had been too taken up with her new life as a VAD. But now, with two girls as friends and three chaps for them to go around with in a group, it was nice to think that there might be someone special for her.

Could Tony be special? She thought of the two of them, heaving the big, hairy stoker about on his bed, giving him enemas and wiping his bottom, and giggled. It wasn't exactly romantic. But that didn't mean romance couldn't blossom away from the ward.

'He's nice, isn't he?' Patsy said as they made their way to their dormitory, and Thursday nodded.

'Mind you, I've never gone so much for the dark ones, but my last boyfriend had fair hair so maybe it's time for a change.'

Patsy looked at her in surprise. 'Dark hair? I was talking about the red-headed one – Roy Greenaway. I thought he was smashing.'

'And *I* quite fancied the good-looking one – Doug,' Elsie said, grinning. 'So that's one each! Things are looking up, girls.'

Laughing and pushing each other, they ran down the corridor to the dormitory. Madam would have a fit if she could see us now, Thursday thought with a giggle. But life had been difficult and serious enough in the past few weeks. It was time they started having fun.

Chapter Nine

The weather began to improve at last and the roads were cleared of their covering of ice. Patsy's bike arrived and Thursday had bought the one that was for sale. Elsie brought hers back from a visit home, so they were now able to go further on their afternoons off and one Saturday afternoon the six of them cycled out through the big gateway, feeling as if they'd been set free. They rode all the way along the road that ran along the top of the seawall to Gilkicker and past the big red-brick fort that had been built almost on the beach.

It was the first time they'd all been out together since the day they'd met in the Swiss Café. It wasn't often that their time off coincided and Thursday and Tony had only seen each other on the ward, but Patsy had been to the pictures with Roy Greenaway a couple of times and Elsie had been to the Forum cinema in Gosport with Doug Brighton, and told Thursday it was like sitting next to an octopus. 'You never know where his hands are going to be next!' she said, but her grin told Thursday she hadn't objected much.

'I wouldn't trust him further than I can throw him,' Thursday said, but Elsie just laughed and said she could handle Doug Brighton. He already knew that he only had to go an inch too far and he'd get a slap.

The road led inland for a little way and then past a row of big, elegant houses and out to the beach again, where it stopped. Away on either side ran the sweep of Stokes Bay, with only a rough track running along the top of the shingle.

'It's all stones,' Patsy said in a disappointed voice. 'There's hardly a patch of sand anywhere.'

'There isn't much sand anywhere along this coast,' Elsie admitted. 'It's all shingle.'

'What, even at Southsea?' Thursday asked teasingly.

'Even at *Brighton*, and nobody seems to complain about that!' Elsie retorted, making a face at her. 'It's good for swimming, though. I've come out a few times, when I've been over to see my gran. Mind you, there's no amusement arcade or fair, like there is at Southsea and Clarence Pier. Not even a prom. It's just beach.'

'There's a pier,' Patsy pointed out. 'But it looks as if something's happened to it – it's all broken down at this end.'

'That was done deliberately,' Tony told her, 'so that the Germans couldn't use it for landing when they invade.'

'*If* they invade,' Thursday corrected him automatically. 'But you can see this would be a good place for them to try.'

It was almost like a spring day, still cold but bright with a pale sun shining, and the sea glittered blue all the way over to the green hump of the Isle of Wight. Gulls swooped on the water, calling in raucous voices, and there were a few people walking their dogs along the shoreline. One black Labrador was rushing in and out of the waves, and a Jack Russell that reminded Thursday of her Auntie Maud's Nipper joined it, barking hysterically. Thursday felt a sudden pang of longing for Patch, who had never even seen the sea. He'd love it here, she thought, and wished she could see him again. But except for girls who lived nearby, like Elsie, none of them had been able to go home yet. They'd been promised some leave at Easter and she was looking forward to it. Only a couple of weeks now.

It must be nice, living by the sea, she thought. She looked at the beach and imagined it crowded with families in the summer, their bikes leant up against each other while the children scrabbled for enough sand to build a castle and the parents lay back on an old blanket in the sun.

Wooden groynes had been built running down the beach to break up the waves and prevent the storms that could blow up along the Solent from doing too much damage. It was almost as if the beach had been divided up into compartments. Probably people had their favourite places and looked on them almost as if they owned them.

'I suppose lots of people come out here in summer,' she remarked.

'Families and so on.' She gazed along the sweep of Stokes Bay. 'I bet it's lovely here on a sunny day.'

'Oh, yes, it's all right,' Elsie conceded. 'It gets quite crowded at weekends. Mostly Gosport people, of course.'

'Well, it's not crowded now,' Doug commented, taking off his round matelot's cap to smooth back his hair. 'There's not another soul to be seen, apart from those people with their dogs. Pretty bleak, if you ask me.'

'Nobody did ask you,' Thursday said a little sharply. 'I think it's nice like this.'

Doug looked at her and raised his eyebrow in the way that always annoyed her. 'Well, pardon me for breathing. Somehow I thought we were all allowed to talk this afternoon, but maybe I was wrong. Maybe we had to have special permission from her ladyship.'

Thursday flushed. He was right, of course, and she shouldn't have snapped at him. But he'd only said it to annoy her. Whatever she said, he had to say the opposite, just because she wasn't taken in by his good looks.

They continued on along the path that had been worn along the top of the beach. Rough, tussocky grass stretched on their right between the beach and the village of Alverstoke with its grey church tower. They turned inland again to cycle on to Lee-on-the-Solent and stopped to look at the pier and the tall, white tower.

'What's that for?'

'It's a sort of entertainment place. You can go up the top and look at the view in summer, and there's a tea-place and a ballroom. They have quite good dances.' Roy Greenaway looked at them, his blue eyes twinkling. 'We could come to some.'

The girls brightened. 'That'd be good. But it's a cup of tea we could do with now. Is there a café or anything here?'

There was a small café opposite the tower and they parked their bikes and went inside, giving little exclamations of relief at the cosiness. The early March sun, cheering though it was, didn't do much to warm things up. The boys took off their caps and stacked them on the table. Doug once again smoothed back his hair, which Thursday thought had obviously been given a liberal dose of Brylcreem, and Tony ran his fingers through his tousled dark curls.

'Tea and toast all round, I reckon,' he said. 'And I'll have cheese on mine.'

The waitress shook her head. 'No cheese today, love. We've got Spam or marmite. Or you could have a sausage.'

'Just the one?' he asked, and she nodded and said, 'They're a bit short today.'

'And there's nothing worse than a short sausage,' Doug quipped, and gave Elsie a nudge and a meaning look. 'Isn't that right, Elsie?'

The other two boys grinned and the girls looked at them reprovingly.

'I hope I don't understand that joke,' Thursday said, tossing her head so that her hair swung like a chestnut bell against her cheeks. 'We're not on the ward now, you know.'

'Bit of a prude, are you?' Doug said with a faint sneer in his voice. He lifted his eyebrow.

'I don't think so.'

'Not much good being prudish when you're nursing sailors,' he went on as if she hadn't spoken. 'No such thing as private parts in a hospital. No such thing as privacy.'

'I said, I'm *not* a prude.'

'Not much fun for Tony here if you are,' he said, looking her in the eye.

Thursday flushed scarlet and started to get up. Tony put his hand on her arm and spoke to Doug.

'That's enough, Doug. Thursday's a nice girl, she doesn't like that kind of talk.'

'Shouldn't have joined the Navy then,' he said. 'You know what they say. If you can't stand the heat, get out of the kitchen.'

'I didn't volunteer to make stupid jokes about men's private parts or to be called a prude,' Thursday said tightly. 'I volunteered to help nurse people who were injured in the war. So that people like you could go back to sea and nurse them on board ship. And if you ask me, it's a pity that's not where you are now.'

'Here, hang on a minute, Thursday,' Elsie said. 'It's not Doug's fault he hasn't been drafted. They're waiting till we're properly trained.'

'They'll wait a long time then,' Doug said, still looking at Thursday. 'Some of the VADs I've seen still haven't found out how to scrub the brightwork.'

'And some of the SBAs I've seen still haven't learnt any manners.'

'All right, you two, all right, that's enough,' Patsy said. 'There's no need to get all aeriated. It was just a joke, that's all.'

'Yes, come on, Thursday, calm down,' Elsie said. 'He didn't mean anything.'

'He did. He's been needling me all afternoon. He never stops.'

'I haven't said a word—' Doug said in an injured tone.

'You don't have to say anything. It's the way you look at me.'

'Well, I won't look at you again,' Doug said. 'Will that be better?' He turned his chair away and gazed across the café at the far wall. There was a large mirror fixed to it and Thursday, following his gaze, saw that his reflected eyes were meeting hers. He put on a soulful expression and then winked at her. She struggled for a moment with her annoyance, and finally burst out laughing.

'Oh, you're impossible!'

'No, I'm not,' he said, still looking at her in the mirror. 'I'm just unusual. Like you, Thursday – remember?'

Thursday sighed and gave in. 'All right, I'm sorry. I shouldn't have reacted like I did.'

'Well, maybe I shouldn't have said what I did. And I shouldn't have laughed at your name the first time we met.' He turned back and reached his hand across the table, his eyes twinkling as he looked directly at her. 'I'm sorry, Thursday. I think it's a nice name – honestly.'

'Well, thank goodness for that,' Patsy said as they shook hands. 'It's not much fun for the rest of us, I can tell you, having to listen to you snipe at each other. Perhaps now we can settle down and be friends.'

Thursday met Doug's eyes across the table and grinned a little unwillingly. After all, what had he really done to annoy her? Put his arm round her waist, that was all. And said something a bit smutty that she shouldn't even have understood. And what if he was too good-looking? He couldn't actually *help* it, could he? And maybe anyone who looked like Gregory Peck was likely to be a bit conceited about it!

'Yes, and keep the party clean,' Roy said. 'Just because we work together on the wards doesn't mean the girls find the same things funny outside.'

'I know,' Doug said. 'But they're going to hear a lot worse jokes than ones about sausages before this lot's over, and see a lot worse, too.' He looked at the three girls and his voice was suddenly serious. 'All you've done so far is take a few bedpans round and wipe a few bottoms. All the patients you've seen are getting better. You wait till we get a crew straight off a ship that's been blown up. You wait till you've got a bloke with no arms landing in your lap, screaming for his mother. You wait till you see some poor bugger with his face burnt away. You wait till you see raw nerves and flesh and a muscle hanging out by its strings. You won't worry about a few smutty jokes then. You'll be glad of *anything* to raise a grin.'

The girls gazed at him. None of them could think of a thing to say. It was quite clear that Doug had seen all these things and more, and that he thought they would be seeing them, too. Thursday looked at the others and felt sick.

'I'm sorry,' she said quietly. 'It's just that it's all new to us, see. We haven't got the hang of things yet. I know we've got to learn to be more broad-minded.'

'You'll have to,' he said grimly. 'None of you will be much use at Haslar if you don't.'

Thursday and Tony cycled without speaking through the lanes of Rowner. The others were slightly ahead, their laughter floating back towards them, but Thursday felt subdued. Mum and Dad always did tell me I was too touchy, she thought.

There were woods and commons on either side, and she thought it would be a good place for picnics later on in the year. There was a golf club, too, but there was still plenty of room for anyone who wanted to come out and enjoy the countryside. I bet there'll be bluebells in those woods soon, she thought. And blackberries in the autumn.

Tony rode along beside her and glanced at her face. 'Feeling a bit better now?'

She nodded. 'I suppose I shouldn't have flown off the handle like that. I can take a joke as well as the next person, I just don't like smut, that's all, and Doug does get under my skin a bit, I don't know why.'

He nodded, then said, 'But you are going to have to get used to it, you know. People like Doug – well, he's seen a lot of nasty things. A few off-colour jokes don't seem very important when you've been through what he has.' He paused. 'He was on the *Grenville*, too, you know.'

Thursday looked at him. 'The *Grenville*? The ship that stoker was on? The one that sank?'

Tony nodded. 'He wasn't hurt but he was brought to Haslar with the rest of the crew. He'll get a new draft soon but he wanted to be with them as long as possible. Haven't you noticed he comes and has a yarn with Stoker Davis most days? He was one of the blokes Davis dragged into the lifeboat. If it hadn't been for Davis, he wouldn't be here now.'

Thursday didn't speak for a moment. Then she said, 'I wish I'd known that before.' She glowered at the gorse bushes they were passing. 'I'm too flipping prickly, that's my trouble,' she said bitterly. 'I've always been like it, but if I'd *known* that about Doug—'

'It's the same with a lot of the blokes,' Tony told her. 'Almost everyone you meet in Haslar's been through something like that. And it'll be true more and more as this war goes on. They might all be heroes, but that doesn't mean you have to like them all.'

'No, but not liking them doesn't mean I've got to make my own judgements on the sort of people they are,' Thursday said. 'Anyway, we're not supposed to let that sort of thing get in the way of the work, are we? They're *patients* – or they're like you and Doug and Roy, people we've got to work with. Maybe that's why we're not supposed to "fraternise",' she added thoughtfully.

'Well, never mind all that,' Tony said, cycling close beside her. 'I've been wanting to get you on your own. I wanted to ask you if you'd got a boyfriend at home. I bet you have – a girl like you's probably got a boy for every night of the week.'

'Hey, what's that supposed to mean?' Thursday demanded indignantly, and he grinned.

'Not what it sounded like! Sorry – what I meant was, you'd have plenty of boys wanting to go out with you. But is there anyone serious?'

'Not at present, no.' Thursday hesitated. 'Well, there never was really. Only a chap I used to knock about with a bit, go to the pictures and that sort of thing. But it wasn't serious, and he took the huff when I told him I was volunteering for the VADs.'

Tony raised his eyebrows but said nothing. They had reached the town again now and were cycling through the built-up streets. The others had got well ahead, Patsy with Roy, Elsie with Doug. Thursday noticed a small cinema on their right. 'We could go to the flicks some time.'

'Yes, I wouldn't mind,' Thursday agreed. 'I expect the others would like to go, too.'

'Well, it's a free country.' He gave her a grin. 'That's what we're fighting for, isn't it! But I don't want to go round in a gang all the time, Thursday. I'd like us to be on our own sometimes. Like now. We can talk better.'

'We can't do much talking in the pictures,' Thursday pointed out, and he gave her another grin, with a wicked glint in his eyes.

'Well, maybe it's not just talking I had in mind.'

Thursday tried to look exasperated. 'You sailors! You're all the same.'

'And aren't you glad of it,' he retorted, and they both laughed.

Thursday glanced around for something to say to change the subject. 'What's this place we're passing now? It looks a bit like Haslar, with that long wall and all those square windows. And that big gateway.'

'It's HMS *St Vincent*. It's a training place for boy seamen. If you look through the gateway you'll see the mast with rigging, just like on a sailing ship. They send all the sprogs up there and one has to stand right on the top. They call him the button-boy.'

Thursday turned her head to peer through the gateway at the tall mast. It seemed impossibly high to send young boys up. 'How old are they?'

'They start at about thirteen.'

Thursday stared at him. 'Boys go into the Navy at thirteen?'

Tony nodded. 'They start us young, you see. I mean, there's a lot to learn when you go into the Navy. All about ships, and girls, and the sea, and girls, and—'

'All right, all right, I get the message. Every nice girl loves a sailor, and all that.' She grinned at him. 'We don't have much chance to do anything else round here – there's nobody else around! And it's harder to tell which ship they're off, now that you can't wear the name on your hatbands. So we don't know whether the chap we're going out with is likely to be around next week or whether he's going to love us and leave us. I thought that was supposed to confuse the enemy, but I reckon it's more confusing for the girls!'

The others had stopped and were waiting for them, their bikes propped against the kerb. 'Doug says why don't we go in the Swiss Café before we go back?' Patsy said, looking at Thursday. 'He said he'll stand us a penny bun each to make up for upsetting you.'

Thursday looked at Doug. 'You don't need to do that. It was my fault as much as yours.'

'Well, I'll do it anyway. Come on, we've just got time and it was a cold ride all the way from Lee.'

Their eyes met and she knew he was genuinely sorry he had upset her. Maybe he's not so bad after all, she thought, and smiled at him. They mounted their bikes again, turning towards the high street, and went into the little café where they had first met. It was as warm and welcoming as ever, and they sank on to chairs and ordered tea and penny buns. Tony sat next to Thursday, pulling his chair a little closer, and they talked quietly together, their voices muted under cover of the chatter all around them.

'I love these,' Thursday said, taking a bun. 'When I was a kid I used to pick off the brown shiny top and save it for last.'

'I did that, too.' Their eyes met and Thursday felt a little shiver brush across her skin. Tony smiled. 'Where's your home? Gloucester, isn't it?'

'Worcester. It's quite different to this.'

'Almost in the middle of the country. Had you ever seen the sea before you came here?'

'We went to Weston-super-Mare a couple of times. But you're lucky if you see the sea there – the tide goes out for miles!' Thursday glanced around the little café. All the tables were taken, and at almost every one there were men in uniform. There were women, too – Wrens in their dark blue, a few khaki-clad ATS and a couple of VADs she recognised from Haslar. 'You're not so aware of the Services in Worcester. We've got an Army regiment – my brother's joining them – but you don't see them around in the city as much as you see people here. Gosport seems to be one big barracks in itself.'

'Well, it was meant to be, I suppose.' Tony reached for another bun. 'It was built like a fort with bastions all around it, so that it could be defended in any direction. And that would defend Portsmouth Harbour.'

'I haven't been over to Portsmouth yet,' Thursday said. 'We haven't had much time off so far, and the weather's been so awful . . . Elsie's asked me and Patsy to go home with her some time. She lives somewhere called Fratton.'

'*Somewhere called Fratton?*' Tony exclaimed in pretended shock. 'You can't say that – Fratton's famous. It's where Portsmouth football team have their ground. You must have heard of the Pompey football team.'

'Well, yes. My dad listens to football on the wireless and does the pools, and Steve's football mad. But I never take much notice.'

'And you look such a nice, intelligent girl, too.' Tony said, shaking his head sadly.

Thursday giggled. 'Do you have to be intelligent to follow football?'

'You be careful, my girl. People have been pushed off the top of Pneumonia Bridge for less than that.'

'Ooh, I'm really scared,' she whispered, putting her hands up to her face in mock terror. Their eyes met again and she felt a shiver touch her skin. There was a moment of silence.

'Come on, you two,' Patsy broke in suddenly, and Thursday glanced up in surprise. She had almost forgotten the others were there. 'It'll be getting dark soon. It's not much fun cycling with no lights in the blackout.'

'Speak for yourself!' Elsie said, with a glance at Doug. 'I think it could be a *lot* of fun!' She gave Thursday a mischievous glance. 'And going by the way you two have got your heads together, I reckon you might think so, too.'

Thursday looked sideways at Tony and blushed at the twinkling look in his eyes. Well, maybe it will be, at that, she thought, and gave another shiver of excitement. I never felt like this with Sidney, she thought, not even when he kissed me. I never felt anything much when he kissed me.

She wondered what it would be like if – *when* – Tony kissed her.

Chapter Ten

Easter came early that year. The week before the end of March, with the snow and ice gone at last from the streets and still no sign of German bombers, everyone wanted some fun. The girls had all got the weekend off but before they went home there was a dance on at Lee Tower ballroom and they were all going, to celebrate.

'Though I'm not sure what we're celebrating,' Elsie remarked, smoothing the golden hairs off her legs with a piece of sandpaper. 'We're still stuck in this hospital and there's still a war on, even if we haven't got all that many new patients coming in at the moment. We can't even wear pretty frocks, we've got to go in uniform. I mean, who's going to want to dance with a girl in uniform when all the local girls can wear their frocks?'

'Well, there's nothing we can do about that. Some men like uniforms, anyway. And we're celebrating spring coming.' Thursday peered into the scrap of mirror over the washstand as she polished her chestnut hair with a silk scarf. ' "*The winter is over and gone, the time of the singing of the birds is come and the voice of the turtle is heard in the land.*" '

The others stared at her. 'What on earth are you on about? Is that poetry?'

'I think it's from the Bible, actually. Our English teacher used to say it to us at school.'

'I didn't think turtles made a noise,' Patsy said, filing her nails. 'A sort of gurgling, perhaps. And do they really come back in spring, like swallows? Anyway, the Bible happened on land, not at sea.'

'There was the Sea of Galilee,' Elsie reminded her.

'That's not a proper sea, it's an inland sea – a big lake.'

'I don't think they were really turtles anyway,' Thursday said, wishing she'd never started it. 'It means turtle *doves*. I'm not ever going to quote bits of the Bible at you two again, you're just philistines.'

'Don't you mean Pharisees?' Elsie asked, and Thursday threw a hairbrush at her.

'Never mind all that. Look, Patsy, have you made up that row with Roy yet? It's going to be a bit miserable if we go to the dance and you two are still at loggerheads.'

'I don't have to go with Roy,' Patsy said. She finished her nails and picked up a black lisle stocking. 'Just look at this hole, it's enormous! Anyway, there are other fish in the sea.'

Elsie groaned. 'Now we're back to turtles again!'

'Yes, but the trouble is,' Thursday said, ignoring her, 'if you don't go with Roy you can't come with us either, because the other two won't go without him.'

'Flipping heck! They're not chained together, are they? They can go out without each other.'

'They won't, though. No more than we will. And it's nice, going round in a group. Come on, Patsy, promise you'll make it up. It wasn't anything serious, was it?'

'S'pose not,' Patsy said reluctantly.

'Well, then. Get up off that bed and do your hair.' Thursday looked at her own in the mirror. It shone like a conker polished on a small boy's trousers. She clipped it back at the temples and let it fall in a shimmering bell to her shoulders. 'And you can use my new lipstick if you like. You know you'll enjoy it when you get there.'

The whole dormitory seemed to be going to the dance at Lee Tower. There would be plenty of young men there – sailors from *Hornet* and *Dolphin*, Fleeties from *Daedalus*, and lots of local girls to supplement the VADs and Wrens. Even Madam had promised to put in an appearance, though none of the girls could imagine her dancing.

'Which just goes to show how wrong you can be,' Thursday remarked a few hours later as they watched Miss Makepeace whirl by in the arms of the Surgeon Rear Admiral. 'She's a smashing dancer.'

'I wouldn't mind being able to foxtrot like that,' Tony admitted.

He slid his hand down Thursday's arm and took her hand. 'Let's go outside for a minute.'

Thursday got up and followed him. It was part of the evening to nip outside for a few minutes with your partner, and everyone studiously avoided looking at you as you went – though they were quick enough to notice smudged lipstick when you came back! She felt in her pocket to make sure she had a hanky to wipe any tell-tale stains from Tony's cheeks.

Hand in hand, they walked slowly along the promenade, passing other couples who were standing at the rails gazing out over the whispering sea. The full moon had thrown down a glimmering pathway which seemed to lead directly to the mysterious bulk of the Island. We could walk across it, Thursday thought, we could walk across it into a magic land where there's no war and nothing to do but be happy.

Tony stopped and took her in his arms. They kissed gently and she sighed and laid her head on his shoulder.

Since the day a couple of weeks before, when they'd all cycled out to Lee together, she'd been feeling different about Tony. Before that, he'd been no more than one of the SBAs she worked with, a pleasant fellow with dark curls and friendly eyes who tipped her the wink when Sister Burton or Matron was about to come into the ward, and sometimes offered to sluice out the bedpans for her. It had been nice to run into him and his mates at the Swiss Café that day but there hadn't really been time to take the friendship any further, although she'd hoped they'd get the chance some time. But as they'd pushed their bikes back in the dark past Trinity Church that evening, he'd stopped suddenly and pulled her against him. She'd felt his lips against her cheek, and then on hers, and she'd felt a great surge of excitement. I never felt like this with Sidney, she thought, I never felt anything like this with Sidney . . . And she'd pressed herself close to Tony and found herself returning his kiss, wanting it to go on.

Since then, they'd found quite a few odd moments to slip away into a dark corner of the hospital grounds for a few more kisses. They'd been to the pictures, too, as Tony had suggested, though they hadn't seen a lot of the film. He'd managed to get seats in the back row, right in the corner, and they'd cuddled close together in the dark, blissfully aware that all those nearby were similarly engaged. Nobody in the back row took any notice of anyone else – or of the film. That wasn't what the back row was for.

'You wouldn't think there was a war on at all,' Thursday murmured. 'It's all so peaceful. And everyone seems so happy, enjoying themselves in there.' She shivered a little. 'I feel sort of excited because summer's coming, and there ought to be so much to look forward to – and then I remember that now the weather's better Hitler will probably start the air raids and we could be bombed or invaded at any minute, and I feel scared instead. What's going to happen to us all, Tony?'

He said nothing for a moment. Then, laying his face against her hair, he said quietly, 'I can tell you what's going to happen to me, Thursday. I'm going away.'

A cloud drifted across the moon, suddenly throwing the promenade and the sea into darkness, blotting out the silver pathway. Thursday lifted her head and stared at him, trying to make out his expression. 'What do you mean? Have you had a draft?'

'Yes. It's partly your fault.' He tried to speak jokingly. 'You're all so well trained now, us poor SBAs aren't needed any more, so we've all got to go to sea. I'm joining a ship at the end of next week.'

'Next *week*?'

'Yes,' he said. 'But I'll be leaving Haslar before that – I've got a few days' embarkation leave. I'll have to go home, see my mum and dad and everything.'

There was a silence. Thursday stood very still in his arms. I knew this would happen, she thought, I knew he'd have to go away. We're not serious about each other. We've just been having fun. We haven't even known each other more than a few weeks. I *knew* he'd have to go away. But . . .

'Oh, *Tony*,' she said, and tears crept down her cheeks.

'Hey,' he said, feeling the wetness against his face. 'What's all this? You're not going to go all soppy on me, are you, Thurs?'

She tried to laugh, but it choked in her throat.

'No, of course not. I just felt – well – you know – it took me by surprise, I suppose.' She felt for her hanky. 'Sorry.'

'It's all right,' he said quietly. 'I feel a bit like crying myself.'

'Oh, Tony.' Now she did laugh. 'You don't!'

'I do. Half of me doesn't want to go away, Thursday. Not now we're just getting to know each other.'

He paused and she said, 'And what about the other half?'

'Oh, the other half can't wait,' he said with a grin. 'Going to sea again – getting the chance to give old Hitler a bloody nose. It's what we all want, isn't it, we blokes?'

'So you don't want to cry too much.'

'Not too much, no,' he said honestly. 'This past fortnight or so's been good, Thursday, and I don't want to leave you. But I can't honestly say I wish I wasn't going. It'll be good to get back to sea, and I've been itching for a crack at the Huns.'

'But you won't actually be fighting. You'll be in the sick bay.'

'When we're in action,' he said, 'we're all fighting. You can't be on board ship and not be part of it.'

Thursday was silent. Then she said, 'You haven't told me which ship you're joining.'

'The *Rodney*,' he said. 'It's a battleship. I can't say where we'll be going.'

'No, I know. Walls have ears and all that.' She shivered against him. 'Oh, Tony . . . Tony, if you want me to wait for you, I will. It doesn't matter that we've only known each other a few weeks—'

'No,' he said. 'It wouldn't be fair to ask you to wait, and not go out with other blokes, and then come back and find we didn't feel the same any more. Look, we don't know how long this war's going to last, or what's going to happen to any of us. It's better not to be tied.'

Thursday felt the tears burn her eyes. 'But I want you to know that when you come back—'

'We don't know that I *will* come back,' he said sombrely. 'Look, I told you about the *Grenville* and what the blokes were like that came off that. You've seen some of them in the wards – they're better now, but there's still that poor blighter who lost both his legs, and the one who was blinded. And I told you about some of their girlfriends – they can't cope with it. They don't know what to do. Some of them stick by their boys, but some of them just walk away. I don't want you to have to make that sort of decision, Thursday. I don't want you to feel tied.'

'I wouldn't feel that.'

'You don't know what you'd feel,' he said soberly. 'Those girls didn't know they'd feel like that either. It's not their fault – they just weren't ready for that kind of thing. Maybe they got engaged without really being sure. Without knowing each other well enough. That's what I feel about us, Thursday. We don't know each other well enough. We haven't had time. I don't want you to feel tied to me. It's too soon.' He kissed her ear. 'It's not goodbye,' he whispered. 'I'll come back, and maybe we can start again. And I'd like you to write to me.'

'I will,' she said. 'I will write. Oh, Tony—'

'It's been fun,' he said firmly. 'It's been smashing, knowing you. But now I've got to go away. Give me a kiss, Thursday, a proper kiss to remember you by.' He bent his head and touched her lips with his.

Thursday clung to him. Their lips met again and she felt him shake. She pressed her lips against his, trying to feel the surge of desire she'd felt when they first kissed, but all she could feel was sadness.

'Don't let's go back inside,' she said. 'Let's just stay out here. Let's find somewhere to sit down and be together.'

'We'll go back for the last waltz,' he said, and with their arms wound tightly around each other's waists they walked slowly along the moonlit prom. 'Let's have one more dance to remember.'

Easter leave for the VADs started on the day before Good Friday. They had the whole weekend off, and didn't have to be back until they went on duty on Tuesday morning. It was their first home leave since they had arrived at Haslar, and they were all wildly excited at the idea of seeing their families again.

Tony came to the railway station to see Thursday off. She and Patsy were catching the same train and Patsy scrambled aboard, taking Thursday's bag with her.

'You two say your fond farewells here and I'll find seats.' Patsy winked at Tony. 'Good luck. See you again soon.'

Left alone on the platform, the two stared at each other. For a few moments, Thursday could think of nothing to say. She glanced down at the wooden platform, with the sea surging beneath it.

'It seems ages since Patsy and I first came here, back in January,' she said with a laugh. 'But it's only just over three months – no time at all, really. And it's even less than that since we first met – you and me.'

'I know,' he said quietly. 'Not long. But long enough to know . . .'

'Know what?' she whispered, when he stopped.

Tony looked at her gravely. 'Long enough to know that I meant what I said last week. I like you too much to want to tie you down, Thursday. If we had a bit longer . . .'

'Oh, Tony,' she whispered. 'I meant what I said, too. I would wait for you – if you wanted me to.'

'No,' he said, and bent his head to her face. 'No, I'm not going to ask you to do that. It isn't fair – not after just a few weeks. But – oh, Thursday, I *wish* we had longer. I wish so *much* that we had longer . . .'

The whistle of the train shrieked in their ears. A puff of steam billowed around them and they clung together and kissed. If we had longer, Thursday thought desperately, if we really did have longer – what would happen? Would we find we loved each other – or would it just fizzle out, like it did with me and Sidney? And will we ever get the chance to find out?

'Thursday, get in the train, for heaven's sake!' Patsy shrieked, leaning out of the window. 'You'll get left behind – come *on!*'

Thursday tore herself out of Tony's arms. 'I'll have to go. Oh, Tony, take care. Please take care. And I'll write – I promise I'll write.'

Between them, with Tony pushing and Patsy dragging at her arms, they got her into the train. The porter came along and slammed the door and Thursday leant out of the window, waving wildly. Her cheeks were wet with tears, and she was half laughing, half crying as the train puffed out of the station and she watched him dwindle away in the distance. Then the train rounded a bend and he was gone, and Patsy hauled her into the compartment where she had saved two seats.

'Well, that's that,' she said, pulling Thursday into the seat beside her. 'Fun while it lasted, but he's gone now and you'll have to look for someone else to go around with. It's no good looking at me like that,' she added, catching Thursday's shocked expression. 'You weren't in love with Tony, any more than I am with Roy.'

'How do you know that?' Thursday demanded. 'You don't have any idea whether I'm in love with him or not.'

'Well, more fool you if you are,' Patsy remarked. 'It's no use falling in love these days, Thurs. Not seriously, anyway. *I* don't intend to – not with Jeff, nor Roy, nor anyone else. I'll be friends with them, I'll have a bit of fun and a few kisses, there's no harm in that – but I'm blowed if I'll let it go any further. You just get hurt if you do that, Thursday, believe me.'

Thursday said nothing. She looked out of the window and thought of Tony, left behind at Portsmouth to join his ship. By the time she came back off leave he might be anywhere. He might even have been sunk.

'I don't know whether I loved him or not,' she said honestly. 'We didn't have time to find out. I just know I *might* have done – if we'd had longer.' She turned to Patsy. 'I don't think I want to just have fun. I want to love someone – really love someone.'

Patsy looked at her shrewdly.

'Well, I expect you will, one day. But don't go looking for it in every chap you meet, Thursday, and don't try to force it either. Just wait till it comes of its own accord. And in the meantime—' she grinned wickedly '—just do what your Auntie Patsy says and have fun. It's good practice, if nothing else!'

It was strange to be at home again. Thursday arrived at the front door, fumbling in her bag for the key she'd been given on her birthday and remembering the big red wooden one her father had given her, but before she could do anything else, the door swung open and her sister Jenny stood there, beaming with delight.

'Thursday! Gosh, you're doing your hair different!'

'It's to get it under my cap more easily.' Thursday stepped through the door and gave her sister a hug. 'And you've got taller, surely.'

'I've grown another inch and a half,' Jenny said proudly. 'I'm taller than Mum now.'

'*Everyone's* taller than Mum.' Steve, who had just completed his first six weeks' training in the Army, was behind her, grinning. 'Hiya, Thurs. How's tricks?'

'Okay, thanks.' She made a face at him and was then nearly knocked off her feet as her mother came flying through from the kitchen and enveloped her in a tremendous hug. 'Oh, *Mum*! Mum, it's so good to see you again. Oh, and here's Patch too!'

'It seems years since you went away. Let me look at you.' Mary's eyes ran over her assessingly. 'Are you sure you're eating enough? They're feeding you properly, are they?'

133

'Mum, we never stop eating! We probably get more than you do. How are you getting on with the ration books?'

'Oh, they're dreadful. You should hear our Jenny go on about them at the shop. Well, you probably will.' Mary took Thursday's bag from her and pushed her into a chair. 'I'll make a cup of tea. What sort of journey did you have? At least there's no snow now, not like when you went. What's Haslar like? And Gosport? Have you been to Portsmouth yet?'

'Don't you read my letters?' Thursday demanded, getting out of the chair and following her mother to the kitchen. 'I've told you all those things.' Patch was leaping at her, and she lifted him into her arms.

'I know, but it's not the same as hearing it from your own lips. What about the other girls – and Patsy and Elsie? They sound nice girls. Have they gone home, too?'

'Never mind them,' Jenny said wickedly, poking her head round the door. 'What about the *sailors*? Have you got a boyfriend yet? And what about that stoker you mentioned, the one that had all the tattoos – is he still there? Is he really tattooed *everywhere*?'

'Jenny, don't be disgusting,' her mother said sharply. 'I don't know why you had to tell us about that, Thursday, it's just given her a lot of silly ideas. Tattoos, indeed! I don't know what that girl's coming to.'

Thursday laughed. 'Well, it did give us all a surprise when we first saw them, but we've got used to them now. A lot of the men have them. They get them done abroad mostly, but there are places in Portsmouth as well – there's one quite close to the harbour. It's a sort of naval tradition, I suppose.'

Mary made the tea and brought it into the living-room. The best biscuit tin was produced, with biscuits in it that Jenny said she'd got from the shop specially, and Thursday was made to sit in the best armchair while they plied her with questions. She told them about everything she could think of – the hospital, the town of Gosport and the city of Portsmouth, the harbour and ships, the sea and the cycle rides she'd enjoyed with the other girls. Finally, she told them about the dance and about Tony.

'So you *have* got a boyfriend!' Jenny exclaimed. 'I knew it!'

'Don't be daft,' Thursday told her sharply. 'It's not serious and anyway, he's going away. We said goodbye this morning,' she added with a forlorn note in her voice as she remembered their parting on the station platform.

'Oh, Thursday. I am sorry,' her mother said. 'But still, if it wasn't serious . . . Young Sidney's home, too, you know. I saw his mother in the street the other day, she said he'd got a bit of leave. Maybe you could pop round and—'

'No,' Thursday said firmly. 'No, Mum, I couldn't. It wouldn't be fair. And, anyway, I don't suppose he'd even be interested now.'

'No, he wouldn't,' Jenny piped up from the floor. 'I saw his sister last week and she told me he's got a new girl. Dorothy, her name is, and he's ever so sweet on her, so there wouldn't be any point in you going round.'

'Oh.' Thursday looked at her sister. So Sidney had a new girl. Well, there was no reason why that should bother her, was there? She'd always said there was nothing serious between them. She hadn't even given him a thought for weeks.

All the same, the news, coming only hours after she had said goodbye to Tony, gave her a cold, lonely feeling and she remembered her words to Patsy. It *would* be nice to have someone to love.

Patsy was right, though. You couldn't go looking for it. And you certainly couldn't force it to happen.

The Tilfords had organised a family party for Easter Day. Everyone was coming to Walter's and Mary's house for tea. Flo and Percy were there with Denise, Albert and Ada had walked round from the next street, and Maudie had come over on the train from Ledbury, bringing Nipper. He and Patch were sent straight into the garden.

'I've brought some flapjacks, too,' Maudie said, taking a tin from her shopping bag. 'Thought they'd do for tea.'

Mary took them, smiling her thanks. 'Oh, yes, we all love your flapjacks. I've made some rock buns and a Victoria, and Flo's brought a beautiful fruit cake. She'd got some sultanas and currants saved up since Christmas. Mum's brought some scones and Jenny's made a pink blancmange in that rabbit mould and put green jelly all round it – looks lovely, it does.'

There was an atmosphere of celebration. Thursday had spent the morning making hot cross buns and Steve had brought bars of chocolate from his allowance. He lounged in his mother's armchair in his new khaki uniform, talking to his father and uncle about his 'square-bashing' while his grandfather sat listening. Like the other men, he had already been through a war, but his had been fought in Africa, against the Boers.

'Thursday's been telling us all about Haslar,' Mary said as the women made tea. 'Says it's a beautiful hospital and in a lovely spot, right by the sea. They'll be able to go swimming in the summer. And Portsmouth's a nice place, too, lots of good shops, like Worcester. Not that you've got much money to spend, have you, Thursday?'

'Not by the time they've deducted most of our pay for rations and uniform,' Thursday said ruefully. 'And we have to pay for any breakages, too. Jeanie Brown was nearly in tears the other day when she dropped a thermometer, but the patients all had a whip-round to pay for another one. I don't know what she'd have done, else.'

'Well, us nurses never do get paid much, do we,' Maudie commented. 'But there's always the chance of marrying some nice young doctor! We'll have to have a bit of a chinwag all to ourselves later on, Thursday. Mary, I've finished this sardine and tomato paste – what d'you want me to use next?'

'There's a pot of bloater over there, look. I managed to get a bit of luncheon meat, too – the men will like that. Pity those pullets Flo and Percy have bought haven't come into lay yet, we could have had a few boiled eggs as well. Still, I think it's a pretty good spread, all things considered,' Mary declared, looking at the piled plates.

Thursday looked at her aunt. 'How's Mike, Auntie Flo, have you heard from him lately? And what about Leslie? I was sure he'd be with you today.'

Flo's mouth turned down at the corners. 'He'll be along later, in time for tea. He stayed home to sort out his things, ready for Tuesday. You know he's been taken in the RAF? Minute he turned seventeen, they took him in. We did our best to stop him, your Uncle Perce laid the law down proper, but there was nothing we could do. He said he'd go whatever we did, and he's so headstrong we knew he meant it. Says he'll never get a chance as good as this, and you know he's always been mad about aeroplanes.'

'Well, they'll never let him fly, surely, a boy of seventeen,' Mary said. 'I mean, he's barely old enough to drive a car.'

'I hope not. But it's out of our hands now, see. This is war, and once their lads are in the Services what parents want just doesn't come into it any more.' She stood with her hand on a pile of sandwiches, ready to slice them into squares, and sighed heavily. 'As for our Mike, he's off to France with the BEF. Looking forward to it, too. Says Hitler doesn't stand a chance against the whole Army. Well, maybe he's right, but it stands to reason *some* of them are going to get hurt and killed. I just pray every night it won't be him – and then I think of all the other mothers praying for their boys, and I feel guilty for doing it.'

'You don't have to feel like that. We're all bound to think of our own.' Mary took the knife from her sister's hand and cut the sandwiches. 'There, put those on that meat-plate – goodness knows when it'll see a joint of meat again – and we'll start laying the table. Tell those men to get up off their backsides and go outside. Walter can show them the garden, he's got all sorts of veg growing out there, planted a lot of stuff over the weekend, he has – beans and carrots, and I don't know what else. If it all comes up, we'll not need to bother the greengrocer all summer.'

Thursday looked at her mother and aunt and thought of the young sailors she had seen at Haslar. Boys no older than Leslie in the wards, brought in off ships that had been sunk by enemy action. The eighteen-year-old who had lost both legs, the one who was blind. As yet, she hadn't seen men with fresh wounds, but she knew it would come, and she knew that many of them would be no older than her cousin and would have had just as responsible jobs.

Of course they would let Leslie fly. They'd let anyone go to war who was willing and soon they would be conscripting even those who weren't. And then they'd be filling the hospitals, too, with their own injuries – broken and torn limbs, shattered bodies, burns. Why else would the Government be recruiting so many VADs?

She went into the back room where the men were now discussing the RAF raid on the German seaplane base at Hornum, in reprisal for the German bombing of Scapa Flow. Maudie was there, too, and she turned and gave Thursday a look which showed that she also understood what it meant. She also knew that youth was going to be no bar to responsibility and to action.

'Fifty bombers!' Walter said. 'You ought to be proud of your Leslie, Perce, volunteering to join that lot. I know he's jumped the gun a bit, going so early, but you can't say his heart's not in the right place.'

'Oh, he's got the right idea,' Percy agreed unwillingly. 'I just hope he'll take a bit more notice of his officers than he takes of me. He'll find Service discipline a bit strict for his taste, I'm afraid.'

'Well, he'll soon get used to that,' Maudie said briskly, and turned to Steve. 'You'll know all about that, won't you? And I hear you've been learning to wash and iron your own clothes – I thought you were supposed to be training to be a soldier, not a washerwoman!'

'A smart soldier's an efficient soldier,' Steve said, obviously repeating what one of his officers had said. 'And the enemy wouldn't be very frightened by a crowd of scruffy oiks.'

'So how are you enjoying it, then? Think you'll like being a soldier?'

'Yes, I do, as a matter of fact. I didn't think I would, really. I volunteered because it seemed the right thing to do – but I'm in with some really good blokes, and once we're through our training and we can get out there and start putting the Jerries to rights, we'll be able to feel we're really doing something. And it's interesting learning to fire a gun and use a bayonet and all that. We were throwing grenades the other day. I tell you what, you don't make any mistakes with those.'

'Real grenades?' Mary asked in horror, coming in from the kitchen. 'You mean they could have exploded?'

He nodded. 'That's the idea of them! Once you've pulled out the pin, you throw as hard as you can. This is the Army, Mum, not a Boy Scout camp. We're going over the Channel soon and we'll need to know what we're doing if we're going to beat Hitler's men.' He finished his cup of tea and looked at his father and uncle. 'Let's go for a walk, over the allotment. You can show me what veg we're having for Sunday dinner.'

The men went out, obviously wanting to get away from the women to talk properly, and the women looked at each other.

'I suppose he's right,' Mary said sadly. 'There'll always be wars. It's human nature, isn't it? But I don't suppose there's ever been a mother yet who's really wanted her own boys to go and fight.'

And they'd want it even less if they could see what I've already seen, and what Doug Brighton says we'll see, Thursday thought.

But she couldn't say so. What was the point of upsetting her mother and aunt even further? What was the point of telling them the truth?

Jenny and Denise had gone upstairs to the bedroom Jenny shared with Thursday. She thought of it as hers now, even though Thursday's bag was in one corner, her nurse's uniform hung in the wardrobe and her pyjamas were laid on her pillow. Denise held them up in front of herself.

'Proper passion-killers, aren't they? I suppose they're to put the sailors off.'

'Don't be daft, the sailors never see them. They're all in different buildings. I like that green jumper, Dizzy. It's new, isn't it?'

'Well, sort of. Mum unravelled one of hers and knitted it for me. It's all right, but I'd rather have had that pink one she wears.' Denise picked discontentedly at the lacy pattern, then reached into the new handbag she'd persuaded her brother Mike to buy her before he went away. 'Look, I've got some nail varnish! Crimson Lady, it's called – want to try it?'

'Coo, yes, it's smashing!' They stared at the little bottle of scarlet fluid. 'I've got some remover here – we'll have to take it off again before we go downstairs.' Jenny began to paint her nails, holding them out to gaze at them. 'It's ever so bright, isn't it?'

Their nails painted, they lounged on the beds and compared notes about their jobs, the boys they'd met or would like to meet, and the films they'd seen.

'I know *Pinocchio*'s a kids' film really,' Jenny remarked, looking into the mirror as she fiddled with her dark curls, 'but it was good all the same. And there's some really scary bits in it, too. I heard quite a few kiddies crying when he got swallowed up by that whale.'

'I didn't like the bit where his nose grew,' Denise said. 'It seemed a bit cruel to me. I went to see *Wuthering Heights* last week with my new boy. It was lovely. Laurence Olivier's a real heart-throb.'

'*What* new boy? You never said you had a new boy. What happened to Brian?' Jenny sat up, agog. Denise was younger than she was, yet had already had a string of boys, all willing to take her to the pictures *and* pay for her to go in, while Jenny had only been out with one boy, and he'd suggested they meet inside. She stared jealously at her cousin.

Denise combed her fair hair with her fingers and looked

nonchalant. 'Oh, he's still around. I just decided I didn't want to see him for a couple of weeks, that's all. I dare say I'll go out with him again some time.'

'He might not hang about.'

Denise shrugged. 'Doesn't matter. Plenty more fish in the sea.' She glanced sideways at Jenny and started to take the nail varnish off again. 'You work in the wrong place, that's why you don't get anyone. What boy's going to come into a grocer's shop?'

'I know, but Dad won't let me get a job at the factory. He says the girls are a rough lot and he doesn't want me associating with them. You'd better give me that remover, they'll be shouting for us in a minute. He wanted me to do a tailoring or dressmaking apprenticeship like our Thursday, but even he can see I'd be no good at that – I can't even thread a needle. And he wouldn't let me work in a hairdresser's either, said the premium was too high.'

'That's daft. He'd have had to pay a premium for you to do dressmaking. Anyway, you wouldn't have had any more chance of meeting boys there than at the grocer's.' Denise preened her hair again. 'I get a lot coming in the garage, of course.'

'I thought you were sweet on that mechanic with the curly hair?' Jenny said with a touch of malice. The dark-haired mechanic was at least twenty and had never shown the slightest interest in Denise. About the only boy who hadn't, Jenny thought, rubbing her nails with a scrap of cotton wool and wondering what her cousin had that she didn't.

'Oh, him,' Denise said dismissively. 'He's going out with that redhead from Larksley's. Talking about getting engaged, she is. I don't think he's so keen, mind. Anyway, he'll be called up soon, bound to be.'

'There won't be any boys left to go out with at this rate,' Jenny said gloomily. 'They're all either getting called up or volunteering. The only ones left will be the ones with flat feet or glasses, and who wants to go out with them?' Denise nodded and made a face, and they sat in silence for a moment before Jenny said, 'Anyway, you still haven't told me who this new boy is. Come on, Dizzy, spill the beans.'

Denise grinned. 'Well, you won't believe it, but it's that fellow from the post office. The one on the parcels counter. Vic Pearce, he's called. I take the post down every afternoon, see, and there's usually a parcel or two to send off – parts for other garages, stuff like that. Well, he's been on that counter for the past couple of weeks and we've got chatting and – well, you know. He asked me out on Saturday and we went to see *Wuthering Heights*.' She rolled her eyes. 'It was ever so romantic.'

Jenny stared at her. 'But he must be over twenty! I saw him when I took that parcel down to send to our Thursday.'

'Twenty-two,' Denise said with some pride. 'He told me.'

'Does he know you're only fifteen?'

'No, and you're not to tell him! He thinks I'm eighteen. Well, I look it, don't I? 'Specially when I've done myself up.' She tossed her head defiantly. 'And don't you tell our dad or mum neither, nor yours. They'd go up the wall if they knew I was going out with someone that old.'

'Yes, but – well, you know what boys are like when they get that old.' Jenny spoke doubtfully, not sure herself what she meant, but knowing that older boys spelt trouble. 'I mean – he'll have had other girlfriends, lots of them.'

'Well, I've had lots of boyfriends. It doesn't matter.'

'Yes, but suppose he wants . . . I mean, what happened? Did he put his arm round you or kiss you or anything? In the pictures, I mean.'

'We sat in the back row,' Denise said shortly. 'You've got to have a cuddle if you sit in the back row.'

'And what about afterwards? You want to be careful, Diz.'

'He saw me home like a perfect gentleman and kissed me goodnight at the door,' her cousin retorted. 'I don't know what you're getting at, Jenny. Vic's a decent boy.'

'He's a man,' Jenny said, feeling that as the older of the two she ought to be responsible.

'Man, then. What difference does it make? You're turning into a proper old woman.'

Jenny had an idea it made a good deal of difference but she said no more. She wasn't sure she knew what the difference was or what the dangers were, she just felt that there must be some in her fifteen-year-old cousin going out with a man seven years older than her. That was nearly half her age again, she thought, aware that her uncle and aunt would have a fit if they had any suspicion. At the same time, she was wildly envious and knew that she would have given her eye-teeth to have gone to see *Wuthering Heights* – or any other film – with Vic Pearce from the post office.

'Tell you what,' Denise said generously. 'I'll get Brian to take you to the pictures next week. He won't be doing anything. They're showing *The Lion Has Wings*, it's about the RAF. We saw the trailer.'

'No, thanks,' Jenny said shortly. 'I'll find my own boys. I don't want your cast-offs.' She got up and stared into the mirror on the wall above the chest of drawers. 'Did you get any new lipsticks this week?'

'Yes, I was going to show you. Here.' Denise produced the familiar Ponds tube. 'Cupid's Bow. It's a lovely bright red. Try it.'

'And have my dad see it when we go down? You know what he's like about make-up.'

'Well, so's mine, but I manage. You can wipe it off before we go down. Come on, I'll show you how to make your mouth into a proper Cupid's bow. And it wouldn't hurt you to go to the pictures with Brian, you know. Boys are much more interested in a girl who's already got a boyfriend. They think she's worth going after, see?'

'I can't see any boy being interested in a girl who's going out with Brian Jones,' Jenny sniffed. 'They'll just think she must be desperate. Anyway, I don't want to see a picture about the RAF. I shouldn't think you do either, what with your Leslie joining up.'

Denise, gazing into the mirror as she began to apply her lipstick, grinned. 'We don't need films at our house! It's all he can talk about – flying aeroplanes. Dad keeps telling him they won't let him train for a pilot, but he's dead set on it. And Mum's almost in tears every time she looks at him. I tell you what, Jenny, the minute I'm old enough I'm going to join, too. They're talking about letting women fly as well.'

Jenny stared at her. 'What, Spitfires and Hurricanes? They never are!'

'Not for fighting. It's transport – taking the new planes from the factories to the airfields. They say Amy Johnson's going to be doing it.'

'The one that flew to Australia all on her own? But she's a really good pilot. She's famous.'

'That's right, and now she's flying for the RAF,' Denise said.

'And there's one who's only twenty-two, and she's an instructor as well. She learnt to fly when she was seventeen.'

'Yes, but they're people who can already fly,' Jenny said. 'They won't train new ones.'

'Who says? Anyway, they'll let women work on planes – be mechanics, and all that.' Denise, who was never happier than when grubbing about helping her brother with his motor-bike, finished painting a Cupid's bow on her mouth and gave Jenny a radiant smile. 'Look, this is our *chance* – our chance to get away and do something *interesting*. You know what'll happen when it's all over, don't you? We'll have to get married and settle down and live dull, dreary lives like our mums, doing what our husbands tell us all the time. We'll never have another chance like this. I'll do your mouth now.'

Jenny opened her mouth and stretched her lips as her cousin directed. There was silence until Denise had finished and then they both looked into the mirror.

'There,' Denise said. 'Doesn't that look smashing? You could also pass for eighteen now.'

'I could, couldn't I,' Jenny said, staring at herself. 'Maybe I will go out with Brian after all. I like the way you've made it turn up at the corners.'

'Makes you look sort of smiling and cheeky,' Denise agreed. 'Tell you what, there's a dance on at the Oddfellows next Saturday. Why don't I get Vic to ask one of his friends to make up a foursome? That's a better way of meeting other boys than going to the pictures. Come on, Jen, it'll be fun. And our dads won't mind if we say we're going together.'

Jenny turned her head this way and that, still admiring the red Cupid's bow of her lips. She felt a quick tremor of excitement. 'All right. But I'll need to borrow your pink blouse. I haven't got anything else to wear.'

'That's OK, I was going to wear my spotted one anyway.' The ring of the doorbell sounded suddenly, and there was a sudden hubbub of voices. 'That'll be our Leslie arriving.'

Mary's voice sounded from the bottom of the stairs. 'Are you two coming down now? Leslie's here and we're all going out for a walk.'

'Better take this lipstick off,' Jenny said with a grimace. 'Dad'll go mad if he sees it. Says it makes a girl look cheap.'

Denise giggled. 'Well, if it does, I bet she has more fun than an expensive one! Most of the boys I know can only just afford the price of a ticket at the pictures. Except for Vic, of course,' she added with some pride. 'He's getting a good wage, being older and in the post office.'

Jenny scrubbed at her mouth, finding with some panic that the stain was more difficult to remove than she'd expected. There was still a trace of scarlet around her fingernails, too. She hoped her father wouldn't notice. She needed to keep in his good books now, if she was to be allowed to go to the dance next week with Denise and Vic, and Vic's friend. The excitement tingled through her again.

'Will you do my lips when we get there?' she asked. 'And can I borrow your black belt as well?'

Chapter Eleven

It seemed to Thursday, in those first weeks after Tony went away, that it was at sea that the war was fought the most bitterly. All through the winter the Navy had been battling it out, from the River Plate in South America to the North Sea, and now Scandinavia was being drawn in as well. There was a sense that the 'phoney' war, as it had come to be called, might be drawing to an end and the real war beginning. The winter might be over and gone, but with the time of the singing of birds came the threat of invasion.

The hospital, too, was imbued with a sense of waiting. Patients arrived in a fairly steady stream, but there had been no further sudden influxes. As the men got better, they got out of bed and sat round the big iron stoves in the middle of the wards, drinking cocoa and strong tea and swapping tales of life at sea. They always fell silent as the nurses came near, not realising that most of the girls had very good hearing and knew exactly what they were talking about. Thursday thought of Doug's joke about sausages and smiled wryly, wondering how she could ever have been offended by such an innocent quip. I didn't know the half of it! she thought with a grin.

The training of the VADs went on, with the girls learning how to take pulses, give injections and apply drips. It wasn't likely that they'd be expected to undertake these skilled tasks as a general rule, the QARNN who taught them explained rather dismissively, but in times of emergency anything could happen.

'You'll all be having your inoculations tomorrow,' she informed them as they ended their duty. 'Don't expect to be let off duty if you feel a bit off-colour. The patients must always come first.'

The girls stared at her. 'Inoculations?' Thursday asked. 'What for? I had my smallpox when I was a baby.'

'Yes, but you have to have more now you're in a hospital. You may come into contact with all kinds of diseases, brought in from abroad, besides which you may go abroad yourselves. Cholera, diphtheria, yellow fever—'

'Yellow fever? But that's from China, isn't it?' Elsie exclaimed. 'We're not going to China, surely?'

The QARNN gave them a cold look. 'You don't know where you might go. Anyway, whatever you have, you're having it tomorrow, so be prepared and *don't expect time off.*'

'I can't say I like the idea of this,' Elsie muttered as they went off duty. 'I never did like needles.'

'You didn't say that when you were giving that poor artificer his injection!' Patsy said. 'You told him not to be a big baby.'

'Well, of course I did. I didn't have to tell him I was even more scared than he was. I wonder if they'd let me off if I said I had a cold?'

'No, they wouldn't, they'd give you a double dose,' Thursday said unkindly, but she wasn't really looking forward to the injections any more than Elsie was, and when her turn came to hold out her arm next day she closed her eyes and turned her head away. Later on, when she started to feel shivery and hot, she wondered if she was getting flu, but one look at Sister Burton's face told her that there was no use in saying anything. She finished her duty feeling groggy and went without supper to crawl thankfully into her bunk as soon as the night staff took over.

'If this is just the inoculation,' she heard Elsie groan, 'I hope to God I never get the real thing. Yellow fever must be absolutely *horrible.*'

They felt a little better next day, and on the third day were back to normal. Some more patients had arrived from a trawler which had had an encounter with a mine in the Solent, and Thursday was able to forget her troubles in looking after them. It was when she came off duty that she found herself thinking of Tony, feeling a mixture of sadness and guilt. Did I really love him? she wondered. Or was it just a passing flirtation? She wrote to him every day, trying to keep his cheery face alive in her mind and feeling angry with herself when she couldn't do it.

'Why don't you come home with me this weekend?' Elsie suggested, coming into the dormitory a week or two after Easter to find Thursday sitting despondently on her bed, staring at a blank sheet of paper. 'There can't be anything to write to Tony about – you only posted a letter yesterday. And you haven't been out since we came back off leave.'

'I know. It just makes me feel better. Closer, somehow.' She sighed and closed the writing pad. 'Thanks, Else, but I don't really feel like it. I'll just stop here.'

'No, you won't.' Elsie went across to the mirror and pushed back her yellow hair. 'Stopping in on your day off won't do nobody no good. You'll come with me. I've told my mum all about you and she thinks you sound the sort of girl she wants me to be friends with. So you come and show her how wrong she is, all right?'

Thursday grinned reluctantly. 'Why don't you take Patsy? I'm no company for anyone at the moment, Else, honestly.'

'Because Patsy's all right. She's going out with Roy, anyway. They've made it up again – till next time they have a row. Come on, Thurs,' she wheedled. 'We can go to Commercial Road and look at the shops on the way.'

'We'd have to go on our bikes,' Thursday said. 'I haven't got enough money for the bus. I spent this week's wages on new stockings for the dance.'

'That's all right, I don't mind the ride so long as it's not raining. And if it is, I'll lend you the fare.'

On Saturday it wasn't raining and the two girls set off as soon as they came off duty, cycling down to the jetty to catch the pinnace. They settled themselves on the wooden seats, gazing down at the water churned by the propeller into pale, sudsy blue. As the boat chugged on its five-minute journey across the harbour, they looked up at the green rampart of the hill that enclosed it, pockmarked by the white chalkpits, and at the Naval ships tied up to the jetties in the dockyard.

They stared at the sharp grey prows looming above as the pinnace circled round to approach the Portsmouth pontoon. Thursday thought of Tony, somewhere at sea, and felt the ache of tears in her throat. She turned deliberately away and thought instead of the day she and Patsy had first come to Haslar. They'd caught the Naval pinnace then and it had been getting dark as they crossed the harbour. There had been snow and ice on the ground and a bitter wind scouring across the water, bringing yet more snow, while underneath the station platform had hung enormous icicles.

Now spring was coming – the time of the singing of the birds – and the tender blue of the sky was reflected in the dancing waves. And apart from the evidence of the warships – some of which were always present in Portsmouth anyway – there was still little to show that the country was at war.

Little – except for the sandbags piled outside every shop doorway the girls passed as they cycled up Queen Street. Little, except for the strips of brown paper criss-crossing every plate-glass window. Little, except for the cardboard gas-mask boxes hung on every shoulder, the tin hats of the ARP wardens, the posters everywhere reminding gossipers that 'Walls have ears' or that they should 'Be like Dad – keep Mum'. Little, except for the recruiting posters, the air-raid regulations, the public shelters on street corners, the sailors with no ship's name-band on their caps, the nervous glances skywards whenever an aircraft passed overhead.

'Blimey,' Elsie said as they came into Commercial Road. 'It's like a flaming army camp. Don't let's bother with the shops, Thurs. We've got no money, and it's too flipping depressing anyway. Let's just go straight home and see if Mum's managed to make any cakes.'

Thursday nodded. They pedalled through the streets and on to Fratton, where Elsie's family lived in a small house in a quiet back street.

She banged loudly on the front door. 'Dad put in a bell but it's stopped working. Hello, our Eddy,' she greeted the small boy who opened the door. 'I've got something for you.'

The boy was about seven. He stared at Thursday and then backed away, shouting over his shoulder. 'It's our Elsie, and she's brought a lady with her.'

'Lady!' Elsie said, laughing. 'He must mean you, Thurs. I thought for a minute someone else had come in behind us. Hello, Mum,' she added, stopping to kiss a tiny, birdlike woman who had popped out of the kitchen like a wren from a nestbox. 'Looking as good as ever. This is Thursday, that I told you about.'

'It's not,' Eddy said. 'It's Saturday.'

'Her *name's* Thursday, silly. Thursday Tilford. She's a nurse with me at Haslar.'

Eddy stared at her suspiciously. 'How can a person have a day's name?'

'My mum and dad liked it, that's how,' Thursday told him. She smiled at Mrs Jackson. 'I hope you don't mind Elsie bringing me home.'

'Mind? Of course I don't mind! You being miles away from your own home and all. You're welcome. Now . . .' she bustled back to the tiny kitchen ' . . . you'll be wanting a cup of tea after that long ride. I'd have had the kettle on ready but I didn't think you'd be here yet. Thought you were going round the shops.'

'We were, but it's so flipping miserable. All those sandbags and things.' Elsie wandered out after her. 'Where's Dad?'

'Down the shed, mending my shoes. Go and give him a call, there's a duck.' Thursday heard the clatter of teacups being arranged on a tray. 'I made a few rock buns 'specially, supposed to be fruit buns but the currants look as if I chucked them in from the top of the hill. There just aren't any to be had, even on ration.'

Thursday looked around the room. It was small and cluttered, with a dining table in the middle and an armchair each side of the fireplace. On the wall was a big map of Europe which had been given out by the *Daily Express*, with blue pins stuck all over it showing where the Allied forces were and red ones where the Germans were. There were an awful lot of red ones, she thought.

Elsie came back in, followed by a large bald-headed man wearing a dirty shirt and braces. He wiped his hand down the shirt before shaking hands with Thursday and gave her a broad smile then jerked his head towards the map. 'Been looking at my arthritic efforts, then?'

'It's all right,' Elsie said. 'He knows it's supposed to be "artistic". Not that a few pins stuck in a map are anything to do with art.' She looked at the map. 'Blimey, it don't half bring it home to you what's going on. We think it's bugger all just because we're not getting the air raids they were on about, but there's plenty of fighting really, isn't there.'

'Language, Else,' her mother said, coming in with a tray of tea. 'You can see Thursday's a decent girl – she doesn't swear and nor should you. She used to work in a laundry,' she told Thursday, setting the tray on the table. 'Learnt a bit more than washing clothes, she did, and none of it much good to her.'

'They were a pretty rough lot,' Elsie acknowledged. 'But hearts of gold, all the same.' She looked at the map again. 'What d'you think's going to happen next, Dad?'

Mr Jackson was filling a pipe. He tamped down the tobacco, set a match to it and drew in deeply before answering. 'Well, it's up in Scandinavia mostly now, see. The Germans going into Denmark took the Allies by surprise a bit. It'll be Norway next, if I'm any judge, and then us.'

'But they were supposed to be neutral,' Thursday objected. 'They shouldn't have been invaded.'

'It's for their "protection",' Mr Jackson said with heavy sarcasm. 'Mind you, they've turned the tables on the Germans a bit by not putting up a fight. That means they're not at war and the Germans can't take over. They've got to recognise their government, see?'

Thursday didn't really see but she nodded. Elsie was more sceptical.

'I don't see Hitler taking no notice of that. He hasn't bothered too much about rules so far.' She passed Thursday a cup of tea and looked at her mother. 'Is our Dave going to be home tonight?'

'Far as I know. You know he's broken up with that Eileen?'

'He never has! I thought she'd got her claws into him proper.'

'So did I, but he came home last weekend and said they'd finished. Wouldn't say why, but I reckon she'd been a bit sharp with him once too often. You know what she was like.'

'She was a real little cat,' Elsie told Thursday. Treated our Dave like dirt. Thought he was a little puppy-dog, and so he was for a while, but it wasn't ever going to last. Dave's not the sort to be ordered about.'

They sat chatting as they drank their tea, and then Mr Jackson went back to his shed at the bottom of the garden to finish his cobbling. Eddy took another bun and ran outside to play, and Elsie's mother got out some sewing. She was doing piece-work for the marine barracks at Eastney, she said. Lots of the women in Pompey and the surrounding towns were sewing various items of uniform. They got paid a bit for it, but it was war work as well and you knew that some sailor or marine was going to be glad of the stitches you put in.

'I wonder if my brother will get something you've made,' Thursday said. 'He's gone into the Army. But his regiment's in

Worcester, so I suppose it'll be people round there who do the uniforms.'

'Oh, your poor mother,' Mrs Jackson said, laying down her work for a moment. 'She must be so worried. Has he gone away yet?'

'He's just finished his training. He'll be going soon – to Belgium or France, I suppose, that's where most of them seem to be going. Or maybe Norway.'

'Our Dave can't join up,' Elsie observed. 'He's got a bad leg, see – had infantile paralysis when he was a nipper and it left him with one leg a bit short. He has to wear a surgical boot.'

'I never thought I'd be glad he had that,' Mrs Jackson said. 'Poor little chap, he was only five, and stuck in bed ill for months – but now look, it could have saved his life. It's funny how life turns out.'

'Here he comes now,' Elsie said as the back door opened and a young man appeared in the doorway. He had fair hair, a few shades darker than Elsie's blonde, and very dark blue eyes. He came into the room, limping a little, and gave Thursday a shy grin.

'This is my friend Thursday,' Elsie said, 'and this is our Dave. He's a bit of a nuisance but we can't get rid of him.'

Thursday grinned, recognising the same brother–sister banter that went on between herself and Steve. She thought Dave looked rather nice. He was a couple of years older than Elsie and although he wasn't very tall his illness didn't seem to have left him badly crippled. The built-up boot was barely noticeable and his limp no worse than as if he'd turned his ankle. He had the sort of face that creased easily into a grin, and the creases stayed afterwards so that he looked permanently amused and friendly.

'They tried,' he told Thursday. 'Elsie's been trying all her life. Put me in the rubbish bin once, she did, nearly drowned me in the bath, left me outside in the snow . . . But you can't keep a good man down.'

'It's all lies,' Elsie said, getting up. 'I couldn't help you slipping when I was washing your hair, and I didn't know that old pram had been left out for the dustmen. And it was you wanted to make a snowman.'

'I didn't want to *be* a snowman,' he retorted, and they both laughed. Elsie went out to help her mother get supper ready and Dave and Thursday were left alone.

'So how d'you like Pompey?' he asked, sitting down in his mother's armchair.

'I haven't seen much of it yet. The weather's been so awful, and we've been going to Lee on our half-days, or round Gosport. Elsie's talking about going to a dance-hall in Southsea some time.'

'Kimballs,' he nodded. 'It's quite good. Or there's South Parade Pier. I don't go dancing much myself,' he added.

Thursday felt awkward. She said, 'What d'you like doing?' She could only think of things he probably couldn't do at all – roller-skating, walking, playing football. She wondered what it had been like for him as a small boy, growing up with one leg shorter than the other. Had the other children picked on him or had they been kind?

'I can ride a bike,' he said, guessing her thoughts. 'I go miles. Over the other side of the hill – there's lots of nice places to go to. Southwick, Hambledon, Rowlands Castle. You ought to get Elsie and your other friend to come, now the weather's getting better.' His eyes were bright and friendly. 'We could go for a whole day somewhere.'

It was a nice idea. But Thursday thought of Tony and shook her head. 'I don't know. I've got a boyfriend, you see—'

'That doesn't stop you having a day out,' Elsie said, coming back into the room to lay the table. 'And Tony told me he didn't want you stopping in. You're not engaged, are you?'

'No, but—'

'Listen,' Elsie said, spreading a blue cloth on the table and getting a set of home-made cork mats out of the cupboard, 'there's a war on. We don't know where we'll be this time next year. We've got to have fun while we can.' She looked at the map on the wall, at all the pins clustered in France, in Belgium and in Scandinavia. 'I reckon Dad's right. Once Hitler's got all that lot under his thumb, he'll be looking across the Channel at us. There won't be much time for bike rides then.'

Mrs Jackson appeared in the doorway with an enamel casserole dish held in a cloth between her hands. 'Have you got that table laid yet, our Else? I've made a nice Lancashire hotpot, with plenty of veg. And there's a bottle of plums for afters, with some custard.'

'Lancashire hotpot!' Dave said, getting up to help Elsie with the knives and forks. 'My favourite. Must be because you're home, Elsie – all we get these days is corned beef. Corned-beef hash, corned-beef fritters, curried corned-beef balls – you wouldn't believe the number of different things our Mum's found to do with a tin of corned beef!'

'Oh, I would,' Elsie said feelingly. 'I can tell you, I would. I reckon the cooks at Haslar could give her a few tips, and all.'

It was getting dark when the girls finally returned to Haslar after an evening spent playing cards and listening to the wireless. They cycled in through the big gateway, waving their passes at the guard and keeping a careful eye open as they rode illicitly along the quarter-deck. As they parked their bikes in the shed, Elsie gave Thursday a sideways look.

'Feel a bit better now?'

'Yes, I do,' Thursday admitted. 'Thanks for taking me with you, Else. It was nice, meeting your family. It was nice being in a home again, if you know what I mean.'

Elsie smiled. 'I think our Dave fancied you a bit.'

Thursday shook her head. 'There's nothing like that. I can't just forget about Tony. We were just starting to get fond of each other.'

'That doesn't stop you going out and having a bit of fun with friends,' Elsie pointed out. 'You can't stay indoors all the time or just go for bike rides on your own. Tony wouldn't want you to do that.'

They walked away from the bike sheds towards the dormitory building. Thursday looked up into the sky. It was quiet, with no aircraft, but she could see the dim shapes of the barrage balloons that floated above them. For an hour or two, while they'd played hilarious card games – Chase the Ace, 99, Devil's Poker – she'd been able to forget the war. But now, back at the hospital, knowing that behind the blacked-out windows men were lying injured and ill, she knew that it couldn't be forgotten for long. And she knew that Elsie and Tony were right – nobody knew what was going to happen next. You couldn't live your life as if you had years and years ahead of you and all the time in the world to enjoy yourself.

You had to have fun while you could. You might not get many more chances.

Chapter Twelve

The war was spreading. Denmark surrendered only a day after being invaded, yet remained neutral despite being occupied by German forces. The newspapers explained this at length, but Elsie complained that she still didn't properly understand it. It was all to do with 'politics', she thought, and ordinary people like her just weren't expected to understand them.

Thursday didn't agree.

'You ought to try to understand them,' she said. 'Ordinary people can change politics. Look at trade unions. Look at the Labour Party.'

'My dad's Labour, always has been,' Elsie said.

'That doesn't mean to say you've got to be one. You can think for yourself, can't you?'

'Of course I can. But how do I know what to think if someone doesn't tell me?'

'Oh, for Pete's sake!' Thursday exclaimed, and Elsie laughed.

'Well, you know what I mean. I can't make up my mind just like that. I need to know a bit more about it.'

'Read the papers, then,' Thursday said, and picked up the crumpled *Daily Mirror* that Elsie had tossed aside once she'd looked at 'Ruggles' and 'Jane'. 'But don't just take what they say as gospel. Think about it.'

'You'd better come over our house again and listen to our dad,' Elsie told her. 'He's a shop steward, and he knows what he's on about.'

Thursday wondered what her own father would say if he knew that she was going to the home of a shop steward. He hated Labour politics and trade unions, despite working in a factory himself.

Worcester Porcelain had always dealt fair with its workers, he said, and you didn't need to go calling strikes when you had a fair employer. But Thursday could see that not all employers were fair, and what else could the workers do but withdraw their labour? What other weapons did they have? She sympathised with Elsie. It was very hard to know what was right and what wasn't, where politics were concerned.

Thursday had been over to Elsie's home twice more now. She felt at home with the Jacksons. Mr Jackson reminded her of her own father – even though his politics were so different – and Mrs Jackson treated her like another daughter. Eddy, having decided that her name was the only interesting thing about her, left her alone, but she got on well with Dave and they'd been for a bike ride together, pushing their cycles up the steep, chalky slopes of Portsdown Hill to coast down the other side to Boarhunt and Southwick. Dave had suggested the three of them take a picnic and make a whole day of it next time they got a Saturday or Sunday off.

'We could go up through Hambledon to Soberton or Droxford. The Meon Valley's nice, you'd like it.'

'Hey, don't get too ambitious,' Elsie warned him. 'We've got to ride back to Gosport afterwards, remember.'

On a bike, you couldn't tell that there was anything wrong with him. He had put wooden blocks on one of his pedals to make cycling easier for his shorter leg, and could cycle much further uphill than either Thursday or Elsie. When they had puffed their way as far as they could and finally dismounted, he would look over his shoulder at them, his face creased with his grin, and ride on to the crest of the hill. Portsdown was the only one he couldn't manage, and even then he was almost at the top before he was forced to give in and limp the rest of the way.

Patsy didn't come to Elsie's. She was spending all her free time with Roy Greenaway. They continued to quarrel but always made up again, and Patsy swung between moods of fury and elation. One day, Roy was a rat and she was never going to speak to him again; the next, she was blissfully in love again. The other girls got used to it and merely shrugged their shoulders and rolled their eyes.

Roy was the only one of the 'Three Musketeers' still at Haslar. Doug had been drafted to the *Rodney* with Tony and they were now somewhere off Scandinavia. Thursday and Elsie had been alarmed to hear that the ship had been damaged in an air attack but letters came soon to tell them that both boys were all right, though it had been 'a bit busy' down in the sick berth for a while.

'They take it so lightly,' Thursday said. 'As if it's a big game.'

'I don't suppose they thought so really. It's just the way they talk. To tell you the truth, I was surprised to hear from Doug at all. There was never anything between us. I suppose they just like to get letters from home. He always asks after you, by the way.'

'Can't think why. He never had a good word to say to me when he was here.' Despite Tony's assurances that Doug was a 'good bloke', Thursday had still never managed to get on with him. 'Anyway, I dare say they'll have both forgotten us by the time they come home again.'

Elsie cocked an eye at her. 'Absence not making the heart grow fonder, then?'

'It's nothing like that! Tony and me weren't serious either. We just write – you know, like you said, they like getting letters from home.' She turned away so that Elsie wouldn't see her colour rise.

Thursday had been dismayed when she first realised she was thinking less of Tony as the days and weeks went by. Missing him at first, she had gradually found her life and thoughts filling with other things. They were busy at the hospital, their training almost complete, and she'd even been allowed to help with one or two minor operations, flushing with delight when the surgeon told her she would make a good theatre nurse. With the spring weather improving every day, a cycle ride with Elsie and her brother was more attractive than staying in the dormitory writing letters and although she still sent him a letter every other day, they were shorter and talked less about 'missing him'.

She felt guilty, but reminded herself that Tony hadn't wanted her to wait. He'd known they hadn't had time to get serious. And she'd still be his friend when he did come back, of course she would. She wasn't serious about Dave either. Probably, she thought, Patsy was right and it was best not to get serious about anyone, the way things were.

I'll go on writing, she decided, but not so often. And I won't sign off with kisses. He won't mind, and we can just be friends.

The Allies landed in Norway, only to depart after no more than a fortnight. It seemed as if the German army was too powerful for them. People began to get anxious about an invasion again. Suppose the BEF, now in Belgium and France, couldn't hold out against them? What was to stop the Germans from crossing that frighteningly narrow strip of water? There were only twenty miles between Dover and Calais. Not much further than it was from Portsmouth to Southampton.

The word *blitzkrieg* was once again on people's lips. Air raids. Bombs. The unthinkable. The unimaginable.

And then, on 10 May, it became all too real.

'They've invaded the Low Countries. Belgium. And Holland. They're *bombing* them.'

Dave came rushing in with the *Sunday Dispatch* soon after Elsie and Thursday had arrived for their bike ride. The girls stared at each other and Mr Jackson snatched the paper.

'They've bombed the harbours – almost all the ships have gone. And they've sent in parachutists, and troops in gliders. And tanks – Panzers. They're overrunning *everywhere*.' He lowered the paper and looked at them. 'You know what this means, don't you. It's the end of the phoney war. It'll be our turn next.'

Thursday felt a cold trickle of fear down her spine. She looked at Elsie, and saw the same dread in her friend's eyes. Dave slapped his leg in frustration.

'Blast this thing! I wish I could go. What use am I, a flaming cripple?'

'Don't talk like that!' his mother said sharply. 'You're doing a useful job at home. I'm thankful you can't go.' She looked at her husband. 'What d'you think's going to happen, next, Bill?'

He was reading the paper again. 'They'll go for France next. Let's hope Churchill will do a bit better than Chamberlain. At least he's got a bit of fire in his belly, for all he's a Conservative.'

'It's going to be a coalition, though, isn't it? That's what they're saying. He'll put the best men in the jobs. Politics isn't going to matter.'

'Well, let's hope so.' He looked again at the paper and shook his head. 'It's looking bad. Mind you, we've got a lot of men in France and they might be able to hold 'em off – but if they can't . . .' He shook his head again.

The cold trickle of fear shivered further over Thursday's body. She thought of her brother Steve and her cousin Mike, both now in

France. She'd been anxious before, of course she had, everyone was anxious all the time – but it was more of a background anxiety, something you were aware of but lived with. Now, it seemed sharper and more frightening. Now, it seemed horribly likely that they might get hurt. Now, it seemed horribly likely that they might not even come home.

Blitzkrieg.

If they could do it to Holland, they could do it to England. Thursday glanced out of the window, almost as if she expected to see parachutes descending at that very moment. All she could see were the blue sky and the silver, floating barrage balloons. But she could imagine the puffball shapes of parachutes. She could imagine the aircraft and the falling bombs.

'Well,' Dave said, sounding subdued, 'it's not going to help anyone if we just sit here staring at each other. We might as well still go for our bike ride.'

He stopped, as if he'd been about to add something else but thought better of it. But everyone could finish his words in their minds.

It might be the last chance they'd have.

Blood, toil, tears and sweat.

It seemed to Thursday afterwards that that Sunday bike-ride was the last carefree day of the war. The three of them, their sandwiches already made and an apple each in their saddlebags, had set off uneasily, feeling almost guilty that they could still enjoy themselves while the people of Holland were suffering so much, but after they had puffed their way up to the top of Portsdown Hill and were coasting down through the narrow, primrose-spattered lanes to Denmead, their spirits lifted. It was impossible to be entirely gloomy on such a lovely May day, with the sun smiling out of a sky of tender blue and the hedgerows bursting into fresh green life. Amongst the soft gold of the primroses were purple splashes of violets, the fields were full of ambling cows and a stream sparkled between drooping willows. The thought of war seemed very far away and the three of them tried to set aside their fears and concentrate on enjoying this day, which seemed to have been handed to them as a gift.

'It's no good everyone being miserable,' Dave said as they sat on the bank of the little River Meon to eat their picnic. 'We've all got to go back to work tomorrow, and you two have got to be cheerful for your patients. Days off are meant to help us stay strong.'

'I know. I just can't help thinking about those poor people . . . What must it be like to be bombed and invaded?' Thursday looked around the peaceful fields, at the flowers in the grass, the trees with their leaves curling out from buds. 'I keep thinking – what if it happens here? How would we manage? The Army's all in France. It would be just us.'

Her answer came a few days later, when the new prime minister made his first speech to Parliament which was reported on the Home Service news. He offered little hope, only '*blood, toil, tears and sweat*' – yet somehow his speech, gloomy as it was, gave them heart. It was his determination that shone through – his determination not to be beaten. Without denying that the country faced an '*ordeal of the most grievous kind*', without offering any easy solution, he drew everyone to him by his confident assumption that the country was with him, that victory would be achieved by every man and woman working together. He made no apology for declaring that his policy was to wage war – war against monstrous tyranny. And that without victory there would be no survival – either for the British Empire or for mankind itself. And somehow he managed to covey his belief that victory was held in the hands of ordinary people, and not something to be left to those in power. And – what was more – his belief that together they could achieve it.

'*I take up my task with buoyancy and hope,*' he ended. '*I feel entitled to claim the aid of all, and I say, "Come then, let us go forward together with our united strength".*'

'He's got a wonderful way with words,' Thursday said soberly when the news ended and Helen Stanway switched off the wireless in the D Block mess. 'What he says makes you feel you really can win.'

'And so we can,' Helen said. Her father was an army major and in France now, and so was her fiancé, a captain. She looked pale and anxious, but the light of determination was in her eye and the set of her jaw. 'And we've got an important part to play. It's up to us to get the wounded men fit and ready to fight again.' She looked grave. 'I've got a feeling we're going to be seeing quite a few of them from now on.'

Again, Thursday felt a small shiver of premonition trickle down her spine. She glanced at Patsy, who had been subdued all day because Roy had been suddenly drafted to a ship – a 'pierhead jump' he'd called it – because of an attack on the convoy it was in, which had resulted in a number of injuries. The sick bay itself had been damaged and two of the SBAs killed. The ship had stayed at sea, helping others which had been struck, and Roy and another SBA had been sent out at less than an hour's notice. But where they were and when they would come back, Patsy had no idea.

Patsy really did love Roy after all, Thursday thought, never mind all her talk about not taking it seriously. She was still writing to Jeff, but – as Thursday wrote to Tony – as no more than a friend. But from the look on her face now, it was obvious to everyone that Roy had become far more than a friend.

His ship might be next, Thursday thought. And there'll be other ships sunk, too. How many of the wounded will make it back to Haslar? Are we really going to be as busy as Stanway thinks?

The atmosphere on the wards was tense. The recovering patients paced up and down, staring out of the windows, obviously itching to be back at sea. Some of them badgered the doctors to let them return to duty, and some succeeded in getting themselves discharged. The other men, not fit to be out of bed, were equally restless. 'How can we win a war when we're stuck here like bloody old women?' one demanded fretfully. 'Blimey, they got sick bays and sawbones on board, ain't they? All I needs is me dressings changed. I could still do me job, couldn't I?'

But as fast as the beds were emptied, new patients arrived to fill them. Ships were still being attacked and sunk in the Channel, and Haslar was the nearest hospital. The patients arrived by launch, ferried from the ships that came in to tie up at the jetties, or lay at anchor in the Solent. Thursday got used to helping them disembark at the hospital jetty and loading them on to trolleys to wheel them along the old, polished tramway. Sometimes she handed them over when they reached the ward, sometimes she came in with them and helped the QARNNs tend to their injuries. Usually, they had been more or less patched up by the doctors and SBAs on the ships that had brought them there and, so far, she had seen few fresh wounds. All the same, the sight of their gashed and broken bodies was enough to subdue her normally bubbling spirits, and she went to bed at night tired and dispirited.

'No use letting it get us down,' Elsie said. 'Remember what our Dave said, we've got to be cheerful for the patients. They don't want long faces round them, do they.'

Thursday smiled ruefully. 'You're right, and so's Dave. It's just – well, I can't help thinking about Steve, and my cousin Mike, in France. Hurt, and away from home.'

'And wouldn't you want them to be looked after by someone bright and cheerful?' Elsie asked. 'Course you would!'

A day or two later, Elsie opened a letter from her mother and told them that her brother Dave was joining the newly formed Local Defence Volunteers. 'It's for all the men who can't join the regular Services to be part of the armed forces. It's a sort of home army. Anyone between seventeen and sixty-five can join and they'll get proper uniforms and guns and things.' She read a bit further. 'They're just getting armbands to start with, but they can start training straight away. Then if we get a parachute invasion like Holland, they'll be ready for them.'

'Well, that's something,' Thursday remarked. 'I bet Dave's pleased.'

'He is, Mum says. He's been fretting at not being able to do anything. Now he'll be as good as anyone else.'

On the following Sunday they were able to hear Mr Churchill's voice for themselves when he made his first broadcast. His rolling voice boomed through the mess, calling the Nazis the '*foulest and most soul-destroying tyranny that has ever darkened and stained the pages of history*'. We must win, he told the listening nation. Together, we *would* win.

'We will,' Thursday said, gripping Patsy and Elsie by the hand. 'We *will*.'

Yet it was only days later that they heard that France and Belgium had begun to fall. The Germans were sweeping through to the Channel coast. Amiens was taken. Arras was surrounded. Boulogne was evacuated. And as Britain watched and held its breath, the BEF, pride of the Army, was forced to retreat to the beaches. Their backs were not even against a wall; only the sea lay behind them.

'What are they going to *do*?' Patsy asked, as she and Thursday walked back to D Block from the ward for breakfast after their night duty. She was almost in tears. 'They'll never get back – they'll all be killed. It's going to be a massacre!'

It had been a bad night on the ward. One of the patients, a young sailor who had been badly burned in an explosion in the engine-room of his ship, had died as Thursday helped the QARNN to change his dressings. They had known he was near the end, and had felt almost relieved that his suffering had stopped at last, but as Thursday had stared down at the young face, raw and reddened by fire, deeply pock-marked by shards of white-hot metal, she had felt a grief that seemed to foreshadow the horrors that were to come. I don't know if I can do this, she'd thought with sudden fear. I don't know if I can stand seeing more and more men come in like this, only to die . . . But the senior nurse, seeing her hesitation, had spoken sharply.

'Stop it, Tilford! You're here to help them, not to think about yourself.'

'I wasn't—' Thursday began, but the QARNN shook her head. 'Yes, you were. You were thinking about what *you* feel. You've been told before, over and over again, you must not, *ever*, allow your own feelings to get in the way of your work. Now, this poor boy needs attention even if he's gone beyond medical help. You can see to the body.'

She marched away down the ward, her back straight, and Thursday looked after her and then down at the still, ravaged body in the bed. She knew that the QARNN was right, and that she must not allow her own feelings to interfere with her work. But she knew too that the QARNN herself had been upset by the boy's death. Otherwise, Thursday thought as she began the task of laying out the wasted body, she would not have used the word 'poor'.

None of the nurses, however hardened they seemed, was totally immune from pity and emotion. And once again she thought of the men who were being driven to the beaches of France, the men who were being beaten back by the enemy they had been sent to conquer.

'I don't know what they're going to do,' she said miserably in answer to Patsy's question. 'I don't see what they *can* do.' She stopped and looked at her friend. 'D'you think – d'you think this is going to be the start of the invasion?'

They stared at each other. Then running footsteps sounded close behind and Elsie, who had been working in the Zymotics Block, panted up to them. 'There's something going on. I saw it from the upstairs windows. Come and look.'

She set off, still half running, for the gate leading out to the sea-wall. The other two glanced at each other and followed. There was already a small crowd of VADs, QARNNs and sailors crowding through the narrow opening, and the girls joined them, pushing their way through to stand in the long line forming at the top of the sloping wall.

'Boats,' Patsy said in wonder. 'Boats of all sorts. But what . . . ?'

'They're going to France,' Thursday whispered. 'They must be. They're going to bring the soldiers back.'

It was still early. Dawn had broken, but there was still a pale rosy tinge to the sky, and the tower and dome of the cathedral glowed softly like mother of pearl. Mist lay in gauzy shreds on the water and muffled the engines of the boats that slid across its surface. There was something ghostly about the long procession of boats, as if they were from another world.

Silently, they watched as the flotilla slid through the narrow neck of water between Sallyport and Blockhouse. Half of Haslar Lake must be there, they thought, as well as all the other creeks and inlets around the edge of the harbour. Boats of every description: family motor-boats and small yachts, used more often for Sunday jaunts in the Solent than for longer voyages; larger boats, owned by wealthy people who kept them pristine and polished but were offering them now on a journey from which they might come back – if they came back at all – battered and bloodstained. And tugs and ferries – one of the Isle of Wight paddle-steamers, and even one of the stubby little Gosport ferries.

'It's the *King*,' Thursday said, staring. 'It's the *Ferry King*.'

'It never is!' Elsie strained her eyes. 'I wonder who's on board. I know the skipper, Ted Chapman – he lives down April Grove, not far from my auntie. And Sam Hardy, his mate, my dad knows him, and their apprentice – Ben something – surely they've never taken him as well. He's only a boy.'

'But why are they going anyway?' Patsy asked. 'They're only little boats – they won't be able to bring many men back. Look at that one, it's not much bigger than a dinghy. What good will that be?'

'It'll be able to get close inshore,' said a sailor with his arm in a sling, standing nearby. 'That's what it is. They must be getting them off the beaches. The ships'll have to stand off, see – too shallow to get close in. So they'll need the little 'uns to ferry them over.'

'But how did they know to go? It hasn't been on the news.'

'Didn't people who owned small boats all have to register them a couple of weeks ago?' Thursday asked. 'I seem to remember something about it. Maybe this was why.'

'You mean they knew the Army would get caught? They knew, and never did anything about it?'

'What could they do? They couldn't bring them back till they got to the beaches, could they? And they did do something – they got all these little boats lined up ready to go and help. And made sure the Navy was ready, too. And the hospitals, like Haslar. I don't see what else they could have done.'

'They could have never sent them there in the first place,' Patsy said bitterly, staring at the passing fleet. 'They could have not had a war.' She was silent for a moment and Thursday saw tears slipping down her cheeks before she burst out again. 'It's not fair! All these boys having to go and fight, and get hurt and killed – their lives ruined, their families pulled to pieces. And why? What for? Because of some horrible man in another country who wants to take over the world. It's not *fair!*'

Thursday put her arm around Patsy's shoulders. 'We know it's not fair, Patsy. But you can't just stand by and let a man like Hitler walk all over people. It'd be us next. We had to stop him.'

'We haven't, though, have we? We haven't stopped him at all. He's taken over Norway and Denmark. He's bombed Holland and Belgium and taken them over, too. And now it's France. He's driving our boys out of France and we've got to send a lot of – of *dinghies* to go and get them back. He's *winning*, Thursday. He's winning, and it *will* be us next. We just haven't got a chance.'

The sailor turned on her. His eyes were angry, his face red. 'And if he wins, whose fault will it be?' he demanded. 'Yours, that's who. And people like you who give in. It's people like *them*, out there—' he jerked his head towards the apparently endless procession '—who're going to win the war. People who *won't* give in. People who're ready to stand up on their hind legs and give him what for, no matter what it costs. Not people like you, staying safe on shore and whining about things being *fair*.'

He drew in a breath and Patsy, her face scarlet and her eyes filled with tears, opened her mouth to answer, but he began again, drowning her voice, '*Nothing's* fair, didn't nobody never tell you that? It ain't *fair* that I broke my bloody arm falling down a companionway so that I can't be going, too, to do my bit. It ain't *fair* that my old dad got killed in the last war, so that my poor mum had to go charring and take in washing to bring up five kids. It ain't *fair* that there's thousands of poor bleeders over there now, waiting for someone to go and fetch 'em home. But *fair* don't have nothing to do with it. We got to forget *fair* and just get on with the job. And the sooner I can get my arm out of this bloody sling and get back to sea, the better. I'll be out of the way of you snivelling VADs for a start.'

Patsy stared at him. Her face was working with her efforts not to cry. Thursday tightened her arm around her shoulders and spoke equally angrily.

'We're not snivelling VADs! We've been up all night looking after patients, and we'll do the same tonight and every night as long as we've got to. And when they start bringing men back from France we'll work night *and* day to look after them. And we're not going to give in to anyone. But you can't blame Patsy for being upset. Her boy's over there somewhere, on a ship, and she's already lost a cousin on the *Grenville*. It's not always easy to keep hoping, 'specially when you're dog-tired.'

He looked embarrassed and shrugged. 'Well, maybe I did come on a bit strong. But you hear of these fifth columnists and so on, trying to lower morale. I reckon it's up to all of us to keep it up, that's all. We've bin through other wars and come out all right. We'll get through this one, too.'

'But not before there's a lot of people killed,' Patsy said in a shaky voice.

The sailor looked at her and made a face of wry sympathy. 'I know, love. But that's war, innit? There's always people killed. We just got to remember that most of 'em volunteered, one way or another. So far, anyway. And it's winning in the end that counts.' He paused and then said, very quietly, 'I reckon most of us'd be ready to give our lives so that the world can be free again. That's what it's for, innit.'

For a moment or two, nobody spoke. Then Elsie, who had been

unusually quiet, said cheerfully, 'Well, that's as maybe, but I'll tell you what I *ain't* ready to give up, and that's me breakfast! And a little bird told me it's sausages this morning, so let's go and get our share before them other greedy-guts snaffles them all.'

The news broke on Monday. Hundreds of requisitioned boats, from ferries to fishing smacks, cockle boats to barges, yachts to drifters, had already left and now others joined the fleet. Dinghies, pinnaces, even rowing-boats all came flocking out of hidden creeks and little harbours. If they were too small to make their own way, they were towed by bigger ships; some of them were swamped by the wash of the bigger boats, some were damaged by the stanchions to which the tow-ropes were tied being ripped away from their bows. But most of them got there, and joined in the great rescue, driving right into the shallows on the beaches of Dunkirk, and ferrying crowds of exhausted, wounded soldiers to the ships that waited to take them home.

The hospital radios were switched on for every news report. Anyone who had time would race to hear it, then report back to the wards so that nurses and patients alike could hear the latest. They heard the call for small ships, for steamers and ferries and motor-boats. Portsmouth Harbour, like every other harbour in the country, became alive with vessels, all setting forth on their mission of rescue. The girls went up to the seawall whenever they had the chance, to watch.

'A lot of them are going to be coming here, you know,' Elsie said quietly.

The other two nodded. Patsy had recovered from her moment of despair and was even more determined that Hitler would be defeated – here at Haslar hospital, if she had anything to do with it. They gazed at the procession of boats and then turned their eyes to the south, to stare past the Isle of Wight to the smudge on the far horizon.

Perhaps it was cloud they saw there; perhaps it was the smear of smoke from the burning town of Dunkirk. But each girl felt a shiver as she watched it, and each girl felt that now the war had truly begun.

From this moment on, nothing would ever be the same again.

Chapter Thirteen

Soon the patients would begin to arrive.

Madam had called all the VADs together and told them that they were to stand by for a huge intake. Her eyes sombre, she had warned them that they must not expect these new patients to be as well presented as those they were accustomed to receiving from ships. There would be severe injuries to deal with, worse than anything they might have seen before.

'These men are coming straight from the beaches of Dunkirk,' she said. 'There are going to be thousands brought home, as fast as they can be shipped across the Channel. There won't be the facilities or the time to give them the treatment they need before they arrive here. We must be ready to do whatever is needed, and we must be ready to work all the hours we can. There will be no time off, except for essential eating and sleeping – and not too much of that either.' Her brown eyes moved slowly over the faces of the silent girls. 'I know I can rely on every one of you to give of your best.'

The girls went back to their duties quiet and a little nervous. Thursday and Patsy found themselves together in the sluice, washing out bedpans. They paused for a moment, unsure of what to say.

'This is it, isn't it,' Patsy said at last. 'The real beginning.' She looked at Thursday a little fearfully. 'I know we've seen plenty of wounds before, but it sounds as if this is going to be just awful. I just hope we can cope with it, Thurs.'

Thursday nodded. 'I hope so, too. But we will, Pats. We will. We've got to, haven't we? It's what we've been trained for all these months.'

She went back to the ward, thinking of her brother and her

cousin, both in France. Were they even at this moment waiting on the crowded beaches? The thought made her feel sick. Perhaps they were on their way back already, she thought. Perhaps tomorrow she'd get a letter telling her they were safe.

The wards had been cleared of all who were fit to leave. Neatly made beds, the blue anchors on their counterpanes all perfectly in line, stood in rows waiting for new occupants. The operating theatres were ready, the medical staff on standby. All leave had been stopped. Thursday, who had been planning to have a few days with the family in Worcester, wrote to tell her mother that she wouldn't be coming.

She received an answer that told her that Steve and Mike were both in France and that nobody knew what had happened to them. Her heart sinking, she read the letter out to the others as they sat in the mess.

'My cousin's hubby's there, too,' Elsie said. 'And the boys – Tony and Doug, and Roy – they're probably mixed up in it somewhere as well, on the ships. And poor Stanway, her dad's a major and he's out there – I reckon nearly everyone's got somebody to worry about.'

'We've just got to do our best for the ones we get here,' Patsy said. Her face was white and the other two realised again just how much she thought of Roy Greenaway, despite their squabbles. 'And hope there's someone, somewhere, doing their best for our boys.'

'They won't *all* be injured,' Thursday said, trying to inject a positive note into the conversation. 'There'll be plenty that are still all right.'

'That's right,' Elsie said. 'No news is good news, that's what my mum always says. And we just got to pull together, like Mr Churchill told us. We can't give way. Mind you,' she added, 'he promised us blood, sweat and tears, didn't he? So I suppose we got to expect to cry a bit as well.'

Thursday thought of her brother, somewhere in France. Somewhere on the Dunkirk beach, perhaps, or already at sea and on his way home. Alive and unhurt, she prayed, and realised for the first time just how much Steve meant to her. She thought of their childhood, of growing up together. Squabbling over who had the skin on the custard, who would lick out the bowl of cake mixture, whose turn it was to have the cat on their lap. Walking to Sunday school together, stiff and clean in their best clothes, arguing under their breath; scrambling for the best biscuit in the tin. I've been greedy all my life, she thought. I've always wanted the best for myself, but if Steve comes back all right he can have everything. Custard-skin, biscuits, cake mixture – they were all things for kiddies. But if he comes back from this, I'll give him the world.

There wasn't time to think any more. Between listening to the wireless, scanning the newspapers and getting the wards ready – as well as caring for the patients still in hospital – there was barely time to think at all.

'Will we be getting soldiers?' Patsy wondered. 'I mean, there won't be that many sailors hurt, will there?'

Almost before the words were out of her mouth, reports were coming in of ships being blown up and sunk. HMS *Wakeful*, torpedoed by a German E-boat – six hundred men lost from below decks, those on the upper decks thrown into the sea to be rescued or drown. Then a drifter, fired on by her own side who mistook her for an E-boat as she picked up some of those survivors. And the Isle of Wight paddle-steamer ferry, *Gracie Fields*, launched by the singer herself only three years ago, sunk with eight hundred men aboard as she plied her way back across the Channel.

The news grew worse with every bulletin they heard. The Luftwaffe were out in force, strafing and bombing. They machine-gunned men on the beach and in the water. They attacked the ships as they stood off, waiting for the men to be brought to them. And then they were forced to defend themselves as the RAF swooped in like a cloud of angry bees and waged battle in the skies, above the heads of the soldiers and sailors struggling in the sea.

Brief as the news items were, they were enough for Thursday's vivid imagination to picture the details. As if she were there herself, she could see the sky which had been so blue and tender obscured by a pall of oily black smoke – smoke from the inferno of Dunkirk, smoke from the bombed and burning ships, smoke deliberately created to block the view of the bombers. She saw the sea, which had been so calm and blue, churned into seething, blood-reddened soup; the beaches strewn with the bodies of dead and wounded soldiers, in grotesque parody of the sunbathers who had once lain on the golden sands, and the boats which came and went a bitter reminder of the pleasure craft of a different world.

News filtered through each day, and each day Thursday felt as if she were living it with the men. She seemed to stand with them during those endless days, as they waited patiently for hours up to their necks or waists in the flowing tide. She seemed to watch them as they stood in the water because there was nothing else to do; as they queued because there was no other way. When the little boats came, she felt the cold, hunger, thirst and exhaustion of the men as they climbed aboard, almost dead with it, and fell into the arms of the sailors who had come for them. She felt their dulled relief as they heaved themselves into the ships and lay on the decks, crammed together, speechless and dazed, some unable to understand what was happening, since so much had happened to them. Some of them were wounded, some barely scratched. Some died.

Others, she knew, waited without patience. Their nerve had broken, their minds gone, and they screamed and panicked, pushing to climb aboard the boats, almost sinking them in their clumsy panic. All reason gone, they clawed at the sailors who shoved them back into the water, knowing that their small craft were too overloaded to float. They fought and raged, and in some cases were threatened with pistols before they would cease. Some were shot, to save the rest. Some simply fell back into the water and drowned.

'The poor bloody blighters,' Elsie said, in tears as they listened to the news late that afternoon. 'Oh, the poor, poor bloody blighters . . .'

'Listen!' Patsy exclaimed, holding up her hand. 'It's the siren! It's an alert!'

'They're coming!' Thursday was on her feet as the wail of the siren rose into the air, almost drowning out her words. She shrieked to make herself heard. 'It must be them – they're arriving already!' She grabbed up her cape and flung it round her shoulders. 'Come on – down to the jetty!' She was out of the door, followed by the others, and as they ran they could see VADs and QARNNs pouring out of every building in the hospital. Doctors and SBAs were there too, running as fast as their legs would carry them for the jetty where the men must land. And as they ran, they could see the boats – the little boats that had not gone to Dunkirk but could now play their own part, going out to the ships or across to the harbour railway station and ferrying the wounded men to the jetty where, for the past three hundred years, such wounded men had been brought to Haslar Hospital to be healed.

Thursday and the other two girls were amongst those receiving the first intake. They stood on the jetty, their capes and headdresses fluttering in the breeze, watching as the first Naval pinnace ploughed through the choppy waves towards them. The men could be seen lying in the bottom of the boat and, as they drew closer, Elsie gave an exclamation of pity.

'Just look at the poor devils! They haven't seen a wash in weeks. And those *bandages* . . .'

'We'll soon have them right,' Thursday said stoutly, but her heart quailed as she began to catch a glimpse of the injuries they must deal with. And the *numbers* – for beyond the first boat she could see another; and, beyond that, another and another and another. A whole line of them, stretching across the harbour. And she knew that as the first was unloaded of its wretched cargo it would turn and go back for more. It was like Dunkirk all over again – in miniature. Not thousands, but hundreds, all coming to this one hospital.

And, she thought, the same scene was being enacted in other naval and military hospitals all over the country. Not hundreds, but thousands.

The pinnace drew alongside. A matelot jumped ashore with the painter and wrapped it swiftly around the bollard. The nurses moved forward, ready to take their patients, and the sailors helped them lift the broken bodies carefully out of the boat.

'Go easy with this one. Got a broken back . . . This un's not so bad, just his arm smashed and a few grazes . . . This feller's eyes are all bandaged up, look, can't see nothing, the ship's doc says he mustn't be moved too rough . . . This one's bad. Burnt all over. Tell you the truth, we didn't think he'd make it across. He don't even like being touched . . .'

The man's screams proved the sailor's words. Thursday flinched as she tried to lift the body without hurting him, but it seemed impossible. She felt a sob rise in her throat as she tried to find a place where she could touch him without causing him searing pain. In the end, she gave up and steeled herself to lift him without paying attention to his cries, praying that once he was in the ward he could be given relief from his agony.

There was no time to think about him again. The stream of

casualties was swift and apparently endless. In the next few hours, Thursday found herself faced with injuries such as she had never seen before – torn and broken bodies, their limbs wrenched away, sightless eyes, heads swathed in rough, bloodstained bandages. There were broken bones, burns and bullet wounds, there were great bleeding cuts tied with hasty tourniquets or heavily padded, there were broken backs and pelvises and once, to Thursday's enduring horror, a man so badly slashed that the dark mass of his liver protruded from his abdomen. Surely, she thought, such a wound could not be survived – but even as it entered her head she thrust the thought savagely away and knew that even the faintest shred of hope must be seized on and used for the patient's recovery.

She didn't know how many hours had passed, sometimes with Patsy and Elsie at her side, sometimes with Vera Hapgood or Jeanie Brown or one of the other VADs. It didn't matter who it was: they all worked with equal determination and equal care in all the tumult. Around them was a cacophony of noise – boats coming and going, men and women shouting orders, patients crying out and screaming. The trolleys rattled back and forth along the paved way, their wheels clattering on the smooth stones. Above them, the late afternoon sky faded into evening and then darkened to night. The blackout was ignored. They had to have light and surely the German planes were too occupied in trying to prevent the rescue from Dunkirk. Occasionally, they were dragged away to swallow a hot cup of tea and a sandwich, but nobody wanted to stop for long and as soon as they had finished they were back at their posts back with the endless stream of wounded men.

It seemed to Thursday as if she had been working almost for ever when Patsy spoke suddenly in her ear.

'Oh, Thursday,' she muttered, 'look at this.'

The sailor they were lifting had a loose bandage over his entire face. He'd groaned, but the groan had had a strange sound to it and, alarmed, Patsy had lifted the bandage.

Thursday looked. The face was so badly damaged that it was almost unrecognisable as human. The nose had been smashed, the mouth torn and most of the the teeth knocked out. One cheek was bruised almost black, and as swollen as if the man had mumps. But above the damage the dark brown eyes were miraculously untouched and as she stared into them she saw recognition and caught her breath.

'*Tony* . . .'

'I thought it was. I couldn't be sure,' Patsy whispered, horrified, but Thursday nodded and so, grotesquely, did the man they were lifting. He groaned again and his torn lips twisted. 'Oh, my *God* . . .'

'He's in agony,' Thursday said. 'You can see. Oh, Tony, *Tony* . . .' She stared at him and felt a strange, twisting agony in her own breast. In the months since he had left, she had come to realise that she hadn't really loved him – but he'd been the first boy she'd felt real desire for, the first boy who had kissed her properly, the first boy who had found a place in her heart. And now, seeing him torn and bleeding and in pain, her heart went out to him in sorrow. 'Oh, *Tony* . . .'

'Come on, you girls,' Helen Stanway snapped, materialising beside them. 'Keep going. We've got to get these poor fellows up to the wards as quickly as possible. What's the hold-up?'

'It's Tony West. SBA West, who used to be on our ward,' Patsy explained rapidly. 'He was Tilford's boyfriend.'

'Oh.' Stanway looked at the mutilated face and it was clear that she was wondering how they could tell. 'Well, all the more reason to get him to the ward quickly. Get him on the trolley and then come with me. There's another pinnace coming in.'

Between them, the girls lifted the stretcher on to the waiting trolley. Tony's eyes were still fixed on Thursday's face and she bent towards him and spoke softly beneath the tumult all about them.

'You'll be all right now,' she said softly. 'You really will, Tony. Haslar's a marvellous place.'

He knew that, of course. He had worked here himself, nursed men through their own injuries. He had seen men recover, he had seen men die. And he knew too, as Thursday knew, that he might – along with so many of the other men who had been brought this far – have come to Haslar only to die. The deaths of Dunkirk had not ended on the beaches, or in the sea.

The phoney war was truly over. The real war was well under way.

It was over at last. The stream of patients slowly came to a stop. There were no more boats. On the ninth day, the doctors and nurses went down to the jetty and received the last few broken men; there was no one left alive to bring back. They walked slowly and heavily back to the crowded wards.

The beaches of Dunkirk were strewn with the last of the dead, some thrust into hastily shovelled graves, some left to the waves and the gulls. Some, who had died before it began, had been buried in the dunes and the fields behind the beaches. Some would be found and identified, some would never be known.

And yet, even in this darkness, Winston Churchill could find words to hearten his countrymen. The girls listened to his next broadcast, weighed down with exhaustion and the grim horror of all they had seen, and heard the words that were to carry them through the rest of the war, the words that once more stiffened the resolve of so many worn and weary people.

'*If the British Empire and its Commonwealth last a thousand years,*' Winston Churchill declared, '*men will say, "This was their finest hour".*'

Their finest hour? To Thursday, thinking of the exhausted men, travelling dazed and bewildered by ship and train to hospital or home, it was difficult to believe. Yet somehow, as he always managed to do, Mr Churchill managed to point to those who had worked so hard and with such courage to bring the men home. This was the spirit of Britain, he seemed to say, this was the spirit that would, despite all setbacks, eventually win the war for Europe and for the world. Once again, he inspired hope, defiance and determination, and as Thursday and the other girls listened, none had any doubt but that he would lead the country to victory.

'*We shall fight on the beaches, we shall fight on the landing grounds, we shall fight in the fields and in the streets, we shall fight in the hills; we shall* never *surrender . . .*'

There was little rest for the VADs, for those first few weeks after Dunkirk.

The hospital was packed with wounded – soldiers as well as sailors, for they had simply been brought to the nearest hospital at first. As their conditions improved they were transferred, until eventually all the patients were naval once more. The girls worked ceaselessly, often continuing long after their duties should have ended, to help the casualties and each other. They tottered back to their mess and dormitories only when they were too weary to carry on, ate without noticing what was on their plates and then fell into bed for a few hours' sleep. Then they were up and ready to go back again.

Thursday could never even have imagined some of the injuries she saw. Dressing them was difficult, sometimes impossible. The men lay awkwardly in their beds, some piled with pillows, some with none at all. Their exhaustion delayed healing and they seemed dazed and stunned by what they had endured. As they slowly got better, some of them talked about their experiences; others turned their faces aside and tried to forget.

'It was the queues in the water that got me,' one sailor told her as she changed his dressings. 'I was in charge of one of the boats, see, that was ferrying them off. Hundreds of them, there was, long queues of men just standing there in the water, waiting. Bin there for hours, tide coming up round 'em, going down again. Gawd knows what state they was in under their clobber. Must've had skin like sponges.' He flinched as Thursday removed the last pad of lint and began carefully to bathe the wound beneath. His little boat had been strafed, several of the men in it killed outright and two or three others, like himself, injured by bullets. 'Them at the front was almost swimming,' he went on. 'And as the blokes behind tried to get near the boats, the poor buggers at the front got pushed in even deeper. Just bloody bad luck if you couldn't swim.'

Thursday paused and looked at him. 'Do you mean some of them couldn't?'

'Stands to reason, dunnit. Not even all sailors can swim – reckon that if they get sunk, they'll be so far out at sea it wouldn't do 'em no good, just prolong the agony. So it stands to reason soldiers won't be no better.'

'But what happened to them?'

'What usually happens,' he asked, 'if you're in deep water and can't bloody swim?'

Thursday felt sick. She went on bathing the wound and then folded a dressing to go over it. The man went on talking. It was almost as if he had a festering boil, she thought, that must be lanced so that the pus could ooze out. The pus of his memories needed to be released or it would remain inside him, poisoning his mind. And she, as a nurse, had to listen, just as she had to bathe the wound to stop it going septic.

'That wasn't all,' he said. 'If you ask me, they was the lucky ones.

It was the poor bleeders on the beach I felt sorry for. Just waiting till they could even get near the water, knowing they didn't have a chance. And even when they did get to a boat, they wasn't safe. None of us was safe. Bloody bombers overhead, ships blown to bits as you climbed aboard. I saw one, just taken a big ferryboat load on, the ferryboat was just pulling away when a bomber flew over and dropped the lot. I never saw nothing like it. Just a huge mass of black smoke and flame, and bits flying everywhere. And the poor bleeders aboard . . .' He shook his head. 'Nothing left. Nothing to speak of. Just bits and pieces. The sea was full of 'em. Arms and legs and Gawd knows what, flying through the air and then floating past.' He was silent for a moment, then said quietly, 'I saw a bloke's head. Just his head, nothing else. His eyes were still open – it was as if he was looking at me. As if he was *asking* . . . I tell you, nurse, I don't never want to see nothing like that again.'

Thursday finished the dressing with shaking hands. Her legs were trembling and she wanted to sink down on the bed beside the man and put her arms around him. She wanted to cry with him, to hold him and feel his warmth against her; two human beings, bewildered and terrified by the reality of war.

Sister Burton's voice cut sharply into her thoughts and she jumped. 'If you've finished that dressing, Tilford, there are other patients waiting.' She was standing at the foot of the bed, her face severe. 'Bed number three needs a bottle, and number five has been asking for his water-jug to be refilled for the past ten minutes. You know it's vital that burn cases have their liquid levels kept up.' Her eyes rested on the sailor for a moment. 'You really mustn't keep the nurses gossiping. They've got important work to do.'

Thursday hurried to fetch the urine bottle, and then to fill the water-jug. As she passed Sister again on her way to the sluice, the older nurse detained her for a moment.

'I know the men have been through a terrible ordeal,' she said quietly, 'and as nurses it's our duty to give them whatever care we can. But it mustn't be at the expense of either other patients or ourselves. And we must never, never break down in front of a patient. You do understand that, don't you, Tilford?'

Thursday nodded, feeling a sudden lump in her throat. She knew that she had been dangerously close to tears as she'd listened to the sailor's tale, and she knew that Sister must have heard at least some of what he had been saying, and seen the effect it was having.

'Yes, Sister,' she said. 'Thank you, Sister.'

Sister Burton's eyes rested on her face for a moment. 'They all have terrible tales to tell,' she said gently, 'and it's only right that we, safe here at Haslar, should listen to them. But we must never let it interfere with our duties. Whatever happens, we must always be able to carry out our work.'

'Yes, Sister,' Thursday said and, perilously close to tears again, escaped to attend to another patient who was calling for a bedpan. I can take it better when she's telling me off, she thought, scurrying round the ward seeing first to this man and then to that. It's when she's being nice to me that she almost makes me cry.

Sister was right, though. The stories the men had to tell, the experiences they recounted, were so horrific that if you dwelt on them you wouldn't be able to cope. And nurses had to be able to cope.

'It's like you've got to grow another skin,' Elsie said when they talked it over later that night. 'Or put on a suit of armour whenever you go in the ward. I can see now why sisters and matrons turn into such dragons. They've been doing it so long they can't stop.'

'But Sister was kind to me really,' Thursday said. 'She knew I was getting upset and she came to put a stop to it. And I could see she was upset, too, inside herself. She'd heard the bit about the head, I'm sure. Anyone'd be upset by that.'

She went to see Tony whenever she had a chance. He was in a different ward and, as a patient, she wasn't really supposed to 'fraternise' with him. But the ward sister knew they'd been friends and allowed her in, on the strict understanding that it was only for a few minutes. 'The poor boys need all the comfort they can get,' she said. 'Just sit and talk to him about happier times. It's all any of us can do.'

Thursday approached his bed the first time with trepidation. She couldn't forget his horrific injuries and didn't know quite what to expect. She knew he'd had an operation and would therefore be bandaged, but was unprepared for the grotesque sight which greeted her.

'His head's all swollen!' she whispered to the VAD who had come with her. 'It's enormous.'

'No, it's just the dressings,' the girl reassured her. 'They've built a sort of wire cage round his face, you see, and then bandaged over that. So that it's kept sterile but the bandages don't actually touch him. It's all raw flesh, you see. The next operation he has, they're going to try taking some skin from his thigh and put it on his face. It's a new procedure but it's been quite successful so far.'

'Skin from his thigh? But that'll leave—'

'A raw patch there, yes. But it'll be very carefully done and looked after. And it doesn't matter if his thigh's a bit scarred, does it – not if it saves his face.'

Nothing was said about his life being saved. But Thursday had seen that appalling injury, and knew just how deep it had gone. She didn't know how Tony had managed to go on breathing, let alone living, during that terrible journey from Dunkirk to Haslar. Someone, she thought, had already saved his life. Now Haslar was continuing with the task, making every effort to ensure that he kept on living.

And Tony was just one man. One sailor, amongst so many.

She crept to the bedside and sat down on the straight-backed wooden chair, looking at the bandaged body. She hadn't realised before that Tony had many other injuries, too, but now she could see the splints and the dressings that covered him. Only one hand seemed unhurt, and she touched it softly, afraid that, however gentle she was, she might be sending ripples of pain through his body. But Tony didn't move. She didn't even know if he were aware of her presence.

She thought of the day she had first seen him on the ward, the day they had done Stoker Davis's enema. She thought of the day they had met in the Swiss Café, the day they'd cycled out to Lee, the night so soon after that when they'd gone to the dance together and he'd told her he was leaving. I'd just begun to fall in love with him then, she thought, but it was too soon to know if it was going to last. And then, while he was away, I began to see that it wasn't real, lasting love – not the sort you need for a marriage. But it's a sort of love all the same. We stayed friends and always will. And she felt the tears burn her eyes and brim over on her cheeks.

'Tony,' she whispered. 'Tony, it's me – Thursday. I'm here with you. You remember me, don't you? Thursday – Thursday you went dancing with, and cycling? Thursday you used to take to the Swiss Café? You remember me.'

There was no movement. The fingers lay limp in her hand. She swallowed back tears and started again, trying to bring back to him all the memories that had been in her mind.

'Remember the day we went out to Lee, and I had that row with Doug? Remember the day we gave Stoker Davis the enema? Remember Pneumonia Bridge and Bemister's Lane? You're back at Haslar now, did you know that? Back here, safe and sound. And nothing more's going to happen to you. Nothing bad. They're going to mend you and put you together again and you'll be as good as new. Everything's going to be all right, Tony. Everything's going to be all right.'

The other VAD came quietly to stand beside her. 'You'll have to go now, I'm afraid. Sister said only a few minutes.'

Thursday bit her lips. 'Does he know I'm here? Does he know anything at all?'

'We don't know.'

'He's in a coma, isn't he?' Thursday said. 'He's not responding at all.'

'It's better that way,' the girl said, her eyes full of pity. 'At least we know he's not suffering.'

Thursday turned and looked down at the still figure on the bed. The eyes were hidden by the cage of wire and bandage. The unbandaged hand lay still and limp. The man on the bed was undoubtedly unconscious, but who knew what was going on in his mind? Who knew for certain that his sleep was peaceful?

'We don't know that,' she said. 'We don't know that at all. But I hope – I really do hope – it's true.'

Chapter Fourteen

Not all men who came back from Dunkirk were injured. Some, like Helen Stanway's father and Roy Greenaway and Doug Brighton, were unscathed.

Others, like Thursday's brother Steve and her cousin Mike, didn't come back at all.

'Missing!' she said to Elsie when she received her mother's letter. 'That's all they know. Missing, both of them. They could be dead, or prisoners – we just don't know. They don't even know how to find out.' She was white-faced, dazed. She looked at the letter again, as if it might say something different this time. Steve, missing. Mike, missing. It couldn't be true. She felt sick.

'Here, sit down,' Elsie said suddenly. Her voice seemed to come from a distance and her face loomed close and then receded. Thursday stared at her, felt herself sway and then felt Elsie's hand on her arm, pressing her down into a chair. 'Put your head between your knees. Take a deep breath. That's right. And another. No, don't try to sit up, just stop there a minute . . .' She heard Elsie's voice talking to someone else. 'Just had bad news about her brother. And her cousin, too. Both at Dunkirk – didn't come back . . .' The voice faded amidst a concerned murmur of voices. She could make out Jeanie Brown's soft tones, and Ellen Bridges's louder Cockney, and then Louisa's commanding voice. Someone pushed a cup of water under her nose and she sipped it, choked a little and then lifted her head, staring at them with bewildered eyes.

'Our *Steve*. He hadn't been in the Army five minutes. He'd only just finished his basic training—'

'Oh, *Thursday*.' Patsy was beside her, putting her arm round her shoulders. 'Thursday, I'm so sorry.'

'It doesn't say they're dead.' Louisa had taken the letter from her fingers and was reading it swiftly. 'It says missing. They might be prisoners of war.'

'The army'll find out,' Elsie said. 'Don't you know where they were, or anything? Didn't they say in their letters?'

'You know they're not allowed to. All we knew was that they were in France.' Thursday stared at the scrap of paper, already stained by her mother's tears. 'Mum must be going mad, worrying, and so must be poor Auntie Flo. And there's her Leslie too, he's in the RAF, training to be a pilot. Oh, if *only* I could go home, just for a couple of days . . .'

'Ask Madam,' Louisa suggested. 'She might give you a couple of days. I'll come with you now.'

They went up the stairs to Madam's office together and knocked on the door, always left ajar so that the VADs felt at liberty to go to her at any time. Madam was at her cluttered desk, working on some papers. She listened with sympathy to Thursday's hesitant request, and then shook her head regretfully.

'I'm very sorry, Tilford. You know as well as I do how busy we are. With so many patients, we're at full stretch. I can't spare anyone, even for a moment, unless for the gravest emergency. If your brother had been killed, for instance . . . But it seems that there's still hope for him. I'm afraid there's no chance of any leave.'

Thursday knew she was right. There was far too much to do on the wards. The girls were kept busy running to and fro all day, at the beck and call of the QARNNS nurses. Their tasks were still mostly menial but they were, during 'specially busy periods, allowed to do more of the skilled nursing work that they had practised, like changing dressings or administering medicine, even injections. In the present emergency, they took on more and more, and Thursday was especially grateful for the extra responsibilities.

'It makes you feel you're really doing something,' she said to Patsy as a group of them sat in the office rolling bandages during what was supposed to be their time off. 'I don't know why I didn't go in for nursing years ago.'

'Probably because your dad said you had to be a tailor's apprentice,' Patsy said shrewdly. 'Dads have got a lot to answer for.'

'Well, he wanted the best for me, I suppose.' Thursday rolled in silence for a moment or two before returning to the subject that seemed to occupy so many of her thoughts these days. 'Oh, Patsy, I *wish* we knew what had happened to our Steve, and Mike. I had another letter from Mum this morning. She says Dad's written to the regiment but there hasn't been any answer yet. She's frantic.'

'They must be in an awful muddle,' Patsy said. 'There were men all over the place. Nobody knew who was where. It'll take ages to sort them all out.'

'Yes, but you'd think the men themselves would be able to get in touch somehow. I mean, if they're prisoners. Aren't there rules about that sort of thing? Aren't the Germans meant to let our authorities know, and let them write home?' Thursday sighed despondently. 'The longer it goes on, the worse it seems. Sometimes I think they must be dead, and sometimes I think maybe they got away and they're wandering round France, lost and starving . . .' The tears came to her eyes again and a picture came into her mind of Steve, aged about three, sitting on the floor with a chocolate biscuit in one hand and getting it smeared all over his face. 'I can't *bear* to think of our Steve like that, I just can't.'

'Perhaps the Germans are in a muddle, too,' Jeanie said. 'They must have taken an awful lot of men prisoner. It's probably taking them a long time to sort them all out.'

They sat in silence for a while. Thursday wiped her eyes and drew a deep breath, determined not to start crying again. She seemed to have done so much of that lately, either about Steve and Mike or about poor Tony, still swathed in his cage of bandages. But she'd managed, on the whole, to stay more or less dry-eyed when on the wards and she didn't want to break down now.

'Well, they're doing their best to get the Army together again,' Louisa said, trying to sound more cheerful. 'At least we're not going to let ourselves be beaten.'

'And how long's that going to take?' Vera Hapgood demanded. 'Months, maybe years – and meanwhile Hitler just marches in and takes us over. It's just the chance he needs, isn't it, while we've got no army to speak of. What sort of defence have we got against all those great big Panzers and things?'

'What do you mean, great big Panzers?' Patsy enquired. 'What d'you think they are?'

'Well, they're tanks, aren't they? Huge big tanks that can go over anything.'

'I don't think so. They're soldiers – German soldiers. What they call crack regiments.'

'Well, whatever they are,' Vera said, irritated, 'they can just march in and take over now, and there's not a thing we can do to stop them.'

Thursday lifted her eyes from the bandage she was rolling. Her jaw was set. 'There is. We can fight them. Like Mr Churchill said – on the beaches, in the streets, in the hills. We shall never surrender.'

'You'd surrender all right if half a dozen German soldiers were holding you down and raping you,' Vera said bluntly. 'Didn't they surrender in Czechoslovakia and Poland? And Belgium, and Holland, and all those countries in Scandinavia? It'd be the same here, too. You can't fight against the sort of army he's got.'

'But we're *British*. We don't get invaded. We haven't been invaded since – since—'

'Since 1066,' Elsie supplied. 'William the Conqueror. We did it at school.'

'Yes, that's right, so did we. Since 1066. That's nearly a thousand years ago.'

'Doesn't make any difference,' Vera said, occupying herself with a fresh bandage. 'Nobody's ever sent such a big army against us since, that's all that means. Look, *nobody* wins against Hitler. It's obvious.'

'And it's also unpatriotic to talk like that!' Elsie said angrily. 'You're as bad as a fifth columnist, trying to make us all miserable. I wouldn't be surprised if you're a spy!'

'Don't be daft,' Vera began, but the other girls were joining in, too, shouting at her and getting to their feet. One even threw a bandage at her. Patsy was almost in tears. The office was in pandemonium when into the midst of it all walked Miss Makepeace herself.

'Girls! Girls! What in heaven's name is going on?'

Her voice cut through the uproar, and the girls stopped shouting and stared at her in dismay. One or two began to cry. Vera looked defiant, and Elsie furious.

'We were just rolling bandages, Madam,' Patsy began uncertainly, and faltered to a stop under the icy glare.

'*Rolling bandages?* It sounded more like a bear-garden. And this bandage looks distinctly *unrolled*.' She bent to pick up the bandage someone had thrown at Vera. 'You realise this cannot be used now that it's been on the floor? A whole bandage wasted! I don't know *what* you were all thinking of.' Her brown eyes snapped with anger as she turned them on each girl in turn. 'Will someone please explain to me exactly what was going on? Tilford, you're a sensible girl – usually.'

Thursday bit her lips, wishing that Madam hadn't singled her out. Whatever she said now, she was going to get someone into trouble, and experience had taught her that she wouldn't be thanked for it. She looked down miserably.

'It was just a silly argument,' she muttered. 'It got a bit out of hand, that's all. I'm sure it won't happen again.'

'*I'm* sure it won't, too,' Madam said cuttingly. 'But I'd still like to know what it was all about.'

'It was Hapgood,' Elsie began furiously. 'It was all *her* fault, she—'

But Miss Makepeace cut her off with the lift of a hand. 'I was asking *Tilford*, if you don't mind.' She looked again at Thursday. 'Well? And just what was this silly argument about?'

'It was about the invasion,' Thursday said desperately. 'If one happens – and whether we could fight them – and what's happened in other countries. Some – someone said we wouldn't be able to and the rest of us said – well, we said what Mr Churchill said—'

'Very well. I think you've given me the gist of it.' Madam looked at Vera Hapgood, who was looking sullen, and at Elsie, who was still red with anger. 'Would I be correct in saying that you suggested we wouldn't be able to resist, Hapgood, and that you, Jackson, said we would?'

'She as good as said we'd let them rape us!' Elsie burst out. 'She's no better than a traitor!'

'*That's enough!*' Madam's voice cut through the hubbub as the other girls joined in, each eager now to give their own version. 'I've never known such disgraceful behaviour. This is a *hospital*. There are sick men here, needing your care. How can you shout and scream at each other like fishwives, when there are men only a few yards away who may be *dying*? Have you forgotten everything you've been taught – everything you should know without *having* to be taught? I'm ashamed of you all. Every one of you.' She paused for a moment, giving each girl in turn a scathing glance so that they wilted before her like flowers. 'You will all sign your names in the book as soon as you go off duty, and none of you is to go outside the gates of the hospital for a week. Is that understood? And if you find yourself bored with all the free time you'll find on your hands, you can go to each ward in the hospital and offer to do whatever tasks they allot you. They may have their own bandages to be rolled.' She turned to Elsie and Vera. 'Hapgood and Jackson, come with me. The rest of you, get on with your work. Without talking *at all*.' She gave them all another severe glare and turned to stalk out, followed by the half mutinous, half frightened figures of Elsie and Vera. The others looked at each other, anxious and embarrassed, and sat down again slowly, picking up their half-rolled bandages. Thursday glanced sideways at Patsy.

'I wonder what she'll do to them.'

'Not let them out again for a fortnight, I wouldn't wonder,' Patsy muttered back. 'Not that it makes much difference, when we're working all the hours God sends as it is. And we'd better not say any more. I wouldn't put it past her to be outside the door now, listening to hear if any of us dares speak.'

Madam did not return, however, and when they had finished their task the girls returned to the ward, where it was clear that Sister Burton knew all about their misdemeanours and was as angry as Madam. She received them coldly.

'You realise that your behaviour reflects directly upon me? And I imagined that I had a ward to be proud of. I thought I could rely on every one of you to be responsible and to carry out tasks usually allotted to trained nurses. Instead, you've shown yourselves to be no better than raw recruits, and as such you'll be returned to orderly duties.' Her icy glance was like a scratch across their faces. 'I hope you understand that this means the QARNNs will be even more hard-pressed, and that you needn't expect any sympathy from them.'

'We're really sorry, Sister,' Thursday said. 'Honestly, it won't happen again.'

'I should hope not, but I'm glad of your reassurance. However, such promises don't mean you won't be punished. I understand that all shore leave is to be stopped for the next week? Well, we'll find you plenty to do here, and if we can't, I dare say they've quite a few potatoes waiting to be peeled in the kitchens. I'm sure the time will fly!'

Her heels clacked away across the polished floor and the girls made rueful faces at each other. They dared not say any more, though, but went about their tasks as efficiently as possible, hoping desperately that their efforts would be noticed. Unfortunately, Sister Burton seemed to have developed the ability only to notice the things that weren't done properly, and for the next few days the wards echoed to her voice as first one VAD and then another fell victim to her irritation.

'What are you doing in the sluice, Nurse? Bed three needs changing . . . What are you doing with those sheets? The blanket baths should have been finished a quarter of an hour ago . . . What are you standing there for? The poor man in bed six needs a bedpan at once . . . Nurse, come here immediately – what sort of a dressing do you call this? Didn't you take in one single word of your training?' She stood with arms akimbo, shaking her head in despair. 'Really, I sometimes wonder what the Red Cross is thinking of, sending us such dimwitted girls. If you ever saw a dream walking . . .'

Her sarcasm reduced the girls to tears. Even Elsie, returning to the ward after her dressing-down in Madam's office, was subdued, while Vera looked at everyone as if it was all their fault and she hated them. Never a popular girl, she now withdrew into her shell completely, carrying out her work with just as much effort as was necessary to keep her out of trouble. She went through the day without the vestige of a smile on her thin, sallow face, and the men began to call her Nurse Sourpuss.

'It doesn't help,' Patsy said as they sat in the mess eating their supper towards the end of that dreadful week. 'She does her work, but she never puts anything extra into it. Sister's bound to have noticed.'

'It's not the men's fault we got into trouble,' Thursday agreed. 'And they're a good bunch – it cheers me up, too, to smile at them and have a little chat. It's about all that's got me through this.'

'You're lucky,' Elsie said morosely. 'You can go out again on Saturday. I've got another week of it, along with that long-faced little cat Vera. And to cap it all, Sister's put us on duties *together*. I won't be able to get away from her for a minute. Pass the bread and marge, Pats, I need a bit of comfort.'

'Perhaps she thinks you'll make friends with each other,' Patsy suggested, sliding the plate along the table. 'Here, have a spoonful of jam as well.'

Elsie snorted. '*Nobody* could make friends with that scaremonger.

186

I still can't get over what she said. It was almost as if she thought we'd *enjoy* being raped by Germans!'

'Oh, I don't think she really meant that—' Thursday began, but Elsie broke in, shaking her head vigorously.

'She jolly well did! You didn't hear what she said to me while we were on our way to Madam's office. She as good as said I was looking *forward* to it!'

The others were silent. Then Patsy said uncomfortably, 'Are you sure of that, Else? You didn't – well, misunderstand her?'

'No, I flipping well didn't. She said it plain. "Of course, they wouldn't have to hold *you* down, would they, Jackson?" I couldn't misunderstand that, now, could I?'

Patsy and Thursday glanced at each other unhappily. Elsie was right, you couldn't misunderstand that. And after Vera's other remarks, it really was almost enough to have her branded as a scaremonger – the sort of talk that could get you into serious trouble.

'Did you tell Madam she said that?' Thursday asked after a moment.

Elsie shook her head again. 'What's the use? She won't want one of her VADs branded as a traitor. She just wants us all to get on with being nurses. She wants us to be a credit to her.'

'Yes, but if Vera goes on saying that sort of thing—'

'If she does,' Elsie said darkly, 'I'll deal with her in my own way. You don't need to worry about Vera-blooming-Hapgood. Vera *No*good, that's what I'm calling her from now on. And if she dares say another word about me, or about us giving in to the bloody Germans, she'll wish she'd never been born. *I'll* see to that.'

Despite all the extra duties, Thursday managed to get in to see Tony at least once a day. She sat beside him, holding his lifeless fingers and murmuring into his ear, reminding him of the fun they'd had together and the things they'd done. The trouble was, there hadn't been all that many of them and so she found herself repeating the same things over and over again. Not that it seemed to matter, she thought, gazing sadly at his face, still swathed in bandages. He didn't seem to hear her, didn't seem to know she was there. In fact, every day he seemed to slip a little further out of her reach.

'He isn't doing well, is he?' she said to Jeanie Brown, who was the VAD on duty when she left on the fifth day.

Jeanie started to deny it, then caught the look on Thursday's face and bit her lip. 'No, not very well. The captain's worried about him.'

The doctors were all officers, most of them lieutenant commanders or captains. Their rounds were conducted like 'rounds' on ships – an inspection to see that all was in order as much as to treat the patients. Nobody was ever allowed to forget that Haslar was as much a ship as any that went to sea, and that patients were effectively on duty. But this didn't affect their treatment – unless it was to make it even more thorough. The naval doctors' code of behaviour was as strict as the men's, and their driving aim was to get them back on active service.

'What does he say?' Thursday asked, and Jeanie looked awkward.

'Well, you know they don't tell us anything much . . . But I heard him tell Sister he thinks there's some brain damage. You can't tell until the patient wakes up – but the longer he stays in a coma, the poorer the outlook is.'

Thursday knew this, but her heart sank at hearing it confirmed. She turned back to look at Tony's still figure, and tears burned her eyes. He'd been so pleasant, so friendly, such good company. And even if they hadn't been really in love, they'd been good friends and he'd made her feel special, just for a while.

'There's still a chance, though,' Jeanie went on determinedly. 'We're doing all we can to bring him round. I sit beside him, too, and talk to him like you do – except that I didn't know him so well before,' she went on hurriedly. 'But I can tell him about what's happening here. He was an SBA so he'd understand about hospital news. I talk about that, and what I do when I'm off duty – that sort of thing.'

Thursday nodded and tried to smile. She went out of the ward and crossed the broad square towards D Block, trying to blink back the tears that stung her eyes.

Poor Tony, so bright and cheerful, so full of jokes, yet so tender on that last night at Lee, when he'd told her he'd got a draft. Poor Tony, his face torn apart, his body wrecked, lying there in a coma, perhaps never to wake – and even if he did, what would life be like for him? What could life be like for a man with a ruined face and a damaged brain?

Oh, Tony, she thought, Tony. It would almost be better if you never did wake up . . .

Chapter Fifteen

Mary Tilford, her greying hair hidden beneath the turban she wore for housework and her everyday frock hidden by a flowered pinafore, opened the front door to find her sister-in-law standing there. They stared into each other's eyes for a moment, each asking the same question and each reading the same answer.

Mary turned away and went indoors, and Flo followed her. She was wearing a cardigan she'd knitted from one of Percy's old pullovers. It was grey and a bit shapeless, not one of her best efforts, and in ordinary times she wouldn't have been seen outside the house in it. Now, Mary knew, she hardly cared what she looked like.

'There's no news, then,' Mary said, going out to the kitchen to fill the kettle. She got two pale green cups and saucers out of the dresser and set them on the small wooden table with its covering of checked American cloth. She'd been making corned-beef rissoles and the ingredients were just ready for mixing – the corned beef flaked into small pieces, the potatoes mashed with carrots, a bowl of bread-crumbs and a bottle of OK sauce. She fetched a pint of milk from the shed, which was the coolest place, and poured some into each cup.

'No news,' Flo agreed heavily. She stood in the doorway and watched as her sister-in-law finished mixing the rissole ingredients together and shaped them into balls, placing them on a baking tray and patting them flat. The gas stove was already hot, and just as Mary slid them in the kettle began to whistle. She poured some hot water into the brown teapot, swished it about and then tipped it out before measuring two level teaspoons of tea into the pot.

'One for each person and *none* for the pot,' she said ruefully.

'That's what Lord Woolton says, isn't it? I must say I don't like it much. I like tea to *look* like tea – and taste like it, too. But we've all got to save wherever we can. Come and have a sit-down for a minute, Flo.'

'I wouldn't mind so much,' Flo said as they went back to the living-room and settled themselves in the two armchairs, 'if we'd got any idea where they were. But we don't know anything at all. All we've had about Mike is that one telegram – "Missing". It could mean anything.'

'I know. We've had the same.' The crumpled scrap of paper was on the mantelpiece now, behind the marble clock that had been Mary's mother's, and Mary got up and took it down, staring at it as if it might say something different this time. 'I just dread that telegram boy coming again. I dread it.' She put the paper back behind the clock.

'I know, and yet you *want* him to come as well. You want to *know*, don't you? And it could be good news next time, that's what you've got to think of.' Flo dropped a couple of saccharine tablets into her tea and took a sip. 'What I keep telling myself is there must be hundreds of soldiers in hospitals who've been wounded and aren't properly conscious yet – can't say who they are. Our boys could be like that. It's not that I want them to be wounded, of course it isn't – but they'd be *alive*, wouldn't they? That's the thing.'

Mary sighed. Flo was clutching at straws, but they were straws Mary wanted to clutch as well. If only Steve could be in hospital somewhere, peacefully asleep, wounded in some way that he could recover from – something that didn't hurt too much ... But her common sense told her that although there must be boys who were like that, and that both Steve and Mike could be amongst them, there were also many more who were dead or taken prisoner. And her mind would not stop seeing the beaches of Dunkirk – beaches she had never seen but imagined as long stretches of sand – crowded with the waiting men, and strewn with the bodies of those whose wait was over.

'They'd have their dog-tags, though, wouldn't they?' she said to Flo. 'If they were in hospital, they could be identified.'

'They could have lost them.' Flo wasn't ready to give up hope. 'They could have taken them off—'

'They're not supposed to take them off, ever.'

'But they *could* have. We don't know. Nobody knows.'

Mary was silent. She wanted to cheer Flo up – heaven knows, she wanted to cheer herself up – but this was a straw that was too fragile for anyone to clutch for long. The boys wouldn't have taken off their identity discs. Walter had told her there were circumstances in which the discs could have been damaged and unreadable – if the wearer had been shot, or blown up, for instance, without actually being killed – but she didn't want to think of Steve or Mike being shot or blown up. The only real possibilities were that they'd been either killed or taken prisoner.

'We'll hear before long, I'm sure,' she said at last. 'They'll have to let us know soon. They're calling all the men in again, those who had leave, so they'll be sorting them all out. They'll know who's still missing. And if they're prisoners, don't the Germans have to tell our people? We'll get some news soon.'

'I suppose so.' Flo sipped again and pulled a face. 'I don't like these saccharin tablets as much as sugar, do you? They're much too sweet. It's a horrible taste.'

'Well, don't put two in, then.' Mary was glad of an excuse to smile. 'Just use one!'

'I suppose I could do that,' Flo said, with the ghost of a smile. 'Funny how you don't think of the obvious, isn't it. I'll just rinse out this cup, Mary, and have another one, only don't tell Lord Woolton, will you. But, you know, I reckon I'll give up saccharin as well as sugar. Percy's always drunk his tea without. He says it's more thirst-quenching that way.'

'I suppose you'd soon get used to it. And how's your Leslie? Jenny said she'd seen Denise at that dance last Saturday and she said he was learning to fly. I told her I was sure she'd got that wrong.'

'No, it's true. They're training all those that have got an aptitude. I don't know what that means, I'm sure, our Leslie's never shown an aptitude for anything much, bar laying in bed on a Sunday morning. He's cock-a-hoop over it, of course.'

'But he's only just seventeen!'

Flo shrugged. 'Old enough to drive a car, old enough to fly a plane, it seems. I don't reckon they'll let him fly in action, though, not so young as that. It'll be a few years yet. No, it's not him I'm worrying about. It's our Denise.'

'Why, what's she been up to?'

Flo pursed her lips and leant forward as if she thought she could be overheard. 'She's been stepping out with a young man from the post office. Thinks I don't know about it, but Mrs Hawkins up the road told me her Rosie had seen them. Those dances she and your Jenny go to, she sees him there, and they've been to the pictures together too.'

'From the post office? Well, what's wrong with that? It's a good job, the post office is – civil service.'

'It's not the job I object to. It's the fellow. Twenty-four if he's a day, Mrs Hawkins says, and I went down to see for myself and she's right. He works on the parcels counter. Nice enough looking chap and a nice smile, but he's a bit free with it. Flirting with a girl from one of the offices, he was. I don't like it, and nor does Percy, and we're going to have it out with Denise tonight. He's too old for her.'

'Twenty-four!' Mary repeated. 'That's nine years older than Denise.'

'I know. I don't even like her having a boyfriend, not a regular one. It's all right going to a local hop, a crowd of boys and girls together, and I didn't mind when she said she was going with your Jenny, but going out steady with a boy – no, not a boy, a *man* – that age, well, that's a different kettle of fish altogether.'

'And what about my Jenny? What's she doing while your Denise is canoodling with this fellow?'

'You'd better ask her that yourself,' Flo said grimly. 'Is that those rissoles I can smell?'

'Oh!' Mary jumped up and ran out to the kitchen. 'Caught them just in time,' she called, lifting the tray from the oven. 'Good job you remembered them, Flo, we can't afford to waste food these days.' She came back into the room. 'I'll have a word with Jenny tonight. See what she's got to say about this chap from the post office – and see what she's been getting up to as well. The trouble with these young girls is that they can make themselves up to look so much older. I know for a fact she's been wearing lipstick and powder, and I'm almost sure I saw stuff on her eyes when she came in the other night. She wipes it off before she comes in, but it won't *all* come off on a hanky.'

'I know. Denise is the same, and she's painting her nails, too. I saw flecks of bright red varnish all round the edges of them the other day. Her dad's told her he won't have her looking cheap, but she takes no notice. It's this war, Mary. It's giving them all ideas.' Her mouth turned down as she thought again of Mike. 'I'll go now. I don't like to be out too long, in case – well, you know what I mean.'

In case a telegram comes. Mary knew exactly what she meant. She, too, was anxious every moment she was out of the house, in case the boy came sweeping down the street on his red bike with that dreaded brown envelope in his bag. She saw Flo to the door and they both looked up and down the street anxiously, as if he might be coming at this very minute.

'We'll hear soon,' Mary said, giving her sister-in-law a kiss. 'I'm sure we'll hear soon.'

'Yes. Yes, I know. And in the meantime . . .' Flo gave her a crooked smile. 'We've got plenty to worry about at home, haven't we?'

Mary watched her go, giving her a wave as she turned the corner, and then went thoughtfully indoors. She stood looking for a moment at the rissoles, cooling on their tray.

Denise, going out with a man of twenty-four. And her Jenny, supposedly out with her but apparently somewhere else instead. So who was she really spending her time with?

I'll have a word with that young lady when she gets home tonight, she thought grimly.

'He's not twenty-four,' Jenny said. 'He's twenty-two.' She tossed her dark curls and faced her mother defiantly. 'And he's really nice.'

'That's still too old for a girl of fifteen,' Mary said sharply, slapping a rissole and some mashed potato on her plate. Jenny was the only one who came home for dinner now that both Thursday and Steve were away. 'It doesn't matter how nice he is. And your Auntie Flo's been down the post office and seen him. She said he was flirting with all the girls.'

'Well, what if he was? Anyway, I don't believe it. He loves Dizzy, he said so.'

'*Loves* her?' Mary repeated in shock. 'What do you mean, loves her?'

'What I say. He told her he wants them to get engaged.' Jenny put her hand to her mouth and gazed at her mother with wide brown eyes. 'Only it's supposed to be a secret. You're not to tell Auntie Flo.'

'Not tell Flo! Of course I'll tell Flo. She's got to know. Denise is only fifteen – she can't be thinking of getting engaged. Her father would never allow it anyway, not till she's at least nineteen. And then only when he's sure the man's the right sort.'

'Well, Vic is the right sort. He's ever so nice-looking, and he's got a good job. What else do you want?'

'There's a lot more than that to getting married,' Mary said. 'And what I want to know is—'

'They're not talking about getting married. Just engaged. *Secretly* engaged. Nobody else would even know.'

'Half Worcester will know, if you've got anything to do with it,' Mary said. 'You've never been able to keep a secret. And getting married is what being engaged is all about, you silly girl. Anyway, Flo and Percy will soon put a stop to all that nonsense. What I want to know is what *you've* been getting up to.'

'Me?' The colour ran up Jenny's face. 'What d'you mean? *I* haven't been getting up to anything.'

'Oh, no? Then why have you gone as red as a turkey-cock? Come on, Jenny, out with it. What have you been doing while Denise and this Vic have been off spooning? Sitting all by yourself in the moonlight? Or did she get him to bring along a mate?'

Jenny's colour deepened. 'We haven't done anything we shouldn't—'

'Who is it, Jenny? What's his name? And how old is this one? About the same age as Vic, I should think, if they're friends.'

Jenny's eyes dropped. She scraped the rug with her toe. 'He's called Sam. Sam Hayward. He's in the post office as well, he's a sorter.' She lifted her eyes. 'He's nice, Mum, he really is. You'd like him.'

'And how old is he? Same as Vic?'

'He's twenty-three,' Jenny muttered, casting her eyes down again.

'Twenty-*three*? Oh, *Jenny*.'

'I don't see what's so awful about that! Why's age so important? Uncle Percy's five years older than Auntie Flo. Vic and Sam are only seven years older than me and Denise. It's not that much different.'

'Your Uncle Percy and Auntie Flo knew each other for a long time before they got married. And Flo was nineteen before they even started going out together. There's a lot of difference.'

'I don't see why,' Jenny muttered.

Mary looked at her. The girl's cheeks were still scarlet. 'You do know why. You know very well why. Now, be truthful with me, Jenny. Have you done anything you shouldn't? I want to know.'

'No! I've already *told* you! What do you think I am, some sort of a – a tart? Sam *respects* me, he said so, and he wouldn't do anything I didn't want him to. He – I – we—' Jenny floundered, and then burst into tears. She turned and pulled open the door, running from the room. 'Oh, it's not *fair*! You always think the worst of me – it's just not *fair*!'

Mary heard her footsteps on the stairs and then her bedroom door slammed. Overhead, she could hear noisy weeping and knew that Jenny had flung herself on the bed. She bit her lips ruefully, feeling tears in her own eyes.

So he 'respected' her, did he? And he wouldn't do 'anything she didn't want'? And Jenny couldn't even look her in the eye when she said so. Her only way out was to burst into tears and cry that it wasn't fair, like a small child caught out, and then run away.

I'll have to talk to Walter about this, she thought. And we'd better go round and see Flo and Percy, too. If we don't put a stop to this straight away, one or the other of those girls is going to be bringing trouble to the house. And Denise isn't even sixteen yet.

Just as if we haven't got enough to worry about.

'I knew this would happen,' Denise said furiously. 'I *knew* some old cat would see us and tell Mum. Why can't people mind their own business?'

Jenny shrugged. She had met Denise from work to warn her that there was trouble waiting for her at home and they'd gone into a teashop to discuss the matter. Denise was wearing a new pink blouse, she noticed a little jealously. It was funny about Denise, even with all the shortages she always seemed to have something new – a blouse, a jumper, a lipstick. She smoothed down her own green frock. It was her favourite and she'd set her hair only last night, but she felt shabby beside Denise in her pink blouse, and with her fair hair done in Marcel waves. 'You know what old people are like. Nosy and spiteful, just because their lives are practically over. Can't stand seeing younger ones having a bit of fun. The question is, what are we going to do about it?'

The waitress, a girl of about fifteen, appeared at their side with a notebook. 'You can have chips and Spam or chips and one egg, but you can't have chips and spam *and* egg, or—'

'For goodness' sake!' Denise snapped. 'We just want a pot of tea, all right? And a slice of cake between us.' She turned back to Jenny. 'Do about it? Why, nothing. We'll just go on same as usual. They can't stop us seeing Vic and Sam. They'd have to lock us in our bedrooms to do that.'

'My bedroom hasn't got a lock,' Jenny said. 'But I wouldn't put it past our Dad to put one on.'

'They can't do it,' Denise said impatiently, smoothing one hand over her waved hair. 'We've got to go to work, haven't we? They can't come with us. They can't watch us every minute. They can't even stop us going out in the evenings. This is the twentieth century, Jen, not Victorian times.'

'There'll be awful rows, though.'

'So what? I'm not scared of a row or two.'

Jenny chewed her lip doubtfully. She'd been in trouble with her dad before, of course, but never seriously, and they'd always made things up with a kiss and a cuddle. She'd never defied him in the way that Denise was suggesting now.

'I don't know . . .'

'Well, I do! I love Vic and he loves me, and we're not going to let anyone stop us seeing each other. We're secretly engaged. We'll be getting married one day. We've got to see each other.'

'Uncle Percy's never going to let you get married, 'specially when he finds out you've been going out with someone seven years older than you.'

'We can wait. We'll wait till I'm twenty-one. He won't be able to stop me then. Or we'll go to Scotland.' She became aware of the young waitress at her side, holding a tray and listening in fascination to their conversation. 'All right, you can put it down.' She poured two cups of tea and looked at her cousin. 'Well, what are you looking so pop-eyed about?'

'*Scotland?*' Jenny gasped. 'Why Scotland?'

'Because you can get married there when you're sixteen, without having to ask anyone. There's a place – Gretna Green. I read about it in a magazine. People who want to get married run away and they get married in a blacksmith's forge.'

'In a *blacksmith's* forge? You're making it up, Dizzy.'

'I'm not. It's true, I tell you, I read about it.' Denise put a lump of sugar in her tea and stirred it aggressively, her reddened lips pushed out in defiance.

'Anyway, you're not even sixteen yet, so you can't even do that.' Jenny looked at her cousin. 'Diz, I'm not sure about all this. I mean, I know you love Vic and he says he loves you—'

'He doesn't just *say* it, he does love me. Are you going to have a bit of this cake?'

'Yes – no, you eat it. Look, you won't do anything daft, will you? I mean – you don't want to take any risks. He *is* a lot older, and—'

'I can look after myself, thank you very much,' Denise said, biting into the slice of dry sponge. 'And Vic's promised me nothing'll happen. Anyway, what about you and Sam?'

'We don't – we haven't – we've never gone all the way.' Jenny's colour scorched her cheeks. 'But he wants to, I know he does, and I – I'm not sure I—'

'Well, me and Vic are in love,' Denise stated. 'And what we do is our business. And I might not be sixteen yet but I will be in a couple of months, and no one – not even my dad – is going to stop me doing what I like. Things are different now, Jen. There's a war on. Vic could get called up and go away, and I might never see him again. Why shouldn't we have what happiness we can while we've got the chance? What right does anyone have to ruin our lives by making us wait?'

'So what will you do? I mean, Scotland's a long way away and you know we're not supposed to travel if we don't have to. There's those posters: "Is Your Journey Really Necessary?" And I don't know what the fare would be, though I suppose Vic's getting a good wage. And where would you live? You couldn't stop at home, and—'

'Oh, for goodness' sake! I didn't say we *would* run away – just that we *could*. Vic hasn't said anything about getting married – not yet, anyway – just engaged. *Secretly* engaged.' She stopped and looked at Jenny. 'You never said anything to your mum about that, did you?' Her eyes widened as she saw Jenny's colour deepen again. 'Oh, Jen, you *didn't*!'

'I didn't mean to! It just sort of came out. I wanted her to know that you and Vic were serious. I'm sorry, Diz. I really am.'

'Oh, that's wonderful, just wonderful,' Denise said bitterly. 'Now everyone'll know. *Dad* will know. And all the old cats in the street will know. They'll all be looking at me. Honestly, Jenny!' She looked round for the waitress. 'We want to pay now.'

'I'm ever so sorry,' Jenny said humbly, looking at her cup of tea. She hadn't even touched it so far. She picked it up and sipped, but it was cold and she put it down again.

'Sorry's not going to help much, is it.' Denise brushed crumbs from her lips and got to her feet. 'Well, better go and face the music, I suppose. And I don't fancy being in your shoes, neither, when your dad hears about all this. And you and Sam aren't even engaged, not even *secretly*.'

Nor going to be, Jenny thought as she walked slowly home. She'd already begun to have doubts about Sam. It had been fun at first, going out with an older boy, but his kisses had scared her a bit. She'd only been kissed once or twice before and those had been fumbling attempts, with lips firmly closed. And Sam had wanted to touch her a bit more than she liked, even though it was exciting, too. She'd been sleeping badly, her body itchy and restless, and she'd worried quite a bit about whether she might be going to have a baby. Someone at school had told her you only had to kiss a boy to find yourself in the family way, and although she hadn't thought this seemed very likely, the way Sam had kissed her had brought the idea back into her mind. Suppose it was true . . .

'Don't neither of you girls never bring trouble to this house,' Mary had warned her and Thursday more than once. 'We've never had nothing like that in this family and we're not starting now.' And Jenny had thought of a girl she knew a few streets away, who'd had to get married suddenly and had a baby five months later. She lived in two rooms with her young husband now, and people said they argued all the time and the baby never stopped crying. Their landlady had given them notice, and her mum and dad still wouldn't speak to her or let her in the house.

I wish Thursday was home, she thought miserably. She could tell me if it's true, what with her being a nurse.

Perhaps it would be better not to see Sam again. Then, whether it was true or not, he wouldn't be able to get her into trouble. If he hadn't already.

She walked the last hundred yards down Waterloo Street slowly and reluctantly. Whatever she and Sam had or hadn't done, there was going to be trouble anyway. Mum would have told Dad about Sam, and about Vic and Denise, and he'd be waiting with a face like thunder. There was going to be a really horrible row.

As it happened, she needn't have worried. By the time she reached home, her mother and father had other things to think about.

'There's been a telegram!' Mary said the minute Jenny walked through the door. 'Oh, Jen, there's been a telegram about Steve – and your Auntie Flo's had one, too, about Mike!'

Chapter Sixteen

'You can have a forty-eight hour leave pass and a rail warrant,' Miss Makepeace said to Thursday. 'That's all I can give you, I'm afraid. You know how busy the hospital is.'

'I know, Madam. I'm really grateful. It's my mum I'm worried about, you see, she must be so upset. She and my auntie are really close.'

'Of course. And I'm very sorry to hear about your cousin. You've a brother missing, too, I believe?'

'Yes, Madam. He's *believed* killed – we don't know for sure. But we know Mike – my cousin . . .' Her voice choked on the words.

'Yes, I see. It's a very sad and anxious time,' Madam said. 'Well, you can go tomorrow morning. There's an early train from Portsmouth, you should be able to reach Worcester by the afternoon if all the connections work. You'll have to be back on duty on Monday morning, so you'll have to leave on Sunday afternoon at the latest. It doesn't give you very long at home, but it's the best I can do.'

'It'll be good just to have a few hours, Madam. Thank you.'

Thursday left the office and walked slowly down the stairs. She paced out to the seawall and stood gazing across the Solent to the Isle of Wight, thinking of Mike.

It didn't seem possible that he was dead. He was too young. He was her *cousin*. He'd only been in the Army for five minutes. It couldn't be true that he would never come home again, never come round to see Steve and sit in Dad's chair laughing at her, never kick a football about with his mates or play charades at Christmas. It couldn't be true that he would never sit at the dinner-table again, pouring OK sauce over his meal until Auntie Flo took the bottle away from him, never go to the pictures at the Scala, never have a proper girlfriend, never get married.

His whole life's gone, she thought, watching a frigate steam out through the neck of the harbour. His whole life's gone for ever.

And what about Steve? Had his life gone for ever as well? Wasn't he ever going to come home again to tease her and argue with Jenny, and go up to the pub with Dad? She remembered how they used to go on the train to Malvern and climb up Worcester Beacon to fly the kite Dad had made him, how they'd go down to Upton-on-Severn on a pleasure steamer on Sunday afternoons, how they'd go on Sunday school outings to Bredon Hill by charabanc. I didn't realise how much he meant to me, she thought. He was just Steve, my brother, a pest and a nuisance – except that he wasn't really a nuisance at all and I'd give anything to have him come home again.

The journey seemed endless. Thursday sat in the hot, stuffy carriage, staring out of the window and thinking of the last time she had travelled on this line, on her way to Haslar for the first time. She'd been excited, nervous, looking forward to her new life and the independence of being away from home. And at the same time, Steve had been starting on his new life, too, joining the Army and setting off for his basic training.

And now he was missing, and Mike was dead.

The train was full. Trains always were these days. Her compartment was filled with soldiers, all talking in loud voices. They tried to draw her into their conversation but she shook her head and they noticed her reddened eyes and left her alone. She sat in the corner, staring out of the window, trying not to feel bitter that they were alive and Mike was dead. Their own lives might not last much longer anyway. They'd come back safe from Dunkirk, but who was to say where they would be sent next?

She stood on the platform at Worcester station at last, her kitbag at her side. There was nobody on the platform to meet her – but she hadn't expected anyone, she told herself valiantly. Trains were so unreliable these days, you couldn't say for certain when you'd arrive anywhere, you couldn't expect people to hang about waiting on railway platforms. She made her way to the exit and handed over her ticket.

'Thursday! *Thursday!*'

'Jen!' Thursday exclaimed, feeling a surge of pleasure and relief. 'Have you been waiting long? There was a hold-up—'

'Only about an hour,' her sister declared with a grin. 'I got some time off from the shop. Oh, *Thursday* . . .'

Their momentary pleasure at seeing each other vanished in the sudden remembrance of grief. They stared at each other, tears welling from their eyes, and Thursday opened her arms to her sister.

'Oh, Jen, Jen . . . I still can't believe it. Our *Mike*. It doesn't seem possible.'

'I know. We can't believe it either. Auntie Flo can't stop crying. I wonder where all the tears come from, I really do. Dizzy says she keeps making cups of tea for her but she lets half of them go cold. She just looks at that photo he had took of him in his new uniform and then she keeps looking at the telegram as if it might say something different, but it never does. And Mum's nearly out of her mind over Steve.'

'There hasn't been any more news?' Thursday asked, knowing that if there had been Jenny would have told her at once. Her heart, momentarily lifted in hope, sank again as Jenny shook her head.

'No. Nothing. We don't know what to think. One minute Mum's convinced he's dead, the next she says she knows he's alive. She thinks he's in a hospital somewhere with a lost memory.'

'Well, I suppose he could be.' They walked to the bus-stop. Thursday wanted to get home to her mother as quickly as possible and it was already nearly four o'clock. She fidgeted impatiently as they stood there, waiting. 'Oh, Jenny, I've felt so awful, being all those miles away.'

'I know. We just want to be together, somehow. Only we – we won't be, will we?' Jenny's eyes filled with tears again. 'Oh, Thursday, it's just *horrible*.'

The bus lumbered along and they climbed aboard and found seats upstairs. The air was filled with cigarette smoke. Thursday tried to find something more cheerful to talk about. 'Did you hear Mr Churchill's broadcast on Monday evening?'

'Yes. We all did.' Jenny sighed. 'We didn't know about Mike or Steve then, but it still made Mum cry. She said it made her feel proud that he'd been there. Now – she just can't stop thinking how cruel it all is. Why can't they go and fight it out between them,

Churchill and Hitler and everyone? Why do they have to send boys like our Steve to do their dirty work? Why can't they just sit down and *talk* about it?'

'Well, I suppose they tried. That's what Mr Chamberlain did, wasn't it? But it doesn't do any good with people like Hitler.'

Jenny sighed and nodded. 'I suppose that's it.' Her voice wobbled. 'And Dad – I've never seen Dad so upset. He was crying the other day, I saw him. Our Dad, *crying*, Thurs.'

'Don't say any more,' Thursday begged her, unable to bear the thought of her father in tears. 'You'll start me off again. Let's talk about something else for a bit. Have you got a new boyfriend?'

Jenny wrinkled her nose. 'You could have picked something a bit more tactful! There was going to be a proper shindig if all this hadn't happened. I suppose there still will be, once they start thinking about it.'

'Thinking about what? What sort of shindig? What are you on about, Jen?' Thursday stared at her sister.

'Me and Sam Hayward. I've been going out with him for a few weeks now. Denise fixed it up for me when she started going out with Vic Pearce. He's one of Vic's mates at work, see.'

'No, I don't see,' Thursday said. 'Who's Vic Pearce, and who's Sam Hayward? I've never heard of either of them. Is he any relation to Mrs Hayward up the road?' She frowned at Jenny. 'What do you mean, you've been going out with him?'

'Well, what do you think I mean? Going out – going to the pictures and things. And I don't think he's any relation of Mrs Hayward. He comes from near Powick. Anyway, they both work in the main post office, him and Vic, and Denise got talking to Vic when he was on the parcels counter and they started going out together, and then she fixed it for me to go, too, with Sam. He's a sorter.'

'Well, what's wrong with that? They're both good jobs.'

'It's not their jobs. It's – well, Vic's twenty-two and Sam's twenty-three.'

Thursday stared at her. 'Twenty-two and twenty-three? No wonder Mum and Dad don't like it! Have they met these chaps?'

'No, but Auntie Flo went down the post office when she found out, and she said Vic was flirting with all the girls. The thing is, Dizzy says they're secretly engaged, only I let it out when Mum was on at me and of course she went and told Auntie Flo. And Dizzy was talking about running away to Scotland to get married, and – well, that's how it was when we got the telegram, so I don't know what'll happen now.'

'Dizzy's talking about getting *married*? But how can she? She's only fifteen. And why in *Scotland*?' Thursday put a hand to her head. 'I can't make all this out. Are you sure it's not some daft story?'

'No, of course it's not. And Dizzy says you can get married there without your parents' say-so when you're sixteen, and she'll be that in a few weeks. Honestly, Thurs, I don't know what to make of it all. She's got some story about a blacksmith's forge, you can get married over the anvil or something. It can't be true, surely.'

'I think I've heard something about that,' Thursday said doubtfully. 'But Auntie Flo and Uncle Percy will never let her go.'

'Well, that's the point, isn't it – she'd be running away.' Jenny shook her head. 'She's really fallen for this Vic. I – I'm a bit worried about her, to tell the truth.'

Thursday glanced at her. 'Why?'

Jenny turned her head away and Thursday's glance sharpened. 'Jen! You don't think . . . ?'

'I don't know.' Jenny gazed unhappily out of the window. The bus was just crossing the bridge. In a few minutes they'd be home and all the talk would be of Mike and Steve. She lowered her voice. 'Thurs, there's something I want to ask you. You know what they say about when a boy kisses you – I mean, is it true you can have a baby from that?'

Thursday stared at her. 'Just from kissing? No, it's not. Of course it's not.' She glanced around the bus, wondering if anyone could overhear their conversation, and felt a sudden twinge of panic. The whole thing sounded like a dreadful muddle and she wondered how her mother was coping with it all, on top of Steve's disappearance. 'Jenny, you and Sam haven't—'

'No more than that,' Jenny said hastily. 'Honestly. But it's the way he does it – sort of deep, if you know what I mean. I just wondered – I mean, people do say – and you being a nurse, I thought you'd know.'

'He'd have to go pretty deep for that to happen!' Thursday said. 'It's all right, Jen, if that's all you've done you're OK. But don't go any further.' She looked at her sister. '*You're* not thinking of getting secretly engaged, or married or anything, are you? Because if you are, I've got to say I think you're being really, really selfish. What about poor Mum, with all she's got to worry about – have you thought about her feelings? I mean, I'm not surprised about Denise, she's always been one for getting her own way, but I thought you had a bit more sense. I hope you're not thinking of running off to Scotland as well.'

'No. In fact, I've more or less decided to stop going out with him. I only went because Dizzy fixed it up for me. It scares me a bit. I don't want that sort of thing yet.'

'Well, all you've got to do is tell Mum and Dad that, then, isn't it.' Thursday stood up. 'Here's our stop.' The memory of her brother flooded back into her mind and she thought of her mother, sitting at home with Steve's photograph, waiting for another telegram, and Jenny's tale was pushed once more to the back of her mind. They were just silly girls, the two of them, she thought impatiently.

She pushed her way down the bus and dragged her kitbag out from the luggage space under the stairs. Jenny joined her on the pavement and they walked in silence the last few hundred yards to Waterloo Street and the house where Mary Tilford sat, gazing at a photograph of her son in his stiff new khaki uniform and the telegram that told her he was missing, believed killed.

'I can't believe it,' Mary said dully for the fifth or sixth time. 'I just can't believe it. My Steve. My *boy*.' She shook her head. 'I just can't believe it's true.'

'I know,' Thursday said gently. She and her mother had fallen into each other's arms, weeping, when she first arrived, but now the initial storm was over and they were sitting with cups of tea and a slice of cake brought in by Mrs Harting next door. Jenny, still subdued, had slipped out to the kitchen where she was scraping potatoes and carrots for tonight's meal.

'He was too young,' Mary went on, talking almost to herself. 'He was just a boy. He had all his life before him, and now it's gone, all gone. I just can't believe it.'

'We don't know yet what's happened to him,' Thursday reminded her, trying to convince herself that Steve could still be alive. 'He could still turn up. Just try to keep your mind fixed on that.'

She was having to try very hard not to cry again herself. The only way she could manage, she found, was to think of herself as a nurse, with the mother of one of her patients. She'd dealt with that often enough in the past few months, she thought sadly. Weeping mothers and sisters, wives and girlfriends, even brothers and fathers. They'd all needed a calm, reassuring presence, someone who would sympathise without becoming too involved in their tragedy. She'd been able to provide it, even though she had often wept afterwards, and it was what her mother needed now.

'Remember what the telegram says,' she went on. '*Missing believed killed.* They could be wrong. It was chaos over there, they didn't know half of what was going on.' But she had a dreadful, aching feeling that it was true. Steve was dead, just as Mike was dead, and he was never coming back.

Patch came and put one paw on her knee. She stared into his anxious face and her control broke. 'Oh, Mum. Oh, *Mum.*' Her heart was a fierce twist of pain against her ribs, spreading upwards into her throat and eyes and tightening across her skull. Tears were the only relief and, unable to hold them back any longer, she sobbed, 'Oh, Mum. *Steve* – our *Steve . . .*'

Jenny slipped back into the room, white-faced. She brought fresh cups of tea and she set them on the table and patted her mother's shoulder. Thursday felt for her handkerchief and wiped her wet face and blew her nose. She gave her sister a shaky smile of thanks and thought how Jenny had grown up in the few months since she'd last seen her. Probably she'd grown up most of all in the past few days.

'Sorry, Jen,' she murmured. 'I'm not being much help.'

'You *are*,' Mary said, hearing her. 'You're all the help in the world – both of you. I don't know how I'd have managed these past few days without our Jen, and it's so good to have you here now, Thursday. I just wish you could stop a bit longer.'

'So do I. But we're so busy in the hospital.' She stopped abruptly, remembering that many of the patients were men who had been brought back from Dunkirk, wounded but alive. 'I couldn't get more than a forty-eight-hour pass,' she finished lamely.

'I know. There's other mothers' sons need you. It's all right, Thursday, I know that. And I want you to go back and look after them. There's got to be *some* good come out of all this.' She wiped her own face and looked at Thursday. 'I'm glad you went to be a nurse. I really am glad.'

Thursday felt her eyes fill again and picked up her cup hastily. 'Drink your tea, Mum. Jenny's made some fresh, look. And she's out there now, getting the vegetables ready for tonight. What a difference! She didn't even know what the potato peeler looked like when I went away.'

'I heard that!' Jenny called. 'And I don't remember you doing all that much in the kitchen, our Thursday.'

'I did! I always helped cook the Sunday dinner, and wash up after it. You made yourself scarce then, if I remember right.'

'I had to go to church,' Jenny said with dignity. 'I'm in the choir.'

'Now then,' their mother said, 'don't you two start squabbling the minute Thursday gets through the door.' But she spoke fondly, as if it was good to hear their banter again. There was a small silence as she drank her tea and then, as if she'd remembered her anxiety all over again, her eyes brimmed over. 'But why did they send all those poor young men to France?' she cried. 'Why didn't they realise Hitler was too strong for us? They must have *known* most of them would be killed. Why did they ever do it?'

'I don't know, Mum. But you heard Mr Churchill on the wireless the other day. Jen said he made you feel proud. Remember what he said about Dunkirk? "*Their finest hour.*" Our boys are heroes. Maybe thinking that will make you feel a bit better.'

'Nothing'll make me feel better,' Mary said, dully. 'Nothing's ever going to make me feel better, except our Steve coming home again.'

When Walter came home half an hour later, Thursday felt her tears flow again as she embraced him, but this time she didn't try to hold them back. Dimly, she understood that although the mothers of her patients needed a nurse who would stay calm, her own parents needed to share their anxiety and grief with their daughters. And she needed to share hers, too. It wasn't right to hold it all back.

Jenny made him a cup of tea and announced that supper would be ready soon. She'd made a meat pie, with mince and carrot and onion, and the savoury smell was filling the house. She started to lay the table.

'I'll do that,' Thursday said, getting up. 'You've been slaving away ever since I arrived.'

'No, you sit and talk to Dad.' Jenny set the knives and forks beside the plates. 'You've only got a couple of days.'

Walter sat down heavily in his chair and received his tea. Thursday saw how drawn he looked, and felt a pang of sorrow. He's aged ten years, she thought. Poor Dad. He thought the world of Steve, and now he doesn't even know if he's still got a son.

'Are we going round to see Flo and Perce?' he asked his wife. 'We said we would, if Thursday managed to get home.'

'Yes, we'll go round about seven. We won't stop long, though. I don't like to be out too long in case – in case a telegram comes.' Her voice shook.

'Perhaps he's been taken prisoner,' Thursday said hopefully, but Walter shook his head.

'I reckon we'd have heard by now if he had been. Bill Brown at work, his boy's a prisoner and they heard last week. Mind, it must have been a real mess out there, with all the men separated from their units and everything. It'll take time to sort it all out.'

'Well, then, he *might* be a prisoner. Or he might even be hiding somewhere in France. Someone could be looking after him. They're on our side, after all.'

'So they say,' Walter grunted. 'I don't know as the French have *ever* been on our side. And they're giving in now, you can see it. Why, the Germans are in Paris now – how can they stand up against them? 'Specially now we're not there. They're being overrun.'

'They haven't surrendered yet. They haven't signed anything.'

'They will. They'll have to.'

Jenny brought the pie and vegetables in and they all sat round the table. Thursday was hungry after her long journey, and Walter, too, after his hard day's work, but Mary only picked at the food and then pushed her plate away.

'You've got to eat, Mum,' Thursday said gently. 'It won't do our Steve any good for you to starve yourself.'

'I can't fancy it. I can't fancy anything.'

'You'll get ill. You've still got Jenny and Dad to think about. What good is it going to do them if you get ill? They'll have to worry about you as well as Steve. And there's Auntie Flo, she needs you, too. And at least you've still got some hope for Steve – it's more than they've got. It's *selfish* to let yourself get ill, Mum. It's *unpatriotic*.'

Mary stared at her daughter and Walter made a movement as if to stop her.

'Don't talk to your mother like that, Thursday.'

'She's got to eat, Dad. She's got to.' Thursday turned back to her mother. 'Come on, try a little bit and it'll give you heart to eat some more. Never mind whether you fancy it or not – just eat some. That's it. And a bit more. It's not so bad, is it, even if our Jenny did get it ready!'

Mary gave a small, shaky laugh. She put some more into her mouth, chewed and swallowed. 'It does make me feel a bit better,' she admitted.

'Of course it does. Now try some more. You don't have to finish it, just eat as much as you can manage.' Thursday watched as her mother slowly ate the pie and vegetables. 'And eat something every mealtime, all right? It doesn't have to be much – just so long as you keep on eating. You mustn't stop.' She finished her own plateful and smiled at her sister. 'That was good, Jen. You're turning into a good little cook!'

After the meal, when the girls had washed up, they all walked round to Flo's and Percy's house. Mary and Walter walked behind and the two girls in front, just as they'd done when they were little. But when they were little, Steve would have been there too, scampering on ahead. Now, there was a gap where he had been.

'I don't know how you dared talk to Mum like that,' Jenny said. 'I've been treating her with kid gloves, frightened of making her cry even more.'

'You have to be cruel to be kind sometimes,' Thursday said. 'I learned that in my training. You can be really gentle with the men sometimes, but other times you have to just buck them up. You should hear the way we talk to the sailors!'

Jenny laughed. 'Don't they swear back at you?'

'Yes, sometimes. They get really narked. But it's better for them to be angry than sorry for themselves and they're usually OK after a bit.'

They arrived at their aunt's house. The blinds were drawn and inside the front room it was quiet and dim, the summer sunshine shut out. But at the back, the window was open and Flo was washing up the tea-things. In the garden, they could see Percy with his sleeves rolled up, hoeing his vegetables.

Mary kissed her sister-in-law. 'How are you feeling, Flo? I didn't think I'd find you doing the chores.'

'Oh, I'm not so bad.' Flo tipped the water down the sink and dried her hands on the roller towel behind the back door. 'I'm better doing something. And it's no use giving way, is it? Life's got to go on. Perce needed his tea, and there's no one else to get it. Our Denise has gone out somewhere – said she'd only be half an hour, but that was over an hour ago so goodness knows when she'll be back.'

'Denise has gone out?' Mary exclaimed, while Thursday and Jenny gave each other rueful glances. 'Well, that's not very thoughtful of her, in the circumstances. I dare say she's off out with that chap of hers?'

'Must be, I suppose.' Flo spoke wearily. 'I can't blame her for going, it's miserable here and she's as upset about Mike as we are.' She looked at Mary. 'I haven't said nothing to Percy about the feller. About how old he is, and all that talk about being engaged. What with – with Mike and everything – well, I couldn't bring meself to even think about it, let alone do anything. I just hope it'll blow over.'

'Well, let's hope you're right. And I won't say anything either. Now, you come and sit down and let me make you a cup of tea. Thursday's here too, look, she's got two days' leave to come and see us all, so we'd better make the most of her. She's done me a bit of good already, I can tell you!'

'Your mum's lucky to have you,' Flo said, giving Thursday a kiss. 'Just a shame you've got to be so far away. While I think of it, Mary, there's half a dozen eggs in that pudding basin, you can take 'em with you when you go. The hens are laying really well. And it'll be currant time soon, too, we must think about going and picking a few for jam and bottling. Mind, I don't know where we're going to get the sugar from – they do say we'll get extra sugar for jam-making, but I'll believe it when I see it. Oh, and I've got a knitting pattern for you, that one out of *Woman's Weekly* for a pullover, I'll look it out now—'

'Come and sit down,' Mary said again, gently. 'We can see to all that later. Come and have a rest and a cup of tea now. It'll make you feel better.'

Flo looked for a moment as if she were going to agree. Then she sagged, her momentary unnatural brightness dimmed. 'Oh, Mary,' she said, sinking into a chair and putting both hands over her face. 'Oh, *Mary*. I don't reckon *anything's* going to make me feel better. I don't reckon I'm ever going to feel better again.'

Chapter Seventeen

There was no funeral for Mike – there couldn't be, without a body to bury – but perhaps one day he'd be given a proper marked grave in a special cemetery in France, like the soldiers who had been killed in the Great War. But on Sunday morning they all went to the little church at the end of the road and the vicar said a special prayer for him, and all the others who had been killed at Dunkirk, and then for those like Steve who were still missing. And they sang 'He Who Would Valiant Be' as a special hymn for them. And afterwards, people who knew the family came up and shook Flo's and Percy's hands and said how sorry they were, and a few went back to the house for a glass of sherry. It was the nearest you could get to a proper ceremony and somehow it did seem to help.

'I can sort of believe it a bit more now,' Flo said afterwards, as she put away the plates and glasses that Mary and Thursday were washing. 'All those people being so nice about it. It makes it seem more real.' She paused. 'Not that I want it to be real. I don't, I don't at all.'

'I know, Auntie. None of us wants it to be real.' Thursday put down the glass she was drying and put her arm around her aunt's shoulders. 'But we've got to go on living, somehow.'

Flo nodded and rubbed her nose with the back of her hand, leaving a tiny moustache of bubbles. 'That's it. There's the rest of the family to think about as well. I wish our Leslie could have got leave, too, but he said it was impossible, they're all on standby even when they're not flying. I suppose you'll have to be going back tomorrow.'

'First thing,' Thursday said regretfully. 'We're so busy. And everyone's expecting the invasion to start any time.'

'Oh, Thursday, and you're right in the front line down there. It's one of the places they'll come, isn't it – the south coast.' Mary's voice shook. 'What will you do? Have they got places for you to go if there's bombs? And suppose they send in ships and troops – how will we ever stop them now that all our boys have been brought home? I can't bear—'

'Well, that's the good thing about it, isn't it,' Thursday said cheerfully. 'All our boys are back here—' her voice shook as she remembered that not all the boys were back, but she went on determinedly '—so they'll be on the spot straight away. They won't let the Germans set a single foot on the beach. Remember what Mr Churchill said. "*We'll fight them on the beaches.*" That's what we'll do. And we'll know when they're coming, too, because the bells will be rung to warn us, and Alverstoke church is only just round the corner from Haslar.'

'But where will you go?' Mary asked again. 'Have they built shelters?'

'There are huge cellars all underneath the hospital. It's all organised, Mum, they've even got operating theatres down there. Honestly, there's no need to worry.'

Mary sighed. 'Well, if you're sure.' She washed a mark off one of the glasses. 'That Mrs Hoskins, fancy wearing bright red lipstick to church! And it's all smeared on this glass. I don't know what the vicar thought. Still, she's a nice enough body.' She was silent again for a moment, waiting as Flo carried a tray of the best glasses through to the front room, and went on in a lowered voice, 'I just wish we could get some news of our Steve now, that's all. And I'm worried about poor Flo. She's bearing up ever so well, but she's got all that worry about with her Denise, too. Has our Jenny said anything to you?'

'About this boyfriend?' Thursday said cautiously. 'Well, yes, she has. He's a lot older than Denise, I gather.'

'Him and his pal, yes. The two of them ought to know better, going around with girls Jen and Denise's ages. Denise isn't even sixteen, you know. And talking about secret engagements, if you please! Well, stands to reason they must know it's wrong, or they wouldn't want to keep it secret, would they? And what's our Jenny been up to? She won't tell me a thing. I don't know what's to be done about it. Me and your dad were going to come round here and have a talk about it, and then the telegrams came . . .' Her voice faded, then she went on despondently, 'I suppose we'll have to think what to do about it now. Only I can't somehow. I can't seem to put my mind to it, and yet I can't stop thinking about it either. Our Jenny always seemed such a level-headed girl. I don't know what she's thinking about, going with a feller so much older, and encouraging her cousin as well.'

'I don't think you need worry, Mum,' Thursday said. 'Jenny told me she's stopped seeing Sam. She didn't really like it, him being so much older. And I don't think she was ever as keen as Dizzy.'

Mary tipped away the water. 'Is that true? Oh, that's a relief! At least she's got a bit of sense. Let's hope Denise sees it the same way. I dare say Flo will be round to see us later on, she said she'd call round before you went back. Perhaps we could have a word about it then. Anyway, we'd better go home now and have a bit of dinner, it's going to be late enough as it is.'

Sunday dinner was liver and bacon without the bacon. It wasn't much of a Sunday dinner, Mary said disparagingly, especially for Thursday's first time home, but there just hadn't been any meat at the butcher's, and what with everything else . . . Thursday declared that it was her favourite meal anyway, and if she'd been asked what she wanted it was just what she'd have chosen. And afters of stewed apple and blackcurrants from the allotment made it a feast. Her voice broke a little as she almost added that with Steve not there, she could have all the skin off the custard, and tears came into her eyes as she thought of why he wasn't there. But luckily her mother didn't seem to notice, and the moment passed. Jenny, however, seemed to realise why Thursday stopped so abruptly and reached beneath the table to give her hand a squeeze. The two girls looked at each other with understanding and Thursday thought with surprise how much her sister had grown up in the past few days.

'You'll look after Mum, won't you,' she said privately afterwards. 'You won't give her anything to worry about.'

Jenny shook her head. 'I know what you mean. And I'm definitely going to finish with Sam. I'm seeing him tomorrow to tell him.'

'And stick to boys your own age, right?'

'Don't think I'll bother with them at all,' Jenny said with a shrug.

'I'm going to join the Red Cross, like you, and learn first aid and nursing. I might even go down the Infirmary and see if I can get in there.' She looked at Thursday with a gleam in her eye. 'And how about you? You haven't said much about what you get up to. I bet you've got a few boyfriends, haven't you, what with all those sailors and doctors around?'

Thursday coloured. 'Don't be daft! Doctors wouldn't look at someone like me. There's plenty of VADs that are quite upper-class, you know. Helen Stanway, her father's got a title of some sort, and someone told me she's an "Honourable" herself, only she never says so, she doesn't put on any side at all. And there's Caroline Stoddart, she's a bishop's daughter, and Louisa Wetherby's father was a general in the last war and got a chest full of medals. I don't think the doctors are going to look at girls like me when they've got people of their own class.'

'It's not what their fathers do that they're interested in,' Jenny observed. 'It's what the girls'll do.'

'Jenny! And you were asking me if you could get in the family way by just kissing!' The girls dissolved into giggles and their mother came out to see what was going on.

'Honestly, I thought you must have got Arthur Askey out here.' She looked at them as they tried to straighten their faces, guilty at having found something to laugh at. 'Don't look so worried! It's good to hear you laugh. I don't think Mike would have wanted us to be miserable all our lives. Anyway, what I came out to tell you was that Auntie Flo's come round and she wants to see you before Thursday goes back.'

Jenny looked alarmed. 'I think I ought to go upstairs and do some mending. My stockings are all holes—'

'You've got to talk to her some time,' Mary said. 'You're the only one that knows about this fellow she's been going around with. Your auntie's worried.'

'I don't like telling on Denise,' Jenny began, but Mary shook her head.

'This isn't a kiddies' game, Jen. It's serious. If Denise is talking about getting engaged, they've a right to know. She's only fifteen.'

'I don't see why that matters so much—'

'Of course it matters! If they've been doing anything they shouldn't . . .' Mary hesitated, her colour rising. 'It's *against the law*,

Jenny. Kissing is all right, though I'd rather you didn't even do that till you're a bit older, but anything more is *against the law* with someone under sixteen. This Vic could be in serious trouble, and so could Denise.'

Jenny stared at her mother. 'Against the law?'

'Yes.' Mary was clearly embarrassed. Such subjects were never discussed, or even mentioned, normally. Thursday herself hadn't know the 'facts of life' until some older girls had told her at school, and when she'd started nursing she'd discovered that half those were wrong. Like Jenny's fear about kissing ... She knew that her mother was finding this conversation difficult, but it was something that had to be made clear. Jenny was over sixteen, but Denise wasn't, and if things had gone further than kissing – well, the 'trouble' that would be brought on Auntie Flo's house might be even worse than what was usually meant by that phrase – an illegitimate baby.

Jenny looked ready to burst into tears.

'But I don't know what Denise and Vic have done! She hasn't told me anything, honestly – only that they wanted to get engaged. I can't tell Auntie Flo anything more than that. I really can't.'

'Well, you'd better come and tell her that, then. Come on, Jen, you can't skulk out here in the kitchen for ever. And she wants to see you, too, Thursday.'

Thursday looked at her sister. 'Come on. You haven't done anything wrong. And Mum's right, you can't lurk out here every time Auntie Flo comes round.'

Reluctantly, Jenny followed her mother and sister into the living-room. Flo was sitting in Walter's chair, looking at the empty fireplace, and when Jenny saw her, tears came to her eyes. She ran forward to kneel beside her aunt, covering her hands with her own and looking up into the worn face.

'Oh, Auntie Flo, I'm ever so sorry. I really am. I never realised – I never knew all that about – about it being against the law and all that. But I don't think they – they *did* anything. I honestly don't.'

'You weren't with them all the time, though, were you? You and the chap you were going with?'

'No,' Jenny admitted. 'But I still don't think they did.'

'Have you asked her?' Mary asked, and Flo shrugged.

'With all the upset about Mike, I haven't had much chance. And when I did, she just flounced out of the room. I don't know what to do with her, Mary, I really don't.'

'I'm sorry,' Jenny said miserably. 'It just seemed fun and – and sort of glamorous, going out with someone older. And they had plenty of money, too, they could afford to pay for nice seats at the pictures – not like when that Freddy Billings asked me to go and then said he'd meet me inside! I never thought about it being against the law.' She looked up with sudden horror. 'We won't have a policeman coming round here about it, will we?'

'Of course not!' Thursday said at once. '*You* didn't do anything wrong, Jen.'

'But Denise? I mean, how would the police know? You wouldn't tell them, Auntie Flo?'

'That depends on what they did,' her aunt said grimly. 'And on whether I can calm your uncle down. He's in such a state about it, he might do anything.'

'But you couldn't have Dizzy put in *prison*!'

'Denise wouldn't go to prison, she wouldn't go anywhere. It's the man who'd be in trouble.'

'But it wasn't Vic's fault!' Jenny cried. 'He's a nice boy, he is really. He'd never do anything to hurt her. And she told him she was eighteen! How was he to know?'

There was a brief silence.

'She did *what*?' Mary said.

'She told him she was eighteen. She told me she had, and he said something about it, too. He didn't know she was only fifteen, he really didn't.' Jenny hesitated and then said in a rush, 'She – we used to put make-up on before we met them. Lipstick and powder and – and eye-shadow and mascara. Dizzy even had some red nail varnish. She *looked* eighteen. She looked older than eighteen.'

The silence this time was longer. Then Mary and Flo looked at each other and Mary lifted her shoulders.

'I reckon that's it, then, Flo. You can't really blame the chap. Denise does look older than her age, and if she made herself up and then told him that – well, I don't see as how we can say it was all his fault.'

Mary folded her mouth and sighed. 'No, nor do I. Not that it helps much when it comes to this so-called secret engagement. I mean, we're going to have to tell them they can't see each other any more. Perce will have to see this Vic and tell him the truth. But we can't watch her all the time.'

'Perhaps when he knows, he'll be scared off anyway,' Thursday suggested. 'He won't want trouble.'

'And what's our Denise going to say about that? You know what she's like. She's so headstrong, she's as likely as not to go off with him anyway. Scotland, they're talking about. We can't go chasing her to Scotland.'

'They'll never do that. Vic'd lose his job for a start, and he could probably get into trouble for taking her away as well.' Thursday shook her head. 'That's just Dizzy talking, Auntie Flo, you mustn't take any notice of that.'

'I suppose you're right.' Flo got up. 'Well, I'm glad we've got a few things sorted out, anyway. I'd better go home and talk to Perce. Denise is up in her room, sulking, and he won't let her go out, so we can have it out with her, too.' She looked at Thursday. 'Why don't you walk back with me, if you've got a minute? It might help to have you there, you having been away from home. And thanks, Jenny – I know you don't like telling tales. But, like your mum says, it's not a game.'

Jenny nodded, subdued. But when her aunt and Thursday had departed and Mary came back into the room, she saw that her daughter's eyes were full of tears.

'What is it, Jenny?' she asked. 'What's the matter? There isn't anything else you ought to tell us, is there? If there is, you'd better say so.'

Jenny shook her head. 'No. Honestly, Mum. It's just that – well, me and Dizzy have always been best friends. And now – now I don't suppose she'll ever want to speak to me again!'

Thursday walked back with her aunt, not quite sure what was expected of her. Being away from home didn't seem much of a qualification for taking her aunt's and uncle's side against her cousin. I hope they don't think I've already forgotten what it's like to be nearly sixteen, she thought, and I hope they don't think that because I've been away from home I'm somehow more 'experienced'. And I hope Denise doesn't think I've turned against her.

All in all, she would much rather not have been involved. But she knew all too well how strained everyone was just now. Mike missing for so long, then confirmed dead. Steve, still missing. And now this problem with Denise and Jenny. It was too much to cope with, all at once.

'It's not that we don't like her having her fun,' Flo was saying as they trudged along. 'Your Uncle Perce and me, we've always taken the view that youngsters should be allowed to do what they like and enjoy themselves, within reason. But it's got to be *within reason*. And going out with a boy seven or eight years older and talking about getting secretly engaged and running away to be married – well, that's not within reason. It's not, is it?'

'No, it isn't,' Thursday admitted. 'But I'm sure it is just talk, Auntie. I don't really think Denise would do it.'

'I don't know so much. She's always been a headstrong little hussy. I wouldn't put anything past her, 'specially if she's really keen on this boy. Boy! I keep saying that. He's a *man* – and he's too old for her.'

'Maybe if they waited a while—'

'Well, I said that, but your Uncle Perce wants them to stop seeing each other right away. He won't have it. He's really angry, Thursday.'

Thursday could see this was true, the minute they walked into the house. Her uncle was sitting by the fireplace with the newspaper held in his hands, but he wasn't reading it. He was glowering at the pages and when Thursday and her aunt walked into the room he turned the glower on them. Thursday stepped back a little.

'Now, there's no need to look at us like that,' Flo told him sharply. 'It's not Thursday's fault all this has happened. She's come round to see if she can help us talk sense into Denise, that's all.'

Thursday couldn't remember having said any such thing but she couldn't really say so. She gave her uncle a doubtful smile and was relieved to see his expression soften a little.

'I'm not blaming you, girl,' he said heavily. 'It's just that everything's such a mess. Your Steve – our Mike – and now this. And worrying about an invasion and bombing and whatever's going to happen next. It's not *knowing* anything, that's the trouble. Not knowing what Hitler'll do, what's going to happen to us all. I mean, suppose he uses gas? We've got our masks, but half the people don't bother about 'em. They carry the boxes, yes, but is there gas masks inside 'em? Sandwiches, that's what half of them use their boxes for!

Sandwiches! Bloody fine use they'll be if the Germans drop gas on us all.' He stared at Thursday and she saw with dismay that his hands were shaking. The newspaper rattled. 'I went through the last lot,' he said. 'I *saw* people with gas. It's not funny. It's not funny at all. And just as if we didn't have enough to worry about with all that, our Denise goes and springs this on us. It's selfish, that's what it is. Selfish.'

'Well, I suppose she hasn't been in love before,' Thursday ventured, and he snorted with disgust.

'*In love!* She's not in love! She's just a silly girl who's had her head filled with nonsense out of all those daft love stories she reads. Mills & Boon! Barbara Cartland! I've seen 'em. She's forever got one in her hand, when she ought to be helping her mother round the house. She thinks some tall, dark, romantic hero's going to come along and sweep her off her feet. So what happens? She falls for the first bloke that gives her the eye and believes every word he says. And because he's a few years older and got a bit more money to spend, she thinks he's bloody Clark Gable. If you ask me, she ought to be still playing with her dolls.'

A sound at the door made them all turn. Denise stood there, her eyes red-rimmed but defiant. She stared at them all.

'I heard you talking. You're talking about me, aren't you? You're planning what to do with me. Well, you're not doing anything, because I'm going away. I'm going to Vic, that's what I'm doing, and you won't need to worry about me any more!'

Flo gave a little cry and put her hand to her mouth. Percy flung down his newspaper. Thursday stood by, uncertainly, wishing she hadn't come. This wasn't her quarrel and she didn't see what she could do to help. And she wanted to be back with her mum, using the little time she had left to comfort her.

'Going away? Denise, you *can't*—'

'And she's not going to!' Percy said grimly. 'You're not going anywhere, my girl. You're under age and under my jurisdiction, and if you go out of this house I can get the police to bring you back. And it won't be just you in trouble, it'll be that boyfriend of yours, too, and he'll be in *serious* trouble.'

'Oh, but there's something else,' Flo broke in before Denise could shout back at her father. 'Something Jenny told us.' She looked at Thursday. 'Tell your uncle what she said, Thurs.'

Thursday glanced unhappily at Denise, who was staring at her as if she were a traitor. She shrugged apologetically and said, 'Well, I honestly don't know much about it, but what our Jen said was that Denise told Vic she was eighteen. And he believed her.' She gave her cousin another apologetic look. 'Honestly, I don't think I can be much help, I ought to go home—'

'No, wait a minute.' Percy stared at his daughter. 'Is this true, Denise? Did you tell him that?'

'Yes, I did. I didn't think he'd want to go out with me if he knew I was only fifteen.' Denise stared back at him. 'What difference does it make, anyway?'

'It makes a hell of a lot of difference, you silly girl! It means we can't take him to court if – if he's done anything he shouldn't have done. And it means—' He stopped abruptly. 'Well, never mind what else it means. Let's just hope it doesn't come to it.'

'I don't know what you're on about,' Denise said crossly. 'All we've done is love each other. What's so awful about that?'

'Love each other!' Percy repeated contemptuously. 'At your age! Well, let me tell you this, my girl, you won't "love each other" any more. You're not to see him again, understand? It's over.'

Denise stared at him. 'You can't do that. You can't stop me.'

'I'm telling you,' he stated. 'You're not seeing him any more. You'll be walked to work every morning and you'll be met every evening. You'll stay in every night. And I'll go down the post office myself and tell this Vic he's not to see you either. I'll put the fear of God into him. *And I'll tell him how old you are.*'

Denise's face whitened. 'You won't! You can't!'

'I will. You see.'

She stared at him, then at her mother, who was looking ready to cry. Finally, she turned to Thursday.

'Tell him he can't do this. We love each other, Vic and me – we'll *always* love each other.'

'Well, you can wait for each other, then, can't you,' he said. 'When you're twenty-one, you can do what you like.'

'But that's years away! Anything could happen!'

'If he can't wait, it means he doesn't love you, and you'll be better off without him. And it might be you who can't wait.'

'It won't be.'

'Your dad's right,' Flo said persuasively. 'You're very young,

Denise. I know you think you love him, but you haven't had a chance to meet other boys yet—'

'I don't want to meet other boys. They're stupid.'

'Just give it time. That's all we're asking. A bit of time.'

Denise gave them a withering glance. 'And just what time do we have? There's a war on, in case you've forgotten. Vic'll get called up. *He* could be the next one to be missing, or killed. What time does anyone have these days?'

There was a short silence. Then Percy said, 'You didn't have to say that. Upsetting your mother. And Thursday here, not knowing what's happened to her brother. You didn't have to rub that in.'

Denise bit her lip. Then she said, 'I just wanted you to know how much it matters to me, too. I'm just as upset about Mike as you are, and just as worried about Steve. But I love Vic, and he matters to me just the same way. If you stop me seeing him now – and he gets called up and goes away – and I never see him again – well, I'll never forgive you, that's what. I'll never, ever, forgive you.'

She turned and walked out of the room, and they heard her going upstairs. Flo looked at her husband and sat down abruptly.

'Oh, Perce. Oh, *Perce* – what are we going to do?'

'I don't know,' he said heavily, shaking his head. 'I just don't know, Flo, and that's the truth.' He picked up the newspaper, stared at it for a moment, then dropped it again. 'I'd better go and feed the hens. Won't do any good to let them starve, on top of everything else.'

'Would you go and have a word with her?' Flo asked Thursday appealingly. 'She might talk to you, you're nearer her age. I know you want to get back to your mum, but if you'd have just a quick word.'

'Well, all right.' Thursday moved unhappily towards the stairs. 'I don't really think it'll do any good, but I'll try.' She went up the stairs and tapped on Denise's door. 'Dizzy, it's me. Can I come in a minute?'

Denise opened the door. She had been sitting on her bed and Thursday saw a photograph lying on the pillow. A thin, friendly face, topped with dark, curly hair, grinned out at her and she had to admit he was attractive.

'Is this Vic? He looks nice.'

'He is.' Denise looked at her. 'I suppose they've sent you up to talk sense into me.'

'Something like that.' Thursday sat on the bed. 'I don't know that I can, though.'

'Nobody's going to change my mind,' Denise told her. She looked down and drew a pattern with her finger on the counterpane. 'I really am upset about Mike. It's awful.'

'I know.'

'But I keep thinking – what if it happened to Vic? They wouldn't even *tell* me. His mum doesn't know me. I just – wouldn't know. I couldn't bear it, Thurs.'

'I know, but you can't get married, you know that. Not even in Scotland.'

'We could soon. It's not that long till my birthday.'

'Think about it, Dizzy,' Thursday said gently. 'What would happen if you ran away together? Vic would lose his job – what would you live on? Where would you live? And if he did get called up – what would you do then? You'd have cut yourself off from your family and everything. You know what your dad's like – he'd probably refuse to have you back. And you'd break your mum's heart.'

'They're breaking *my* heart.'

'They're not. They're trying to look after you.'

'I might have known you'd be on their side,' Denise said bitterly.

Thursday sighed. 'I'm not on their side. I'm not on anyone's side. I'm just trying to see reason. They love you, Dizzy—'

'They've got a funny way of showing it!'

'No, they *are* showing it. They're trying to look after you—'

'I can look after myself!'

'Can you?' Thursday asked. 'When you're somewhere in Scotland, away from everyone you know, with a man you've only known a few weeks or months, who's got no job and has cut himself off from *his* family as well – and might start to blame you for everything going wrong? Will you be able to look after yourself then?'

'It won't be like that.'

'It might be. And in any case, he's bound to get called up sooner or later. You'll be on your own then.'

Denise was silent for a while. She twisted her fingers in the counterpane and said at last, 'What am I going to do, Thurs?'

'Well . . .' Thursday had been thinking about this question. 'Why don't you ask your mum and dad if you can bring Vic to meet them? Ask him to Sunday tea or something?'

'They'd never agree! You know what Sunday tea means. Dad would go mad.'

'All right, then, one evening during the week. Just ask if you can bring him round. They ought to meet him before they decide what sort of chap he is.'

'I know, but they won't. I've tried.'

'Try again,' Thursday advised. 'I think maybe they'll agree now. They're in a sort of corner, you see – you all are. Nobody will back down or make the first move. But if you say you're sorry you've worried them, and promise you won't do anything like get secretly engaged or try to run away and get married, and if they can see for themselves that Vic's a nice chap—' she looked at the photograph '—and he does look a nice chap, I can see that, well, maybe they'll let you go out together again. And if you're still keen on each other in two or three years' time, they might let you get engaged. Or even married. People do get married at eighteen.'

Denise chewed her lips and stared frowningly at the creased counterpane. 'Well, I suppose I could try. But—' she looked up at Thursday again '—suppose – suppose we *have* to get married?'

Thursday stared at her, feeling cold. 'What do you mean? Dizzy, you don't think – you haven't—?'

'I didn't come on this week,' Denise said in a small voice. 'That's the first sign, isn't it? I asked someone at work and she said it was. And – and yesterday I felt sick.' Her face crumpled. 'Oh, Thursday, I've been so scared. I didn't know what to do. And what with Mike – and then hearing about Steve – I don't know which way to turn. I can't tell Mum, I can't. It would break her heart. And Dad would kill me! Thursday, what am I going to do? I can't have a baby! I *can't*!'

Chapter Eighteen

Thursday sat on the train and gazed out of the window at the passing countryside. She felt, she thought, as if she had been wrung out through her mother's mangle. The two days at home, which would have been hard enough to bear if there had only been her cousin's death to think about, had been a nightmare, and she felt guiltily thankful to be returning to Haslar.

At least Jenny seemed to have seen sense and decided to finish with her boyfriend, but Denise was in a very difficult position. If she really was expecting, she was going to have to tell her parents, as well as Vic. Thursday had no way of knowing whether Vic would stand by her – the photograph showed a nice enough looking young man, but you never knew what anyone would do when things got tricky. It wasn't his fault that Denise had lied to him about her age, but the fact was that she *was* under age and not knowing might not be a proper defence. And Thursday had an idea that a doctor, once he knew about it, would have to report it to the police. Even if he didn't – and she knew there were rules about confidentiality – she still wouldn't put it past Uncle Percy.

'If you're only a few days overdue, it might not mean anything at all,' Thursday had told her cousin. 'It could be just that you've been upset. Are you always regular?'

'Not always, no. But suppose it is?'

'You'll have to tell your mum. That's the first thing to do. And Vic,' she added.

'And how do I do that, if they won't let me see him?'

'You can write to him. Anyway, you're going to ask if you can bring him round, aren't you? Look, you don't know that anything's happened, and you won't know for a few more weeks yet. Feeling sick yesterday isn't anything to do with it.' Thursday had only a hazy idea of what went on in pregnancy – it wasn't considered necessary to give detailed information to VADs who were going to nurse sailors – but she was doing her best to dredge up from her memory any scraps of knowledge that had come her way. 'You'd better just hope for the best,' she concluded at last. A clock struck downstairs. 'Look, I've got to go now. I'm catching the six o'clock train. Write and let me know how you get on, and for heaven's sake, don't do anything silly.'

Denise nodded tearfully and Thursday gave her an awkward kiss. She went downstairs and shrugged at her aunt's and uncle's questioning looks.

'I don't think she'll run off, or anything like that,' she said, hoping it was true. 'But she's got something to ask you. And – and I hope you'll agree.' She caught her uncle's look and flushed, knowing that he was about to say something caustic about being advised by a 'bit of a girl' even though she was a nurse. She went on hastily before he could speak. 'I've got to go now. Mum'll be wondering where I've got to. And – and I really am sorry about Mike.'

Her aunt nodded and gave her a kiss. 'Thanks for coming round, Thursday. You've been a real help.'

'I don't know that I have really,' Thursday said. 'But I dare say it'll turn out all right in the end.'

I hope it does, Thursday thought as she hurried away. And again, staring out of the train window a few hours later, I really do hope it does.

Leaving her mother had been even worse. Mary was tearful again when Thursday had got back to Waterloo Street, and her father didn't seem to know how to comfort her. He had his own feelings to deal with, and he and Mary had never faced anything like this before and weren't prepared for it. How did you prepare yourself for the death of your child?

'It just doesn't seem right,' Mary said sadly. '*You* expect to be the ones to go first, not your children. I know it's different in war – but we've already been through one lot in our lives. We didn't think it was going to happen all over again.'

'You don't know it is going to happen,' Thursday said. 'Steve's only missing – nobody knows for sure he's dead.'

'Not yet. But the longer it goes on . . . We've got to face it, Thursday. We've got to admit it's possible.' She sighed. 'It doesn't seem fair.'

'I don't think "fair" comes into it,' Thursday said. 'It's not up to people like us to decide when there's going to be a war. And we couldn't just stand by and let Hitler walk all over Europe.'

'Hitler never ought to have been allowed to get so much power in the first place,' her father said. 'He ought to have been stopped years ago.'

'But the Germans thought he was so good,' Mary said. 'Setting up the youth movement, and getting the country back on its feet. And nobody seemed to realise what he was doing to the Jews.'

'They didn't want to realise. They shut their eyes to it.'

'Well, we're doing something now,' Thursday said. 'And whatever's happened to Steve, we know he was doing something. He was doing his best for us all.'

'I'd rather he was at home,' Mary said, but the weeping seemed to be over, for a while at any rate, and she gave Thursday a shaky smile. 'You're a good girl, Thurs. I'm sorry you've got to go back, but at least you're safe where you are. And you're doing a good job.'

Jenny had been sitting quietly on the rug at her father's feet. They seemed to have made up their differences, Thursday thought thankfully, and got back to their old relationship. Jenny had always been her father's favourite – perhaps that was why he'd been so angry and upset about Sam. Now she looked up.

'I'm definitely going to see about nursing, too. I'm going round to see the Red Cross lady tomorrow, and ask about training for first aid, and I'm going to go down the hospital as well and see if I can train as a proper nurse.'

'I don't think you're old enough,' Thursday began doubtfully, and Jenny made an impatient noise.

'I'm not old enough for anything, it seems! But I will be soon. And there's no harm in finding out. There must be *something* I can do.'

'You can do first aid. It's nursing I think you have to be seventeen for, and they're not taking VADs till they're twenty-one. But you could probably get a job as an orderly or something, in the meantime.' Thursday hesitated. 'It's hard work, mind, and not very nice. Cleaning floors people have been sick on, taking round bedpans and washing them out, scrubbing the sluices – you'd get all the worst jobs.'

'I don't care. I'd be learning as well. And I'd be doing something to help – I'd be getting ready to do better things.'

Walter put down a hand and ruffled his daughter's hair. 'You're a good girl, Jenny. You go and do your nursing, if that's what you want. It's good training and it doesn't seem to have done our Thursday any harm. You might even end up in the same hospital together!'

'And talking of ending up in hospitals,' Thursday said, getting up and looking round for her kitbag, 'I'd better get moving or I won't be ending up in Haslar tonight. And if I'm late back, the ship will sail without me and Madam will have my guts for garters!'

Mary looked alarmed. 'What ship? You never told us you were going to sea!'

Thursday laughed. 'It's just the Navy, Mum. Haslar's a naval hospital, so it's counted as a ship, and Navy time's five minutes early, wherever you are, because if it was really a ship it would have gone. They don't wait, you see. It's a real crime to be adrift – late, I mean.'

They all followed her to the door and kissed her goodbye. 'You'll be careful, won't you, love,' Mary said, holding her tightly. 'You won't do anything silly.'

'Don't worry, Mum. We're safe as houses there, and they really look after us.' She hugged her father. 'Look after Mum, won't you.' She saw that his eyes were full of tears, and she buried her face against his shoulder for a moment. 'Oh, *Dad*—'

'Go on,' he said gruffly. 'Time to go. And don't worry about your mother or me, we'll be all right. It's your Auntie Flo I'm bothered about now, what with Mike and young Denise and all.'

'I know.' Thursday looked at her sister. 'You go and see about the Red Cross, Jen. You'll be all right. They're crying out for girls like you. And – don't do anything daft. You know.'

Jenny grinned a little crookedly. 'I won't. Don't you either.'

'Cheeky!' Thursday said with a grin, and hefted her kitbag on to her shoulder. She walked away and strode with a firm step to the corner of the street before turning back to wave.

They were all there – her mother, her father, her sister. But there was a gap where her brother should have been and, for a moment, as her eyes misted over she seemed to see him there, tall and proud in his stiff new khaki uniform, smiling and waving. And then he was gone, like a ghost vanished, and she had a dreadful, heartbreaking feeling that she would never see him again.

The train pulled in at last at Portsmouth Harbour station. Thursday dragged her kitbag out on to the wooden platform and made for the steps and the pontoon. The pinnace was there as usual and she scrambled aboard.

'Been home on leave?' the sailor asked. She knew him slightly, a big, broad-shouldered matelot with a cheery grin, and she nodded and smiled. 'Family OK?'

'Yes,' Thursday said. There was no point in regaling him with the troubles she had left behind. 'Anything happened here?'

He shrugged. 'They reckon the French are going to surrender any day now, and Mussolini and Hitler are going to get together. But I dare say you heard that anyway.'

Thursday nodded. None of it was good news. With France occupied and submissive, the threat of invasion was very real indeed. And with Italy – who had been their allies in the 1914–18 war – joining forces with the enemy, it didn't look as if there was anyone left to fight on Britain's side.

'We're on our own,' she said. 'And it's only twenty miles across the Channel – not much further than from here to Winchester. How can a little island like us stand up to all that?'

'Same as we did before,' he said stoutly. 'Show 'em what Britain's made of. Land of hope and glory, they say, don't they? Well, that's what we are and what we'll always be. And don't forget the Navy.' He tapped his chest. 'Best navy in the world, we are. Britannia rules the waves. It's being an island that keeps us safe. It might be only twenty miles – but it might as well be a thousand, for all the good it'll do Hitler. We'll never let him in!'

Thursday looked at his sturdy body and cheerful, determined face, and smiled. With men like him to fight, and men like Churchill to lead them, maybe a little island like Britain *could* stand up to the might of the forces that were massing across that narrow strip of water. Maybe Britannia could still rule the waves, and maybe Britain would once again be a land of hope and glory.

Hope and glory. Two words that seemed to express what Britain stood for. The hope that all would once again be well with the world. The glory of knowing that it was true.

Her grief for Mike and Steve was no less. Yet when she walked into the dormitory at Haslar and dumped her kitbag on the floor, she was still warmed by the glow that the sailor's words and cheery grin had given her. She looked at the other girls, who were lounging on their beds, mending stockings, knitting, reading or writing letters, and smiled.

'I'm back! And what have you lazy lot been doing while I've been away?'

They turned and stared at her. She saw the stillness in their faces, and the sadness in their eyes, and a terrible premonition gripped her heart. She opened her mouth to speak, but no words came.

Elsie got off her bed and came towards her, and Patsy followed and reached for her hand.

'What is it?' she whispered. 'What's happened?'

'Oh, Thursday,' Patsy said in a voice full of tears. 'Oh, Thursday – it's Tony.'

'Tony? What do you mean? What's happened to Tony?' But she knew already. There was barely any need for them to say the words.

'He died,' Elsie said in a small, flat voice. 'He died last night. It was very sudden and he didn't suffer, they told us. But – his heart gave out – he just *died*.'

Chapter Nineteen

It hadn't been entirely unexpected, the naval surgeon told Thursday. Tony had been very ill and his treatment had necessitated several operations. Each one had been a danger to him, yet there was nothing else they could have done. And, finally, his heart had given out under the strain.

'He fought a brave battle.' Surgeon Commander Kirkpatrick looked at her. 'Was he your sweetheart?'

'I don't really know,' Thursday said honestly. 'We went out together when he was stationed here, but when he was drafted he said he didn't want me to wait for him, he didn't want me to be tied. And we hadn't known each other all that long anyway. I don't know if it would have got more serious or not. But we were fond of each other – and we had fun – and I'll miss him.' Her voice quavered.

The surgeon nodded. He looked about thirty-five, tall, with curly light brown hair that gave him a boyish appearance. He looked tired, as if he'd worked a long time to try to save Tony and the other sick sailors under his care, and she felt suddenly sorry for him. How many other wives and sweethearts had he had to talk to like this?

'I'd better go,' she said. 'I'm due on my own ward in five minutes.'

He nodded again. 'I've seen you there. Miss Makepeace says you're a good nurse.'

Thursday blushed with surprise and pleasure. The girls always supposed that the doctors didn't even notice them, except as pieces of equipment standing ready to do their bidding on their rounds. She couldn't imagine that such august beings actually bothered to talk to Madam about the girls.

'Madam's wonderful,' she said. 'We all think the world of her.'

'And we think the world of you,' he said. 'All you girls, coming here and turning to doing all the worst jobs and never complaining. It makes a big difference to the hospital, having VADs here.' He gave her a sudden grin that made him look more boyish than ever. 'Mind you, I shan't talk to you like this when I'm on your ward! I shall be all stiff and starchy again then.'

Thursday met his eyes and saw the twinkle in them. She smiled back and wrinkled her nose.

'Yes, sir,' she said demurely, and turned to walk away. But as she passed the bed that had been Tony's and saw a different sailor there, her sadness returned and she felt a surge of misery and resentment.

Her mother was right. It *wasn't* fair that all these young men should suffer and die. It *wasn't* fair that their lives should be snatched from them before they'd had a real chance to live at all.

Land of hope and glory? She shook her head, and wondered if it would ever really come about. And how many more young men would have to suffer and die before it did.

Gradually, the Dunkirk wounded recovered and were sent to convalesce at home or in other hospitals, or went back to their ships or to other drafts. There was no lack of new patients, however. The Luftwaffe were in the skies every day, bombing convoys and ports, with the RAF on constant alert, ready to 'scramble' their aircraft to go and do battle overhead. Ships were sunk, some of their crews to be recovered and some to be lost. Of those who were saved, a large number came to Haslar.

'We may get patients of all nationalities,' Madam told the girls as they attended one of her lectures. 'Dutch, German, Italian – anyone who needs treatment will be brought here. Obviously—' she fixed them all with a stern eye '—they will receive the same care, *whatever* their nationality. They are our patients, and we will not engage in hostilities. Our job is to care for the sick – not fight a war.'

'But suppose they've sunk one of our ships?' Elsie asked doubtfully. 'Suppose they've shot down one of our pilots? I don't know as I can feel the same about looking after a man that might have done that, Madam.'

'You must try, Jackson. You *will*.' Madam was quite unequivocal about it. 'I say again, these men will be our patients, they'll be brought here for our care. We're nurses, and ours is not to question

232

or do anything else but our utmost for the patients, whoever they are and wherever they come from. Is that understood?' She swept her gaze around the rows of scrubbed faces. 'Very well. And there will, of course, be absolutely *no* fraternising. You don't have to talk to them – even if you can. All you have to do is care for their bodies.'

'So no getting friendly,' Patsy muttered as they filed out. 'Not that we'd want to, if they're the enemy.'

'I still don't feel right about it,' Elsie said. 'I mean, there's poor Tony, with that awful injury to his face, dying right here in Haslar, and there's Thursday's brother Steve missing, and her cousin dead, and all the others we know about – and now we're expected to look after Jerries and Eyeties. It just doesn't seem right. One minute we're trying to kill them, next minute we're trying to make them better. Just so they can go back and do it all again!'

'Well, they won't be able to do that,' Thursday said. 'They'll be POWs, won't they.'

'I suppose so. I still don't see why—'

'It's the rules,' Patsy said. 'The Geneva Convention and all that. You'd want them to look after our boys, wouldn't you?'

'Well, yes, but—'

'Well, then. We've got to look after theirs. And I bet that's all they are, too, lots of them – just boys, made to go and fight like our lads being called up. I bet they don't know what it's all about, half of them.'

They walked out to the seawall and stood looking out towards the Spithead Forts and the Isle of Wight. As usual, the broad strip of water was busy with ships and tugs. The girls sat down and gazed at the smooth blue sea.

'It still doesn't seem possible there's really a war—' Patsy was beginning, when Elsie gripped her arm and exclaimed, 'What's that?'

They stared where she was pointing. A small cloud of black objects, not much bigger than houseflies, had appeared on the horizon. They approached rapidly, growing to the size of blue-bottles, then bumble-bees. And that was what they sounded like, too. A low, snarling buzz, and then a drone. A rising, falling drone, like the snores of an evil man.

'It's German planes,' Thursday whispered. 'It's bombers. Patsy – Else – it's the invasion!'

They clutched each other's arms, staring. The planes came nearer and although the girls had no real idea of what the difference was between German and British planes, they were certain that these were the enemy. Transfixed with horror, they watched, waiting for the bombs to fall.

'We ought to get under cover,' Elsie whispered. 'We ought to get back inside somewhere—'

'No – wait. Look at that! There's another lot coming from inland somewhere. Who are they?'

'It's our boys,' Patsy cried, leaping up and down. 'It's the RAF! They're coming to see them off. Hooray, hooray, hooray!'

'It *is*. It must be. There's an airfield not far away, isn't there? Near Chichester?'

'Tangmere,' Elsie said briefly. 'Oh, look at that, *look* at that! They're starting to fire. They're all over the place, look. See, those little puffs, that's smoke from the guns. They've got them in the tails of the planes. Oh, *look*!'

'One's been hit,' Thursday whispered. 'One of the planes has been hit.'

There was a silence as they watched one of the aircraft drop away from the mêlée and fall towards the sea. A stream of thick black smoke billowed from one wing, and then there was a sudden burst of flame and the whole plane was engulfed and spiralled in a black and orange ball towards the sea. It hit the water in a huge spray of boiling steam.

The girls were silent, and then Elsie said in a shaking voice, 'Was that one of ours or one of theirs?'

'Whichever it was,' Thursday said, 'there was someone inside it. I didn't see anyone bale out, did you?'

The others shook their heads. They looked again at the spot where the plane had hit the water, but there was nothing to be seen from this distance but a slight surge in the glassy surface. Whoever had been in the plane must be dead by now. Probably, they'd been dead even before the plane reached the sea.

The air battle was still going on. Aircraft were swooping and diving, performing all the aerobatics that once they'd performed for entertainment at air shows. They twisted between each other, jockeying for position, and all the time guns were firing. Another two planes went down, and then the raiders seemed to vanish. Two or three could still be seen as diminishing black dots, and then they were gone. The remaining aircraft circled around for a few minutes, then headed back inland, a couple doing victory rolls as they disappeared.

'We beat them!' Elsie exulted. She punched Thursday on the arm. 'We *beat* them! *We* saw 'em off, we showed 'em, *we* sent 'em packing all right. *They* won't come back in a hurry.'

'They will, you know,' Thursday said. 'They won't be put off that easy. Anyway, they don't have a choice, do they?' She looked at the sea, smiling under the June sunshine, and shuddered as she thought of what lay beneath it. 'And we still don't know if it was ours or theirs that went down. It could be our lads down there.'

'Yes, it could,' Elsie agreed soberly. 'But even so, Thurs – we did send 'em off with a flea in their ear, didn't we? They never got anywhere near Pompey.'

'No, they didn't.' The girls turned and walked back through the gate into the hospital grounds. 'What was that name you said, the place near Chichester where the airfield is?'

'Tangmere. Why?'

'I think that's where my cousin Leslie is,' Thursday answered quietly. 'He's been training as a pilot. Mum told me at the weekend he'd passed out. I was just wondering if he was in one of those planes we just saw.'

Dogfights became part of everyday routine. The raiders would appear as black dots, their droning sound increasing as they approached, and then the RAF defenders would swoop on them and the battle commence. There were nearly always two or three aircraft destroyed, some RAF and some Luftwaffe, and if the pilots were lucky they could be seen baling out, their parachutes appearing to rise from the falling plane to drift down like pale, floating mushrooms to the sea beneath where – if they were even more lucky – they might be picked up by a fishing boat or perhaps a naval ship.

Some were, as Madam had foretold, brought to Haslar.

'He's got terrible burns,' Elsie reported when a young German pilot had been brought into her ward. 'All his hair and eyebrows have been burnt away, but mostly it's his hands. He's got to have operations or he'll never be able to use them again.'

'Is he going to stay here for them?'

'Seems like it. For the time being, anyway. He's in that little side room at the end of the ward.'

'Poor chap,' Thursday said. 'It must be awful, being away from all your own people in an enemy hospital. I bet he wonders what we'll do to him.'

'Poor chap nothing,' Elsie retorted. 'He shot down one of our planes before he went down, and our boy was lost. He's bloody lucky we're looking after him. I bet the Jerries wouldn't bother with our lads the way we're bothering with him – washing his face for him, spoonfeeding him, wiping his bum and all. I'm surprised at you, Thursday, what with losing your brother and Tony. And with your cousin one of the pilots at Tangmere too.'

'I don't think he's actually flying yet. Not in operations.'

'Well, he will be soon,' Elsie said grimly. 'There's a hell of a lot being lost.'

Thursday knew that was true, but she didn't want to think about it. She didn't want to think about Steve either. He came into her mind every night when she went to bed, and the realisation that he surely must be dead hit her afresh every morning when she woke up, and she was afraid that if she thought about him during the day as well she just wouldn't be able to do her work. The only way she could manage was by putting him out of her mind, and then she felt guilty, as if she didn't care as much as she ought to. And she felt guilty, too, when she thought of Tony, who seemed to be no more now than a part of a distant past. Too much has happened too soon, she thought, and I just haven't got time to think about them all . . .

There was nothing she could do about it, and no point in talking to anyone else. Everyone had the same griefs and worries these days. You could help each other, but when it came down to it, in your bed at night, in your mind and in your heart, you were on your own and had to find your own way through.

Denise and her parents had declared an uneasy truce over Vic. As Thursday had suggested, Denise had asked if she could bring him round one evening and her father had eventually agreed, saying that he wanted to have a word with the young man anyway. The problem then had been persuading Vic to come. She tried the next evening as they sat by the river, eating two pennyworth of chips out of newspaper.

'He's going to knock my block off. You said he was really up the pole about us.'

'I know, but I do think he'd calm down if he met you. He'd know what a nice boy you are then, he'd be able to see for himself. And Mum'll love you, I know she will. You've only got to smile at her!'

Vic wasn't so sure, but he couldn't see any way out of it. If he refused to come, Denise's father would be round at the post office like a shot, demanding to know why he was letting his precious daughter down. It didn't seem as if Vic could win. He took another chip and chewed thoughtfully.

'Maybe they're right. Maybe we ought to stop seeing each other for a while. Make sure of our feelings, like.'

Denise stared at him. 'But we *are* sure! *I* am.' Her lip quivered. 'I thought you were too. You said you loved me.'

'I do,' he said hastily. 'I do love you, Dizzy. It's just that – well . . .'

'Just that what?' She stared at him suspiciously. 'Has anyone been talking to you about me, Vic?'

'Talking to me? No, why? What would anyone have been talking to me about?' He poked about in the newspaper for a last chip, but could find only scraps of batter. 'D'you want these crispy bits, Diz?'

Denise shook her head impatiently. She said nothing for a moment, then she sighed and said, 'You might as well know. Mum and Dad'll tell you anyway. It's just that – well, there's something I told you when we first started going out together. Something that wasn't quite true.'

'What wasn't true? What are you talking about, Diz?'

'It's about how old I am,' she said uncomfortably. 'I told you I was eighteen, and I'm not.'

He looked at her. As usual, she was wearing lipstick and powder, with a touch of eye-shadow. Her hair was done in the latest Marcel waves. She could have passed for twenty-one, easily.

'What are you, then? Forty? Fifty?'

'Don't be daft! I'm younger – not older.' She looked at him appealingly, in the way that had first melted his heart.

'You're not!' He stared at her in astonishment. 'How much younger, then? Seventeen? That's not much. *Sixteen?*'

Denise shook her head. 'I'm fifteen,' she whispered. 'I'll be sixteen in August, but—'

'Fifteen?' His exclamation made her jump. 'You're *only fifteen*?'

Denise nodded. She saw his face whiten, his eyes grow dark. She put out her hand to touch him, but he flinched away. He screwed the newspaper into a tight ball and flung it into the water. His hands were trembling.

'Vic—'

'You told me you were eighteen and you're only *fifteen*? What the hell did you do that for?'

'There's no need to swear—'

'There's every need! I'm entitled to swear! Don't you realise, I could be had up for rape?'

'*Rape?*'

'Yes. Rape. *Statutory* rape, they call it. I could be put in prison.'

'But surely it's rape when the girl doesn't *want*—'

'Not when she's under sixteen,' he said grimly. 'She can want it all she likes, she can flaming *beg* for it, but it's still rape and it's still the poor bloody bloke who gets sent down for it.'

Denise was silent for a moment. 'Well – but it was you kissed me and – and touched me – and—'

'And you're telling me you didn't like it? You didn't exactly stop me, did you?'

'Well, I didn't know what you were going to do, did I? I've never been with a boy before – not like that. I didn't know you were going to – to . . .' She blushed crimson and floundered on. 'And I've been so worried ever since.'

'Worried?' he said, suddenly still. 'What about?'

'Well – about babies. Someone told me you could get a baby from kissing – a special sort of kissing, she said. And someone else said it was if you were out after eleven o'clock at night, and that was why fathers always wanted their girls in by ten. And then, when we – when *you* – did that, I thought that must be the way. I asked my friend and she said it was, but not the first time. And she was right, because I came on the next week, but then we did it again – three *times* – and – and, Vic, I haven't come on again and I'm over a week late now and I'm scared stiff! Suppose I'm having a baby? What am I going to do? My mum'll kill me, and so will my dad. You've got to come and see them, Vic!'

He stared at her. 'And they won't kill me, I suppose! Diz, I've told you, they'll get me put in prison.'

'No, they won't, not if we tell them we're secretly engaged and want to get married.' She grabbed his arm and shook it. 'Vic, they'll have to let us get married! They'll *have* to!'

Vic shook his head.

'They don't *have* to do anything, Dizzy. They'll never let us get married – not that we can, anyway, till you're sixteen.' He drew in a shuddering breath. 'I'll tell you what they'll do. They'll go to the police for a start and get me had up in court and put in prison. Then they'll find some nice quiet home for unmarried mothers, out in the country somewhere, and put it about that you're going away to work. You'll be sent there before you start to show, and you'll have your baby there and . . .' He stopped and looked at her white face, then continued in a ragged voice, 'And then they'll make you give it up for adoption. And that'll be that.'

Denise stared at him. 'Give it up for adoption? But why not just let us get married?'

'Because everyone would *know*,' he said. 'We couldn't get married for at least three weeks – that's even if they agreed to it straight away – and the baby would be born seven months later at the very most – more likely six, or even five, by the time they'd agreed to it – and everyone would know you were expecting when you got married. Your mum would never get over the shame and, come to that, nor would mine.' He rubbed his hand across his eyes. 'God, what a mess.'

Denise's eyes filled with tears. 'But I don't want to give my baby up. I want to get married to you and be a *family*.'

'I told you, they won't *let* us.'

'We could go to Scotland—'

'*No*. We couldn't. What would we live on? I'd lose my job, don't you realise that?' He sighed again. 'I'm going to lose it anyway. And what sort of a job am I going to get after I've been in prison? Nobody'll have me then – not for anything decent. Oh, God, why did I have to be so bloody *stupid*?'

'You didn't know I was only fifteen,' she said in a small voice. 'It's not your fault, Vic.'

'It's my fault I went with you,' he said roughly. 'It's my fault I never used anything. I took a chance. And now I'm paying for it. I'll go on paying for the rest of my life.'

'We can still get married. After you come out of prison—'

'For God's *sake*, Denise! Don't talk as if it's a foregone conclusion!'

He took a deep breath. 'Listen. How sure are you that you've fallen?'

'I don't know. I don't know anything about it – what happens and all that. But my friend says that if you don't come on – that's the first sign. And then there's morning sickness, and I did feel sick last Saturday morning, so that's the second sign, and—'

'*I* felt sick on Saturday morning, too. I thought it was the fish and chips we had on Friday.'

'Oh. Well, it did taste a bit funny.' She gazed at him hopefully. 'D'you think I might be all right, then?'

'How the hell do *I* know?' He rubbed his forehead again. 'Look, it seems to me it's a bit early to tell. Aren't you ever – you know, a bit late?'

'Well, sometimes,' Denise said, blushing. She had never discussed this sort of thing with anyone except her mother and a few friends – never with a boy. 'And I've missed a whole month once or twice.'

'Well, maybe this is just the same. It might not be anything to do with – with us.'

'But how am I going to *know*?'

'You'll have to wait and see.' He put his arm round her. 'Look, it's no use worrying till we know for certain, is it? There might be nothing to worry about. Let's just try and forget it for a while, shall we?'

'*Forget* it?'

'Well, you know what I mean,' he said. 'Wait another two or three weeks. It might be perfectly all right. And if it isn't – well, we'll get something sorted out then, I promise.'

Denise stared at the water flowing past.

'Doesn't that make sense?' he persisted gently.

'Well, I suppose so. But you'll come round and see Mum and Dad?'

'Yes, sure. Only not this week, because I've got to go and see my auntie in Birmingham.'

'Your auntie? You never said.'

'No, well, you were so upset over your brother, and then this, I couldn't, could I? But she's not well and I've always been her favourite, and – well, she wrote to Mum yesterday asking me to go and stop for the weekend, and I couldn't think of any way out of it. I'm sorry, Diz, I'll have to go.'

'Well, you'll come next week, then, won't you? Just for a cup of tea. They will like you, Vic, I know they will.'

Vic wasn't so sure. Fifteen! He looked again at the girl beside him and saw past the make-up and the hairstyle to the naïve child she truly was. I ought to have seen it in the first place, he thought. I ought to have been more bloody careful.

Chapter Twenty

The invasion was expected any day. Nobody was allowed on the beach any more – even the seawall was out of bounds, although the inmates of Haslar Hospital could still look out from the windows and see the activity in the harbour and on the Solent. There were gun emplacements all along Gilkicker and Stokes Bay, and the golf course was strewn with rubbish – old bedsteads, broken prams, even a car with no wheels. It was to stop enemy gliders landing, someone said. Apparently they had really big ones that could carry troops, not like the little two-seaters you used to see soaring up from Lee airfield on Sunday afternoons.

'They've taken down all the signposts along the roads, too,' Elsie reported after she had been home for her afternoon off. 'Our Dave went over to Southwick on his bike and he said if he didn't know the roads so well he'd never have got home. And the nameplates on the railway stations are all painted over, so the Germans won't know where they are.'

'That's daft,' Patsy said. 'The stationmaster always shouts the name out.'

'Well, he won't when the Germans are in charge, will he?' Elsie said in exasperation. 'Honestly, Pats, you are a twerp sometimes!'

'The Germans aren't going to *be* in charge,' Thursday said stoutly. 'We're going to fight them on the beaches, remember? And in the streets, and in the hills—'

'And on the railway stations,' Patsy said with a grin. 'And since they won't be able to find their way anywhere, with all these signs taken down, all we've got to do is point them in the wrong direction – back to Germany!'

The hospital was braced for the invasion. Although it wasn't a civilian hospital, it would have to take in local casualties if the Gosport War Memorial Hospital couldn't cope and people were too ill to be taken on the long journey round the harbour to Portsmouth. And there were always naval patients coming in, from ships that had been in action or sunk.

The girls were becoming more proficient at their work and found themselves with added duties. Sometimes they were given patients who were their special responsibility. Thursday found herself assigned to look after the young German pilot with the burnt hands.

'I've got to treat him as my own special patient,' she reported, bringing a tray of food to the table where the others were eating lunch. 'Me and that young Nurse Petty, turn and turn about. So that we get to know him without having to talk to him.'

'I never heard anything so daft,' Vera Hapgood said. She had taken the last vacant seat at the table. 'As if any of us would *want* to talk to him, even if we could!'

'Well, I feel a bit sorry for him,' Elsie said. 'All on his own in a strange country, with nobody to care about him. I shouldn't think he's a day over nineteen – just a kid, really. What's his name, Thurs?'

'Schmidt – Sister told me it's German for Smith. And his Christian name's Heinz – sounds like a tin of baked beans, doesn't it?'

'I think it's a cheek, calling it a Christian name,' Vera said. 'How can a German be a Christian?'

'Well, they are, aren't they. Not the Nazis, I know, but the ordinary Germans. They're not so different from us.'

'Not different from us? Of course they are! My dad says the only good German's a dead German.' Vera stirred her tea fiercely. 'It's unpatriotic, talking like that.'

'He's quite nice-looking,' Elsie said, just to annoy her.

And Patsy chimed in with, 'I don't see why he has to be horrible just because he's a German. I mean, they can't *all* be bad.'

'Why not?' Vera demanded. 'They're taught to be – it stands to reason.' She gave them a defiant look. 'He's the enemy, and if it was me looking after him, he'd soon know what *I* thought about it. You don't have to be able to speak the language to let a man know what you think.'

'And that's just why Madam didn't assign you to be his special nurse,' Thursday told her bluntly. 'You'd torture him, that's what you'd do.'

'I wouldn't. I just wouldn't put myself out for him, that's all, and if you do it's as good as collaborating.'

Thursday drew a deep breath. 'Take that back!'

'Shan't. And it's not just you, it's her as well.' Vera pointed her fork at Elsie. 'Saying he's good-looking and all! You're nothing but tarts, the pair of you.'

Elsie jumped to her feet. 'And you're nothing but a spiteful little bitch—'

'Stop it, both of you!' Patsy grabbed Elsie's arm. 'You know what happened last time, we all got our shore leave stopped. Just calm down and don't be so daft.'

Elsie glowered but sank slowly back into her seat. Vera speared a piece of fried bread with her fork and put it into her mouth, glancing coolly around the table.

'I'm not saying a word,' she said. 'I just think you all ought to be more careful what *you* say, that's all.'

'And I think *you* ought to shut up,' Elsie muttered. 'It's all right, Thurs, I'm not going to scratch her eyes out, even if she does deserve it. Someone else'll do that for her one day, and I'll be there to cheer 'em on.'

'Me, too.' Thursday gave Vera a withering look and then got up and marched out of the mess to go to the ward. It was time to change the young German's dressings. She collected everything she needed on a trolley and wheeled it into the small side room where he'd been put. He was lying on his pillows, staring out of the little window at the bright summer sky. He turned his head as Thursday came in and gave her an uncertain look. She smiled at him.

'Hello. My name's Thursday. I'm going to look after you during the day from now on.' She had no idea whether he could understand her or not, but Vera's words rankled. Collaborator, indeed! Just because she talked to the man like a human being. And Elsie was right, he was a nice-looking boy, and probably had a nice home with a plump, loving mother and a dad not so very much unlike her own . . . She gave him another grin and lifted up his hand.

'Now then, how's this burn getting along? You haven't been doing anything you shouldn't, have you? No dirty work, no shovelling coal or gardening? Got to look after burns, you know,

244

mustn't let any infection in. That blister now, that doesn't look so good, but as long as you don't let it burst you'll be all right. Let's get this nice clean dressing on it – and then a bit of bandage. I spent all yesterday afternoon rolling these bandages, I did, just for you . . . that's right, that's it, that's more comfy, isn't it? Now the other hand . . .'

She chattered away as she changed the dressings and gently washed the boy's face. He had been burnt about the forehead but his cheeks were unmarked, a smooth golden brown as if he had been sunbathing before he was shot down. There was a faint golden fuzz, as if he'd only just begun to shave, and she wondered again just how old he was. She met his blue eyes. He was just a kid, no older than her cousin Leslie, she thought. Probably longing for his mum or his girlfriend. For anyone who would be able to talk in his language, anyone who would be friendly and warm and loving towards him. He must be scared stiff here in England, not knowing what was going to happen to him when his hands were better.

'There,' she said at last, and stood back a little to beam at him. To her dismay, she saw his eyes fill with tears and he lifted his bandaged hands helplessly, as if to brush them away.

'Hey, what's all this, then? You don't have anything to cry about. You're safe here – no one's going to hurt you. And I bet they've let your family know where you are, so you'll be getting letters from home soon. Here . . .' She picked up the towel and wiped his eyes gently. 'It's all right,' she whispered. 'Thursday's here. Thursday'll look after you.' And before she knew what she was doing, she bent and kissed him on the smooth, golden cheek.

The German made a soft sound in his throat and Thursday jumped back as if he had stung her. She covered her mouth with her hand and stared at him, biting her lip against the nervous giggles that threatened to bubble forth.

'Oh, I'm sorry! I shouldn't have done that. I don't know what came over me. It was just seeing you, so – so sort of helpless, not even able to wipe your own eyes.' She backed away, pulling the trolley with her. 'I'm sorry – I really am sorry.' Without looking to see if anyone was coming, she fled out into the ward, then paused to draw in a deep breath and glanced around anxiously. Suppose anyone had seen her. Suppose *Sister* had seen her . . .

But apart from the patients in the nearest beds, who were both too concerned with their own troubles to worry about those of a German, no one else was taking the slightest notice. Instead, they were all engrossed by something that was happening by the window at the far end of the ward, where some of the up-patients were gathering around and reporting on what was going on. Another dogfight, she thought, and heaved a sigh of relief.

You'll have to be more careful, Thursday Tilford, she thought. Vera Hapgood would have had every right to call you a collaborator if she'd seen that. *And* a tart. Kissing a patient – any patient – was bad enough. But kissing a *German* patient! Thank God no one had seen, or heard.

'What are you all looking at over there?' she called, pulling herself together and wheeling her trolley down the ward. 'I've got a load of dressings here to do. What's going on, another dogfight?'

The men turned and the nearest shook his head. 'We thought it was at first. But it looks more like a raid. It's bombers – Jerry bombers – and they're coming in fast.'

'Jerry bombers? But why hasn't there been an alert?' Thursday left the trolley and ran to the window. She stared at the black shapes, rapidly approaching, and saw the cloud of RAF planes rise from the Sussex coast to intercept them. And as she gazed, she heard the first wail of the siren split the air. 'Oh, my *God*!'

A raid. An air raid.

'It's the invasion . . .' she whispered.

It wasn't the invasion, but it was the first of the real air raids. The hospital was placed immediately on yellow alert, and then purple. That meant that everyone must be indoors and anyone not on duty was to take cover. If a red was announced, the up-patients would have to be moved down to the cellars, and a double red meant that everyone must take shelter, and the bed-patients taken down below as well.

'I don't know how you're going to get us all down there,' a sailor who had his leg in traction said fretfully. 'I mean, you only got to loosen it off a bit and I go through the roof.'

'We'd better give you a gun, then, and you can shoot down a few Jerries while you're up there,' the man in the next bed suggested. 'You can be our secret weapon.'

The yellow alert stayed yellow, and no one was required to leave the ward. It seemed as if most of the action was over Portsmouth. They were probably targeting the dockyard, Thursday thought as she continued to change the dressings, trying to ignore the cacophony outside. She could hear the snarl of the German bombers wheeling over the harbour, and the lighter sound of the Spitfires and Hurricanes attacking them. Every few moments a tremendous crash signified yet another bomb hitting its target, and there was a constant rattle from the anti-aircraft guns dotted all around the two towns. The floor shook, and she tried not to glance too often towards the rattling windows, knowing that the sky was filled with swooping and diving aircraft. I wonder if Leslie's up there, she thought, frowning as she endeavoured to concentrate on her work. I wonder—

A cheer went up from the men who, contrary to all orders, were still clustered round the window. 'There goes one! He's hit, he's on fire! Bloody hell, what a sight, what a *sight*! Look at the flames – cor, bet his pants are feeling a bit warm!'

Thursday turned and stared. There, spiralling down into the stretch of water between Haslar and the Isle of Wight, was a ball of flame. Transfixed, she stood as still as a rock, both hands clutched to her chest. She saw a tiny puff of white lift itself from the fiery mass and float slowly down in its wake. The pilot, she thought, he's baled out. I wonder if he's badly burnt . . . And then the burning aircraft hit the water in a great, boiling plume of steam and spray, and the parachute disappeared.

The men burst into laughter and thumped each other's shoulders. 'Did you see that? Thought he'd got away with it, didn't he? Thought he'd parachute all the way back to bloody Germany! I bet he couldn't believe his eyes when he found himself landing in that lot. Couldn't believe his bloody luck!'

Thursday stared at them. She thought of her cousin Leslie, who might even now be circling up there, waiting his chance to attack. Who might be the next one to be shot down in a ball of fire. She thought of the young German pilot with his bandaged hands and his smooth golden-brown cheeks. She thought of her other cousin Mike, caught and killed on the beaches of Dunkirk, and her brother Steve who was probably dead, too.

'Stop it! *Stop it!*' Her voice startled everyone. They turned and stared at her and she faced them, too angry to remember that they were her patients, too furious to care. 'What do you think you're doing – laughing and cheering when you've just seen a man *die*? Don't you realise, that was a man on that parachute, probably no more than a boy – like that poor boy back in the ward here – and he was *burning to death*. Can't you imagine what that must be like? Hasn't any of you ever burnt himself? It *hurts*. Even a burnt finger hurts. And he was burning all over. And you're *laughing* about it.'

They gazed at her, then at each other. One or two dropped their eyes. A burly torpedoman glowered and spoke up.

'It's all very well for you to talk like that, Nurse. You never bin in action. We have – that's why we're here now. *We* got hurt, too – by blokes like that one you're so sorry for. We got shot and bombed on our ships, yeah, *and* burnt, too, some of us at Dunkirk. You don't have to tell us nothing about getting hurt, we does it for a bloody pastime.'

Some of the men murmured their agreement and Thursday bit her lip. She bowed her head a little in acknowledgement.

'I know. I'm sorry – shouldn't have said that. But I still don't see why you have to laugh. It isn't funny, whoever it happens to.'

'Yeah, but look at it this way.' The torpedoman seemed to have become spokesman. 'We don't think of them like human beings, see. We can't, can we? We got to go out there and kill people. We can't feel sorry for them.'

'But *laughing*—'

'It's not that we think it's funny,' another sailor said. He was smaller, with untidy fair hair and large ears. 'It's just that it's a fight and we're winning. We're pleased – aren't you? Aren't you glad when you see one of our blokes winning? They're risking their lives up there.'

Thursday bit her lip again. 'Yes, I know. Yes, of course I'm pleased. It's just that – well, my cousin's a pilot and it could have been him up there. I couldn't help thinking—'

'Yes, well, you're a woman, ain't you, and a nurse, what's more. And that's why men fight wars and women kiss them better,' the torpedoman said. He turned back to the window. 'Looks like we seen 'em off for the time being, anyway. But they made a bit of a mess of Pompey, by the look of it.'

They all gazed out again. There was a huge black cloud, shot with orange flame, billowing from somewhere near the dockyard, and smaller clouds rising from all over the area. There was a tug on fire in the middle of the harbour. It looked as if the dockyard had been hit, but some of the explosions and fires seemed to be further into the city.

Elsie! Thursday thought with a stab of fear. Her family lived in Fratton. Was that one of the places hit? She stared doubtfully at the city across the water, not sure enough of its geography to know if the flames were burning in Fratton. She thought of Mr and Mrs Jackson, of Eddy, of Dave, and hoped they'd all managed to get to a shelter in time.

'When you've quite finished admiring the view,' Sister Burton's acid voice said behind her, 'there's a trolley full of dressings here that don't appear to have been changed. Were you thinking of doing any work today, I wonder?'

Thursday whipped round guiltily, her face reddening. 'I'm sorry, Sister. We were all watching – and I was thinking of Nurse Jackson's family, they live in Portsmouth. There'll be people hurt there – she must be terribly worried.'

'And your job is to nurse the patients we have here.' Sister Burton's face softened very slightly. 'I've already seen Jackson and told her she can have an extra two hours to go and see her family. But I won't be able to give her or anyone else such a concession every time there's a raid. We've work to do – and I'd be grateful, and so would the patients, I'm sure, if you'd just get on and do it!'

'Yes, Sister.' And as the all-clear sounded its more comforting wail, Thursday turned back to her trolley.

Sister was right. There were dressings still to be done, and a few bombs and aircraft shot down wouldn't be any excuse for not having got on with the allotted tasks.

Thursday consulted her list and then looked over at the burly sailor, a glimmer in her eye.

'Come on, Torpedoman Sellers. Let's have a look at that knee of yours. And now you've told me how used you all are to getting hurt, we won't have any of that yelling we had yesterday – *will* we?'

The raid had killed a number of people in Portsmouth and injured many more. The huge pall of smoke and flame had come from the gasholder at Rudmore, which had been struck by one of the first bombs. Another casualty had been a first-aid post, occupying a school in Drayton Road. It wasn't far from Elsie's home.

'Everyone's all right,' she reported when she got back from her hasty journey. She'd gone on her bike, knowing that the buses and trolleys would be disrupted, and arrived in the dormitory breathless and shaken. 'Dave and Eddy were already home and they all got down the shelter. Dad was on his way home from work and went into a street shelter – he got home just before me. Mum cried her eyes out when she saw him – she thought he was dead. But the damage is awful. Houses just smashed to bits, you wouldn't believe. Walls ripped out and roofs torn off, bricks and stuff all over the place, people's furniture all broken up and laying in the gutter. You can't get down some of the roads at all. And dust and smoke everywhere – the stink's horrible. And they don't know how many people have been killed. They're going through all the rubble, looking for people. They got a little girl out of a house just when I was going by, her mum was in hysterics.'

'I bet she was.' The girls listened in horror. They had been in different stages of preparation for bed – Patsy filing her nails, Thursday brushing her hair, Vera Hapgood lathering Pond's cold cream all over her face. Some of the others crowded round as well to hear Elsie's story, and they looked at each other in dismay.

'Are they going to keep on doing this?' one asked in a whisper. 'Are they going to keep on and on bombing us till we give in? Or till we're all dead?'

'We're not *going* to give in,' Patsy said stoutly. 'We're going to fight. We *are* fighting – we brought down some of those planes. We sent 'em back with a flea in their ear.'

Elsie sank down on her bed. Thursday looked at her and saw tears well up in her eyes. She moved across quickly and sat beside her, putting her arm round the other girl's shoulders.

'Elsie, you're shaking all over.'

'I know. I can't help it.' Elsie's voice trembled. 'I was all right till I got back here and – and started to talk about it.' She started to cry. 'Oh, Thurs, it was awful. All those bombed buildings, and the smoke and flames – a lot of them are on fire – and fire engines everywhere, and ambulances. And people just wandering about, crying or looking lost. I felt I ought to stop and help, but I only had that two hours Sister gave me, and I just had to get home and see that everyone was all right.' Her words became incoherent and she leant her head on Thursday's shoulders and gave way to huge, wrenching sobs. 'And then . . .' she went on with a gulp, 'then I saw this little baby, couldn't have been more than a year old, just *laying* there in the gutter, and I knew – I knew it was dead – it was all – all – oh – and then a fireman came along, and he pushed me out of the way and I told him I was a nurse, and he said there wasn't nothing we could do for the kiddy – I already *knew* that, but I couldn't leave it there in the gutter, could I, not a little *baby* – and he said he'd see to it and I ought to go and do something for the ones that was hurt. And I didn't. I *didn't*. I just got on me bike again and went the rest of the way home. I was so worried about Mum, you see, and Eddy and Dave. I just went home. And they were all right, so I *could've* stopped and helped. But then I had to get back here. I only had the two hours – and Navy time and all – I had to come back. And I know I'll *never* get that baby out of my head and I'll *always* be sorry I didn't stop and help.'

Thursday held her closely in her arms and rocked her to and fro, while the other girls sat round and gazed at them in dismay. Watching the raid from the windows of the hospital had been frightening, but also exciting as the RAF aircraft had swooped and dived in their efforts to drive the raiders away. The sight of flames rising from the city had been sobering, for they knew that there must have been people hurt and even killed. But Elsie's story gave them a different picture – a picture of what had been happening on the ground, in people's homes and the streets where they lived. They saw in their own minds the rubble-filled roads, the clouds of smoke and dust, the flames. They saw the dazed and injured people wandering amongst it all, searching for their families. They saw the baby, lying dead in a gutter.

'It had lovely fair hair,' Elsie said in a broken voice. 'And a little blue romper suit, all covered in blood.' And she began to cry all over again.

The girls were all in tears. The dead baby seemed to be a symbol of all that was most dreadful about this war. Until now, they'd thought of the conflict as being waged between adults – men, albeit some of them were not much more than boys, going off voluntarily to fight. Women staying at home to take on the work they had left behind, or to work in munitions factories to supply them with the equipment they needed to fight. Grown-up people with a choice, people who could listen to the news and read the papers, who understood – to some extent, anyway – what was going on.

None of them had ever thought of the war being waged against babies.

'We ought to have realised it,' Thursday said later to Patsy in the washroom. Elsie had been coaxed into bed and now lay fast asleep, exhausted. 'We've seen enough men hurt already. We knew there were going to be air raids. We ought to have realised there'd be kiddies killed. But what Elsie said – it made it so *real*. It sort of hit me, like it never has before. Not even when I heard about Mike and Steve being missing.'

'What I want to know is, why hadn't it been evacuated?' Patsy said, rubbing her toothbrush on her tin of Gibbs' toothpaste. 'I thought all mothers and babies had been sent to the country.'

'They didn't all go, though. Elsie said the woman next door to her mum wouldn't go because her hubby works in the dockyard and there'd be no one to give him a hot meal. And a lot of them have come back since Christmas, thinking nothing was going to happen.'

'Well, they know different now, don't they,' Patsy said grimly, and began to scrub her teeth.

Thursday looked at her reflection in the mirror above the washbasin. She saw a face that looked graver and older than it had done that morning. The raid had shaken them all, and none of them would sleep quite so easily at night now. Portsmouth had been attacked, and its streets lay in rubble.

The next time, it might be Gosport. It might be Haslar. It might be the hospital itself.

Chapter Twenty-One

The next time seemed a long time in coming. It wasn't for another month, and by that time other things had happened, too.

In Worcester, Denise was now certain that she was pregnant. She had missed two periods and if she didn't come on soon, that would be three. She'd never missed this many before. And she'd definitely been feeling a bit off in the mornings.

'It's not much,' she told Jenny as the two girls sat on Jenny's bed. 'But I do bring up some sort of yellowy stuff every morning. It tastes horrible – all bitter. What d'you suppose it is?'

'I think it's bile,' Jenny said doubtfully. 'I had it once, when I had a bilious attack. It's when your stomach's got nothing else in it. But hasn't your mum noticed, Dizzy?'

'I don't think so. I do it in the outside lav, and it really isn't much. Maybe it's something else. I've heard people feel bad all morning – it doesn't seem enough, d'you think?' Denise looked hopeful.

'I don't think it matters how much it is. You've missed nearly three times and you're sick in the mornings. It does look as if you're expecting, Diz.'

'Oh, flipping heck.' Denise flung herself back on the pillows. Tears welled from her eyes. 'What am I going to do, Jen, what the flipping heck am I going to *do*?'

'Well, you're going to have to tell them soon.' Jenny looked at her helplessly and thanked her lucky stars that she'd finished with Sam and wasn't in the same boat. 'It'll start to show in a month or two. What about Vic? What does he want to do?'

'He just wants to pretend it's not happening,' Denise said

drearily. 'And I hardly see him anyway. He seems to get an awful lot of overtime, and he's got this auntie in Birmingham, she's poorly and he—'

'Dizzy! He's not trying to get out of it, is he?'

'No, of course not! He loves me, he says so every time we see each other. And it'll all come right, I know it will, he'll stand by me. I'll be sixteen in October and we can get married then, and—'

'Suppose your mum and dad won't let you? Have they met him yet?'

'No.' Denise leant up on one elbow and fiddled with the fringe along the edge of the bedspread. 'It's because of this auntie, he's been her favourite ever since he was little, and he says—'

'Dizzy, he's making excuses! Can't you see it? He's trying to get out of it. Pretending he's got overtime. Pretending he's got to go and see this auntie. It's weeks since Thursday said you ought to take him home to meet your mum and dad, and you still haven't managed to get him to go. One of these days, you're going to go in the post office and he won't be there any more – he'll have been called up. It's bound to happen soon anyway, and then he'll go off heaven knows where and you'll be left all on your own, holding the—' She stopped abruptly and bit her lip. 'Well, you *will*.'

'Jen – do you really think so?' Denise whispered, her face white.

'Well, yes, I do. I'm sorry, Diz, I don't want to upset you – but it seems so obvious. And now he knows how old you are, he must be scared stiff. It's not just a matter of having to get married, Diz. He could be in real trouble.'

'I didn't know. I didn't know that.'

'Well, nor did I. I mean, nobody's ever told us much about the facts of life, have they? We've had to learn them for ourselves. But that doesn't mean we've got any excuse. We're still the ones who'll get into trouble over it, and we're the ones who'll have to carry the can.' She looked soberly at her cousin. 'You're going to have a baby, Diz. It's not a doll that you can put in a cupboard when you're fed up with it. You're going to have to look after it, all day and every day, for years and years and years, and you can't do it all on your own. You've got to have a husband.'

'Vic. I want Vic.' Denise looked at her piteously. 'We really do love each other, Jenny. We *do*.'

Jenny reached over and took her hand. 'I know, Diz. I know.'

Privately, she was sure that her cousin was in love – but she wasn't so sure about Vic. 'But you can't let him go on making excuses. He's got to face up to it – you both have. And you've got to tell your mum and dad.'

Denise nodded. She looked down at the bedspread and a large tear fell on the back of her hand. Jenny watched her with pity. It was the worst situation either of them had ever been in, she thought, the worst a girl *could* be in. Having a baby meant you'd been a 'bad girl', and everyone was going to know about it. Even if you got married, like Gladys Watson up the street who'd had a hasty wedding and then a 'seven-month baby'. The old gossips had had a field day with her. It would be even worse with Denise, who wasn't even sixteen.

'I'll tell Vic he's got to come and meet them,' Denise said at last. 'I'll tell him it's definite, there's no mistake and we can't hang about any longer. And – and I'll tell Mum first and ask her to tell Dad. I just – I just can't face them both together, Jen.'

Jenny nodded. It was what she and Steve and Thursday had always done, if they wanted something or had some small misdeed to confess. Get Mum on your side, and you had a better chance with Dad. And Mum nearly always *was* on your side.

I'm not so sure Auntie Flo's going to be on Dizzy's side over this, though, she thought. But she's got to start somewhere. They've got to know.

'You make sure you get Vic round there soon after,' she said. 'You can't let him leave you in the lurch.'

'Oh, he wouldn't! He'd never do that.' But Dizzy's voice was uncertain, and more tears were falling. She looked up at Jenny and her eyes were wide and frightened. 'I don't know what I'd do if he left me, Jen. I just don't know what I'd do . . .'

As it happened, Percy was out that evening at a fishing club meeting. Denise and her mother sat knitting and listening to the wireless. It was the new Tommy Handley show, *ITMA*, and when it finished Flo turned off the wireless and looked at her daughter.

'You didn't seem to find much to laugh at, Denise.'

Denise bit her lip and concentrated on her knitting. Her heart was thumping. 'I didn't think it was as funny as usual.'

'That's funny, because the audience laughed as much as ever.' Flo waited a moment, then said, 'Put that knitting down a minute.'

'I'm just turning a heel—'

'It won't go bad. I want to talk to you. And I've got an idea you want to talk to me, don't you?'

Denise looked up, her eyes filled with tears. 'Oh, *Mum . . .*'

'I'm right, aren't I,' Flo said after a moment, her voice flat. 'You're in the family way.'

Denise burst out crying. 'Oh, Mum, I've been so frightened! I've been nearly frantic, wondering what to do. I didn't know what ought to happen, you see, and someone at work told me there was morning sickness and I *have* been a bit sick in the mornings – not much, and I still didn't know for certain – and I haven't come unwell for nearly three months now so I thought it must be, and I – I just don't know – I don't know what to do, and I didn't know how to tell you, and – and – oh, Mum, what am I going to *do*? Will you throw me out? Will you and Dad throw me out?'

Flo stared at her. She'd been prepared to be angry, she'd been afraid she might even hit her daughter when the fears that had been growing in her over the past few weeks were finally confirmed. She'd been dreading this moment ever since she knew Denise was knocking about with a boy so much older than herself. But now, seeing the girl's fear and distress, she couldn't be angry after all. It was just the same as when she'd fallen out of a tree and broken her arm, even though Flo had warned her it would happen, the same as when she'd broken her china doll through making that cradle to hang from the same tree, and anyone could have seen it wasn't strong enough. Denise had always been the same, rushing headfirst into trouble, but you couldn't be cross with her somehow. Not when she was your little girl and turning to you for comfort.

She crossed the little space between the chairs, and knelt in front of Denise to put her arms around her. Denise leant against her, sobbing.

'You silly girl. You silly, *silly* girl. I thought that's what it was. You being so quiet lately – and slipping down to the lav early every morning – and not using your pads. I wondered a few weeks ago when you missed, and thought, no, it couldn't be, she wouldn't be so daft. But the past few days – oh, Denise, you silly girl. You *naughty* girl.' The anger she'd expected to feel was beginning to come through, like the pain when your hands had been very cold and were now warming up. 'You bad, *naughty* girl!'

'I'm sorry, Mum. I really am. I didn't know – I thought it wouldn't happen, not to me—'

'And why should you be any different to anyone else?' her mother asked. 'Whatever did you want to go and do it for? Haven't we always tried to teach you right from wrong? Haven't I always said what'd happen if you brought trouble to the house? And here you are, not even sixteen. We can't even get you decently wed. And that Vic – whatever was he thinking of? He's old enough to know better. He shouldn't ever have been going out with you in the first place.'

'He didn't know,' Denise whispered. 'He didn't know I was only fifteen. He thought I was eighteen.'

'Well, I know that. You told him, didn't you? You made your face up to look older and spun him a line. You lied to him, as well as me and your dad.' Flo sighed. 'I'm sorry, Denise, but I'm ashamed of you, ashamed and disappointed. I never thought you'd let us down like this. And how we're going to break it to your father, I don't know.'

'I thought – would you tell him, Mum? I can't face him on my own.'

'Well, you're going to have to, aren't you? You're going to have to face a lot of people over this. And so'm I, more's the pity. Everyone will know, everyone in the road. I wouldn't be surprised if that Mrs Hawkins never speaks to me again.'

'Well, I don't see as that'd be much loss,' Denise said with a flicker of her old spirit. 'You don't like her anyway.'

'That's not the point! The point is, she's always tried to set herself up as better than me, and now she'll do it more than ever. *Her* daughter never got into trouble, they had that nice white wedding before the war started, and now she's got a baby grandson, born a decent year after.' Flo herself was crying now. '*You* won't be able to get married in white, even if you ever do get married. Not that anyone'll want you now. Soiled goods, that's what you'll be.'

'Mum! Don't say that! That's horrible – and anyway—'

'It's true, though,' Flo said drearily. She put her arms round her daughter again. 'It's what people'll say, see. And we've tried so hard, me and your dad, we've always given you a good home, seen that you went to Sunday school regular – you're even in the church choir with Jenny.' A fresh thought struck her. 'What's the *vicar* going to say? You won't be able to go on going there, you'll have to leave.'

'Well, I would have done anyway,' Denise said. 'Because I'll be getting married – I'll be getting married to Vic. And *he* won't call me "soiled goods".'

Flo stared at her. 'Getting *married*? But you're only fifteen—'

'I'm not going to be fifteen for ever, am I? I'll be sixteen in a couple of months and we can get married then.'

'Your father'll have something to say about that.'

'No, he won't – because we won't be here!' Denise stared at her mother defiantly. 'We've talked about it, we've been talking about it for months. Before – before our Mike got – before Dunkirk. If you won't let us get married, we'll go to Scotland, they let you get married at sixteen there without anyone's permission. You won't be able to stop us.'

'Denise! Don't you dare talk like that! And don't be so silly. Of *course* you can't go to Scotland. And as for getting married or not, your dad and I will have to have a talk about that. We haven't even met this Vic yet. There's places girls like you can go, out in the country – places you can have the baby and give it up for adoption, and come back with no one any the wiser. That might be the best thing all round.'

'Give my baby up to *strangers*?'

'Yes. There's hundreds of people, *decently married* people, wanting a baby but can't have one. They'll take a baby like yours and give it a good home, better than what you could do, and you could start fresh. Nobody'd ever know.'

'I'd know. And you'd know, too. It's my *baby*, Mum. It's your *grandchild*. How can you even talk about giving it away? Would you have given *me* away? Or our Leslie? Or *Mike*?'

'Denise!' Flo put both hands to her mouth and tears flooded down her cheeks. 'How can you *say* such things? Your brother—'

'I know. He's not coming back, he's never coming back.' Denise dropped to her knees and stared at her mother's distorted face. 'And you know how you feel about that. *I* know how you feel about that. Because that's what it would be like for *me* if I gave up *my* baby. Can't you *see*?'

Flo pulled a hanky from her sleeve and wiped her face. She looked at her daughter pleadingly. 'But your baby would be alive still. It would have a better life. Wouldn't you want that for it, Denise? Wouldn't that be best? We could say you'd gone away for work, or something, got a job in the country, or gone to stay with a relative – anything. And you could come back after a few months, when it was all over, and start again. You'd probably find yourself a decent young feller in time and get married, and then you could have your family in the proper way. And—'

'But I'm going to marry *Vic*,' Denise broke in. 'I've told you, Mum. And it's his baby, too – he ought to have some say. He might not want me to give it away. I don't know as I want to give it away myself. And there won't be any need to, anyway, not if we're getting married—'

'For goodness' sake, Denise!' Flo cried. 'Stop going on about getting married! I've told you, your dad and I will have to talk about that, we haven't even met him yet, and I very much doubt if we'll like him when we do – a chap his age, leading a young girl like you astray. And—'

'He didn't *know*!' Denise shouted. 'I told you, Mum, he didn't *know* I was under sixteen. It wasn't his fault! It was my fault, all of it – I *wanted* him to do it! And I want my baby! I'm not going to give it up – me and Vic are getting married. And that's it and all about it!'

She was on her feet, shouting at the top of her voice. Flo stared at her, appalled. And as Denise's voice finally died away, the door to the passageway opened and Percy himself stood there, his fishing things in his hand, staring from one to the other. Flo and Denise stared back, and Flo put her hand to her mouth and started to cry again.

'What in the name of all that's wonderful's going on here?' he asked at last. 'What the hell's all this shouting and yelling? I could hear you halfway up the street. And what's all this about getting married – and *babies*?'

Thursday was still nursing Heinz Schmidt. He had still never spoken, and she had never given way to any sudden impulses again, but a strange kind of rapport grew between them. His eyes looked relieved when she came in to take over from the night staff, and he gave her a cautious smile. Thursday smiled back and chatted as she changed his dressings or tidied his bed.

'I know you're German and supposed to be the enemy, but to me you're just a patient, see, and you get the same treatment as everyone else. And I talk to the others, so why not you – even though you don't understand a word I'm saying. And you can't have any breakfast this morning because you're having an op later on today, and Surgeon Commander Kirkpatrick says that'll be the last one, and your hands should be OK once everything's healed up. And then I suppose you'll be sent off to a prison camp for the rest of the war.' She straightened up and looked down at him. 'To tell you the truth, I'll be sorry. I'll miss you – and I suppose that's something else I shouldn't say, but you can't understand so what does it matter?'

The German gazed up at her. He was much stronger now, despite his operations, and although his face had lost its golden tan his eyes were still very blue. A strange expression came into them then, and his mouth widened in a broad grin.

'But I do understand,' he said clearly, with only the smallest trace of an accent. 'I've understood everything you've said to me.'

Thursday stared at him.

'You understand? You speak *English*?'

He tilted his head a little. 'As you can hear.'

'But – why didn't you do it before? Why didn't you *tell* me?' Thursday thought of all the things she'd said while she was attending to him and flushed scarlet. She'd talked freely, almost as if he'd been another VAD – grumbling about Sister, commenting about some of the other patients, letting off steam – things she would never have said if she'd known he could understand. And it wasn't just hospital gossip, she thought with sudden horror – had she said anything else? Anything she really shouldn't have said to the enemy?

She racked her brains. Not that she actually knew anything much, and not that he'd be likely to get the chance to pass it on to anyone while he was stuck here, but he was the enemy nonetheless. And he got letters from home and answered them, too, or someone did, writing at his dictation. Could he have passed on any information that way?

I don't think I've said anything, she thought, it's all been hospital gossip, but if I'd known he understood . . . And I definitely talked about the air raid.

A feeling of anger began to grow, pushing the embarrassment aside. Silly, girlish indiscretions didn't matter. Things that might help the enemy did.

'Why didn't you say before?' she demanded again. 'Are you a spy? Because if so, I think you've been really mean. I could have told you *anything*.'

He laughed. 'But that's what spies are – mean people! And you would expect one of your own men to behave in just the same way. We all have to fight for our own country, don't we, in whatever way comes possible to us.' He looked at her angry face and shook his head gently. 'No, *Donnerstag*, I'm not a spy. How could I be, lying here? And there is nothing you have said that I could pass on, anyway. You have been careful – and very, very illuminating.'

'*Illuminating?*'

'Yes. You've talked to me of your life, your days, your pleasures and your pains. You've made me laugh and you've made me want to cry.' His eyes were serious. 'You've made me understand that the English are just like the Germans – ordinary people, with ordinary hopes and fears, wanting nothing more than to live ordinary lives. If I were to pass on anything of what I have heard from you, that is what it would be.'

Thursday gazed at him doubtfully. 'But Hitler – the Nazis . . .'

'Not all Germans are Nazis,' he said. 'Many of us live in small villages in the country, sometimes high in the mountains. Politics are not important to us. We farm the land, we take cows to the pasture for the summer, we scarcely move from our homes. We are not all a part of Hitler's Youth Movement or his Nazi Party, and we don't all agree with what he has done to a people who have shared our lives for centuries yet retained their own race and customs. But I think we have been wrong in taking so little notice, for he has grown in power, and his party has grown with him, and now we can do nothing against him. We must join his army and fight his war . . .' he glanced ruefully at his bandaged hands '. . . whether we want to or not.'

'Did you live in a village?' she asked.

'Yes, in Bavaria. My father is a farmer. He thought I would work with him and take over the farm when he grew old, but my schoolmaster said I had a good brain and should go to a university. My father decided that I should have this chance and so I went to Berlin. I came to England, too.' He glanced at her, almost apologetically. 'I spent a year in Cambridge. It's a beautiful city and England is a beautiful country.'

'So that's why you speak English so well.'

'Partly. But I learned it when I was very young, from an Englishman who used to come and stay in my village, to walk and climb. He was a professor and he became friends with my schoolmaster. Perhaps, if he had not, I would never have left the village.'

'Would you rather that had happened?'

'How can I say? I have gained so much from all that I've learned. I've had wonderful opportunities. I've met wonderful, kind and loving people.' He sighed again and added, very quietly, 'And now I've been sent to kill them.'

'Couldn't you have refused? We have conscientious objectors—'

'In Germany,' he said, 'one cannot refuse. And besides – it is my country.'

Thursday was silent. She became aware that she had spent too long in this room and must go before Sister came in search of her. She saw the torment in the young face before her, and felt a wave of compassion.

'You're right,' she said. 'This war's being fought by ordinary people, who would rather be at home with their families, doing their ordinary jobs.' She hesitated. 'My cousin was killed at Dunkirk, and my brother's still missing. Neither of them ever set out to be soldiers, but when it came to it they were proud to go.'

'They died in a good cause,' he said. 'We all die in a good cause, if we are defending our country.'

'Even if it was our country that was wrong in the first place?' she challenged him. 'Even if it's done horrible, evil things?' And then she felt ashamed, as she saw his eyes cloud and his head droop. 'I'm sorry – but it's true, isn't it? The things they've done to the Jews – making them live in ghettos and wear yellow stars, and give up all their money – they're evil.'

'Let's not talk about it any more,' he said. 'We can't know it all. We can't decide.' He lifted his eyes again. 'That first morning, when you came to me – do you remember it?'

Thursday blushed, remembering the kiss she had given him. He smiled.

'It was the first tenderness I had known since I left home to join the Luftwaffe.'

'I shouldn't have done it,' Thursday said quickly. 'I don't know why I did. I just felt so sorry for you.'

'Do it again,' he said softly. 'Do it again, just once. I go for my operation this afternoon. It will be the last, and then I shall be moved to a camp. We may never see each other again. But I want to tell you how much you have meant to me, all these weeks – how your tenderness has helped me. Please, *Donnerstag* – do it again.'

'What was that you called me? *Donner*-something?'

He smiled. '*Donnerstag*. It's the German word for Thursday. You told me that first day that it was your name, and I've always thought of you so. *Donnerstag*,' he repated softly. 'A pretty name. A very pretty nurse.'

Thursday stared at him. She felt a lump in her throat and knew that tears were not far away. She could no longer deny that caring for him had meant something to her, too. His quiet face, his bright blue eyes, his smile of gratitude and welcome – all these had become part of her daily life, and she knew suddenly and unexpectedly that she was going to miss him.

'I must go,' she whispered. 'I've been here too long already.'

'A moment.' He lifted his hand towards her. 'One moment more. Please.'

Thursday looked at him and bit her lip. She could hear footsteps coming down the ward, the unmistakable clatter of a nurse's shoes. Sister Burton was on her way, and in a moment would be here, her eagle eyes missing nothing.

The footsteps were almost at the door. Swiftly, she bent and brushed her lips against his skin, then touched his cheek with her fingertips, and gathered up her things. She turned away, giving him one last glance, and walked out of the door, nodding brightly at the senior nurse.

'He's all ready for his pre-med, Sister. I've told him it's his last – but, of course, he doesn't understand a word I say.'

Sister nodded and went on her way. Thursday made for the sluice and stood just inside the door, shaking a little, and felt the tears slip down her cheeks.

Poor boy, she thought, poor, poor boy. He could be our Steve, injured and alone in an enemy country.

Well, if Steve were, by some miracle, still alive and in a foreign hospital, she hoped that he had found a nurse who would care for him as she'd cared for Heinz Schmidt. A girl who would look on him as if he were indeed her brother. And she knew then just why she had felt that extra tenderness towards the young German, and why it was she was going to miss him.

Chapter Twenty-Two

It was only a few days after Heinz Schmidt had been taken away from Haslar that the Portsmouth area was bombed for the second time.

This time, they hit Gosport as well. Screaming out of a blue August sky, two dozen bombers swooped over the beaches and the seawalls to hurl hundreds of black sticks of death and destruction on the city and town which stood on either side of the harbour. To the wail of the sirens, people ran and dived for cover, and the hospital went rapidly through all the colours of the alert, ending up on double red.

Thursday wasn't in the hospital. She and Elsie had been over to visit Elsie's family, and were walking down the ferry slipway when the sirens went. They stared at each other in dismay.

'Where should we go?'

Dave had come with them, for the ride and to have a look at the harbour. He grabbed Thursday's arm. 'There's a shelter up the road – we'd better make for that.'

'I don't like those over-ground shelters,' Elsie said, hanging back. 'I can't see they're any better than anywhere else. Let's get on the pinnace, Thurs – we'll be back in five minutes and we can go down the cellars. You go to the shelter, Dave, we'll be all right.'

Dave was staring at the sky. 'Look at that! There must be a couple of dozen of them. Stukas, I reckon. Look at *that* one, shooting up all the barrage balloons! I always knew they'd never be any good.'

Thursday stared, too. The planes were coming in fast, quick and lithe as silverfish in the sky, swooping and soaring between the lumbering balloons – and, yes, Dave was right, one of them was shooting the barrage down, clearing the way for the bombers to fly in low. One was coming right at them now – right at the nearby dockyard, right at the railway station.

'Get down!' she shrieked. 'He's going to bomb us – Dave, Elsie, get *down* somewhere.'

'The shelter—'

'There isn't time! Under the steps – up against the wall – anywhere!' It didn't make sense, she knew it dimly, for a wall or a building could fall on you and kill you, but somehow nobody wanted to be in the open. Instinctively, everyone dived for cover, however fragile. One woman even put up an umbrella.

A bomb fell somewhere in the dockyard and the ground shook. Almost immediately there were two separate explosions on the other side of the station, towards Old Portsmouth. Thursday, crouching against the station building, put both hands over her ears. She peered upwards and saw the bombers diving towards Gosport. Haslar, she thought, agonised, don't let them hit Haslar . . . Another explosion rocked the hard, and she heard Elsie scream. She started to scramble up but Dave was beside her, gripping her arm and forcing her to stay down. She felt his breath, warm on her cheek, and then a blast of hotter air and a huge roar that seemed to knock her flying. Pain shot through her head, and she was conscious of a blur of sight and sound; of flashing lights, of thick black smoke and grey, choking dust; of screams and shouts and yells and shrieks; of the tearing crash of bricks and stone and plaster; and the thudding, pounding, thundering beat of her own blood as it surged in her ears.

She fought for breath, but it was as if the air had been sucked away and there was none left to breathe. Then, like a wave crashing on the shore, it roared back at her and it seemed there was then too much. Her lungs screamed and she gasped and heaved, until heart and lungs and pulses seemed to have won some kind of synchronisation once more, and then she opened her eyes and looked into Dave's anxious face.

'Was that a bomb?' she gasped, thinking with a strange, detached portion of her brain what a silly question that was. 'Have we been hit?'

'I don't know. It was pretty close, I know that.' The roar of the aircraft was diminishing, although explosions could still be heard over the city and harbour. 'I think they got the station with incendiaries.'

'I should just think they bloody did!' Elsie was crawling towards them, her face and shoulders covered with grey dust. 'It's on fire!'

'On *fire*?' Thursday turned her head and saw that Elsie was right. The station was already in flames and the fire engines were coming down the hard, their bells clanging through the din. A squad of ARP men were running from the pavement, shouting to everyone to get out of the way, while the Stukas were still roaring overhead and explosions could still be heard in different parts of the city.

'Get home!' Elsie said urgently to Dave. 'Get *home* and see if our Mum and Eddy's all right. Me and Thursday have got to get back to the hospital.'

'But how—'

'The pinnace'll take us,' Thursday said, and threw her arms around him suddenly. 'Elsie's right, Dave, you ought to get home. We'll be OK.'

'I dunno. Oh, Thursday, I don't like leaving you here in all this—'

'We'll be all *right*. We *will*. You get back home.' She kissed him quickly and gave him a push. 'Go *on*.'

Without watching to see that he went, she turned away and gripped Elsie's arm. She felt it shake, and hardly knew whether it was Elsie shaking, or herself, or – more probably – both of them. For the first time, she realised that she, too, must be covered in dust. Her dress and sleeves were grey with it, and her eyes and nose felt gritty. 'D'you think we ought to stop and help?'

Elsie shook her head. Her face was white under the grime. 'They'll have plenty of first-aiders. Our job's to get back to Haslar while there's still some boats. The pinnace is there, I saw it, but it won't be hanging about, not in this lot. Come on, Thurs, we'll have to run for it . . .'

Hand in hand, they raced down the slipway to the pontoon. The Gosport ferry was there, rocking on the waves that had been driven in by a bomb that had dropped into the water, but there was nobody on board. The naval pinnace lay against the pontoon's other side, a matelot at the wheel and two anxious VADs and an officer crouching on the seats. The matelot saw Thursday and Elsie, and shouted at them to get a move on.

'I'm not hanging about here any longer. It's too bloody dangerous.'

'All right, you can go now,' Elsie panted, almost falling over the gunwale. 'The most important ones're here.'

'Slowest ones, you mean,' he grunted, spinning the wheel so that the boat moved away from the pontoon. 'Whatcher bin up to, then, loitering around talking to soldiers? Oughter know better.'

'We do,' Elsie said, with an attempt at a wink at Thursday. 'It's marines we're interested in.' She sank on to the seat and pulled Thursday down beside her. Despite her brave attempt at humour, there were tears making dirty runnels down her cheeks and she choked a little.

'Marines!' The pinnace surged away into the harbour. 'Blimey, I'der thought you'd have more taste. And who put that match to the poor old harbour station, eh? Tell me that.'

They looked back over their shoulders. The station was blazing now, smoke and flames billowing into the sky. As they drew further from the shore, they could see smoke rising from all over Portsmouth and Southsea, and when they looked ahead at Gosport they could see that there had been explosions there, too.

'Have they hit Haslar? Don't say they've hit Haslar.' Thursday felt her mouth begin to tremble. 'Oh Elsie . . .'

'It's all right, Thurs. It's all right. And they seem to be going away now.' The planes had disappeared, and only one or two RAF Spitfires were left, circling to make sure none were about to come streaking from the sun. 'Blimey, that was short and sweet, as they say.'

'Twenty minutes.' The officer moved over towards the girls and Thursday saw that it was the young surgeon who had spoken to her about Tony. His uniform was covered in the same dust that had laid itself over the entire harbour station and ferry pontoon; it had smothered itself over his curly light brown hair, making him look as if he had turned suddenly grey, and the gold braid on his cap and sleeves was dull and dingy. 'Are you all right?' he asked them.

Elsie nodded. 'We're OK, sir. We were up by the station when the siren went. I reckon they've done a bit of damage.'

He nodded ruefully and looked at the black, flame-spattered smoke rising from all around the harbour. 'There'll be a fair number of casualties, I should think. We'd better be prepared for some in the hospital.' He looked at Thursday, his hazel eyes puzzled. 'I know you, don't I?'

'Tilford, sir. You talked to me about my friend SBA West. He – he died a few weeks ago. He was badly hurt at Dunkirk.'

'So he did. And you've been nursing the young German pilot, haven't you? He spoke very well of you.'

'Did he?' Thursday said in surprise. The pinnace lurched suddenly as the steersman gave the wheel a sharp twist to avoid some floating debris, and she reached out involuntarily and caught the surgeon's arm. 'Oh – I'm sorry, sir.'

'Yes, he did.' Commander Kirkpatrick smiled as she regained her balance. 'He told me you didn't realise he could speak English till that last day.'

'I don't know why he pretended he couldn't,' Thursday said. 'I must have driven him mad, nattering away about this and that all the time. I never said anything I shouldn't have, though,' she added hastily.

'I know. And he wasn't trying to catch you out. He told me that he thought if you'd known he could understand, you wouldn't have chatted to him as you did. He was enjoying it!'

'Blimey,' Elsie said ironically, 'must be the first time anyone's ever said that to you, Thurs.'

'Funny, ha-ha.' The 'raiders passed' signal began to sound over their heads and the matelot gave the engine an extra burst of throttle to celebrate. Thursday glanced at the commander. 'Did – did his last operation go all right, sir? He went to a different ward next day and I didn't see him again.'

'Yes, it went very well. He'll live to fly again – but not until the war's over!' Commander Kirkpatrick grinned and she saw again how boyish that made him appear. 'He's been sent to a POW camp in Derbyshire. Used to be a health and beauty centre – seems appropriate, in a funny kind of way.'

The pinnace was drawing alongside the Haslar jetty. Commander Kirkpatrick nodded at the girls and sprang up on to the jetty, setting off at a run towards the hospital. The girls climbed out, too, and walked quickly along the paved way where trolleys had once been run to take wounded men from the boats to the hospital wards. The slabs were smooth and polished under their feet. They paused for a moment and stared along the quarter-deck, with its avenue of trees, towards the little church of St Luke. They had stopped shaking now and were beginning to recover themselves. The talk with

Commander Kirkpatrick had helped, too. He was nice, Thursday thought. Strong and comforting, and friendly with it, the sort of man you could just talk to, without any side or rank getting in the way.

'I'm glad they didn't hit Haslar,' she said softly. 'It's awful to think of it being bombed and torn to pieces. It's so peaceful – so sort of healing.'

Elsie gave her a sideways glance. She had got over her shock quickly and was always at her most robust when Thursday went what she called 'all poetical'. She gave her friend's arm a punch.

'Well, that's what it's meant to be, isn't it? Healing. It's a bloody hospital, after all. And if you ask me, we'd better go in and sign our names in the book, or Madam'll be after us to know why we're late – and then it'll be *us* what needs healing! And I reckon your friend the Commander's right and all – we're likely to get a few more patients coming our way. Better be on the spot, ready for them.'

She set off quickly through the arcade, leaving Thursday no chance to ask what she'd meant by calling Surgeon Commander Kirkpatrick her 'friend'.

The raid had been a bad one – as well as the fire at the station, the church of St John at Portsea was completely destroyed and a lot of houses were too badly damaged to be occupied. The people who had been made homeless were sent to temporary accommodation, salvaging what possessions they could from their ruined homes. They did their best to sort themselves out, and then went back to work as usual. There was, they said, nothing else they could do.

At Lee, HMS *Daedalus* was bombed. Three hangars were destroyed and over forty aircraft lost. Miraculously, nobody was killed, but the devastation shocked everyone. No longer did the residents of Portsmouth and Gosport glance up casually and shrug when the air-raid warning went, assuming it was yet another false alarm – now, at the first rising wail, they grabbed what valuables they could and scurried into their shelters, either the sunken Andersons that had been built in most gardens, or the over-ground ones that stood on street corners.

It looked as though the 'fighting in the streets' was about to begin.

As the daylight raids continued, the VADs at Haslar swiftly got used to the yellow, purple and red alerts. If a double red was announced, everyone possible had to be taken down to the basements, and they quickly developed a routine of getting the stretcher cases into the big, creaking lifts. Once, as the hospital shook to bombs falling in the nearby town and thudding into the harbour, the lift got stuck.

'For God's sake,' panted the seaman orderly who had just got in with two beds and four up-patients. 'This is a bloody fine time to be stranded. Who's on maintenance this week?'

'Whoever it is, he's probably all snug and safe down in the basement,' one of the patients said bitterly. 'And mind your language – ladies present.' He nodded at Elsie, who had helped wheel in the beds.

'Oh, don't mind me, I learnt all the words at me mother's knee, and what I didn't know when I come here I've picked up since.' Elsie knelt by one of the beds. 'You OK, mate? It's all right, I reckon we're as safe here as anywhere. Bloody *hell*!' she added as an explosion rocked the big, metal cage. 'That was a bit close.'

'We're a sitting target here,' the patient said. 'That bleeding water tower, it's like a guide for the planes to know where they are.'

'Maybe they won't bomb it, then,' the orderly said, trying to cheer them up. 'Too useful, see. Anyway, they're more interested in the dockyard than a hospital, stands to reason.'

'Oh, yeah? And us right alongside *Dolphin* and all them subs? Use your head, mate, we're front line here and no mistake about it.' Another explosion shook the building. 'Flippin' heck, ain't no one going to try to get us out of here?'

'I'm bothered about my mate in the ward,' said the man on the other bed. He had both arms in slings and a heavy bandage round one thigh. 'Strapped up to one of them Balkan-beams, he was, leg up in the air like a can-can dancer, and they just *left* him there. Three of 'em there are, strung up like that, left all on their tods, and what happens to *them* if the hospital gets hit? Tell me that.'

'We did leave a knife to cut them down, if they got to be rescued,' Elsie said. 'I mean, what else can we do? It'd be murder to unstrap them now, and their legs'd break all over again. They could even lose 'em altogether. It's like being between the devil and the deep blue sea.'

'Yeah. And I reckon that's where we are now,' the gloomy patient complained. 'Stuck in this bloody lift. I'm going to need a bottle soon, too. D'you reckon they'll ever get it going again?'

'Course they will,' Elsie said stoutly. 'Don't be such a misery. I can hear people outside now – they're trying to do something. They'll have us out in no time, soon as the raid stops, and then you can have your bottle. It won't be long.'

'That's one thing,' the orderly remarked, backing her up, 'they never seem to last long. Twenty minutes, half an hour, and it's all over. They got our boys chasing 'em by the tail.'

'What's left of our boys,' the misery grumbled. 'Shooting 'em down left, right and centre, they are. My cousin's in the RAF and he says some of the boys coming in now've had hardly any training, and only last a couple of days before they're blasted out of the sky. It's like the Great War over again, cannon-fodder, that's what they were then, and sky-fodder's what they are now. And I'll tell you another thing—'

'No, you won't,' Elsie interrupted. 'You won't tell us anything more at all. You've told us too much already. We're supposed to be keeping our peckers up in this war, not spreading alarm and despondency. That's treason, that is. You just shut up, and be grateful you're here in a nice safe hospital with me and the others to look after you, even if we *are* stuck in a lift for the time being.'

'Now, you listen to me—'

'I've told you, I'm not listening to another word, and nor's anyone else.' Elsie looked round at the others, who were nodding agreement. 'I'll tell you what we're going to do, we're going to sing a few songs—'

'Songs! I've sung enough bleeding songs to be at Covent Garden.'

'You don't have to join in if you don't want to. But it'll let people know we're here and we're OK, and it's better than yelling for help. Now then, who's going to start?'

Thursday, struggling down the cellar stairs with a 'special watch' patient on a stretcher, heard the voices and grinned. Trust Elsie to get a party going! She tightened her grip on the handles of the stretcher as another explosion rocked the building above. They really were close today, she thought, nodding at the orderly on the other end to keep going, and she felt a pang of anxiety for the patients left behind. But it was the patient on the stretcher who mattered now. Once he was safely below, she would go back and at least be with those still strapped to their Balkan-beams, helpless and alone.

The vast maze of cellars had been fitted out for occupation months before. There were benches all around the walls, space for stretchers and even some beds. A full operating theatre had been set up for emergencies, although there was talk of it being used full time if the raids continued. There were emergency food supplies and a small galley where mugs of tea and wads of cake or sandwiches could be given out.

'Home from home!' Thursday declared, setting the stretcher down. 'It'd take a bomb as big as the moon to get us here.'

She set off towards the stairs, intending to return to the patients left above, but as she slid through the big doors Miss Makepeace materialised from the shadows and put out her hand.

'And where do you think you're going, Tilford?'

Thursday stopped, startled. 'Oh – Madam! I – I was just going to make sure there was no one else who should be brought down.'

'There isn't. I checked that myself.' The bright brown eyes regarded her. 'There are only the trauma patients left. You wouldn't have been going up to stay with them, by any chance?'

Thursday gazed at her helplessly. 'It seems so awful just to leave them there on their own. With all these bombs dropping around them. It doesn't seem right. We're supposed to be looking after them.'

'I know.' The eyes were kind. 'It's a dilemma – which patient needs us most, which to choose when there's a decision to be made. It always will be. But our choice is made for us, Tilford. Our orders are to remain under cover. Remember, the men we treat here are all on active service – even when they're strapped to a Balkan-beam.'

Thursday nodded reluctantly and then glanced at Madam again. They were standing just outside the first big pair of doors, in the space of the stairwell. The lift doors were to one side, and they could hear Elsie exhorting her fellow prisoners to pack up their troubles in their old kitbags and smile, smile, smile. Another explosion shuddered through the ground.

'You weren't thinking of going up yourself, were you, Madam?' Thursday asked innocently, and watched the older woman's face break into a smile.

'Thursday Tilford, you're too clever for your own good! Well, I suppose since you've caught me out, I might as well admit that I *was* just going to slip up to see that they were all safe. Only for a moment, mind – I don't intend to break any rules.' She caught Thursday's eye again and Thursday could have sworn she winked. 'Just bend them a little, perhaps. And now I suppose you'll tell the Surgeon Rear Admiral on me!'

'Not if you let me come, too,' Thursday said demurely, and the two of them ran swiftly up the stairs together and into the ward.

It was oddly peaceful up there, in the lull. Almost all the beds were empty, the up-patients' chairs scattered untidily where they had been left when the warning had sounded, and a curtain blew in at an open window. There were three beds still occupied, the men shackled by their ankles to the pulleys.

'Blimey, just when we was getting a bit of peace and quiet,' one of the men remarked when Madam and Thursday appeared. 'Thought we'd seen the back of you lot for a bit.'

Thursday gasped, expecting Madam to reprimand him, for the patients were as much in awe of her as the VADs, but instead Miss Makepeace shook her head and went to close the window, drawing the curtain in case of flying glass. She then went to each bed in turn, looking down at the men.

'You know we can't stay here, don't you?' Another bomb, landing somewhere in Gosport, thundered above her voice. 'We have to go below. But either I or Tilford here will come up every half-hour to see that you're all right. We haven't forgotten you.'

'You're angels, you are,' a skinny, monkey-faced mechanic told her. 'Ruddy angels. But we don't want none of you coming up here, risking your lives, see? What could you do if the roof fell in? Bugger – I mean, nothing. You're better off stopping down below and having a bit of a sing-song. We can hear one goin' on now, sounds lovely, too.'

'That's Elsie – Nurse Jackson,' Thursday said. 'They're stuck in the lift.'

'Stuck in the – well, I'm buggered!' The man forgot to moderate his language and laughed. 'Only happen to her, it could. Wonder who she's got in there with her, then?'

'I'm not sure, but I think I saw Writer Donkett going in.'

'Blimey, she's in for a jolly time, then. Don't say she's got *him* singing an' all!' The man called over to the patient opposite. 'Hear that, Knocker? Old Eeyore's stuck in the lift with Nurse Jackson, and she's got him singin' a roundelay! Wonders'll never cease.' The building shook again. 'Look, love, you'd better get cracking and go below. We'll be all right, and if we ain't we got these knives you so thoughtfully left to cut our throats with!'

Thursday scurried across the ward to where Madam was waiting impatiently, and they both descended the stairs. Elsie and her choir were now embarking on a medley of romantic songs – 'The bells are ringing, for me and my gal' and 'You made me love you', its effect rather spoilt by a raucous voice declaiming 'You woke me up to do it! Woke me up to do it!' at which the entire company in the lift apparently broke down in giggles. Thursday, biting her own lip, glanced sideways at Madam and saw her smile.

'She's a good girl, Nurse Jackson. Understands the importance of morale. And you're a good nurse, too, Tilford. I shan't forget today.'

Neither will I, Thursday thought as she went back to her stretcher patient and made sure he was comfortable before sitting down beside the others. Because today's the day I decided to go for proper training, the minute I can. I'm going to be a registered nurse – perhaps a QARNN – and make nursing my career.

How funny, she thought with amused surprise. Before the war, I never even thought of a career – I did my tailoring apprenticeship because that's what Mum wanted me to do, and so that I'd have a trade to follow if I needed to work when I was older. But I never thought of a *career*.

Girls didn't, did they. Not before the war started, anyway.

Chapter Twenty-Three

Once Percy had walked in on Flo and Denise in the midst of their argument, the whole story had had to be told again. As everyone had known he would be, he was furious and declared that he was going to go round and sort that young man out now, this very minute, no hanging about.

'You can't, Dad! You mustn't.' Denise was in floods of tears again. 'Anyway, you don't know where he lives.'

'I'll find out! I'll go to the post office, that's what I'll do. I'll see his boss and tell him what's been going on. I'll see him sacked from his job, just for a start, and then I'll give him the hiding of his life. He'll not get away with this!'

'It wasn't his fault—' Denise began, but he silenced her

'Oh, made him do it, did you? I bet you hardly knew what it was all about. Me and your mum have made sure you never heard any filthy talk, pure as the driven snow you were till you started knocking about with that bloke. What was he thinking of, that's what I'd like to know, picking a girl hardly out of school? Aren't there enough girls his own age to go with?'

'He didn't—' Denise began, but this time it was her mother who interrupted.

'He thought she was eighteen, Perce.'

'Thought she was eighteen? Why would he think a thing like that? Couldn't he see for himself?'

'Perce, you know our Denise can make herself up to look older when she wants. She told him that's how old she was, that's why he thought it. You can't blame the chap entirely.'

'I can blame him for doing what he done, whatever age he thought she was. It's not decent behaviour, Flo, and you know it.

People should wait till they're married, same as we did.' He glared accusingly at his daughter.

'We *love* each other—'

'So did your mum and me love each other! But we never went together till your mum had my ring on her finger. I wouldn't have asked it.'

Denise said nothing, and Flo knew she was thinking that they couldn't have loved each other like she and Vic did. All young couples thought that. They all thought they'd invented it, that nobody else had ever felt this way. But telling her that wouldn't help matters.

'It's no good arguing about it now, anyway,' she said. 'What we've got to do is think what to do next.'

'I've told you what I'm going to do next,' Percy growled.

'No, you're not. Sit down, Perce, and let's talk this over like we always do. I'll make a cup of tea. I need one, and I'm sure you do too, and Denise is looking as white as a sheet. She's still got to be looked after, whatever she's done.'

She went out to the kitchen and filled the kettle, then stood trembling beside the stove. I've been expecting this, she thought, ever since Mary told me her Jen had let out that Denise and that feller were talking about secret engagements. I've known it might happen, but I've tried to tell myself I was being silly. I wasn't, though, and I ought to have done something about it before it got this far.

Denise came out and stood beside her. She was crying again.

'I'm sorry, Mum.'

Flo put her arm round her. 'I know, love. I know.'

'I never meant it to be like this.'

'I don't suppose you did,' Flo said with a little sound that was half laugh and half sob.

'It wasn't Vic's fault, honestly.'

'Well, you say that, but it takes two, you know. And he's a lot older than you. He could at least have been careful.'

'Well, he was,' Denise began, and then stopped, embarrassed. 'I mean, he always – he – well, he *said* it'd be all right. Safe. You know.'

'Well, now you know it isn't,' Flo told her. 'There's only one way to know you're safe, and that's to say no. And if you weren't going to do that, he should have been *more* careful. But you never ought to have done it in the first place.'

The kettle began to whistle and she turned to make the tea. Denise slipped past her and went outside to the lavatory. Flo fetched the milk from the meatsafe outside the back door, and poured three cups of tea. She put them on a tin tray and carried them into the back room.

Percy was sitting in his chair, staring at the empty fireplace.

'This is a bad job, Flo,' he said as she set down the tray. 'Just as if we hadn't got enough to bear, with losing our Mike.'

'I know, love.' She handed him a cup of tea. 'Here, drink this. I've put extra sugar in.'

'Sugar! I thought we could only have saccharin in our tea now.'

'Saccharin's no good for shock. It's sugar we need.' Flo sat down in her own chair opposite and faced him. 'What are we going to do, Perce?'

'I dunno, I'm sure. It's her age that bothers me. I mean, are the police going to be getting involved? That's what I've been wondering.'

'Perce!' Flo's hand went to her mouth. 'You don't really think they would, do you? I mean, they don't put girls in prison for—'

'No, but they might put the bloke in, and our Denise would have to go to court and testify, and I expect they'd have to have a doctor's report and all that, and—'

'Oh, Perce, no! That'd be awful. We can't let our Denise go through all that.'

'We might not have any choice. Once a doctor sees her . . . Has she been to one yet, d'you know?'

'I don't think so. She'd only just told me about it when you walked in. D'you mean a doctor'd have to tell the police?'

'Well, I don't think he'd have any choice. I don't really know, Flo.' Percy rubbed his hand over his face. 'It's not the sort of thing you take much notice of in the ordinary way.'

The door opened and Denise came in. She looked uncertainly from one to the other and sat on one of the dining-chairs that stood against the wall. Flo nodded towards the table.

'Cup of tea there for you, Denise. Drink it while it's hot.' She waited while Denise sipped and then said, 'Your dad and me've been talking about this.'

'Well, I didn't suppose you'd been discussing the weather,' Denise said in an attempt to lighten the atmosphere, and jumped as her father brought the flat of his hand down hard on the arm of his chair.

'And that's enough of that! I won't stand any cheek from you, my girl, we've got trouble enough without any of your funny jokes. There's a lot to think about, and it won't help if you take that attitude.'

'I wasn't—'

'Don't start arguing again, please,' Flo begged. 'Let's just try to sort it out.' She looked at the clock. 'It's getting late. We've missed the nine o'clock news and everything. Why don't we all go to bed now, and get some sleep, and talk about it properly tomorrow?'

'Sleep!' Percy said. 'I don't reckon I'll sleep a wink, and neither will you, Flo.'

'Well, our Denise ought to anyway. Whatever the rights and wrongs of it are, she *is* expecting and she's got to look after herself. You're looking worn out,' she said to her daughter. 'You go on up now, and get some rest. Your dad and me'll think about it.'

Denise nodded. She finished her tea and stood up. Awkwardly, she bent and kissed her mother, then looked at her father and hesitated.

'Oh, come here, for goodness' sake!' he said, reaching up a big hand. 'I've never been that angry with you that I wouldn't give you a goodnight kiss, and I'm not now. You do as your mother says and get a good night's sleep, and me and your mum will think what's best to do. All right?'

Denise hesitated. 'Well . . .'

'Well what? What's biting you now?'

'Well – you won't go round and see Vic, will you, Dad? And you won't get him sacked, or put in prison? Please. Because if you do . . .' Her voice shook. 'If you do, I don't think I'd ever forgive you.'

Percy stared at her. Then he pulled her down and kissed her.

'Just you go to bed,' he ordered her. 'We'll talk about it tomorrow. I won't do anything till we've done that. But don't you try telling me what to do and what not to do, my girl. Just remember you're still under my jurisdiction, and so you will be for the next five years, and *I'll* be the one to decide what happens. All right?'

Denise stared at him. Then her lips trembled again and she

turned and ran from the room. They heard her footsteps on the stairs and then her door slammed and they heard the sound of muffled sobbing.

'It's not going to be easy,' Flo said. 'Deciding what to do and making sure it's done – it's not going to be easy, Perce.'

'Nothing's easy these days, Flo,' he said heavily. 'Seems to me, nothing's ever going to be easy again.'

'I know,' she said. 'And while we've all been talking, something else has come into my mind, Perce.' She hesitated, then said, 'Things are so queer these days – with the war and all, none of us knows what's going to happen from one day to the next. And with our Mike going so sudden, and Leslie risking his life every day, and all the bombing – well, our Denise is all we've got, isn't she, in a way. I mean, she's the only one we've got at home. We *can't* turn her out, Perce, we just can't.'

'I know, love. I don't reckon I could have done anyway. Not really.'

'And there's another thing. This baby. It's not just Denise's baby. It's our *grandchild*, Perce. Our first grandchild.' Flo looked at him and tears slid from her eyes and rolled down her cheeks. 'It might even be the only grandchild we're ever going to have,' she whispered. 'We can't let it go to strangers.'

The raids continued throughout the autumn. Once they had started there seemed to be no stopping them. At first they were mostly during the day, but as the days grew shorter they started to take place after dark, and then late into the night. You never knew when they would come over, except that on clear nights people would look at the sky and say it was a 'bomber's moon' that night. No longer a harvest moon or a hunter's moon, Thursday thought sadly, but a bomber's moon. It didn't sound nearly so romantic.

The bright moonlit nights of the autumn were good for Allied bombers, though, as well as the enemy. You could hear them going over – the steady, determined note of the RAF Lancasters, heading off to wreak destruction on Germany. And then the whining, sonorous note of the Luftwaffe Stukas, bringing revenge. London was being especially badly hit, and the news every morning was of fresh destruction. It was as though the whole of Europe would be smashed and destroyed before the conflict was over.

You never knew, when you came out of the shelters after the 'raiders passed' signal, what you would find. A mountain of rubble at your own front door – you might be lucky just to find your front door. The house next door, gone as if it had never been, with nothing but a gaping crater in its place. A changed skyline – a church spire missing, a shop flattened, a fire blazing.

In Gosport, the Market House above the Dive Café was gutted and the electricity company's offices in the high street reduced to a splintered mass. Two houses in Forton Road were smashed to smithereens and every window for a hundred yards on either side blown out, yet a car in next door's front yard remained untouched. At Elson, eight houses were completely demolished and one Anderson shelter blown apart – yet the seven people inside were unhurt, and so were all those who had hidden in the dozen other shelters within a few yards of the wreckage. It just showed, people said when they came to look at it, that the shelters did work, and they gave thanks to Mr Anderson who had designed them.

In Worcester, it was still fairly quiet. The sirens sounded often enough, but it was generally planes going over, heading for Birmingham and the other industrial cities. Places like Worcester and Gloucester, with nothing much but a few local factories like the porcelain or such, wouldn't be of much interest to the Germans. Mind, there were the docks at Gloucester, but Worcester would be all right. Even so, quite a few people took to leaving their homes every evening and trekking down to the riverside and racecourse to sleep out under the stars. They thought that was safer, but it wouldn't be much fun when winter set in.

Vic had finally run out of excuses not to come and meet Denise's parents. Denise hadn't seen him for nearly ten days when she finally caught him, waiting outside the post office until he left work. He looked guilty and uncomfortable when he saw her, but kissed her and let her slip her arm through his and they walked away together, towards the river.

'I was beginning to think you didn't want me any more,' she said after a few moments.

'Don't be daft. Of course I still want you.'

Denise took a deep breath. 'Well, you might not when you've heard what I've got to tell you. Vic – you know what I said about thinking I might be – well, having a baby?' She looked at him. 'I am. It's definite. Next February, probably.'

Vic stopped dead. 'Oh, God. Oh, *God* . . . Denise, are you sure—?'

'I've just told you, haven't I?' Her voice rose shrilly and he glanced uneasily around him. 'Look, I wouldn't make a joke about it, would I? It's not funny. I'm having a *baby*, Vic, and it's *yours*. And we've got to decide what to do about it.'

Vic ran his hand nervously through his dark hair. 'Denise, I don't know, you can't just spring it on me like this—'

'I haven't. I told you weeks ago I thought I might be. You wanted to forget about it, and ever since then you've been either working overtime or going to visit your auntie in Birmingham.' Her glance sharpened. 'I suppose you *have* got an auntie in Birmingham?'

'Yes, of course I have. Auntie Aggie. She's my mum's aunt, actually, so she's really my great-aunt, but I always call her—'

'Vic, I don't care what you call her! What I care about is what you're going to do about me and our baby, and when you're going to come round and see my mum and dad about it.'

'See your mum and – God, Denise, they'll kill me! Your dad'll go up the flipping wall. Here, you haven't said anything to them, have you?'

'Well, of course I have. And Dad was all for going straight round and killing you straight off, only Mum persuaded him not to. And they've been on about it ever since, only I said we'd got to talk to you about it before – before I go to the doctor.'

'You haven't been to a doctor yet? So it's only your family that knows?'

'Mum and Dad know, and so does Auntie Mary, so I suppose Uncle Walter does, too. And Jenny, and—'

'And all the rest of bloody Worcester, by the sound of it,' he said bitterly. 'And all of them wanting my guts for garters. Well, thanks for finally getting round to telling *me*, Denise.'

She stared at him. 'Vic, don't be like that. What was I supposed to do? You're never around – either working late or off up to Birmingham. It seemed to me as if you were avoiding me.'

'Don't be daft.'

'I'm not being daft. Just remember, it was you kept on about secret engagements and said you loved me. But where have you been lately, eh? You knew I was worried, you knew there was a chance, but I've hardly seen you for the past few weeks. It seemed as if you were just trying to get rid of me. What else was I to think? And don't tell me not to be daft again,' she added as he opened his mouth. 'It doesn't matter now anyway. You'll have to make time for me, never mind all this overtime and going to see your auntie. *I'm* the one that needs you, not some old lady thirty miles away.'

Vic ran his hand through his hair again. He looked scared, she thought, and remembered what her parents and Thursday had said.

'They won't really put you in prison, will they, Vic?' she asked anxiously. 'I mean, they wouldn't do that, not if – if we were to get married.'

'*Married?*' he yelped. 'But we *can't* – you're not—'

'I *know* I'm not bloody old enough! D'you think everyone else hasn't told me that till I'm sick of hearing about it? But I will be in October – well before the baby's born. And I think – well, I've got an idea Mum and Dad are coming round to the idea. Look, the police won't do anything to you if we're married, surely – what would be the point? You'd have a wife and baby to support, they couldn't be so cruel. Anyway, you'll probably be called up soon, it would be better to have you in the Army than in jail, I'd have thought.'

'Well, ta very much,' he muttered. 'That's *my* future mapped out – jail or dead. Blimey, not much of a prospect either way, is it.'

Denise was silent. They started to walk again and after a few minutes she said in a very small voice, 'Don't you want to marry me, Vic? Don't you love me any more?'

Vic stopped again and looked into her face. He sighed and put his arms around her and rested his cheek against her hair. She felt small and slight against his body and he felt a sweep of tenderness.

'Of course I love you, you daft ha'porth,' he said. 'Of course I do. And I want to marry you. It's just – well, it's come as a shock, that's all. And I didn't want it to be this way. I didn't really.'

Denise lifted her face and looked at him with shining eyes. He could see the relief in them, the relief and the certainty, and he felt ashamed, and bewildered, and trapped. I can't go back on my word now, he thought. I can't ever go back.

'I don't mind which way it is,' she whispered. 'Just so long as we're going to be together, I don't mind anything.'

282

Portsmouth fared even worse than Gosport in the raids. It was true that on some nights no one was killed and hardly anyone injured, but on others the casualties were heavy. The gasworks at Hilsea was hit, and nobody could cook anything for days. One of the churches in Copnor, not far from Elsie's home, was destroyed. Pickford's Furniture Store was set ablaze, and so was Government House. An unexploded bomb in the mud of the harbour, where once little boys had begged for pennies to be thrown, stopped the Gosport ferry for nearly a week.

In the middle of November, twenty high-explosive bombs were dropped around the Copnor and North End districts, and one of them fell on Elsie's home.

'They were down the shelter, Mum and Dad and Eddy,' she told Thursday through her tears. 'They were safe. But our Dave – he'd gone up to the house to make a jug of cocoa. It was a quiet spell – they'd almost thought of going back in, the lot of 'em. But Dad said no, and Dave said he'd go and make a hot drink. Mum had a cold or she'd have gone, and then it would have been her. But it was *Dave* – our Dave.'

'Oh, *Elsie*.' Thursday was crying, too. She had been to the house so often, cycling up from the ferry through Portsmouth and North End. Now it was in ruins, all of it. The railway had been hit, Copnor Road was closed, and so was Milton Road. You couldn't get up nor down, Elsie said. 'Oh, Elsie, your Dave – oh, it isn't *fair*!'

They all knew it wasn't fair, and they all knew it was no use complaining about it. But when it was a young chap like Dave, already crippled by illness yet bravely carrying on and living his life, when it was boys like Steve and Mike and Leslie – and even Heinz Schmidt – well, it *didn't* seem fair, and you couldn't help saying so.

'I don't seem to be able to take it in,' Elsie said, shaking her head. 'Our Dave, gone, just like that. We oughter be getting used to it, but – I can't believe it's true, Thurs, I really can't.'

'You've got to go and see for yourself,' Thursday told her. 'That's the only way you'll be able to believe it. And you must want to go and see your mum and dad anyway. D'you want me to come with you?'

'Oh, Thurs, would you? I'd be ever so grateful, and so would they. I've asked Madam if I can have an extra couple of hours tomorrow, and she said I could ask you or Patsy, too. I don't know what I can do, but I just want to *see* them – you know.'

'I know. Like I wanted to see my family when we heard about Mike. I'll come, Else, whenever you like.' She hesitated. 'There – there'll be the funeral too, I suppose.'

'I suppose so. I hadn't even *thought* about that. Next week some time, probably.' Elsie blew her nose and rubbed her face with her hanky. 'I don't even know where they're going to live. Or how much they've managed to save. It might all be gone – all our clothes and stuff, the wireless Dave made out of crystals, all his Glenn Miller and Ambrose records, and my Frank Sinatras – and Mum's glass ornaments and things what we brought back from the Sunday school charabanc outings – and our Eddy's collection of train numbers – it'll all be gone, Thurs, all of it!'

'I know, I know.' Thursday stroked Elsie's yellow hair. 'It doesn't bear thinking of. We'll go tomorrow and see them. D'you know where they'll be?'

'The lady I spoke to on the phone told me to go to the church hall,' Elsie said dully. 'They're all stopping there, apparently, all them that's been bombed out, while they sorts out places for them to go. I hope they don't get sent too far off, Thurs. Mum's never left Fratton in her life, she just wouldn't settle down anywhere else.'

'She'll be all right.' She'll be too upset about Dave to worry about where she was living, Thursday thought. She went back to the ward, her heart heavy, thinking of the fun she and Dave and Elsie had had together. The bike-rides over the hill, to Southwick and Hambledon and up the Meon valley. The day they'd stopped for a drink at the White Horse at Droxford, and Dave had persuaded Thursday to try a local beer. I'd hardly been able to ride straight the rest of the way home, she thought, half smiling and half weeping at the memory. And there were the summer afternoons at Hilsea Lido, where Dave proved that having one leg shorter than the other didn't have to stop you being a good swimmer and diver. He was like a fish, she thought, remembering how he would disappear beneath the surface and how you wouldn't know where he was till you felt his hand on your ankle . . . Oh, Dave – Dave . . .

She went with Elsie the next day, and found her parents and young Eddy sitting on camp beds in the church hall, their faces grey with misery. It seemed as if everything had been taken away from them – everything but their remaining two children. Mrs Jackson leapt up when she saw Elsie and flung her arms around her, bursting into tears on her shoulder. Elsie, crying too, held her tightly, both patting each other's shoulders as if to give comfort as well as to receive it, while Mr Jackson hovered nearby, anxious for his turn, and young Eddy sat on the flimsy folding bed, staring dully into space, barely seeming to know that they were there.

Thursday dropped on her knees beside him. 'Hello, Eddy.'

He didn't answer. She took the hand that lay limply on one knee and held it to her cheek. It was like ice.

'Eddy, it's me, Thursday. You know me, don't you?'

He shrugged a little but still didn't answer. Thursday gazed at him and then touched his colourless cheek. It was as cold as his hand. His body was shivering.

She pulled a blanket from the next bed, and wrapped it round his shoulders, holding him against her. He turned his head and his eyes searched her face. He seemed totally bewildered, like a baby thrust into a strange environment. She stared at him, feeling pity well up within her, and then drew him close again.

'Oh, Eddy. Poor, poor Eddy. What have they done to you, then?'

He didn't answer; he couldn't answer. Nor did Thursday expect him to answer. She knew that he was in deep shock, that it would take time, and warmth, and comforting words for him to come slowly out of it. But what comfort could you give to a boy who had sat night after night in an underground shelter, listening while bombs pounded the streets where he lived? What comfort could you give to a boy who had come out of the shelter one morning to find his home smashed to rubble and his brother killed?

Thursday held him against her. She rocked him gently to and fro, feeling the ice of his body freezing her own heart, when all she wanted to do was give him some of her warmth; when all she longed to do was give him comfort, although she knew that there was only one thing that would comfort him. And that was the return of the world to the way it had been yesterday.

Chapter Twenty-Four

Things could never be as they had been yesterday. 'Yesterday' meant so much – a day before, a week, a year, a century. Whatever it meant, things could never be the same again. The world changed a little each day, and some days it changed a lot.

Elsie's parents and brother were allotted a house to live in, a small terraced house whose tenants had been evacuated. Mr Jackson tried to persuade his wife to be evacuated too, but she wouldn't hear of leaving him. Who would give him a hot meal when he came home from work, she asked, and who would wash his clothes? But she agreed to Eddy being sent away to the country.

'Mum never liked the idea of Ed going to live with strangers,' Elsie told Thursday as they measured out pills one morning. 'But she says she can't stick the idea of losing another boy, so he's got to go. Tell the truth, I don't think he's all that keen to stop in Pompey anyway. He ain't bin the same boy since the raid, jumps at his own shadow now, he does.'

'It's a shame.' Thursday thought of the bright, cheeky little boy who used to rush to meet her and was now so pale and subdued. 'People don't realise what it's like for kiddies. Some of them are scared stiff.'

'Not all of 'em, though. Most of the nippers in our street think it's some sort of glorified firework display, and they're out after every raid, looking for souvenirs. Boy next door's got half a ton of shrapnel under his bed! I don't reckon it's the bombs that've upset Eddy, it's what happened to our Dave. Thought the world of Dave, Eddy did.'

'I know.' Thursday worked in silence for a while, then said,

'What d'you think of the moves, Elsie? I'm looking forward to going into Theatre.'

Elsie chuckled. 'Fancy your name up in lights, then? You sound like a starstruck actress!'

Thursday made a face. 'Don't think I'm going to get a chance to be a star, down in the basement. Surgeon Commander Kirkpatrick does all his ops there now.'

'You going to be working with him?' Elsie rolled her eyes enviously. 'Coo, some people are jammy!'

'Not at all,' Thursday said defensively, aware of a warmth in her cheeks. 'I don't expect him to take the slightest notice of me. Anyway, I should think he's already spoken for.'

'Yeah, I heard one of the QARNN sisters had got her eye on him. That one with the long ginger hair.'

'She wouldn't like to hear you say that – she thinks it's auburn,' Thursday said. 'Anyway, how d'you know it's long? I've never seen her with her cap off.'

'Yes, you have, she was at that dance at Lee Tower. Here, are we going to the dance at Grange next week? There's invites for anyone that wants to go.'

'I don't know . . .'

'Come on, Thurs,' Elsie said persuasively. 'You haven't been out for weeks. We can't sit indoors and mope for ever, you know.'

'I know.' Thursday washed her hands, staring at the scrap of pink Lifebuoy soap in her hands. Elsie was being braver than she was, she thought. She had cried bitterly over Dave and then just got on with things. Thursday didn't seem able to do that. Maybe there'd been too many young men gone already: Mike dead; Steve still missing and almost certainly dead, too, one of those whose bodies would never be found and whose fate never known; Tony, so horribly wounded, going through operation after operation only to die at the end of them; and now Dave, who had ignored his limp and gone cycling and swimming, always with a joke on his lips and a smile in his eyes.

It wasn't just that. Thursday was worried about her mother. With the weeks and months going by with no news about Steve, Mary Tilford was growing more and more depressed. Her letters were short and, although Thursday could see she was trying hard to be cheerful, there was a thread of sadness through them. It was as if she was losing hope, not just about Steve but about everything. The war's getting her down, she thought. It seemed awful to think it, but it wouldn't be so bad if they knew for certain that Steve was dead. It was this not knowing, the constant wondering, that ate away at your heart.

And then there was her cousin Denise, who was getting married next week. Her mother had written to tell her about it. There wasn't going to be any white dress or cake, and hardly any guests, just the family, and it wasn't even going to be on a Saturday, which was the proper day for weddings – instead, it was going to be a hole-and-corner ceremony on a Friday morning. No one seemed to be looking forward to it – Auntie Flo and Uncle Perce hardly talked about it at all. Denise had brought Vic round to meet Thursday's parents one day and they'd liked him all right, and thought Flo and Percy would too, in time, but it was all the wrong way round, and not the way Flo had wanted it at all.

'Come on, Thursday,' Elsie urged, watching her. 'It'll do us both good. After all, you're luckier than I am. *I'm* not going to be the one down in Theatre with the gorgeous Commander Kirkpatrick. *I'm* going to be in Zymotics, with all the nasty infectious diseases!'

Thursday laughed. 'It doesn't sound so romantic, I agree.'

'It's not. Madam's slipped me the wink that I'm starting on VDs. Nasty little bugs that the boys have picked up on shore leave. You know the Rear Admiral made a stink about VADs working with them, but Madam, bless her cotton socks, put up a fight and said we were as good as any QARNN and ought to be allowed to work anywhere.' She grinned. 'She must have thought she was doing us a favour, I suppose! Truth is, he didn't even like the QARNNs nursing VD cases, said it wasn't right for women to have to do it, but he had to give in since any blokes that are still left are likely to be drafted at any time. Can't leave 'em to fester all on their own, can we!'

'Well, you just watch you don't catch anything,' Thursday warned, and Elsie hooted.

'Only one way to pick that up, didn't you know? It don't come off a lavvy seat, you know. Not like crabs, anyway.' She giggled. 'Someone wrote on the wall in the men's the other day, "Do not sit upon the seat, The crabs in this place jump six feet!" I cleaned it off right away, of course, but I had to laugh.'

Thursday laughed, too, and thought that a year or two ago she wouldn't have even known what the joke was. I've learned a lot since I became a VAD, she thought, and not all of it to do with nursing!

'That's better,' Elsie said, watching her face. 'So you'll come?'

Thursday nodded. 'Oh, OK, Elsie – I'll come.'

Fort Grange stood at the entrance to the local aerodrome and dances were often held there, in one of the empty hangars. A lorry was going from Haslar and the girls scrambled over the tailgate, laughing and looking forward to their evening's fun. Thursday, who had almost backed out at the last moment, had been dragged out by Elsie and Patsy. She climbed aboard quietly and huddled in one corner.

'I'm getting worried about her,' Elsie murmured to Patsy. 'I thought she was cheering up a bit when we talked about coming, but she seems to have slipped right back. It's as if she just starts to feel better and then it all comes over her again. It's almost like she feels she didn't *ought* to be happy any more.'

'Well, we'll just have to do our best to put some life back into her. Maybe she'll find some nice chap here tonight. That's what she needs, you know. There's been nobody since Tony went.'

'I don't think she was all that serious about him, really,' Elsie observed. 'It was only that he came back in such a mess, and then popped it. Flipping shame, but she can't live like a blooming nun because of it.'

The lorry arrived at Grange and they all piled out and trooped into the hangar. The band was playing Victor Sylvester tunes and the floor was crowded with dancers. The big space had been decorated for the occasion with flags and bunting, and looked very festive. Elsie nodded with approval.

'That's the kind of thing we need. A bit of patriotism to remind us what it's all about. King and country! Land of Hope and Glory! Kick old Hitler up the—'

'All right, Elsie, we know what you mean!' Patsy giggled and gave her friend a push. 'Madam's just over there, look, with Commander Kirkpatrick – you don't want her hearing you, do you?'

'Why not? What's wrong with a bit of patriotism? And I was only going to say "backside". I don't know what sort of a girl you think I am, Patsy Martin.'

'A smasher, that's what *I* think,' said a new voice, and they turned to see a sailor standing close behind them. He was an electrician and had been checking the wiring in Elsie's ward, so they'd already exchanged a bit of banter. He grinned and held out his hand. 'Want to dance?'

'That's what I'm here for,' she responded, and they swung away into a foxtrot. Another sailor pulled Patsy into the throng and Thursday was left alone.

She stood hesitating for a moment, then slipped along the wall to an empty chair and sat down. She felt lonely and out of place. I shouldn't have come, she thought. I'm not in the mood for dancing. I don't seem to be in the mood for anything just lately.

Someone came and stood in front of her, and she looked up. It was Commander Kirkpatrick, and he was smiling down at her.

'Will you give me the pleasure of this dance?'

'Oh . . .' Thursday scrambled to her feet. 'It – it's very kind of you, but I'm really quite all right – I mean, my friends will be back soon and—'

'I'm not taking pity on you,' he said with amusement. 'I'm asking you to dance because I'd like it.'

Thursday felt her blush rise. Thank goodness the lights were dim! She went into his arms and they moved off into the fast, intricate steps.

Thursday loved dancing, and Commander Kirkpatrick was good at it. He led her firmly into manoeuvres she had never attempted before, but because his guidance was so sure, she found them easy and fun. She liked the way he held her, too – lightly but confidently, with none of the clumsiness of some of the partners she'd had at other dances. She smiled at him as he took her back to her seat, and thanked him.

'That was lovely.'

'I enjoyed it, too. I hope you'll give me another dance before the evening's over.'

Patsy and Elsie were already there. They gazed at her, and Thursday coloured.

'There's no need to look like that. He was just being kind.'

'Looked as if he was enjoying it, all the same. And what lovely manners! "Hope you'll give me another dance before the evening's over." Not like my bloke, he just said "Ta, see you later" and sloped off.'

'Well, some of us attract a better class of partner,' Thursday said innocently, and Elsie hooted.

'That's one in the eye for you, Pats! Anyway, he seems to have bucked our Thursday up a bit, so it's all to the good. Listen, that's a quickstep. Look lively, or we won't get asked.'

There was no question of not being asked to dance. The hangar was crowded with sailors and local boys who were all eager to hold a girl in their arms for a few minutes. The girls found themselves besieged, and by the interval they were all breathless and ready for a rest.

'It's a smashing dance.' Elsie declared. 'Just what we needed to take us out of ourselves a bit. I saw you dancing with Kirky again, Thurs.'

'Only once. It was another foxtrot. He's a good dancer, I'll say that.'

'Maybe you could take a turn or two round the theatre in a quiet moment,' Patsy suggested. 'You're moving down there on Monday, aren't you?'

'Yes, and I don't suppose he'll even recognise me, so you can take that look off your face, Patsy Martin! *And* you, Elsie Jackson. You notice I'm not making a lot of remarks about your partners.'

'Well, they're not as interesting as yours. Except for that tiffy I did the square tango with, he was a bit of all right. Radio ops, he is, from *Collingwood*. I wouldn't mind doing a bit more with him.'

'Well, I expect you'll get the chance, there's another two hours to go.' The band was striking up again and Thursday looked up as Commander Kirkpatrick approached and held out his hand. The other two girls watched as the couple moved away, Thursday almost floating in the commander's arms.

'I don't care what she says,' Patsy remarked, 'I bet he *will* notice her in the theatre. Three times in one evening – and two hours still to go! Don't tell me he's just being kind.'

The dance was a waltz, and there was more time for partners to talk to each other. Thursday, feeling suddenly shy, said nothing but after a moment or two the commander spoke in her ear.

'You're a very good dancer, Nurse Tilford.'

'Thank you,' she said. 'I love it – always have. I wanted to be a ballet dancer when I was little, but I dare say most little girls want that.'

'I don't know. My sister always wanted to be a circus rider!'

They laughed. Then he said, 'D'you have any sisters? Or brothers?'

'Yes.' Thursday paused for a moment. 'A younger sister, Jenny. And – and a brother. But he was reported missing at Dunkirk and we haven't heard any more about him.'

He looked at her. 'You mean you don't know if he's alive or not?'

'He was "missing, believed killed". And now it's five months and we still haven't heard, so . . .' She shrugged. 'It'd be better in a way if we knew for certain that – that he was dead. It's not knowing that's the awful part.'

'Of course it is. I'm really sorry.' They danced in silence for a few moments, then he said quietly, 'I had a brother at Dunkirk, too. He was on one of the ships that was sunk. So we're in much the same position over that.'

'Oh that's awful. I'm sorry, too. Was he a doctor as well?'

'Yes. Runs in the family – our father was a surgeon captain when he retired. He went into general practice in Devon then, and lives in a village on the edge of Dartmoor. Pillar of the local community and all that – he's very involved in local defence, Home Guard and so on. And my mother's a leading light in the local WVS, so they're both doing quite a lot in the way of war work. It's a good thing – takes their minds off Stephen.'

'Stephen? Was that your brother? My brother was called Stephen, too, only we always shortened it to Steve.'

'Well,' he said, 'that's a coincidence, isn't it? We seem to have quite a bit in common.'

Thursday didn't think that their both happening to have a brother with the same name exactly counted as having a lot in common, even if both had been lost – or missing – at Dunkirk, but she smiled anyway, and they went on dancing. After a few moments, just before the dance came to an end, he spoke again.

'You're coming into Theatre next week, I believe.'

'Yes, sir.'

He glanced at her. 'Why the "sir" all of a sudden?'

'Well – I didn't realise you knew me, before. I was just a dancing partner. But now you know who I am, and you know I'll be working for you, so it's different.'

'Not while we're off duty and dancing together,' he said. 'And that reminds me, I don't like calling you "Nurse Tilford". You must have another name.'

'Well, yes,' she said reluctantly, and then, as he looked at her expectantly, 'It's Thursday, actually.'

'*Thursday?*'

'Yes. I was born on Armistice Day, you see, in 1918, so my parents thought they ought to give me a special name. My first name's Rosemary – for Remembrance – but they've never used it, and I've always been Thursday.'

'So it's your birthday the day after tomorrow – and you'll never be able to hide your age!' He grinned at her, and she laughed. 'Thursday,' he repeated, as if tasting the word. 'It's a nice name. And it's certainly unusual.' The music came to an end and they stood for a moment looking at each other. Then he smiled.

'And my name's Connor. So now we're equal, all right? When we're dancing, anyway.'

'Yes,' Thursday said uncertainly, wondering if he really meant her to call him by his name, and he smiled again and led her back to her seat. But this time he didn't leave her there. He stayed with her and asked her for the next dance as well, and the one after that.

Towards the end of the evening, he gave her a rueful smile and said, 'I'll have to go and do my duty again, I'm afraid, Thursday. But I've really enjoyed dancing with you. We fit very well together.'

Thursday coloured and smiled. 'I've enjoyed it, too. Thank you . . .' She hesitated.

'Don't you dare,' he said, reading her mind. 'Don't you dare say "sir". I've told you my name. You haven't used it at all, but you might do it now. Just to say goodnight.'

Thursday bit her lip, feeling the colour rage into her cheeks. She took a deep breath. They might have been dancing all evening, but it still took a bit of daring to use an officer's first name.

'Goodnight, Thursday,' he said, smiling, and held out his hand. 'And I hope you have a happy birthday.'

She took it, feeling suddenly shy, and felt the warm strength of his fingers. It was oddly comforting and her shyness fled.

'Goodnight, Connor,' she said, and smiled back into his eyes. 'It's been a lovely evening.'

He nodded and took her back to her seat, and this time he left her there and a few minutes later she saw him dancing with the QARNN sister with the long, auburn hair.

Connor Kirkpatrick, she thought. It was a nice name. Different. Classy. But, then, he *was* a commander – way out of her class. And on Monday he would be her boss, and there would be no question of first names or special smiles. They would be there to do a job, and he wouldn't take the slightest bit of notice of her.

She wouldn't even expect him to.

There hadn't been a raid over Gosport or Portsmouth for nearly two weeks, and even over London the raids didn't seem to be quite so bad. People began to think that perhaps the Germans were slowly giving up, or maybe even running out of ammunition. Or perhaps, as Elsie said, just getting ready for the real invasion – the one that would come by sea.

'And all that barbed wire they've put up along the beach won't stop 'em,' she said as they collected their lunch in the mess. 'Few pairs of wire-cutters'll soon sort that lot out.'

'Oh, yeah, and we're going to stand by and let 'em, aren't we!' Patsy argued. 'What about the gun emplacements? What about the Army and the Marines? And the RAF? They won't get within an inch of Stokes Bay, nor anywhere else round the coast.'

Thursday listened in a dream. She was still thinking of the dance at Grange the night before, still whirling round the floor in the arms of Connor Kirkpatrick – *Commander* Kirkpatrick, she reminded herself sharply. From tomorrow, he was going to be her boss and she'd better put paid to any other dreams she might have had. It was a dance, nothing else, and he wouldn't even know her in her mask and gown.

'Coming for a bike ride this afternoon?' Elsie asked. 'We could go round Stubbington and Titchfield, maybe call in on Gran for a cuppa. It's a nice afternoon, hardly cold at all.'

Thursday nodded. The trees had turned a glorious golden brown but the leaves would soon be gone and winter beginning. She loved autumn – it was her time, after all – and a day like today, with the sun lighting up the mellow colours and a soft blue sky fading into an early dusk, was far too good to stay indoors.

She ate her lunch absently, thinking of all that had happened during the past year. It was her birthday next day – she would be twenty-two. It seemed far more than a year since the party at home, when Dad had given her that huge key and everyone had sung over the cake Auntie Flo had iced. She had never dreamed then that she would be a nurse, here in Haslar Hospital, or that her brother Steve would be missing somewhere in France, her cousin Leslie flying Spitfires, Mike dead and Denise getting married.

Mum'll be feeling it even more tomorrow, with me away as well, she thought. I ought to have tried to get home this weekend. I ought to have told Madam it was my birthday and that things are difficult there. I ought to have done something about it . . .

The wail of the air-raid warning split the air. The girls looked at each other and hesitated. Was this going to be red, a double red or just a yellow? But almost before the sound had died away, the signal came for a double red, and they leapt to their feet and made for the wards.

On duty or not, everyone turned to for a double red. There were patients to be got out of their beds, on to stretchers if they couldn't walk, and down into the cellars. Meals were left on the table, books and newspapers flung down to be retrieved later, and the entire hospital thrown into orderly turmoil. Almost before the first planes came over, everyone who could be got down below was there, safe from the bombs that would soon begin to fall.

'Sunday bloody dinnertime,' a patient grumbled as a friend helped him down the stairs. 'Don't we never get no peace?'

'Not flaming likely in wartime, mate!' his pal said caustically. 'That's what it's all about, innit? And our lads are givin' as good we get, you can depend on that. I bet there's Germans havin' to leave their Sunday dinners an' all.'

Thursday, still in the ward with some of the trauma patients, looked out of the window. She could see planes coming in fast over the Island, a black cloud of them. Fascinated, she stared as they came nearer, so low that she ducked instinctively as they passed almost directly overhead. She dropped to the floor and froze, waiting for the explosion. Surely they wouldn't pass a complex like Haslar without bombing it. But the planes roared overhead, so close that she thought they must brush the roofs with their undercarriages. And then they were gone and, almost immediately, the expected explosion rocked the building.

'Blimey,' said a nearby sailor with his leg strapped up. 'That was bloody close.'

'It was.' Cautiously, Thursday raised her head. The planes were coming round again and she flattened herself once more. What were they aiming at?

'*Thursday!*' The voice jerked her head up again. 'What the hell are you doing here? Why aren't you down in the cellars?'

'Connor!' She remembered where she was, in a ward if not officially on duty, and hastily amended it. 'Sir! I was just—'

'You were just being a bloody heroine!' he said angrily, and then dropped to the floor beside her as another explosion rattled the windows. 'Makepeace told me about you, slipping back up here during the raids. What good's it going to do the patients if you're killed? You ought to be down below, with the others.'

'I was going to. They came so quickly.' She looked into his face. It was oddly intimate, lying here beside him on the floor. 'Where are they bombing, sir? It sounds ever so close.'

'Grange,' he said briefly. 'That's what it looks like, anyway. You could see them from the other side of the hospital, making their run in along Cambridge Road. They're after the aerodrome.'

'But there's a big ammunition dump there too,' she gasped. 'If that goes up—'

'I know. And if people are hurt, they'll be brought here. They're going to need nurses – live ones. So for God's sake, get down below. *Now*.'

'They'll need doctors, too,' she said boldly, and gave him a challenging look. 'Are you coming as well?'

'For crying out loud,' said a voice above them, 'either go or shut up about it. It's Sunday afternoon, for Gawd's sake – can't a bloke have his blooming siesta?'

Thursday and Connor looked at each other in surprise. They'd almost forgotten there were other people around them. Connor's lips twitched and Thursday began to giggle.

Commander Kirkpatrick stood up and regarded the sailor. 'I could put you on a charge for talking to an officer like that,' he said severely. 'But I'll let it go – just this once. Provided you can persuade this recalcitrant VAD to be sensible and go down below. Because *I* don't seem to have any influence with her.'

The sailor grinned back at him. 'With all due respect, sir, I'd say you had. And I'd say she was right, too – you ought to be below as well.' Another violent crash shook the ground. 'Bloody hell, it *hurts* when they do that!'

Connor grabbed Thursday's wrist. She shook herself free angrily. 'I can't, sir! Not when the patients are suffering.'

He grabbed her again. 'You can't do anything to help them. You can't stop the bombs shaking the place about. What use are you going to be if you end up in a hospital bed yourself – or worse?' Another bomb fell. 'Tilford, if you don't come down below this minute, I'll put *you* on a charge! And never mind what your Miss Makepeace says. And it'll be insubordination, and nothing less.'

Thursday stared at him. Their eyes locked. She felt fury blaze up from her breast, flaming brightness into her cheeks and eyes. She wanted to defy him, to jerk her wrist from his grip, but his fingers were tight and strong and she knew she was beaten. He had rank, power and sheer brute strength on his side. She turned and gave the patients an apologetic look. The one in the nearest bed grinned and gave her a thumbs-up.

'You go on, love,' another one called out. 'Get down below, where it's safe. And give the rest of the buggers our love while you're there.'

'I'll be back the minute it stops,' she promised, but Connor gave her arm a fierce jerk.

'Come *on*, Tilford.' He hauled her out of the ward and along the corridor to the landing. They ran down the wide stairs to the cellars, and he paused and looked at her. 'I hope to God you're going to be a bit more disciplined when you're on theatre duties,' he said harshly. 'I can't work with nurses who won't do as they're told.'

Thursday stared at him. It was as if their encounter on the dance floor had never happened. The man who had held her in his arms and talked softly in her ear and seemed to understand about Steve and Mike had disappeared, leaving a coldly efficient surgeon who was prepared to cut out anything that didn't work – including his theatre nurses. Including her.

Her eyes filled with tears and her lips trembled. Connor sighed and put his hand on her arm.

'Don't look like that, Thursday. It has to be this way, don't you understand? We're here to do a job, and we've got to look after ourselves so that we can go on doing it. Not for selfish reasons but because we're pieces of *equipment*, if you like. *And you must obey when an officer gives you an order* – whatever it is. Yours is not to reason why – haven't you heard that?'

'Yes, sir,' Thursday said, staring at the floor. 'Ours is but to do or die.'

'Exactly. Except that I don't want you to die. I really don't.' He put one finger under her chin and lifted her face so that she was forced to meet his eyes. 'That isn't in my plan at all,' he said quietly.

Another bomb rocked the floor. Thursday jumped and Connor's hand slipped down to her shoulder and gripped her tightly. They stared at each other and then he said, 'Get below. And this time, *stay there*.'

Chapter Twenty-Five

Getting the patients back to the wards when the 'raiders passed' signal sounded was even worse than getting them out. Everyone was tired after the ordeal of getting them down to the cellars, the sense of urgency was gone and the men were fractious and upset. For some of them, any movement meant pain of some degree, and to think that there had been no need for it, as they arrived back in wards that looked just the same as when they'd left them, seemed to be an added insult.

Even worse was the fact that those who had been left strapped to their beams had the laugh on them. 'Here they come, out of their burrows . . . Been nice and peaceful up here without you lot . . . Had a nice afternoon down in the mines, have you? Brought us up a shovelful of coal for the stove?'

But the news that Grange had been bombed and that there was a hangar ablaze beside the moat that separated it from Fort Rowner subdued everyone. 'We were there only last night,' Elsie whispered to Thursday. 'A few hours earlier and we could've been in that hangar.'

'You mean it was the one they had the dance in?'

'So they say.' Elsie shivered. 'I dunno, Thurs, what with this and the raid over the station, we seem to be getting nearer and nearer to these bombs. About as near as I want to get, too. I hope we don't get a double red tonight. I couldn't face hauling them all down below all over again.'

However, Elsie was to be disappointed. Just as she and Thursday got into bed a few hours later, the scream of the siren rose yet again. Everyone groaned and waited for the alert – yellow, purple or red –

and then stared at each other as the sound of bells took over from the dying wail.

'That's church bells!' Thursday whispered. 'It must be Alverstoke – they've got bells there, haven't they?'

'St Mary's, yes.' Elsie nodded. 'You know what this means!'

'*Invasion* . . .'

The whisper ran round the dormitory, and then the whole room exploded into life. The girls leapt from their beds, grabbed shoes and coats, ran for the doors. Clad in an assortment of pyjamas and nighties, they scurried along the corridors and downstairs, out of D Block and across the quarter-deck to the main hospital. No matter that they were off duty – the patients came first. No matter that the Germans might even now be landing on the seawall and Stokes Bay beach – the sick and injured must be made safe. No matter that the girls themselves might be at terrible risk – the men who had put their own lives at risk, weeks or months before, must be cared for and protected.

They arrived to find people already thronging the stairs – up-patients, doctors, VADs and QARNNs, all working to carry the stretcher cases to safety. Thursday caught sight of Miss Makepeace and the Surgeon Rear Admiral struggling with a huge stoker on a stretcher that looked as if it had been stretched just as far as it could go. Connor passed without seeing her, an injured man's arm looped over his shoulders. Patsy was guiding a sailor whose eyes were bandaged, and Helen Stanway was helping Sister Burton to manoeuvre a trolley into the lift. But there was no more time to notice who was passing. Swinging into a routine that was becoming all too familiar, Thursday and Elsie went into the ward and began getting men out of bed again, men who had already been hauled out once that day and were now becoming bitterly resigned to being dragged up and down the stairs and in and out of the lifts at the behest of a screaming, banshee siren.

At last they were all safely below. The men rested on their trolleys and stretchers, the doctors and nurses found spaces to sit where they could. And then they waited.

They didn't know whether they were waiting for the signal that the skies were clear and it was safe to emerge again, or whether they were waiting for the invaders that were expected to storm the beaches. They didn't know whether they were waiting for life, or for death.

There was nothing else to do but wait.

There had been no invasion. Nobody ever really knew who had given the signal for the bells to be rung, but St Mary's was not the only church to have sounded its warning. And the rumours next day told of hundreds of German soldiers, drowned and washed up on Stokes Bay beach. Or down in the New Forest. Or perhaps it was Brighton.

Or perhaps all three. Or none of them at all. Whatever the truth, the rumour persisted, yet strangely the fear of invasion receded. It was as if everyone felt that the invaders had indeed been beaten off, and a small feeling of victory lifted Gosport hearts. People told stories of having gone out with guns, to fight as Churchill had said, on the beaches and in the streets. The Pioneer Corps and Home Guard, pitifully unarmed, had marched up Clayhall with broomsticks and garden tools. You could do a lot of damage with a spade or fork or hoe in hand-to-hand combat, one elderly allotment-holder remarked cheerfully. ''Specially if you'd been in the last lot, and trained with a bayonet . . .'

Those children still at home came out into the street, too, with scraps of red, white and blue ribbon fastened to sticks; one or two even had real Union Jacks. They marched the streets singing 'Rule Britannia' and 'Land of Hope and Glory', and 'Run, Rabbit, Run'. They shouted 'God Save the King' and stood to attention, their grubby hands held to their foreheads in salute. They got as near as they could to the gun emplacements and begged to be allowed to climb on the guns, and have a go at firing them.

None of the soldiers had the heart to tell them to go away. Everyone was too well aware of what might have become of these same children if the invasion had really happened.

Thursday, reporting for her first duty in the operating theatre down in the cellar, felt both elated and subdued. It's as though we've actually won, in some queer way, she thought. Yet we haven't won at all, really. We're in as much danger as ever we were. In other ways, it feels as if we've hardly started.

By the end of the week, she knew just how true that thought was. For on Friday, 15 November, the day of Denise's wedding, the city of Coventry was razed to the ground and its great cathedral left nothing but a shell.

'I had an auntie and uncle in Coventry,' Patsy said, her face white. 'I don't know what'll have happened to them. You say it's all gone, Thurs?'

'So the papers say. Look at these awful pictures – street after street, just knocked to bits, and people picking their way through the rubble like refugees. Well, I suppose that's what they are, really. They say there's thousands just walking out of the city, with nothing but a few bags or a pram or barrow with their things in, looking for somewhere to stop. They've got nothing left, nothing. It's terrible.'

'My Uncle Tom would never be able to do that,' Patsy said. 'He's got arthritis in both knees, he can hardly walk. And they can't afford a wheelchair. They don't even go down the shelter . . . What's he going to do, Thurs? Whatever's he going to do?'

Thursday didn't know. She couldn't begin to imagine what the citizens of Coventry were going to do, with their homes torn away from them, their great church smashed to pieces, their city nothing more than rubble. And it didn't help to know that people in Germany were being bombed in the same way. That there were families trudging the ruined streets in Berlin and other cities, their homes destroyed, all that they loved gone for ever. Furniture they'd scrimped and saved for. Best teasets. Sheets and blankets, tables and chairs. Photos. Pets. All blasted away to nothing – and for what?

Because of one man's greed for power. And because none of the men and women who were supposed to lead the world had been able to stop his onslaught.

There ought to be another way, she thought. There *must* be another way.

'I don't know, Patsy,' she said sadly. 'I don't know what your uncle's going to do. But there'll be people to help him and your auntie. They won't be left to stay out in the streets.'

A few days later, Patsy heard that her uncle had survived the bombing, crouched beneath the stairs of his little two-up, two-down house, and had managed to stagger down the ruined street in search of help for his wife, trapped beneath a beam. But by the time they got back, she had died, and now Patsy's heartbroken uncle had been taken to stay with Patsy's parents in Evesham. 'Where they ought to have gone in the first place,' Patsy said through her tears. 'Mum asked them often enough, she begged them to go, but the obstinate old man wouldn't have it that Coventry was in any danger, no German was going to make him run away, he said. And now poor Auntie May's dead.'

There were tears in plenty as November dragged on. Only a few days after Coventry's destruction, Haslar found itself on red alert again as planes snarled overhead and dropped more bombs on the town. Shops and offices in the high street were ruined, and a house in Alverstoke village reduced to rubble. And a Wrens' billet in Lee-on-the-Solent was destroyed, killing eight young Wrens sleeping inside and injuring others.

They were brought to Haslar, and Thursday found herself assisting at operations on several. She looked at the young faces with sorrow. As Madam had said when they first began their training, the VADs would learn to get used to seeing people in pain, but this was different. Until now, their patients had been mostly serving men, wounded in action. These were girls, some of them no more than seventeen or eighteen, and their injuries seemed all the more cruel.

'Will you be going to the funerals?' Commander Kirkpatrick asked her as they watched the last young patient being wheeled out of the theatre. 'The ones who died – they're being buried in our cemetery, you know.'

'Yes. They've asked us all to go, if we can. I want to – but I'm afraid it will make me cry.' She gave him a wavering smile. 'I just hope no one looks at me.'

They had had no conversation since Thursday had begun work in the theatre – there had been no time. After his words during the raid, Thursday had been determined to prove her worth as a nurse, and had striven to remain cool and efficient, waiting for the theatre sister's orders and carrying them out swiftly. Although they were in the same room, her work with the autoclave kept her away from the operating table and she had barely encountered Connor himself unless they had passed in the doorway or stood together at the basin as Connor scrubbed up. And although she knew that at those times he was remote from everyone, concentrating on what he had to do, she couldn't help feeling hurt by his lack of attention and had begun to believe that the warmth she had felt in him on the dance floor had been no more than a dream.

Now, suddenly, she sensed that warmth again.

'I think it will make a lot of us cry,' he said quietly. 'Young girls like that, thinking they were safe to sleep . . . it seems so unfair.'

'It *is* unfair,' she said passionately. 'All these people being killed – nearly all of them are young, too. My brother, my cousin, these Wrens – and hundreds of others. Thousands, probably.' She looked up at him with angry eyes. 'What do they do, count them and see who's got most left – if there are any left at all? And who's supposed to build the brave new world they talk about, when all the young people have gone? It'll be just old men and children. Where's the *sense* in it?'

'Shh,' he said, touching her arm. 'Don't let yourself get upset, Thursday. You're tired. And we all wonder these things, but there's nothing we can do about them. We just have to grit our teeth and carry on. Eventually, they'll sit down and talk, and it'll be all sorted out. Eventually.'

'Yes,' she said, 'that's what they did last time. On the day I was born. And what happened on my birthday this year? Grange was bombed, just a few hours before, and we spent the night in the cellars, waiting for an invasion. And that's how well they sorted it out the *last* time!'

Connor sighed. 'Well, let's hope they do better when they finally sit down to sort this lot out.' He looked at her. 'And did you manage to celebrate your birthday at all?'

'She shook her head. 'I forgot all about it, till the end of the week. When Coventry was bombed, I looked at the date, and realised . . . So much had happened . . . I just didn't have any heart for it. What does a birthday matter, when people are being killed?'

'I know,' he said, 'but you ought to celebrate it, all the same. Birthdays do still matter. Why not come out and have some tea with me?'

Thursday looked at him, startled. 'But – I couldn't do that, sir! I mean, you're a surgeon and a – an officer, and I'm just a VAD. And I'm one of your theatre nurses.'

'I don't think that need matter. What about tomorrow afternoon – after the funerals? I have a feeling you're going to need a little cheering up.'

Thursday bit her lip and looked down. Tears crept into her eyes. She had seen funerals already, in the cemetery close to the hospital grounds, and she had even attended some, when the person had been a patient she had nursed, but the funeral of eight young women, even though they were unknown to her, was something she knew would be hard to bear.

'I don't know if I'll want to go out,' she said in a small voice. 'I think I might just want to go – go to bed or something.'

'And cry,' he said. 'And brood. No, Thursday, it'll be better if you come out with me. Just for a little while, just to be somewhere different, between different walls. It'll do you good.' He paused, and then added, 'I could make it an order if you like. And so I will, if you insist on calling me "sir" when we're off duty!'

Thursday smiled. She looked up at him and nodded.

'All right. I'll come out with you.' She paused, then added with a straight face, 'Sir.'

Their eyes met. He inclined his head and smiled back, and the warmth was there in his eyes once again.

Thursday looked at the trees, standing with bare branches around the graveyard as the funerals of the eight young Wrens was conducted by the Haslar chaplain. The leaves had fallen without her even noticing them. It was almost as if the trees had wept them away during that terrible fortnight.

Grange. Coventry. The Wrens. And countless other casualties, too. Portsmouth, Southampton, Bristol, Birmingham, Liverpool – all the major cities had been bombarded. And poor London – you wondered how the people there were managing, with the city being blown to pieces night after night, never knowing where the bombs would fall or the fires blaze. Thursday had heard that everyone just went to their shelters as a matter of course every night now, and since many of them didn't have shelters they went to the Underground stations instead and slept on the platforms. Bunks, they'd got down there, she'd heard, and tea-urns and even little libraries so you could get a book to read if you couldn't sleep . . .

She heard the chaplain's voice saying the Grace and came back with a start to the cemetery. The coffins had been lowered into their graves, and the earth scattered over them. A few flowers had been tumbled in last, and as the mellow voice faded, there was silence.

A woman sobbed somewhere, and a blackbird burst into

unexpected song. Someone whispered that it was the girls' souls being received into heaven, and then everyone began to move. Thursday, her eyes full of tears, turned away from the graveside and found herself face to face with Surgeon Commander Kirkpatrick.

'Oh – sir, I'm sorry, I didn't know you were there.'

'It's all right.' He touched her arm. 'Are you all right, Thursday?'

'Yes.' She brushed away her tears. 'Just – you know.'

'I know. It seems so cruel – eight young women, killed as they slept. I went in to see the others this afternoon – the ones we've been operating on, and another couple who are still in bed. They're being very brave, but it's hit them hard. They just want to get back to service as soon as possible.'

'You'd think they'd be frightened,' Thursday said, but he shook his head.

'It doesn't seem to work that way in wartime. Seeing your mates killed . . . just makes you all the more determined. And now, what about that cup of tea?'

Thursday drew back a little, aware of the other people moving around them. Patsy and Elsie were there somewhere, and the other VADs and QARNNs. And there were officers, too, who must be wondering why Commander Kirkpatrick was so interested in a little VAD. She started to shake her head.

'I don't know. Perhaps it would be better not—'

'Now, don't start having second thoughts. Remember, I said I'd make it an order if I had to! Come on, it's a pleasant enough afternoon, we'll walk out to Lee. You've got time, haven't you? We can catch a bus back.'

'Yes, sir – I mean . . .' She floundered into silence and he smiled.

'All right, I'll let you off that one. While we're on the premises. But as soon as we're safely out of earshot, I expect you to stick by our agreement yesterday. It's Connor, all right?'

They walked down Clayhall Road to Angelsey and then along to Lee. Thursday thought of the day she and the other girls had cycled out here for the first time, and met Tony and Roy and Doug. That had been the first of many teas in the little café opposite the Tower. She remembered the time she'd lost her temper with Doug about some silly joke, and had flounced out, and wondered how she could ever have thought such a thing important enough to lose her rag over. Now Tony was dead, and Roy somewhere in the Mediterranean, and Doug – she'd lost touch completely with Doug, had no idea where he was.

'Penny for them?' Connor asked, and she jumped and came back to the present.

'Sorry. I seem to keep drifting off this afternoon. I was just thinking how much has happened in the past year. I volunteered straight after my birthday – they only take you once you're twenty-one, so I couldn't before – and then I had to do extra training before I was posted here. And since then . . .' She shook her head. 'Sometimes, I just can't believe it all – can't seem to take it in, somehow.'

'I know. It was all so quiet to begin with – the war was being fought mostly at sea, and the threat of invasion and the bombing just didn't seem to happen. But now they've started, it's even worse than we thought. And there's more to come, I'm afraid.'

She looked at him. 'D'you think we're going to be invaded? Last week – did it really happen? Were there really hundreds of bodies washed up on the beaches? I don't see how—'

'I think it was just rumours. How could it be hidden – *why* should it be hidden? If there really had been so many, something would have had to be done about them, and it's something we'd want the Germans to know about. A victory for us.' He shook his head. 'But there's no doubt that the bombing happened. We've seen that for ourselves.'

Thursday thought of the eight young Wrens who had just been buried, and nodded soberly. No older than she was – some even younger. It was so tragic. So cruel. And we're doing the same over there, she thought. Somewhere in Germany, there are people walking away from the funeral of other young men or women, and wondering just what was the point of it all.

'How long is it going to last?' she asked. 'How long can we go on like this, being bombed day after day – night after night? I don't see how people can stand it.'

'I don't think we have much choice,' he said. 'And that's the point of it, isn't it? Go on hammering us until we can't take any more. What we've got to show the world is that we *can* take it.' He looked down at her. 'I had to go to London a few days ago – you remember, when Commander Peters took over my duties. The damage there is just incredible, yet all over the bombed and boarded buildings people have painted signs. Slogans like "Go Home, Hitler" and "Britain Can Take It", or jokes like "No Milk Today". They're cocking a snook at him, you see. They're determined not to be beaten – absolutely determined.'

'But how many people are going to die before it's all over?'

'I don't know,' he said quietly. 'I just don't know.'

They walked in silence for a while. The gorsy heath of Browndown rolled away to their right, the sea lay to their left, beyond the strung-out huts of the military establishment. There's barbed wire everywhere, Thursday thought, barbed wire and War Ministry notices. Yet in a strange way this must be just what Gosport was used to. It had always been a garrison as well as a naval town. Look at all those forts, those so-called 'follies' that had been laughed at because Napoleon didn't invade after all – but which were proving so useful now.

'How are you enjoying working in Theatre?' he asked suddenly.

Thursday turned to him, relieved to have something different to talk about. 'Oh, it's great! It's so interesting. Seeing all the different injuries being put right – it's almost like magic. Actually . . .' she laughed a little '. . . it's not so very different in a way from what I did before the war started. I was a dressmaker – sewing's what I was trained to do!'

'Really? We'll have to ask you to demonstrate a bit of fine stitching some time.' They discussed some of the operations that had been done that week, and then went on to talk about what they'd done before the war. Connor had already been a naval surgeon, of course, and had served in the Far East and Malta. He told Thursday stories of Singapore and Hong Kong, and she listened in fascination.

'I'd love to go to places like that.'

'Well, maybe you will, some time. I wouldn't be surprised if some of you VADs didn't get posted abroad. They did in the last war, after all.'

'It's the only chance I'd ever get to go to those sort of places,' she said wistfully. 'People like me don't travel much.'

'Why not? What stops you?'

'Well, we just don't. My dad's never been anywhere, except France in the last war, and that wasn't exactly a holiday. He and my mum would never think of going abroad. The furthest we've ever been is Tenby!'

'Well, that's practically abroad,' he said teasingly. 'Wales – they speak a different language after all, don't they.'

She laughed. 'Yes, but you don't have to go overseas to get there. That's what makes the difference. And we didn't need passports.'

Connor looked at her. He said, 'You'd like the Far East, Thursday. It's so different from here. The weather, the people, the buildings, the whole way of life – everything's different. I'd like to see you there, enjoying it all.'

Thursday laughed. 'Well, you'll have to put in for a draft for me. Maybe they'll take VADs in the hospitals there.'

'Oh, they will,' he said. 'Perhaps we'll meet there. I'll take you for tea in a real teahouse. Just like this afternoon. We'll pretend that's what we're doing, shall we?'

Thursday laughed. 'There's some difference between a cup of tea in Lee-on-the-Solent and a trip to the Far East!'

'Well, maybe,' he said with a grin, 'but it's only a difference of distance. If Singapore was just over the harbour instead of Pompey, you wouldn't bat an eyelid.'

'Well, it's not,' she said firmly, 'so stop talking nonsense. We're going to Lee, not the Far East, and we're going to have a cup of tea, not – not . . .'

'A cup of tea?' he supplied helpfully. 'It really is what they drink there, too, you know – China tea. Or did you think they drank some exotic brew flavoured with foreign spices and poppy-seeds? Actually, they do that as well – maybe we could try those. D'you think the café at Lee will have any on the menu today, or will it be "off" this afternoon?'

'Oh, stop it! You're just an idiot!' She heard her words with amazement. I can't be talking to him – a commander – like this, she thought, as if he were no more than an ordinary seaman or an artificer. Someone of equal or lesser rank to herself. But it seemed as if rank had disappeared somehow. They were just two people, a man and a woman, out together for a walk, and exchanging the sort of banter that helped you get over those first awkward moments.

Not that there seemed to be any awkwardness between her and Connor Kirkpatrick. It was as if they had known each other for years.

She was aware of a glow spreading through her body. He likes me, she thought. And I like him. I've liked him, from that very first moment, even though I was so upset over Tony.

She smiled up into his face.

'Let's go and have that cup of tea,' she said. 'But not in Singapore. We'll just go to Lee – it's nearer!'

Chapter Twenty-Six

After their wedding, Denise and Vic went back to live with Flo and Percy. There didn't seem to be much point in getting rooms anywhere else, since Vic was sure to be called up soon and the boys' room was empty now. The two beds were put together and Denise moved her things into their cupboards. Her room would now be Leslie's – if Leslie ever came home again.

Flo had decided to make the best of things and make Vic welcome, but Percy found it more difficult. He couldn't look at Vic without thinking of what the young man had done to his daughter, and the sight of Denise's swelling body brought it home even more harshly. It was even worse that Vic started work early in the morning, and the two men were falling over each other as they tried to get ready, both wanting to shave at the same time or both heading for the lavatory door. As for sitting down to breakfast with him, Percy just couldn't stomach it.

'I'll have to take a bite to eat when I get there,' he said to Flo. 'A sandwich or something. I tell you, I just can't sit across the table from him eating cornflakes like a – a married couple! It can't be expected.'

'Well, if anyone's going to take a bite to eat on the way, it ought to be him,' Flo said. 'But can't you try a bit harder, Perce? He's our son-in-law now, for better or worse, and we've got to make the best of a bad job.'

'Better or worse is right,' her husband growled. 'And it's the worse we're getting now. I'm still not sure we've done the right thing, Flo. That girl's much too young. Sixteen! It's a daft age to get married. And seeing them go off to that bedroom together every night – well, it's embarrassing, that's what it is.'

'So you'd rather we had a by-blow in the family? I've told you, Perce, I won't countenance her giving it away—'

'No, love, I know that. And I dare say it'll be different once the kiddy's born, and once they've got a place of their own. Or once that feller's called up. At least we won't be tiptoeing round each other of a morning.'

It was no easier for the newly-weds. The whole of their wedding day had been clouded by the news of Coventry's bombing. They'd had no honeymoon, just the brief wedding in a chilly, badly lit church and then a stilted, uncomfortable meal at home, with Mary and Walter and Vic's mum and dad. Mrs Pearce had been as upset by it all as Flo, although not too upset to give the house a thorough going-over with her sharp eyes, and Mr Pearce, who was a tax officer, looked as if he suspected them all of smuggling. They'd picked critically at the shepherd's pie Flo had made, using a whole week's meat ration, and refused second helpings of stewed apple, even though there were a few of Flo's precious bottled blackberries in it. They'd left at the soonest possible moment, and after Denise had helped her mother to wash up nobody knew quite what to do next.

'We mustn't stop too long,' Mary said after they'd had a cup of tea. 'It's so dark these nights, with the blackout and everything.'

'Oh, don't go yet!' Flo was dreading the long evening ahead before they could decently go to bed. The thought of Denise and Vic going to bed together, even though it was now quite legitimate, was so embarrassing she hardly knew how they would all face it. 'It won't be any darker at nine o'clock than it is now. Stop and have a game of cards, and we'll have some supper before you go. I've got some sardines, we can put them on a bit of toast.'

'I don't know,' Walter said. 'I think we ought to be getting back. There was that raid last night . . . we don't know where they might choose next. I think we ought to get home. It could be us next time.'

'You could come in our shelter,' Flo urged. 'Anyway, I don't suppose our boys will let them come this way again.' She thought of Leslie, one of 'our boys', and the fear that was always present clutched a little more tightly at her heart. 'Stop for a while, do,' she pleaded. 'We need to do something to make the day a bit special.'

A game of cards, making a wedding day special! Mary thought pityingly, and nodded. 'We'll stop till after the nine o'clock news,' she said firmly. 'Flo's right, we're as safe here as we are at home, and anyway they won't bother with Worcester. What have we got to interest them here? A porcelain factory! They're not going to bother about smashing a few cups and saucers.'

They all knew that Worcester and its porcelain factory had more than cups and saucers to interest the enemy – not least, the army barracks just outside the city – but nobody pointed it out. The day had been a strange one and would be a complete anticlimax if it was just allowed to dwindle into nothing more than an evening listening to the wireless. At least a game of cards usually produced a few laughs.

The game did ease the tensions a little, but nobody could forget the poor people of Coventry, trudging away from their ruined city with their possessions piled into prams and barrows and carts. It was like something you heard about in other countries. Refugees, fleeing from an oppressor. Where would they go? What would they do?

'Some of 'em have come to Worcester,' Walter said. 'People that have got relatives in other places are all right. The rest – well, I dunno. There must be hundreds – *thousands* – got no homes now. And the state Coventry's in, I don't reckon they ever will have. There's nothing left. No gas, no electricity, no water – it's all been smashed to bits. There's no telephones, no buses running – nothing. It'll never be rebuilt, not like it was.'

'But what are people going to *do*?' Flo asked. 'What about their jobs – what about all their papers, their insurances and bank books and things?'

'Well, anyone with any sense takes all that down the shelter with them, same as we do. But the banks are bombed as well.' Percy shrugged hopelessly. 'I dunno. It's a bad job.'

Denise looked around the table. The cards had been stacked in the middle of the table after the last round, and nobody had bothered to pick them up. She shoved them suddenly, so that they scattered over the table.

'Come on,' she said shrilly, 'whose turn is it to deal? It must be someone's. We're playing a game, if you remember. It's my *wedding* day, if you remember. If this is the only celebration I'm going to get, you might at least try to make it a decent one, and not all sit there with chins down to your knees. I know it's awful – I know people have got killed – I know there's lots of people having a horrible time because of it – but can't you just think about *me* for once? Just for one evening?'

The family stared at her. Vic put his hand on her knee. Flo's eyes filled with tears and Mary gave her an anxious glance. The two older men looked at each other, and Walter cleared his throat uncomfortably.

'Think about you?' Percy said. 'Think about *you*? Isn't that what we've been doing all day? Haven't we had to think about you for the past three months, wondering whether the police were going to press charges against this – this young chap what ought to have known better – and wondering if you were going to have to go to court and have your shame dragged up in the papers for everyone to know about? Haven't we had to think about whether it was best to let you get married only a month after your sixteenth birthday, to keep you out of all that and give the baby a name? Blimey, I don't think I've done anything *but* think about you, all that time! And I won't say it's a relief to think about Coventry and the poor buggers there – I'm sorry, Flo, but I can't help it, she's been getting my goat for weeks, I've got to say what I think – I won't say it's a *relief* to think about them – but at least it makes a change! And it'd make a change if you thought about someone else for a bit, too. You've got a selfish streak in you, our Denise, and always have had.'

Denise stared at him. Her face reddened and her mouth turned down. Tears sprang to her eyes and she jumped up, tried to say something and then ran from the room and up the stairs. Vic gave them an uncomfortable glance and stood up awkwardly.

'I'd better . . . ' He followed her, and they heard the bedroom door close and then muffled sobbing, interspersed with Vic's low voice.

Percy looked defiant. 'I'm sorry, but it had to be said. It's been boiling up inside me for weeks.'

'Well, it's a pity you couldn't have just let it simmer a bit longer, instead of letting it boil over tonight of all nights. She'll never forget this, Perce, never, none of us will.' Flo drew in a deep breath. 'Well, there's no use going on about it, we can't call the words back. Why don't you take Walter down the shed and show him what you've been making?' She gave Mary a crooked smile as the two men went out, then reached out and scooped the cards together.

'Well, that's the end of *that* game, I suppose. I'll make a cup of tea, Mary. I don't know about supper. I don't feel hungry somehow.'

'Nor do I.' Mary touched her sister-in-law's arm. 'I'm sorry the evening had to end like that, Flo.'

'Well, it had to come. And I dare say it won't be the last time either. But it's mostly talk, you know. Perce thinks the world of Denise, always has. He's upset that this happened and even more upset that it happened so quick, but he'll get over it, same as she will. Walter'll tell you.'

'Walter? Why?' Mary looked at the other woman's face. 'What *is* it Percy's making down in the shed, Flo?'

Flo smiled. 'Only a cradle, for the baby! You see? It's all talk, really.'

By Christmas, the family was beginning to settle down. Denise's pregnancy was obvious now, although everyone knew about it from the hastiness of the marriage. But Denise had always been a favourite in the street as well as the family, and Vic had a pleasant, open face that endeared him to most of the women. And things were different in wartime, you had to be a bit more open-minded. They'd been silly, but Vic had stood by the girl and everything would come out all right in the end.

Thursday managed to get home for two days just before Christmas, and Mary and Walter decided to bring Christmas forward to give her a proper family celebration. They had one of Percy's cockerels, 'specially fattened, and a Christmas pudding that was more black treacle and grated carrot than anything else, and they gave out Christmas presents just as if it were Christmas Day itself.

Most of Thursday's presents were light and easy to carry back to the hospital: a warm scarf in bright red, knitted by Flo; a new pair of stockings from Denise and Vic; a pair of mittens knitted by Jenny; and a writing case in dark blue mock leather from Mary and Walter. Inside were a brand-new pad of Basildon Bond, a packet of envelopes, a new fountain pen and six twopenny stamps. Thursday looked at them and grinned.

'Is this to remind me to write to you more regularly?'

'Don't be silly, you're a good girl for keeping in touch. Not like Mrs Jeffers's girl that's gone in the Wrens – they're lucky to hear once a month from her.' Mary was busy unwrapping Thursday's present to her and Walter. 'Oh, look, Walter, it's a record. Ambrose and his Orchestra, playing "Stardust". That's my favourite song!'

All Thursday's gifts were records – she had slipped into the shop in Worcester as soon as she'd got off the train and done her Christmas shopping all at once. For her sister, she had bought Dinah Shore singing 'Maybe'; for Vic and Denise, Count Basie's 'Louisiana'; for her uncle and aunt, a recording of Winston Churchill's speech 'This Was Their Finest Hour'. She watched anxiously as they unwrapped it, half-afraid that she had done the wrong thing, and her heart sank as she saw Flo's eyes fill with tears.

'Oh, Percy, look. The speech he made after Dunkirk. Oh, what a lovely thing to have. It's like a memorial to our Mike. Oh, thank you, Thursday, love, it's a lovely present.'

'I nearly didn't buy it,' Thursday confessed, with a sigh of relief. 'I didn't know if it might upset you . . . I'm glad you like it, Auntie.'

'We won't play it now,' Flo said as Walter began to wind up the gramophone. 'We'll wait till we get home. Let's just have the music now. But we really are pleased with it, aren't we, Perce?'

Percy cleared his throat and nodded. Walter looked at the little pile of records as if deciding which one to play first, but before he could speak Thursday produced another parcel wrapped, like the others, in brown paper with holly leaves and berries drawn on it in green and red crayon.

'I brought a present for Steve, too,' she said, meeting her mother's eyes. 'I know we might never find out what's happened to him – but there's still a chance he's alive somewhere. And if – if he doesn't ever come home again, I want you to have it, Mum. In his memory, like Auntie Flo's record is in memory of Mike.'

Mary reached out slowly and took the thin, square package. It was obviously another record. Her eyes questioned her daughter.

'It's Hutch,' Thursday said. 'You know he always liked Hutch. It's a song called "There'll Come Another Day". And I think there will, too. There'll come another day for all of us – Steve as well. He'll be back, Mum, you just see if he isn't.'

'Oh, Thursday,' Mary said softly, and took the parcel. 'Thanks, love. I'll put it with the others.' She smiled. 'We've bought him presents, too, all of us. He's going to have a real pile to open when he comes home!'

With the gramophone cranked, they began to play the records, old ones as well as the new ones Thursday had brought, and Walter produced an old favourite which they played every year – a noisy, sing-song party called 'Jolly Old Christmas', with Billy Cotton's Band and Tommy Handley. At last Denise said she was tired and wanted to go home.

'You don't have to come,' she said to her parents. 'Vic and me can go on our own.' She looked at Thursday. 'Don't suppose we'll see you again if you've got to go back tomorrow. I dare say I'll be a mum when you get home again.'

'I suppose you will. It's due in February, isn't it?' Thursday looked at her cousin's blossoming figure. 'What do you want?'

'I don't care what it is, so long as it gets born,' Denise said. 'I just want to get it over with. Not that I think about that more than I can help,' she added. 'It scares me too much!'

'Well, we've been through it and survived,' her mother said a little tartly, and Thursday knew she had only just stopped herself from adding that Denise hadn't been forced into it. Quickly, she thought of another question to ask.

'Got any names yet? I was thinking of some on the train yesterday.'

'Vic's mum wants us to call it John if it's a boy, but I think that's a boring name. I'd rather have something a bit different – Robin, or Mervyn, something like that. Or Jacqueline if it's a girl. I saw a new baby in the paper the other day called Jacqueline, I think it's a lovely name.'

'It'll get shortened,' her mother said disapprovingly. 'You want something that can't get shortened, and nothing too unusual.'

'Why? Why shouldn't it be shortened? Jenny's name's shortened and nobody complains about that. And look at *Thursday* – you couldn't get anything much more different than that.'

'Well, it's for you to decide, of course, but if you ask me—'

'We're not asking you!'

There was an awkward silence. Flo looked upset and Denise ready to burst into tears. Vic, who had been quiet all through the evening, put his arm round her shoulders.

'Come on, sweetheart. Let's get you home. You're tired out.' He fetched her coat and helped her into it, talking soothingly all the time. 'There's plenty of time to think about names. We don't have to decide anything now. And we don't have to call it anything we don't want to. Now, where are your things?' He gathered together their bits and pieces, including the Count Basie record. 'Thanks, Thursday.' He bent and, to her surprise, kissed her lightly on the cheek. 'It's been smashing, seeing you and having a bit of Christmas with you. And thank you, Auntie Mary and Uncle Walter, we've had a really good time. Will we see you on Boxing Day?'

Mary nodded, knowing that he and Denise had promised to go to Vic's parents for Christmas Day itself. The family waited until the young couple had gone, shutting the front door quickly behind them so that no light escaped, and then turned to each other.

'Well!' Flo said. 'Now you see what I mean, Mary, about our Denise. Flies off the handle at the slightest thing. And those names she's on about. Robin – I ask you! And Mervyn – what sort of a name's that?'

'It's an old Cornish name, she told Jen. She's been looking it up.'

'Well, this isn't Cornwall. And *Jacqueline* – well, I know it's quite popular just now, but think what the kiddy'll get called. Jack, just like a boy! I don't think she's given it any thought at all.'

'Well, it is her baby, Flo,' Mary said. 'For all she's no more than a kiddy herself, she does have her rights. And anyone gets a bit aeriated when they're expecting, you know that. Is she very frightened?'

'She doesn't say much about it, not to me anyway. I don't know what she tells him. I suppose I come second now, being only her mother.'

Thursday looked at her aunt's aggrieved face and felt sorry for her. It had all happened too quickly and too soon.

'He seems a nice chap, though,' she said. 'He looks after her, and he didn't forget to say thank you to us all. I should have thought she could have done a lot worse.'

'Oh, I'm not saying that. I've got to admit he's all right – so far. It's just the way it's all happened.' Flo sighed. 'Well, we don't want to spoil your Christmas with it all, Thursday. It's been a nice day, and it's been good to see you again, and looking so well too. I dare say you're being kept busy in that hospital.'

Thursday nodded, thinking of the constant air raids, the victims of the bombing, the Wrens who had been killed. Like everyone else at Haslar, she seemed to be permanently on duty these days, and permanently exhausted. It was as if rest and sleep had been postponed somehow. Rest, and sleep, and time off – except for the hasty visit to the Swiss Café, or the Dive – were little more than memories. And since that day after the Wrens' funeral, when she and Connor Kirkpatrick had walked to Lee together, she had seen him only in the theatre, when they had once again become 'Nurse Tilford' and 'sir'.

She yawned and then smiled apologetically. 'I'm sorry – just thinking about it reminded me how tired I am! I'll have to go to bed soon, I'm afraid, or I'll fall asleep on the floor.' As Flo and Percy stood up and began to say their own goodbyes, she got up too and kissed them both. 'Thanks for coming. It's been a lovely Christmas. And just think, we've still got the real one to come! Let's hope it's a happy one for everyone, and we don't have to eat our dinners in an air-raid shelter!'

'I know what'd make it a happy one for me,' Mary said wistfully, and she looked at the packet that Thursday had given her to keep for Steve. 'Just one little brown envelope, telling me my boy's all right. That's all I want now.'

Chapter Twenty-Seven

I t seemed as if there was to be an undeclared truce for Christmas. No German bombs fell anywhere in Britain either on Christmas Day or Boxing Day. The sirens were mercifully silent and nobody had to eat their Christmas dinner in an air-raid shelter. Presents were opened in peace, games were played and carols sung, and people went to church to give thanks and to pray for an end to the war.

Thursday went to the little church at the end of the quarter-deck. St Luke's was full of nurses, doctors and patients, and the chaplain led the service and gave a short but moving sermon about the men who were at sea, and the families who waited. They came out to bright, cold sunshine, and Thursday found Connor Kirkpatrick walking beside her.

'Did you have a good trip home?' he asked her. Thursday had had to ask his permission to go. 'Family all well?'

'Yes. Mum's still looking for the telegram boy every day, but I think she's slowly coming to accept that Steve must be dead. He must be, mustn't he?' she added, turning her head to look at him with troubled eyes. 'I mean, what else could have happened to him? We'd have heard by now if he was a POW. He must be just one of those thousands who were killed and never found.'

'I'm afraid it does seem most likely. But strange things do happen. It must be a help to your mother to think that there's some hope.'

'I don't know if it is or not,' Thursday said. 'I think it's sort of holding her back. She's going to have to admit it some time, and the longer it goes on the harder it's going to be for her.'

They had come to the end of the quarter-deck. Thursday made to turn left, but Connor reached out and touched her arm. 'Don't go yet, Thursday. I haven't wished you a happy Christmas.'

'Happy Christmas,' she said, smiling. 'But I've got to go, I'm helping on the ward.'

'I'll probably see you then. I'll be doing the Christmas rounds with the rest of the doctors. Armed with a pair of garden shears to demonstrate my calling! But look here . . .' He reached out a hand as if to detain her. 'Can't we make some arrangement to see each other on our own? It's a long time since we walked out to Lee that day.'

'Well, only three weeks,' she said, thinking that it seemed much longer. 'Not all that long, really.'

'A long time,' he repeated firmly. 'What are you doing the rest of the day? We've got no operations.'

'We've got a special tea for the VADs. Madam's gone to a lot of trouble – I couldn't miss it.'

'Tomorrow? Boxing Day?'

'Well, Elsie's asked me and Patsy to go round to her gran's. She lives in Gosport. Her mum and dad are going to be there, too. And I'm on the ward in the morning, so that another girl can go home. I don't know when—'

'Thursday,' he said as sailors and nurses streamed past them, 'there must be a minute in these two days that you can spare for me. Can't you leave early? Go a little late? Well, what about after this special tea? That's not going to go on all evening, is it? You can slip out for half an hour.'

'But – won't you be having your own – I mean, isn't there a dinner in the wardroom?'

'Yes,' he said, 'and nobody's going to miss me if I nip out before it starts. Say about seven.'

'But it'll be dark.'

'Well, that's all right,' he said. 'I'll have you to look after me.'

Thursday stared at him and burst out laughing. She looked into his dark blue eyes, thinking what a different man he was outside the operating theatre. At work, he was self-contained, stern, concentrating on what he was doing. There was no time for the odd smile or moment of communication. The only eye contact was made when an instrument or dressing was required, and it was required instantly. Commander Kirkpatrick could be very sharp with any nurse who didn't immediately provide him with what he needed.

Thursday's job was to look after the autoclave, where instruments, dressings and everything else needed for the operations were sterilised. She wasn't involved in the operations themselves, though she hoped that one day she would be. The thought of standing beside Connor – or any other surgeon – and handing him the instruments directly, taking swabs and even being allowed to do the stitches when they were particularly busy, was a thrilling one. Back to sewing, she'd thought with a giggle when she'd first realised how fascinating theatre work was. But more interesting sewing than ever it could be making frocks or suits.

'Well?' Connor repeated with a touch of urgency. 'Can you slip out for a while tonight? *Will* you?'

'Yes,' she said, smiling into those dark blue eyes. 'Yes, I will.'

'Coo,' Elsie said as they went into the ward to help serve the Christmas dinners. 'You've made a bit of a hit with the gorgeous Kirkpatrick. I saw you, holding hands after church.'

'We weren't holding hands! We were just discussing an – an—'

'Don't tell me you were discussing an operation, 'cause I won't believe you! Even a surgeon commander doesn't discuss operations on Christmas Day, not with that look in his eye, anyway. He fancies you, Thurs.'

'Don't be daft!' Thursday retorted, feeling the heat in her cheeks.

'And you fancy him,' Elsie said, observing Thursday's blush. 'You'd better be careful, my girl.'

'I don't know what you're talking about,' Thursday said with dignity, and Elsie hooted.

'Well, I've a feeling you're about to find out! When are you seeing him?'

'Oh, for goodness' sake!' Thursday caught Elsie's eye and grinned. 'Well – this evening, actually. After tea. But it won't be for long – he's got a wardroom dinner to go to. Anyway, it'll be dark and there's nowhere to go on Christmas Day.'

'Oh, you'll find somewhere. Some secluded little corner. I must say, I'm surprised at him, a commander and all, leading an innocent young nurse astray—'

'Shut up, Elsie,' Thursday ordered. 'It's time to go to the ward. And you needn't go spreading gossip all over the hospital either.

He's my boss. He probably wants to talk about bandages or something.'

'Oh, yeah,' Elsie said, rolling her eyes, 'and Mr Churchill's coming to tea at my gran's tomorrow. Pull the other one, Thurs.' She smiled and nudged Thursday's arm. 'It's all right, kid. I'm not going to go blabbing. You go and have a nice little cuddle somewhere. You deserve it. I just wish it was me, that's all – he's a real smasher!'

Connor was waiting at the corner of D Block when Thursday slipped out, her cape thrown hastily round her shoulders. It was a cold, clear night and the stars gave a faint, silvery light, just enough to see their way. They walked together through the avenue of trees along the quarter-deck, decorously apart at first until Connor took Thursday's hand and slipped it through his arm, where he held it closely against his side. She trembled and then relaxed. His arm felt warm and strong, and her own fitted against his side as if it was meant to be there.

'What a lovely night,' she said after a moment. 'It's so quiet. You can't imagine bombers coming over, can you?'

' "*Silent night, holy night*," ' Connor quoted from the carol they had sung that morning. 'There really is something special about the stillness you get on Christmas Day. I suppose it's because there isn't any traffic on the roads, no trains or ferries running, the ships in the harbour are all tied up and, best of all, no aircraft! And in homes all over the country, people are enjoying their Christmas with the family. In homes all over Europe, I suppose.' He was silent for a moment, then added sombrely, 'But not enough of them. There are too many homes that have been torn apart by this war, Thursday.'

'I know.'

He glanced down at her and she saw the shine of his eyes. 'I'm really very sorry about your brother, Thursday.'

'Yes. It's all the worse because Mike – my cousin – must have been near him, they were in the same regiment. And then there's Leslie, my other cousin, Mike's brother – he's a pilot in the RAF. He's on bombers now.'

'But he's all right, isn't he? Last time you mentioned him—'

'Oh, yes,' Thursday said, 'he's all right. So far.'

Connor said nothing. They both knew that the odds were stacked high against the young pilots. Leslie himself, managing to get home for a couple of days' leave just before Thursday, had told his parents that there were none left in the squadron who had joined with him. He had already won several medals, but brushed them aside, saying that there were so many to go round that you couldn't help getting the odd one or two. Flo turned them over in her hands, marvelling that her son could have become a hero in such a short time, but Percy, although just as proud, shook his head over them. The boy was flying on borrowed time, he said gloomily, but Leslie just laughed and said that he was like a cat, had nine lives and every one of them charmed.

Mary, telling Thursday about this, had said that his laughter didn't ring true. It sounded like fragile glass being broken. She said that Leslie was living on his nerves, and Flo lived in daily terror of another telegram.

'Thursday,' Connor said suddenly, 'I've got something to tell you. I've got a draft.'

'Oh!' She stopped and turned to him, trying to see his face in the darkness. 'A ship, you mean?'

'Yes. That's why I wanted you to come out tonight. One of the reasons, anyway. I didn't want you to hear it on the grapevine.'

Thursday didn't know what to say. They'd had so little conversation really – the time when Tony had died, the short trip across the harbour in the pinnace during an air raid, the dance at Grange and the walk to Lee after the Wrens' funerals. It was true that they had seen each other every day in the operating theatre, but that was different. They hardly knew each other – and yet, she felt again that they had always known each other. And at the thought of him going away, it seemed as if cold fingers touched her heart.

'I can't tell you where we're going,' he said, 'but I can tell you that we may be gone a long time. I've got another three or four weeks. I want to be able to see you during that time – so that we can get to know each other a bit better. Can we do that?'

But we already know each other, Thursday wanted to say. Instead, she nodded and said, 'Yes. Yes, we can do that.'

'Provided we don't get too many more raids,' he added with a wry grin. 'If we do, we'll probably be in the theatre all the time, which isn't quite what I mean.'

He's going away, she thought desolately. He's going away for months – maybe longer than that. He may never come back. The realisation of what it meant to her shook her heart. She reached up and laid her hands on his lapels.

'I'm right, aren't I?' he said quietly. 'We do want to get to know one another, Both of us.'

She nodded, then realised he couldn't see her, and whispered. 'Yes. Please.'

His arms wrapped themselves suddenly around her and he drew her close against him. The doeskin of his jacket was soft against her cheek. She felt his face against her hair, and lifted her head. Their lips met and clung.

'Thursday,' he whispered. 'Thursday . . .'

It was like no other kiss she had ever received. His lips were gentle, barely touching hers at first, yet there was something, almost an electricity, that transmitted itself between them and she could not have broken away. It was like the tender brightness of a candle-flame, trembling in the darkness yet shining a soft, true light into her heart. She closed her eyes, losing herself in the leaping delight of a wild, sweet emotion such as she had never known, and when she felt his lips break away softly and his fingertips touch her cheek she sighed and opened her eyes to look up at his face, dark against the frosty stars.

'Connor,' she whispered.

'Thursday.' He looked down at her and then kissed her again, and this time the kiss deepened and he caught her fiercely against him. She clung to him, feeling as if they were sweeping together into the starry skies, wheeling far above the cold earth and riding the high, soaring wind of the night. She felt his body against hers, hard and urgent, and let herself melt against him. 'Connor. *Connor* . . .'

They broke apart at last, breathing quickly. He held her close and she laid her head against his chest, wanting nothing more for the moment. This is what I've been waiting for, she thought. This is what I wanted all the time . . .

'What was the other reason you said you wanted to see me?' she asked at last. 'You said there was something else.'

'Good heavens, I almost forgot!' He let go of her with one hand and felt in his pocket. 'Here. It's nothing much,' he added quickly as she stared at the little box. 'Just a little Christmas present. You'll have to open it when you get back – you won't be able to see it now. But I hope you'll like it.'

Thursday looked at him, and opened the box anyway. She could barely see its contents, but her fingers traced the shape of a crown. A naval brooch, such as sailors gave their sweethearts. She looked up at him again, doubtfully.

'It's just a token,' he said quietly. 'Something to remind you of me while I'm away.'

'It's lovely. I can tell it's lovely. But—'

He took her in his arms again, silencing her with a kiss, and they stood for a moment, close in each other's arms, before he drew away. 'I've got to go in soon. The dinner – we have to be on time, curse it. Can I see you tomorrow?'

'I'm going to Elsie's gran's . . .'

'All day?'

'I'm helping on the wards first. We're covering for other girls. But we're not going to Elsie's gran till about three o'clock. After lunch—?'

'Before lunch,' he said firmly. 'Listen, I can have the loan of a car for the afternoon. I've managed to scrounge some petrol. We'll go out the minute you come off duty, get away from this place for a couple of hours. I'll have you back here in time to go to Elsie's gran, never fear. And we'll take a picnic with us – of sorts, anyway. I can get a few sandwiches from the wardroom, or some sausages from breakfast – something, anyway. You won't starve!'

Thursday stared up at him, her heart beating quickly. Go out in a car? She'd only ever been in one once before. And with Connor – away from Haslar, away from sharp eyes, from wagging tongues. She felt a little dizzy. 'But . . .'

'But what?'

'But – why *me*? There must be lots of other girls – better-looking girls, girls of – of your own sort. I don't understand . . .'

'Girls of my own sort? What on earth to do you mean?'

'You know what I mean! I know a lot of VADs are quite posh, but I'm just an ordinary girl, from an ordinary family. My dad's a foreman in a factory. I was apprenticed to a tailor's shop. I'm not like Helen Stanway, been to a smart boarding-school and all that. I'm just *ordinary*.'

Connor put one finger beneath her chin and tilted her face up to his. She could just see his expression and the glimmer of his eyes. 'Now, let's just get a few things straight,' he said. 'For one thing, Thursday Tilford, there's nothing ordinary about you. How could there be, with a name like yours? And your family can't be ordinary either, or they wouldn't have had the nerve to give you such a name. Or the imagination. And for another, you're talking rubbish and you know it. You know very well why I want to see you again. Don't you?'

Thursday caught her breath. She swallowed a little and then whispered, 'Yes.'

'Yes. I should think so! So we'll have no more nonsense about *why me*, all right?' He looked down at her gravely. 'I'm not asking you to make any promises, Thursday. I'm not asking you to hand your life over. I just want this time with you, just to see if I'm right about what I think – what I think about us. D'you understand that?'

'Yes,' she whispered again. 'Yes, I do.'

He laid his lips on her forehead and then trailed them down her cheek to her mouth. 'Then we both understand,' he murmured, 'and for the time being, that's enough. That's all we need.'

He took her out through Fareham and over to Boarhunt before swinging up the road which led along the top of Portsdown Hill. Thursday sat at his side in the rattling Austin Seven, remembering bike rides with Dave. The tears came to her eyes as she thought of him, limping up to the house to make cocoa during a lull in the air raid. And then hearing another plane come snarling over – the bomb falling . . . Only they said you didn't hear the one that hit you, didn't they? So what had he heard? What had it been like for him? Sudden unbearable pain as his body was torn apart – or just nothing? Just, suddenly, nothing. No more Dave. No more anything. And was that it, just nothing left, for ever and ever? Or was he truly somewhere else now, perhaps even able to see her, to know what she was doing, to know what everyone was doing . . . ?

'Thursday!' Connor said in alarm. 'Thursday, what on earth's the matter? You're crying your heart out. What is it? Is it your brother – have you had bad news?'

He drew the car into the side of the road and stopped. He took her in his arms and Thursday leant her head against his chest and sobbed. He held her close, his hand moving on her hair, cradling her head against him, waiting until the storm began to diminish. He produced a large white handkerchief and when Thursday looked at it helplessly, he mopped her face and then held it over her nose.

'Blow.'

'Connor, I—'

'*Blow*. It's all right, I've got another one. One to show and one to blow, as they say. Come on. Now, tell me what it is. What's happened to make you cry like this?'

She shook her head and gulped. 'It's nothing – nothing that's only just happened, I mean. It's Dave – Elsie's brother. We – we used to come for bike-rides together up here. We used to go to Southwick and Hambledon, and the Meon Valley – all over the place. And then – and then he was killed. In an air raid, only a few weeks ago.' She blew her nose again. 'I haven't been up here since, and it all just reminded me.'

'I see.' Connor watched her for a moment. She was wearing his brooch, a small, naval crown worked in silver and gold. 'And this Dave – was he special to you?'

'I don't know. We hardly had time – it was like Tony – there's never time. But, yes – he was special. You see, he'd had infantile paralysis and one of his legs was shorter than the other. He couldn't serve in the Forces, but he could swim and cycle, and he'd just joined the LDV. He was going to ride a motor-bike, be a dispatch rider. And then there was a raid one night and they were in the shelter, him and Elsie's mum and dad and Eddy – he's the youngest – and Dave went up to the house to make a cup of cocoa for everyone and – and a bomb hit it. There was nothing left.' She drew in a great, shuddering breath. 'They – they never found him, properly. Just – just—'

'All right, Thursday,' he said quietly. 'You don't have to go on.' He glanced ruefully at the slope of the hill, the harbour lying spread beneath them. 'And I thought this would be such a good place to bring you.'

'It would have been,' she whispered. 'It's just that it brought everything back. Poor Dave – he was so thrilled to be in the LDV. He wanted to do something. And instead – it was such a *waste*.'

She began to cry again and Connor held her, one arm around her shoulders, the other stroking her hair. His face was grim and after a while he said, 'I think we'd better go back. You're in no fit state to enjoy a picnic.'

'I'm sorry,' she said miserably.

'No need.' He started the engine again and turned the car. 'Maybe we'll try again some time.'

Thursday stared at him. His face was closed and his jaw tight. He didn't look at her as they cruised along the top of the hill.

'Connor—'

'There's no need to explain. I got the wrong idea, that's all.'

'*Connor*—'

'Please,' he said, 'don't say any more. I'm sorry. I've been rather a fool. I just thought . . .' He glanced swiftly sideways at the brooch. 'I did tell you it was just a token, didn't I?'

Bewildered, she touched it. 'Yes, but – Connor, are you angry with me?'

'Angry with *you*? No, of course not! With myself, for being such a blundering fool, but never with you.' He drove fast, the little car almost leaping along the road. 'I'm only sorry that you've had so much to put up with. One boyfriend dying before your eyes – another blown up in an air raid. And then a fool of a doctor making himself a nuisance—'

'Connor, *no*, you're *not* a nuisance.'

'Well, it's good of you to say so, but—'

'Connor, stop it! What's the matter with you all of a sudden? You're not jealous, surely – not of Dave?' She looked at him in sudden anger. 'If I can't cry for a friend . . .'

She saw him bite his lip, and then once again he pulled the car in to the side of the road. He turned and looked at her gravely.

'I'm sorry, Thursday. I'm behaving abominably. And I'm ashamed to say that yes, I think I am jealous. Of Dave – of young Tony West – of anyone else who's special to you. And I know that when you've lost so many people you love – well, it takes time to recover. You can't let anyone else be special, perhaps for a long time. So I'm sorry I—'

'Connor, I don't know what you're talking about,' she broke in. 'Dave was special because he was, well, because he was so brave and so willing, and just when he'd got the chance to help it was snatched away from him. And Tony was special because he was the first boy I'd ever felt anything for at all.' She thought of Sidney, who had been her boyfriend for so long and for whom she'd felt hardly anything. He'd been at Dunkirk, too, her mother had told her, and had come home safely, ready to go again. 'But neither of them was special in the way that you are. That's quite different.'

He stared at her. She saw his eyes darken, and her heart leapt. He put out one hand and touched her cheek. She turned her head and laid her lips against his palm.

'Thursday—'

'We haven't got much time,' she said quietly. She lifted one hand and touched the brooch he had given her. 'I know you said it was just a token. But when I got back to D Block last night and looked at it – I knew it was more than that. It is, isn't it?'

'It's whatever you want it to be,' he said.

'And what do *you* want it to be?'

He kept his eyes on hers and laid his fingers over hers so that their hands both covered the little brooch. She felt the pulse beating in his fingertips.

'I would have liked it to be a ring,' he said.

Chapter Twenty-Eight

The respite was brief. On the day after Boxing Day, a raid on London left six hundred people dead or injured. And just two days later, on the Sunday evening, the worst attack yet left London almost entirely in flames.

'Look at this picture of St Paul's on the front page of the *Daily Mail*,' Elsie said at breakfast. 'Standing there amongst all those fires. "The War's Greatest Picture", they're calling it. It's like the whole city's on fire.'

'How will people manage?' Patsy wondered. 'I mean, how can they get to work? Even supposing there's any work to get to. It doesn't look as if there's going to be much left of London.'

'Oh, I don't know. It's a big place,' Thursday said. 'I went once with Mum and Jenny, and we went to the Tower and Buckingham Palace and the Houses of Parliament, and it was miles between them all. We went to St Paul's as well,' she added, looking at the picture of the great dome standing amidst the smoke and the flames. 'It's a lovely church. You can go right up high in the dome and look down at the people down below, just like tiny little dolls they are, and there's a whispering gallery and all sorts. It'd be terrible if that was ruined.'

'Well, it's not.' Elsie poured milk on her bowl of Force. 'And it's not going to be. There's some things even the Germans can't smash.'

In the next few days, it seemed as if the enemy had heard Elsie's words and were determined to disprove them. It wasn't only London that was under attack. Cities such as Cardiff and Bristol were being relentlessly bombed, and although the weather on New Year's Eve prevented any planes from reaching England there was little time to celebrate. The streets were full of rubble, fires were still smouldering and, as Patsy had said, just getting to work was difficult. The damage was almost unbelievable, with the papers full of pictures of devastation. And you never knew where the enemy would strike next.

It was Portsmouth's turn ten days later.

Connor, with only days to go before joining his ship, had been working at full stretch and his theatre staff had worked with him. It sometimes seemed to Thursday that this would be the pattern of their relationship for ever – clad in green or white gowns, only their eyes visible as she passed the instruments from the autoclave to the nurse who would, in turn, pass them to the surgeon. Will we ever get a chance to be together again? she wondered. Will we ever get more than just a few moments, snatched between duties?

'We've got to get away for an hour or two,' Connor said as they met at what had become their 'special' corner. 'I've only got a few more days. Look, neither of us is in Theatre this evening. Let's go out. I can borrow Freddy's car.'

Driving at night wasn't easy, with the streets blacked out and only a sliver of light allowed to shine through the covered headlights. Cautiously, Connor drove on to the slope of Portsdown Hill, as far as you were allowed to go, and pulled on to the verge. They sat looking down over the darkened city. Somewhere above them were the anti-aircraft gun emplacements and the searchlights. As yet, they were switched off and there was no sign of a light anywhere. If you hadn't been up there in the daytime, Thursday said, you wouldn't believe that there were buildings and streets and thousands of people down below.

'You can see why they're so keen for people not to show a light. It really would show up.'

'Yes, but wait till the moon comes out. It's like daylight then, and not a darned thing we can do about it.'

The moon had been behind a cloud. The edges showed silver against the blackened sky and then the cloud drifted past and the moon shone down, throwing the harbour and coastline into sharp relief. Portsmouth, Gosport and the Isle of Wight lay below like a relief map in black and silver, ready and waiting for any enemy bomber that chose to pass over.

'Gosh, look at that,' Thursday said in dismay. 'They might as well turn on the streetlights and have done with it!'

Connor looked down soberly. Then he turned to Thursday and put his arms around her.

'Listen, darling. We haven't got long. I'm going on Monday. That's only two days, and we may be busy.' He kissed her. 'We haven't had as long as I wanted to get to know each other.'

'I know,' she whispered.

'And yet – it doesn't seem to matter somehow. I feel that I *do* know you, Thursday. I know all the important things about you.' He paused and laid his lips against her ear. 'I know that I love you.'

Thursday felt a shock run through her body. I wanted him to say this, she thought, I knew he would say it, yet it still comes as a strange kind of surprise. Like something I've dreamed about but never really thought would happen. Something I knew, yet didn't know.

'Oh, Connor,' she breathed. 'I love you, too.'

She felt him relax against her, as if he had been tense and anxious. But he must have known, she thought, he must have known I'd say it. Perhaps it was the same for him as it was for me – we both knew, yet didn't dare believe it.

'Thursday, I want to say so much. I want to plan – I want to talk about the future, our future, together. But I'm going away on Monday and God knows when I'll be back. There might not *be* any future, for us.' He was kissing her as he spoke, small, passionate kisses that covered her face. 'Oh, my darling – if only we had more time. If only we *knew* . . .'

'We *will* have time,' she said. 'You *will* come back, Connor, and we'll have all the time in the world. The war *will* be over one day. We do have a future.'

'I believe it. We have to believe it. But . . .'

'What?' she said, disturbed by his change in tone.

'I wanted to give you a ring. I wanted to give you an engagement ring.' He laughed suddenly. 'No, what I really want to give you is a *wedding* ring. But we haven't had time for any of it, and I'm not sure it's right to ask you to wait.' He looked down at her soberly and she could see his face, pale in the moonlight. 'I'm not asking you to wait for me, Thursday. I could be gone for a long time. I'm not tying you down.'

'And what if I want to be tied down?' she asked with spirit.

His teeth glimmered as he smiled. 'I can't stop you tying yourself down, can I! But I don't want you to sit in the mess, moping and knitting, while the other girls go out and have fun. I don't want you living like a nun. I want you to be the Thursday I know and love – the one that's always got a smile and a laugh, who goes out on her bike and has tea at the Swiss Café or a cup of coffee in the Dive – yes, I know all your haunts! – and goes dancing. All we've got, these days, is *today*. So I want you to make the most of every today, you understand? And then write and tell me all about it!'

'I'll write to you every day.'

'And I'll write back,' he said, 'but you may not get a letter every day.'

They sat quietly for a while, their arms about each other, their cheeks close. And then a different sound broke into the silence. The distant snarl of German aircraft.

'A raid,' Thursday whispered, and as she spoke the sirens began their wail and the searchlights sprang into life. Their long, bright swords lanced into the sky, criss-crossing it with a latticework of light. A plane was caught in the brightness and there was an instant rattle of ack-ack fire. The city below seemed bathed in light. It was so bright that Thursday and Connor could see the aircraft; they could see the bombs, falling away.

'They're bombing *Portsmouth*!'

'*Christ!*' Connor said, but anything further was drowned by the blast that followed. In that moment, it was as if the entire city were exploding. Searing white light, shot orange and black with flame and smoke, erupted somewhere in the centre. Splashes of brilliance flashed, like the graphic pictures in a comic strip. Fires began to burn, searchlights fanned the heavens and the gun emplacements all over the area spattered shots like spots of brightness into the darkness. A plane fell in a ball of flame, another trailed a plume of fire at its tail as it streaked, comet-like, across the sky. The drone of aircraft, the thunder of the explosions, the violent rattle of the guns were almost visible in the flares of scorching light. And then, in the centre of it all, in the city itself, the flames began to burn, blazing orange and white-hot heat into the darkness. The city and the waters that surrounded it were lit by an unearthly, pulsating glow, as if some devilish beast had been woken from a long sleep and was breathing a deadly fire.

'They can see every bloody ship in the harbour,' Connor whispered. 'Every shed in the dockyard. Every last street and every smallest house . . . It's all laid open to them, Thursday.'

'The whole city's going up in flames,' she said in a small voice. 'Oh, *Connor* . . .'

'We should get back.' He started the engine. 'We shouldn't be here anyway, on the hill. There'll be casualties . . .' He turned the car and began to drive down towards Fareham. 'The whole place is likely to catch this. It's going to be as bad as London.'

As bad as London. Or Bristol, Manchester, Cardiff. As bad as Coventry . . . Thursday remembered the photographs she had seen in the newspapers – of Coventry Cathedral left no more than a burnt-out shell, of the miles of devastated buildings in London – and felt sick. Was there going to be any city left unravaged? What of Worcester, her own home town? Was it, even now, being bombed as Portsmouth was being bombed? Was this happening everywhere tonight?

There was no need to drive cautiously now. The whole area was lit by the burnished glow. You could have read a newspaper by its light, Thursday thought as they came down into Fareham and turned down the Gosport road. Bombs had fallen all over the surrounding area and there were damaged and destroyed buildings at almost every turn. The fire engines were out and ambulances, many converted from vans, raced along, demanding right of way. As Connor, avoiding a street which was blocked by fire engines, drove down a side street, a man rushed out of a flaming building and yelled at him to stop.

'We'll have to help,' Connor said. 'We can't just go by.'

'But Haslar – they'll be needing us.'

'I know, but we're here now and there are people who need us here as well.' He was out of the car and running with the man. Thursday leapt out and followed them.

'Connor, don't go in—'

'It's all right, I'm not going to. There's a child here.' He bent, and Thursday saw the figure of a small girl lying on the pavement. Her body was twisted and her clothes in shreds. Blood matted her hair and covered her face with ugly splashes so that it was impossible to tell where it came from. Her eyes were closed and her mouth twisted in a grimace of pain.

'Oh, the poor little mite!' Thursday was on her knees immediately, brushing the blood-soaked hair back with tender fingers. 'Connor, we must help her.'

'Of course we must.' His fingers were moving swiftly over her body. 'She's badly hurt, I'm afraid. Is she your child?' he asked the man, and added, 'I'm a doctor.'

'A doctor? Oh, thank God. She ain't mine, no, she's my sister's kiddy. Our Meg – she was in the house when the bomb hit, getting the youngsters out of bed. Her other little 'un's been poorly, see, and she didn't want to take her down the shelter if it was a false alarm.' He drew in a long, shuddering breath and wiped his sleeve across his face. 'They were in the house – I tried to get 'em out, but . . .' His face crumpled. 'Oh, God. Oh, *God*. Our Meg. And young Rosie – they're both gone. I couldn't get near 'em, see. I tried. I *tried*.' He gazed at Connor as if expecting to be blamed. 'I managed to drag young Susie out, but when I tried to get back in . . . She ain't dead, too, is she? You can help her?'

'I'll do my best.' Connor turned to Thursday. 'We've got to get her away from this building – it could topple on to us at any minute. But we'll have to be careful – she's got broken bones, and there may be internal injuries as well.' He looked back at the man, who was staring down at the child, lying like a rag doll amongst the debris on the pavement. 'Can you find something – a door, perhaps – that we can use to carry her away?'

'A door . . .' Susie's uncle looked helplessly about, then darted away. He came back a moment or two later, staggering under the weight of a door that had been blown from its hinges. It was torn and splintered at one end, but it was still large enough to carry a child. He laid it down and, very carefully, Thursday and Connor lifted the broken figure on to it.

'God knows what harm we're doing,' Connor muttered. 'But what choice do we have? Well done, Thursday. Now, let's get her away from here and find an ambulance.'

But there were no ambulances to be had. The streets were filled with people needing help, and as many as possible had already been carried away. Thursday looked at him.

'We can use your car.'

He frowned. 'It's hardly big enough. We'd never get this door in, and I don't want to do her any more damage. And I want to get her out of the street – there could be more bombs.'

'There's a street shelter round the corner,' Susie's uncle said. 'We could get her in there.'

'Right. You help me carry the stretcher. Keep it as level as possible. Thursday, my emergency bag's on the back seat, fetch it out and bring it along. I'll do whatever I can once we're there.' The two men set off, carrying their fragile burden, and Thursday ran for the bag. By the time she caught them up, they were manoeuvring the makeshift stretcher through the narrow door of the street shelter, and the people inside were pressing back to make room.

'Hurt kiddy, is it? Poor little mite. Here, ain't that Meg Jones's little Susan? Where's her mum, then? And where's young Rosie?'

'Gone,' the man said brokenly. 'Direct hit. I managed to get Susie out, but the other two . . . The flames was just too much. I tried. I *tried*.'

'Lay her down there,' Connor ordered, and then looked round for Thursday. 'Oh, good girl. Now then, let's have a look. Can someone get some light over here, please?'

A hurricane lamp was brought and held over the child, and Connor began a more thorough examination. Thursday crouched beside him, holding his bag open. She watched as he gently lifted away the torn and scorched clothing – a little red kilt, it looked like, and a red jumper with a yellow teddy-bear knitted into the front. Her mum probably knitted that, she thought, and felt a lump come into her throat.

'We've got to get this stuff off her,' Connor muttered. 'Can you help me, Thursday? Very gently, now – it's going to hurt . . .'

The child had been unconscious, and as far as Thursday could tell was still unconscious, yet even through the depths of her numbed mind the pain was still enough to penetrate. Her cries brought a collective sigh from the others in the shelter, a whisper of sympathy and a sob or two from those who knew her. Somewhere behind Thursday, the little girl's uncle was telling his story, and she heard his own sobs and the soothing murmurs of the neighbours as they tried to comfort him. But all he could say was, 'I tried. I *tried*,' over and over again, as if his failure would haunt him for ever.

'How is she?' she asked Connor in a low voice, and he shook his head.

'Not good. It's not just the burns. They're fairly superficial, as far as I can tell, though they're more extensive than I like. But it's this leg – see? It's a bad compound fracture, and the bone's splintered and piercing a deep vein. She's losing too much blood, and there's nothing I can do to stop it. If something isn't done quickly, she won't survive.'

'Oh, Connor . . .'

'It's an amputation,' he said quietly. 'And it needs to be done as soon as possible.'

'But we'll never get her to the hospital! The War Memorial's the nearest, and they must have hundreds of patients coming in . . . Can we take her to Haslar?'

'It'll be the same there,' he said, 'and it's further away. We just don't have the time, Thursday.' He was fumbling in his bag as he spoke and she realised with horror what he intended to do. 'Clear a space. I don't want spectators.'

'*Connor—*'

'You'll have to help me,' he said. 'You've seen amputations before. It's a straightforward enough procedure. But you've got to be able to give me what I need without delay.' He didn't ask if she felt capable of it. He started to make up an injection while Thursday quickly pushed back the crowd. As they understood what was about to happen, most of them dropped back quickly, while two or three pressed forward, offering help. One said she was a member of the Red Cross and had done first aid, another said he'd nursed his old mother through her last illness and didn't mind the sight of blood, and a third had been a stretcher-bearer in the Great War of 1914. Thursday stationed them beside her and around Connor, and asked a couple of the other men to keep the rest back.

'She's got to have enough air. We can't have everyone breathing all over the poor little thing.'

'Choke her with carbon dioxide, that would,' the first-aider said knowledgeably. 'It's oxygen she needs.'

Thursday spread a piece of clean cloth on the ground and laid out Connor's instruments. She looked at the saw and felt faintly sick, then reminded herself that she was a nurse, and just because this wasn't a proper theatre it didn't give her any excuse to be squeamish. She looked at Connor, and their eyes met for a moment.

'All right?' he asked, and she nodded, knowing that he wouldn't see her as herself again until the operation was over. From this moment, she was a nurse – as much a piece of equipment as his scalpel.

A sudden thundering explosion shook the ground and reminded her that there was an air raid going on outside. She thought briefly of the fires she had seen, of the devastation of Portsmouth and its surroundings, and wondered what would be left when morning came and the raiders were driven away. And then she forgot everything in the concentration of the moment. There was nothing in the world now but the three of them – herself, Connor and a little girl called Susie, who was about to lose her leg. There wasn't even time to feel sad. From this moment it was a job of work, which must be properly done.

It took a surprisingly short time. There was a silence in the shelter, a lull in the bombing and in the roar of aircraft. The only sounds were those of Connor's steady breathing, the whimpers of the child, now deeply unconscious, and other sounds, the inevitable sounds of the operation, that grated in her ears. The pain of the child seemed to trickle through the entire shelter, to be shared by everyone present. The uncle was quiet now, numbed by his own pain. He crouched just within Thursday's sight, his head cradled on his knees, and whimpered softly like a hurt animal.

'That's it,' Connor said quietly at last, and straightened his shoulders.

Thursday looked down at the child and felt the tears come at last. The stump of the little leg was bandaged just above the knee – or where the knee had been until just a few minutes ago. The stretcher-bearer reached forward and lifted the remainder in his arms and carried it to the door of the shelter.

'We'll get her to the hospital as quickly as we can,' Connor said quietly to the little girl's uncle. 'You'd better come, too. Are there any other relatives? What about her father?'

'In the Army,' the man said tonelessly. 'I was stopping along with our Meg, see, they won't have me on account of me eyesight. There was only her and the two kiddies. Now there's just me and Susie.

And how'm I going to look after her when I've got to go to work in the dockyard every day? I dunno what we'll do, I don't straight.'

'Hasn't she any grandparents?'

'Our dad's dead, got flu after the last lot, and Jack's mum and dad are up north. Manchester. I dunno what we'll do.' He started to cry again. 'I tried to get 'em out, I did, I tried. But it was the flames, see, the flames, they was just . . .' He shook his head blindly. 'I couldn't get past 'em, I couldn't, and our Meg, she was *in* there, her and young Rosie, and I just couldn't get to them.' He stared at them piteously. 'I *tried*.'

'I know.' Connor touched his shoulder. 'Look, we should get this little girl to the hospital as soon as possible. I'm a doctor at Haslar, and if my car's still all right out in the street I'll take her there straight away. Will you come as well?'

'Haslar?' the man said doubtfully. 'But that's a naval hospital.'

'That doesn't matter. We'll take her there. She's my case now, and if necessary we'll enrol her as a Wren!' He nodded at Thursday. 'You'll sit in the back with her, so go and get in, and I'll get this useful chap here—' he glanced at the stretcher-bearer '—to help me carry her out. And you can sit in the front and direct me,' he said to the uncle. 'We may not be able to go by a straight route.'

They couldn't. They had to go round through Stubbington and back along the seafront at Lee and through the village of Alverstoke. Everywhere there was damage – houses on fire, incendiaries flaming in the middle of the road, shrapnel flying through the air. Connor twisted the wheel this way and that to avoid hoses and rubble, and finally they were driving down Clayhall Road, past the long, high wall of the hospital and in through the gate.

Connor leapt out and ran into the hospital, calling for help, and two QARNNs came running out. They looked into the back and lifted the child carefully away from Thursday's lap. The uncle got out and stood uncertainly for a moment before following them in, and then Thursday got out, too, her legs shaking. She also stood still for a moment or two before going inside.

The sky was lit with the glow of the fires burning in Portsmouth. The raddled light flickered on the walls of the buildings and lit the straight narrow road of the quarter-deck as if it ran with blood. The roar of the aircraft was dying away, slowly vanishing into the distance as the planes, their deadly loads disposed of, returned home. She thought very briefly of her cousin Leslie, wondering if he had been up there, trying to fight them off in the darkness, and then she turned and followed Connor and the QARNNs into the hospital.

It had not occurred to her once that she and Connor could themselves have been injured during those hours as they'd driven through the burning streets and crouched over the injured child in the street shelter. It had not once entered her mind that she could be in any danger. Now, suddenly, the realisation hit her, and she reeled and put out a hand to steady herself.

'It's all right,' Connor's voice said in her ear, and she felt his arms wrap themselves around her. 'It's all right, Thursday. You're safe. And little Susie is going to be all right.' He held her close and rocked her gently in his arms. 'It's all over, sweetheart, all over now. You're safe. You're safe with me.'

Thursday turned her face into his coat and felt the tears seep from her eyes. Her body shook, and he tightened his hold on her. For a few moments they stood quite still, aware only of each other, while around them the light of the flames flickered bright and crimson on the walls, and the scarlet colour of blood lay flung like a discarded cloak upon the ground.

Chapter Twenty-Nine

Thursday and Connor had returned to Haslar to find the place in as near chaos as the Navy would ever allow. Because the raid was so huge, all military and naval personnel had been called out to help, and inevitably there were countless injured, many of them ferried straight across to Haslar despite the bombs that rained down on the harbour as well as the city. Everyone was on duty; those not in the underground shelters with their patients were at the jetty, bringing in new ones. There was a constant coming and going along the paved way into the hospital.

'Take Susie down below,' Connor said to Thursday. 'Make sure she gets immediate attention – that amputation's got to be watched. And you stay with her – I want you safe.'

I want you, safe too, Thursday thought, but what use would it be to tell you that? She caught a passing QARNN and together they manoeuvred the makeshift stretcher down the stairs. Swiftly, she explained what had happened.

'Poor little soul,' the QARNN said. 'But she seems to be all right. We'll take her over there – there's a couple of Wrens who've been brought in, they're not too badly knocked about. She'll be best if she can just sleep now. I'll keep an eye on her, if you've got others to see to.'

Thursday nodded and dashed back up the stairs before anyone could stop her. There were plenty of people down here, looking after the patients from the wards, and she had no intention of obeying Connor's orders to stay safe. Not while he was up there, amongst the bombs, and not at all safe.

She found him on the jetty, examining the injured as they were brought ashore. The whole of the harbour was lit by the fires that raged all through the city only half a mile away, and new ones broke out with every fresh explosion. From Portsdown Hill came a constant, deafening roar as the huge guns there fired at the planes that circled the city. More firing came from the other emplacements all around the area, and a massive barrage from the *Corbet*, the French battleship impounded at Hardway. You could only hear what someone shouted at you if they put their mouth to your ear, yet people were yelling anyway, gesturing to make themselves understood. For the first time, Thursday fully understood the effects of the strict Naval discipline. You just knew, from intensive training, what the slightest movement of hand or head meant and you knew almost from instinct what to do. All the apparently petty and irritating rules came into their own when emergency demanded action.

Connor straightened up and saw her beside him. He shouted at her, his mouth forming the words 'What the hell are you doing here?', but Thursday shook her head impatiently and there was no time for argument. Together, they slipped into their routine, surgeon and nurse, and as the planes and the bombs and the guns all roared about their ears, they worked together as if in an oasis of their own calm, receiving their patients, examining them, giving them immediate treatment or handing them on to an SBA or QARNN.

The bombs were not confined to Portsmouth. Many of the planes flew low over Gosport, and every now and then there was an explosion close by. At some point, one came so low that Thursday ducked and Connor flung his arm across her shoulders. They staggered together and fell, and as they lay on the paved slabs they felt the rocking thud of an explosion nearby. Connor swore in Thursday's ear and she felt him cover her body with his own. Debris rained around them; she heard a cry as someone was hit, and prayed that it wasn't Connor. Not now, she begged, not now . . . And then the shuddering of the earth slowly ceased and, cautiously, she lifted her head.

Connor rolled off her. He looked back at the hospital buildings. 'Haslar's been hit.'

'Oh, no. The patients. *Susie* . . .' Thursday was on her feet. She could see flames, people running.

'It's not the wards. And she'll be all right, down in the basement.' He screwed up his eyes against the burning light. 'Looks like the stores to me. Or the museum.'

'The museum!' It was full of medical specimens and oddities.

A skeleton, used for anatomy lessons. Jars of organs, preserved in formaldehyde. A duck with four legs. But there was no time to worry about that now. Another pinnace had arrived, bringing more casualties, and Thursday turned back with Connor and the other doctors and nurses to bring them ashore and race them into the safety of the cellars.

The raid lasted for seven hours. It was four in the morning before Thursday finally crawled into her bed, sent there by Miss Makepeace who had caught her swaying beside a patient and immediately ordered her away. 'You'll become a danger to yourself and others if you don't get some sleep. Haven't you been on duty since early this morning – yesterday morning, I mean?'

'Yes, Madam.' Thursday didn't mention the drive up Portsdown Hill, or the amputation in the air-raid shelter. 'But really, I'm quite all right—'

'*Bed*,' Madam repeated forcefully, and Thursday, more thankfully than she would have admitted, obeyed her.

She slept until ten, then got up and went back on duty. There was plenty to do, but her first thought was for Susie. Eventually she tracked down the QARNN who had taken her over, and was told that she'd been transferred to the War Memorial Hospital in Gosport.

'She'll be all right there. There was a man asking for her—'

'Her uncle. I think he's almost all she's got left.'

The QARNN nodded. 'He's gone to see her. He seems very fond of her. Poor little mite, losing her leg.' She sighed and then looked at Thursday again. 'You helped with the operation, I hear. You did a good job.' Her hand rested a moment on Thursday's shoulder. 'You should think about training properly once all this is over.'

Thursday went down to the basement, thinking sadly of the child who would go through life with only one leg. At least she had survived, but how was she going to adapt, not only to her physical problems but to the loss of her mother and sister as well? Poor little Susie, Thursday thought, and made up her mind to go and see the little girl as soon as she possibly could.

The operating theatre was already in full swing. Thursday reported to the theatre sister and waited until she was called.

'Hullo,' said Ellen Bridges, spotting her as she wrapped herself in

344

her green overall. 'Bit of a night last night, wasn't it? Heard about the duck?'

'The *duck*?' Thursday stared at her uncomprehendingly. 'What duck?'

'The one in the museum. *You* know – the one with four legs. Apparently it got lost when the museum was hit, and they want everyone to go and look for it.' Ellen's voice rose with a touch of hysteria. 'Just as if we hadn't got enough to do, we've got to go and pick through the rubble for a bloody duck with four webbed feet! You can't help laughing.'

There wasn't a lot to laugh at, however. The raid had been the worst yet known in the whole area – a blitz every bit as bad as those on London. Gosport and Alverstoke had both been badly hit, with incendiary bombs close to Haslar itself, damaging houses in Clayhall Road, Foster Road, Bury Crescent and the bridge, and many others falling in Stokes Bay and on the allotments. Fires had broken out almost simultaneously all over the town, and over eighty fire engines, with almost five hundred men, had been sent to deal with them. The raddled glare could be seen for miles.

Portsmouth itself had been devastated. The first stick had fallen on the electricity station, plunging the entire city into darkness. The fires that Thursday and Connor had seen had started in Palmerston Road, one of the main shopping centres, and it wasn't long before Commercial Road and King's Road were also alight. The next planes to come over attacked the Guildhall (which was still on fire days later) and so many other public buildings that it was almost impossible to count them. Six churches had gone, the Eye and Ear Hospital, part of the Royal Hospital, Clarence Pier – its blackened ruin visible from Haslar – three cinemas and the Hippodrome theatre, a hotel and drill hall, the Royal Sailors' Rest and the Salvation Army citadel. Amongst these were countless small ships and businesses, together with over three thousand private homes, an underground shelter with nearly fifty people inside, which had received a direct hit, and most of the gas and water mains. There were nearly two and a half thousand fires.

And they want us to look for a four-footed duck that's been dead for years anyway, Thursday thought with an echo of Ellen's hysterical laughter as she tied her green theatre gown and answered the sister's call. All this, and they're worried about a flaming *duck*!

Connor left two days later. He went at first light, catching the early pinnace across the harbour to board his new ship, which was at the Southern Railway jetty. She was due to sail on Friday, and he would not be able to come ashore again.

Thursday came down to the jetty to see him off. She stood, shivering a little in her scarlet cape, her throat aching but her eyes dry. They stood together, gazing into each other's eyes, unable to think of the right words. Perhaps there were no right words.

'I've got something for you,' Thursday whispered at last, and felt in her pocket. She handed him a small package. 'You can open it now, if you like.'

Connor unwrapped the little packet and took out the small cloth badge that lay inside. He stared at it for a moment, and then his eyes went to Thursday's sleeve, where her VAD badge should be proudly displayed. The sleeve was bare, with only a few small needle-holes to show where it had been.

He looked at the badge again. It was black, with a golden, jewelled crown above a circle of gold. Within the circle was the word 'Mobile' and in the centre was another gold circle, with the letters 'VAD' in gold on a red background. It was the badge that all mobile VADs wore, the badge they wore with pride.

'Won't you get into trouble?' he asked with a smile, and Thursday grinned.

'I'll just have to pay for a new one and sew it on. It was all I could think of to give you.'

'It's all I want,' he said quietly, and slipped it into his breast pocket. 'I'll keep it with me always.'

'Take care, won't you?' she begged with sudden desperation. 'Come back to me. I love you, Connor.'

'I love you, Thursday,' he said gravely and then, regardless of the sailors in the waiting pinnace, bent his head and kissed her. 'And you take care, too. No freewheeling down Pneumonia Bridge on that old rattletrap of yours!'

'As if I would,' she said, and laughed, but her laughter was dangerously close to a sob. She gave him a little push. 'One last kiss and then go, Connor. Please.' They clung together for a moment and she tried to believe the unbelievable, that he was here in her arms now, his lips on hers, and that in a few moments he would be gone, out of her reach. She would see him step down into the pinnace and she wouldn't be able to call him back, she wouldn't touch or kiss or even see him until – until when?

Nobody could tell her that. Nobody knew. It could be a year. It could be years.

She stood on the jetty, where so many sailors had in the past been brought from their foundering ships, and watched the pinnace draw away. It turned into the waves and began its short, choppy journey across the harbour to the still smoking city. Connor stood in the prow, his cap off, his hair ruffled by the wind. He lifted his hand, and Thursday lifted hers in farewell.

When she could no longer see him clearly, she turned and made her way back to the block. She would be on duty in half an hour, and before then she must wash away her tears. She could not go on duty without a smile.

The bombing went on. Sustained raids, lasting for hours, and lightning strikes with the planes making a swift dash across the Channel to hurl their bombs into the cities below, and swooping away like lightning itself, ready to reload and return next night – and the next – and the next.

In Worcester, the raids were mostly 'hit and run', a few bombs dropped as the planes flew over on their way to Birmingham or Liverpool. It was still enough to force people to take shelter, or trek into the countryside or down to the open ground around the racecourse and on the riverbank.

Vic and Denise were settling into a more stable but still uneasy relationship with Flo and Percy. The problems of two men trying to get ready for work in the mornings had been sorted out by Flo, who had pinned up a rota for the lavatory and the washbasin. Percy had glowered at this, muttering that he didn't see why he couldn't use either just whenever he liked in his own home, but Flo had been sharp with him and pointed out that she was sick and tired of his grumbling, and it wasn't good for Denise. The girl was expecting, and needed a peaceful home.

'You don't have to tell *me* she's expecting,' Percy growled. 'That's just why we're having to put up with having this bloke in the house. Calling us Mum and Dad, and all.'

'Well, he has to, doesn't he, he's our son-in-law now for better or worse.' She went on quickly, biting off Percy's inevitable retort. 'Look, Vic's not so bad. He's a decent lad, and if you gave him the chance you'd see it for yourself.'

'So decent he gets a fifteen-year-old girl in the family way,' Percy said. 'You and me must have different ideas about "decent", Flo.'

'I know they did wrong, but they've put it right now, and she could have done a lot worse for herself. And it was her fault as much as his, telling him lies about her age. Not that it would have been any excuse if she really had been eighteen,' Flo added fairly. 'I must say, I'm disappointed in her, same as you. But it's happened now and we've got to make the best of it. So it's your turn in the lav first, and don't sit in there for half an hour, keeping the boy waiting. He's got to be down the post office at six, for the sorting.'

It was easier in the afternoons, when Vic came home first. He was often home before Denise, who had managed to get a cleaning job at the school for the last couple of months of her pregnancy, and it was on one of these afternoons that he came in to find Flo sitting at the table, staring at a scrap of paper, her face like a stone.

'Mum! What's the matter? You're as white as a sheet.' He saw the piece of paper. 'What's that?'

'It's a telegram,' she said tonelessly. 'It's what I've been waiting for. I knew it was going to come, some time. I knew he couldn't go on and on like that, flying night after night, and since he's been on bombers, going all that way to Berlin and places, I knew it was going to happen. I knew it. He was the only one left out of all those boys, the only one. He couldn't go on much longer.'

'It's not Leslie!' Vic said. He picked up the telegram and read the few words. 'Oh, *Mum*. When did this come? How long have you been sitting here like this, all on your own?'

'I dunno. About half past two, I think. I dunno what time it is now, I dunno how long it's been—'

'It's a quarter to five. Haven't you moved in the last two hours?'

Flo shook her head wearily, as if to ask why it should matter. 'He's *dead*,' she said, breaking into tears at last. 'My *Leslie*, shot down and killed. That's both of them now, both my boys gone, and what for? It hasn't stopped the Germans coming, it hasn't stopped us getting bombed and killed and blown out of our own homes. What's it all for? What good has it done? Oh, Leslie, my *Leslie* . . .'

She raised both hands to her face and began to rock to and fro, great choking sobs forcing their way up from her breast and breaking, like waves on the shore, in a storm of tears. Vic put both his arms around her and held her. He didn't know what to do. He only knew Leslie slightly, and hadn't had a chance to make friends with him, but he had taken it for granted that Denise's brother was a likable young man and they would be friends once the war was over. Now he would never have the opportunity.

'I'm sorry,' he said, thinking how useless and inadequate the words were. 'I'm really sorry.'

'He always wanted to fly an aeroplane,' Flo wept. 'We used to tell him not to be so daft, people like us don't fly planes. You've got to have money and education . . . Even when he joined up, we never thought he'd be able to be a pilot, but he was so set on it, he did all the classes and exams and everything and next thing we knew he had those wings on his shoulder . . . He was so pleased with himself, and we were so proud of him. And he got all those medals that he showed us last time he came home . . . And now he's dead. He's dead. *My Leslie's dead.*' Her voice rose in a little scream, and Vic began to wonder what he would do if she got really hysterical and couldn't stop, started throwing herself about and banging her head on the wall like he'd heard about. He didn't want to have to slap her face, not his own mother-in-law . . . He held her tightly and murmured things in her ear, silly things that meant nothing. 'There, there . . . it's all right, everything's all right . . .' Stupid things, he thought savagely. Everything was *not* all right.

'I'll make you a cup of tea,' he said. 'You haven't had anything all afternoon, have you? You've just been sitting here.' He let go of her cautiously, as if she might start to thrash about, but Flo sat still, her head on her arms, sobbing. 'You have a good cry, and I'll make some tea.'

When he came back with the pot and a bottle of milk and two cups on a tray, she was sitting up a bit and mopping her face with a sodden handkerchief. Vic set down the tray and went back to the scullery. He found a clean teacloth and gently wiped her face. Then he poured the tea and put in three teaspoonfuls of sugar.

'I've been having saccharine,' Flo objected weakly. 'And I never have that much anyway.'

'Sugar's better for you when you've had a shock. It can come out of my ration. Sweet tea's what you need.' He put the cup into her hands and she bent her head to it, as if she didn't have the strength

349

to lift it. Vic poured a cup for himself, adding no sugar, and then pulled a chair round the table and sat down beside her. He put his arm around her shoulders and she leant against him.

'I've been sitting here all afternoon,' she said, between hiccuping sobs. 'Waiting for someone to come. I didn't know what else to do. I couldn't take it in, somehow.'

'Of course you couldn't. It was a terrible shock for you, here all on your own.'

'If our Denise hadn't got that job round the school—'

'I know. But you know what she's like, she won't sit about, and we do need the money for the baby.'

'She's never been one to sit about,' Flo agreed. 'And she's so self-willed anyway, we couldn't have stopped her. You couldn't ever stop our Denise doing something she'd set her mind on.'

Vic said nothing. He held her firmly, comfortingly, and poured another cup of tea.

'Don't put all that sugar in,' Flo said. 'I'm all right now.'

'You still need it. Shock doesn't wear off that soon.' But he only put in two this time. 'Denise won't be long now.'

'Oh, I'm all right now you're here.' She gave him a shaky, watery smile. 'You're a good boy, Vic. Good as a – a . . .' Her voice broke and she began to cry again. His own face twisting with sorrow, he held her close. 'Oh, Leslie, Leslie! And Mike – both of them gone. Both my boys, that used to be together all the time, both gone. My boys, my lovely, lovely boys.' She looked at him with reddened, streaming eyes. 'I used to be so proud of them when they was little. They had little red knitted suits, I made them myself from a pattern in *Woman's Weekly*, little round hats and everything, and we'd take them out for a walk on a Sunday afternoon and they'd run on ahead, looking so smart and lovely. People used to admire them. I was so proud. And now they've gone, and I'll never see them again. Neither of them. Oh, *Vic*!'

'Shh,' he whispered, both his arms holding her close as she wept against his chest. 'Shh, shh.'

He knew she wouldn't stop crying. He knew she couldn't. But the soft, hushing sound seemed to offer some small comfort, if only to reassure her that there was someone here, someone who would share her grief and listen to her words, and wipe away her tears.

It was all he could do. It was all anyone could do.

Chapter Thirty

Denise's baby was born two days after the telegram about Leslie had come. The doctor said the shock could have brought it on, but Denise had never been too sure of her dates anyway, and when the baby was born he didn't look more than a couple of weeks early. Because they thought it was more than that, Denise had been taken into hospital and stayed there for two weeks. She came home in the middle of February, on St Valentine's Day.

Thursday had managed to get leave again, four days this time. Miss Makepeace always tried to let the girls go home if there had been a loss in the family, and with a new baby arriving as well, she made no objection to the request. As before, Jenny met her at the station and they hugged, tears coming at the thought of Leslie, and then walked along the platform together.

'How are Denise and the baby? Does he look like her or Vic?'

'He looks like Winston Churchill at the moment,' Jenny said. 'Mum says she can see a likeness, she thinks he's like Mike when he was a baby, but Dad . . .' she shrugged. 'You know what Dad's like. He couldn't tell one baby from another if he was paid for it.'

'How are Mum and Dad? The news about Leslie must have upset them.'

'Yes, it did. Set them off thinking about Steve again. But Mum writes to you, doesn't she?'

'Yes, but you can't always tell from letters, can you. She tries to be so cheerful . . . I'm sure she's not, really.'

Jenny was silent for a moment, then she said, 'No, she's not all that cheerful, not all the time. Tell you the truth, Thurs, I think Dad's worried about her, and I am, too. She seems to have sort of gone back into herself. I can't explain it, but it's as if she's not really *there*. D'you know what I mean? She goes all quiet and you can see her trying not to cry.'

'She's bound to be still worrying about Steve,' Thursday said. 'It's not surprising, 'specially now. If we could just *know* what happened.'

'I know. I think about him, too. I say my prayers for him, Thurs, do you?'

'Yes, I do.' If I don't fall asleep first, she thought ruefully. But God would know that she meant to.

'Anyway, I've done what you said and joined the Red Cross, and I've applied for a job at the Infirmary as an orderly. I've put in for nursing training as well, but there's a waiting list. You wouldn't believe that, would you. You'd think they'd be taking all the girls they can get. But a lot of older women have come back into nursing to let the younger ones join up.' Jenny sighed. 'I've thought of applying to the QARNNS or the Army nurses. At this rate, the war'll be over before I get a chance to do anything.'

'Well, I hope it is. I don't want it to go on a minute longer than it's got to.' Thursday's hand went to the little naval crown she wore on her lapel, and Jenny looked at it.

'Oh, that's pretty! Where d'you get it, Thurs? Special boyfriend?' She saw Thursday's colour rise and gave a crow of delight. 'It is, isn't it! You dark horse, you! You've never breathed a word. Who is he, what's his name? Is he in the Navy? Is he one of your patients?'

'We're not allowed to fraternise with the patients,' Thurs said austerely, not mentioning the fact that, to her own knowledge, at least three VADs had regular assignations with some of the up-patients, in the sluices or the little galleys where late-night cocoa was prepared. 'And I don't know that I'd call Connor a boyfriend. We've only been out together a few times, for a walk or a drive.'

'Connor! That's an Irish name, isn't it? Is he Irish?'

'I think his family is, but he was born in England. He's a doctor. A surgeon.'

'A *surgeon*? So he must be an officer!'

'Yes, he's a commander,' Thursday admitted, feeling embarrassed.

'A *commander*? Whew!' Jenny rolled her eyes. 'Bit out of our class, isn't he?'

Thursday said nothing. This aspect was one which had bothered her the most, yet when she was with Connor the difference in their backgrounds didn't seem to matter in the least. They shared so much in their work, and when they were off duty they fell into an easy, comfortable companionship that was shot with passion when they touched. She ached to be with him again, yearning for his kisses and dreaming of a future together. It didn't matter that they had grown up in different kinds of houses, with different people. They had the Navy, the war and the hospital in common, and that was their true background.

'Well, good luck to you,' Jenny said after a moment. 'I think it's smashing. And it's time we had a bit of good news in this family. When are we going to meet him? Have you got a photo?'

'I've got one photo,' Thursday said. 'It's one he had taken for his mother before the war started, so it's two or three years old. He got her to send him a copy for me. And I don't know when you can meet him, Jen. I don't even know when I'm going to see him again myself. He's on a ship and I think they're going to the Far East.'

'Oh. Oh, so he'll be gone a long time, then.' Jenny squeezed her sister's arm. 'I'm sorry, Thurs. You must miss him ever so much.'

'Yes,' Thursday said, 'I do.'

They had walked the length of the main street and were now crossing the bridge over the River Severn. Thursday paused to set down her kitbag for a few moments and to watch its steady flow, and looked downstream to the soaring tower of the cathedral.

'I'm glad they haven't bombed it. It's awful to think of churches being smashed to pieces. We've had a horrible time around Portsmouth.'

'It's been bad here a few times,' Jenny said. 'Mostly, it's planes on their way to Birmingham. They drop their leftovers on the way back. People have been going down to the racecourse to sleep.'

'What, out in the open? They must be freezing.'

'Well, they take blankets and things, but I suppose they think it's better than being bombed.' Jenny tugged at her sister's sleeve. 'Come on, Thurs. Dizzy's waiting to show you the baby.'

Thursday hefted her kitbag again and they trudged on. The February sunshine was pale and weak, glimmering on the river, and a few early almond trees were showing their delicate blossom. Spring was coming again, the second spring since the war had begun.

'Have they chosen a name for the baby yet?'

'You'll have to ask her that yourself. When she heard you were coming, she said she'd wait till you were here before she told anyone. We're all going round to Auntie Flo's this evening to see them.'

'How do they feel about it now? Auntie Flo, and Uncle Percy?'

Jenny shrugged. 'Dunno. They don't say much. Uncle Percy doesn't anyway. Auntie Flo cries whenever she looks at the baby and it's as Uncle Percy can't bear to see the poor little kiddy. I mean, it's not *his* fault, is it? He didn't ask to be born.'

'But that's awful,' Thursday said. 'I mean, I know they must be ever so upset about Leslie but, like you say, it's not the baby's fault. I don't suppose they think it is, not really. They can't do.'

By the time they reached home her arms were aching, and Jenny carried the kitbag the last few hundred yards. Mary was sitting at the window, looking out for them, and as they approached the front door it flew open and she rushed out, her arms held wide. Patch raced out, too, leaping with delight at sight of his mistress.

'Thursday! Oh, Thursday, I'm so glad to see you!'

'It's not all that long since I was home,' Thursday protested, laughing as she hugged her mother and bent to pat the dog. 'It was only just before Christmas.'

'I know, but it seems ages. So much has happened since then.' Mary held her away and inspected her anxiously. 'You're all right, are you? You look a bit washed out.'

'We've been working hard. There's been a lot of bombing around Pompey. We've had hundreds of new patients in.'

'I was worried stiff about you in all that blitz and everything. I mean, they might just as easily drop bombs on the hospital. It's right on the harbour, isn't it – no distance at all from the city. You must have been able to see it all.'

'We're down in the cellars during the raids. We don't really see much at all.' Thursday hadn't told the family about her night with Connor during the worst of the blitz, when they'd amputated little Susie's leg. The child was out of hospital now and had gone to stay in the country, but she still wrote to Thursday every week, short letters with big, scrawled capitals and rows of kisses. 'One bomb did drop on the hospital, though – just a small one. It hit the museum and we lost our four-footed duck.'

'You lost *what*? You're having us on!'

'No, honestly, they had this duck with four legs, and we all had to look for it next day. I think someone found one foot, but that was all.' They were indoors by now and Thursday unwrapped her big coat and dropped thankfully into her father's armchair. 'Oh, it's lovely to be here!' Patch leapt up on to her lap and she hugged him close against her as he licked her face.

'It's lovely to have you here.' Mary was bright-eyed and animated, with no sign of the depression she'd been suffering. She bustled about, making tea and getting out a packet of custard creams she'd been saving specially. She came in with the tray. 'Did Jenny tell you, we're all going round to Flo's after tea to see the baby?'

Thursday nodded, but before she could speak, Jenny butted in excitedly. 'Thursday's got some news, too, Mum. Haven't you, Thurs?'

Thursday gave her an exasperated look. 'You don't have to go blurting that out the minute I get through the door.'

'What's that, then? What news? You're not going away, are you? They're not sending you overseas?'

'No, nothing like that – in fact, it's nothing at all, it's not news—'

'Oh, yes, it is.' Jenny was determined to have her say. 'She's got a boyfriend, Mum, a serious one. He's given her this lovely brooch, see?' She held up Thursday's coat. 'He's an officer and he's a doctor – a *surgeon*. What d'you think of that, then?'

Mary sat down and looked at Thursday. 'Is this true?'

Thursday sighed. 'Well, yes, I suppose so. Only we're not engaged or anything. We haven't known each other long enough. But we've met a few times, and we've been working together, and – well, we like each other, that's all.'

'It's not all,' Jenny said. 'You must like each other a lot for him to have given you this lovely brooch.'

'Well, maybe we do, but it hasn't gone any further than that.' Thursday gave her mother a reassuring look, knowing what was going through her mind. 'And it won't, because he's gone to sea now and I don't—' she felt a sudden, unexpected ache in her throat '—I don't know when we'll see each other again.' Her mouth trembled.

'Oh, Thursday. Oh, you poor girl.' Mary got up and gave her a hug. 'It's all right, lovey, we know how you feel.' Her face grew grave. 'It's how all of us feel these days – all of us who've got men away.'

There was a little silence. Then Thursday said, 'Is Auntie Flo taking it very badly? About Les?'

'Well, she's better than she might be, considering. She told me Vic was ever so good to her, he was the first one home when she had the telegram and he looked after her really well, made her a cup of tea and let her cry, and was a proper help. She says it's really made her see what a good chap he is. And I think the baby's helping. He might have come at the wrong time, but he's here now and you can't help loving a baby, can you. Denise has only been home a day or two, of course, so it's early days, and Percy'll take a bit of bringing round, but what can you do? You've got to put up with things the way they are, haven't you. It's no good wishing for what you can't have.'

There was an odd note in her voice and Thursday looked at her. Mary met her eyes and nodded.

'I've taken it in at last,' she said quietly. 'I've decided I've got to accept it. Our Steve's dead – he must be. We'd have heard by now if he wasn't. The Army should have let us know, but I suppose it just got overlooked, what with everything . . . But I'm going to ask your father to write to them and get it sorted out. There's a bit of paper we ought to have – a certificate . . . ' Her voice broke and now it was Thursday who went to her. 'That's three, just from this one family,' she said, the words muffled by Thursday's shoulder. 'Mike, Steve, and now poor young Leslie. That's why I don't want you to go away, Thursday – not overseas. Don't let them send you away, will you? Please don't let them.'

'I won't, Mum,' Thursday promised, holding her and stroking her hair. 'I won't.'

By the time Walter came home, the tears and the teacups had been cleared away. The table was laid with a clean checked cloth, the fire was lit and an appetising smell was wafting from the kitchen. His face brightened on seeing Thursday.

'Well, you're a sight for sore eyes, I must say. I wondered if you'd get here, with all the trains going doolally. And what's that I can smell – your mother killed the fatted calf, has she?'

'She'd have a job,' Mary remarked from the kitchen. 'They

haven't even had any thin calves round at Huggins' lately, let alone fat ones. It's curried corned beef balls and potato jane, with carrots.'

'Potato *who*?'

'Jane. I got the recipe off the wireless. One of Gert and Daisy's. It's layers of sliced potato and cheese and leeks, with some breadcrumbs, only since we're having corned beef I left out the cheese. Well, I did just put a spoonful in, for the taste,' she added a little guiltily.

'Well, it smells good, whoever it is. And what's for pudding, apple betty?'

Mary poked her head round the door and made a face at him. 'It's bread pudding. I made a big one so it'll see us through the week.'

'As the little boy said when he went to the butcher's for a sheep's head. Leave the eyes in, so it'll see us through the week.' Walter winked at Thursday and she grinned back. She knew his old jokes off by heart, but it was good to hear them again, and good to hear her mother responding. Perhaps it was a good thing that she'd finally made up her mind that Steve was dead, even though it did seem sad, almost a betrayal in a way. She'd hoped against hope for too long.

Do I think he's dead? Thursday asked herself, and didn't know the answer. It was too difficult. How could she know, how could anyone know, if nobody had told them – made it official? I don't know if I'll ever believe it, she thought sadly, and wondered if her mother did even now, in her heart of hearts.

The meal was warming and substantial. When it was all cleared away, they set out for Flo's and Percy's. Flo would be sure to offer them a cup of tea, Mary said, so there was no sense in having one first, and besides, Denise would probably be tired and wanting to go to bed early.

'She won't be having good nights yet, what with having to feed the baby every four hours. It's that two o'clock one that's the worst, breaks the night in half, it does.'

'Does the baby sleep all right apart from that?'

'Far as I know. Course, they've only been home a couple of days, you can't really tell. I didn't like to ask too much when Flo was round here yesterday. She's still all at sixes and sevens over Leslie.'

It was queer, Thursday thought, going to see an aunt and uncle who had lost their one remaining son and acquired a new grandson, all in the space of a couple of days. What were you supposed to do first, offer condolences or congratulations? And how was Dizzy feeling, having lost her brother? And Vic, who had hardly known him? It must be even more awkward that they were all having to live together, with all their different feelings.

They came to Flo's door and Mary lifted the knocker. Percy answered it. He looked grey and drawn, and somehow his clothes looked too big on him, as if he had shrunk. He nodded at them all, put his hand on Thursday's shoulder for a moment, then led the way indoors.

Denise was sitting in her mother's armchair. The baby was in her arms, wrapped in a white shawl that Thursday thought she remembered from when Jenny was a baby. Vic was beside her, and Flo came in from the kitchen, where she had gone to put on the kettle.

'Thursday, love! It's good to see you.'

'Oh, Auntie Flo,' Thursday said, her awkwardness vanishing as she kissed her aunt. 'I'm so sorry about Leslie. I was ever so upset when I heard.'

'I know, love. But we're getting over it now, a bit. At least I don't have to worry about him any more.' Her mouth twisted a little, but she went on determinedly, 'And have you seen our new little boy? He's a real smasher, he is.'

'Let's have a look.' Thursday grinned at her cousin and crouched down beside her. 'My, isn't he lovely! Look at those curls already. What did he weigh?'

'Seven pounds six ounces,' Denise said proudly. She looked different, Thursday thought. Plumper, which was inevitable really, since she was nursing, but different in herself. Grown-up, that was what it was. She looked more grown-up.

'He's gorgeous,' Thursday said. The baby's eyelids fluttered open and the milky blue eyes gazed at her. 'Look, he knows me already. It's your Auntie Thursday,' she crooned, and then laughed at herself. 'No, it isn't! I'm his cousin, aren't I? Second cousin – or is it first cousin once removed? I can never—'

'It'll be *removed* all right, if you don't stop talking nonsense,' her father told her, pushing her gently aside. 'Come on, Denise, love, let the dog see the rabbit.'

'Well, that's nice, I must say! Calling my son a rabbit.'

Walter took no notice. He touched the baby's cheek with the tip of one finger and then glanced round at Percy. 'Fine lad, isn't he, Perce? What d'you think of your grandson, then?'

Percy grunted something and Thursday saw Denise's eyes go to him. There was a pleading look on her face, but her father didn't return the glance. He was busying himself with his bootlaces and didn't look up. *Wouldn't* look up, she thought with sudden anger.

'Where's the proud father, then?' Walter went on, apparently determined to make his brother-in-law acknowledge the baby's presence. 'Thursday was hoping he'd be here.'

Percy flushed a dull red, but before he could speak Denise said, 'He'll be in soon. He had to do some overtime. We're hoping to get a place of our own,' she said to Thursday, although the words were obviously meant for her father. 'Somewhere we feel a bit more welcome.'

Percy dropped the boot he was holding. His face was red and his eyes angry. 'Now, look here, my girl—'

'*No!*' Flo darted in from the kitchen, where she and Mary had gone to make tea. She put her hands on her hips and faced her husband. 'No, *you* look here! We're just about fed up with this, all of us. What good's it going to do, treating our Denise like something the cat brought in? Eh? Tell me that. Isn't it enough we've lost both our boys? Isn't it enough that she's the only one we've got left, and this might be the only grandchild we ever have? I've told you and *told* you, Perce, we've got to look on the little mite as a gift from God. And I thought you agreed with me, yet ever since she came back from hospital you've been acting like a bear with a sore head. Why? *Why?*'

Percy's glance shifted sideways. He stared down at his feet in their thick socks, and muttered something. Mary and Walter looked at each other in embarrassment and Thursday knelt down again beside Denise.

Flo sighed and put her hands on her husband's arms. 'Come on, Perce,' she said more gently. 'It's not like you to take it out on an innocent little baby. What is it, now?'

'Well, what do you *think* it is?' he said miserably. 'It's everything. This war – the bombs – our Mike, and now our Les. Steve, not heard of since last June. Everything's upside down. And on top of it all, I've got to come to terms with – well, you know. The whole street whispering behind their hands. Blokes at work sniggering. And we were lucky to get away without a court case, you know. It was touch and go, that was.'

'I know, but we did get away without that, and thank heaven for it. And thank heaven for this little chap as well.' Flo moved over to her daughter and laid a tender hand on the white shawl. 'I know it's not happened as any of us wanted it, Perce, but the little boy's here now and we've got to forget all that. He's our flesh and blood. And Vic's as good a boy as you'd wish to meet. What's more, he'll be gone himself before long, so why don't we all try to make this a happy home for him and Denise in whatever time they've got left.'

Thursday stared at her cousin. 'Has Vic got his papers, then?'

Denise nodded and bit her lips. 'He got them yesterday. They let him defer it till the baby was born, but he's got to go in a fortnight.' She looked at her father. 'Please, Dad. Do what Mum says – let bygones be bygones. We're sorry for what we did, but I can't say I'm sorry to have my baby. And I'm not sorry me and Vic had to get married neither. At least when he goes away, I'll know he's mine, and I'll have a bit of him left to look after.'

Percy stood irresolute for a moment, then he came over to her, bent and kissed her awkwardly.

'All right, love. I can't say I've enjoyed feeling like I have. And Vic's done his best, I'll give him that. But about you finding a place of your own . . . ' He shrugged and looked at his wife. 'I don't see as how we can allow that, do you, Flo? 'Specially if Vic's going away. We've got to have a bit of life about the place.'

Flo gave a sigh of relief. 'Well, that's settled, then, and thank heaven for it. I was beginning to think you'd never see sense. Mary, did you put the whistle on the kettle? It must be boiling itself dry out there.'

They hurried out to the kitchen again and Thursday sat on the chair beside Denise and held her arms out for the baby. She looked down into the tiny face and thought she'd never held such a small one before. Jenny sat beside her, playing with the baby's tiny fingers. Percy went to have a wash, and Walter sat down and picked up the evening paper. Mr Churchill was going to broadcast again tomorrow, it said, and there would be one of J.B. Priestley's 'Postscripts'. He liked them, the man was down to earth and didn't mince his words.

Vic came in just as Flo brought the tea through. He came straight over to kiss Denise, and then gave Thursday a quick peck before bending to his son.

'Well, what d'you think? Isn't he a smasher? Look at those legs, he's going to be a footballer for certain.'

'He's lovely,' Thursday said. 'But what we all want to know is what you're going to call him. Nobody seems to have any idea.'

Vic grinned. 'Dizzy wanted to wait till you were here and we were all together before telling anyone. But I reckon we can now, eh, Diz? I must say, I can't wait much longer myself!'

Denise smiled. She held out her arms for her baby and Thursday laid him carefully back on her lap. Vic sat on the arm of her chair and they both looked at the expectant faces around them.

'I hope you'll be pleased with what we've decided,' Denise said. There were tears in her voice. 'It's partly because of – of when he was born, and partly because we just wanted to keep their names alive.' She looked at her parents and added quickly, 'But we won't do it if you don't like the idea. We don't want anyone to feel upset about it.'

'Upset about what?' Flo began, but Thursday had already guessed what Denise was going to say. She laid her hand swiftly over her aunt's and waited.

'We want to call him Leslie Michael,' Denise said, and then she looked at Mary and added, 'Leslie Michael Stephen. After all three of our boys. That's what he's going to be, because he's like that man said on the wireless the other day – he's our hope for the future.'

There was a silence. Flo drew in a long, shuddering breath and put her apron to her eyes. Mary patted her arm, heedless of her own flowing tears, and Thursday squeezed her hand. Percy, across the room, cleared his throat.

'Well, I think that's a very nice thing to do, our Denise. A very nice thing to do. And I think we all ought to have a drink to mark the occasion and celebrate. Flo, where's that bottle of sherry we had at Christmas?'

Half crying, half laughing, Flo hurried to the sideboard to get it out. Jenny produced glasses and when they all had one, Percy cleared his throat again and called for silence.

'I want to propose a toast,' he said, and held his glass towards Vic and Denise. 'To Denise, Vic and little Leslie. May they always be a happy family. And to all the rest of us as well.' He looked at his glass and added quietly, 'To families everywhere.'

'To families everywhere,' they echoed softly, and clinked glasses.

Percy set down his glass and moved across the room to his daughter. He held out his arms.

'Well,' he said, a little gruffly, 'what about it, our Denise? Aren't you going to let me hold my grandson?'

Chapter Thirty-One

Every major city seemed to be on the Germans' list. As spring advanced, so did the Luftwaffe. City after city found itself devastated by raids which left thousands dead or homeless. London, the main target, was hit night after night, with even Buckingham Palace struck by two bombs.

Portsmouth had its second blitz exactly two months after the first. Thousands of bombs were aimed at the naval dockyard and its ships, the shore establishments and the marine barracks at Eastney. Once again, Haslar found itself besieged with wounded sailors and marines, and the QARNNs and VADs were run off their feet looking after them. Thursday was too busy to worry very much about Connor. She scribbled a page or two to him every night when she went to bed, and sometimes managed more, and she lay for a few minutes every night longing for him and praying that he would be safe, but sleep overcame her so quickly that she felt almost cheated when she woke next morning. I want longer to think about him, she thought, I want more time. But time was another luxury that the war had taken away.

In April, they heard that Portsmouth's sister naval port, Plymouth, had been almost flattened. There was nothing left of the centre but rubble, with a lone clock tower standing in its midst and services still being determinedly held in the shell of the city church. Coventry was attacked again, and in May it was the turn of Liverpool, with over a week of bombing that left nearly four thousand people dead and seventy thousand homeless. The brilliance of another 'bomber's moon' brought more devastation to the North-East and then London's worst raid yet.

'I don't see as they *can* get any worse,' Elsie said, staring at the pictures in the newspaper. 'Look at it. Just look at it. The only comfort's that we're giving as good as we get. They reckon we've done just as much damage to some of them German cities – Kiel and Berlin and everywhere. If they knock us flat, we'll do worse to them and no mistake!'

'So there are people being bombed out of their homes there, just the same as here,' Thursday said. 'People losing their families and everything they've got, little children being killed, people looking for somewhere to live . . . It can't be right, Elsie. There ought to be another way.'

But it seemed that there was no other way. The fighting continued, spreading across the world. Russia, Yugoslavia, Hungary, Greece, Italy, Africa – all were being drawn into the conflict. Only the Far East and America still stood apart, and even Japan had begun to wage its own war with China.

A few days later came the first good news. Italy, after less than a year allied to Germany, had surrendered. That made one less country to fight – even if it also brought thousands of prisoners to be fed and looked after. And at least they could be made to work . . . But almost before this had sunk in, the country was stunned again by the news of the sinking of HMS *Hood*, the world's largest battle cruiser. It had gone down in only four minutes, with only three out of the fourteen hundred men aboard surviving.

At Haslar, any naval loss was keenly felt. The patients were depressed and gloomy, and the nurses were hard put to it to stay cheerful. In fact, as Patsy said, it seemed wrong, in a way, even to try. Nobody should be ashamed of being upset about that lovely ship and all those brave men.

'They say Mr Churchill's told them to go all out to sink the *Bismarck*,' Elsie said. 'He's taken it personally – says he'd go and fire the guns himself, if he could.' And indeed it was only three days before the German ship went the same way, chased across the Atlantic by over a hundred ships. She finally sank a few hundred miles from the coast of Brittany, losing over two thousand men.

It seemed a fitting revenge. But Thursday couldn't help adding the two crews together. Nearly four thousand men lost altogether, all sailors, all brave and mostly young. Four thousand families left to grieve. Four thousand wives and sweethearts, and heaven knew how many children, parents, brothers, sisters, friends. What was happening to the world?

'It's no good thinking like that,' Elsie told her. 'You'll drive yourself mad with it, Thurs. You've just got to close your mind to it.'

Thursday knew she was right. But it seemed so wrong, almost wicked somehow, to close your mind to all that suffering. Yet what good would it do to anyone if you didn't, if you tried to take all the suffering into yourself and, as Elsie had warned, drove yourself mad doing it? You wouldn't be able to do anything. You wouldn't be able to nurse the men who needed you. You'd need a nurse yourself, and what help would that be?

Why, it was practically treason.

'We need something to cheer us up,' Elsie decided, and on their next half-day they cycled over the patched-up Pneumonia Bridge and went to the Swiss Café for tea. They debated going 'over the water', as Elsie's gran called it, to Portsmouth, but the thought of the devastation there put them off. It was bad enough in Gosport, with bombsites like missing teeth along the high street, and the market hall no more than a shell.

They had tea and penny buns, and then left their bikes propped against the wall and strolled down to the Esplanade. The harbour was as active as always, with the ferryboats bustling to and fro and ships moored up in the dockyard. The girls leaned on the railings and gazed at the busy scene.

'It's a wonder there's so much left,' Patsy remarked. 'The Semaphore Tower's still there, and HMS *Victory*, and the cathedral, *and* the station, even though it was on fire that time. You'd have thought with all that bombing there'd be nothing left standing at all.'

'There isn't much in the middle,' Elsie said. 'Commercial Road and all around there are just nothing. McIlroys was all burnt out, you know, and the Landport Drapery Bazaar. I dunno how they're ever going to build it all up again.' She sighed.

Thursday put her arm around her. 'How are your mum and dad, and Eddy?'

'Oh, much as you'd expect. Getting on with it. Mum's managed to get a few bits of furniture together – lucky she'd got all the savings certificates and things down the shelter with her – and the house they've got's not bad. There's no electric, though, and not even any gas upstairs, they have to use candles . . . And Eddy seems to have settled all right, out near Winchester he is with the school, so he's got his mates around him. As Mum says, you mustn't grumble.'

Patsy was staring down at the pontoon where one of the ferryboats was just pulling away, allowing the next to take its place. 'Look, isn't that the one that went to Dunkirk?'

'So it is,' Thursday said. 'The *Ferry King*. Let's give her a cheer – she deserves it.' They waved and cheered at the little boat and the skipper, standing on his bridge, waved back. The little exchange lifted their spirits and as they turned away Patsy said, with a sudden, shy little smile, 'I've got some news for you.'

'What?' The other two stopped and stared at her. 'What news? What haven't you been telling us, Pats?'

'You've got a funny look on your face,' Thursday said. 'Come on, out with it. What have you been up to?'

Patsy's twitching mouth broke into a broad grin and she laughed. 'Can't you guess? It's me and Roy – we're getting married!'

'Getting *married*? But you're not even engaged.'

'Yes, we are,' Patsy said, smiling.

'Since when?' Elsie demanded. 'You've been holding out on us, Patsy Martin, and us supposed to be your best friends.'

'Since last week. I never said anything because of all the *Hood* and *Bismarck* business – there just didn't seem to be a good moment. But the ship's going to be in Plymouth next week for repairs and they're all getting a bit of leave. He says we can get a special licence and get married at the weekend, and then we can have a honeymoon. I've seen Madam, and she says I can go. I can have a whole week! A whole *week*.' She sighed blissfully. 'I can't believe it's true.'

'Nor can I,' Elsie said. 'I can't believe you've gone and got all this fixed up and never said a word about it. Didn't we have breakfast together yesterday? Haven't we just had tea in the Swiss Café? Don't we sleep in the same dormitory every night? What d'you mean, never been a good moment?'

'Well, I wanted to tell the two of you when we were out of the hospital, not when there were lots of other people waggling their ears. And I never got a chance in the Swiss Café, you were going on about that tiffy you met at the dance last Saturday.' Patsy giggled. 'Anyway, guess who's going to be best man.'

The other two stared at her. 'Not Doug Brighton!' Thursday said at last.

'That's right. You know Roy and him have always been good mates, and Doug's been on the same ship this last twelvemonth. He asks after you now and again,' she said slyly to Thursday.

'Oh, yeah? Pull the other one,' Thursday said scornfully. Even after Tony had told her about Doug's heroism, she'd never been able to take to him and although they'd accepted one another on the jaunts the six of them had had together, they'd never become real friends. 'More likely to be Elsie he asks after.'

'No, it was never more than a bit of fun between us,' Elsie said. There had been a number of young men since for her to have fun with, mostly matelots, but she'd not found anyone to be serious about. 'Trouble is, there's never time for anything more than that. You just start getting interested and it's off to sea again, like the song says. And you know it's probably true, a wife in every port. Sweetheart, anyway. Well, you can't blame 'em, can you, after weeks at sea.'

They strolled back up the high street and collected their bikes. Cycling back up Stoke Road to the White Hart, and then along Avenue Road to Alverstoke, Thursday thought longingly of Connor. He was in Singapore now and there was no knowing when he'd be back. He was keeping her VAD badge like a talisman, he told her in his letters, always close to his heart, to keep him safe. She hoped it would – but how could a cloth badge, even if it bore the King's crown, keep a man safe in these perilous times?

Already there was anxious talk of the Japanese threat to Singapore, and Mr Churchill was known to have asked America for help, but so far the United States was unwilling to become involved. Like Switzerland, it seemed, it would stay neutral unless threatened itself. And Singpaore was British, not American. Suppose the Japanese invaded? Suppose Connor's ship was lost, as the *Hood* had been lost . . .

Her thoughts refused to take her any further and she came back with a start to the present.

'When is this wedding, then?' Elsie asked. 'And where's it going to be? You're not going to go to Plymouth and leave us in the lurch, are you?'

'No, Roy and Doug can get warrants to come to Pompey, so it makes more sense to do it here.' She looked up at the little grey church they were passing. 'I'd like it to be here at Alverstoke, but if the rector can't do it, we'll have to make it the registry office in Gosport. There's so many weddings now, with men going overseas, that the churches are all booked up. We don't mind too much, the main thing is to get married. We're hoping it'll be next Friday,' she added. 'Sixth of June.'

'Next *Friday*? We'll never be ready in time! I suppose we are asked, aren't we?' Thursday added.

'Of course you're asked. I want everyone to be there. Mum and Dad can't make it, so I want all my mates. Anyway, you two're going to be my bridesmaids.'

'Oh, are we? Thanks for telling us! What are we supposed to wear?'

'Oh, anything,' Patsy said carelessly. 'Something pretty. A frock'll do.'

'Well, I wasn't going to wear slacks and a jumper,' Elsie retorted. 'Honestly, Pats, I do think you could've told us before. And where's this honeymoon going to be, then? Lee?'

'Not on your life! We're going to Cornwall. See,' she explained as they coasted along Clayhall Road, 'Roy's warrant will be a return, and I can get one to go down there, and that'll be a return too, so the fares as far as Plymouth and mine back here won't cost us anything. We can get a train to Cornwall – Penzance or somewhere – and find a room there for a few nights.' She stretched out her arms, cycling no-handed for a few yards. 'It'll be lovely.'

'Even lovelier if you've got both arms in plaster!' Thursday said. 'What about a wedding dress?'

'Shan't bother. I'm just going to get a couple of new summer frocks that I can wear any time. Well, one really nice one and a more ordinary one, I expect. I thought I'd go over to Pompey and do some shopping next Monday. We could all go, we're not on duty in the afternoons.'

'I am,' Thursday said. 'You know how busy we are in Theatre.'

'Oh, yes, I forgot. Well, you don't need to buy anything anyway, you can make yourself a frock. Go down that shop in Stoke Road, they've got some nice materials in there, even with the shortages.'

'And when am I supposed to do all this sewing?' Thursday enquired. 'In between passing the boss his scalpels and things?'

They swept in through the gates, waving cheekily to the sailor on guard, and then dismounted to walk down the quarter-deck. Thursday had once been seen cycling along its length, when she was late back from a trip into town, and had been severely reprimanded by Miss Makepeace. Next time, she'd been told, it would be gates for a week. They didn't dare take that risk, with Patsy's wedding so close.

Next morning, she slipped in early, taking Elsie's advice to go to the haberdasher's and buy some material for a new frock. She had just enough money, and chose a fine, pale blue cotton. The woman measured it out for her and told her she was lucky to have it. 'We've got hardly anything left now. It's a wonder they haven't put clothes on ration, like everything else. I don't know what we're supposed to live on, now there's almost nothing to sell.'

Thursday pedalled back with her parcel. Even on Saturdays, operations were still carried out and she was to be on duty at nine. A year ago, she thought, men were being brought back from Dunkirk. A year ago, we were just hearing about Mike, and Steve. And we still haven't heard anything about Steve. He must be dead. He must be.

Tears came to her eyes as she pushed her bike up the steep slope of the bridge. She paused at the top and gazed over Haslar Lake towards the church tower and the big blue gasholder. The little boats were there, the flotilla of yachts and sailing dinghies that had set off so bravely to cross the Channel a year ago. A few of them hadn't returned, but the rest lay beneath her, rocking very gently on the calm waters. Hundreds, perhaps thousands of men had been saved by those little boats. Mike could have been brought back in one. So could Steve. Instead, both had been left behind to die.

Oh, Steve, she thought sadly. Oh, Steve, I miss you so much . . .

It was lucky that Thursday had bought her material on Saturday, because on Monday it was suddenly announced that clothes would be rationed. Patsy and Elsie stared at each other in dismay, and Thursday tried not to feel smug. Her frock was already half-made, and she was pleased with it. Her pleasure was spoilt when she saw that Patsy was near to tears.

'Can't we buy anything new at all?'

Elsie was studying the *Daily Express*. 'It says we've got to use our margarine coupons till they can issue special ration cards. We'll get sixty-six coupons, to last us a year.'

'So what does that mean? What does a coupon buy?' Patsy demanded. A fresh thought struck her. 'We don't even *have* our own ration books, the hospital's got them! They're not going to hand over our marge coupons, are they – stands to reason.'

'There's a list here. Examples. A man's overcoat needs sixteen coupons—'

'Never mind men's overcoats!' Patsy broke in. 'What about a frock?'

'Well, a woollen dress will be eleven—'

'It's the middle of flaming June, you twerp!'

Thursday giggled and Patsy turned on her. 'It's all right for you, sitting there all pleased with yourself because you've got yours. How am I going to get anything now? I'll have to get married in my uniform, that's what! And spend my honeymoon in it, too, more than likely.'

'Oh, come on, Pats, you've got some civvy clothes, haven't you? What about that red skirt you wore to Kimballs?'

'If you remember,' Patsy said coldly, 'I wore a black blouse with it and it got torn when the wardrobe door stuck. I am *not* getting married in a red skirt and a black blouse with a tear in one sleeve.'

'If it's not wool, you can get a frock for seven coupons,' Elsie said on a note of triumph. 'There, that's better, isn't it? And you can get a new blouse for five, and a pair of stockings for two, and a couple of nice hankies to wipe away your tears for just one. So you can be fitted out for fifteen coupons and still have enough marge for Christmas!'

Patsy gave her a withering look and turned to Thursday, who was giggling helplessly. 'You're useless, the pair of you. I might as well forget about getting married at all. Roy's not going to want to walk up the aisle with a nurse, he'll feel like a flipping invalid. Oh, why did this have to happen now? Why couldn't they have given us some warning?'

'Because everyone would have rushed out and bought up every

scrap of clothing in the shops, like they did when food was put on ration,' Thursday said. 'Look, Patsy, it's not the end of the world. You can have my frock.'

Patsy stared at her. 'What frock? I thought you didn't have anything decent either.'

'The one I'm making, goof! We're much the same size, I can easily do any alterations to fit you. And it's a really pretty blue. What do you say?'

'But it's for you. You chose the material and the pattern and everything. I can't take it off you.'

'You're not going to. I'm lending it to you – not giving it. You can wear it for your wedding and you can take it away for your honeymoon, and then I want it back, all right? Look, it's the ideal answer – something borrowed, something blue!' Thursday jumped up. 'Anyway, I haven't got time to argue about it – I'm due in the theatre. It's settled.' She grinned at Elsie. 'Don't think I can find anything to fit you as well, but if you've got anything we can alter I could have a go.'

Elsie didn't have anything, but when the other VADs heard what was happening they sorted through their few civilian clothes and produced an assortment of garments which they spread out on the beds. When Thursday came off duty she and Elsie inspected them thoughtfully.

'Blimey, it looks like a blooming jumble sale in here,' Elsie commented. 'Whose is that enormous grey thing? I'd look like a barrage balloon in that!'

'I don't know, I've never seen anyone wearing it. What about this pink? No, perhaps not,' Thursday added hastily. Pink was definitely not Elsie's colour. 'Tell you what, suppose we all wear blue, all three of us? Patsy'll be in my new frock, and I could wear my blue check skirt and this white peasant blouse of Annie Gardner's, and you could – you could . . .'

'Yeah? I could what?'

Thursday shrugged helplessly. 'There doesn't seem to be anything else blue here.' The real trouble was that Elsie was the fattest girl in the dormitory, and even if there had been something blue, it was hardly likely it would have fitted her. 'Hang on a mo – what's this?'

'It's a nightie,' Elsie said scornfully, looking at the flowing garment Thursday was holding up. 'I am *not* wearing a blooming *nightie*.'

'I don't see why not. It's perfectly respectable. And it's quite pretty, too – look at these little flowers embroidered all round the neckline.' Thursday held it against Elsie. 'I bet it'd fit you, too, it looks nice and loose. Look, we could make a belt with that blue wool Jeanie got to make a baby coat with – she could knit that up in no time – and if we both wear little caps made of flowers, we'd look all sort of countrified. And Vera Hapgood's got a waistcoat you could borrow, just to set it off. You don't need to do it up. You'll look a real stunner, Else!'

'Vera Hapgood won't ever lend me her waistcoat,' Elsie said, grudgingly allowing Thursday to drape the nightdress around her body. 'She wouldn't lend her own mother tuppence.'

'Yes, she will, we'll make her.' Thursday wasn't going to take no for an answer. 'Look, Elsie, it's either this or your VAD uniform, and *I* think it'll look very nice, so what about it?'

'Oh – all right. Maybe it won't look so bad. At least it'll be comfy.' Elsie giggled suddenly. 'And if I get too tired, I'll be ready for bed, won't I!'

Thursday sighed with relief. She was going to have enough to do, she reckoned, finishing the blue dress and altering the peasant blouse so that it wouldn't slip too far off her shoulders. The last thing she wanted to do was to have to dismantle something with enough turn in the seams – even if you could find such a thing – to fit Elsie.

'That's settled, then,' she said. 'Now let's get to work ... '

Everyone was on tenterhooks that nothing would happen to prevent the wedding. To Patsy's delight, she had managed to book the church for half past four on Friday afternoon. Saturday was all booked up, the rector said, but he would be very happy to marry her and Roy on Friday.

'We'll just have to hope the train from Plymouth isn't held up. Roy and Doug are leaving at eight o'clock, so they ought to make it.'

All the VADs and even some of the QARNNs who were able to get off duty were going to attend. Miss Makepeace would be there, and so would at least two of the doctors. Patsy rolled her eyes when she heard this. She hadn't thought they'd even known she existed, she said. VADs were invisible, weren't they?

'Unless something goes wrong,' Elsie said. 'Then they can see us plain enough.'

'Mind you,' Patsy said with a wink at Thursday, '*some* of 'em know we exist. How *is* the Commander these days, Thursday?'

'Shut up,' Thursday said, laughing. 'As a matter of fact, he's very well, thank you. I had a letter this morning.' She touched her breast pocket, where the letter crackled beneath Auntie Maudie's watch. It had come with the first post that morning and she'd slipped away through the gate to the seawall to read it alone, looking out over the crinkled blue waters of the Solent.

My Darling Thursday,

It's so different here in the Far East, and yet I seem to feel you with me with every step I take. Perhaps one day, when all this is over, we'll come here together and I can show you this strange land, with the narrow, bustling streets filled with rickshaws and Chinese pedlars, and the rivers crammed with sampans and Chinese junks. The sun is hot by day and the moon is a soft, saffron gold by night, and I miss you every moment, more than I can say, more than I can ever show you – but oh, how I long to show you and to love you, and when this is over I swear we'll never be parted again, never. I love you, my darling, and I shall always be yours, your very own, your deeply loving Connor.

Thursday had sat for as long as she dared, holding the letter in her hands, reading the words over and over again until she knew them by heart. She stared at the hard blue of the sea and thought of a softer light, a mellow saffron moon that threw a golden carpet down upon the gently moving waters of the river, and she gazed at the great grey warship that was steaming out of the harbour and thought of the sampans and junks of a more ancient world.

Connor had said nothing about the Japanese threat to Singapore, perhaps because he didn't want to worry her, perhaps because it had no place in his words of love. Most of his letters were more prosaic, telling her as much as he could about their work, although all spoke also of his love. But this was the first he had ever written that was so poetic, and through Thursday's tender love there wove a cold, narrow thread of fear. It was almost as if he were saying goodbye . . .

Suddenly she remembered where she was. The other girls were

looking at her with sympathy, and Patsy's bantering tone changed to a more compassionate one. 'You must miss him ever so much.'

'Yes, I do. But I'm not the only one, am I? And your Roy will be going away again soon, so we'll be back in the same boat. Again. We've just got to put up with it.'

'That's right. And it's the same for naval wives even when there isn't a war on, when you come to think about it. They're always being left on their own.' Patsy made a humorous face. 'Maybe we should think again while we've got the chance – find some nice young motor mechanic who works in the local garage to marry!'

Friday was bright and sunny. The girls were on duty most of the day and came off at three, with just time to have a quick bath – 'no more than five inches, mind, even if it is your wedding day!' Elsie said with a grin – and get changed. By ten past four they were arrayed in their finery, and Patsy was in a blind panic.

'How do I look? Suppose he takes one look and changes his mind. We haven't seen each other for nearly a year! What if we're making a mistake? Thursday, I feel sick—'

'No, you don't. It's just butterflies. All you've got to do is get them flying in formation. And you look smashing.' Ruefully, Thursday surveyed the dress she had intended to wear herself. It suited Patsy, with its slim waist and flared skirt and the pretty, sweetheart neckline. Someone had produced a blue necklace that went just right with it, and Miss Makepeace had given Patsy a bunch of blue and white flowers from the hospital garden. Thursday had woven circular headdresses from some raffia, with more blue flowers poked into them, and she, Patsy and Elsie set these on their heads.

'You look the bee's knees,' Elsie agreed, adding wryly, 'Dunno so much about me in this nightie!'

'Don't be daft, you look lovely, and nobody would ever know it was a nightie. It looks more like a ball gown – really posh.' Patsy gave one last look in the mirror. 'Well, come on, we'd better go. It'll take us a good ten minutes to walk there.'

Thursday gave herself a last, hasty glance in the mirror and then, as an afterthought, snatched up the little silver watch Auntie Maudie had given her. She pinned it on to her dress, her fingers shaking a little. It's been lucky for me so far, she thought. It'd be a shame to leave it off today.

All the VADs and nurses who were able to come were waiting outside, and they cheered as Patsy and her bridesmaids emerged. They were all in uniform, and they made a protective group around the three for the walk through Clayhall to Alverstoke. Laughing and excited, they made their way towards the gate.

The sailors on guard saluted smartly, and then one of them held up his hand for attention. They all fell silent.

'I hope you're not going to make a speech,' Patsy said. 'No funny jokes, mind.'

'I'm not going to say anything,' the matelot said. 'There's a phone message for someone. A telegram. VAD Tilford, it says here. Isn't that the girl they call Thursday?'

'Yes!' Thursday stepped forward, her heart thudding. 'A telegram for me? A phone call?'

'Well, I can't make out which it is, but you've to go back to D Block straight away and see the Red Cross Commandant.' He looked at her. 'It sounded pretty urgent.'

'Oh, no!' She looked frantically round for Patsy. 'Pats, did you hear that? I've got to go—'

'It's all right. We – we'll wait for you.' Patsy stared at her fearfully. 'Roy won't mind.'

Thursday shook her head. 'You can't do that. It could be anything. Mum – Dad – our Jen – I might have to go home. Madam wouldn't have sent a message down to the gate if it hadn't been serious. Anyway, she's supposed to be coming to the wedding, too.' She put a hand to her face. 'It might be Connor . . .' She turned away.

'I'll come with you,' Elsie said, but Thursday pushed her away.

'No. *No*. You go with Patsy. I – I'll come if I can.' Her voice made it plain that she didn't expect to be able to. 'Oh, Pats, I'm sorry. I'll have to go—' She was off, running back along the road, heading for D Block.

The others gazed after her.

'Poor Thursday,' Patsy said. 'I wonder what it's about.'

'Whatever it is,' Elsie said, 'there's nothing we can do to help her now. Madam's with her, she'll see to it all. You've got a wedding to go to.'

'I know,' Patsy said, turning to go through the gate. 'But it won't seem the same, somehow, without Thursday there.'

＊

Thursday arrived panting at the top of the stairs. Miss Makepeace's office door was open and she was inside, pacing anxiously to and fro. She turned as Thursday skidded to a halt at the door, and gave her a warm smile.

'Tilford, child, you'll have an accident if you race about like that. There's been a telephone call for you.'

'Yes, Madam. Is it a telegram?'

'Not exactly, but I gather there's *been* a telegram. It was your mother. She's ringing again in five minutes, from a telephone kiosk, I gather.'

'Yes, Madam. That'll be at the top of the street. We don't have a telephone at home.'

'No, I understand. Well, she said she would ring back to see if we'd managed to catch you.' The phone on her desk rang and she picked it up quickly, listened for a moment and then handed it over to Thursday.

Her hand shaking, Thursday held the receiver to her ear. She heard her mother's voice, made small and unfamiliar. Almost without thinking, she lifted her other hand to touch the watch at her breast.

'Thursday? Is that you?'

'Yes, Mum, it's me. What's happened? Is it Dad? Or our Jen? It's not the baby, is it?'

'No, no, none of them. It's all right, Thursday.' For the first time she realised that the strange tone in her mother's voice wasn't grief, but excitement. 'Thursday, it's our *Steve*! He's *alive*! He's a prisoner of war somewhere in Germany, but he's *alive* and we've had a telegram to say so, and we'll be getting a letter soon. Thursday, did you hear me? It's our Steve! He's *alive*, he really is, he's not dead after all, he's *alive*! Our Steve!' Her voice went on, repeating the words over and over again, while Thursday stood, holding the receiver tightly against her ear, unable to speak, her other hand fastened tightly over the watch. Slowly, her eyes filled with tears. She looked at Miss Makepeace and realised that she already knew, that she'd wanted Thursday to hear it from her own mother, and she gave her a trembling, tearful smile. At last, Mary Tilford's voice faded into silence, and Thursday took a deep, wavering breath and managed to speak.

'Oh, Mum. That's wonderful. It's *wonderful*.' There must be other words, but she couldn't think of them. 'Oh, Mum, you must be so pleased. But where's he been all this time?'

'We don't know yet. The letter will tell us. Oh, Thursday, I can't tell you – can't think straight – I just had to ring up.' Thursday heard a little sob, then her mother seemed to take a deep breath and went on more steadily. 'Here, aren't you supposed to be at a wedding?'

'Yes. You just caught us, we were on our way out of the gate. It's in ten minutes!'

'Well, you'd better go, then, hadn't you.' Mary's voice sounded suddenly brisk, though there was still a betraying tremor in it. 'Go on, Thursday. I'll write as soon as I get some news. You go on now, and enjoy yourself – I want to go round to Flo's. And there's your gran too, I must go and see her. And—'

The phone suddenly cut off. Mary's money had run out. Thursday handed the receiver back to Miss Makepeace and felt a huge smile break out over her face, even though tears were pouring down her cheeks.

'Oh, Madam. It's my brother. We thought he was lost at Dunkirk, and he's turned up as a POW. Isn't it wonderful?'

'It is indeed.' Miss Makepeace came round her desk and gave Thursday a kiss. 'I'm so pleased, my dear. And now we'd better get our skates on or we're going to be late for this wedding. Come along.'

Thursday glanced at the clock on the wall, above the big world map that showed where the war was being waged and where VADs were already being sent. 'We're going to be late anyway. It's in ten minutes' time – we'll never get there now, even if we run.'

'There's no need for that.' Madam led her briskly out of the office and down the stairs. 'Sister Burton has organised a taxi for us. It should be waiting now.'

'A taxi!' Thursday caught her breath as she saw the car waiting at the gate. Together with Madam and the sister, she scrambled in and the car swept down Clayhall Road, to arrive at Alverstoke Church just as the organist was beginning to play 'Here Comes The Bride'.

Patsy and Elsie stared as Thursday arrived, breathless, beside them.

'What was it? What's happened?'

She shook her head, smiling. 'Tell you afterwards. Look, Roy's there, he's waiting for you. Let's get you married off, Pats. Let's make this the happiest day of your life!'

It already was, for her, she thought as she and Elsie followed their friend up the aisle. Maybe there would be others as happy, even happier, in the future, but she couldn't remember any that soared higher than this. Her brother, thought dead in the sea and the bullets and bombs of Dunkirk, was alive. After a year – a whole year – of waiting, and just as they had finally given up their last shreds of hope, he had been returned to them. He wasn't coming home, he wouldn't be coming home until the war was over – whenever that might be – but he was safe. They could write to him, send him comforts. They could get letters from him, letters that he had written on paper that he had touched.

He was alive.

Thursday stood beside Elsie and watched as their friend stood beside her groom and made her marriage vows. Will this be me one day, she thought, me and Connor? Will it all come right in the end after all?

She didn't know, nobody knew, how long this war would last. Already, it had been nearly two years. It might be another two, perhaps even longer. But there could still be moments like this – this moment of soaring joy that her brother was alive after all, that people like Patsy and Roy could still find happiness for even a little while, that the sun could shine and a church be full of friends who wished each other well. She glanced round and saw their faces – Jeanie, Ellen and Louisa, all of them. Even Vera Hapgood who had, after all, agreed to lend Elsie her waistcoat.

They're lovely people, Thursday thought. They're all good friends, and together we're doing a good job, a worthwhile job. And we'll go on doing it, as long as the war goes on.

She sent a thought to Steve, and another to Connor, and to all the men who were still serving or who, like her brother, had finished their war and had to wait. Not all of them would survive, she knew – there would be many more deaths before it was all over. But here in this little church, on a sunny June day, seeing the radiance on Patsy's face and the joy of all her friends, she could not doubt that the war would be won in the end.

However long it took, the struggle would one day be over. The world would, once again, walk free.

A Promise to Keep

For Aidan

FOREWORD

Once again, I owe a debt of gratitude to Helen Long, whose book *Change Into Uniform* inspired both this novel and the previous 'Thursday' story, *A Girl Called Thursday*.

Helen Long was a remarkable woman. A debutante in the 1930s, she volunteered as a Red Cross VAD and served in Haslar Royal Naval Hospital in Gosport, Hampshire, and then in Egypt. She was one of the first members of the RN Blood Transfusion Service, and after the war became one of the first BEA air hostesses, before marrying Dr Aidan Long, whom she had met at Haslar.

Helen wrote several other books, the most significant being *Safe Houses Are Dangerous* – the story of her uncle, Dr Georges Rodocanachi, and his wife, Fanny, whose flat in Marseilles was the headquarters of the O'Leary escape line, bringing many Allied servicemen to safety from occupied France. She contributed frequently to such magazines as *The Lady* and in the last year or so of her life was awarded the Silver Rose Bowl of the Society of Women Writers and Journalists for her writing. Sadly, she died in 2001 while I was writing *A Girl Called Thursday*, and I was never able to meet her. I have, however, had the pleasure of meeting both her husband, Aidan, and her son, David, who have been most helpful and encouraging.

As the Royal [Naval] Haslar Hospital features strongly in both books, some readers might like to know its situation today. Unfortunately, although the hospital is still functioning, it is on a much reduced scale. Currently run by all three Services and the NHS it serves local as well as Service patients, but its excellent Accident Treatment Centre is confined to dealing with injuries only. Patients with life-threatening conditions have to make the twelve-mile journey through the bottleneck of the Gosport – Fareham road to the Queen Alexandra Hospital at Portsmouth – a journey that can take well over an hour. The town of Gosport is in constant fear of its complete closure, which would be a sad end to an historic and still desperately needed hospital. The Save Haslar Task Force has been working to prevent this, and I wish it all success.

I would also like to thank Surgeon Captain Jarvis and his staff at the hospital who gave me so much assistance with my research and kindly allowed me to use their marquee as a launch venue for *A Girl Called Thursday*.

A WORD OF EXPLANATION

Some terms may be unfamiliar to new readers:

VAD: Voluntary Aid Detachment – volunteer nurses (mostly unregistered) who served as assistants with the armed forces
QAIMNS: Queen Alexandra's Imperial Military Nursing Service
QARNNS: Queen Alexandra's Royal Naval Nursing Service
SBA: Sick Berth Attendant
BGH: British General Hospital (Egypt)
DUKW (pronounced 'duck'): wheeled amphibious personnel carrier
Pompey: local name for Portsmouth

Chapter One

'*Thursday!*'

Thursday Tilford, enveloped in a mass family embrace, laughed and cried and kissed all at once, and finally begged for mercy.

'You're suffocating me! I can't breathe!' They stepped back and she found herself with just her mother's arms still around her. Tears brimming from her eyes, Thursday held her close for a moment.

'Oh, love,' Mary said at last, pulling a hanky from her sleeve and wiping her wet cheeks, 'it's *so* good to have you home again.'

'It's good to be here. But it's not for long, mind,' Thursday warned her. 'I've only got a few days' leave and then it's back to Haslar. The war's not over yet by a long chalk.'

'No, but it could be soon,' Jenny piped up. She had gone back to her favourite position on the hearthrug where she had been playing with little Leslie. 'They say there's something really big going on all along the south coast – tanks and all sorts heading for the beaches, and—'

'And you didn't ought to be talking about it!' her father said sharply. 'For goodness sake, our Jenny, the war's been going on for nearly five years; you ought to know by now about walls having ears and all that. I hope you're not opening your mouth like this when you're working down at the hospital.'

'Course I'm not,' Jenny said in an injured tone. 'It's just in the family. Anyway, Thursday'll be there to see for herself soon. I bet Portsmouth's one of the main places the invasion's going from—'

'Jenny! That's *enough*.' Walter gave her an angry glance. 'Family or not, we didn't ought to discuss it. It's too easy to let something slip when we shouldn't – not that *we* know any secrets,' he admitted, 'but you just don't know who might be listening or what they might pick up on. Least said, soonest mended.' He opened his tobacco pouch and stuffed his pipe, pressing the baccy down hard with his thumb. Jenny folded her lips wryly and shot Thursday a comical look. Thursday felt her lips twitch. Not much had changed at home, she thought. They might all be two years older than when she had last seen them, and Jenny training as a nurse at the Royal Infirmary, but Dad was still doing his best to rule the roost and Jenny still cheeking him and getting away with it.

'Never mind all that,' Mary said, giving Thursday's arm a little shake. 'Come and sit down, love, and I'll make a cup of tea. We're all pleased to see you back safe and sound, and that's the main thing. I can't tell you how worried I was, all the time you were at sea.'

'We're all waiting to hear about Egypt,' Jenny added. 'Aren't we, Dizzy?'

Denise nodded. She had pulled Leslie back on to her own lap and he leaned into her and slid his thumb into his mouth. Thursday knelt beside her cousin and gazed at her little godson, marvelling at his soft cheeks and long lashes. 'I've missed two whole years of him,' she mourned. 'He was still a baby when I went away – he's a real little boy now.'

'Three years old,' Denise said proudly. Her face clouded a little. 'His daddy hasn't seen him since he really was a baby.' She looked at Thursday. 'How was Vic when you saw him? He's hardly told me anything.'

Thursday hesitated. She'd still not decided how much to tell Denise about the injuries her young husband had received in Africa. 'I'll come round and have a chat tomorrow,' she said quietly. 'We can't talk properly in this scrum. But he's all right, Dizzy, and he talked about you and Leslie the whole time. You don't have to worry about that.'

Her Uncle Percy cleared his throat. 'The main thing is, he's safe, or as safe as anyone can be these days. And Denise knows she's always got me and her mother to turn to.'

'That's right,' Flo agreed. 'It's just as well she stopped at home with us when Vic was called up. She can carry on with her job and I can look after the baby. Not that he's any trouble at all, the dear little soul,' she added, chucking her grandson under the chin so that he giggled and curled himself more deeply in his mother's lap.

Thursday smiled and turned to take a cup of tea from her mother. 'How about our Steve, have you heard from him lately?'

'Oh yes, he writes regular. He doesn't say a lot, mind you, they're not allowed much paper for a start, but he seems to be going on all right and I don't think they treat them too badly either in prison camp. They have football matches and get up concerts and that sort of thing, and we're allowed to send parcels, when there's anything to send, which isn't all that often. I don't think the food's very good but at least he's alive and more or less safe.' She shook her head. 'I don't like thinking of him treated like a criminal, but I don't mind admitting I'd rather that than have him fighting.'

Thursday nodded. The Tilfords were lucky that Steve was a POW. She thought sadly of her cousins Mike and Leslie – Mike posted missing, believed killed, at Dunkirk and Leslie shot down in his Spitfire. No wonder poor Auntie Flo thought the world of her grandson, named after them. He and Denise were all she had left now.

It was obvious that Leslie was the apple of everyone's eye. It seemed almost impossible to believe that Uncle Percy had refused to look at him when he was born. He and Flo had been horrified when Denise, at only fifteen, had admitted that she was pregnant, and furious with Vic even though he'd believed her to be eighteen. The fact that Denise had lied to him didn't excuse him taking advantage, Percy had raged. They weren't married, not even engaged, nor likely to be if Percy had anything to do with it. He'd wanted the girl sent away somewhere quiet to have her baby and get it adopted, but at this Flo had put her foot down. Out of wedlock or not, she told Percy, this was their grandchild, and it could be the only grandchild they'd ever have. They couldn't, they just *couldn't*, let the baby go to strangers.

Walter and Mary had been just as dismayed. Girls who had babies without being decently married were ostracised, and the whole family tainted. Flo's stance had surprised them – she'd always been one to worry about what the neighbours would say – but she'd been so determined that everyone had had to accept it, and with Denise flatly refusing to give up the baby, Percy had been forced to agree to their marrying as soon as Denise turned sixteen. And, as Mary had observed, babies brought their love with them. Even if they hadn't been wanted, they all seemed to make themselves a place in the

3

family, and little Leslie Michael Stephen – named after his two uncles and Thursday's brother Steve – had been barely a fortnight old when he'd won his grandfather round. Even Vic, who had got his call-up soon after his son's birth, had been accepted, especially by Flo who had never forgotten the way he had comforted her when she'd got the news about Leslie. 'As good as a son to me,' she'd said, and refused to let Percy say another word against him.

As Mary handed round the tea and a plate of biscuits, Thursday sat in her mother's armchair, trying to get used to the feeling of being at home again after two years in Egypt. She looked round at the familiar room and the faces she'd missed so much. There'd been changes while she'd been away. The saddest was that her little dog, Patch, had died. Mary had written to tell her he was ill with distemper, and Thursday had known at once what the next letter would say. When it arrived, she'd left it unopened for a whole day, waiting till nightfall to read the bad news. Oh Patchie, she'd thought, the tears dripping on to the sheet of paper, oh Patchie. And she'd remembered how he'd come to her as a puppy on her twelfth birthday, struggling out of the cardboard box in which her father had brought him home and licking her face as she lifted him into her arms. He'd been with her during all her growing-up years, her special friend, rushing to meet her when she came home from school or work, sleeping on her bed whenever he could sneak up the stairs, keeping so close to her that Steve had once said he was glued to her leg. And now he was dead. Patchie. Her Patchie.

Thinking about him brought the tears to her eyes again. Now she was home, it was as if he'd only just died, and the sorrow of knowing he would never rush to her again came as fresh as on the day she'd received her mother's letter. Then, catching Mary's eye, she blinked back the tears and smiled. I've cried for him once, she thought. I'm not going to spoil this homecoming by doing it all over again.

'Is Auntie Maudie coming over? I want to see her before I go back.'

'She's on duty a lot this week. I thought we'd pop over to Ledbury on the train one afternoon. Day after tomorrow, if that's all right with you.'

'I'll come too,' Jenny suggested. 'We can talk about operations and things.'

Mary frowned. 'You know I don't like—'

4

'It's all right, Mum, I'm only teasing. But you can't expect three nurses to get together and not talk about their job! I always have a natter with Auntie Maudie when I go over, and she's sure to be interested in what Thursday's been doing.'

'Of course she will,' Thursday said. 'And I want to thank her again for the little nurse's watch she lent me. Uncle Bill gave it to her in the First World War, and I've worn it all the time. It's been a godsend on the wards.'

'Well, so long as you don't start talking about blood,' Mary said, and everyone laughed. 'Now look, we didn't know just what time you'd be getting home today so I haven't done anything special, just a few Spam sandwiches, but we're all here again for Sunday dinner. Your father's going to kill one of the hens—'

'Not Aggie!' Thursday broke in, and her mother gave her an exasperated look.

'No, not Aggie, I daresay she'll outlive us all if you've got anything to do with it. It's one of the others, that you don't know so well. And don't go down the garden giving them all names – you know once they've got names nobody likes to eat them. There's plenty of veg from the allotment, and some soft fruit for pudding, so it'll be a real old-fashioned Sunday dinner. When d'you have to go away again?'

'I knew you'd ask that,' Thursday said. 'I'm just surprised you've waited so long – usually you ask the minute I walk through the door. "Hello, Thursday, nice to see you, when are you going again?" Can't wait to get rid of me, as usual.'

'You know I didn't mean that!' Mary's face was pink as everyone laughed again. 'Oh, you're awful, the lot of you. I can't say a word without getting picked up on it . . . I only want to know so that I can make arrangements. And so I don't wake up one morning to find you've gone.'

Thursday gave her mother's arm a squeeze. 'You know I wouldn't do that. And I'm only teasing, you know that too. I've got a week – so that's next Wednesday, thirty-first of May.' She stretched her arms, nearly knocking her cup off the arm of her chair. 'A whole week at home! Luxury.'

'Time to tell us all about Egypt,' Jenny said wistfully. 'I wish now that I'd volunteered as a VAD, instead of going for State

Registration and getting stuck here in Worcester. Would have done, if I'd known you could go to places like that.'

'You're better off as you are if you want to be a real nurse. We're just dogsbodies most of the time, doing all the dirty work, though we do get to talk to the patients a bit more – the QARNNs just don't have the time. But we'll never be trained like you are.' Thursday took another ginger biscuit to show her appreciation, aware that her mother would have saved these specially for her return. 'Anyway, what I want to know now is what's been going on while I've been away. How about Mrs Hoskins – is she home or is she off with that fancy man of hers again? And that boy who got sent to approved school – is he back terrorising the neighbourhood? I've got a lot of catching up to do.'

Jenny giggled. 'You certainly have! Freddy Barnes went into the Army and he's won two medals already – his mum's like a dog with two tails. As for Mrs Hoskins, she's had so many fancy men even she's lost count, and—'

'Pipe down, Jenny!' Mary said sharply. 'You know what we think about that sort of gossip. I'm surprised at you for encouraging her,' she told Thursday. 'I'd have thought you'd have learned better, being with those other girls. They tell me a lot of the VADs are real upper-class.'

Thursday grinned. 'They are. But they like a good gossip as much as anyone else. It's just upper-class gossip, that's all. You should hear what they say about the lords and ladies they know and what goes on in big houses with all those bedrooms. Why, Louisa Wetherby once told me—'

'*Thursday!*' her mother expostulated, and the girls dissolved in giggles.

Thursday winked at her sister and cousin, and whispered, 'Tell you later,' and then said aloud, in a demure voice, 'Sorry, Mum. Let me get you another cup of tea, and then you can tell me all the things you want to tell me about, all right?' She got up and took her mother's cup, then bent suddenly and kissed her. 'D'you know what? It feels *much* more like being at home when you tell me off than when you treat me like an honoured guest. So just carry on that way, will you? Because that's what I've missed most.'

Mary shook her head at her. 'Stop it do, or you'll have me in tears again. As if I've ever told you off! Didn't tell you off enough, that's what your father always used to say.'

Thursday smiled and went out to the kitchen. She filled the kettle and put it on the stove, then stood leafing through the pile of cookery books and pamphlets her mother had collected. *Potato Pete's Recipe Book: Two Ways of Reconstituting Dried Eggs*, and *Try Cooking Cabbage This Way* ... She turned to find her Cousin Denise standing beside her. The younger girl looked at her.

'You will tell me the truth about Vic, won't you – what happened to him and – and how he is now. I'm sure there's more than he's told me, and I've got to know.'

Thursday laid her hand on her cousin's arm and nodded. 'I will, I promise. But you mustn't worry, Dizzy. He's just the same as he ever was, really. And he misses you and Leslie all the time.'

Denise nodded and sniffed, brushing her hand across her eyes. 'I miss him too. I really do love him, Thurs, I always did. It wasn't just a – what did they call it? – infatuation. We really did love each other. That's why I lied to him about my age. I was so scared I'd lose him if he knew the truth.'

'Well, that's all over now.' Thursday warmed the teapot with a drop of hot water from the kettle. 'You're married and you've got your little boy, and one day soon Vic'll come home and you'll be able to get a place of your own and settle down properly.' The kettle boiled and she made the tea. 'Go and get the cups, Dizzy. I'll come and see you tomorrow and tell you all about when I saw him in Egypt.'

She stood for a moment alone in the kitchen, listening to the chatter from next door. There would be a lot of talking to do in the next few days, a lot of stories to swap and a lot of reassurance to give. And then she would be going back to Haslar, the Naval hospital on the shore of Portsmouth Harbour where she had first become a VAD. Another kind of homecoming, in a way. I wonder how much will have changed there, she thought. And I wonder what's going to happen next. Something big, Jenny said – perhaps even an invasion. Can this really be the beginning of the end of the war, after all this time?

Denise came back with the cups and Thursday began to fill them with tea. Just for now, she'd forget all about it. Just for now, it was enough to be at home in Worcester with her family.

During those few days' leave, Thursday saw Denise only a couple of times. She was working long hours at the glove factory, making khaki gloves for soldiers, navy-blue ones for sailors, grey ones for airmen and leather ones for officers. 'Once this is all over I'm never going to look at a glove again,' she declared, coming in for a late supper after three hours' overtime when Thursday was round at her aunt's the next evening. 'I'd rather have chilblains!'

She lay back in her mother's armchair, her eyes closed. Thursday looked at her pale face and thought of Vic, lying in his hospital bed. They're just kids, the pair of them, she thought, and they're not the only ones either. This whole war's being fought by kids.

'I had a letter from Vic today,' Denise said, opening her eyes suddenly. 'I told him you were coming home. He says you just about saved his life, Thurs.'

Thursday coloured. 'I didn't do much. I just sat beside him at night. I think it helped that I could talk about you and Leslie, that's all.'

'Well, whatever you did he thought a lot of it. And so do I.' Denise closed her eyes again. 'I'm glad you were there.'

Thursday bit her lip and nodded. 'I'm glad I was there too. It was strange having someone from the family out there in Alex. We hardly knew each other before – when you got married – but we got to know each other quite well in the hospital. He's a nice chap, Dizzy. You're lucky – you've got a good husband.'

'Well, I always knew that!' Denise said, with a flash of her old spirit. 'Knew that right from the start. But then you do, don't you – when it's the right one.' She closed her eyes again. 'That's if he still thinks I *am* the right one.'

'Oh, he does!' Thursday hesitated, then took a breath. 'Look, it's a long time since I saw him and I expect it's different now, but – well, he was wondering if you'd still fancy him. You see—'

'But of course I'll fancy him!' Denise exclaimed. 'I fancied him the minute I first saw him. Why on earth shouldn't I?'

'Because he doesn't look quite the same.' Thursday searched for the right words. She'd known for a long time that this moment must come, that she would have to prepare Denise for her first meeting with Vic. 'Dizzy, he was badly burned. His face was blistered all over – and parts of his body too. It's probably not so bad now as when I last saw him, but he's bound to be scarred.' She looked

8

helplessly at her cousin. 'I'm sorry, but you ought to know – so that it isn't too much of a shock.'

There was a short silence. Then Denise said in a small voice, 'Is it very bad?'

'Quite bad,' Thursday said honestly. 'I'm really sorry, Diz.'

Denise bit her lip. She looked at Leslie, who was on the floor engrossed in a game with some old lead soldiers. Then she took in a deep breath and shrugged.

'I don't see that that's so awful – so long as he's not still hurting from it. He'll still be the same old Vic underneath, won't he?'

'Yes,' Thursday said with relief. 'He'll be the same old Vic. He was in Egypt, anyway. We got on really well.'

'That's all right then,' Denise said. She lifted her chin a little and looked Thursday in the eye. 'You know what Gran says – handsome is as handsome does, and I reckon my Vic will always be handsome to me, no matter what other people think. But thanks for telling me. I wouldn't want to look as if I was upset by it, the first time we see each other again.'

Thursday nodded, relief washing through her. It had been one of the things that had haunted her about coming home – the necessity of telling Denise about Vic. Even now, she wasn't sure that she'd really prepared her for the puckered, dead-looking skin that covered all one side of Vic's face now and stretched down his body. Perhaps later on she'd tell her more, but she'd learned that such shocks took time to absorb. Denise would ask for more information when she was ready.

'He really does love you, Dizzy,' she said quietly. 'He told me that. He just wants to get back to you and Leslie. Nothing else really seems to matter to him.'

'It doesn't matter to me either,' Denise said. 'Just to have us together again, a proper family – that's all we want.' She paused. 'All anyone wants, I suppose. Funny that it takes a war to bring it home to people what's really important about life.'

The brief leave over, Thursday set out on the familiar train journey to Portsmouth. And as she walked down the pontoon from the railway station and stepped aboard the waiting pinnace, she felt herself jerked back four years, to the moment in 1940 when she had first stared out over Portsmouth Harbour.

Four years! Four – no, *five* – years of war, years that had torn her and millions of other young men and women from their homes and families and thrown them into lives they could never have dreamed of. Thrown many of them to their deaths, she thought sadly, remembering the long lists of names in newspapers, the reports on the wireless, the soldiers and sailors she had herself nursed, both here in England and during her years abroad. And here she was, home again, and still it wasn't over.

'Come on, love,' urged the matelot waiting to cast off. 'You're not here on your holidays, you know. Mind you,' he added, glancing at her, 'you look as if you 'ave been. Look as if you've been in the South of France sunning yourself, you do. And what's that ribbon you're wearing? Been serving overseas?'

Thursday nodded a little self-consciously. She'd been proud to be presented with the medal that indicated her service abroad, but reluctant to display it until her father had told her, bluntly, that it was her patriotic duty to do so. 'That's an encouragement to others, that is,' he'd said, knocking his pipe out on the fender. 'It's good for people to know what girls like you have been doing to serve your country. It gives 'em summat to hold up their heads about, summat to hope for. You wear it, and be proud to.'

'So where you been, then?' the matelot asked now, still eyeing the ribbon. 'Africa?'

Thursday nodded. 'Egypt. I've been there two years. But I was at Haslar before that, and now they've sent me back. It feels queer, coming home again after all this time and the war still on. Somehow I always thought we wouldn't come back till it was over.'

'Maybe it won't be too long now,' the sailor said cryptically, looking out over the busy scene. Thursday followed his glance. The harbour was thronged with ships – some tied up at the main jetties in the dockyard, others moored out in the harbour, with smaller boats, ferries and tugs bustling between them. And as the Naval pinnace made the short crossing to the Gosport side she could see through the entrance that the Solent itself was just as crowded. Something was obviously going on – something big.

'What is it?' she asked curiously, but the sailor glanced at her sideways and tapped his nose.

'What we don't know can't hurt us. But you must've seen the roads, all jammed up with Army stuff. Been coming in for the past few weeks, so I've been told – lorries, tanks, DUKWs, you name it, it's there. American, too, a lot of it. Second Front, innit? And they say it's all being master-minded from just over Portsdown Hill.' He seemed to remember his first words and shut his mouth firmly. 'Shouldn't have said that.'

Thursday looked at him. There was nobody else in the boat, but everyone knew that you had to be careful what you said, especially about anything military. *Careless Talk Costs Lives* – the notices had been everywhere at the beginning of the war, and there had been cases of people put into prison for making casual remarks that could have been helpful to the enemy. A girl only had to be overhead in a teashop, telling a friend that her sweetheart's ship was sailing that night, and it could end in the ship's being torpedoed and sunk. Spies and Fifth Columnists, it seemed, were everywhere.

She turned her eyes again towards the crowded harbour. There was clearly a big 'flap' on, and from the look of the ships and the determined air of the smaller boats hurrying between them, it was obvious that the matelot was right – it was the long-awaited Second Front. Everyone was expecting it, had been for months – it was why she and the other VADs had been brought home. The theatre of war was moving back to Europe.

Jenny had been right too. It was the invasion. The invasion of Europe by Britain, and by her allies – America, Canada, Australia and the rest. This was what the country had been waiting for.

'I came by train,' she said, 'and it was packed with Navy types. But you're right, we did see a lot of Army vehicles on the roads, and all along the country lanes. You mean they're planning to take them all on ships? But how?'

He shook his head. 'We don't talk about it, not more'n we can help. There ain't no need. Everyone can see what's going on, and we all know the beaches have been closed for months. Gawd knows what they've been doing there, building bloody great concrete towers it looks like – not that you can see much past all the barbed wire. We might have our own ideas what they're for but we don't ask. And if you take my advice, you won't neither.'

Nothing's changed, Thursday thought, remembering how she and Patsy Martin – Patsy Greenaway now – had come to Portsmouth by train on that bitterly cold, snowy day in 1940, not daring to talk about where they were going or why, in case there was a spy in the carriage with them. It all seemed a very long time ago: the train getting stuck in huge snowdrifts so that the passengers – mostly soldiers – had climbed out to help dig a way through; their surprise at the harbour station with its wooden platform and glimpse of the sea surging beneath them; the massive icicles that had formed beneath the structure; the sloping pontoon to the Gosport ferry crowded by the workmen swarming out through the dockyard gates.

And the ships! It was like a different world, different from anything either she or Patsy had ever seen, except in pictures or at the cinema. The frigates, the destroyers, the enormous, towering bulk of the aircraft-carrier *Ark Royal* looming over them in their tiny pinnace. One of the greatest ships of the Royal Navy, she thought sadly, remembering the flight of aircraft it had taken to the beseiged island of Malta, the battles it had fought, the pride everyone had felt in its name. And now it was gone, sunk by a U-boat off Gibraltar.

The sailor brought the pinnace alongside the Haslar jetty, and Thursday turned her head and looked up at the hospital where she had begun her days as a VAD. How ignorant we were, she thought. We knew nothing about the Navy, nothing about nursing. We had no idea of Haslar's history: nearly two hundred years old and one of the first real Naval hospitals. And we certainly had no idea of what we were to face. The ships coming back from Dunkirk. The wounded sailors, some of them no more than boys. The men who would die before our eyes.

She thought of Tony West, who had kissed her before he went to sea and then come back with his face so badly damaged he would never kiss again. And Susie, the little girl whose leg had been amputated on the night of the big Blitz. And all the others who had passed through Haslar's wards – Stoker Davis, with his amazing tattoos, who had been a hero at sea yet made a fuss like a baby when he was given an enema; the young German, Heinz Schmidt; the sailor who had told her about the great queues of men standing in the water at Dunkirk, being shelled and machine-gunned as they waited for rescue, watching their comrades die around them. And that brought her back again to Tony, one of the first to arrive with his terrible injuries, his torn and broken face . . .

We didn't have a clue what war could be like when we first arrived, she thought, gazing along the paved way that led from the jetty straight through the entrance and under the arcade. We had no idea that these tramlines would be used for trolleys to bring men from the boats to the wards, just like they'd been used for the past two hundred years. We didn't know anything about the Navy or the way it worked, or the words it used; we didn't know what the matelot meant when he told us to "turn starboard" – we didn't even know what a *matelot* was. Her lips twitched again, and she gave the sailor who had brought her over – a matelot himself, in his square rig uniform – a sudden grin.

'Well, thank Gawd for that,' he said, raising his eyebrows. 'Thought you'd been turned into stone. I was just about to pinch you to see.'

'You'd have found out pretty soon I wasn't,' she said, laughing. 'I can pack quite a punch when I'm pinched! Sorry, I was just taking it all in – thinking about the first time I came here. It seems so long ago.' She bent to hoist her kitbag on to her shoulder. 'Thanks for bringing me over. I'd better go and find out where I'm supposed to be. I wonder what changes there'll have been.'

'Not many. A place like this don't change much. Pity we can't say the same about the town.' He glanced past her at the buildings of Gosport across the creek, and Portsmouth on the far side of the harbour. 'Taken a fair battering round here – but you'd know about that, if you were here in forty-one.'

'Yes,' Thursday agreed, thinking again of the Blitz. 'Yes, I do.'

She climbed on to the jetty and walked slowly along the marble-smooth paved way that had been trodden by so many thousands of feet over the past two centuries. Haslar Hospital, so difficult to reach by land from Portsmouth, had been ideally situated for bringing wounded sailors from ships in the harbour and the Solent. Standing on the very edge of a low cliff, now retained by a steeply sloping sea wall, it looked straight out across the Solent to the Isle of Wight, yet here on the other side it was sheltered by the neck of the harbour and its own twisting, narrow creek. The phrase 'Up the creek without a paddle', she'd been told when she first came here, had actually originated in Haslar Lake, as it was called, and probably came from the days when sailors brought here had had only a small chance of surviving.

Treatment was better now, especially with the wonderful new drug, penicillin, which had just been brought in – but there had still been plenty of deaths. All the same, Thursday felt proud as she passed under the low, vaulted roof of the arcade and remembered how she and the other new VADs had stood here and cheered so loudly that Madam had come to see what all the noise was about, and reminded them that they were in a hospital. And even prouder when she recalled those dark days after Dunkirk when the wounded men had poured in, coming by boat and being trollied up the tramlines just as in the old days, and coming into this arcade to be sent to the wards . . .

So many memories, she thought, pausing at the other side of the arcade to gaze across the wide quadrangle at the avenue of trees leading to the little church, and at the gracious Georgian façades of the buildings that stood at each side. So many friends, so many patients. I wonder where they all are now. I wonder if there are any still here . . .

'Tilford!'

Thursday jumped. The voice was unmistakable and, when she turned, the woman striding towards her seemed to have stepped straight out of her thoughts. The tall, elegant figure emphasised by the belt clipped round its narrow waist, the thin, aristocratic face, the bright brown eyes and, most of all, that crisp, clear voice.

'Madam!'

'So you haven't quite forgotten us, then.' Miss Makepeace, the Red Cross Commandant at Haslar, who had been in charge of all VADs there since the war began, surveyed her just as she had done on that cold, snowy afternoon when Thursday and Patsy Martin had first arrived. It was a cool, assessing look, as if she were sizing you up and considering your fitness for the job, and once again Thursday found herself holding her breath and hoping she would not be found wanting. Then that familiar warm twinkle came into the bright eyes, the firm lips twitched into a smile, and the smooth brown head nodded as if some test had been passed. 'It's good to see you again, Tilford.'

'It's good to see you too, Madam.' Thursday glanced around the big open space. 'It's good to be back.'

Miss Makepeace gave another sharp nod, as if that were only to be expected. Where else would one want to be, but at Haslar? But Thursday felt a small twinge of guilt as she spoke, for her words weren't entirely true. It *was* good to be back, in a way, but the past two years had been filled with so many new sights and sounds and experiences, that coming back to where it had all begun seemed to be something of an anti-climax. There was nothing new to discover here in Haslar. She knew it all so well. And she was so much older now than when she had first arrived – so much more experienced, so much wiser, so much sadder . . .

Worst of all, Dr Connor Kirkpatrick wasn't here – and Haslar without Connor was an empty place.

Madam was watching her, those bright brown eyes as keen as ever, missing nothing. 'You won't have much time for nostalgia, Tilford. There's plenty of work on its way, as you may have guessed. You'll find some of your old friends here, I dare say, so there'll be lots of news to catch up on, but the first priority is to find out where you'll be working. Sister Tutor will decide that, but you can have a meal first and get settled in. You're in your old dormitory – I expect you can remember the way.' She turned, as if Thursday were already dismissed from her mind, then turned back and gave her that warm, well-remembered smile. 'I've had excellent reports of your work in Egypt. Of all my girls, in fact. Well done – I'm proud of you.'

Thursday blinked back the sudden tears. 'Thank you, Madam.' She hefted her kitbag on to her shoulder and began to climb the familiar stairs to the dormitory. Nothing had changed here either, she thought, treading the old brown linoleum between the brass strips on the edge of each step. She wondered who would be in the dorm with her. Old friends, Madam said, but the last she'd heard of Patsy, she was in Scotland. And Jeanie Brown had been posted abroad at the same time as Thursday, only two or three months after Patsy's wedding to Roy Greenaway in June 1941, and someone had told Thursday that they thought she'd been killed. And what about Helen Stanway, who had shown them all around the hospital on their first day, tall, bony Ellen Bridges from Dorset, Anne Davis from Kent, and Susan Morrison from near Guildford? Where were they all now? Would she find any of them waiting for her in the dormitory?

And of course, there was Vera Hapgood, she thought with a wry smile. The least popular girl at Haslar, sallow-faced and brooding, with a sarcastic and bitter tongue. What had happened to *her* in the past two years? Would she be back at Haslar?

The only ones Thursday knew about were her great friend Elsie Jackson, from Portsmouth, and Louisa Wetherby – Louisa who was 'posh' and had been to boarding school in Great Malvern, not far from Thursday's own home in Worcester. She, Elsie and Thursday had been together in Alexandria, working side by side in the same wards, and had become good friends despite the difference in their backgrounds. We've been through too much together not to be, Thursday thought. It doesn't make any difference when you're emptying bedpans together. And we've all learned a lot since we started here as VADs together, way back in 1940.

The sense of having stepped back into the past was even stronger as she came to the door of the dormitory. How many times had she climbed those stairs, worn out after a day on the wards or a night on the town? How many times had she run out, still fastening her cap, terrified of being late for duty? *'Navy time is five minutes early, nurse . . .'* She could hear Sister Burton's voice now, reproving any girl who was even a few seconds late, and she remembered the jokes about the ship sailing without you if you weren't on time. And Haslar *was* a ship, in Navy terms – a ship where every man, however badly wounded, was on active service, and every nurse's task was to get the patients fit to return to sea. In order to maintain the atmosphere and discipline of a real ship, the terminology was the same: 'deck' for floor, 'heads' for lavatories, 'quarterdeck' for the long, tree-lined avenue leading to the little church of St Luke.

The familiarity of it all flooded back and, as she pushed open the door, Thursday almost expected to see exactly what she had seen on that first January day and so often afterwards – the rows of beds with their neat counterpanes, each with a blue anchor embroidered on its centre, and the girls either sitting or lying on them or clustered around the stove in the middle of the long room, drinking cocoa. Elsie Jackson, half asleep as usual. Patsy, darning her stockings. Jeanie knitting a navy-blue balaclava or socks. Ellen Bridges reading *Woman's Own*, Louisa Wetherby writing a letter home, Vera Hapgood sitting apart from them all, as if she were better in some way. And Anne and Susan playing draughts or snakes and ladders, looking up to suggest a game of Ludo with some of the others . . . The picture was so clear in her mind that it came as a shock to see the beds replaced by two-tier iron bunks, and an even bigger shock to see the different faces turned towards her. The strange, unknown faces.

Thursday stopped abruptly, feeling almost as if she'd been thrown into a different world. The faces blurred before her, swam a little and then settled again into sharp focus. She was able to see their expressions – enquiring, friendly, smiling. And then, with a sense of joyful relief, to recognise one or two.

'Elsie, you bad penny! And *Patsy* – I didn't think you'd be here! Oh, and Ellen and Susan too – oh, it's lovely to see you all again.' She found herself enveloped in hugs, returning them with tears running down her cheeks. 'Look what you're doing, you're making me cry! Oh, it's so *good* to be with you, you horrors.'

'You're making us cry too,' Patsy said, grinning through her own tears. She'd hardly changed at all, Thursday thought, still as small and bright-faced, her dark curls as exuberant as ever. 'Just shows how awful it is to think we're all back here where we started.' She turned and held Thursday's hand high in the air, as if showing her off to the rest of the girls in the long room. 'This is Thursday Tilford. She was here with us in 1940 and 1941, all through the Blitz. Not a bad nurse, all things considered, and she makes a smashing cup of cocoa.'

The girls looked at her with varying expressions. Some of them must be quite new, Thursday decided, for they looked no older than twenty or twenty-one, the age at which VADs were taken on. Others were her own age or older, and clearly at least as experienced as she. Thursday wondered where they had been serving and what stories they could tell. She smiled around at them, and they grinned back and waved or lifted their cocoa mugs in salute. It's all right, she thought with relief. We'll be friends. And then, catching the dark, sardonic eye of Vera Hapgood – well, most of us will.

For the time being, however, it was her own old friends she was interested in. Patsy had saved her the bunk above her own – 'you being so much taller than me' – and Elsie's was next to it. The three of them sat down together and gazed at each other. Two years – it wasn't so very long, really. You wouldn't expect many changes in that time. And yet, even though Patsy seemed much the same, there *were* changes – a splay of tiny lines at the corners of her eyes, and around her lips, lines that made her look as if more than two years had passed. And when you studied her more closely you could see a haunted expression in her eyes. Thursday, staring at her, felt a sudden stab of fear.

'What's happened?' she asked. 'Where've you been these past two years? I seem to have lost touch. Is everything all right, Pats? Is – is Roy all right?'

Patsy nodded. 'He was, last time I heard. But there don't seem to be any letters getting through now, and you've seen what's happening – all the troops coming south, the ships crowding into the Channel. People say it's the Second Front – the invasion. And Roy's ship . . .' To Thursday's dismay, she saw tears gather in her friend's eyes. 'I don't know if I can take much more of all this worry,' she said defeatedly. 'He's been sunk twice – caught in an engine-room fire, nearly drowned. I mean, for God's sake, he's not a *cat*, with nine lives. He's just an ordinary sailor. How lucky can anyone be?'

'I don't know,' Thursday said. She thought of the day they'd met Roy Greenaway and the other two sick-berth attendants they'd gone around with – Doug Brighton and Tony West. Three breezy young sailors, looking forward to getting back to sea as soon as the VADs were sufficiently trained to replace them on the wards. Three cheeky, bantering young men who had cycled over Pneumonia Bridge into Gosport and taken them to tea at the Swiss Café or gone dancing at Lee and Grange. Three young men with their whole lives to look forward to – and now Tony was dead and the other two still facing peril. 'I just don't know, Pats. I can't say he'll be all right, because none of us knows what's going to happen. But we can think about him – pray, if you like. They say it helps.'

'Do they?' Patsy said tonelessly. 'It didn't help Tony, or all those other young chaps who got killed, did it? They're just as dead as if nobody'd given them a thought.'

They were silent for a moment, then Elsie spoke in her old, brisk, matter-of-fact tone. 'Come on, Pats. No use looking on the black side. We're here to do a job of work and we're not going to be much use if we sit about grizzling.'

Patsy looked at her and then grinned. She reached out and took Thursday's hand. 'It's all right, Thurs. I'm not the only one with a bloke out there. And at least we've had our share of happiness. And now we three are back here together, and there's a lot of hard work coming. It's the best thing, hard work – especially our sort.' She straightened her shoulders and went on determinedly, 'It's going to be good, us being here together again. It's going to be really good, Thursday.'

'Yes.' Thursday squeezed her hand and then got up and went to the window. She looked out over the hospital grounds, at the wall that ran alongside the top of the sloping sea wall. She could just see the green bulk of the Isle of Wight across the Solent. The sea was crowded with ships, some at anchor, some steaming for the harbour entrance. She gazed at them and thought of Patsy's words and of the sailor who had brought her across in the pinnace.

Something big was about to happen. And when something big happened in wartime, it always meant casualties.

There would be plenty of hard work to do in the coming weeks and, as she thought of what lay ahead, Thursday braced her shoulders and lifted her chin. Whatever had happened to them since they had last been here, she and the other VADs would be ready for it.

And I'm looking forward to it too, she thought. Not to the wounded men, but to helping them get better. And to working here with Elsie and Patsy, and whoever else is here too.

Patsy was right. It was going to be good.

Chapter Two

Sister Tutor was as brisk as Madam had been. 'Let me see, you did some theatre work when you were here before, didn't you? And you've done mixed ward nursing and theatre while you've been away. Well, we're going to need plenty of good theatre nurses in the next few weeks, so unless you've any objection to working underground I'd like you to go there. There's a Naval training course you could do as well, with qualifications if you pass the examination. I understand you were considering going in for full State Registration after the war. Are you still interested in that, or have your experiences in Egypt put you off the idea?'

Thursday hesitated. Her experiences in Egypt, she thought, ought to be a qualification in themselves but she knew there was far more to nursing, especially in peacetime. Tending wounded men was no preparation for illnesses such as cancer or heart disease, or any of the multitude of other complaints that could bring patients into hospital. She thought of the years of training that she would still have to do, and felt suddenly weary.

'I don't know, Sister,' she said honestly at last. 'I've spent such a long time as a VAD, I'm not sure how I'll feel about it after the war.' *After the war.* The words sounded strange, almost meaningless. They'd been spoken for so long, and yet the end of the war seemed as far away as ever. Further, in fact, for when they had first been spoken, everyone had been expecting the war to be 'over by Christmas'. And then the following Christmas . . . and then, slowly, hope and expectation had been put to the back of the mind as the nation gritted its teeth and resigned itself to years of endurance.

Sister Tutor regarded her for a moment, then nodded slightly, as if recognising the weariness of Thursday's heart. Perhaps she had seen it before, in all the girls who had come back to Haslar after their service abroad; in all the men and women who had suspended their lives five years ago to fight this war, who had lost friends, relatives and lovers. Perhaps she too felt the deep fatigue and longed for it to be all over.

'Well, there's no need to decide that now,' she said at last. 'I'll put you down for the Naval course anyway. There'll probably be plenty of others wanting to do it, too, so there's no guarantee you'll get a place.' She glanced down at her list again. 'Meanwhile, I'd like you to report to Ratings' Medical. Sister Burton is in charge there – you'll remember her, I'm sure, and I've no doubt she'll remember you.'

I bet she will, Thursday thought as she thanked the Sister and made her way to the ward where she had begun her days as a VAD. Once again she felt she had come full circle, but she was no longer the innocent she had been then, and she felt slightly resentful at the thought of meeting Sister Burton again. Just what *would* she remember about Thursday? The day she'd taken nearly an hour over her first blanket bath? The day she and some of the other girls had got into a heated and noisy argument while rolling bandages? The day she and Tony West had colluded to give Stoker Davis an enema he'd never forget?

Tony. He'd died on this ward. Thursday hadn't been looking after him herself – Jeanie Brown had been specialling him – but she'd been to see him as often as she could get away, holding his hand and gazing down with tears of pity in her eyes at his ruined face. And it was here, she thought, that she'd first met Connor. Connor Kirkpatrick, who had given her his smile and walked away with her heart.

Connor, somewhere between Africa and the Far East.

Connor, who had given her the little Naval brooch of a silver crown. Connor, who wore her cloth VAD badge next to his heart.

Connor, who was, as her sister Jenny had remarked, a 'bit out of her class' but who didn't seem to care. Connor, who wrote her such loving letters, who had – almost – made her a promise.

Did I do that too? she wondered as she tapped her way swiftly through the polished corridors. Did I really make him a promise? *Did* we promise each other anything with that little brooch, and that cloth badge? Or was it just wishful thinking, something that couldn't possibly last for years of separation? And how will we know whether it's lasted or not? Won't we be different people, when we meet again at last?

And had there been anyone else for him during all that time – as there had, perhaps, been someone for her?

Sister Burton was in the ward, looking exactly as she had two years before. She was on Captain's rounds when Thursday came through the double doors, walking smartly a step or two behind the Naval doctor, with a QARNN and a VAD close behind them. The Queen Alexandra nurse glanced briefly at Thursday and walked on, but the VAD gave her a warm grin and a wink behind Sister Burton's back. Thursday felt cheered. At least somebody wasn't trying to give her the impression she wasn't welcome any more.

To be fair, neither did Sister Burton when the doctor had departed and she was able to give Thursday her attention. She took her into the little office and sat down behind the desk, indicating that Thursday should take the other chair. 'Well, Tilford. So you've come back to us. I dare say it feels rather strange, doesn't it?'

'Yes, Sister.'

The smooth head nodded. 'Coming back always does. But you'll soon settle in again, I'm sure. Your overseas experience will have taught you how to do that.' She smiled suddenly. 'In fact, it might be a good idea to treat Haslar as a foreign country, accepting the differences instead of letting them upset you. Just until you get used to it.'

'It isn't Haslar that seems different,' Thursday said. 'Not the hospital itself, I mean – that all looks just the same. It's – it's – I don't quite know what it is,' she finished helplessly, and Sister Burton smiled again.

'It's you who are different, Tilford. And the people here too – some of them, anyway. So many of the nurses and VADs are new to you – it's odd to see all those strange faces in the places you know so well, doing the jobs you remember others doing. But I'm the same and so is Miss Makepeace, and I believe there are a few of your old friends here too – Greenaway, or Martin as she then was – and Jackson, and Hapgood. And you'll soon make friends amongst the others, I know.' There was a moment's silence and then she spoke more briskly, in her old, rather terse voice. 'Not that you're here for socialising. There's work to be done, Tilford, and there'll be more very soon. I want you to give your all to my ward, just as you did before. There are sick men to be nursed and, as usual, neither enough time nor enough nurses to do it. Come with me and I'll introduce you to the QARNN who's my staff nurse, and she'll tell you what to do.'

She rose to her feet, and Thursday stood back automatically to allow her to pass. The Sister paused once more and looked her in the eyes, and once again Thursday saw the warmth behind her cool gaze.

'You're very welcome here, Tilford,' she said quietly, and nodded. 'Very welcome indeed.'

'So how did you get on?'

The girls were back in the dormitory, lying on their beds after their first day's duty. Elsie had worked in the Zymotics block, where infectious diseases were treated, and Patsy had been sent to Officers' Medical. Like Thursday, she had applied for the course in theatre work and Thursday hoped they would both get it. It would be good to work with Patsy.

At Elsie's question, she rolled over to face the yellow-haired girl. Elsie was looking tired, she thought, but then so did they all. Scarcely back in England a week, after the long journeys from their foreign postings, they'd hardly had time to find their feet before being rushed off them. And the Second Front hadn't even begun yet. When the invasion took place – and everyone said it must be soon, now – they would be lucky to lie on their beds at all.

'I don't really know,' she said thoughtfully. 'I keep feeling as if I'd stepped back into the past and yet it's different – as if it's out of focus. It's like a dream, when you sort of know the place you're in but it's all different and you can't find your friends in the crowd. And I can't make out who all the strangers are.' She paused. 'I keep thinking of the ones who used to be here.'

'Like Jeanie,' Patsy agreed soberly. 'It was dreadful, what happened to her. She'd not long arrived in Singapore when the Japanese bombed Pearl Harbor. They just overran the whole place – nobody had a chance.' Her eyes were full of tears. 'The ones that got away in ships were bombed and sunk, and you can imagine what happened to those who were left behind – the same as in Hong

Kong, raped and murdered.' Tears spilled over and ran down her cheeks. 'It's awful to think of Jeanie being treated like that. She was always so sweet and gentle.'

'Patsy!' Thursday stared at her, appalled. 'Nobody told me that. I knew she was supposed to have been killed, but I thought it was in a raid or something. Not like *that*.'

'Are you sure, Pats?' Elsie asked, as shocked as Thursday. 'Some of them were taken prisoner, weren't they? I mean, does anyone know for certain?'

'Well, I don't know – I've always thought she was killed. But even if she was taken prisoner,' Patsy shuddered, 'they treat them just as badly, don't they? I mean, we've heard some dreadful rumours about the Japanese POW camps.'

'Let's hope that's all they are, then – rumours.' Thursday felt shaken. She knew a little of what had happened in Singapore, through Connor's letters as well as through the news that had leaked out. Suddenly she felt that she couldn't lie here any longer. She swung her legs off her bed and stood up. 'Let's go into Gosport. I want to see if the Swiss Café's still there. And good old Pneumonia Bridge, and Bemister's Lane. Come on – it'll be like old times, and we might not get many more chances for a while.'

'We'll have to walk.' Patsy got up too. 'I left my bike in Scotland. It was such a wreck it wasn't worth dragging back.'

'I sold mine when I went to Egypt,' Thursday said. 'How about you, Elsie?'

'Mine's at my auntie's in Portsmouth. I thought I might bring it over sometime. But I don't mind the walk now. It's not that far.'

They brushed their hair and set off, feeling better for having something to do. As they crowded through the door, Thursday glanced over her shoulder and saw Vera Hapgood sitting alone, her face sallow under the fading tan, her mouse-coloured hair hanging straight on either side of her thin cheeks, her eyes brooding and unhappy.

Thursday felt a twinge of guilt. 'Come on, Vera. Come into Gosport with us.'

The other two turned and stared at her in surprise. Vera caught their glances and shook her head, a small, bitter smile twisting her lips. 'No, thanks. I don't want to push in where I'm not wanted.'

Thursday opened her mouth, but before she could speak Elsie

had hustled her through the door and down the wide stairs. At the bottom, Thursday pulled her arm away and flung them both an accusing look.

'What did you want to do that for?'

'Why do you think? Why on earth did you ask *her* along? Talk about a wet blanket! You know what she's like, Thursday, we were never pals with her.'

'That was two years ago.' Thursday followed them out of the door. 'We've grown up a bit since then. She's still nursing, isn't she? Doing the same sort of work as you and me and the rest of us. She's not as bad as you think, Elsie.'

'I'll believe you, thousands wouldn't.' Elsie gripped her arm again as if afraid Thursday was going to run back to the dormitory and fetch Vera down by force. 'Some day we'll ask her along again and see if it's true, if you want to. But not today, eh? Today, it's just the three of us, the way it always used to be. A walk down Memory Lane, see? A look round Gosport to see if it's changed much since we were here last. A cup of tea and a bun in the Swiss Café and a stroll down the High Street. Wander round Woolworth's and Littlewood's. See if they've still got that parrot in the window of the Isle of Wight Hoy. Lean on the ferry railings and look at the ships. Why, we could even go over on the ferry and have a look at Pompey.'

Thursday laughed. 'We'll never have time to do all that! All right, Else, it's just the three of us this time. I won't push Vera on you if you really don't want her, but you ought to give her a chance, all the same.'

'We will,' Patsy said as they swung out through the gates, giving the sailors on guard a cheery wave. 'We will. Only not just yet, all right? Let's get to know each other again first.'

Gosport had changed more than they expected. Somehow, they had forgotten the bomb damage of the Blitz and remembered the town as it had been when they'd first arrived. The overgrown jungle of the bombsites took them by surprise, and the sight of the burned-out shell of the Ritz cinema, still standing beside the moat that surrounded Walpole Park, shook them. They gazed at it, remembering the films they'd been to see, remembering the young men who had taken them there.

'Roy and me used to sit in the back row,' Patsy said at last, turning away. 'I don't know that we ever saw much of the film, but we enjoyed ourselves!'

They walked down the High Street, popping into the sweetshop to furnish themselves with bags of sherbet bonbons and toffee crunch. Although the hospital kept their ration books, they were able to use their own sweet coupons and had enough for a few ounces of sweets each. Chewing happily, they sauntered past the Swiss Café where they had enjoyed so many teas and buns, and went into Woolworth's.

'Everyone always comes into Woolworth's,' Elsie remarked as they browsed around the counters. 'It's nice to be able to just look, without feeling you've got to buy something. Not that I've ever managed to come out without buying something,' she added, stopping to examine the array of Pond's lipsticks and face creams. 'This is quite a pretty colour.'

'It would suit you too,' Patsy said, narrowing her eyes at the pale pink. 'Better than that red you're wearing now. It's too bright for you, that is.'

'I like a bright lipstick. That one wouldn't look as if I'd got any on at all.'

'Yes, it would, it just wouldn't be so bright. That red sort of drains your colour. Why don't you get it, Else?'

'I might. I was thinking of some new scent. *Evening in Paris* – I like that one. I wore it a lot in Egypt. Mind you, you needed scent there, didn't you, Thurs? It was more like *Evening in Sewers* sometimes. Specially when it was hot.'

They laughed and strolled on. It was strange to be back, Thursday thought, struck once again by a wave of the feeling that all this had happened before. They'd wandered round Woolworth's like this so many times, discussing the few lipsticks and scents available – not that there'd been much to discuss. The shortages of rationing had just begun to bite then, and there was little in the way of luxury goods. Factories had better things to do than produce cosmetics – or maybe they weren't better things, she thought wryly, remembering the injuries she and the other nurses had to deal with day after day. Maybe it *was* better to produce frivolous things like lipstick and cold cream than bombs and bullets.

There was even less to choose now. It had been one of the shocks of their returns to find that five years of war meant that luxuries were in shorter supply than ever before; everyone had become expert at making things last. Lipsticks were used down to the very last smear in the tube, and scraps of soap gathered together in jars to be melted and hardened into a lump. Washing-up soda was swished in the hard water and then taken out so that it wouldn't dissolve too quickly. Stockings were darned to within an inch of their lives, jumpers unpicked and reknitted into mittens or socks, and shirt collars turned and turned again. New clothes were something you saved your clothing coupons for, and then struggled to find something to buy with them. Make do and mend had become a way of life.

They walked down to the ferry and leaned on the rails, gazing out over the harbour. As always, it was full of ships, some of them moored to the jetties of the dockyard opposite, others riding at buoys in the middle. The harbour stretched away towards the green bulwark of Portsdown Hill, pocked with the white craters of the chalkpits, and other ships could be seen in the upper reaches. The girls stared at them.

'It's going to happen soon, isn't it?' Patsy said at last. 'I mean, look at them. They're not here on their holidays.'

'I still don't understand it,' Elsie said. 'I was round my gran's over near Ann's Hill last weekend – my mum's been stopping with her since she got poorly – and there's long queues of Army stuff pouring in, just clogging up all the roads and lanes. I walked up Leesland Road and there were tanks coming through; the kerbstones were all squashed and marked with their tracks. It's not just our boys either, it's Canadians, and American GIs, thousands and thousands of them. Gran told me they came through in jeeps one morning, chucking bars of chocolate and chewing gum, and even money, out at the kids on their way to school.'

'Where were they going?' Thursday asked.

'Stokes Bay, apparently.' She shook her head. 'All those thousands of men and tanks and lorries and God knows what, all heading for the beaches. What are they going to do when they get there, that's what I want to know. How can they get all that stuff on board ships? I mean, they're huge, those tanks, and there's DUKWs and—'

'Ducks?' Thursday interrupted. 'What are they, for goodness sake? The coxswain on the pinnace mentioned them.'

'Oh, you know, those amphibious things – look like a cross between a tank and a flaming great lorry, and they can go on land and water. It's *DUKW*. I can never remember what it stands for. I suppose they can drive them across the Channel, but I can't see how they'll get the rest over.'

'Well, ours is not to reason why,' Thursday said, stepping away from the railings. 'We probably shouldn't even be wondering about it. They must know what they're doing.'

Elsie nodded. 'Gran says the beaches have been wired off for months now; nobody can get near without a permit, and there's been no end of building work going on there. The man next door to her says they've been constructing a bridge but that's daft. At least,' she added doubtfully, 'I suppose it is.'

'I heard it was a tunnel,' Patsy said. 'That would make more sense, wouldn't it? A tunnel right through to France and then our boys could pop up right under the Germans' noses.' She bit her lip and turned away abruptly. 'Whatever it is, I just hope it gets this horrible war over as quickly as possible, and without thousands more people getting killed, too.'

Sober again, they walked back to the Swiss Café and pushed open the door. Once again, Thursday felt that sense of *déjà vu*. The first time I ever came in here, she thought, was with Tony West and we sat at this very table and had toasted tea-cakes. Oh, Tony . . .

For a little while, she'd thought herself in love with the merry-faced SBA. Then he'd gone away, and although she had written to him the feeling had faded – until he came back, so grievously wounded, and died of his terrible injuries. It had taken her a long time to get over the mixture of grief and guilt she had felt then, and it wasn't until she had met Connor that she'd been able to let herself think of love again. And then Connor too had gone away . . .

'Penny for them?' Elsie said, watching her, and Thursday blushed.

'Oh, you know – I was just thinking about all the times we used to come in here. It hasn't changed at all, has it?' She looked around the walls. 'Got a bit shabbier, that's all.'

'It needs a lick of paint,' Elsie agreed, 'but so does everywhere. I think they're only making grey now, for battleships.'

They were silent for a few minutes, until the tea and plate of buns arrived. Then Patsy glanced at the other two. 'Well? What have you been doing all this time? How was Egypt?'

'Sandy,' Thursday retorted with a grin. She smiled reminiscently. 'You know, I never thought I'd get sent anywhere like that. I mean, me going to Egypt with all those camels and pyramids and things. My mum's never been further than Weston-super-Mare! Dad was in France, of course, in the First War,' she added, 'but that was no picnic.'

'And Egypt was?' Patsy asked. 'You mean you had a good time?'

Elsie glanced sideways at Thursday, then grinned. 'Well, of course we did, whenever we got the chance. What do you take us for? Weren't going to sit in the mess with our knitting and pass up all the dances, were we? *You* wouldn't have!'

'No, I wouldn't.' Patsy smiled. 'I didn't even in Scotland. You've got to have a bit of fun, and Roy never minded.' She winked. 'So tell us what it was like, out there under the desert stars. Did any tall, dark and handsome sheiks carry you off to their tents and have their wicked way with you?'

Elsie laughed outright. 'Think I'd be here now if they did? I always fancied myself sitting on a gold cushion being fed with dates . . . But there were plenty of soldiers about, just waiting for a bit of home comfort.'

'Soldiers?' Patsy said. 'But we're Naval VADs.'

Thursday nodded. 'Yes, there were a few Navy people there because it was a Naval base, but the hospital itself was a military one. And I can tell you, they don't half do things different. No nice china plates like we've got here, with a pretty blue anchor on them – they use *tin* ones! And tin mugs, that nearly burn your lips off if you're not careful.'

'Not that we had all that many of them,' Elsie added. 'Not enough room on the merchant ships for stuff like that, see. Some of our blokes had to make mugs out of old beer cans. But it wasn't just that kind of thing, it was the way they wanted things done – like hospital corners. I mean, you'd think the way we tuck the sheets in at Haslar would be good enough for anyone, wouldn't you, but no, it had to be done different, the *Army* way, and woe betide you if they weren't right on Colonel's Rounds.'

'*Colonel's* Rounds? But they have Captains in the Army, don't they?'

'Yeah, but an Army Captain's not like a Naval one. And that's another thing we had to learn – all the ranks. I tell you, it was like going back to flaming school. And now I'm back with the Navy I've got to start all over again and I just *know* I'm going to get in a muddle at the wrong moment.'

The other two laughed at Elsie's woebegone face, and then Thursday said, 'Still, we enjoyed it. We had a good time.' Her face clouded. 'But there were plenty who didn't. We got the casualties from El Alamein, and all those desert battles – pretty knocked about too, they were. You know the sort of thing.'

Patsy nodded. They had all seen plenty of battle injuries, here at Haslar and on their postings. Nobody needed to be told about the limbs blown away, the terrible abdominal injuries, the faces ruined beyond repair, the agonised and lingering deaths.

There was another silence. Thursday glanced at Elsie's face and poured another cup of tea. She pushed it gently closer to Elsie's hand. They had all seen too much suffering and death, and although you were supposed to develop a suit of armour and not allow it to upset you, nobody could ever be truly protected.

'Let's forget it for a while now,' she suggested. 'We're going to see it all again pretty soon, unless I'm much mistaken. Tell Patsy how many boyfriends you had out there, Elsie.' She winked.

'Quite a few, I'd guess,' Patsy said with a grin.

Elsie brushed a hand across her eyes and tried to look coy. 'I don't know why you should think that, I'm sure. Well – maybe one or two. *You* know.'

'Yes, *we* know,' Patsy said. 'One or two hundred, that's what you mean.'

'No, I don't! Anyway, I never counted,' Elsie said, reducing both the others to giggles. 'Well, all right, there *were* quite a few. But there's bound to be, isn't there? They keep going away. And you've got to give a bit of comfort to the boys while they've got the chance.'

'So long as it's not too much comfort,' Patsy said with a grin at Thursday. 'Or was it a case of, if you can't be good, be careful?'

'Not at all,' Elsie said with unaccustomed dignity. 'More a case of, if you can't be careful, be good! Look, it's different out there under the desert stars, ain't it, Thurs?'

'I think you'd better tell Patsy about your romantic adventures when we're somewhere a bit more private,' Thursday told her, glancing around the crowded café, and then, noticing the wall clock, 'Hey, look at the time! We'd better get our skates on or we'll miss supper.'

'Thursday! And you've only just eaten a whole tea-cake. I don't know where you put it, I honestly don't.' Elsie looked at her friend's slim figure and patted her own stomach ruefully. 'It's not fair. I don't eat half as much as I used to, and I still can't shift it.'

'It's puppy fat,' Patsy told her solemnly. 'It'll go when you grow up.'

'Well, if I'm not grown up at twenty-six, I don't reckon I ever will be. Puppy fat indeed! Must be a blooming big puppy, that's all I can say.'

The girls laughed as they paid the bill and scurried along the High Street to dive into the narrow opening of Bemister's Lane. Pretty soon, they were panting up the steep incline of Pneumonia Bridge, the narrow walkway that had been built to replace the original bridge destroyed early in the war. They ran down the other side and between the high brick walls to the hospital entrance, passing the sailors on guard to arrive at their quarters in D Block just in time to sign in for supper.

We did this so many times, Thursday thought as she sat at the table, eating shepherd's pie. And yet we've changed a lot, since the last time we sat here together. We've been through all kinds of experiences, some we'll never even be able to tell each other about.

We're different – every one of us.

Chapter Three

Elsie's reminiscences about Egypt brought Thursday's own memories to mind as she lay in bed that night, aware of the other girls around her on the iron bunks. Some were already asleep, breathing steadily or snoring gently. Patsy was making that funny little snuffling noise she sometimes made when she was dreaming, and Elsie was clicking her tongue at the back of her throat in the way that had sometimes nearly driven Thursday mad, and which she had missed so much when the other girl was sent to a different hospital in Cairo.

It wasn't only the other VADs that she'd missed, of course. Her family had been very much in her thoughts while she was in Egypt. She'd lain awake like this on so many nights, thinking of them and wondering what they were doing at that precise minute. Her father Walter, working at the porcelain factory where they were now making parts for aeroplanes and military vehicles; her sister Jenny, who had volunteered as an orderly at Worcester Royal Infirmary and was now halfway through her SRN training. Her mother Mary, who struggled to hold the family together, who had wanted Thursday to marry Sidney Fletcher. And her brother Steve, whom they'd thought killed at Dunkirk with his cousin Mike and heard – on the very day of Patsy's wedding, almost three years ago to the day – was still alive and a prisoner of war in Germany.

Patsy's wedding! With a shock, Thursday realised that the anniversary was only a few days away. Friday 6 June, it had been and now it was Saturday 3 June. She thought of that day, of the service in the village church only a mile away from the hospital, of the sunshine and the pretty dresses that had been somehow cobbled together, of the joy in Patsy's and Roy's faces. They never seemed to have stopped bickering during their courtship, but there was no doubt, when you looked at their radiant happiness, that they were meant for each other.

Thursday's heart ached. The tears rose to her eyes and she turned her face into the pillow so as not to disturb anyone with her weeping. Connor, she thought, Connor. We never even got as far as being married before you went away, and that was even longer ago than Patsy's wedding. And then she scolded herself for her selfishness and self-pity.

So much had happened since she had first come to Haslar and learned what nursing was all about, what war really could mean. It meant courage, too. Thursday and the other VADs had had to call upon more reserves of courage than they'd ever thought possible. She thought back to the air raids, when they had had to help patients down from the wards to the basements and wait for the bombing to stop – except that Thursday hadn't always waited. A small smile touched her lips as she recalled the day she'd crept back up to the wards to be with the men with broken limbs who'd had to be left there, strapped to Balkan beams and unable to move, and found Madam there as well. And the time the big, creaky lift had stuck and Elsie had got a sing-song going inside. Then there was the Blitz itself, on 10 January 1941 . . .

I wasn't even in Haslar that night, she thought. I was up on Portsdown Hill with Connor in a borrowed car, and when we heard the sirens go and the planes come over, it was like fireworks night. Getting back to the hospital was a nightmare of bombs and explosions and incendiaries. She remembered the frantic dash through streets that were already aflame, the desperate pleas of injured people, the flying debris and the thick, acrid smoke. And then she remembered Susie.

The little girl's uncle had been almost mad with distress. He'd been looking after his sister and two young children and he'd gone out as soon as the raid began, on fire-watching duty. His sister had stayed in the house with the baby, who was poorly, and when the house had been hit it had caught fire immediately. He'd managed to get little Susie out, but there was no chance for the others, and Susie herself was so badly hurt that Connor had had to amputate her leg there and then. Thursday had helped him and then they'd taken the little girl back to the hospital in the borrowed car. Connor had said afterwards that his friend, whose car it was, would never be able to get the bloodstains out.

Oh, Connor, she thought. *Where are you now?*

It all seemed so very long ago. It was only two days later that Connor had gone away, leaving Thursday with the little brooch in the shape of a Naval crown. She'd stayed another six months at Haslar before being posted to Egypt, and her life had taken a new turn. Images swirled in her brain, half memory, half dream. She could see a succession of faces passing in front of her. Connor . . . Susie . . . Denise and Vic . . . her brother Steve and her cousins Mike and Leslie . . . her mother and father. Then Connor again. She jerked awake suddenly, her heart thudding. She had woken so abruptly that she felt sick and dizzy, and she lay still, trying to steady her breathing, to calm down.

I've got to stop this, she thought, listening to the quiet breathing all about her. I've got to get to sleep. There's a big flap due any day now, and I'm going to need all my strength. I haven't got *time* to lie here going over the past.

Feeling calmer, she turned over again and then felt under her pillow for the little brooch. She felt its shape, the points of the crown, the smooth surface. It had been given her with love, she knew that. Connor had said he wished it could have been a ring. And then they'd been plunged into the Blitz, and there had been no more time. He was gone, leaving Thursday in a mist of tears before she wiped them away, pulled back her shoulders and found a smile to take on duty with her. Neither of them had had any idea that their separation would last so long.

Three years. Three years of hard work, of the fascination of a new land, of unexpected joys and sorrows. We're different people now, she thought, fingering the tiny brooch. What will it be like when we meet again?

And what of the other brooch, packed in its little white box at the bottom of her case? The brooch that was shaped like a star.

With questions still echoing in her mind she drifted away, at last, into sleep.

Connor had sailed for Singapore in January 1941. A British Crown Colony since 1867, it was a major port in the Far East and a popular 'draft' for sailors. Ratings and officers were able to take their wives for the two- or three-year tour of duty, and they lived a pleasant way of life, with servants and nannies, and plenty of time to meet for lunch or cocktails.

Not all the wives took an easy life, however; some were working as VADs in the Naval hospital, and Thursday had hoped that she might get her own posting there, and so be able to meet Connor again when he was in port. But what had happened to Singapore in February 1942 put a cruel end to all such hopes.

The threat from the Japanese had been growing all through the previous year. Now, first Hong Kong and then Singapore were overrun, the men, women and children who had thought themselves safe, raped and murdered. In the hospitals, nurses and patients were bayoneted to death; in the streets, women and children were cut down or shot. The island was in chaos, with casualties flooding into the hospitals while those same hospitals were desperately trying to evacuate. As the Japanese soldiers arrived in their tens of thousands, the British, Australians and Indians who had been prepared to defend Singapore to the death, were ordered to leave.

Connor wrote to tell Thursday about it much later, from Java. His own ship, the *Livid*, had been one of those which left Singapore in the second week of February, loaded with civilians. It was one of the last of the Naval ships to do so. As it steamed away from the island, those on board looked back to see a thick black plume of smoke rise from the oil terminals in the dockyard, and knew that the Naval base had been deliberately fired, and abandoned.

It was one of the worst moments of my life, he wrote, *to see that great Naval base, the whole reason for Singapore's existence, scuttled like a ship and left deserted. If Dunkirk was a defeat, what could you call this? I felt so terrible about those poor souls left behind. We'd heard a bit about the awful things the Japanese had done in Hong Kong and we knew they'd show no mercy. And we couldn't do a thing about it – all we could do was get our own people to safety, and hope for the best for the others.*

Even this simple hope was doomed. Every ship leaving Singapore, whether it be Naval or Merchant, had to run the gauntlet of the Japanese bombers. The *Empire Star*, carrying over two thousand people, was hit three times but managed to limp to safety in Batavia. Others were sunk and their cargo of refugees either drowned or were washed up on the shore, to be captured or to die.

They kept evacuating to the last moment, Connor wrote. *By 14*

February they were down to little coastal steamers. They were loaded with civilians, as well as nurses still trying to look after the sick and wounded. They set up sick bays wherever they could – on the decks, in the holds – but all to no avail. Thursday, reading his letter, could sense the long pause while he tried to find words to tell her what had happened; she could almost hear his heavy sigh as he finally wrote, quite baldly: *They were bombed out of the water – almost all the eighty or so vessels that left Singapore that day. We don't know what happened to the people – how many were killed or drowned, how many struggled to land on one of the hundreds of little islands, nor what befell them if they did. We don't know what the Japanese did to those who were left in Singapore, but we fear the worst . . .*

Chapter Four

Thursday woke next morning with a headache and heavy eyes. She felt as if she'd been crying all night, and perhaps she had – crying in her dreams for the hundreds of women and children who had been killed trying to escape from Singapore, for all the soldiers and sailors who had gone with them, for all those who had died since the war began.

She leaned over her bunk and looked down. Patsy was just waking in the bed below her. She opened her eyes, frowned a little as if wondering where she was, then closed them again, squeezing them tightly. She's thinking about Roy, Thursday realised, drawing back quickly. She must go through it every time she wakes up – thinking about him and then remembering he's somewhere at sea on one of those ships, waiting to go to France. She's wondering where he is and if she'll ever see him again.

After a moment or two, she heard the other girl move and peeped down again. Patsy glanced up at her and grinned. 'Hello, you.' Her eyes were damp but the anxiety had gone, pushed resolutely aside. 'Talk about flaming June, eh!'

Thursday looked towards the tall windows. Someone had removed the blackout and she could see the sky, grey and overcast. It was very different from the blue, sunny skies of Egypt, but the work, she knew, would be the same. She dropped down from her bunk to the floor. Elsie was already up and heading for the washroom, her dollybag, made from an old towel, swinging from her wrist. Thursday followed her and found herself at the row of washbasins with Vera Hapgood between herself and Elsie.

The sallow girl gave her a brief glance. 'So you've come back at last.'

Thursday was determined to be friendly. 'Yes, here we all are, just like a purse full of bad pennies. Did you get posted anywhere interesting, Vera?'

The glance turned to a sneer. 'You know flipping well I didn't. It was all right for you lot, swanning about in Africa. *Some* of us had to stay here and hold the fort.'

'You mean you've been at Haslar all this time? But I thought all the mobile VADs—'

'Well, you thought wrong,' Vera told her bluntly, and pushed past. 'Excuse me. *Some* of us have got work to do, if you don't mind.'

As she stalked out of the washroom, Thursday met Elsie's eye and grimaced. Elsie made a face back. 'You surely didn't expect her to have changed. She's got an even bigger grudge now – thinks we've had it easy, sunning ourselves while she and the others have had to stay in England.'

'Or Scotland,' Patsy remarked, taking Vera's place between them and turning on the tap. 'I can tell you this, some of us think it's the people who stayed at Haslar who had it easy. It's darned cold up there!'

'I don't think anyone's had it easy, wherever they've been,' Elsie said soberly. 'Not nurses, anyway. It stands to reason, doesn't it? We've been sent to the front line, wherever it is, because that's where the casualties are. And even if we weren't near the front line we were still busy getting sick and wounded men fit to go back into action. It hasn't been a rest cure for nurses, whoever they are.'

'No,' Thursday agreed. 'I was thinking last night about the ones who were in Singapore. Hundreds of them died then. As for the ones who got away – most of them ended up in Japanese hands.' She shuddered. 'Connor's told me a bit about it, but no one knows exactly what's happening to them. It doesn't bear thinking of.'

The others looked at her. Patsy said, 'So he's still all right, then, Surgeon Commander Kirkpatrick? I didn't like to ask before.'

'Oh yes,' Thursday said. 'He's all right. Had a few close shaves, and I suppose there'll be more, but so far, *Livid*'s managed to stay in one piece. Goodness knows how.' She opened a round tin of toothpaste and rubbed her toothbrush across the pink block inside. 'He tries to write as often as possible, but of course when they're in action . . .'

The others nodded. Thursday saw Patsy bite her lip and knew she was thinking again of Roy, somewhere at sea. The familiar terror clutched again at her own heart. Even now, something similar might have happened to Connor. Any day, she might switch on the wireless to listen to the news and hear that his ship had been sunk, but she wouldn't know if he had survived until someone wrote to tell her. He might be killed by bullets or bombs, or drowned in the sea he loved so much, and she wouldn't know; she would have no idea.

I *would*, she thought, scrubbing her teeth fiercely. I *would* know. I'd know the minute it happened, I'd feel it inside, I'd feel his pain . . . But she couldn't be sure, and the dread had been with her so long, it was now a part of her.

She picked up her washing things and went back to the dormitory. In silence, she began to make her bed, stretching up over Patsy's to smooth out the white counterpane and make sure the blue embroidered anchor was exactly in the middle. That was something that wouldn't have changed, here at Haslar! And neither had the strict Naval discipline, the demand for punctuality – 'Naval time is five minutes early' – nor the consistently high standards expected of the Queen Alexandra nurses – the QARNNs – and the VADs.

The dormitory was bustling now with girls getting ready for breakfast before going on duty and relieving the night staff. Thursday jerked herself out of her musing, and gave her counterpane a final tug. It was time to stop being self-pitying and get back to work. She put on her cap, made sure the white kirby grips were holding it firmly in place, gave a last twitch to her apron and checked that the little silver watch her Aunt Maudie had given her was pinned to her bib. Thursday had promised to take care of it and return it to her aunt when the war was over. She looked on it as a talisman, to keep her safe and to remind her of home.

Ready at last, she hurried across to the ward. She was almost at the door when she heard brisk footsteps behind her and turned quickly, her face lighting up with pleasure.

'Louisa! I wondered where you'd got to.'

'I had a few days' extra leave because my father's ill.' The tall blonde girl caught her up and they smiled at each other. 'It's good to see you again, Thursday. I was wondering if there'd be anyone here that I knew.'

'There are plenty. Patsy's here, and Elsie, and Ellen Bridges, and Susan – and Vera Hapgood,' she finished with a grin.

Louisa made a face. 'Well, it can't be all good news, I suppose! Or maybe she's improved with time.'

'I don't think so. She and Elsie have already had one dust-up. But what about you, Louie? Is your dad better now?'

Louisa shook her head. Her thin, aristocratic face was sombre and her blue eyes shadowed. Her father had a title of some sort – an Honourable, Thursday thought – but she never talked about it and had always mucked in with the rest, and while they were in Alexandria the two had become good friends.

'He's not going to get better. It's his heart, you see. He just has to rest as much as possible, but you can see he's getting weaker all the time.'

'Oh, Louie – I'm sorry.' Thursday touched her friend's arm. 'It must have been awful, having to come away and leave him and your mum.'

'Yes, it was, but I'm not the only one with problems at home. And we're going to be needed here.' Louisa glanced at her. 'Have you seen all the troops?'

Thursday nodded. 'The place is full of them. Lorries and all sorts, clogging up all the roads, and thousands and thousands of soldiers. It's like a massive queue, stretching right out into the country.'

'It's the invasion,' Louisa said soberly. 'It must be any day now. And d'you know, down in Falmouth they've got another fleet – of *cardboard* ships! Well, wooden ones anyway, knocked up out of plywood or something, and painted to look like real ships. My brother told me about them. And all round the east coast they've got planes and ships racing about like mad, pretending they're a crowd, to make the Germans think we're invading from there!'

Thursday stared at her. 'It sounds daft. It'll never work, surely. Mind you, there are some funny stories going round about what's happening at Stokes Bay. Someone told me they've been building some huge concrete things out there for months. And then they just disappeared. I heard they'd been towed out to sea and sunk but I can't believe that, can you? It doesn't make sense.'

Louisa shrugged. 'Nothing about this war makes sense. And I suppose we shouldn't be talking about it, even here. Anyway,' she moved forward briskly, 'we'd better get our skates on and get into the ward or Sister Burton will have our guts for garters.'

'Mind you,' Elsie said as they scrambled through their lunch a few hours later, 'it wasn't all bad in Alex, was it, Thurs? To tell the truth, it was pretty good a lot of the time.' She grinned wickedly. 'Specially when the Yanks arrived! They were so different from our lot – fresh from home, raring to go, plenty of money to spend, and—'

'And you all ready to help them spend it,' Vera Hapgood butted in. 'You always were a tart, Elsie Jackson!'

There was a sudden silence. Elsie's skin flushed a bright red and her eyes darkened with anger. She shot her hand across the table, grabbed the edge of Vera's plate and tipped it over, depositing gravy, meat and vegetables in the girl's lap. Breathing hard, she followed it with Vera's glass of water, and then she jumped up to face her old enemy, who by now was also on her feet and screaming abuse. The other girls sat by, horrified.

'Stop it, Elsie, for goodness *sake*!' Thursday grabbed Elsie's arm. 'And you stop that noise, Vera or you'll have Madam in here and you know what'll happen then. We'll be up before the Captain. Look, it was an accident, all right? If anyone asks, it was an *accident*. We'll settle this afterwards but for now just get the mess cleaned up, both of you, and stop behaving like children!'

The two enemies glared at her. 'What do you mean, an accident?' Vera demanded. 'She did it deliberately, you all saw it, and I don't care if we do come up before the Captain. I'll tell him what happened, and I'll tell Madam too. I'll get her thrown out—'

'Get *me* thrown out?' Elsie squawked. 'What about you, and what you called me? You'll be the one to get chucked out and I'll tell Madam myself!'

'You won't,' Thursday stated. 'You won't tell anyone, either of you. You're not babies in high chairs – you're twenty-six-year-old *women*, for goodness sake, far too old to throw food at one another. And neither of you is getting thrown out. You're VADs, remember? Nurses! You're needed here, and you're going to be needed even more when D-Day comes.' She stared at them. 'How can you even *think* of getting each other thrown out when there are men to be nursed, men who've risked their lives? What does it matter *what* she calls you?' she asked Elsie, and then turned to Vera. 'Not that you didn't deserve it. You'd better go and get yourself cleaned up and into a decent uniform before Madam does see you. *She* won't have the patience to listen to tale-telling and you'll *both* be for the high jump!'

Vera gave her a furious glance and then ran from the room. Elsie, looking mutinous, took the dustpan and brush from the girl who had run to fetch it, and set about cleaning the floor. She dumped the mess into the swill-bucket where leftover food was collected for the pigs at the farm along Clayhall Road, and came back to the table.

'Lucky we're near the door,' she said. 'Not too many people noticed, what with all the racket going on in here anyway. Sorry, Thurs, maybe I did fly off the handle a bit, but she just caught me on the raw. I mean, I was just trying to jolly things along a bit, that was all. We *did* have fun out there, but there was no harm in it. And I was never – well, what *she* called me.'

'No, of course you weren't,' Thursday said. Elsie had certainly kicked over the traces a bit during her time in Egypt, but that wasn't being a tart. 'But we've got to rub along together here, Else, just like we used to. And like we had to abroad, too,' she added, thinking of other 'Veras' she had met. 'There's always someone we won't get along with.'

'Nobody gets along with *her*,' Elsie muttered, but she sat down again and took a sip of water. Then she grinned. 'Well, there's one good thing come out of it – there'll be a spare helping of pudding at this table! What do you reckon, girls? Shall we save it for Her Ladyship, or shall we share it out amongst ourselves?'

'It's got to be soon.'

The thought was in everyone's mind, the words on everyone's lips. Thursday, taking a patient's temperature later that day, glanced out of the window at the Solent and blinked. The strip of water between Portsmouth and the Isle of Wight had been busy before – now it was packed with ships, crowded so thickly that she felt she could have walked to the Island across them. American as well as British, they floated at anchor, a solid grey mass of steel bulwarks on the grey swell of the sea, shifting beneath an iron-grey sky. And above them, hovering just below the swollen clouds, a vast flock of silver barrage balloons, each tethered to a ship by an almost invisible steel cable.

They look like kiddies going to a party, Thursday thought, then bit her lip, realising the kind of party it would be. There were thousands of them there. Thousands. She remembered what Elsie had said about the tanks and lorries and – what was it? – DUKWs. And all sorts of other queer vehicles that had been seen driving through Gosport. They must be intending to take them across on all these ships. But how did you get things like that on a ship, straight off the beach? And what would happen when they reached the other side? Surely it would take ages to disembark, and the Germans would be certain to find out. It could be Dunkirk and Dieppe all over again.

She shivered and turned away, hoping the authorities knew what they were doing. Mr Churchill, Field Marshal Montgomery – 'Monty' – General Eisenhower and the French leader, General de Gaulle – they must have thought it all out and decided it would work. The men she'd seen sitting by their vehicles at the roadside seemed cheerful enough, too cooking sausages on Primus stoves and chatting to the people from the nearby houses. They seemed ready to go, and keen to get into action.

And in a few days' time they'd be back again, some of them, she thought. Wounded and injured and dying too, the boys who were laughing and joking on their way to Stokes Bay today. On their way to D-Day and the invasion . . .

A muffled gurgling sound from the patient she was checking made her jump, and she turned back to see him pointing to the thermometer in his mouth. Catching her breath, she whipped it out quickly and held it up to the light.

'Blimey, nurse, I thought you'd turned to stone and I'd got that thing stuck in me gob for the duration,' he said. 'What's so interesting out there? Jerry climbing up the sea wall, or your boyfriend waiting to take you to the pictures?'

Thursday looked at him guiltily. For a few moments, she had forgotten where she was, forgotten everything in her amazement at the sight of all the ships. Then she smiled and shook her head.

'Sorry. I lost track for a minute. Your temperature's up again, Stoker Morrison. You'd better lie down and rest for a while, and no getting out of bed, all right? No excitement until it's gone down again.'

He wrinkled his face in disgust. 'And there was me thinking I'd be able to get out and 'ave a look at the sea. Oh well.' He slid down between the sheets again and gave her a rueful grin. 'I got to admit, I 'ave got a bit of an 'eadache. Spot of shut-eye won't do no 'arm. And I don't suppose there's all that much goin' on, is there?'

Thursday glanced again out of the window, at the massing fleet of ships. 'No,' she said, 'not all that much, really . . .'

The gliders began to come over early in the morning, two days later. It was 6 June.

There had been a growing tension in the air for days now. All the nurses and some of the patients were aware of the flotilla packing the Solent, but nobody dared speak of it. It was as if they felt that to talk about it might make it vanish, as if it weren't really there at all but was just a dream. They went about their work, glancing out every now and then to reassure themselves, and dreading the sound of the air raid siren and German bombers. Surely they must know . . . Or perhaps the diversionary tactics of the wooden ships at Falmouth and the frantic activity off Dover had tricked them into thinking the danger was coming from those areas instead. You wouldn't think they'd be so easily fooled, Thursday thought. You wouldn't think they'd even try such schoolboy antics! But maybe it was their sheer, childish simplicity that had made them so successful. Or perhaps it was the unseasonal weather – wet, cold and windy, not at all the sort of conditions when an invasion might be expected.

She was standing at the dormitory window after a restless night when she saw the first flight of bombers approach, each towing a great, silent aircraft across the skies. For a moment, she stood transfixed, staring in disbelief. Then a swarm of them appeared, the bombers growling their deep, threatening note and the gliders like huge birds of prey. She turned to the other girls, some of them still asleep, some yawning and stretching and beginning to climb reluctantly from their bunks.

'Look! *Look!* It's the invasion – it must be – it's started. It's *started*!'

Louisa was at her side at once. Elsie, rubbing her eyes, stumbled over in her nightie and gazed blearily out. The other girls crowded round, pointing and exclaiming.

'They're so quiet! Haven't they got engines?'

'Course not – they're gliders, silly. The bombers'll take them nearly over to France and then let go.'

'I know what gliders are, thanks very much, Ellen Bridges. But these are enormous – how can they stay up there without engines?'

Nobody seemed to want to explain the theory of aerodynamics at that moment. They stood in silence, watching as the aircraft swooped across the Solent and disappeared over the Isle of Wight, and then Elsie gave a yelp.

'The ships! They've gone!'

'Good heavens,' Thursday said wonderingly. 'So they have.'

'I don't believe it,' Louisa Wetherby said. 'It's not possible – so quickly. They were there yesterday, masses of them. The order must have been given in the night and they all just – went.'

'Or very early this morning,' Thursday agreed. She stood on tiptoe, straining her eyes to see through the slanting rain. The sea was grey and bleak, the waves tossing and breaking, spraying white foam into the air. 'Look, you can just see their shapes, out past the end of the Island. They're on their way now.' Excitement welled up in her and she turned and flung her arms around Louisa, hugging her and jumping up and down. 'They're on their way to France! The invasion's started! We're going to win the war at last – we are, I know we are! Oh, Louie, Elsie, Patsy—' She stopped abruptly. 'Where's Patsy?'

'Here I am,' said a quiet voice, and Patsy appeared from the washroom. She looked pale and her eyes were rimmed with pink. 'Sorry, Thursday – I just had to nip into the lav. What's going on?'

Thursday stared at her. 'It's the invasion, Pats – it's started. The ships have all gone.' Realisation dawned, and her hand flew to her mouth as she pushed past the other girls to her friend's side. 'Oh, Patsy – I almost forgot. It's the sixth of June, isn't it. Your wedding anniversary.'

Patsy nodded as the other girls stared uncomprehendingly, and then those who had been at Haslar three years earlier crowded about the two. Patsy was enveloped in a sea of comforting arms and for a few moments she stayed there, then she pushed them gently aside.

'I'm all right. It was just – you know, waking up and realising. I

needed to be on my own for a minute or two. I'll be all right now.'
She moved to the window. 'What did you say? The invasion? How
d'you know?'

'The ships have gone, see?' Thursday stood beside her, her arm
laid lightly across Patsy's shoulders as she pointed. 'And there were
huge gliders going over – look, there's another lot. What d'you think
they're carrying? They look almost big enough to carry tanks and
lorries, but it doesn't seem possible, does it?'

Patsy nodded. Then, after staring for a minute or two more, she
turned and gave them a triumphant smile.

'You know what this means, don't you? It means we're going to
win the war! That's a real invasion, that is. And,' her voice sobered,
'if there are troops on those ships about to land in France, a lot of
them will be coming back wounded. It'll be Action Stations here at
Haslar, just like after Dunkirk. And we'll do our best for them, just
like we did then. Now I don't know about you, but I'm going to get
a good breakfast inside me, because if last time is anything to go by,
we might not get time for a good square meal again till heaven
knows when!'

Chapter Five

The official announcement came soon after breakfast. Today was D-Day and the hospital was at Action Stations. No patients were expected for twenty-four hours but it might be less, and everything must be ready. The operating theatres in particular must be on standby.

With the VADs gathered together, Sister Tutor read out the names of those selected for the theatre course. 'Bowden, Cockroft, Tilford, Wetherby and Mears will report immediately to Surgeon Commander Sharp. The rest of you, return to your wards at once. There'll be plenty to do to prepare for our new patients.' She looked down from her dais and her calm gaze rested upon their upturned faces. 'I know that we can all rely upon your hard work and dedication in the days ahead. Some of you are new and may feel a little nervous about what you may be called upon to do. Others were here after Dunkirk, and many of you have served overseas and in other hospitals where emergencies have stretched you to the limit. I know you will all work together as a team, remembering that the patient must always come first and orders must be obeyed without question. That's the way the Royal Navy has always functioned, and that's the way we shall succeed now. Good luck to you all.'

The girls filed soberly out of the room. Thursday found herself beside Patsy and gave her arm a squeeze. 'All right, Pats?'

The other girl gave her a faint smile. 'To tell you the truth, I'll be glad to have something to do. It'll take my mind off – you know.' Her voice wobbled a little but she drew in a breath and continued, 'It seems awful to say it, somehow. It's our wedding anniversary – I *ought* to be thinking of him. And I am – deep down, I always am.'

Thursday nodded. She thought she understood. Connor too was

far away, and before he left he'd told her that he didn't want her to consider herself tied to him. 'I don't want you moping while the other girls have fun, Thursday. I don't want you living like a nun – I want you to be the Thursday I know and love, the one who's always got a smile and a laugh, who goes out on her bike and has tea at the Swiss Café and goes dancing. I want you to make the most of every day, because all we've got, these days, is today. And then write and tell me all about it!' he'd finished with a grin.

At least Roy and Patsy were married; at least they'd had a little time of happiness together. Thursday looked at her bare left hand, and wished there had been time for that. She and Connor had never had the chance, and perhaps never would. As he had told her, three long years ago, life was too uncertain these days to be sure of anything.

Thursday had done as he had told her. After a time during which she hadn't wanted to do anything or go anywhere, she had begun to go out with the other girls again, to go dancing. It had been good to be held again in a man's arms, if only for a few minutes, and she'd felt comforted and hoped that Connor was finding the same comfort. And when she'd been posted to Egypt it had been impossible to hold herself apart. It was a different world and friendships, flirtations and even romance blossomed under the African skies. But always – always, at the back of her mind – there had been Connor. As Patsy said, deep down you were always thinking of the man you loved.

'I'm glad I'm going to be in theatre,' she said. 'And Louisa, too. But I'll miss being with the patients on the wards.'

'That's why I didn't volunteer,' Patsy said, and Elsie, coming up behind them, agreed.

'I did a bit of theatre in Egypt, remember, and decided it's not for me. I'm better with the patients when they're awake. They seem to appreciate a joke better then!'

The other two laughed. 'Even yours?' Thursday asked wickedly, and Elsie thumped her arm. 'Well, you'll be able to keep us up to date with what's happening up above, then. We're going to be like moles, down there in the dungeons.'

Although Haslar had normal operating theatres in the main hospital, there was also a vast network of cellars beneath the buildings, and several of these had been fitted out as emergency theatres. Others were used as air raid shelters, and there had been so many evacuations during the raids and Blitz of 1940 and 1941 that the men had begun to joke ruefully that they might as well stop down there for the duration.

Thursday and Louisa made their way down the wide stairs beneath the arcade. There was a large lift which could be used for bringing down patients, but to save electricity it was used only when absolutely necessary. There were two large theatres here and the girls who were to take the course and work here made their way to the first one, where Surgeon Commander Sharp held court. They did not expect to meet the man himself, knowing that he would almost certainly be operating at this moment, but when they saw the QARNN who was waiting for them their faces lit up.

'*Stanway!*' Thursday wanted to hug her old friend, but didn't quite dare. 'We weren't sure you were back.'

Helen Stanway smiled at them. She'd been at Haslar when they'd first arrived as raw recruits, and had shown them round the hospital. Thursday remembered how they'd all cheered as they stood under the arcade, so loudly that Madam had come to see what all the noise was about. Helen had been a rock for the younger girls, firm and cool but always sympathetic – as long as you did your job well. She had neither time nor sympathy for sluggards.

'I'm glad to see you all again,' she said, her grey eyes moving over their faces. 'We must get together one day and talk about all our experiences. But that won't be for a while, I'm afraid – for the next few weeks we'll be at crisis level. There'll be a lot of patients arriving here very soon, and we're all going to be stretched to our limits.' She smiled again. 'I know not one of you will mind that at all!'

Briskly, she went through the list of names. Some of the girls, including Thursday, had already done theatre work and their experience would be valuable. Others barely knew a scalpel from a suture and would have to be taught – and taught quickly. They were here not merely to learn, but to assist, and there would be no time for mistakes.

'We'll be working a three watch system, eight hours at a time, over twenty-four hours, and we expect operating to be continuous. Each theatre has three tables, which will be running simultaneously, so at any one time you'll find six operations in progress. Each table has the complete team available, of course – a surgeon, anaesthetist, Sister and two VADs, or sometimes SBAs if they're available; most of them are at sea, of course, aboard ships.' She looked at them gravely. 'If you haven't encountered battle casualties before, you may find the sights and smells a little upsetting to begin with, but remember that these men are war heroes, *every one of them*, and they deserve our best attention. *We* haven't been to war, we haven't had to land on foreign beaches and face enemy attack, we haven't fought and been shot or bombed or bayoneted. All we've had to do is wait in comparative luxury for them to be brought to us. A few unpleasant moments are nothing – *nothing* – compared with what they've endured, and it behoves us to do our absolute best to bring them back to health. So we do *not* think about ourselves, but about them. At every moment.' She paused and there was a silence as she let her eyes move over their faces again, and then her smile broke out once more. 'I know I can rely on every one of you,' she said simply, and gave a quick, firm nod.

The girls were then assigned to their duties. Each would work at a certain table in one of the two theatres. Thursday found herself in 'A' with Louisa, while Ellen Bridges and Joy Cockroft were at the next table. Ellen had done a little theatre work, but Joy was completely new to it and by the end of the morning she was looking flustered and bewildered.

'I don't think I should have volunteered for this,' she said in distress. 'I'm going to be absolutely useless. I'm terrified I'm not going to be able to give the surgeon the right instruments.'

'You won't have to give him anything, not at the beginning,' Ellen told her comfortingly, 'and we all find it a bit strange to start with. You'll soon get used to it.'

'I hope so,' Joy said. 'I don't know what I'd do if someone died because I was so useless.'

'Go on, nobody'll die – not because of you, anyway.' Ellen looked at her. Joy, a diminutive redhead, was two or three years younger than most of them and new to Haslar. 'Where were you before you came here?'

'Well, I started as a Nightingale at St Thomas's Hospital in London. It's Florence Nightingale's hospital, so the nurses there are called after her. But then I got ill and had to leave, and when I was better I thought I'd volunteer. I want to go back to training as an SRN after the war,' she added. 'If they'll have me, that is.'

''Course they'll have you! They'll jump at anyone who's done

Naval nursing, especially if you'd already been there before the war. Look, you needn't worry about the theatre work. Madam and Tutor wouldn't have put you down for the course if they hadn't thought you could do it.'

'But how would they *know*?' Joy asked worriedly. 'Suppose they've made a terrible mistake?'

Ellen smiled at her. 'Madam and Sister Tutor *never* make mistakes. Now, come on – we'll go through the instruments again. Scalpel?'

'That's the knife the surgeon uses to cut into the patient's flesh.'

'Right. Forceps?'

'They're little pincers used to pick up swabs or take out organs – like sugar tongs.'

'Right.' The lesson continued as they made their way to the mess for lunch. Ellen beamed at her pupil. 'You see? You know all that. You don't need to worry at all. You'll be an excellent theatre nurse.'

Joy grinned. 'Well, if you really think so . . .'

'I know so. And I'll tell you something else.' Ellen leaned close to her as they queued for their helping of toad-in-the-hole and cabbage. 'I'm like Madam and Sister Tutor – I'm *never* wrong!'

The first casualties began to arrive next morning. Thursday, taking the chance of a breath of air along the sea wall before going on duty, saw the ships heading back across the Solent in grim convoy and turned at once to run back through the gate.

'They're coming! I've seen the ships – they'll be here any minute.' She burst into the dormitory and snatched up her cap and apron, pinning on her watch with shaking fingers. 'Come on, Ellen – Lou – we'll be wanted in theatre.' She ran out again, followed by the others, and together they scurried across to the arcade to the basement while the other girls ran on to the jetty where the pinnaces would arrive.

The theatre staff were already gathering at the theatre doors when the alarms began to sound. Helen Stanway gave the girls a nod of approval. 'Good. Get yourselves scrubbed and ready. Tilford, Wetherby, Bridges and Cockroft, you'll be on Surgeon Commander Sharp's team. Bowden and Wetherby, you can man the autoclave; there'll be plenty of sterilising to do. Tilford, you'll be dirty nurse. Bridges, Cockroft and Mears, go through to B Theatre where Sister

Weston will give you your orders.' Her voice was calm and clear, steadying the jittering nerves of the girls.

I oughtn't to feel like this, Thursday thought. I should be used to it by now. Once the flow had begun, there would be no time to worry, no time to think of anything other than the work to be done. But those last few moments, waiting for the first casualties to arrive, not knowing just what their injuries might be, were always nerve-racking.

Down by the jetty, the other girls were equally tense. Elsie had gone over to Zymotics, but Patsy, Susan and Vera Hapgood were amongst those who were to receive the patients as they arrived and get them to the wards they were assigned to by the Naval doctors. The trolleys were already in place on the tramlines that had been laid when Haslar Hospital was first built, and matelots stood ready to push them through the arcade, while the walking wounded would be helped by VADs.

'Blimey, this takes me back,' Patsy muttered as they stood there, watching the grey battleships steam slowly through the narrow harbour entrance. 'It's just like it was after Dunkirk, except that they're being landed by Naval pinnaces instead of ferry boats.' Her voice was taut with strain and Susan Morrison squeezed her arm.

'Your Roy'll be all right. He's lucky, you know he is.'

'*So* far,' Patsy said under her breath.

'It's not going to be like Dunkirk,' Susan told her. 'That was all such a rush, and nobody expected it. A lot of planning has gone into D-Day. I mean, all those things they were building out at Stokes Bay – we used to wonder whatever was going on out there. And look what they turned out to be – concrete *harbours*! I mean, who'd have dreamed that was what they were? Who could have thought of it? I bet the Germans never had the slightest idea. And even if they did realise we were going to invade, they didn't know where we were going to go. I reckon we'll have really caught them on the hop.'

'I hope so.' Patsy thought of all the defeats that had been suffered so far – Dunkirk, Dieppe, Hong Kong, Singapore. Yet there'd been victories too – El Alamein, Monte Cassino, Tobruk. And this new invasion could be the greatest victory of all. 'Oh, Susie, I really do hope so.'

The first pinnace was forging towards them across the choppy water. Patsy's eyes scanned it anxiously. 'Oh, those poor blokes, they'll be getting bounced about all over the place. Couldn't they have picked better weather for an invasion?' She moved forwards, her heart skipping. If Roy was in one of these boats . . .

He wasn't. And once the casualties began to come off, there was no more time to think about him. Just as they had done after Dunkirk, Patsy and the other girls were soon embroiled in a state of ordered chaos as the pinnaces came and went, each unloading its cargo of wounded men. Men, some of them no more than boys, boys who had been too young to fight when the war began, with broken arms or legs, bandaged heads, torn and shattered bodies; men and boys whose flesh had been shot or burned away, men with injuries that would maim and cripple them for the rest of their lives; men and boys who had been sitting by their lorries and tanks in the roads and lanes leading to Stokes Bay and other beaches only a day or two before, cooking sausages over Primus stoves and telling tales to the children who gathered around them.

Patsy felt a moment of grief for the young soldiers who had gone off so bravely and been wounded so soon. But there was no time for sorrow. There was too much work to be done. She moved into place and reached out her arms to a young, bewildered Tommy with a uniform caked in blood and salt. 'It's all right, love. It's all right. You're safe now. We'll look after you. It's all right . . .'

'There've only been a few so far,' Helen Stanway told Thursday and the others as they scrubbed their hands at the washbasins, 'but we're expecting a steady flow from now on. The ships are bringing them back as fast as they can.'

It sounded ominous. Thursday recalled Dunkirk – the thousands of men brought home weary, injured, defeated . . . But there were bound to be wounded, she reminded herself. They were going into battle. There would be men injured and killed right from the start. At least they *could* be brought back. They didn't have to be taken prisoner, or left to die in a foreign field.

She took her place at the operating table. The team was in position and the first patient under anaesthetic. She looked down at the prone body. It was a sailor who had been badly gashed by some jagged lump of metal; his torso was torn and shredded, his liver protruding and a white fragment of bone piercing the wall of his chest. Thursday felt a quick pang of pity and then, with resolution, she thrust aside all emotion and concentrated on simply doing her job, just as Sister Tutor had taught her when she had first come to Haslar.

'Right,' the surgeon said quietly, and turned to the nurse who stood at his side. 'Scalpel . . .'

They lost all sense of time. With their work taking such deep concentration, the girls found that the hours could tick by like minutes, and it wasn't until the watch was over that they realised just how exhausted they were. Thursday came off duty after each watch feeling dazed, her legs aching from the hours of standing, her mind numb from concentration. Spare time became a thing of the past; they ate their meals like automatons, washed and fell into bed to sleep like logs. The time went past in a blur and as Thursday came off duty one sunny afternoon, she was startled to realise that five days had gone by.

She climbed the stairs and stood outside for a moment, drawing in great lungfuls of fresh air. The light was dazzling, and she had the same feeling of surprise as when she came out of an afternoon in the cinema to find it was still daylight. Blinking, she put out a hand to steady herself against the wall and found Louisa at her side.

'What we need,' the tall girl said, 'is a cup of tea.'

'What I need is eight hours' sleep,' Thursday said. 'Or maybe a swim. Or a long country walk. But a cup of tea's a good start, and I don't suppose the others are very likely anyway.'

They walked back to the mess together, not speaking. Both had worked in operating theatres during their time abroad, and Thursday had worked here at Haslar, with Connor. They were accustomed to the concentration, to the continuous flow of patients, to the numerous different injuries. But it always took a while to adjust, to return to real life. Thursday remembered going back to the mess one day after assisting at a double amputation and finding leg of lamb being served for dinner. The very word 'leg' seemed offensive, but she'd been sharply taken to task by one of her colleagues, who had told her that if she wanted to be a 'real' nurse she'd got to learn to leave such fastidiousness behind. 'You won't be any use to the patients if you're going to turn into jelly because animals have got legs as well as us, and we eat them. It's the patients who matter – not your silly feelings.'

Thursday, abashed, had taken the warning to heart. She didn't want to find herself back on the wards, taking temperatures and pulses, even though she knew that was just as useful in the general nursing of the patients. And it wasn't as if she didn't *like* leg of lamb . . .

All the same, she always needed those few moments of adjustment from the theatre to the outside world, and she'd learned to accept this and allow for it.

'What d'you think you'll do once the war's over?' she asked Louisa. 'Will you stay in nursing – go for State Registration? I don't suppose they'll want VADs any more.'

Louisa shook her head. 'I don't think so. I think I'll have had enough of it by then. Besides,' she blushed a little, 'there's Andrew.'

'Oh.' Thursday looked at her friend. 'It really is serious, then?'

'I think so. We've been writing to each other ever since he left Alex. Well, it was serious even before then, only we didn't somehow want to commit ourselves – everything's so uncertain, it seemed almost like asking for bad luck. But since we've been apart – well, you know how it is.'

Thursday nodded. She knew exactly how it was. It had been the same for herself and Connor – the brief courtship, the exchanged messages, the promise. Only he hadn't wanted her to make any promises. He hadn't wanted her to tie herself down; he'd wanted her to live her life, go out and have fun while she had the chance.

All the same, he hadn't – she was sure – wanted her to fall in love with someone else. And she *had* promised – she'd made the promise to herself, that she would keep faith with him, that she'd wait until they were together again. She'd promised him in her heart, and it was a promise she wanted desperately to keep.

'I want to marry Andrew,' Louisa said, 'as soon as he comes home. We've been talking about it, in our letters. He'll leave the Army then – he isn't a regular – and go back into his father's business. They run a car manufacturing company in the Midlands. There'll be plenty of new vehicles wanted once things settle down again – cars and buses, lorries, all sorts. He'll need a wife who's at home, not working nights in a hospital.'

'Oh, that's lovely,' Thursday said. 'I'm so pleased. So really you're engaged, aren't you?'

'Not officially.' Louisa blushed again. 'I mean, there isn't a ring yet, and I think Andrew will want to propose properly when he gets back. We don't want to rush things. We'll have to get to know each other again. Everything's going to be different after the war, isn't it? Life will change completely. We'll have to get used to peace all over again.'

'Yes, I suppose we will.' Thursday rubbed her chin wryly. I can't even cope with coming out of the theatre without a bit of time to adjust, she thought. How am I going to manage to come out of the war?

Peace seemed, suddenly, to be rather a frightening idea.

'Well, it won't be for a long time yet,' she said. 'There's going to be a lot more spilt milk going under the bridge, as Elsie would say, before we have to cross that particular one.'

'Or a lot of spilt blood,' Louisa said soberly, and they pushed open the door of the mess and went to get their tea.

The medical wards were just as busy. Patsy, Susan, Vera Hapgood and the others were almost run off their feet, yet they still managed somehow to spend a little time with each patient, chatting to them as they carried out their mundane tasks and trying to give them what comfort they could. Unburdening themselves of their experiences seemed almost as important to the men as having their wounds attended to, especially as few of them could receive family visitors. The ban on visiting the coast, together with the difficulties of transport, made travelling from other parts of the countries almost impossible.

'It was bloody mayhem,' one of the Commandos said. With other Royal Marines and American Army units, he'd been in the first landings and now, less than a day later, he was back in England, with Patsy beside his bed helping the QARNN to change his dressings. 'Dozens of poor blighters were shot down in the first wave, but there were so many of us coming off the landing craft, and with the blokes at the guns firing away like madmen, see, they just couldn't get us all. I reckon our boys saw a few of them off an' all,' he added with satisfaction. 'And once we got to the beachhead, we could take cover under the Atlantic Wall. That's the dirty great concrete walls they put up as sort of fortifications,' he explained, seeing Patsy's mystified face. 'Any road, once you could get under the lee of that, you were out of the way of enemy fire, see, and there were so many of us, we took the Jerries by surprise. They never expected such a mass.' He lay back, wincing as Sister Burton began to clean the gaping wound in his thigh. 'Here, you're not putting that iodine muck on that, are you? It bloody stings, that does.'

Patsy grinned at him. 'Don't tell me you're frightened of a little bit of iodine! Not after you've just been in an invasion!'

'Yeah, well, that's men's work, innit. Iodine's what women put on their kiddies' knees when they falls over in the playground.' He gave a little yelp as Burton swabbed the wound. 'Here, you done that on purpose!'

'I'll do worse than that if you don't behave yourself,' the QARNN told him calmly. 'You're in a Naval hospital now, remember. We expect our patients to be tough. You won't get your Sergeant Major coming round to bring you tea and sympathy.'

The Commando looked entreatingly at Patsy, and she grinned again and winked. 'Never mind, if you're good *I'll* bring you some tea. That's what we VADs are for.'

'Not until you've finished with dressings and bedpans,' Sister said smartly, winding a bandage around the muscular thigh. 'And then only if I haven't found some other jobs for you to do.' She stood back and regarded her work. 'You'll do. A week or so in here and you'll be fit to go back again.'

'Well, if that ain't the best news I've heard since my brother told me Father Christmas wasn't real,' he said morosely, watching her walk briskly away down the ward. 'Still, it'll be better than being in here with that martinet ruling the roost. How d'you put up with it?'

'It isn't Sister Burton we have to put up with,' Patsy told him. 'It's you patients! Just think how nice it would be in here without you lot – nice tidy beds, no newspapers all over the place, nobody cluttering the place up with mugs of cocoa.' She gave an exaggerated sigh of wistfulness. 'That's why we do our best to get you fit again – just so we can have a bit of peace.'

'Peace!' he said, and lay back on his pillows, looking suddenly white. 'Peace, that's what we all want.'

Patsy touched his hand for a moment, then slipped away. The wards were filling rapidly now; as well as by sea, men were being ferried back to England by air. The man in the next bed to the Commando was one of the parachutists who had been dropped from a glider, and parachuted straight into a clump of trees.

'Just hanging there, I was,' he told Patsy in a whisper as he looked up at her from his prone position, 'with all the cords and silk and stuff tangled up round me like a bloody cat's cradle, and then these German soldiers appeared out of nowhere and started machine-gunning me. Thought I was a goner, I did straight, and then some Tommies come out of the trees and shot *them*! Well, you should have seen 'em skedaddle – wasn't expecting it, see. So the Tommies cut me down and took me off to the field hospital, and then this Dakota landed in a field nearby and they loaded me on board with some other blokes and here we are in Haslar.'

'My, you were lucky,' Patsy observed. 'If those Jerries had been better at shooting . . .'

'Well, you can't aim a machine-gun all that accurately, see. I mean, it sprays out bullets all over the place, doesn't it? You just trust to luck one of them will hit something vital – and generally one does. So I guess I *was* pretty lucky, when you think about it. Just got a few cuts and bruises and that, and my arms almost torn out of their sockets, and this bit of back trouble, that's all. And I tell you what,' he winked painfully, the deep scratches on his face pulling at the scraped skin, 'there was this real little doll of a nurse on board that Dakota. Got a date with her, I have, the minute I'm out of here.'

Patsy gazed at him. The 'bit of back trouble' he referred to was a fracture that might leave him paralysed from the waist down for the rest of his life. Nobody had told him yet. She wondered if the nurse in the Dakota had realised it.

'I didn't know they had women nurses flying into France,' she said.

'Only just started, see. Nightingales, they call 'em.' He closed his eyes, exhausted, and Patsy went on to the next man, her heart full of sorrow for the waste of so many young lives, and with a deep gnawing anxiety for Roy.

'It must be nice to be able to talk to the patients,' Joy said a little wistfully when they all met at suppertime. 'Chat to them, help to cheer them up and all that. Ours are either fast asleep or just nodding off.'

'Take it from me, they're better off that way,' Patsy advised her. 'You've seen patients who are in pain all the time. It's a lot worse, I can tell you, when they're straight from the battlefield. You have to get used to seeing men with their arms and legs torn off, or hanging by a thread – men with their insides almost ripped out – men going mad with it, screaming in agony, crying for their mothers and dying in front of your very eyes. *You* see them when they're out of all that. You can tidy them up and do whatever's necessary without hurting them, without hearing them scream. If you'd ever tried changing the dressings of a man who's been badly burnt or had half his face torn away, you'd know what I mean,' she added.

Joy turned pale. 'I don't know whether I'm going to be any use as a nurse either way,' she said. 'I'm so scared of doing the wrong thing. And the amputations – all those poor boys having their arms or legs cut off.' She laid down her knife and fork. 'I've been thinking of going to Madam and telling her I'm no good.'

The others stared at her. 'You don't mean it,' Thursday said at last.

'I do.' The little redhead was close to tears. 'I nearly dropped the scalpel this morning when Sharpie gave it back to me. *Dropped* it! It would have got dirty on the floor and – and –'

'And had to be sterilised. Which is what was going to happen to it anyway,' Ellen pointed out. 'Look, all you need to do is try to relax a bit. Forget about yourself and how frightened or useless you are – just think about what you're doing. We all go through this, you know, when we're new. And you've been thrown in right at the deep end. We haven't stopped for the entire watch, ever since it started. It's as if they were coming in on a conveyor belt.' She slipped her arm round Joy's shoulders and gave her a squeeze. 'You'll be all right. You're just tired, that's all.'

'We're all tired,' Thursday said. 'I'm exhausted! I feel as if I haven't seen the outside world for months.'

'It's the smell, too,' Joy went on. 'Gas gangrene – I've never smelt anything so horrible. I don't know how I stop myself being sick when I go down those stairs.' She leaned her elbows on the table and put her face in her hands. 'Honestly, I'm no good at it. I'm a rotten, rotten nurse.'

The others glanced at each other. Then Ellen got up. 'I'm going to go and see Madam, ask if you can have a bit of time off. You're all right, really, Joy, you just need a break.' She glanced at the others. 'Maybe we all do. Even a walk along the sea wall would do us good.'

Madam agreed. 'You've been working at full stretch for nearly a week. You need a good blow of sea air. The barricades have been removed from Stokes Bay and Gilkicker now – run down there and have a few hours on the beach. I dare say there'll be plenty of other people doing the same, now that the weather's cleared up.'

The girls went out in a gang. Most of them had bikes now, and they pedalled along Clayhall and into Anglesey Road to reach Stokes Bay. The wind and rain of the previous week had cleared away, leaving blue skies and warm June sunshine, and as Madam had said, there were plenty of local people making their way there too. It was so long since anyone had been allowed out to the beach, and now that the great rolls of barbed wire had been removed everyone wanted to see the sea again. For Gosport people, the sea was a part of their lives; you couldn't help but be aware of it, either out at the Bay or Lee, or down at the ferry when you wanted to cross the harbour to go to 'Pompey'. They knew it in all its moods – grey-green under cloudy skies, swelling ominously as the wind got up, slashing against the jetties and sea walls when it was stormy. And blue and calm, as it was today, with just a few 'white horses' far out where a summer breeze blew the tops off the waves in a spray of foam.

The girls propped their bikes together on the shingle and gazed at it.

'It looks so peaceful,' Thursday said at last. 'You wouldn't believe that only a week or so ago, there were hundreds of men here with tanks and lorries and heaven knows what else, going aboard all those ships. And look – those must be the Mulberry Harbours! They've brought them back.'

They stared at the huge concrete blocks anchored just off the shore. Now that they knew what they'd been used for, it was easy to see that they could have been slung together to make artificial harbours where the troops could land. 'Mind, I still don't see how it is they float,' Elsie said, shaking her head. 'I mean, they're *concrete*. I just don't understand it.'

'Just as well you weren't in charge, then,' Ellen said cheerfully. She linked arms with Joy. 'Come on. Let's have a walk along the beach. I want to paddle!'

They set off, but within moments the walk had turned into a run and then a wild chase along the shingly beach. Shedding all their responsibilities, the nurses became children again, racing each other along the edge of the waves. Then Thursday sat down and pulled off her shoes, tying the laces together to sling them around her neck.

Holding her skirt above her knees, she waded into the water, gasping a little at the first icy shock, then laughing with delight as she went deeper. The others followed, lifting their faces blissfully to the sun, and emerged at last to sit on the shingle while their feet dried. Patsy lay back and stretched her arms above her head.

'We'll have to get out our bathers,' Thursday said. 'We'll be able to swim off the sea wall again. It must have been miserable for people not to be able to go for a dip.'

'Mm.' Patsy sounded uninterested and Thursday glanced at her. Patsy had been the keenest swimmer of them all.

'Didn't you do any swimming while you were in Scotland?' she asked idly, letting some sand trickle through her fingers. Stokes Bay was mostly shingle but there were occasional patches of sand, jealously commandeered on Sundays by families with small children.

Patsy sat up and picked up a handful of seaweed. She started to pop the little bladders. 'Not really. We couldn't swim in the harbour and the coast was too far away to go there often – and the water was freezing. And sometimes there were really big jellyfish.' She dropped the seaweed as if it was of no further interest, and stared towards the Island.

Thursday glanced her. She knew that Patsy was worrying about Roy. There had still been no word from him. 'But it must be lovely up there, surely,' she persisted. 'I've seen pictures of the coast – all the little islands. They looked beautiful.'

'Oh yes,' Patsy said, shrugging. 'The scenery's lovely. And the water's so clear, you could see the bottom even when it was quite deep. And the coast is beautiful. We had a couple of trips out there, but that was all.' She looked at the other two. 'I dare say you got plenty of swimming in Egypt. It must have been like being on holiday, when you got time off.'

'*When*,' Elsie said sardonically. 'It wasn't no beach holiday, I can tell you, even if we did have plenty of sand.'

'Bet it was nice and hot, though,' Patsy said wistfully. 'I could've done with some of that sunshine. I don't reckon there's *anywhere* colder than Scotland.'

Thursday thought of the skies above Alexandria. They had been a hard, metallic blue, quite different from the gentle azure of this English afternoon, and the sun had burned with a relentless white heat. But the Mediterranean had been delicious to bathe in, just cool enough to refresh sweating skin yet warm enough to stay in for hours. She thought of the girls and men who had gathered there during their off-duty hours, sometimes during the day, sometimes in the evening. The stars had hung above them, huge and brilliant, almost close enough, it seemed, to touch. Like diamonds . . .

She moved sharply, dropping her handful of sand back on to the shingle of Stokes Bay beach. 'Isn't it time we were getting back?'

Patsy glanced up, surprised by her tone, but Elsie looked at her watch and nodded. 'I suppose it is. We don't want Madam thinking we've forgotten about our next duty.' She heaved herself to her feet. 'It's been good, though, hasn't it? Being able to come out here again and behave like kids let out of school.'

Joy got to her feet too, nodding. 'It has. I feel a lot better.'

'There,' Ellen said, 'you see? That was all you needed, a break and some fresh air. So no more talk about not being any good as a nurse, all right?'

'Well – maybe.' Joy brushed back her auburn curls. 'I'll see for sure when we get back to the theatre. And I hope someone's cleared away all those amputations. It was seeing that big heap of arms and legs piled up outside the theatre door, that started me off in the first place. I mean, they're bits of *people*, and they're treated just like so much rubbish.'

'And that's all they are,' Elsie said firmly. 'No use to nobody. You've got to forget that side of it, Joy. Get your suit of armour on, like the rest of us do.'

Joy nodded a little doubtfully. Thursday watched her, remembering how hard it had been for her too, in the early days. And even now, she was sometimes caught unexpectedly by some sight or sound that reminded her that these patients were men who had home lives – wives, children, parents, brothers and sisters. And a lifetime to go through, without the arm or leg – or both – that had been lost in Normandy or here in Haslar Hospital. It was hard to remain objective when you thought of that.

It was like remembering the sun-soaked days and starlit nights of Alexandria. You just had to push the thoughts and memories away. You *had* to – or you wouldn't be able to carry on.

Chapter Six

The suit of armour was certainly needed after D-Day. Haslar was the first port of call for many of the most severely wounded – military and Air Force personnel as well as Naval. Once any emergency treatment had been carried out and the patients were fit to be moved, they were sent on to other hospitals and their beds freed for the next wave of casualties.

The VADs on the medical wards found themselves listening to more horrific tales as the men recovered. 'You wouldn't credit some of the stuff we took over,' the Commando told Patsy. Mostly silent and withdrawn, he seemed to find relief in talking to her and Sister Burton didn't chivvy Patsy away when she saw her standing by his bed. 'Not just tanks and jeeps, I don't mean, but all those contraptions they call Funnies – crab tanks, and crocodiles, and flame throwers. There was swimming tanks too, supposed to float – and some of them might have but all the ones I saw sank like bloody stones.' He shook his head. 'Tested 'em in calm water, see, but when we actually made the landings we had all those storms, didn't we, the wind whipping up the bloody waves like the sides of houses. Total bloody nightmare. Poor bleeding sods inside didn't stand a chance, not a chance.'

Thursday nodded soberly when Patsy reported this. 'We had a patient in the theatre today. He was rambling as he went under, but we all thought that what he said must be true. It was horrible. Men shot the minute they landed on the beach, and nobody to help them. You couldn't stop, he said, you just had to go on, even if it was your friend, even if it was your *brother*. He saw his best friend with almost all his face blown away . . .' She shook her head. 'He said the medical orderlies tried their best to get all the injured back on the

63

ships, but there were crowds of men still coming off, trying to land. And there were *hundreds* drowned, weighed down by all their equipment. Bodies everywhere, he kept saying, bodies everywhere . . . It was so horrible to hear him, poor man; we were all thankful when he went under the anaesthetic. At least he could forget for a few hours.'

Most of the VADs and the QARNNs had seen war wounds before. They knew that bullets, bombs and grenades could tear through the body, ripping it apart, shredding muscle and shattering bone. Often, it seemed impossible to repair the horrific damage; often, a patient who had miraculously survived the journey back across the Channel died even as he came into the theatre, or while the surgeon was operating. Some died later, as if unable to fight any longer.

'But we save a lot,' Louisa said as they sank on to their beds one day after a particularly grim watch. 'Even if they've lost a leg or an arm, they'll get better. They'll still be able to have their life.'

'And they're not all amputations,' Ellen agreed. 'Even though it does seem like it, when you see those arms and legs piled up outside the theatre door.'

'I just wish the porters would take them away,' Joy said again, but everyone knew that they were so busy transporting the incessant stream of patients in and out of the theatre that there was barely time to clear up the detritus of the operations. Now and again, it got too much for anyone to tolerate for another moment, and then there would be a frenzy of cleaning up; the rotting body parts would be removed to the hospital incinerator and the floors scrubbed and disinfected. But nothing could disguise the overpowering smell of gas gangrene that permeated the basements.

The first German casualties took them all by surprise. Thursday was sitting by with the autoclave, sterilising the vast array of instruments that had been used in the latest wave of operations, when she heard the first scream. A thrill of fear ran through her and she looked up, wondering what could be happening to make a man scream like that. Surely, after all that had happened, the enemy couldn't be invading now . . . And then the screams came closer and the doors swung open to admit a patient on a trolley.

The theatre staff froze. They were used to patients in pain, and did their best to ease it as quickly as possible. Even before they arrived in theatre, they would have been given injections to calm them, yet this patient wasn't calm at all. And his screams didn't seem to be of pain.

He's terrified, Thursday thought. He's frightened to death – but why?

The man was yelling words she didn't understand, and then she had a sudden memory of young Heinz Schmidt, the German she had nursed here at Haslar in the early days of the war, and realised that this man too was a German.

'Whatever's the matter with him?' she asked Louisa in a low voice.

'He thinks we'll operate without an anaesthetic,' Louisa whispered back. 'Apparently that's what they've been told. He's got an abdominal injury and a broken leg, and lacerations, and he thinks all that will be done without any anaesthetic at all. No wonder he's frightened, poor man.'

The anaesthetist approached the trolley and the screams intensified. Even though they all knew that in a few moments he would be unconscious and the screams would cease, everyone in the theatre was affected by the fear that radiated from the injured man. Accustomed as they were to terrible injuries, they were also accustomed to men who either tried to hold back their groans or, if they couldn't do that, at least had a basic trust in the doctors and nurses around them. By the time the noise died down, half the nurses were trembling and the surgeons were even more brusque than usual. Outside the theatre, other patients waiting their turn were shocked and anxious.

'What's going on in there, nurse?' Thursday heard one ask as she slipped outside to fetch something. 'It sounds like a pig's being killed.'

'It's a German patient. He thought we wouldn't use anaesthetic on him.'

The man snorted. 'Blimey, it's a pity we do. They probably treat our boys that way, that's why they think we do it too. Too soft, that's what we are.'

Thursday went back to the theatre, the words echoing in her mind. Was the man right? Were the Germans really so inhumane to their prisoners? She thought about her brother Steve, whom the family had thought dead for almost a year before they discovered that he was actually in German hands. Had they operated on him without anaesthetic?

'Of course they don't,' Louisa said when Thursday admitted her fears later that day. 'They've signed the Geneva Convention, haven't they? There are rules about that sort of thing. They might not treat prisoners like royalty, but they're not that brutal. Anyway, you've had letters from him, haven't you? He hasn't said anything?'

'No, he hasn't,' Thursday said, relieved. 'You're right, Lou. He hasn't even had any operations, as far as we know – never got injured.' She grinned a little shamefacedly. 'It was that man screaming like that – it got me in a panic.'

'Yes, and that's how they brainwash us,' Louisa said soberly. 'All that propaganda we used to hear, about Germans eating babies and that sort of thing – it frightens everyone and when people are frightened they lose their heads and can't fight. It's like another sort of weapon.'

Thursday thought for a few minutes. 'Yes, but what about all those things we've been hearing about Hong Kong and Singapore? For all we know, the Japanese *are* treating people like that. We don't know what's happening to their prisoners. They never signed this Convention, did they?'

'No, they didn't. But they're human beings, just the same. Surely, once people are prisoners and can't do them any more harm, they won't behave like animals. Surely . . .'

But her voice was less certain and they looked at each other with fear, thinking of Jeanie Brown and the other nurses and civilians now in Japanese hands. Nobody knew what was happening to them – but everyone feared the worst.

'It's horrible, this war,' Thursday said at last. 'Horrible. And I can't even remember now why it all started. Hitler, taking over a few countries in Europe – and now it's spread all over the world. When's it going to stop, Louie?'

The other girl put her arm round Thursday's shoulders. 'We're on the last lap now. We must be. We may be getting a lot of casualties here at Haslar, but most of the men who went over on D-Day are still there, fighting and driving the Germans back. We've got them on the run. And when we've finished with them we'll sort out the Japanese too. You'll see. We're winning now, Thursday – we really are.'

It was almost a fortnight before the flood of casualties began to ease off. 'They say there's thousands dead,' Elsie said, coming over from Zymotics, 'and I don't know how many have come through Haslar. However many did they send over there in the first place?'

'Thousands more, I suppose.' Thursday was in a strange state of fatigue and exhilaration. The constant demands of the work in the hot, steamy underground theatres with their lack of fresh air and sense of being cut off from the outside world kept her and the others on a rush of adrenalin, so that they felt almost as if they were floating an inch or two above the ground. They did their work in a dream of efficiency, working on a different level of consciousness, and it was only when they came off duty that they began to realise how utterly exhausted they were. Yet even then, there wasn't time to relax – apart from the odd walk along the sea wall or swift dash into Gosport; their whole beings were wrapped up in the theatre and what must be done there. And those brief moments off duty seemed unreal. Walking round Woolworth's one day, looking for oddments of toiletry or cosmetics, Thursday was overtaken by a sudden exasperated impatience. She flung down the lipstick she had been examining and stalked out, wanting only to get back on duty.

But most of their off-duty time was taken up either with sleep, or with writing letters. Everyone had husbands, sweethearts or family at home to write to. Thursday divided her time between her mother and father, back home in Worcester, and Connor, somewhere in the Far East. Yet even as she covered the sheets of paper with her sloping handwriting, she knew that she couldn't tell her family what she could tell Connor, for the descriptions of her work and her stories of what the men had endured were beyond their imaginings. Even her letters to Connor, who was himself a surgeon, must run the gauntlet of the censor.

Writing to Connor, whether the letters reached him or not, was a safety valve. Thursday and the other girls could talk together about what they were seeing and hearing, but what they really wanted to do with their off-duty time was forget it. At the same time, it would have preyed too much upon their minds – in spite of the suits of armour – if they hadn't been able to express their thoughts and feelings to someone else.

'It's Saturday tomorrow,' Elsie said. She was stretched on her bunk in her underclothes, her skin still faintly golden from the tan she had acquired in Egypt. 'We've got the night off. Let's go out – have a bit of fun.'

Thursday rolled over and peered down. 'Where shall we go?'

'Kimball's? The Savoy?' They were the two best-known dance halls in Portsmouth. 'Or we could go to South Parade Pier, they get some good bands there. They had Joe Loss the other week. Come on. We've been working flat out ever since we got here. It's time we let our hair down a bit.'

Still hanging over the edge of her bunk, Thursday looked down at Patsy. 'What d'you think, Pats?'

'I don't know. I don't know if I feel like it.' Patsy sounded weary, her voice flat and depressed. Thursday and Elsie glanced at each other.

'Come on, Pats,' Thursday said gently. 'Elsie's right, it'll do us good. We haven't had a proper night out since we got here.'

'I don't know if I want a night out.'

Thursday hesitated. She knew how Patsy was feeling – as they all were, suddenly flat after the sustained effort of the last two weeks. She knew, too, that this was the very moment when they most needed to relax – to go somewhere with bright lights and music and dancing, to laugh and make jokes and kick over the traces. Just for one evening.

'Come on, Pats,' she said again. 'It'll do you good.'

'There's only one thing that'll do me good,' Patsy said, staring out of the window. 'And that's a letter from my Roy.' She sat up. 'It's a fortnight now since D-Day and I haven't heard a word. What's happened to him? Why can't he write?'

Thursday gazed at her helplessly. 'You don't even know for sure he was there. His ship could be anywhere—'

'It's bound to have gone there,' Patsy said. 'You know it is. And what about that man you told me about, Thursday, the one who said the medical orderlies were going ashore, trying to get the men back? Roy could have done that, he could have got shot, or drowned, or *anything*. If I could just get a *letter* . . .'

There was a short silence. The girls looked at each other.

'Look,' Elsie said at last, in her commonsense voice, 'you know as well as I do there's going to be no letter coming tonight. Tomorrow morning's the soonest the next post can come, and it's not going to come any quicker for you sitting here moping about it. Come on, come out with us – the time'll pass all the quicker. I don't see how they've got time to write letters anyway,' she added. 'You know what it's been like over there. I don't suppose there's anywhere they can buy stamps!'

Patsy stared at her and then burst out laughing. Her laughter had an hysterical edge to it, but Elsie took no notice. She put her arm round Patsy's shoulders and held her tightly. 'That's it, Pats. You have a good laugh. Have a cry, if you want. But come out with us tonight. A bit of jitterbugging, that's what you need. A bit of a cuddle with some nice bloke. It won't do any harm, and it'll do a hell of a lot of good! Is that agreed, then?'

Patsy nodded, sniffing and reaching into her sleeve for her hanky. She smiled a rather watery smile.

'All right, Elsie, you win. I'll come and jitterbug with you. I ought to get back into practice anyway, for when the war's over and Roy comes home. He was always a good dancer. We used to talk about going in for championships, you know.'

'That's right,' Elsie said, giving Thursday a nod over Patsy's head. 'You get some practice in. It won't be long now, and you'll be jitterbugging champions of Pompey – you and Roy together!'

The Savoy dance hall was almost opposite South Parade Pier, in Southsea. To get there, the girls crossed the harbour via the 'floating bridge' – the chain ferry which carried cars from Gosport to Old Portsmouth. From there, it was only a mile or so to cycle to Southsea, mostly along the seafront.

'It's strange to think that this was all wired off just a week ago,' Thursday commented as they pedalled along. She gazed out across the strip of water between the mainland and the Isle of Wight. There were people on the beach even now, enjoying the long June evening. It would be late tonight before the light faded from the sky – double summer time kept darkness at bay until gone eleven. Yet nobody could doubt that the country was still very much at war. The Solent was still busy with ships, crossing to and fro to take fresh troops to France and bring back the wounded. More injured men for us to nurse, she thought, more young soldiers and sailors with their lives changed for ever . . .

'People still can't come here from other places, though,' Patsy said. 'You still need a permit to come to the south coast. There was a woman the other day in one of the pubs in Gosport, she was caught in a spot check and didn't have her identity card on her – they arrested her and took her off to the police station. She was all night in a cell before her hubby came in next day and got her out, but she's still got to go to the court and pay a fine.'

'Well, as long as they're still sending men over I suppose they've got to be careful,' Elsie said. 'There's plenty of information for spies to pick up. Which ships are going out, and that sort of thing. Wonder if there'll be any decent blokes at the dance tonight?'

'I don't care what they're like, so long as they can dance,' Patsy observed. 'That's all I'm interested in.'

Thursday said nothing. She felt suddenly lonely, and wondered why she'd come. Like Patsy, she really only wanted to dance with one man but Connor was thousands of miles away and it would still be a long time before he could hold her in his arms. She remembered the dance they'd been to at Grange, in Gosport, and how they'd swirled round the floor together. And next day, Grange had been bombed and some of the people who had been there with them had been killed.

And yet, although she was missing Connor desperately, she still wanted to feel the closeness of a man's body against hers, the warmth and strength of male arms around her. It would satisfy at least a pang or two of the hunger that seemed a part of her these days. I'll be twenty-six in November, she thought, and I've never made love with a man, not properly. By the time my mother was this age, she had three children. I'll be an old hag of thirty before I start a family – if then!

They arrived at the Savoy and propped their bikes together. It wasn't very romantic, arriving by bike, but the only other way was to walk, or go by pinnace to the main jetty and catch a bus. And there was getting back to consider too. It would still be light enough to cycle, if they left by eleven, and they could catch the floating bridge on its last crossing.

If they missed that, it meant a wild dash round to the main ferry – a ride of over a mile – for the last of the boats, or the pinnace. And if they missed *that*, it meant a long wait until 5 a.m. when the boats began to run again, and a severe reprimand from Madam. Being 'adrift' was a serious offence, in the Navy.

The dance had already begun as they walked into the hall and people were swirling around the floor. Like the Pier, the Savoy boasted some of the best-known bands for its dances, with leaders like Ambrose, Joe Loss and Nat Gonella. The Squadronnaires, recruited from the RAF, came sometimes, as well as The Skyrockets and their Naval equivalent The Blue Mariners. Both Thursday and Elsie had seen some of these bands during their foreign service, as well as singers and entertainers like Vera Lynn, Gracie Fields, and Tommy Trinder with his broad grin and catch-phrase, 'You Lucky People!'

The band tonight wasn't a famous one, but it played all the favourite tunes of the day – 'I Know Why and So Do You', 'Tangerine', 'In the Mood' and 'Moonlight Serenade'. There were plenty of partners available and the girls were snapped up as soon as they came in. Thursday found herself in the arms of a tall, fair-haired American, dancing a tango that left her breathless. Their bodies were close and she could smell a mixture of coal-tar soap and sweat that was oddly attractive. A very male scent, she thought, inhaling it; a very *exciting* scent. She closed her eyes, letting herself float in his arms, then flicked them open again as he bent her backwards to the swoop of the music, and found herself staring up into his face.

'Say, you're quite a mover,' he drawled, letting her come upright again and finishing the dance with a flourish. 'Will you do the next one with me as well?'

Thursday nodded. Dancing had been a major pastime in Egypt, and she loved the feeling that she could let her body mould closely to her partner's without any sense of betrayal towards the man who held her heart. Even the kisses exchanged during the last waltz, passionate though they might be, were only for that evening – a mutual recognition that love could last for as much as a lifetime, but as little as an evening. It was just as real sometimes, she thought, as they swung into a fast foxtrot, but it would be over by the time she reached the ferry, and no hard feelings on either side. That was the trick of it, like putting on your suit of armour at the hospital. You could let yourself feel, let yourself love a little, but it had to come to an end, just as the dance itself came to an end. With the playing of the National Anthem and that last goodnight kiss, your little holiday from real life must be finished, and real life resumed. But you felt refreshed by your evening. It helped everyone to carry on.

Of course, if you were like Elsie, still single and heartwhole, you could let the romance continue. Elsie looked as if she was going to do so tonight, Thursday thought, catching a glimpse of her friend drifting by, her arms wound round the neck of a sturdy matelot, eyes blissfully closed.

'So you're a nurse, are you?' her partner said, walking her back to her seat at the end of the foxtrot. 'Here in Portsmouth?'

Thursday shook her head, then nodded. 'Well, almost. I'm at Haslar. It's in Gosport, on the other side of the harbour. A Naval hospital.'

He nodded. 'I know it. Buddy of mine finished up there a week or so ago. Went over in the first wave of landings and copped a packet, but he's going to be OK. Lost a foot, unfortunately, so his war's over. He's in one of our hospitals now.'

'Oh.' Thursday looked at him, wondering if she might have assisted in the operation the man must have had. 'I'm sorry.'

The GI shrugged. 'Could have been worse. At least he's still alive, and a guy can do a lot with an artificial foot. Even dance!' The music was striking up again and he grinned at her. 'Feel like doing something more lively?'

Dancers were already crowding the floor and Thursday found herself twisting and gyrating in time to the jazz, her feet tapping wildly as her partner twirled her around. He pulled her close, caught her by the waist and swung her high in the air, then down again and between his legs. Thursday gasped with shock and exhilaration, tried to anticipate his next move and then gave up as she found herself almost on his shoulders. Just don't let him drop me, she prayed, and then forgot even that in her elation. Oh, this was wonderful, this was marvellous; it was exciting and arousing, it was like flying, it was like being a part of the music, a part of the dance, a part of the tall, fair GI who was her partner . . .

The music ended so abruptly that she felt dizzy. She swayed and felt his arms around her, firm and strong as they had been during the dance but with an added tension that transmitted itself to her body. She stood still, close in his embrace, and then looked up into his face.

He had very blue eyes. Clear blue eyes. Honest, direct eyes, with very wide pupils. She looked into them and caught her breath.

There was a moment of silence.

'I don't even know your name,' he murmured.

'It's Thursday.'

'Thursday?'

She nodded. Her voice was low, shaking. 'What's yours?'

'Earl.'

'Earl?' She laughed. 'That's like being called Duke. Or Prince.'

'Well, it's no stranger than being called a day of the week.' He gave her a quizzical glance. 'Let's go outside for a minute. Get some fresh air.'

'I . . .' Thursday hesitated. She flicked a look around the big room, wondering where the others were. She spotted Elsie, now sitting on the sailor's lap, but Patsy was nowhere to be seen. 'I ought to stay with my friends,' she said lamely.

'Aw, come on. They're OK. You all came for a bit of fun, didn't you? A night off from the war?' He took her gently by the arm and drew her towards the door. 'I'm not going to make a pass at you – not unless you want me to, anyway!'

That's just the trouble, Thursday thought as she allowed him to guide her outside. With the exhilaration of the dance still fizzing through her body and the warmth of his embrace still lingering about her, she might well want him to make a pass at her. I'm only human, she thought, and I'm nearly twenty-six, and it's such a long time since Connor went away. And there've been other men to dance with since then, other men to hold and kiss me, other men to love a little – and every time it gets more difficult not to fall all the way in love. Sometimes, it had been almost impossible.

Once, it had been quite impossible. It was only the thought of the promise she had made, the promise she knew she must keep even though it had been made only in her heart, that had kept her from taking that final step.

Earl led her out into the soft light of the evening and they walked across the road to the promenade. The shingle beach was washed now by soft wavelets, a clear turquoise laced with creamy foam – a far cry from the grey, sullen swell and crashing waves of D-Day. Thursday stared at it, remembering the great armada that had massed here, each ship like a child at a pre-war birthday party with its big grey balloon floating above. She remembered the thunder of the aircraft as they passed overhead, wave upon wave of Spitfires, Hurricanes, Dakotas and the huge American Flying Fortresses. And the silence of the gliders, carrying troops and vehicles to land beyond the shores, to take the enemy by surprise.

'I guess that's where I'll be heading soon,' Earl murmured, breaking into her thoughts.

She turned and looked at him. 'To France?'

'Sure. They won't leave any of us behind, not as long as we're fit and ready for action.' He grinned at her and flexed his muscles. 'Gee, I hope not, anyway! I'm sure ready for it. Teach those bastards – sorry – a lesson. It was plenty time for us to come into the war.'

'I suppose that's something we can thank the Japanese for,' Thursday said, and then thought of Jeanie Brown. 'I wish they hadn't done what they did, though. It wasn't anything to do with them – why did they have to join in?'

'The way it was explained to us, they'd been after China for years. I guess they saw a chance and took it, and then found Russia getting in their way. That meant they'd got to take Hitler's side, and get rid of our bases in the South Pacific.' He snapped his fingers. 'Pearl Harbor!'

Thursday nodded. It sounded simple enough, put like that, yet it was terrible that the world was at war simply because of greed. Why did leaders want more and more power? Why couldn't everyone be satisfied to live simply in their own homes, peaceful and content?

The sun was going down slowly, turning the sky to the colour of apricots with a soft green shadow merging into the far horizon. A shimmering path lay like a carpet of gold leaf across the sea, shifting gently with the swell, broken in places as a ship crossed. A few people were bathing, reluctant to let the day end, and couples were walking arm-in-arm along the prom.

'It's hard to believe they're fighting over there,' Thursday said softly. 'Men killing each other. The wounded just lying there helpless while others run past and leave them.'

'There's nothing else you can do,' Earl told her. 'You're there to fight, and if you stop you're likely to get killed as well. You can prop a bloke up, put a cigarette between his lips, but any more than that and you're risking others' lives as well as your own.' He stared out over the crowded waters. 'It might be your best buddy shot down, and you still can't do more than that.'

Thursday glanced at him. 'Is that what happened to you?'

'It has done,' he said briefly, and then took his eyes away from the ships. He turned to look down into her face. 'Don't let's talk about it now, Thursday.' He grinned. 'I still can't get over that name of yours! Come on – let's forget it for a while. Real life'll come back soon enough. Let's do what the song says – let's face the music and dance!'

She laughed, and then reached up and touched his face. 'That's what it's for, isn't it – dancing? To help us forget, for just a little while. It does us good.'

'It'll do me good,' he said seriously, 'to have this evening to remember when I'm over there.' He nodded out towards the sea. 'It'll do me good to remember you, Thursday, and think of the dancing we had together. And maybe a kiss or two as well.' He bent his head and touched her lips with his.

Thursday stood quite still. She closed her eyes. Earl's arms were warm and hard about her body, his lips tender yet searching. She let her own arms creep up round his neck, and pulled him suddenly tight against her, caught by a rush of desire. I want to be loved, she thought, letting herself relax against him. I want to know what it's like to be loved, to love someone. I want to *feel* it . . .

Earl lifted his lips away at last. They pulled slowly apart. She slid her arms down from his neck and rested her palms against his chest. He reached up and took her left hand and looked at it.

'You're not married? Not engaged?'

She hesitated. 'Not exactly.'

'There's a feller, though? Someone you think a lot of?'

She nodded. 'He's in the Far East, on a ship. He's been away for three years now.'

'Three years,' he said. 'That's a hell of a long time to wait.'

Thursday looked down for a moment, then raised her eyes to his. 'He didn't ask me to wait,' she said. 'I wanted to. I made a promise – to myself, really. But it is a long time. I didn't know it would be so long – I didn't know what it would be like.'

There was a little silence. She could feel her heart thudding. She didn't really know what she was saying to him – that she wanted to keep her promise, or that it had been too big a promise to make? Suppose he asked her to break it, on this lovely June evening, with the peace of the seafront disturbed only by dance music sounding from the pier? Had she kept her promise long enough?

'I want you to have fun,' Connor's voice said inside her head. 'I want you to be the Thursday who goes dancing – who always has a smile and a laugh. I don't want you to stay at home moping.'

He must have known the risks. He must have known the temptations. That was why he hadn't wanted to tie her down, hadn't wanted her to make any promises. He hadn't wanted her to face the dilemma that such a promise could cause.

But I made it, all the same, she reminded herself. I made it to him even though he didn't know it. And a promise is a promise.

Earl was watching her face. He cupped his hand against her cheek and lifted her lips to his again. His kiss this time was tender, but he withdrew before it became deep again. He smiled into her eyes.

'Let's go back inside,' he said quietly. 'I've got a girl at home myself. I don't want to have any shadows between us when I get back home. I don't think you want shadows either. Not really.'

Their arms around each other's waists, they went back across the road and into the dance hall again. The band was playing 'That Lovely Weekend' and couples were moving slowly around the floor, arms wrapped tightly around each other, the girls with their cheeks resting against their partners'. Earl held out his arms and Thursday went into them and, like the others, laid her head on his shoulder.

They would never spend a weekend together, nor even a night. They would probably not even meet again. But for this one evening they could give each other comfort – and leave no shadows.

The dance finished at ten, an hour before blackout, and the girls kissed their partners good night and collected their bikes.

Patsy sighed happily. 'You know, I really enjoyed that. It was lovely to dance again. That GI I was dancing with was so good – almost as good as Roy. He was nice, too.' She grinned. 'Gave me a lovely good-night kiss!'

'Mine was nice too,' Elsie said dreamily. She was clutching a small bar of chocolate that she and the Naval rating she'd met in the Paul Jones had won in the Spot dance later on. 'And yours looked a real dish, Thursday!'

Thursday smiled, but she felt a little sad. Earl was a nice man, an attractive man, and one she felt she could have fallen in love with, had things been different. But he was right – he was going away in a few days. Neither wanted a shadow in their life. I wonder how many men a girl could fall in love with, she thought as she started to pedal down the road. In the ordinary way, you probably wouldn't meet more than one or two, but these days, with so many people moving about all the time, you could meet a dozen or more. Could any one of them be 'Mr Right'? If she hadn't known Connor, would Mark Sangster whom she'd known in Egypt, have been the one for her? And if she hadn't met either of them, could it have been Earl – or half a dozen other men she'd met in the past few years?

If it hadn't been for the war, she mused, following the other two girls, would I really have settled down with Sidney, like Mum wanted me to, and lived happily ever after?

The thought made her giggle, and Patsy looked over her shoulder. 'Come on, slowcoach, we'll miss the last ferry if you don't get a move on.'

'Coming,' Thursday said, and put her musings out of her mind. It didn't do any good to wonder. Life was what it was, and you just had to go along with whatever did happen.

By the time the girls reached Gosport again and were pedalling as fast as they could past Trinity Church on their way to Pneumonia Bridge, it was almost dark.

'Oh, that did me good,' Patsy said again. 'Thanks for making me come. It was a smashing evening.'

'We're only just going to make it back in time, you know,' Elsie said, puffing as she got off her bike to push it up the steep slope. 'I bet Madam's there now, looking at the signing-in book and checking her watch.'

'We've still got seven minutes.' They reached the top of the bridge and freewheeled down the other side to swoop round the corner and into Clayhall Road. The high brick wall of the hospital rose beside them and they skidded to a halt at the gate, fishing for their passes to show the sailors on guard. Waved through, they puffed into the sheds, threw their bikes into the racks and rushed into D Block.

Miss Makepeace was waiting on the landing. Her face was grave, and Thursday felt a lurch of her heart. She paused, one hand on the banister, one at her throat.

'We're surely not late, are we, Madam?' Patsy gasped. 'We came as fast as we could.'

'My watch says there's still three minutes to go,' Elsie panted. 'We're really sorry—'

'You're not late. At least, I don't think so.' Miss Makepeace's voice was serious. She turned to Patsy. 'Greenaway, I'm very sorry. I'm afraid there's a telegram for you.'

'A telegram?' Patsy's voice was a whisper. She looked at her friends, then back at the Red Cross Commandant. 'A *telegram*?'

Madam handed it over. Patsy's fingers closed about the little brown envelope and she stared at it. Thursday moved closer and put her arm about Patsy's shoulders.

'Would you like me to open it for you?'

Patsy shook her head uncertainly. 'No. No, I'll do it.' With shaking fingers, she began to tear at the flimsy paper. It seemed to take an age before she had it open and drew out the greyish scrap inside with its letters stuck unevenly across it. She frowned at it, her lips moving slowly, not seeming to understand what it said, and then, shaking her head in denial, read it again.

'It's not true,' she said blankly. 'It's not true. He was going to send me a card. We're going to be dancing champions. It can't be true. It *can't*!'

Thursday reached out and took the telegram from her fingers. She read it quickly and felt the tears fill her eyes.

'Oh, Patsy,' she said. 'Oh, Patsy . . .'

Chapter Seven

Miss Makepeace wanted her to take a few days' leave, but Patsy shook her head. 'What's the point? What would I do? There's no – no *funeral* to go to. And there are patients coming in all the time. I can't leave now.' She spoke in a dull, flat voice, and Thursday caught Madam's brown eyes resting on her anxiously, but the Commandant said no more. She sighed a little and nodded.

'Very well. But if you do decide you want a few days, you must come to me immediately, do you understand? There's to be no bravely carrying on if you don't feel up to the job. I won't have the patients' lives put at risk.'

It sounded rather harsh, thought Thursday who had gone to Madam's office with Patsy early next morning, but perhaps it was the best way. Madam was right – everyone who worked in the hospital must be 'on top line'. A moment's carelessness could cost a man his life.

'I'm looking to you to keep an eye on her, Tilford,' Madam said as Patsy turned to leave the office. 'Come to me the moment you think she needs help. The shock's numbing her at the moment and it may carry her through several days, but the grief's bound to hit her eventually. We can't afford any breakdowns.' The bright brown eyes regarded Thursday. 'I'm as much concerned for Greenaway as for the patients, you understand. She's been an exemplary VAD and this is a terrible blow. We must all take care of her.'

'Yes, Madam.' Thursday hesitated. 'She seems to be in another world, somehow. Almost as if she's decided not to believe it. I listened in the night but I don't think she cried, not at all.'

Miss Makepeace nodded. 'Some people do react in that way. It can mislead us into thinking they don't care, or that they're dealing with the whole thing very bravely. It usually means that, as you say, they just won't accept the truth, and that can be very dangerous. Because one day they *have* to accept it, and it can trigger a much worse reaction than if they began to grieve straightaway. You must keep an eye on her, you and Jackson especially. I know you've always been good friends. Don't forget – come to me the moment you feel any anxiety.'

'Yes, Madam.' Thursday felt the familiar warmth of knowing that she could rely on and trust the Commandant implicitly. It had been like that from the beginning, she thought, from that very first snowy evening when she and Patsy had arrived at Haslar as new and rather scared VADs. One glance from those brown eyes, one word spoken in that clear, steady voice, and they had known that they had come, like the ship Haslar Hospital operated as, into safe harbour.

All the girls were equally concerned for Patsy. Several of them had also lost husbands or sweethearts, and all of them knew some young man who had gone off to war and never returned. Thursday's cousins Mike and Leslie had both been killed in action, Elsie's brother Dave by a bomb, Louisa's cousin in Bomb Disposal had been blown up by a mine, Helen Stanway's father lost at sea . . . the list was endless. But Patsy had been married from Haslar, and Madam and a number of the VADs had been present at her wedding. They'd all known Roy, right from the moment he and Patsy had met, and so the blow seemed all the harsher.

For Patsy, it was as if she had been turned to stone. The shock, hitting her like a blow, ran like ice through her body, and froze her heart. After that first moment of denial, she was swept by a feeling of inevitability. It had always been going to happen. Roy had escaped death twice, three times, already. Perhaps even more. But now his luck had run out and he was gone.

She refused to talk about it, even to her friends. When the letter came a few days later from the First Lieutenant, she read it almost as if it were about someone else. Roy had gone with two other SBAs on to the beaches, working with the wounded, trying to treat them where they lay and get them back on to the ships that had only just landed them. Under heavy fire, he had refused to take shelter and continued to work, saving a number of lives before disappearing in a blast from a storm of grenades. In the confusion, two other SBAs had been killed as well as the ship's doctor, and men were ordered to return to any ship they could reach. It was days before it was known just who had been saved and who killed or injured, and Roy's death had only been confirmed when his identity tag had been discovered. The letter gave no other details, but Patsy had heard enough from other sailors to know that this meant there had been no body; only pieces.

Her Roy, blown to pieces. She tried the words out in her mind and they meant nothing. She couldn't imagine it. It was as if a steel curtain descended between the words and their meaning. It was a curtain she almost welcomed, knowing that beyond it lay a pain too sharp to face.

'I don't want time off,' she repeated tonelessly when Thursday tried to urge her to go home for a few days. 'It won't do anyone any good. I've got a job to do here. Leave me alone.'

She went back to the ward and concentrated fiercely on the men she was nursing. They needed her. They were still alive. Like Roy, they had escaped death. Like Roy, they might not escape next time, but for now they were in her charge and she could do something for them. She could make them comfortable, give them medicine to make them better, tend their wounds, listen to their stories and make them laugh again. With them, she could be in control, and as long as she was in control she could manage.

If she went home, she wouldn't be in control. She would be the one who was being looked after, and then that steel curtain might lift and she would have to face what lay on the other side.

The worst time was when she came off duty.

'I just don't know what to do for her,' Elsie said to Thursday as they walked along the sea wall together during another brief spell off duty. 'Work's all right, but she's got to have some time off as well. But what can she do? She won't want to go dancing or to the pictures, I can understand that, but it's not good for her to sit on her bed and just do nothing.'

'She doesn't even cry,' Thursday agreed. 'She just sits there, looking at his photo, or going through his letters. I wouldn't want to stop her doing that, mind, it seems right to want to go over it all – but she ought to cry as well. It's not natural.'

'It's like Madam said. Some people can't cry, not at first.'

Thursday thought of her mother, waiting month after month for news of Steve after Dunkirk. She'd refused to believe he was dead, even though everyone knew he must be, and she hadn't cried either. She'd held in all her grief, keeping her lips tight, until they'd really begun to fear for her. If she didn't crack soon, Thursday had thought, she'd break into a million pieces, like a glass shattering. But in the end she'd been proved right – Steve *wasn't* dead, he was a prisoner of war in somewhere called Colditz Castle, and one day he'd be home again. Mary's grief had turned to joy and then to practicality as she'd set about sending him cakes and other comforts. It wasn't going to be like that for Patsy.

'I don't think there's anything we *can* do,' she said to Elsie now, 'except just let her go the way she wants and be around when she needs us.'

The road ran under the high brick wall of the hospital and along the top of the sloping sea wall. At high tide the sea lapped halfway up the steep incline, and you could swim straight into deep water. Even at low tide, it revealed only a strip of shingle at the foot. The girls walked as far as they could, along to where the road turned inland towards Anglesey and tarmac gave way to the scrub of the golf course. Like the rest of the beach, this strip had been wired off during the past few months and the smooth greens of the golf course allowed to revert to scrub. The old moat still ran around Fort Gilkicker and there were defences and gun emplacements all the way along.

'This would have done Patsy good,' Thursday remarked as they turned to walk back. 'A bit of sea air and exercise. We'll have to make her come out with us next time.'

They sat down on the top of the slope and turned their faces to the sun. The brief spell of fine weather had cheered them a little, although there was a steely look to the sky now that threatened rain. The Solent was still crowded with ships plying back and forth, still protected by their silvery barrage balloons, and they watched them silently. Above the balloons there was a steady stream of aircraft, each squadron on its way to France both to give air cover to the invading troops and to ward off any air raids the Germans might make on England. D-Day had been only the beginning of an invasion which was still under way.

Thursday gazed out over the scene, then frowned. Her heart gave a sudden lurch and she gripped Elsie's arm. 'Look! Look, Else –

look over there, just past the Island. It's a plane – at least, I think it is – all by itself. I've never seen anything like it. Look at its tiny wings. What d'you think it is?'

They stared, shading their eyes against the brightness. The aircraft was small and black, flying like a dart towards the coast. Thursday felt a knot of fear low down in her stomach. She gripped Elsie's arm more tightly.

'I don't like it,' Elsie said in a low voice. 'I don't think it's one of ours. What can it be? It's too small to be a bomber.'

'It's very high,' Thursday said uneasily. 'Maybe we can't judge its size properly.'

The plane seemed to be flying in a dead straight line, purposefully heading north. It crossed the coastline and disappeared, apparently without having been noticed. Thursday and Elsie looked at each other.

'Let's get back.' Elsie got to her feet. 'There was something about that thing that scared me, Thurs. The way it flew – as if it knew just where it was going, and nothing and nobody was going to stop it. And I reckon it was one of *theirs*. I'm sure it was.'

'The secret weapon people have been talking about?' Thursday suggested doubtfully. 'Hitler's secret weapon?'

'I dunno. All I know is, I want to get back to the hospital. We've been out long enough, Thurs. I want to get back where we know what's what and who people are. I want to get back where I feel *safe*.'

Nowhere was really safe. But Thursday, following her friend as she half-ran along the sea road, knew just what Elsie meant. Out here, in full view of every ship in the Solent, of any plane that came over, they felt exposed and vulnerable. Attack could come from any quarter. People had been strafed and machine-gunned in their own streets, at their own front doors.

Terror gripped her heart as she scurried back to the hospital gates, and although the day was still as bright, she felt as if the hounds of darkness were snapping at her heels.

Over the next few days, the truth emerged.

The strange aircraft was indeed a new weapon – and the most terrifying one yet. Officially, it was called the V1 but it soon acquired more common names – the buzz-bomb or doodlebug because of the noise it made and, most accurately, the flying bomb.

For that was exactly what it was – a pilotless aircraft which was wholly bomb, packed with explosive and with just enough engine power to reach its target.

Its target, on the whole, was London. Anywhere in London. There was no pretence now that the targets were military. The flying bombs were aimed at a city full of people confident that the war was almost over, that air raids were a thing of the past and it was safe to come home. Suddenly, it wasn't safe at all. Death could flash out of a blue or stormy sky, day or night, too quickly for a siren to be sounded and giving no time to take cover. The country was once again on permanent alert, and all you could do if you heard it was pray. If the engine stopped above you, it simply fell and you had just fifteen seconds before the explosion to throw yourself on the ground. If you stayed on your feet, you could be flung across the street by the blast, peppered with debris or simply scattered in small pieces. If the bomb fell directly on you, there was no chance at all of surviving.

'I dunno,' Elsie said as they sat outside the next evening. Even at nine o'clock the sun was still high and warm and they had dragged chairs out in front of the block. 'It's like two steps forward and one back. They're sending these flaming things over all the time. They said on the news that there was over seventy hit London yesterday, and what about that one that killed all those people in that Army chapel just by Buckingham Palace? Over a *hundred*, it said on the news.' She shook her head. 'They're worse than ordinary planes – at least you get some warning when there's a proper raid on, and you know it's people up there. It seems worse, somehow, knowing that there's no one flying these ruddy things. It's as if there's nothing anyone can do. I mean, there could be one coming over at this very moment and we wouldn't know till it was almost here.'

They all glanced uneasily up at the sky. Elsie was right, Thursday thought, there was something horribly menacing about these new weapons. It was because the Germans weren't taking any risks, she thought. There was no pilot, so nobody could get killed. And there seemed to be hundreds of them, perhaps thousands. Would they be the weapons that finally won the war? Had the invasion and all the injuries and loss of life on the Normandy beaches been in vain?

The flood of casualties had eased a little, although there were still plenty of new cases arriving. Many of them were smothered in the sand of the beaches where they had lain for hours, waiting to be rescued. The wards and operating theatres were busy, and off-duty time precious. Thursday spent much of hers writing letters, either to Connor or to her family in Worcester.

It seems an age already since I saw you all, she wrote to her mother. *Madam says we shall all have a week sometime during the summer, if things go on as they are doing, but I don't know when it will be. We're still flat out here, although the first wave has slowed down a bit. I'll probably just turn up on the doorstep one day with my suitcase! Take care of yourselves and give my love to Denise and my godson.*

She folded her letter and slipped it into an envelope. It was funny, she thought, she missed her family more now that she was back in England than she had while she was in Egypt. The few days she'd had at home had been all too short, giving her no more than a tantalising glimpse of the family life she'd left behind when she first volunteered as a VAD. Too short to get used to the changes – the fact that she'd never see her cousins Mike and Leslie again, nor her dog Patch.

She remembered the day the letter had come, telling her about Patch's death. Louisa had come into the room and found her crying. She'd sat down beside her, her arm around Thursday's shoulders, asking what had happened. 'Is it your brother? Or one of your parents?'

Thursday shook her head and held out the single sheet. 'I shouldn't be crying. Not when so many awful things are happening. But he was *my* dog. He understood—' Her voice choked and Louisa's arm tightened about her.

'It's all right, Thursday. You can cry. I know what it's like – I lost my own dog a little while ago. He was a Labrador and he loved everyone, but he was my dog just the same. He was special.'

'That's just what Patchie was – special.' Thursday drew a sobbing breath. 'But it seems wrong all the same. I mean, my auntie's lost both her sons, and we thought our Steve was dead too, and I was really upset, I really was, but I never cried like this for any of them. And when Tony died – I *wanted* to cry for him, but I couldn't, not like this. It seems wrong – as if I thought more of him than I did of them.' She choked again, the tears streaming down her face. 'I don't know what's the matter with me, Lou. I just can't seem to stop.'

'It's all right. It doesn't matter. Just let it go – let it go.' Louisa kept her arm around Thursday's shoulders, murmuring soothingly to her all the while. 'Just cry. Cry as much as you want. It doesn't matter.'

Later, Thursday realised that she had been crying for her lost cousins, for her first sweetheart, Tony West, for her brother, and – perhaps – for all the young men and women she had nursed through the past few years, just as much as for her dog. Patch's death had given her the right to let go of all the grief she had kept pent up inside her, and the pain of all the years of war had been lanced like a boil by the loss of one small mongrel dog. And it had done her good; when the first searing anguish was over, she'd been able to face the war again and return to her duties with a calmer heart.

She and Louisa, already friends, had forged a special bond that evening. From totally different backgrounds, they had discovered common ground in the fact that Louisa had gone to a boarding school in Great Malvern, only a few miles from Thursday's home in Worcester. On the way out to Egypt, with plenty of time at sea for talking, they'd discovered more about each other. Thursday had told Louisa about her home and family and Louisa had in return given Thursday a glimpse into her own, very different, life.

'People think that someone like Daddy's got pots of money, of course,' she'd observed, 'but he has to work for it, just like anyone else. I mean, he did inherit all the land and everything, but it has to pay its way. The farms are what we live on – the rent from the tenants and the income from Home Farm – that's the one Daddy runs himself. And all the tenant farms have to be maintained and looked after – they're not exactly a gold mine.'

They sounded like one to Thursday, whose father had worked all his life in the porcelain factory and wanted nothing more for his children than an apprenticeship to a decent trade. She tried to imagine living in a huge house, with separate bedrooms for everyone and still some to spare, and enormous gardens and not one farm but half a dozen. 'Will your brother take it over one day?' she asked.

Louisa nodded. 'It'll go to Robert – he's the eldest son. It has to – there's an entail on it. There's a trust for me as well, and one for Dominic, and he'll probably take over one of the farms. He loves being on the land.'

'Why didn't you stay at home, then?' Thursday asked. 'You could have been a Land Girl and lived in comfort, instead of roughing it as a VAD and spending all day emptying bedpans.'

Louisa laughed. 'And it wouldn't have seemed like war work at all! Not that we live in luxury, Thursday. I'm sure it seems like it to you, but at home we live quite simply. Well, all right, we do have maids and gardeners, we could never manage the house and garden without. But we don't dine on caviar every night and drink champagne for breakfast. Mummy does most of the cooking and gardening, and we all had to help. And Mummy and Daddy have always insisted that we must be able to look after ourselves. I've always washed my own undies, for instance, and we had to do that at school too. And *that* wasn't the lap of luxury either; in fact, it was just like being at Haslar!'

It still seemed a luxurious way of life to Thursday. 'But you used to go to balls and society parties in London, didn't you? And do the "Season"?'

'Oh yes,' Louisa said carelessly, as if it didn't much matter. 'I was presented at Court and all that kind of thing. That was quite fun, especially meeting the King and Queen – he's sweet, very shy but really nice, and she's lovely – but it all seems a bit unreal now. Like playing at life instead of living it. In fact, now I come to think about it, that's really what we were doing.' She turned her head and looked at Thursday gravely. 'This'll probably sound funny to you, Thursday, but I'd rather be doing what we're doing now – helping to nurse men who've been wounded in war, even if it does just mean emptying bedpans – than going to all those dinners and balls. It's as if all that was a dream and now I'm awake and can get on with real life.'

Thursday nodded. 'I know what you mean. Being a VAD has given me the chance to do things I'd never have been able to do before. I suppose the war's done that for a lot of people,' she went on thoughtfully. 'Especially girls. Without it, we would have been expected to just settle down and get married and have a family, without ever moving further away from home than the next street. But now – well, women are doing all sorts of jobs. Driving buses, flying aeroplanes, being wireless operators, doing important jobs in offices – there's no end to what women can do now.'

'There's no end to what women can do, full stop,' Louisa said with a smile, and then added, 'but I wonder what will happen after the war. When the men come home they'll want their old jobs back again, won't they? And what will we women do, now we've tasted freedom? Are we just going to give it up? Or are we going to fight to keep hold of it? It'll be interesting to see.'

Louisa's words stayed in Thursday's mind. Sitting by the autoclave in the hot, steamy underground theatre, sterilising the instruments, she thought about the end of the war and what it would bring. For so long, it had stretched ahead without any promise of a conclusion, but now, with the Italian capitulation assured and the invasion forging ahead, everyone was beginning to think about the possibility and to make plans. Many of the beaches were open again – although the ban on visitors to the forbidden ten-mile zone was still in force – parents were calling for the evacuated schools to be returned to the city and there was even talk of rebuilding the blitzed city centre. What a job that would be, Thursday thought. She'd been over to Portsmouth with Elsie, to visit the Jacksons, and had noticed that although a lot of the rubble had been tidied up, the gutted Guildhall still stood in ruins, along with most of the big shops along Commercial Street. It would take years to put them all back the way they had been.

However, the important thing was that they were thinking about it. Making plans. And perhaps that was what she ought to be doing too.

Thursday fished out the sterilised instruments and put in a fresh load. Did she want to continue nursing? There'd been a time when she'd been determined to go for state registration as soon as the war was over, like her sister Jenny and their Aunt Maudie, but now she wasn't so sure. I wouldn't have missed it for the world, she thought, but what will it be like afterwards? It'll still be worth doing, I know – nursing will always be worth doing – but will it be quite the same without the urgency of war?

It was only the war that had brought her into nursing; on leaving school, she had been apprenticed to a tailor in Worcester. But did she want to go back to tailoring or dressmaking? Would she even want to go back to Worcester?

Louisa's right, she thought, we've seen and done a lot more than our mothers ever did, or ever even dreamed of. And it's changed us.

We're different people – and we don't know quite what people we're going to be when all this is over.

We're *used* to war, she thought with a kind of horror.

In the dormitory, when they had finished their morning shift, she tried to explain her feelings to the others. 'I don't know *what* I'm going to want to do. It's all going to be so different. People trying to settle down – to get the country back together. Men coming home and wanting their old jobs back – or maybe not being fit enough to work at all. It's not going to be like it was in 1939. We're all older, for a start, and we've done so much. Look at Elsie and Louisa and me – we've been abroad, and not just on holiday – we've *lived* there. We'd never have done any of that – well, you might, Lou, but *we* never would. We'd have been stuck in backstreets all our lives. Marrying the first boy we went out with, renting a few rooms or a little house somewhere near our mums and having three or four kids. And nothing else to look forward to at all. We're not going to settle for that now, are we? *Are* we?' She looked around at them.

'Well, I would,' Patsy said tautly. 'I'd settle for it any day of the week.'

Thursday thumped her forehead with her palm and stared at her friend, horrified. 'Oh, *Pats*! I'm sorry – I never thought. Trust me and my big mouth, every time I open it I put my foot in it! I'm really sorry, Pats. I'm so *stupid*.'

Patsy shook her head. Her eyes were bright and her lower lip was folded in tightly between her teeth. She reached beneath her bunk suddenly and groped for her shoes. 'I'm just going out for a walk.'

'I'll come too.' Thursday slid down from her own bunk but Patsy turned on her sharply.

'*No*! No, I don't want you to come. I don't want *anyone*.' She was making for the door, and although her head was high they could all hear the break in her voice. They looked at each other in alarm and Thursday, her own shoes in her hand, stood helpless and dismayed.

'She looked awful,' Elsie said. 'White as a sheet. Oh, *Thurs*!'

'It's all my fault,' Thursday said. 'I don't know what I was thinking of. Saying all that about getting married and settling down as if it was something no one in their right mind would want. Oh, I'm such an *idiot*. Poor Patsy. What are we going to do? We can't just let her go off on her own like that.'

'Maybe it's what she needs,' Elsie said. 'Maybe she'll have a good cry and let it all out. You know she's been bottling it up. It's not good for her.'

'But she's on her *own*,' Thursday said. 'She needs someone with her. I'm going after her.' She thrust her feet into her shoes and bent to lace them up. 'I won't say anything, I won't even stay with her if she doesn't want me, but I can't just let her go off like that, all upset. I'm her *friend*. At least,' she added dolefully, 'I was. She may never want to speak to me again, after this.'

'Of course she will. It's not that bad, Thurs.' Elsie touched her arm. 'She knows you didn't mean it. Something was bound to set her off sometime.'

'Well, maybe. But I've got to go after her, anyway. Just to make sure . . .' Thursday ran to the door and hurried down the stairs. At the entrance to the block, she stood for a moment looking to see where Patsy had gone. There was no sign of her heading out towards the sea wall, nor along the quarter deck leading to the little church. Then her eye caught a flicker of movement and she saw the familiar figure walking rapidly towards the Clayhall Road gate. Of course! She was going to Alverstoke, where she and Roy had been married. Swiftly, Thursday ran after her, then slowed as she realised that, as Elsie had said, Patsy might want to be alone. I won't let her know I'm here, she thought. I'll just go along to keep an eye on her, just in case she needs me . . .

Patsy was walking quickly. She could feel the tears building inside her, pressing against her heart and her throat like a dam about to burst. They had been building ever since the telegram had arrived, but the steel curtain had kept it back. Now the curtain was dissolving, turning to glass, and she could sense, almost see, the grief that lay on the other side. Soon the glass itself would shatter . . .

She knew only that she had to get away from the hospital before she could let the dam shatter the fragile glass. She had to be somewhere that meant something special to herself and Roy. There were a hundred places – the sea wall where they had walked, holding hands, the road past Gilkicker Fort where they had cycled to Stokes Bay, Lee Tower where they'd danced, Pneumonia Bridge where they'd crossed Haslar Lake into Gosport to have tea at the Swiss Café or a bun and mug of cocoa in the Dive. The ferry to Portsmouth, where they'd huddled against the funnel on cold nights, coming back from the pictures. The entire place was filled with memories, memories she hadn't dared face until now.

She walked down Clayhall Road and along the old railway line, stopping on Jackie Spencer's bridge to lean on the iron parapet and gaze across the head of Haslar creek towards Alverstoke and the church tower. The day was fine and clear, and the tide was in; the water lay like a blue lake and the tower was pale grey against the cloudless sky. You could almost imagine, she thought, that there was no war on at all.

It was just like this the day we were married, Patsy reflected. A warm, sunny June day, three years ago. She remembered what fun it had been getting ready for the wedding – the other girls' panic as they discussed what to wear, the excitement of planning. Most of them had been in uniform, of course, but for Thursday and Elsie as bridesmaids and herself as a bride there had got to be something pretty. Thursday had made herself a lovely frock and then, because Patsy had no wedding dress, insisted that she wear it instead. And Elsie had worn a nightie, with Vera Hapgood's waistcoat over it!

I felt like a film star, walking up the aisle to marry Roy, she thought. Nobody could have been happier than me that day. And we had such a lovely honeymoon, those few days in Cornwall. And since then too, whenever he managed to get some leave. It was all like a dream. And now . . .

Now the dream had come to an end, and with it had ended their dream of a future together. Nothing special. Nothing glamorous. Just an ordinary, quiet life, in a little house somewhere with a family of their own – children, grandchildren, the two of them growing old together. Darby and Joan.

And now it would never happen. It was over. The dream had been destroyed and with it all their hopes and plans, and the children and the grandchildren would never be born.

For a moment, Patsy seemed to see the wedding procession – herself, her friends, the nurses and VADs, Madam and even two of the doctors – walking along the road that led beside the creek to the church. The picture faded and she saw just herself and Roy, a few years older, walking arm in arm, while in front of them ran three or four children. It was a hazy picture and the figures seemed to blur into each other as she peered through the mist that had gathered before her eyes. And then those figures too shimmered away, and there were others – grown men and women she only half recognised, and yet more children, running and calling and laughing. Children who should have belonged to the future; children whose very existence had been snatched away from them.

'Oh, *Roy!*' she cried, reaching out as if she could gather them all to her breast. 'Oh, Roy! Roy! *Roy.*' And as the last fragile barrier of glass shattered in her mind, the pictures dissolved and the tears burst at last through the dam, and she laid her head on her arms and began to weep.

Thursday, following at a distance, had stopped when she saw Patsy on the bridge. She raised one hand to her mouth, biting her knuckles anxiously, praying that Patsy wasn't going to do anything silly. People had jumped from that bridge in the past, she'd heard, knowing that although the water wasn't deep, an outgoing tide would sweep them rapidly out into the deeper waters of the creek and the harbour, beyond rescue. As she heard Patsy's cry, she started forwards, afraid that if Patsy were indeed that desperate, she wouldn't be able to reach her in time. And then she saw her friend's head droop on to her arms and saw the shaking of her shoulders as she began to cry.

Elsie had said that was what she needed – to let out all those tears that had been building up, to face up to her sorrow. And Madam had said the grief would hit her eventually and that Thursday and the others must be ready to help her when it did. Thursday felt a great wave of thankfulness wash over her that she had followed her here. Patsy was crying now as if her heart had broken – as indeed it had – and she needed to be allowed to do it. But she also needed a friend, a pair of loving arms about her, someone who would share her grief.

Quietly, Thursday came nearer and waited. She laid one arm across Patsy's shoulders and whispered in her ear. 'It's Thursday, Pats. I'm here with you. Cry all you want. Just cry. It'll do you good.' Her voice broke and she felt the tears come to her own eyes. 'I'll cry with you.' A sob rose in her throat. 'Oh, Patsy – poor Roy. Poor, *poor* Roy.'

Patsy turned towards her. She put her arms around Thursday and laid her face against her shoulder. They held each other tightly and their tears mingled, while below them the water lay cool and still, and at the head of the creek the church tower stood calm and grey against the blue sky.

When at last their tears eased, they walked on across the bridge, their arms around each other's waists. They walked beside the creek where Patsy had seen the dream figures, the sons and daughters and grandchildren who would never be, and they walked to the church where Patsy and Roy had been married. There, looking up at the altar, they wept again but, when they left the church to make their way slowly back to the hospital, the anguish that had frozen Patsy's heart had been released. She would never forget Roy – they both knew that. But while the memories would always be precious, the grief would slowly grow more bearable, and she would be able to live and laugh again. The steel curtain had gone for ever.

When the two girls came back to the hospital and met the others, Elsie gave Thursday a questioning look but made no comment on their reddened eyes and treated Patsy with the quiet gentleness that Thursday had sometimes seen her using on the wards, when nursing a patient who was particularly ill. It was what made her such a good nurse, she thought – that ability to know when to soften her laughter, when to soothe a man instead of jolly him along. It was what made her the friend that both Patsy and Thursday needed today.

'She's had a good cry,' she told Elsie privately later. 'I dare say she'll cry again, now she's started, but it'll be good, healthy crying. And she's going to ask for a few days' leave when she feels ready for it. Just now, nursing the men's better for her than time off.'

'It's good for her to do something for other people,' Elsie agreed. 'Perhaps she'll take up nursing permanently – once the war's over, I mean. She'll need to have something worthwhile to do, to fill up the gap Roy's left. I reckon we're all going to need something. It won't be easy to go back to what we used to be.'

Thursday nodded. But when she went to bed that night she lay for a long time staring into the darkness, thinking about Patsy and thinking again about the end of the war. I don't think I'll be able to go back to being the old Thursday, she thought, I really don't. I *am* different now. I'm going to want to do something else with my life – and I'm not sure it'll be getting married and settling down. Not straight off, anyway. I'll need some time to find out about myself, and to see what the world's going to be like when there isn't any more war.

And what about Connor? Would he be different too? Would he be as attracted to the new Thursday as he was to the old? Would she still feel the same about him, when they met again, or would the years have made too much difference?

I still feel I love him, she thought, but will it last? We only knew each other for a little while. And he's a doctor – properly educated, from a nice house with parents that people look up to. Is he really still going to be interested in a little VAD from a backstreet in Worcester with a dad who works in a porcelain factory and a mum who helps make soldiers' uniforms?

Her inner panic grew and tightened. I almost wish the war wouldn't come to an end, she thought, and then felt horrified with herself. That's a wicked thing to think, Thursday Tilford, she told herself angrily, and you're a wicked girl to think it. If that's the best you can do, you'd better stop thinking altogether and do what Louisa says – just wait and see.

She turned over, punched her pillow as if it were responsible for her thoughts, and fell asleep.

The initial crisis was almost over. By the time the casualties reached Haslar, the journey had proved almost too much for some of them, even though they'd been nursed all the way. The QARNNs and VADs took them in briskly but tenderly, made them comfortable and did whatever they could.

Thursday enjoyed her theatre work but occasionally found herself longing for a conscious patient, one she could talk to and offer comfort to. She understood Elsie's preference for the wards and wondered if she should ask to go back to them herself.

'Not at the moment,' Miss Makepeace said briskly when Thursday discussed it with her. 'You're a good theatre nurse and you're needed there. I know you're a good ward nurse too, but if we take you out of the theatre we'll have to put someone else in, and that could mean a loss of efficiency while she learns the procedure.'

'It's not as if I'm doing anything really important,' Thursday ventured. 'I mean, you know we VADs just do the ordinary things – sterilising and that sort of thing. We're not helping with the operations themselves.'

Madam stiffened and fixed her with her bright brown gaze. '*Everyone's* task is important in a theatre. You're part of a team, Tilford, and a team can't function properly if one of its members isn't fully effective. I hope you're not going to tell me that your work isn't up to scratch.'

'No, I'm not, Madam,' Thursday said hastily. 'Of course I'm not. I always work as well as I can. I just felt—'

'You feel restless,' the Red Cross Commandant said, her tone softer. 'You're back here at Haslar after having been abroad for two years, people are beginning to talk about the end of the war and you're feeling uncertain. It's understandable, but you mustn't let it affect your work. We still have many casualties and we don't know what may happen next. The war is by no means over, and your work is as vital now as it was at the beginning. Remember that, Tilford.'

'Yes, Madam.' Thursday left the office, feeling a little better but still aware of the questions in her mind.

The flying bombs were coming over every day now. Mostly, they were aimed at London but you never knew, as they flew over, whether their fuel might run out at any moment. Some dropped on Portsmouth and other towns, and everyone felt the same dread when they heard the unmistakable sound of the engine. And even if it didn't stop right overhead, the blast could cause damage for a quarter of a mile all round. In less than two weeks, over fifteen hundred people had been killed and nearly five thousand badly hurt. They really were weapons of terror.

Gosport and Portsmouth were still busy, their beaches a constant scene of activity as ships reloaded with men and provisions. The strange tension of the week before D-Day had mostly evaporated, but the flow of soldiers ready to go over and fight seemed endless. They knew now what they were going to, knew that the Atlantic Wall had been breached and the beaches captured, but they were still very aware that the battle had only just begun. The whole of occupied France waited for liberation and peace and, after that, the rest of Europe. There was a lot more fighting to do before peace could be declared.

Peace. It was a strange word, stranger still after five years of war. For a little while, you heard it everywhere – '*when peace comes*' – and then it stopped as people began to realise that it was still somewhere in the future. Another Christmas, at least, would come and go before peace became a reality.

Thursday pushed her restlessness away. There was work to do, casualties to be nursed and operated on, and dreams and memories must take second place. She went through the days, working her duties, walking along the sea front, writing to Connor and to her family. It was a good day when a letter came, a disappointing one when none arrived. Sometimes she would go a week or more without hearing from Connor, and then a bundle of letters would arrive together. This had happened so many times that they had agreed on a numbering system, so that the letters could be read in order. After two years apart, Connor's letters had reached number 275.

My darling, he wrote, it seems such a long time since I saw you – and England. I miss the seasons almost as much as I miss you. When I think of the short time that we knew each other – from autumn into winter – I realise that I can only associate you with the bitter cold of January, and the terror of the Blitz. We didn't even have a Christmas together. I don't know you with the spring breezes ruffling your hair, nor with the summer sunshine on your face. We've never swum together in the sea, nor walked in meadows or on the moors, nor sailed in the little tub of a dinghy I kept in Haslar Lake. But we WILL do those things, my dearest. When all this is over and we're free to live our lives again, we'll do all those things. I'll take you to Devon, to see my family, and we'll walk on the moors and beside the sea, we'll swim and cycle and ride the two old horses that live in the paddock, we'll do all those things together that we ought to have been able to do when we were young and carefree. And we'll love each other again, as I loved you before I left you – as I love you now.

Thursday folded the letter and put it in her pocket. The words and the passion made her heart beat faster, yet she was aware of a touch of uneasiness. Suppose they *didn't* love each other when they met again? Suppose the changes were too much?

'Don't be daft,' Elsie said robustly, 'of course you will. Anyone could see you two were made for each other. Once he's home again and you've had a proper kiss, it'll all be just like it was before, you'll see.'

'But suppose it isn't?' Thursday repeated, and Elsie shrugged.

'Well, it won't be the end of the world, will it? You're not married – not even engaged. If it doesn't work any more, you can just say goodbye. There'll be other fellers, Thurs. There's plenty more fish in the sea.'

There were indeed, Thursday thought. Plenty. She'd already met some of them, both in Egypt and on the way out there . . .

Chapter Eight

It had been strange, on that day in 1942, to find herself on board a luxury liner, setting sail for some unknown destination. Along with Elsie, Louisa and a dozen other girls from Haslar, Thursday had been instructed to report to the dock at Avonmouth, with her luggage carefully marked with the code number which would, she hoped, ensure that it arrived at her destination with her. None of them had any idea where they were going, and were told that if they did begin to guess they mustn't put any hint in their letters home. They weren't the only ones to be going in the convoy, and if any ship were lost, information could be picked up by the enemy and used to destroy the rest. 'You don't want thousands of deaths laid at your door.'

'Makes us sound as bad as Hitler!' Elsie had said as their train from Paddington tore through the countryside. 'As if we'd be so daft.'

'Well, some might. And it's easy enough to let something slip. That's why they don't tell us anything – we might give it away without even realising it.'

'Fat chance,' Elsie remarked, 'when our letters'll be censored anyway. Where on earth d'you think we are? We could be halfway to Scotland for all we know, now they've taken away all the nameplates on the platforms.'

The train snorted its way into the terminus at last and they crowded on to a coach, its blinds drawn. 'Just in case we recognise anywhere and tell the Jerries!' Elsie said with a grin as they rattled through the streets. At last they stopped, but instead of being at the docks as they had expected, they were told to get off. 'Embarkation won't take place until tomorrow,' the Red Cross official informed them. 'You'll all be staying the night at various small hotels and guest houses. I'll need to check off your names as you get off, so that we'll know where you are, and you must be ready and waiting just here at seven a.m. tomorrow. Don't be late.'

'Or the ship will sail without us!' Elsie murmured, in the phrase that had become a byword at Haslar, where they'd been taught that 'Naval time is five minutes early'. 'Only this time, it really will!'

'This is Bristol,' Louisa said, staring round at the buildings. 'I thought it would be. I came here once on a school trip. The dock's called Avonmouth. You can see the ships over there, see?'

They glanced across and saw the usual tangle of dockyard paraphernalia – cranes, masts, derricks – and the funnels of the ships lying alongside. Thursday felt a little leap of excitement within her as she gazed at them. 'They look different from the ships in Portsmouth. Bigger. And their funnels are different.'

'That's because they're passenger liners. I've heard nearly all the Cunard liners have been requisitioned for service – even the *Queen Mary*. Wouldn't it be a hoot if we were to sail on her?'

Their hotel was a tall narrow building in the middle of a terrace a street or two away. They approached it rather warily, watched by a few girls in civilian clothes who leaned against a wall, smoking cigarettes. Business girls, I suppose, Thursday thought, for they'd been told that most of the buildings in this area were actually hostels where working girls or businesswomen lived. These looked as if they were dressed for an evening out, with low-cut blouses and plenty of make-up. They eyed the three VADs with some suspicion.

Louisa stopped and looked up at the doorway. 'Can you tell us if this is the Pleasant View Hotel?'

At the sound of her voice, with its cut-glass accent, the girls glanced at each other and raised their eyebrows. A couple of them began to snigger and one, with a cloud of red hair and a scarlet blouse, took her cigarette from her mouth.

'You stopping here, then?' she asked brusquely.

'Only the one night,' Thursday said, disliking the way they had sneered at Louisa's voice. 'We're—' She stopped abruptly, remembering that they were under strict instructions not to divulge information. 'We're going on tomorrow.'

'Nurses?' the girl asked, staring at their uniform.

'Look, is this the Pleasant View, or ain't it?' Elsie butted in. 'Not that it's a very pleasant view from where I'm standing!' She stared at the civilians. 'Still, I suppose you do some sort of war work as well, doncher?'

At this, the sniggers erupted into loud guffaws as the Bristol girls turned to each other, their faces red with mirth, punching each other on the arm and repeating, 'War work! Blimey, that's rich! War work!' until the VADs, staring at them with increasing exasperation, shrugged and turned away.

'It's no good talking to them,' Elsie said. 'Anyway, I've just seen a notice in the window – see? *Pleasant View – Vacancies Day and Night* – that's a funny way of putting it, isn't it? – *and Services Offered*. Wonder what they mean by that?'

'Well, never mind, it doesn't affect us.' Louisa lifted her kitbag and mounted the three steps to the front door. 'Come on – I want to get rid of this luggage and find something to eat. That Red Cross woman said there's a restaurant round the corner that we can use.'

Their room was cramped, with one double bed and a single camp bed that had obviously been hastily pushed in along the wall. There was a tiny washbasin, one chair and a small cupboard where the girls could hang their clothes. They looked at it in some dismay, then Louisa shrugged. 'I dare say we'll see worse than this before we're through. Anyway, since all I intend to do is sleep, what it looks like isn't going to bother me too much.' She felt the bed. 'Gosh, this is as bad as boarding school. One lump or two?'

By nine o'clock they had eaten fish and chips at the café round the corner and were back in the room, getting ready for bed. Thursday and Elsie decided to share the double bed and Louisa took the rickety single. They had just begun to undress when they were startled by a knock on the door.

Thursday, who hadn't yet removed anything, opened the door and peered out. 'D'you want something?' She could see a large man, lit dimly by the faint bulb hanging unshaded over the landing.

The man stared at her and she felt a small twinge of unease. 'Who're you? Ain't Rosie in there?'

Thursday shook her head. 'No. You must have the wrong room.'

There was a brief pause, then the voice said, sounding dissatisfied, 'She must be. Thass her room. Where is she?' He began to push the door further open.

Alarmed, Thursday pushed back. 'It isn't her room! It's ours. Stop it – you can't come in. Go *away*.'

'Go away?' He stopped pushing to stare at her again, and Thursday took the opportunity to close the door. Before she could close it fully, he had his foot inside. 'Whatcher mean, go away? I'm a customer. If Rosie ain't here, I'll have someone else.' He peered at her. 'You look all right. You'll do.' And he started to push again.

'No!' Thursday shouted, and looked over her shoulder desperately at Louisa and Elsie, who were staring open-mouthed. 'Go away! Go *away*! You can't come in – you *can't*! Oh, help me, for goodness sake, help me!'

The other two leaped to her side. Elsie lent her weight to the door and Louisa took one look at the foot stuck in the way and stamped on it hard. The man yelped and jerked back, and they shoved the door shut and looked for the key.

'There isn't one! There isn't even a bolt.' He was still pushing from the other side, shouting words even Elsie had never heard before. 'Oh, what shall we do, what shall we do?'

'Use a chair.' Louisa grabbed the kitchen chair that stood beside the bed and pushed its back under the door knob. Cautiously, they stood back and saw with relief that it was holding, although Thursday thought it looked pretty flimsy and wouldn't hold if the man became really determined. However, after one or two more desultory pushes he gave up and they could hear him talking to someone else on the stairs. There was a brief conversation and then his footsteps sounded, going on up the next flight. They heard another door close and the mumble of voices overhead.

Thursday sat down suddenly on the bed. Elsie fixed the chair more securely under the door knob and Louisa sat down beside Thursday and put her arm round her shoulders. 'Are you all right?'

'Yes, I think so. What a horrible man. I wonder why he thought this was Rosie's room? I can't believe she'll be very pleased to see him when he does find her.'

'Oh, I dunno,' Elsie said, surveying the chair grimly. 'I think she'll be pleased enough to see him. Depends what he pays, of course.'

'Pays?' Thursday echoed. 'What d'you mean, *pays*?'

'Well, didn't you hear what he said? Customer, in't he? And that's what that notice means – *Services Offered*. This place ain't a working girls' hostel at all – well, it *is*, but only in a manner of speaking.' She caught Thursday's still bemused glance. 'It's a bloody knocking shop, ain't it!'

'A knocking—?' Thursday began, and Louisa interrupted.

'A brothel, Thursday. That's what Elsie means. A place where men can come and pay girls to have sexual intercourse with them. Prostitutes. That's what those girls outside were.'

'And that's why they screamed their heads off laughing when I said that about war work,' Elsie said. 'I had me doubts about them then. But I never thought the Red Cross would stick us in a place like this!'

'I suppose they didn't know,' Louisa said. She glanced at the chair. 'We'd better keep that there all night – we may get some more callers asking for Rosie. And I'll tell you one thing – I'm not going to undress! I'm not taking any chances.'

'Undress?' Thursday said, still feeling shaken. 'I don't think I'm even going to lie down. And I'm dead certain I'm not going to sleep.' She groaned as more footsteps came up the stairs and someone else knocked loudly on the door. 'Go away!' she shouted. 'Rosie's not here – and neither is anyone else!'

'We're not open for business tonight!' Elsie yelled, banging back. 'Try next door!'

The caller left, grumbling. But the next one was not so easily persuaded, and it took several minutes of bitter argument before he too departed. The girls wedged the chair more firmly and looked at each other with resignation.

'It's going to be a long, long night,' Elsie said, flopping on to the bed. 'I don't think there's much chance of us missing the boat tomorrow. I reckon I'm going to be first aboard!'

'Blimey,' Elsie said in awe, 'it might not be the *Queen Mary*, but it's not far off!'

They stared up at the great ship, its prow rising sleek and elegant above the dock. The familiar Cunard colours had been covered with battleship grey, but there was no mistaking this for a Naval ship. The girls gazed at her in awe.

'We're not really going on that,' Thursday said. 'It's a joke. They're going to let us look at it for a bit and then take us away and shove us on a ferry boat. That's for special people.'

'What d'you mean, *special* people?' Elsie demanded. '*We're* special people – we're VADs! Anyway, I'm not taking any chances – I'm getting aboard before they realise they've brought us to the wrong place. Come on!'

Giggling with excitement, they dragged their luggage closer to the dockside. With the dozen other girls, who had emerged from various establishments nearby (most of them apparently more respectable than the one Thursday and her friends had been allocated) they piled it all together and then sat and watched as a long line of soldiers and sailors made their way up the gangplank. Embarkation had obviously begun some time ago, the men were filing on to the ship like ants and there were still yet more to come. 'Hundreds of them,' Thursday said in amazement. 'Thousands! How many people can a ship like this hold, Lou? It'll burst if many more go aboard.'

'Well, in peacetime they'd have a bit more room, I suppose. I don't really know. Daddy was going to take us to America but then the war came along, so we didn't go. I've never been to sea on a ship like this.' She gazed up at the towering prow. 'And look at all the military stuff they're lifting on board, too! Tanks and lorries, and all the luggage . . . I hope ours doesn't get mixed up with that lot, we'll never get it back again.'

Thursday giggled. 'We'll find ourselves with rifles and grenades, and some poor soldier will have a bag full of navy-blue bloomers! Oh look, someone's calling us over. It must be our turn to go aboard.'

Suddenly subdued, they picked up their cases and kitbags and made their way over to the gangplank where a Red Cross officer was standing with a list. As each girl drew near, she asked her name and ticked it off. Thursday waited for the inevitable comment but it didn't come; instead, the woman made a swift pencil stroke and nodded her past.

'Well, this is it,' Thursday said quietly to Louisa, who was just behind her. 'Goodbye to England. I wonder when we'll be back.'

'And what will have happened by then,' the other girl nodded. She hefted her suitcase a little higher. 'Go on, Thursday. No backing out now!'

Thursday shook her head. She had no intention of backing out. She was too excited at the thought of going abroad for the first time, too intrigued by the mystery of their destination. All the same, she couldn't quite bring herself to take that final move away from

English soil, and she hesitated, touching the dockside with her foot until the very last moment.

'Go *on*, Thursday, for heaven's sake,' Louisa said again from behind her, and gave her a gentle push. With a little sound that was half gasp, half sob, Thursday stepped hurriedly up the narrow ramp. In a moment, she was on the deck and then inside the ship. I'm on my way, she thought, dazed. I'm on a ship, a *liner*, and I'm going abroad . . .

Elsie was just in front. She turned and gave Thursday a broad, though slightly wavering, grin. 'Well, here we are, Thurs. Proper sailors at last. We joined the Navy to see the world –'

'And what did we see?' Thursday finished. 'We saw the sea! Well, I hope we're going to see some land again, because—'

'Never mind what you want to see,' a voice broke in. 'What you're going to see now is your cabins. We got a lot of personnel to get aboard today, so if you don't mind, ladies . . .' The sailor, looking remarkably like the matelots they were accustomed to seeing around Haslar, swung their kitbags on to his shoulder and set off at speed along the steel-lined passageway. The girls followed him, squeezing past the people who wanted to come the other way, people who all seemed to know where they were going. It seemed that the whole of the Army and Navy were trying to cram aboard this ship which, big though it was, was surely never built for a crowd this size. We're going to be crammed in like sardines in a tin, Thursday thought as they followed their guide along gangways, up and down steep ladders and then through more narrow passages and past door after door until at last he stopped and threw their bags into an empty cabin.

'There you are. This one'll do. Four bunks, see, so the next one that comes along'll be in here with you. This is deck E and you'll find the mess deck is on C. Better get yourselves up there pronto and see what time your meals are – they're being served in rotation, see. This here's sea-water soap. There'll be a roster for baths as well. It don't lather up like the Palmolive you're used to, but it's the best you'll get. Fresh water's like gold on board ship, so don't go splashing it about, all right?' He glanced behind him into the passageway to where a tall, slender girl with a cloud of pale blonde hair was standing. 'All right, love, you're in here with these three. They'll give you the gen.' He gave them all a brisk nod and a sudden grin: 'Have a good cruise, girls, and if you want to hand out any tips, I'm your steward for the trip, OK?'

'What did he mean by that?' Elsie said, staring after him.

Louisa laughed. 'A joke, I should think! We won't get stewards and we'll probably never set eyes on him again.' She looked at the newcomer. 'We're from Haslar Royal Naval Hospital. Where are you from?'

'Plymouth. Devonport Naval Hospital.' The girl had a firm, confident voice, with no hint of a west Country accent. She talked like Louisa, and Thursday knew at once that she came from the same kind of background. 'My name's Priscilla Lacock.' She came into the cabin and looked round, raising her fine eyebrows humorously. 'Good Lord, is this the best they can do? Bunks? I thought we'd get cabins to ourselves at the very least!'

The girls stared at her. She was wearing the same uniform as they wore – dark-blue costume with VAD badge sewn on the sleeve, black tie and white blouse, but somehow, on her slender figure, it looked more elegant.

'I think they want to get as many people as possible aboard,' Thursday said at last. 'It isn't a luxury cruise.'

Priscilla grinned. 'We're lucky not to be travelling in the hold, like slaves always used to.' She dumped her suitcase on the deck. 'I suppose you've already picked your bunks?'

'Not really,' Elsie said. 'We've only just got here, see. But I always have a lower one if I can – no one'd want to risk sleeping under me anyway, in case I bring the whole lot down,' she patted her full hips ruefully, 'and Thursday here has the one over me because she's tall and can get up easier. So it looks as if it's between you and Lou for the other two.'

'First come, first served,' Priscilla said cheerfully. 'You were here before me. Only thing is, I get claustrophobia in small spaces so I wouldn't mind having the lower bunk so that I can see out of the porthole.'

'OK by me.' Louisa glanced around the tiny cabin. 'Look, let's leave our unpacking until later – not that we've got much room to unpack anyway. I want to see what's happening on deck – we'll be sailing pretty soon, I wouldn't wonder. Come on, let's see if we can find our way back.'

'It's finding our way back *here* that'll be the clever part,' Thursday remarked. 'Perhaps we ought to take a ball of string and unwind it as we go, so that we've got something to follow.'

'And if everyone else does that too, we'll be knitting a Fair Isle jumper between us!' Elsie grinned and they crowded out of the door and made their way through the busy passageways. They emerged on to the top deck and stared around eagerly. 'Oh, look – they're putting up a barrage balloon!'

'Let's find ourselves a place out of the way,' Louisa suggested. 'How about over here, under this lifeboat? We won't be in the way and we can see everything that goes on.'

They squeezed into the niche together and watched eagerly as the huge balloon was fastened to the deck by a wire hawser. Like a silver airborne whale, it floated high above, a protection against enemy aircraft when the ship put to sea. There was a bustle of activity as it was secured and the sailors and dockyard workers removed all the gangplanks and the moorings, until at last only the bow and stern lines remained. Then they too were removed and the ship began slowly to move, nudged on its way by the tugs that fussed around it. Thursday's heart gave a leap as she realised that they were really on their way.

'I came down here once to see my aunt off to America,' Priscilla murmured. 'You should have seen it then. The ship all festooned with little flags, and people throwing coloured paper streamers to each other, a band playing and everyone singing, everyone excited – some people laughing and cheering, others crying because they were going away, or being left behind.'

'What were they singing?' Elsie asked, but her voice was drowned by a sudden great wave of sound as the thousands of men aboard the ship, joined by those still on shore, broke into song, and the girls fell silent to listen.

' "Now is the Hour",' Thursday said softly when the song ended. 'It's what people always do sing, isn't it? And "Wish Me Luck, as You Wave Me Goodbye" . . . I couldn't join in, could you? It would have made me cry.'

'I'm crying anyway,' Elsie said, feeling for a hanky. 'Oh God, Thurs, do you realise we're going abroad? I've never been further than the Isle of Wight before! And we don't even know where we're going. It could be Africa, India, *anywhere*! I can't believe it.'

'Well, you did volunteer to be mobile,' Thursday retorted with a grin. 'You didn't expect to stay at Haslar for the rest of the war, did you?'

'I dunno. I dunno what I expected.' Elsie looked down at the dockside, now drawing further away as the ship moved out to the open sea. 'I just know it feels funny now, to think of going away from England and not know where we're going or how long we'll be gone.'

'Yes,' Thursday said, thinking of her family at home, of her mother and father, of Jenny starting work in the local hospital, of Steve in his prison camp, of her aunt and uncle and Cousin Denise with her new baby . . . Keep them safe for me, she prayed suddenly, clasping her hands together. And keep all the brave soldiers and sailors and airmen safe as well – though obviously they can't *all* be kept safe, not in wartime – but please, Lord, please keep as many safe as possible, and let me and Elsie and Louisa and the others come home when it's all over and find our families still all right . . . and let us win this war, please, so that the world can go back to being peaceful and happy once again . . .

Chapter Nine

The voyage had taken several weeks. Along with the other girls, Thursday had soon slipped into a pleasant routine – meals taken in the big dining-hall, PT every morning, boat drill, card games, draughts or chess to while away the time or, as the ship sailed into warmer waters, sunbathing in the little portion of deck allocated to the VADs.

'Tell you what,' Elsie said, stretching herself out with her kapok lifejacket as a cushion under her head, 'this might not be a luxury cruise, but it's flipping well nearly as good. Getting waited on at mealtimes, nothing to do but enjoy ourselves – and five thousand men to help us do it! I think I've died and gone to heaven, that's what.'

Thursday chuckled. 'I must say, it's rather nice to have all this attention. And they're all so polite! Why, at the Housey-Housey last night one of the Corporals insisted I share his card, wouldn't take no for an answer, and then made me take the prize we won. He was really nice,' she added reminiscently.

Elsie gave a hoot of laughter. 'We could see that! And what happened when you went out on deck with him, Thursday, eh? Tell us that. Though I bet you won't be telling the dashing Commander Kirkpatrick next time you write!'

Thursday blushed. 'There's nothing between me and Johnny.'

'Johnny, is it? A minute ago he was just "one of the Corporals". And you were looking very pleased with yourself when you came to bed – *eventually*.'

Thursday gave her a sideways glance and folded her lips demurely. She had no intention of telling Elsie how the young soldier had stood beside her on the upper deck, his head close to hers as they gazed down at the phosphorescent shimmer of the waves. Behind the ship its wake foamed and glittered so that despite the stringent blackout imposed, it seemed impossible that they weren't visible for miles. Around them, they knew, were all the other ships of the convoy – a dozen or so more troopships carrying thousands of soldiers, airmen and Marines to their next theatre of war, accompanied by a protective ring of Naval battleships; yet each was completely darkened, no glimmer of light betraying the crowds within.

Above, clustered as thickly as blackberries on a bush, hung the stars, their formations strangely different from the ones Thursday had been used to. She'd never been particularly interested in the constellations, knowing only the familiar shape of the Plough, but she was aware, nevertheless, that these were different. She felt that she could stand here and gaze at them for hours, or at the moon which, as it seemed to rise from the depths of the ocean, was like an enormous globe hung there to light them on their way.

If only you were here, Connor, she thought sadly, her heart aching. It would be so lovely to stand at the rail with you, watching the phosphorescence and the stars, holding your hand and waiting for you to kiss me. Or perhaps I wouldn't wait . . . A tingle of desire ran through her as she thought of being in Connor's arms, held close to that body which had become so familiar, so precious. I've never had any real loving, she thought regretfully. There was only Sidney, who never did more than give me a peck, and Tony who was killed before we'd even begun to fall in love – and Connor, who went away so soon. I'm twenty-four and I've never done more than kiss a man – and even those kisses have been pretty demure.

And now here she was on board ship, a little world of its own – one of just a dozen girls amongst five thousand men. It was unreasonable not to expect the girls to pair off with some of the men – indeed, Elsie had remarked with a grin that she hoped the voyage would last long enough to get round them all – and it was also unreasonable not to realise that among these five thousand there would be more than one who might prove a sore temptation. But all I want is a kiss or two, Thursday thought longingly, acutely aware of the soldier at her side. There can't be any harm in that.

She hung over the rail, gazing at the sea. It was a continual fascination, this shifting, shimmering swell of brilliance, and there was always the chance of a school of flying fish, attracted by the paravane which was hung beside the deck to deflect mines and hurling themselves through the air to land gasping on the deck. One of the sailors had gathered the girls around him a few days ago, showing them a dozen or so of the strange creatures and fanning their 'wings' out to show how they really could glide through the air after leaping out of the water.

'I wonder where Horace went,' she said dreamily. Horace had been their name for the barrage balloon which had accompanied them out of Bristol and then gradually detached itself and floated away through the sky alone as if on its own mysterious errand. A few still flew above the convoy, but several more had managed to escape their ships and gone off after Horace, like a school of airborne whales determined not to be shackled.

'Dunno.' Johnny stood very close, his shoulder touching hers. 'Hope he's enjoying himself, wherever he is. As much as I am,' he added softly.

'Mm. It's like a dream, isn't it, this voyage? It's like time out of the war, out of the world itself. I know we get the daily bulletins so we know more or less what's going on, but it doesn't seem to affect us much. Even though we know it could all change, and we could be attacked at any moment.'

'That's why we have these boat drills every day,' he said. 'Just to make sure we don't forget what we're going for. And we blokes have a lot of training to do, to keep our fitness up,' he added. 'Wouldn't do for the Tommies and Marines to come off the ship too weak and flabby to carry their own kitbags!'

'The boat drills are so boring, though. You should hear what Elsie says about them! I hope we don't ever have to use them. Did you know, if we do have to take to the boats, we VADs all have to go to a separate one? We'd be all on our own in a boat with nearly forty men. We're supposed to *inspire* them, if you please – in the middle of the night, our hair all in curlers and wearing navy-blue bloomers! I don't know what sort of inspiration that would be.'

'It would inspire me,' he said, 'if you were the one in our boat.'

There was a tiny silence. Johnny slid his arm around her shoulders. Thursday turned her face towards him and found him very close, his breath warm on her cheek. She opened her mouth a little, but the words were lost in his kiss and, after a moment of surprise, she found herself kissing him back.

'Oh, Thursday,' he said at last, 'you are a lovely girl.'

Thursday said nothing. Her thoughts were whirling, but the response of her body had shaken her even more. She stared at him, wanting him to kiss her again. Oh, I've missed this, she thought. I've missed it so much . . . Then she put her hands lightly against his chest and held him away.

'I'm sort of engaged,' she said. 'Not formally with a ring, or anything – he said he didn't want to tie me down – but I'm trying to keep my promise.'

'That's all right,' he said. 'I'm not going to do anything you wouldn't want. And I don't want to mess anything up for you – I've got someone myself, back home. But it seems an awful waste to be out here, with all this,' he gestured at the deep black sky, peppered with stars, at the glittering spray beneath them, 'and not have a little bit of romance to remember. It's like you said – it's a different world out here, on board this ship.' He kissed her again, and Thursday wound her arms around his neck and relaxed against him. Oh, this is good, she thought, so good, to feel a man's body close to mine. And Connor wouldn't mind, I'm sure he wouldn't. We had so little time, and this will only be an interlude. A lovely, happy, innocent interlude . . .

She knew that she did look different when she returned to the cabin at last. The other girls were all in their bunks, and only Elsie was awake. She had looked at Thursday in the tiny light cast by Thursday's small torch as she undressed, and raised her eyebrows in question.

But Thursday wasn't going to tell her about those moonlight kisses. Not now. Not ever. They were just a shipboard romance. All the same, when the ship arrived at Cape Town and Johnny disembarked, the two of them had cast away all pretence and, like a dozen others, clung together sadly in the knowledge that their romantic interlude was over and they might never meet again.

Life on board ship wasn't, they all agreed, a luxury trip. The food was good, and well served, but apart from that facilities were basic. With so many more people on board than the liner was built to accommodate, conditions were cramped, particularly for the men, but the greatest adversity was the shortage of fresh water which was strictly rationed and turned on only twice a day. During these two periods, the girls were allowed to take as much as they could carry, and they arrived at the taps with every container they could think of – billycans, tooth mugs, empty shampoo bottles – and, if they were lucky enough to be there without an impatient queue behind them, took the opportunity to wash their hair. Apart from that, their washing was limited to the saltwater baths and the soap that lathered reluctantly and left them feeling as sticky and hot as they'd felt before.

'I'd give twenty pounds for a decent shampoo,' Elsie remarked, brushing hopelessly at her long yellow hair, 'and some setting lotion. All me curls are dropping out in this heat.'

'Well, you certainly work hard enough at keeping them in,' Priscilla said. 'Sitting in your bunk every night wrapping those rags round it. I thought it was only little girls who wore ringlets.'

'Well, now you know it's big girls as well,' Elsie retorted. 'We can't all have natural waves.'

Priscilla tossed her head and her cloud of fine, pale hair wafted like a mist around her head. It wasn't exactly wavy, Thursday thought, but it seemed to settle naturally into a nice shape. Her eyes were nice too, a light grey that could look blue or even green to reflect the sea and, although her face had the aristocratic features that could sometimes look a bit snooty, the minute she gave you that wicked grin of hers you knew she would be all right.

'Got to admit I thought you might be a bit of a snob, when I first saw you,' Elsie remarked one day as they tried to get dressed all at once in the tiny cabin. 'You looked so posh, what with your smart leather suitcase and all.'

'You should have known me when I first went to Devonport,' Priscilla told her. 'I was OK with the girls who'd been to boarding school like me – we were used to iron beds and lousy food – but I couldn't get used to the working-class girls at all. They'd only ever shared with their sisters; they didn't like undressing in front of the rest of us, they hated the food and they cried all night for their mothers! We were accustomed to being away from home, you see, so it came more easily. And I'm afraid some of us *were* terrible snobs. We thought that just because we'd had an expensive education we were God's gift to wounded sailors. We soon learned differently about *that*!'

'I was surprised to find girls like Elsie and Thursday in the VADs,' Louisa admitted. 'The pay's so awful I thought it would be only girls like us, who had families who could send us a bit extra, who'd be able to do it.'

'Doesn't make any difference to us,' Elsie said. 'Shop wages aren't up to much. We're not used to getting a lot of pay anyway, and we do get all found now – all our clothes, food and a bed to sleep in. And if we can find a bloke to take us out we don't even have to pay to go to the pictures. I mean, that's the way it is, isn't it? Girls never do get much pay.'

'Not even if they do the same job as a man,' Thursday agreed. 'Shift over a bit, Elsie, I haven't got room to put my stockings on with you taking up all the space.'

The rest of the VADs – most from Haslar, two or three from Plymouth – had settled down well too and become good friends. They sunbathed together in their private portion of deck, did their PT and boat drill and mourned the possibility that if the ship did have to be abandoned, they would be split up.

'It don't bear thinking of,' Elsie said. 'I mean, on our own in a boatload of men, how are we going to manage about spending a penny and all that? Nobody bothers to tell you that when we do boat drill.'

'Let's hope we never have to find out,' Thursday said. They were on deck, carrying their bulky kapok lifejackets as usual, making for their sunbathing spot. 'We're pretty well looked after by all these ships. Mind you, it cuts both ways – with so many steaming along in a gang, it's a wonder the Germans don't find us easy.'

Each morning the girls went out on deck to make sure their companion ships were still there. They counted them carefully, able by now to recognise each one by name, and there was inevitably consternation when one was missing. Mostly, the errant one returned during the day having been off on some mission, and they breathed a sigh of relief.

Every evening there was some kind of entertainment. The men got up concerts and Thursday was surprised to find how talented many of them were. Some of them formed a choir and sang songs that varied from Victorian ballads to all the latest hits; others did their turns alone, or performed sketches together. There was Housey-Housey too, and the girls joined in with enthusiasm, marking their cards to the calls: 'Clickety-click – number six. Nelson's eye – number one. Two fat ladies – eighty-eight. Was she worth it – seven and six.'

'I don't know how you can do it so quickly,' Priscilla complained. 'I'm always half a card behind the rest of you. It's so hot and stuffy down there too, I can't breathe – all that cigarette smoke, and no portholes open.'

'Well, we can't, can we,' Thursday said reasonably. 'We've got to keep the blackout. And you smoke, in here.'

'That's different. There are only four of us in here. There are hundreds in that lounge.' She put on what Elsie called her snooty look and drawled exaggeratedly. 'The First Class Lounge is bad enough, darlings – but *Second* Class – ugh!'

'Never mind,' Louisa remarked from the bunk where she was lying in her panties and camisole. 'Nobody would expect you to lower yourself to go in there, so they don't have to lay on anything special for you.'

Priscilla made a rude face at her. 'I don't know why I had to find myself sharing a cabin with you,' she declared. 'Elsie and Thursday are all right, but you upper-class girls – well!' She got off her bunk and pulled on her white dress. 'It's so *hot* in here. I'm going up on deck – see if I can find some fresh air.'

'She's a card, she is,' Elsie said as Priscilla wafted out of the cabin. 'I tell you what, Lou, if it hadn't been for the war and being a VAD I'd never have met people like you and Priss. It's opened my eyes a bit. I never thought I'd be able to even talk to anyone who'd been to a posh school and had pots of money, and I never thought they'd bother to talk to me either.'

'It's the same for us, I suppose,' Louisa said. 'We wouldn't meet people like you – not to live and work with. We wouldn't even have got jobs at all, we'd just do the Season and find a husband to keep us. It's been an eye-opener for people like me and Priscilla too. It's done us good.'

'Yes, but you weren't ever snooty,' Elsie said. 'Priss was to begin with, she's told me that herself. And that girl who knew her at Devonport, Daisy Roberts, she says she was a real pain in the you-know-where. Thought anyone who came from a house with less than six bedrooms was straight out of a slum. Daisy says she treated them like dirt at first. *You* never did that.'

'My father would shoot me if I did. He's always told us that anyone who does a decent day's work for a living is worthy of respect, whatever the job is. And those who do the most disgusting jobs – taking away rubbish or working in the sewers – are entitled to the most respect of all.'

'Blimey,' Elsie said, 'he sounds more Labour than my dad.'

'I don't think it's a matter of politics,' Louisa said thoughtfully. 'Just realising that everyone's human and we can't all live in big houses – but that doesn't make some of us better than others.'

'But why *do* some live in big houses and have more money?' Thursday asked. 'Your father – or someone a long way back – must have been better in some way, to get it in the first place.'

'I don't think so. We just got handed a parcel of land by William the Conqueror. We're probably the last people to deserve it, if the truth were known! And look at all the people who made their money from slavery. Not much to be proud of there. Anyway, having land and money means responsibility too. What we've got is a sort of – of *trust*. We've got to look after it. It's not really ours, all that land and money; it's just been passed to us to take care of while we're here, and pass on to the next generation of the family. We're lucky, that's all.' She sat on Prisiclla's bunk to peer through the porthole. 'D'you think anyone knows where we are yet? Someone said they thought we were heading for Cape Town, but we could be anywhere. This endless sea – we could be like the Flying Dutchman, steaming around the ocean for ever, totally lost!'

Thursday laughed. 'Perhaps we are. Perhaps the war's over and nobody's told us because they've forgotten we ever existed.'

'They'd better not forget,' Elsie said darkly. 'I don't mind playing Housey-Housey or draughts and getting up concerts for a few weeks, but I'm blowed if I'm going to do it for ever! Even Mr Churchill can't expect *that*.'

The convoy steamed on. The dozen troopships were still accompanied by their protective ring of destroyers and battleships, all now easily recognisable to the VADs. The girls hung over the rail, gazing at them.

'They're glorious, aren't they,' Thursday said softly. 'Beautiful ships, and yet so sort of *formidable*, with all those guns and things. I feel absolutely safe with them there. Nothing can hurt us while they're looking after us.'

She knew in her heart that this wasn't really true. It would only take a few German bombers to come over, or some submarines to skulk under the surface of the smooth blue sea, for all hell to break loose. She closed her eyes, imagining for a moment the battle that would ensue, the shells exploding, the aircraft shot down, the ships sinking in a mass of flames . . . Dear God, don't let it happen, she prayed. Please, please don't let it happen.

'I don't want to scare anyone.' Elsie said suddenly, frightening Thursday so much that her heart seemed to fall like a stone right through her body, 'but could that be land over there?'

Thursday craned her neck. 'It's a smudge. It's probably smoke.' Her heart thumped again. 'You don't think it's ships?'

'No,' Louisa said, 'it's not. It *is* land. We're arriving somewhere.'

They stared anxiously, still uncertain, and then Thursday noticed something else. 'What's that? Look – over there. There's something in the water.' Her fears seemed to surface with the sudden turbulence only fifty yards or so away. 'Oh, my God, it's a sub!'

'It's not! It's a whale! It's a *whale*!' Louisa was almost jumping out of her skin with excitement. 'I saw one once when we went to Norway. Look, it's coming right up – it's going to spout! Oh, did you ever see anything more glorious!'

They watched, enthralled, as the huge creature rose to the surface like a black, glistening mound and sent a fountain of water high into the air. By now, word was being passed round the ship and men were running from everywhere to hang over the rails on that side of the decks. Aboard other ships, people could be seen doing the same, so that the whale had an audience of thousands on every side. As if enjoying the attention, it dived and rolled to the surface in a series of glittering displays, then with an almost wicked look in its eye, stood on its head and flourished its tail like a magnificent flag of victory.

'Oh,' Thursday said, tears in her eyes at the beauty of it. 'Oh . . .' The next second, her ears were blasted by the sound of the ship's sirens. 'Action Stations!' she gasped, and stared in terror at her companions. But there was no time to do more than give each of them a swift hug, and then race to her position by the lifeboat. Thank heavens for all that drill, she thought as she panted along the decks. At least everyone knows where to go. But what could it be?

There were no planes, so it must be subs, or maybe that smudge they had seen was smoke from German ships after all. She reached her lifeboat and scrambled into place beside it, waiting to hear the sudden rattle of gunfire or the shattering roar of an explosion, and then saw that the sailor in charge of it was grinning.

'What is it? What's so funny? Are we being attacked?'

'Not on your life,' he said cheerily. 'It was the only way to trim the ship, see? What with the whole five thousand of you all rushing over to one side to see that blooming whale, we were in a fair way to keeling over. This was the quickest way of getting you all away, I reckon.' His voice was drowned by the siren, sounding the return to normal. 'See? And didn't you notice you had to run uphill to get here?'

Thursday felt the deck shift beneath her feet. He was right – the ship *had* been listing as everyone raced to see the whale. She grinned, a little ashamed of her fear, and he patted her arm. 'It's all right, nursey. The good old J25 ain't going down yet. And if I'm not much mistaken, we're about to make landfall too. Be smashing to get some terra firma under our feet again, won't it!'

Thursday turned again. The smudge that Elsie had pointed out had become clearer. It was definitely land. But she knew better now than to race to the rail to stare at it. The call to Action Stations had been a false one, but nobody wanted another.

'Well, that was exciting, wasn't it!' Elsie said when they met again. 'And it *was* land I saw – it's getting clearer every minute. The question now is—'

'What land is it?' Thursday finished. 'And is this where we'll leave the ship, or will we go even further?'

The land had been, as they'd suspected for some time, the coast of South Africa. The prospect of firm ground beneath their feet was, as the matelot had said, an exciting one and the atmosphere on the ship was almost like the end of term at school as last-minute concerts were arranged, parties held in various corners and addresses exchanged with newfound friends. With so many men available for so many weeks, the girls had had as much choice of partners as any girl could possibly ask – yet it was surprising, Thursday thought, that there hadn't been more real, full-blown love affairs. Romance there had been in plenty – she recalled her own lingering hours spent at the rail with Johnny – but for the most part they'd known it couldn't be serious. As soon as land was reached, they would be separated, the girls going on to destinations yet unknown, the men to be plunged back into battle. Their brief idyll would be over and they would never see each other again.

For two of the VADs, however, it had turned out to be more serious. Daisy Roberts, a small, quiet girl from Devonport, had struck up a friendship on the very first day with a young airman and by the time the ship docked at Cape Town, they'd announced their engagement. And Priscilla had stunned them all by arriving in the cabin one evening flourishing a sparkling diamond ring on her left hand.

'A *ring*?' Thursday exclaimed, staring in astonishment. 'But who is it? And how on earth did he come to have a ring with him?'

Priscilla grinned. 'He's one of the ship's officers – Lieutenant-Commander Hillier. I met him the night we were asked to "take wine" with them. And it's none of your business why he had a ring with him.'

'Pardon me for breathing,' Thursday said. 'It's just a natural question. You've kept it jolly quiet, all the same. I suppose all those little jaunts up on deck to get some fresh air had something to do with it!'

'Well – maybe.' Priscilla stretched her hand out and admired the flashing stone. 'Aren't you going to wish me happiness?'

'Of course we are, you goof!' Thursday flung her arms around Priscilla. 'Even though you don't deserve it, after keeping it all so secret. We hope you'll be very happy. And Lieutenant-Commander Hillier too,' she added. 'What's his Christian name, by the way? Or haven't you got that far yet?'

Elsie gave a hoot of laughter and Priscilla shot her a withering look. 'His name's Quentin.'

'Quentin,' Elsie repeated expressionlessly, her lips twitching.

'Yes, *Quentin*, and you needn't say it like that – just because it's the sort of name your family would never dream of using! Oh,' as they all began to giggle, 'it's simply no use at all talking to you three! For heaven's sake, stop *laughing*, will you!'

'Sorry,' Thursday said, trying to straighten her face. 'Honestly, Priss, we're all pleased for you. We're not really laughing at you. It's just such a surprise, that's all.'

'Mind you,' Elsie said, her face twitching again, 'I'm not sure you've really given it enough thought, Priss. You know what your name is going to be, don't you? Priscilla Hillier. It's a bit of a tongue-twister.'

'It's not such a bad name as all that,' Louisa defended her. 'Neither's Quentin. I've got a second cousin once removed called Quentin. It's a very old name. There's a saint in Scotland, I think, and Walter Scott used it in one of his novels.'

'All right, you've convinced us.' Thursday said, and rolled off her bunk. 'Come on, let's see if the water's on. All my bottles are empty, and I want to wash my hair before tonight's concert.'

'Don't say *you're* going to try to trap a nice Lieutenant-Commander,' Elsie said slyly, and ducked away from Priscilla's punch. 'Well, *I* am! I'm not letting our Priss outdo me.'

Laughing, they squeezed out through the narrow door and into the passageway. As they went, Thursday gave a quick glance out of the porthole. The land was definitely getting closer. Africa! she thought. Whoever would have thought that Thursday Tilford, from backstreet Worcester, would ever go to Africa?

Chapter Ten

Back at Haslar in August 1944, Thursday found it hard to believe that she'd actually lived in the elegant house where she, Louisa and Elsie had been put up while waiting to start the next stage of their journey. Dreamily, she recalled their first sight of Table Mountain, draped in its white tablecloth of cloud, their first tentative venture into the town, the dances and parties they'd been invited to, the strange and delicious foods – fruits she had never heard of, like mangoes, lychees, guavas and passion-fruit – and the beautiful flowers and trees that grew in the gardens. They'd been treated like queens, she thought, and hadn't they just lapped it up! After the cramped conditions on board ship and with the prospect of yet another voyage, a touch of luxury was what they'd craved.

And the food parcels they'd been able to send home! Thursday had hugged herself with glee, imagining her mother's face when she found dried fruits, jams and sugar such as she hadn't seen for months. There was chocolate too, to be tucked into the corners, and a bar or two to be kept for themselves in this land of plenty, and no rationing. She ordered another box for her aunt, and marked one of the bars of chocolate specially for Denise and little Leslie.

'I could do with one of those food parcels now,' she remarked to Elsie when they met after their duty for a stroll round the grounds. 'You know, the ones we sent from Cape Town. The shortages seem worse than ever here now. Everything on coupons or points – what use is two ounces of sweets to anyone? And one egg? They might as well not bother at all.'

'Did you reckon we'd be this long in the VADs when you first volunteered?' Elsie asked. 'I know we all knew by then that it wouldn't be over by Christmas, but I don't think we believed it'd go on like it did. And look at us now – four flipping years since we first came to Haslar, and here we are again, wiping men's bottoms and changing their dressings, just as if we'd never been away.'

'You're not sorry you joined though, are you?'

'Flipping heck, no! Best thing I ever did. I mean, how else would I have ever got to go to Egypt? I know it wasn't no picnic, but we had some good times too, didn't we, Thurs? Remember the Pyramids that night? And the poor old Sphinx with sandbags up to his chin? At least they didn't have no trouble getting the sand! Oh, yes – and remember that camel, the one what stood on Prissy-Cilla's foot?'

Thursday laughed. 'You'd have thought it had broken her leg, the way she screamed. It hadn't even broken her toe. I never knew their hooves were all soft and warm till that Arab boy showed us.' Her face saddened. 'Poor Priscilla . . .'

Elsie nodded soberly. After a few moments she said casually, 'Ever hear from that Army chap again? What was his name – Martin, Malcolm?'

'It was Mark,' Thursday said, colouring. 'As you very well know! No, I haven't heard from him. I don't expect to, either. We said goodbye when he went away, and that was that. I don't even know where he is now.'

'Daresay you could find out,' Elsie suggested offhandedly. 'You know his unit.'

'I don't want to find out!' Thursday caught herself up, surprised herself by the sharpness in her voice. 'Sorry, Elsie – I didn't mean to snap. But when we said goodbye, we knew that was what we meant. It was never more than a friendship, anyway.'

Once again, Elsie didn't reply. They walked along the avenue of cherry trees, each lost in her own thoughts. Then Thursday sighed and said, 'I haven't forgotten him – how could I? I haven't forgotten any of them – Johnny on the way out to Cape Town, Tom and Peter when we were going to Egypt, and all the men we got to know while we were in Alex. They were all special, but they could never take Connor's place, any of them.'

'Not even Mark Sangster?'

There was a brief silence. Then Thursday shook her head. 'Not even Mark.'

They arrived at the door of D Block and stood for a moment in the late-afternoon sunshine. Thursday closed her eyes and lifted her face, letting her thoughts waft back to those hot afternoons and cool evenings in Alexandria, where she had met and nursed so many young men. And back, inevitably, to Mark.

No, she told herself as Elsie touched her arm and she stepped aside to let a group of other VADs come through the door. Nobody has ever taken Connor's place in my heart. Not even Mark Sangster.

Troops were still arriving daily to embark for France, and in August the *Portsmouth Evening News* showed a photograph of hundreds of ATS girls boarding a troopship bound across the Channel. Since they would certainly not be sent to any fighting zone, this was considered the most hopeful sign yet, although it still seemed at times as if the war were a matter of two steps forward and one back. You could feel confident at one minute that the Allies were winning, and then in despair the next over some other defeat. And still being waged, as viciously as ever, was the war in the Far East.

Thursday lived for Connor's letters. She never really knew where he was, just that his ship was out there somewhere, in the Indian Ocean or the South China Sea. She wrote every day, adding a little to her letters each evening and posting them two or three times a week. Some news, she knew, would be censored, so there was no point in telling him that the ban on travelling to the Isle of Wight had been lifted at last so that relatives could see each other for the first time in eighteen months, nor that the ten-mile forbidden zone all around the south coast had been removed, but she could tell him that Paris had been liberated and that the defence against the V1s was succeeding and that out of almost a hundred launched that month, only four had got through.

Our boys go up in their Spitfires and tip their wings to turn them off course, she wrote, wondering if this would be crossed out but determined to pass the news on if she could. *As often as not, they go straight down into the sea. Hitler must be hopping mad!* And one evening, after a walk on the sea wall with Patsy: *We've just seen the most amazing thing. The sun was going down into a fairly clear sky when we saw some enormous crimson V signs high up above it. Everyone saw them and nobody can talk about anything else. Louisa thinks the Air Force has sent some planes up to lay a coloured trail, like the sky-writing they used to do before the war, and Elsie reckons it's an omen – a miracle, sent by God, to tell us we're winning. I never realised Elsie was so religious! What do you think it could have been?* A day or so later, giggling to herself, she added a postscript: *Hundreds of people saw the V signs in the sky and wrote to the local paper about them. The Air Force won't have it that it was anything to do with them, and pass it off as just cloud formations. But a lot of people agree with Elsie that it was an omen – and even if it wasn't, it's done a lot of good. Patsy's been a different girl since then, and if it's helped her it's probably helped a lot of others too, so who cares what it was really! And it really does look as if the war MIGHT be coming to an end – some of the Home Guard have been stood down and we're having 'dim-out' instead of 'blackout'. That means we can have ordinary curtains up on the windows instead of those horrible black ones (that's if anyone has still got their old ones, and hasn't cut them up to make clothes or had them eaten away by moths!) and there'll even be a few streetlights to show us the way home!*

After her breakdown on Jackie Spencer's bridge, Patsy had begun to emerge from her shell. Still a pale, subdued ghost of her former self, she could at least be persuaded to come for a walk or a cycle ride, and once she'd been with Elsie and Thursday to the Theatre Royal in Portsmouth, to see to see the new Walt Disney cartoon film *Snow White and the Seven Dwarfs*. Glancing sideways as the dwarfs heaved their shovels on to their shoulders and marched off to work, singing, 'Hi-ho, hi-ho, it's off to work we go,' Thursday had seen Patsy giggling helplessly, and blessed Walt Disney for his ability to make people laugh.

The sight of the V signs in the sky had stopped Patsy short as she walked along the sea wall, and the flush in her cheeks, as if the sunset had touched her as well, as she stood with upturned face and brightened eyes, made her look more like the old Patsy than Thursday had seen for weeks.

'I'm going home for the weekend,' she said a few days later. 'Madam's given me some leave, and Mum's been on at me to go home ever since . . .' her voice shook but she went on determinedly, 'since Roy died.'

'Oh, Patsy, I'm glad. You need to get away, and be looked after for a while. Pity it can't be longer than a weekend, though. You need a couple of weeks at least.'

Patsy shrugged. 'Who gets a couple of weeks' holiday? Two or three days'll be enough for me. Anyway,' she lowered her voice, 'I've got an idea something big's going to happen. Madam didn't exactly say so, but I got the impression we're going to be on standby again.'

Thursday stared at her. 'Why? What d'you think's going to happen? The Germans can't be going to push us back again, surely. We're well into France now.'

'I don't know,' Patsy said. 'I just got the feeling, that's all.'

'Well, we'd better not talk about it then,' Thursday said, glancing round the busy mess-hall. 'Anyway, you don't need to worry about it, Pats. You go home and have a good time. Me and Elsie and the others will hold the fort.'

Patsy went off a day or two later, crossing the harbour in the Naval pinnace to catch the London train at the station built out on its stilts above the edge of the harbour.

'I hope she'll be all right,' Joy Cockroft said anxiously. Since Patsy had taken her under her wing when she'd first arrived, she'd followed the older girl around like a puppy. 'There've been a lot of reports about gas explosions. All over London, they reckon. I can't help wondering if it's not some new secret weapon Hitler's got.'

'Don't be daft,' Thursday said briskly. 'If it was anything like the doodlebugs you'd hear them coming – and you know they've told us there won't be any more of those. These are just explosions, and Patsy's not going anywhere near a gas main, anyway. She's only going to change trains for Evesham. Tell you what, we'll go over to Southsea tomorrow afternoon – they say there's lots of shops open and people are coming from all around, even from London. Poor souls, they haven't been able to come down to the seaside all summer.'

The shopping centre at Southsea had been virtually reduced to rubble, with the big shops Handley's and Knight & Lee's taking the brunt of the Blitz, yet, as Thursday said, there were still plenty of shops which had managed to stay open. Mostly, women were looking for household utensils which were beginning to appear again – pot scourers, wooden spoons, mops and china. It was all utility, of course – not bone china, Thursday thought a little critically, remembering the porcelain her father had made in Worcester – but it was selling in huge quantities. People had been making do with old china for years now, having to salvage whatever they could from their bombed houses, and it wasn't at all uncommon to be offered tea in a cup with no handle.

The girls were more interested in stockings and make-up. A fortnight earlier there had been a consignment of nylon stockings from America and the queue had stretched for half a mile. They made for the lingerie counters and were lucky enough to come away with two pairs each.

'Well, that's my week's pay gone,' Thursday said ruefully. 'D'you know, one of the best things about peace coming will be getting paid a decent wage again. It's no wonder it's mostly upper-class girls who volunteered to be VADs – nobody else could afford it. If my dad hadn't sent me the odd Postal Order, I don't know what I'd have done.'

'Well, we do get fed, and have our uniforms provided,' Elsie said fairly. 'But you're right, Thurs, it's never left much for our bits and pieces, or going out. But at least there's always been plenty of blokes around, ready to buy a drink or take us to the flicks!'

It seemed a waste to be going to Southsea on a Saturday afternoon and not go on to a dance at one of the three popular venues, the Savoy, Kimball's or South Parade Pier. They'd looked in the paper to see which had the best band, and decided on the Pier, so they collected their bikes from the rack and cycled out to the front to find a café for some tea.

'Beans on toast and a pot of tea,' Thursday said, 'and then I'm cleaned out till next week.'

'You've got enough for the ferry, in case we miss the pinnace?' Joy asked anxiously.

'Oh yes – and a penny for emergencies!' Thursday grinned. 'Listen, it says in the paper there's going to be a big RAF parade to the cathedral tomorrow – it's September the seventeenth, Battle of Britain Day. There'll be Navy and Army people there too. Wish we could go and see it.'

'They'll be having a special service in St Luke's, though,' Elsie said. 'It don't seem possible it was four years ago, does it? Remember how we used to watch the dogfights from the hospital? And that day we had the first big air raid and you went for the men because they were cheering when a Jerry plane got shot down? Cor, I reckon you'd have stood up to Madam herself that day, you were in such a blazing temper.'

'Well, it seemed so awful to laugh because some poor man was being burned to death, even if he was a German. But they never thought of it that way, did they? It was just a fight to them. They didn't seem to realise there were human beings in those planes.' She sighed. 'I suppose they were right, in a way. We wouldn't have a chance of winning if the men all started to feel sorry for the enemy. But I couldn't help thinking of my Cousin Leslie, who was probably up there in the thick of it – and that young German we had in the ward. He was just an ordinary boy, like ours, and he didn't have any real quarrel with us. It was just Hitler, telling them lies and working them all up.'

'Your cousin did get shot down later on, didn't he?' Elsie said, and Thursday nodded.

'Yes, he was killed. Poor Auntie Flo – she lost both her boys. Leslie shot down and Mike at Dunkirk. At least our Steve's still alive, in the POW camp.'

'I remember coming over to Pompey to see if Mum and the family were all right,' Elsie said quietly. 'It was the first time I'd seen what an air raid could do. I couldn't believe it – houses smashed to bits, furniture all broken and lying out in the gutter, everyone scrabbling in all the rubble looking for people that had been buried . . . Fire and smoke all over the place – ambulances and fire engines rushing about . . . And that little dead baby, just lying in the gutter, covered in blood. That was the worst of all. A *baby*.'

The other two nodded. They'd seen many more sights as bad since then, but the first time was always the worst. It was always a shock, to see what war could do.

'It's got to be over soon,' she said. 'It's just got to be.'

And it seemed, the next morning, as if she was right. The word ran round the hospital again – 'by Christmas'. Field Marshal Montgomery himself had said so. The girls had seen the evidence themselves, as they crossed the grounds from D Block to the hospital to go on early duty, and heard the sound of a steady roar from above. They stopped, staring upwards, and then caught at each other's arms. 'Look! Look at that!'

Yet again, the sky was almost black with aircraft, moving steadily towards the sea. Elsie shaded her eyes with her hand. 'It's planes. And *gliders* again! Enormous ones. But why would we be sending gliders over now? We're not invading France again, surely.'

'Well, we're invading somewhere, that's for sure,' Thursday said slowly. 'That's the same sort as went over before, remember? What was it they were called? Horsas – the ones carrying troops and tanks and things. And look at those huge planes towing them – they must be carrying men as well.' She dropped her hands and turned to them, her face alight. 'This is what Madam was hinting at! This is the new flap – what we're on standby for. It *is* an invasion – I don't know where, but it is, all the same – and they're expecting casualties. They always do.'

'Well, it won't be for a day or two,' Elsie said, staring up again. 'They're only just setting out. There won't be any casualties yet.'

'They won't be long coming, all the same,' Thursday said grimly. 'They're bringing them back by air now, remember, in those Dakota air ambulances. And going by the last lot, Haslar's going to need all the nurses it's got. We'd better get on duty now, anyway. There won't be any news for a few hours and we've got men here now, waiting for us. There's a long list of ops in the theatre this morning and your bed patients will be wanting their bedpans!'

For a few days there was little news. The whole country was aware that something big was happening – the biggest operation since D-Day itself – and there were numerous rumours. But most people were still too aware of the dangers of gossip to take too much notice. They watched the steady flights of planes and gliders heading out over the south and east coasts, and kept their lips tight.

Thursday concentrated on her work. In a day or two, the first casualties would begin to arrive, she thought. But she wasn't prepared – nobody was prepared – for the number that began to arrive, nor for the number of those who would never come back.

To begin with, the news had been good. When Thursday came off duty on the third or fourth day, it was to find people hurrying towards the blocks, calling out that there was a special broadcast, that Field Marshal Montgomery himself was making an announcement. She raced up the stairs from the basement and joined the throng hurrying back to the mess, where other VADs and QARNNs were already gathering. Glancing around, she caught sight of Louisa and Elsie, clustering with the others round the wireless. Thursday joined them and craned her neck to listen.

'It's Monty himself!' Louisa whispered, making room for her. 'He's making the announcement now – Operation Market Garden, it's called. They're going to capture all the bridges over the rivers between Holland and Germany. They've dropped thousands of American and British paratroopers at Maas and Arnhem, and tanks as well – that must be what we saw going over in those planes and gliders – and they're going to take the bridges over the Rhine itself, and then the land troops will be able to advance. He says if it all goes well, the war will be over by Christmas!'

Thursday stared at her. 'By Christmas?'

'Yes!' Louisa cried jubilantly. 'Just think, of it, Thursday – all this, over by *Christmas*!'

'But they said that before,' Thursday said blankly, thinking of all the times when that very phrase had been used in the past. Could it possibly be true this time?

Within another day or so, they knew that Operation Market Garden had gone disastrously wrong. On the first night, the Germans had captured the battle plans from a crashed glider and, wherever the troops went after that, they were expected. The bridges and their surrounding towns were defended and the paratroopers, who had expected to land in secrecy, found themselves machine-gunned as they floated down from the sky. The forces trying so desperately to hold the bridge at Arnhem surrendered at last, and the whole operation was abandoned.

Of the ten thousand men who had crossed with such brave hearts and high expectations, less than a quarter returned. Over a thousand were killed in those few terrible days, the rest taken prisoner.

The war would not be over by Christmas. Monty's daring plan had come to nothing – worse than nothing, for so many men had been either killed or taken prisoner, each one a highly trained soldier or paratrooper, each one a desperate loss to the Allies. And of those who had escaped, so many were wounded, either shot or burned, and once again Haslar, barely recovered from the D-Day crisis, was one of the receiving hospitals for wounded men straight from the war. Arriving by sea through Portsmouth or by air through various RAF stations, the familiar stream of bandaged, bloody and dirty soldiers and airmen were carried in and the nurses and doctors worked with scarcely a pause to tend them. Thursday and Louisa scoured tables, scrubbed floors, sterilised instruments and laid them out ready for the surgeons, and wheeled in the patients on their trolleys, tending them in their last few moments of consciousness before the surgeon began his work.

'You know,' Thursday said as she sat for a few moments beside Louisa at the autoclave, 'I sometimes think that's the most important thing we ever do. Just holding their hands when they come into the theatre, and giving them a smile. It's the last thing they see before they go under – and I'm sure it must do them good to see a smile, to think for that last few seconds that there's someone there who cares.'

'But we all care,' Louisa said. 'The QARNNs and the surgeons care. They wouldn't be doing it if they didn't.'

'I don't know. Sometimes, I think some of them just see the patients as interesting jobs to do. Like mending a clock and being pleased that you've got it going again. They don't really see them as people who are going to sit up in bed again and walk about and do all the things real living people do. They're just – jobs.'

Louisa thought for a moment. 'Well, maybe some of them are like that,' she admitted. 'Surgeon-Lieutenant Brown, he's a bit cold, I admit. But Connor wasn't like that.'

'No,' Thursday said. 'He wasn't. But how do I know what he's like now, Lou? This armour we're supposed to put on – some people forget to take it off again, and that's what makes them seem so hard. How do I know Connor hasn't become one of those people?'

'Can't you tell from his letters?'

'I don't know,' Thursday said sadly. 'It's been so long, and there've been so many letters. Sometimes I think we've just learned how to write them – we've got so used to it that the things we say have turned into a habit. I just don't know any more.'

Louisa stared at her in dismay. 'You're not having doubts again, are you, Thursday?'

But Thursday could not answer. She turned away. No, she told herself fiercely, I've never doubted what I feel for Connor, *never*. I love him. And he loves me. I know it's true. I *know* it . . .

The men continued to come, and once again they had terrible stories to tell. Stories of paratroopers being riddled with bullets as they hung, helpless, on their floating parachutes. Others coming down in trees, too tangled in their 'chutes to be able to escape the jeering Germans. Dying men hanging in hedges or on fences, bleeding to death. Ground troops walking into ambush, fighting desperately amongst the houses of terrified civilians. Soldiers attacked with flame-throwers as they struggled to hold the bridges that were so vital for success.

'It gets worse and worse,' Thursday said despairingly. And by now it had been admitted too that the 'gas explosions' in London really were yet another terrible weapon, sent by Hitler to kill and terrorise the capital. 'V2s, they're called. They come so fast all you hear is a double thunderclap, and then a noise like an express train rushing past – and then the explosion. There's nothing you can do about them. Our boys can't even go and tip them off course, like they could the doodlebugs. They go too fast, faster than anything's ever gone before.'

'They're talking about evacuating everyone out of London,' Elsie said. '*Everyone*. My auntie lives at Putney. She's always said she'd never leave, but she's so frightened now she'd go anywhere just to get away from them. It's awful.'

'I don't know if this war's ever going to be over,' Thursday said gloomily. 'Sometimes I think we're going to be here for ever, Elsie, until there are no men left to send away.'

'They ought to put Mr Churchill and Hitler into a boxing ring and let them slug it out,' Elsie said with an attempt at a joke. 'I bet I know who'd win – Churchill! He'd only need to fall on Hitler to squash him!'

Thursday went back to her duty. She was feeling low today, as if she truly believed that the war would never end. And yet she knew that she would never give in. However much of a struggle it was, however low she felt, she only had to look at the next patient to know that she would carry on to the bitter end.

The theatre was ready again. She stood by the door, waiting for the trolley. It came through, and she looked down at the face of the man who lay there, ready as always with her smile of comfort.

As the dark eyes met hers, she saw the recognition, felt her own like a flash of blinding light in her brain, and in that moment the years swung away from her and she was back in Alexandria. Her heart kicked, and she gave a small gasp and laid her hand on the edge of the trolley to steady herself.

'Nurse?' said a sharp voice behind her. 'Nurse? Are you all right?'

'Yes,' Thursday said dazedly, as she looked down again and saw the same shock reflected in the wide dark eyes. 'Yes – yes, Sister, I'm all right.'

She touched the hand that lay on the trolley and summoned up her smile. 'It'll soon be over now,' she said, as she always did. 'You're going to be all right. You're here in Haslar Hospital, and you're going to be all right . . .'

The trolley moved on, away from her, and she watched as the patient was moved carefully from the trolley to the table. She saw the nurse begin to unwrap the dressings and remove the splints, the anaesthetist prepare his instruments. She saw the man on the table close his eyes as the medication took its effect.

Mark, she thought. *Mark . . .*

Mark Sangster. The only man who had ever come anywhere near making her doubt the promise she had made to Connor.

Chapter Eleven

From Cape Town, the convoy had sailed up the east coast of Africa and through the Red Sea to Suez, stopping briefly only twice, at Aden and Durban. There, they had stood at the rail staring at the blaze of lights.

'D'you mean to say there's no blackout here?' Elsie asked in disbelief. 'After all the rules and regulations we've had on board – sentries posted at every doorway and all hell let loose if you dare light a fag? Don't they know there's a war on?'

'Perhaps it's all over,' Thursday said. 'Perhaps the war's finished and they've forgotten to tell us.'

'It's a mirage,' Louisa grinned. 'It's the heat – we're seeing things.'

Everyone on board was suffering from the heat. For the men, living in such cramped conditions with areas like the ship's swimming pool and billiard rooms packed with bunks six or seven tiers high, it was particularly bad and the ship's hospital was full of cases of heat exhaustion and sunstroke. Thursday had suggested that the VADs volunteer to help with the nursing, and the girls found themselves reporting for duty, wearing their new white tropical dresses, and discovering for themselves just how difficult it was to nurse patients in the confined quarters below deck.

'It's making the beds that's the most awkward,' Louisa commented, rubbing her back. 'I know they've got to be like boxes, to stop patients rolling out in high seas, but it makes it jolly tricky to do hospital corners!'

'Still, it's nice to be working,' Thursday said. 'I was getting fed up with Housey-Housey and ship's concerts. It's good to feel useful again.'

'Keeps our hand in too,' Elsie agreed. 'I was beginning to think we'd have been at sea so long we'd have forgotten what to do when we arrived wherever it is we're going!'

Everyone had been pretty sure by then that they were heading for Egypt. As Louisa, who had been good at geography at school, had said, where else could they be bound? And with the war in the African desert getting worse, there were sure to be lots of casualties. The nursing Sisters in the hospitals there were going to need VADs to do the menial tasks.

At Suez, there was just time to rush into town and send telegrams home. Mum and Dad will be wondering where on earth I've got to, Thursday thought, for no news of the convoy's position would have been broadcast and there had been no way to receive letters from home, although they'd been able to write from Cape Town. She stared at the list of standard texts which could be sent. There was so much she wanted to say, and almost all of it forbidden. It seemed such an anti-climax to their long voyage to be able to say no more than: *Safe and well. Fondest love, Thursday* – but she knew that it would be thankfully received at home.

'The last leg, thank God,' Elsie said as they set off for Cairo. 'At least, we hope so. I tell you what, Thurs, I'll be jolly glad now to get back on dry land and be in a proper hospital again. The only ship I'm ever going to go on again when we get home is the Gosport ferry!'

The 64th British General Hospital in Alexandria was a military one situated in a Naval base, although in peacetime it had been a public school. Like Haslar, it was set in broad grounds with an avenue of trees leading from the central doors, but there the resemblance ended.

It had been hard enough, when they'd first arrived at Haslar, to get used to Naval discipline and jargon – calling the floor the 'deck', the lavatories the 'heads' and so on – but now they had to adjust all over again, this time to Army procedures and different ways. The Wardmaster on Thursday's ward was a Regimental Sergeant Major and the ward Sisters, all members of the Queen Alexandra Royal Military Nursing Service – QARMNS, as opposed to the QARNNS the Haslar girls were used to – were inclined to be disparaging towards the new arrivals and found fault with every small misdemeanour. Even bedmaking became an issue – the 'hospital corners' which had become second nature were suddenly all wrong and had to be done in a different way. Thursday raged inwardly at what seemed to her to be an unnecessary fussiness – how could it *really* matter how the sheets were tucked in? – but, like the others, she knew that even the smallest point of discipline mattered in the Services, and it was easier in the end to do as you were told. And as Louisa reminded her one day, Miss Makepeace, back at Haslar, would be relying on them to make a good impression. 'We can't let Madam down,' she said, and it became a byword whenever the going seemed especially difficult. However, they were all too pleased to be working again at last to allow small irritations to disturb them for long, and soon got back into the hospital routine.

'Blimey, it's a bit different here to Haslar,' Elsie said, encountering Thursday in the sluice where she was washing out bedpans. 'I've never even heard of half the things these poor sods have got. Dysentery, malaria, diptheria, typhoid—'

'Typhus,' Thursday continued, 'and jaundice, and enteritis, and desert sores—'

'And God knows what else. You name it, these poor blighters've got it. And there never seem to be enough bandages or dressings or medicines to treat 'em all. They say the boss carries his sulphaguanidine about in his pocket all the time, won't let it out of his sight and only gives it to the blokes who've got really bad dysentery.' She shook her head. 'It's the gas gangrene that gets in my craw. I think that's the worst stink I've ever smelled. I don't reckon those cones we burn to get rid of the pong do all that much good either – I'm not sure but what they aren't worse! And you know, soon as you feel those little bubbles under the poor bloke's skin, that he's a goner. They can't do nothing for that.' She was silent for a moment, then straightened her shoulders. 'And the *sand* – don't nobody *never* suggest going to the beach again. Sandcastles! I've seen enough sand to build *Windsor* Castle.'

Thursday nodded. The desert sand seemed to get everywhere. It came in on the bodies of the patients and it didn't matter how often you bathed them, they still seemed to have it in their beds. 'It's like laying between sheets of bloody sandpaper,' one of them complained. 'Can't you do nothing about it, nurse?'

'Well, I've tried,' Thursday said helplessly. 'I've bathed you three times already, and there's all the others to do as well. I just don't know where it all comes from.'

'We're made of it,' the Sergeant in the next bed said lugubriously. 'Spend enough time out in the Blue and that's what happens to you. Your skin turns to sand. You never get rid of it. I had an uncle in the First War, he come home covered in sand, and my auntie said she wouldn't sleep with him no more because it was like he needed a shave all over. Never got rid of it, he didn't.'

'Well, if I don't get rid of this,' the first man said, 'I'm going to go right round the bloody bend. I tell you, it's bad enough being riddled with bloody bullets, but this is adding insult to injury. If I'd wanted a beach holiday I'd have gone to bloody Brighton.'

'I'll give you one more bath,' Thursday said, 'and that'll have to do till tomorrow.' Tenderly, she washed the soldier's bony buttocks. The men were all so thin, she thought, and burned almost black by the sun. How could they have survived out there, not only under fire but prey to all these horrible diseases as well?

She patted the soldier's skin dry. 'There. I hope you'll feel more comfortable now.'

'Oh, I will,' he said, and winked. 'It's worth a bit of desert sand to get a cuddle from a pretty young nurse.'

Thursday gave him a reproving look and moved on to the next patient. He had a leg in plaster from toe to thigh, and a look of extreme suffering on his face. She stared at him in alarm.

'What is it? Are you feeling ill?'

'Blimey, I almost wish I was,' he groaned. 'It's the flaming bed-bugs, they're driving me mad. They're bloody hell, they are. Worse than flaming vampires. Talk about Dracula.' He shifted awkwardly in his bed. 'Can't you have a feel down me plaster? I'm sure there's one down there. Just up above me knee, it is. Look, try this knitting needle, see if you can't catch the little blighter.'

Thursday took the needle and poked it under the plaster. Whether she was reaching the bed-bug or not, she had no idea, but after a few moments the Corporal grunted with satisfaction and she withdrew the needle. 'That better?'

'Well, you've either killed him or frightened him to death, love. He's stopped biting anyway. Cor, they're bleeding hell, they are. I dunno what God made them for, no good to man nor beast. Thanks, love, I'll give you a shout next time I wants a bit of a scratch, shall I?'

'Not if Sister's about, please. I don't know what she'd do if she saw me poking a knitting needle down your plaster!' Thursday looked at the implement. 'What are you doing with a knitting needle, anyway? Making balaclavas for your mates?'

'Blimey, they don't want no balaclavas out here!' He grinned. 'Sister give me it. Got fed up with me asking for a scratch, she did, and give it me so I could do it meself. But it's much nicer when a pretty young nurse does it!'

Thursday stared at him, then laughed. 'You mean you could have done it yourself? Well, of course you could – you old rascal, you! You got me here under false pretences.'

He winked. 'Is there any other sort? Come on, Nursey, you got to allow us a bit of comfort – specially after what we bin through for our country, eh?'

Thursday shook her head at him and hurried away. She was behind with her routine now and the next two patients got their baths in double-quick time. By the grins on their faces, though, she could see that they didn't mind. The whole ward had enjoyed seeing her poking about with the knitting needle in the Corporal's leg plaster, and for the next three days she had to endure a barrage of teasing about knitting, and requests to kill bed-bugs in various delicate parts of the men's anatomy.

There seemed to be no way of getting rid of the bugs. The school buildings had been taken over so quickly for use as a hospital that there had been no time for proper fumigation and the hydrocyanic acid which would have been used was too dangerous when the wards were occupied. All that could be done was to stand the legs of each bed in tins of paraffin to stop them climbing up, and apply a blowtorch to the beds of the up-patients. Even that only got rid of them for a short while.

Bed-bugs were mostly a problem at night, hiding in even the tiniest cracks and crevices during the day. But that didn't mean the men – or the nurses – were free from irritation, for as soon as dawn broke the sandflies arrived, clouds of them searching voraciously for flesh to bite. They were especially fond of open wounds, however small, and nearly all the men suffered from the 'desert sores' they caused, but the greatest danger they brought was diphtheria and there had been an epidemic not long before Thursday and the others arrived.

'I'd never even heard of half the diseases we get here, when we were at Haslar,' Elsie said. 'I must say I'm jolly glad of my mosquito net to sleep under, though. Once you get malaria, you've got it for life, Sister told me – and that's if you survive the first lot!'

'Just think yourself lucky not to have been sent out to the desert,' one of the QARMN Sisters told her. 'I was there for three months. We slept in tents and had to iron our uniforms with a flat-iron that we heated up on an oil stove. And you didn't skimp the ironing – it was the only way to kill off the bugs that had got through the wash! It wasn't just bugs and flies and mosquitos, either – we were absolutely overrun with rats.'

'Rats!' Priscilla said with a shudder. 'Oh, how revolting.'

'You don't have time to be revolted,' the Sister said. 'There are too many. They're everywhere. We had to take sticks with us when we went to the latrines, to beat them off, and they used to nest right down beside the tent walls and come in and run over the beds. It was worst of all for the patients who were in plaster – the rats would come in and chew it. They'd gnaw holes in the mosquito nets to get at it. We had to give the men sticks to beat them off with.'

The girls listened in horror. They'd all seen desert rats by then, but the hospital itself was largely clear of them. A few bed-bugs seemed a mild kind of torture in comparison.

'It's luxury here,' the Sister went on. 'You grumble about the sand, but out there in the desert the wind never stopped blowing, so it was like having sand kicked into your face the whole time, and we only got one bucket of water each a day – for *everything*! And when all you wanted at night was a long, cool shower to get the sand and the sweat and the bugs off you, that really *was* torture.'

'I'll never moan again,' Elsie promised, but the Sister smiled.

'Yes, you will. There'll be plenty of other things to grumble about – you'll find out! But there's plenty to enjoy as well, and we're doing valuable work, so I don't think it'll seem too bad.'

The biggest surprise to the girls was to find themselves nursing men with such everyday diseases as chicken-pox, mumps and measles. The Australian soldiers, who weren't accustomed to these childish illnesses, caught them almost as soon as they boarded the troopships that had been British liners in a previous life, and a lot of them arrived at Suez covered in spots or with painfully swollen necks. After several weeks at sea, many of them were over the worst and more than a little disgruntled to find themselves told they must stay in quarantine. Priscilla, going round her ward at midnight, would find their beds stuffed with pillows while the men were out sampling the nightspots. 'And spreading a few spots of their own around the locals,' she reported with irritation. 'Honestly, how selfish can you get!'

'Well, they've been cooped up at sea for weeks, they must be really fed up,' Elsie said. 'Poor sods, they're desperate for a bit of fun.'

'It won't be much fun for us when the other regiments go down with measles,' Priscilla said, but Thursday shook her head.

'They'll have had all those things when they were children. Why, my mum invited all the neighbours' children in when me and our Steve had chicken-pox, just so we could all get it over with. And she was dead keen for him to catch mumps. They say it's really bad for boys if they don't get it till they're grown up.'

Apart from Diggers' Plague, as some of the girls called it, most of the men they were nursing now were either serious medical or orthopaedic cases, kept at the hospital until they were fit to be moved to the canal zone. It was more like civilian nursing in a way, Thursday thought – an even routine of bathing, dressing, bedmaking and bedpan duties. She knew that there had been a good deal of fighting out in the desert but just now there seemed to be a moment of abeyance. It would start again, of course – they hadn't accompanied all those thousands of troops out here for nothing – but just for a while there was time to breathe. Time to wander out at night and look at the myriad stars; time to wonder at the tales the men told of creatures they encountered out in the desert – chameleons, scorpions, tarantulas; time to make new friends, to explore their surroundings and get to know the night-life of a town that was full of bars and restaurants, with plenty of British and American uniforms to be seen, and plenty of offers to take a pretty young nurse to dinner or for a drink.

'Come on, Thurs,' Elsie urged. 'That smashing young Sergeant says he can find a partner for you and we'll go dancing. Let's make the most of what fun there is around here. We might never get the chance again.'

Thursday pushed her writing-pad aside and went to get ready. Elsie was right – you didn't know what life held. Only a few weeks ago there had been a serious panic in Alexandria, when it was thought that the Germans were about to invade, and the Navy had been evacuated. In the British Embassy, the staff had burned all their papers to prevent their falling into enemy hands, and the Eighth Army had been pushed back as far as El Alamein, only sixty miles away. Although so far the Allied troops had managed to hold the defence, you never knew what was going to happen next. It was foolish not to snatch at what fun and happiness there was.

I'm not breaking my promise to you, Connor, she thought as she changed into a clean white dress, examining herself closely for any fleas or bed-bugs that she might have collected during the day, but it's going to be so long until we meet again, and life is here and now. It seems almost like tempting Fate to think about the future, when we don't even know if there's going to be one.

So she went out with Elsie and her Sergeant and the young soldier who had been brought along as her partner, and danced in his arms, closing her eyes and her mind against tomorrow. And later, they walked under the stars, their arms about each other's waists, and when he paused beneath a palm tree and took her in his arms she lifted her face for his kiss and allowed him to hold her close.

'It's been a marvellous evening, Thursday,' he whispered. 'I wish I could ask you for another date, but we might not be here much longer. I'll look you up when I get back, OK? See if you still remember who I am?'

'OK,' she whispered back, and wondered if he ever would – indeed, if he would ever even come back. So many young men were going away, out into the desert, literally into the 'Blue', and how many would come back? And of those who did, how many would be whole and undamaged, with two arms and legs, two eyes, and a face that wasn't seared by flames or smashed by bullets? She gripped him tightly in her arms and kissed him again. 'It's been a lovely evening. I won't forget you. Good luck – wherever you go.'

'Thanks.' They stood in silence for a moment, warm and close under the gently sighing fronds of the palm. 'Thanks, Thursday. And good luck to you, too.'

Later, as she ducked under the mosquito net and climbed into bed, Thursday noticed the half-finished letter to Connor. And good luck to you too, my darling, she thought. Good luck to all the men out here in the desert, or wherever you are, good luck to those still in Europe and those in the Far East – especially those in Japanese POW camps. Good luck to the nurses too, and all the civilians everywhere who have been caught up in this horrible war that's spread like a sore over the world.

Good luck. It's what we all need.

In the third week of October, almost before the VADs had become acclimatised to their new surroundings, they were thrown once more into battle stations as General Montgomery ordered the attack on El Alamein and gunfire roared once more in everyone's ears.

'Oh, my goodness!' Thursday clutched her friend as the ground shook beneath their feet. 'What's that?'

'It's the guns.' Louisa was pale. 'It's all right – they're miles away. It's just that the sound travels, and the vibration carries a long way too.'

'Well, I hope you're right. I feel as if we're in the front line.' Elsie took out a packet of cigarettes and lit one, her fingers shaking. 'Want one, Lou?'

Louisa took one but Thursday shook her head. She'd never taken to smoking – her father had always said he didn't like to see a woman with a fag hanging out of her mouth, and anyway it turned your fingers yellow and your teeth as well. Why I should think about all that now, in the middle of a big battle, heaven only knows, she thought, but the smallest things could remind you of home. Like that little dog she'd seen in Cairo that had looked just like Patch. And the white cat that had reminded her of her Auntie Maudie's Snowy. A fresh burst of gunfire broke into her thoughts and she reached out involuntarily for Elsie's hand.

'It's as bad as the Blitz,' Elsie said as the girls crowded together, listening to the distant thunder and staring, fascinated, at the brilliant flashes of light along the horizon. 'There must be hundreds of guns.'

'A thousand, I heard someone say,' Thursday said. 'It's a terrific attack. And they've got armoured cars and tanks and God knows what to back them up. They were brought over in the holds of the convoy.'

'I felt sorry for the men, having to set off on a route march the minute they landed,' Elsie observed. 'I mean, all that PT and training on board just isn't the same as marching off into the desert with a heavy pack on your back.'

'Well, we'll be seeing some of them soon,' Louisa said, drawing on her cigarette. 'It won't be long before the casualties start to arrive.'

They had been busy ever since early that morning, when the order had come through to prepare the hospital as a casualty clearing station. As swiftly as possible, all the patients who were fit to be moved were packed on to the trains that waited at the hospital gates, and those who were left shifted so that there could be empty wards for the new arrivals. Here, beds were rapidly remade and everything made ready for wounded men – dressings and bandages newly sterilised, medicines and lotions lined up in cupboards and on shelves, stretchers stacked along the walls in case there were too few beds. One ward was set aside for blood donating, and in between their duties, Thursday and the others queued up to give their pint, barely resting for five minutes afterwards before they were up again and scurrying about to carry out the Ward Sister's demands. One, coming upon Thursday as she made gallon after gallon of fresh lime juice, paused to speak to her.

'You're doing very well, you girls,' she said. 'I must say we thought you were going to be something of a burden rather than a help, but you're all working very hard. What's more, you can think for yourselves – you don't have to be *told* all the time. Well done.' And she marched away, leaving Thursday staring after her open-mouthed.

'What did she think we were, morons?' she asked indignantly, telling the others about it now. 'As if we hadn't already been through the Blitz! The trouble is, they think if you're not State Registered or in the QA, you can't be a proper nurse at all!'

'Well, we'll soon show 'em their mistake,' Elsie said stoutly. 'Won't we, Lou?'

Louisa nodded. 'Some of them think we're either mindless shopgirls or mindless debutantes! Sister Freeman told me the other day that she hoped I hadn't wasted space bringing out my ball gowns, because I wasn't going to get much chance to use them. I didn't like to tell her I'd already been dancing at Shepheards, when we were in Cairo!' She chuckled. 'Or that the very attractive Lieutenant Colonel who took me was my cousin!'

Within a few hours, the casualties had begun to arrive. The first of the exhausted men, their wounds roughly bandaged or splinted at a First Aid post just behind the front lines, were Australians, quickly followed by New Zealanders, South Africans and the Scottish Highlanders who had sounded the call to arms on their bagpipes. And once they had begun, there was no chance for conversation for many hours, many days. Once again, the girls were plunged into the heartbreaking exhilaration of receiving a long line of injured soldiers, knowing with one glance that many of them were not going to survive and doing their utmost to give them comfort as they tended their terrible wounds.

It was a long, long night, that first of the El Alamein attack. It ran into daylight and then again into darkness, and Thursday scarcely knew when one began and the other ended, nor where the hours went. She worked without stopping, removing bloodstained bandages to reveal deep and jagged wounds – some already showing signs of infection or the dreaded gangrene – or easing a splinted limb with pillows. She washed faces and bodies that were encrusted with desert sand and gunpowder, mixed to a glutinous paste with congealed blood. She smoothed back matted hair from brows that were creased with pain, and smiled into eyes that begged her to put an end to the misery. 'You'll be all right,' she said over and over again, knowing that for many it was not true. 'You're safe now. You'll be all right . . .'

'Stay by this boy, Tilford,' Sister Carrington said, straightening up by one of the new arrivals. She lowered her voice. 'He doesn't have long, I'm afraid. We can't let him go without a friendly face by his side.'

There was a chair nearby and Thursday pulled it close to the bed. She looked down at the young face, ashen beneath the desert tan, and her heart sank. Sister was right, he was barely more than a boy – no more than nineteen, surely – and it was obvious that he was sinking fast. But his eyelids were fluttering and she thought he knew she was there. She took his thin hand in hers – the bones no thicker than a sparrow's leg, she thought and smiled although she knew her lips were trembling and the tears were hot in her eyes.

'It's all right,' she whispered. 'You're safe here in Alexandria. You don't have to fight any more. You're going to be all right.'

The boy's head, covered with a thatch of thick fair hair, turned restlessly from side to side. 'Mairi . . . where's Mairi? I want Mairi.'

Pity swelled up in Thursday's heart. She stroked the hand that trembled in hers and whispered again, 'It's all right. You're going to be all right.'

'Mairi! Where's Mairi? Mairi . . .'

'She'll come soon,' Thursday said desperately. She was giving him no comfort, she knew it. It wasn't her he wanted, it was Mairi – his girlfriend probably – and no one else would do. She stared down at him helplessly, taking in the body that was so thin that she could see his ribs, see the fluttering of his heartbeat just beneath the stretched, sunburned skin. 'Mairi will be here in a minute. Someone's gone to find her.' He wouldn't live long enough to know that she was lying. If it could give him just one small crumb of comfort . . . But he was twisting on the bed, each movement clearly an agony, yet his mental agony all the greater. 'Mairi! Mairi!'

I can't do a thing, Thursday thought. I can't help him at all, and he needs it so much. Oh God, please let me help this poor, poor boy. Please give me strength to help him, please let me say the right words, do the right thing . . . But all she could do was hold his hand, whisper in his ear and watch the twisting restlessness and the rapidly weakening flutter of his heart. 'It's all right. Mairi's coming.' And then, with a final desperate attempt at relieving his anguish, 'She's here now. Look – she's coming through the door. Mairi! Mairi! Over here . . .' And what am I going to do now, she wondered, appalled by her recklessness. I've just made it all worse. And she looked down again, tormented by guilt, knowing that she must tell him the truth and that the truth was the last thing he wanted to hear.

The dark-blue eyes looked up into hers. There was a moment of perfect clarity, of joy. He believed her lie, she thought, dazed, and opened her mouth to confess the truth. And then their expression altered; the pupils widened and the fluttering eyelids faltered. And Thursday looked away and at the fragile chest, just in time to see the final throb of his heart as it stopped for ever.

She sat very still, holding the limp, bony hand. As Sister had said, he had had very little time, and Thursday was not the person he wanted by him in those last few moments. But perhaps she had, after all, given him comfort at the last. Perhaps he had believed that his Mairi was with him. Perhaps, in some strange way, he had actually seen her.

She got up a little stiffly. She had been sitting there longer than she should, as the boy was dead and there was nothing more she could do. Her task now was with the living.

It was on the second, or perhaps the third day, when she was almost dropping with exhaustion, that a new group of casualties arrived. During all that time, Thursday and the other VADs had worked almost ceaselessly, eating when food was thrust in front of them, returning to their quarters only when ordered to go, falling on to their beds for a few hours' sleep then getting up to stumble back into the wards. There they spent hours in the sluice, washing blood-stained bandages, for there would be no more sent out from England while the present emergency continued. They took them into the gardens and festooned them over shrubs and bushes for the sun to bleach them white, and when they went back in there was a new supply waiting to be washed. They began to feel as if their hands would be bloodstained for ever.

'They're giving us some Italian POWs to help out,' Louisa said as they worked. Louisa was always first to get news. The others looked at her in some dismay. 'They're all right really, you know.' She hesitated. 'I went to Italy a couple of times before the war. I knew quite a lot of Italians. They're not like the Germans. They never really wanted to be in the war anyway. And they'll be guarded all the time.'

'I dunno,' Elsie said dubiously. 'Eyeties . . .' But when they came, dark-eyed and black-haired, almost pathetically anxious to help, her heart melted; and like pet dogs they adored the yellow-haired girl and followed her about, vying to carry out her wishes so that the other girls teased her unmercifully about her male harem.

Thursday found herself sitting beside several other men who were obviously not going to survive. With each one she felt more miserably helpless, tortured by the knowledge that it was someone else they cried out for – their wife, their girlfriend, their mother – and more than once she made up her mind to ask Sister not to give her this particular task again. But she could never bring herself to do so. If it isn't me, it'll have to be someone else, she thought, stroking the rough, hairy hand of a man who was surely too old to be a soldier, or the smooth skin of a lad even younger than Mairi's lover. And none of us is going to be the one they want.

'You should go and get some rest, Tilford,' Sister said when Thursday went to report that the latest one had slipped away. 'Go now.'

'But we've got a new batch just arriving – I can do a few more hours,' Thursday said, though in truth she felt dizzy with fatigue. 'I'll stay as long as you want me.'

'An hour, then,' Sister said firmly. 'No more. You're on your honour to leave the ward when the time's up, do you understand? And you mustn't do any more than just sit by their beds.' Her face softened a little. 'It's what you are best at, you know. I don't quite understand why, but they seem to draw a kind of calmness from you – a touch of peace. It's a wonderful gift.'

Thursday stared at her, then stumbled to the nearest bed. A wonderful gift? A calmness – a touch of peace? She shook her head, dismissing the words, and then looked down, expecting to see what she had now so often seen; the blurred grey shadow of death flung like a cobweb across the body that lay there.

Instead, she saw a thin, narrow face with deep brown eyes and a wide mouth, tightened just now with pain. Straight dark hair, dusted with sand, swept across a high forehead. Blood was clotting over the slashed wounds that had laid his cheeks open. A rough splint had been bound on each arm and stained bandages were wrapped around his body.

How badly injured he was, she couldn't at that moment tell. But he was not dying. This man, Thursday knew, was still full of life and energy and determination. It was, perhaps, a good thing that she didn't know then just how determined he could be when he saw a thing he wanted. Nor that in that first brief glance, in pain though he was, he had decided that he wanted her.

Chapter Twelve

Mark Sangster was an Army doctor. He was young for the rank of Lieutenant Colonel, and as his injuries – mostly superficial – healed, he became the star of the ward, his dark eyes gleaming and impertinent as he teased the nurses. He led the rest of the patients in counting loudly whenever a VAD was trying to take a pulse, he deliberately dropped his book or writing-pad on the floor by his bed so that a passing nurse would have to bend over to pick it up, to the accompaniment of cheers and wolf whistles, he distracted Thursday by pointing out of the window and then dipping his thermometer into a cup of hot tea, and he pestered them all for a good night kiss. 'Come on, I know you've got the best kisses in Alex. It'll help me get better. You are *supposed* to help me get better, aren't you?'

Despite his teasing, or maybe because of it, he was a popular patient with the nurses and not least because of his dark good looks and easy manner. It wasn't surprising that they all fell in love with him.

'I'll have to be very careful about Lieutenant Colonel Sangster,' Louisa remarked one day as they washed bandages in the sluice. 'He's the sort that could turn a good girl into a very bad one.'

'Go on, you'll never be a bad girl,' Elsie told her. 'Now me, I could be *very bad indeed*, specially when he gives me one of those looks of his. He's got eyes like a filmstar!'

Thursday said nothing. She was aware of a powerful electric current running through her whenever she caught one of Dr Sangster's dark glances, and it wasn't a joking matter. He looked at her as if they already shared a secret, she thought, and a guilty one at that. It wasn't a feeling she liked. As Louisa had said, he was a man to be wary of, and Thursday made up her mind not to have any more to do with him than she had to.

Lieutenant Colonel Sangster, however, had other ideas.

'So what made you volunteer as a VAD?' he enquired one night, lounging against the end of his bed as Thursday set her hurricane lamp and primus stove on a rickety table and spread a white sheet over her chair to keep off the lurking bed-bugs. 'You're bright enough to have taken State Registration, or gone into the QARMNS.'

Thursday gave him a look. 'It's not a matter of intelligence,' she said crisply. 'I wanted to do something to help.'

'But couldn't you help more if you were properly trained? I mean, you're not much more than a dogsbody here. I wonder you can stand it.'

Thursday faced him. 'I can stand it because someone's got to do these jobs, and I'm not too proud to be the one to do them. I also happen to think that keeping people as comfortable as they can be in hospital is important – whether it means operating on them, giving them medicine or bringing them a bedpan. In fact,' she added with a challenging glance, 'on the whole, they're probably more grateful for the bedpan than for anything else!'

Mark Sangster laughed. 'You're probably right! But don't you ever wish you could do some of the more interesting work? Not have to spend *all* your time emptying bedpans and washing used bandages?'

Thursday stopped to think. In fairness, she had to admit that she had considered training as a Registered Nurse once the war was over. But the war had gone on for so long that, like many other people, she'd almost given up planning for life in peacetime. You couldn't look ahead when you didn't know when peace was going to come, or even if it was going to come. For thousands, perhaps millions, of people, it never had and never would. How could you know that you wouldn't be one of those thousands, those millions? How could you know that you would still be alive this time next week?

'I'll think about that when there's more time,' she said finally. 'Just for the moment I'm quite happy to be doing what I am doing. I know I'm being useful, and that's all that matters. Now, perhaps you'd be kind enough to go to bed. We're keeping the other patients awake, and if Sister comes in she'll be furious to find you still up.'

He made a comical face. 'Oh dear! Mustn't risk Sister's fury, must we?' He winked and lowered his voice. 'I'll tell you what, I'd rather go back to Alamein and face the German guns than face Sister Carrington in one of her furies.' With a smile that turned Thursday's heart over, he climbed into the bed that was uncomfortably close to her chair. 'Come and hold my hand for a while.'

'Certainly not,' she said indignantly, and he put his head on one side.

'Oh, why not? Don't tell me you've already got a sweetheart.' He groaned comically. 'Though it's obvious a pretty girl like you would already be spoken for. Are you engaged?'

'Not exactly,' she admitted. 'Not that it's any of your business – *sir*.' She bit her lip. It wasn't always easy to remember rank with men who were in their pyjamas.

Dr Sangster gave her a bright-eyed look. 'What do you mean, not exactly?'

'Connor's in the Navy,' she said, exasperated. 'Somewhere in the Far East. He gave me a brooch and said he wished it was a ring. But he didn't want to tie me down—' She stopped, wondering why she was telling him this. It was between herself and Connor. 'Look, I think you ought to be asleep. And anyway, I'm not supposed to sit here talking all night.' She sat down and picked up a book.

'You won't mind if I just lie here and look at you, will you? Just to help me fall asleep and give me sweet dreams?'

'So long as you realise that's all they can ever be – dreams,' she answered crisply. As it happened, she minded very much. She was acutely conscious of his gaze, of his nearness. I'm sure he's moved that bed, she thought. I'm sure it wasn't that close last night. She turned away, determined not to let him disturb her, although the way that her heart was thumping told her he'd disturbed her already. Tomorrow, she thought, I'll ask if I can be moved to a different ward.

Next day, however, Mark Sangster was ill, more ill than he'd been even when he had arrived. One of his wounds had been infected by the bite of a sandfly and his temperature shot up. The wound itself turned into a desert sore, a suppurating ulcer that refused to heal, and on top of that he developed jaundice and the dysentery that the sandflies were believed to carry as well as diphtheria. Thursday was told to special him, and spent much of her time by his bed, dressing the sore, keeping his other wounds clear of flies, stamping a damp cake of soap over his sheets to catch bedbugs, monitoring his pulse and temperature and supplying him with a seemingly endless succession of bedpans. Once, through his haze of delirium, he grinned weakly and muttered, 'You were right about the bedpans, Tilford. Just keep 'em coming, won't you!' And Thursday felt the tears come to her eyes.

Allied servicemen weren't the only ones to be brought to Alexandria. There were Germans and Italians too, nursed separately from the others in huts guarded by Indian sentries in turbans. Elsie found herself sent to work there and reported that the Germans were a grim, unyielding lot, angry about their defeat and bitter about their capture. 'Not like that young Heinz Schmidt we had at Haslar that time after Dunkirk,' she said. 'You rather fell for him, didn't you, Thurs?'

'I did not!' Thursday felt a flush of anger and embarrassment, and Elsie looked taken aback. 'I felt sorry for him, that's all. He was just an ordinary boy – too young to be in a war.'

'Sorry, Thurs. I didn't mean anything by it. But these are young too – just kids. Not much over fifteen or sixteen, some of 'em, but they still won't give in. Anyone would think we were going to eat 'em alive.'

'Perhaps that's what they do think,' Louisa said. 'Remember how the ones at Haslar screamed because they thought we were going to operate without anaesthetic? They'd been told all kinds of horror stories, just to make them hate us.'

'Like we were told the Germans ate babies,' Thursday said thoughtfully. 'I'm sure that wasn't true – just people starting rumours.'

The Italians, who had been British allies in the First World War, were allowed to help in the wards. They lived in tents in the grounds and planted flowers in between them, so that their camp looked more like a garden than a POW camp. At night they sang together, often arias that were familiar to those like Louisa who knew about opera, and to girls like Thursday, whose father was fond of classical music and had collected quite a lot of records which he played in the evenings on the gramophone he'd built himself. The sound of the liquid voices floating across the hospital grounds in the darkness brought memories to many of them, and even those who had never heard an operatic aria paused to listen.

'Them Tonis can certainly sing,' Elsie commented. 'I was never much of a one for posh music before, but I reckon I'll go along to the King's Theatre when I get back to Pompey – they have whole weeks of opera there. That's if the King's is still there then,' she added wryly.

Thursday, who hadn't after all asked to be moved, found herself shifted anyway to do night duties on a different ward. She left Mark's bedside with an odd mixture of relief and reluctance and handed him over to Priscilla, who was to special him next, with a list of instructions.

'He likes his lime juice really sharp – hardly any sugar. When you wash him, look out for his right arm – it wasn't broken but it was badly bruised and it's still tender. His temperature tends to go up at—'

'Yes, *all* right,' Priscilla interrupted. 'I have specialled patients before, you know.' She gave Thursday a quizzical look. 'You seem very concerned about Lieutenant Colonel Sangster.'

'No more than I am about any of our patients,' Thursday answered stiffly. She handed over the sheet of paper on which Mark's temperature was recorded. 'There you are, then. I'm not going to be away for long anyway – I'm just relieving for a couple of weeks while Nurse Dawson's getting over that bug she caught. I expect I'll take over again when I come back.'

'Oh, I doubt that,' Priscilla said sweetly. 'He'll be used to me by then – he won't want to change back again.'

Thursday made a face at her. I hope he is, she thought. Anyway, with any luck he won't need a special by then. He'll probably be moved somewhere else. I'll be thankful if he is.

'You shouldn't take any notice of him,' Louisa advised when Thursday told her this. She stretched a pair of rubber gloves over her hands and examined them for holes. 'He's just a natural flirt – can't help it.' She took off the gloves and fished about in a tin box until she found the right-sized patches to stick over the holes. 'Mind you, he does seem to watch you quite a bit more than the others. These gloves are in a terrible state, you know. Good thing I got lots of practice at home, mending my brother's bike punctures!'

Night duties were a strange, lonely time. With no Colonel's rounds to prepare for and only a few medicines to be given out, there was little to do and until the men fell asleep they would talk amongst themselves. A lot of their talk was about their war experiences, and Thursday listened sadly to the stories they told – stories that seemed to grow more horrific as the war progressed. Tanks bombed or mined and set on fire, their crews trapped inside, burning with them. 'You can smell it, nurse, just like roasting meat of a Sunday dinnertime, it is.' Men mown down by enemy tanks, the wide, implacable tracks crushing them into the sand so that there was almost nothing to be salvaged. Men who were still just alive, their bodies booby-trapped by the enemy so that when the stretcher crews ran to pick them up they were all blown to oblivion together. Men in aircraft, shot down and found days or weeks later, still strapped into their seats, having either bled, fried or starved to death. 'You never seen nothing like it. You don't want to, neither.'

'We didn't oughter tell you these things, I know,' a Sergeant said to Thursday one night as she sat by his bed listening to his outpourings. 'But we gotta tell someone, see. It's like it's all festering inside and if we don't talk about it we'll go clean round the bend.' He chuckled. 'You heard what they call blokes what do that, doncher? Harpic – clean round the bend, see?'

Thursday smiled but her heart felt close to breaking. And as she sat through the night in her white-sheeted chair, in sole charge of the ward, she felt the desolation of the desert creep eerily close. All around her were men in varying stages of suffering, some of whom would not survive, all of whom were desperately missing their homes and families. 'It ain't so bad when yer doin' the actual *fightin'*,' one of them explained as she paused by his bed to soothe him with cool water on his parched lips. 'You can't think about nothin' else then, see. But layin' here of a night, with nuffin' to think about but blasted bed-bugs – well, you can't help yer mind wanderin', can yer? An' then when you hears about all them Yanks over in Blighty, you gets to worryin', see. What's the old woman doin' with herself? I mean, I bin away nigh on three years now. She must wonder if she'll ever see me again. And if some bloody Yank swaggers by with a pocket full o' dollars, lookin' for company, well . . .'

'I'm sure you've nothing to worry about,' Thursday tried to

reassure him. 'With a fine man like you for a husband she won't look twice at an American.'

'I ain't so sure,' he said restlessly. 'I ain't so flamin' fine these days, I can tell yer. There's this bloody great scar right across me chops for a start – what's she goin' ter say when she sees that, eh? She was always one for a good-lookin' bloke, was my Edie. What am I goin' ter do if she won't even kiss me, eh? Tell me that.'

'Of course she'll kiss you. I would, if you were my husband. In fact, I'll kiss you now, just to prove it!' And with a swift glance around the ward to make sure that Sister hadn't crept in unnoticed, Thursday bent and laid her lips on the sweating face. She rested her cheek against his for a moment, feeling the puckering of the scar, and just for that instant, poured into him all the love she wanted so desperately to give – to her cousins Mike and Leslie, to poor dead Tony West, to Patsy's Roy, to all the men who lay in hospitals. And, most of all, to Connor.

After that, good night kisses became a part of her duties – albeit unofficially, and always discreetly. Nothing was ever said, and it never became a habit, but always there were one or two men who seemed especially in need for some reason – a worsening in their condition, bad news from home, or sheer aching loneliness. A kiss was the least she could give them – a kiss, a touch on the cheek, a whispered word or two. It was all the comfort there could be.

And then Thursday, having finished her rounds and made sure they were all at least resting, if not asleep, would sit in her chair in the middle of them all, sharply aware of the loneliness all around her and piercingly aware of her own.

Gradually, Mark Sangster's dysentery began to improve and when Nurse Dawson returned to duty Thursday came back to the ward to find him sitting up again, the yellowness fading from his skin and eyes. His thin face lit up when he saw her.

'I thought you'd abandoned me. Was it something I said?'

'It was everything you said,' Thursday replied crisply, dismayed to feel the tingle that went through her as she rested her hand on his shoulder to help him lean forward. 'Just let me shake out your pillow . . . There, is that better?'

'Just seeing you makes me feel better,' he said. He lowered his voice, beckoning, so that she had to move closer. 'You are going to special me, aren't you? You're not going to let Nurse Lacock loose on me again?'

'It doesn't look to me as if you need specialling any more. Anyway, what was wrong with Nurse Lacock? Didn't you get along with her?'

'Get along with her?' He rolled his eyes. 'It was *her* getting along with *me* that was the problem! Honestly, if I'd been able to walk she'd have had me out of here and walking up the aisle in the local church! A man's not safe with her around.'

Thursday laughed. 'Don't be silly! As if she'd look at you, with all these other men in the ward to choose from. Anyway, she's already engaged.'

'Well, she doesn't act like it,' he said, and then added with huge dignity, 'I'll have you know that I've been voted The Man Most Likely To by all the nurses in the ward, so put that in your pipe and smoke it!'

'Most likely to what?' Thursday asked unkindly, and he gave her a haughty look.

'You'll have to ask them that. And much as I like having you stand there with your hand on my shoulder, I think perhaps you ought to remove it, because I've just seen Sister go past the window and she'll be in at any minute.'

Thursday leaped away, her face burning. Hastily, keeping her face turned aside, she began to tidy his locker. Mark chuckled. 'You needn't look so guilty. There's nothing to be ashamed of in giving a man a cuddle.'

'I was not cuddling you!' Her voice came out as a squeak and she lowered it to repeat forcefully, 'I was *not* cuddling you. I just forgot what I was doing for a minute.'

'How unflattering,' he murmured. 'I didn't forget it, not for a second. Most enjoyable. Do it again, sometime.'

Thursday shot him a murderous glance and moved away. Sister had come in by now and was clapping her hands for attention. The nurses stopped what they were doing to listen.

'Colonel's rounds will be early today,' she announced, sending a wave of panic through the ward. 'I want this ward spick and span in ten minutes. All up-patients in bed, please, and no newspapers or magazines or other clutter on show.' She looked around with disfavour. 'The whole place is in the most disgusting mess. Ten minutes, mind!'

Ten minutes! The nurses erupted. Panic-stricken, they scurried around, gathering up overflowing ashtrays, used mugs and plates, orange peel and bags of dates. The patients opened their lockers and thrust in books and half-written letters, and stubbed out their cigarettes. 'Put it in there, nurse. That's right, just give the door a good kick, it'll close. Mind you don't take Major Rodway's teeth, now, he'll need them later for cracking nuts. Don't you go losing that photograph of my best girlfriend, will you.'

'We'll never get rid of it all in time,' Louisa panted, passing Thursday with an armful of assorted bits and pieces. 'I don't know where it's all come from.'

'Shove it under Captain Barry's cradle,' Mark suggested, indicating the man in the next bed, who had a large wooden frame over his leg to keep the bedclothes from touching it. 'He won't mind.'

Louisa hesitated. Thursday whipped up the sheets, revealing the space beneath, and Louisa shoved her load under, taking care not to touch the bandaged leg. Thursday dropped the counterpane back into place and smoothed it down rapidly, and the girls snapped to attention as the Sister came briskly back into the ward, the Colonel beside her.

Two pairs of piercing eyes swept about the room. Thursday, glancing covertly from under her lashes, wondered how they had ever managed to achieve so much in so short a time. Every bed was immaculate, the openings of the pillowslips all turned away from the door, the patients sitting up straight with pyjama jackets neatly buttoned and the sheets folded over to the same depth. The tops of the lockers each had a jug of water and glass placed precisely in the middle and the chairs were exactly at right-angles to the beds. The floors had been swept clean and there was not a bedpan or a urine bottle to be seen anywhere.

Does the Colonel really suppose the ward looks like this all the time, she wondered. Doesn't he realise that there are books and papers strewn around, half-eaten bars of chocolate, mugs of tea? Does he really think the patients just sit to attention all day long, doing absolutely nothing?

The Colonel advanced into the ward. He paused by each bed, shooting gimlet glances but treating each man with the respect to which, as an officer, he was entitled. He asked a few questions, which Sister answered promptly in a deferential voice, and he glanced at the charts. Once or twice, he stopped for several minutes, talking to the patient, until with a nod of satisfaction he proceeded on his way.

He came to Mark's bed. Thursday and Louisa, standing stiffly at the foot, moved aside to allow him to see the chart hung on the end. He glanced at it and pursed his lips.

'You've had a bad dose of dysentery and jaundice, I see. Getting over it now?'

'Yes, sir. Thanks to the good offices of these nurses.'

The Colonel gave Thursday a sharp glance. 'Been your special, has he?'

'He was at the beginning, sir, but I was moved over to C Ward for a fortnight. Lacock's been looking after him since then.'

'But it was Tilford who set me on the road to recovery,' Mark added helpfully, ignoring Thursday's imploring expression. 'I keep telling her, she ought to join the QARMNS.'

The Colonel looked at her from under his brows. 'Well, why didn't you do that? Prefer the Navy, do you?'

'I just wanted to help,' Thursday began helplessly, but he was already moving on. He stopped beside Captain Barry's bed and looked at the hump made by the cradle.

'Burns and a break, hm? Let's have a look.'

Thursday caught her breath and cast Louisa an agonised glance. Louisa was biting her lips and looking as if she was ready either to laugh or to burst into tears. The Sister, standing nearby, gave them both a suspicious stare. Thursday, meeting her eye, saw light dawn and drew in another breath as she stepped forward.

'Sir, you do have a number of patients to see. I don't think there's any need——' But it was too late. The Colonel had motioned to Louisa to draw back the covers, and Louisa had no choice but to obey. Slowly, her face crimson, she pulled down the sheets and revealed the treasure house within.

There was a long silence. Thursday stared at the floor, willing it to open up beneath her feet. She knew that every eye in the ward was riveted upon them. She could imagine exactly the livid fury on Sister's face, the half amused, half appalled guilt on Captain Barry's, the suppressed chuckle on Mark's. I'll kill you for this, she promised him silently. I'll smother you with your pillow. I'll make you eat boiled rice for every meal. I'll load your lime juice with sugar. I'll confiscate your bedpan—

The sound of laughter broke into her murderous thoughts and she lifted her eyes, astonished, to see the Colonel throw back his head and roar with mirth. He flung back the cover, grinning broadly, and turned to Sister.

'That's what happens when you take people by surprise,' he said. 'You force them to use their initiative.' He gave Louisa a nod. 'Well done, girl. But perhaps you'd better clear out some of the rubbish now, hm? And I think we'll call rounds over for this morning, shall we, Sister? As you say, I do have other patients to see, and this lot look disgustingly healthy. Taking up beds!'

He strode out of the ward, followed by the Sister, and the men erupted into laughter. Louisa, her face still scarlet, hastily removed all the offending articles from Barry's bed, aided by suggestions from Mark. Thursday, almost as embarrassed, turned on him. 'That was all your fault! You could have got us into real trouble.'

'I didn't know he was going to want to examine old Barry's bad leg,' Mark protested. 'It's not something I'd want to examine myself, and I'm a doctor! Now if it was yours . . .'

'Oh, for goodness sake! You're impossible!' She turned on her heel. The men were already getting out their papers and books, strewing them about the ward so that it looked just as untidy as it had before. She paused and shook her head. 'What's the use? What *is* the use?'

'None at all,' Mark said cheerfully from behind her. 'It's just so that we don't forget our discipline, that's all. And to stop us degenerating into total chaos. But you must admit, it does look more homely like this, now doesn't it?'

Thursday ignored him. She knew that Sister would be back, and would have some sharp words to say about the clutter hidden under Captain Barry's cradle. In any case, it was time to take the bedpans round again, and after that would come the daily bathing routine. And when that was done, there would be no shortage of bandages to wash, roll and sterilise – and by then they'd be calling out for bottles and bedpans again, and then it would be lunch . . .

Thank heaven Mark Sangster's getting better now, she thought, going to the sluice to collect an armful of pans. At least I don't have to special him any more. With any luck, I can stay at the other end of the ward and keep right out of his way.

Chapter Thirteen

It seemed very strange, with the sound of gunfire in the distance and the knowledge that wounded men were arriving daily at the hospital, to realise that outside the gates quite a different life was being lived.

'You wouldn't think there was a war on at all, to see the way they carry on round here,' Elsie observed as the girls snatched a few hours' relaxation in the town. 'Look at that lot getting out of that Rolls Royce, all dressed up to the nines as if they were going to dinner with the King hisself. I suppose they're going to that posh hotel. And look – there's some Yanks. I didn't know they were here.'

'They look as if they've only just arrived,' Thursday said, gazing at the group of American Army officers, relaxed and fresh-faced in their clean uniforms. 'There's not a speck of sand on them! And don't they look keen and eager.'

'Think they've come to win the war for us,' Elsie said a trifle sourly. 'Pity they didn't join in a bit earlier, it could've been over by now.'

Louisa shook her head. 'You have to be fair. Why should they get involved, when nobody'd actually threatened them?'

'Well, *we* did, didn't we? Come in just to protect Poland and all those little countries. Stand up for our friends, we do, but the Yanks wait till someone knocks them on the head before they'll lift a finger, and then come breezing in like Sir Galahad on a white charger and expect us all to fall about with gratitude.' Elsie threw a disparaging glance in the direction of the Americans, who were lounging on the verandah of one of the restaurants, sipping beer. 'And they all seem to think they're flipping film stars, too! Look as if they're posing for their blooming pictures all the time.'

Thursday laughed. 'You do seem to have it in for them. But you ought to remember they did do all that Lease-Lend, and send us food parcels and things. And you've got to admit we are glad of them now.'

'I bet you won't say no if one of them asks you out for a drink or dinner, either,' Louisa said slyly. 'They *are* rather good-looking, after all – and they have plenty of money. And some of them might even *be* film stars! I've heard people like James Stewart and Clark Gable are joining up.'

'I don't know what you're suggesting,' Elsie said with dignity. 'As if money and good looks would mean anything to me! And I don't know what you think is so funny about that, Thursday Tilford. If you laugh much more, your face'll get stuck.'

'Well, what shall we do anyway?' Thursday asked, trying to control her giggles. 'I don't feel like just sitting in a bar. Let's get a gharry and have a drive out.'

'Or we could have a camel ride,' Elsie suggested. 'We haven't done that yet. The camel park's over there, look. Come on, it'll be fun.'

If fun was to be had, it didn't seem to be shared by the camels. Groaning and complaining, their rubbery lips curled with disdain, they squatted in the sand so that the girls could clamber aboard and then rose grudgingly to their feet and lurched off into the desert. All along the road they were passed by gharries and taxis, each one ringing a little bell or hooting so that the camels snorted with bad temper and hunched their shoulders as if to toss their passengers on to the rough, gritty sand of the track. Thursday, clinging to the hump for dear life, wondered why in the world anyone had ever come to think about riding camels in the first place, and how they'd managed to catch and tame the first ones. Even now, it didn't seem to be a matter of co-operation or mutual enjoyment, like it did with horses. For two pins, she thought, if you let go of these beasts for more than a second they'd be off into the desert and never come back.

'Ships of the desert,' Louisa said. 'That's what they're called, because they can travel miles on the sand. Did you know they can go for days and days without drinking? They store water in their humps, or so I've heard.'

'So do the humps sort of shrink as they get thirstier? And what about those camels without humps?' Elsie asked, but Louisa didn't know. She'd never heard of a camel with no hump.

'It wouldn't really be a camel at all then, would it,' she said thoughtfully. 'Perhaps they don't store the water there after all.'

The desert was a strange place. At first glance, it seemed quite empty, nothing but dunes stretching away endlessly beneath the harsh blue sky, but when you looked more closely you could see that the dunes were rippled by the wind, and that they were continually changing. It really was a bit like the sea in slow motion, Thursday thought, a huge rolling swell of sand, with waves creasing its surface. And in a storm the motion would quicken, the sand swirling up into the air and sweeping into a different shape altogether, so that when it was over the landscape would have completely changed. No wonder people got lost out here in this vast emptiness, far away from habitation with no trees or buildings or landmarks of any kind to guide them.

'Let's go back,' she said suddenly, a strange sense of oppression sweeping over her. 'All this space – it's making me feel queer. I don't like it much.'

Back amongst the buildings, she slid down from the camel's back and grinned a little shamefacedly. 'Sorry, I just felt a bit peculiar out there, I don't know why. I've never been anywhere as *empty* as that before. I felt a bit sick and dizzy – stupid, I know.'

'It's not,' Louisa said. 'I've heard other people say the same thing. It's like the opposite of the claustrophobia Priscilla has. It's all so different from what we're used to – it's bound to affect us a bit.'

Thursday sighed. 'I know, but what about the poor men who feel the same way and have to go anyway, and fight? Oh, Lou, it just makes it all seem so much worse. We don't think about these things when we're at home. We send our boys off to war and we never really know what they're going to have to face. All those terrible stories they tell us in the wards – men being killed so horribly, lying there wounded for hours without help, perhaps dying out there all alone with nobody to look after them. And having to go to sea when they never wanted to, or out into the desert or the jungle. And what for? What's it all *for*?' She shook her head. 'Why did it all start, Lou? Did anyone have any idea it was going to spread like this? Didn't anyone ever *realise*?'

'I don't think they could have done,' Louisa said soberly. 'No one could ever have imagined all this. It's like a machine you don't know how to stop. You press a button, and it starts going and doing all sorts of things you didn't want it to and sucking other things in, and you can't find the button to press to stop it. That's what this war seems to be now. A machine that can't be stopped.'

Mark Sangster was an up-patient now and, since he was a doctor, able to be more helpful than most about the ward. He seemed to be always at Thursday's elbow, ready to hand her whatever instrument she needed, or leaning against the door of the sluice as she embarked yet again on a 'dhobey' of soiled bandages. Disturbed by his presence at first, and annoyed with herself – and therefore him – by her discomfort, she gradually became accustomed to it, but never felt as easy as she did with some of the other patients, nor the servicemen who invited her and the other girls out for a drink or a meal. She knew that this reluctance was unreasonable, but she couldn't explain it to herself, let alone to the other girls.

'I don't know what you've got against him, I really don't,' Elsie told her. 'I mean, he's the best-looking bloke on the ward, he's a good laugh and a perfect gent – and *those* two don't always go together, mark my words! What's more, he obviously fancies you. Why don't you kick over the traces and have a bit of fun?'

'You know why.' Thursday waved the pad of paper on which she was writing her daily epistle to Connor.

'Huh!' Elsie said scornfully. 'Didn't stop you having a bit of a kiss and cuddle with that NCO at the pictures the other night. *I* saw you. And what about all those good night kisses you handed out when you were on nights? I heard about them too. Gave the rest of us a bit to live up to, I can tell you.'

Thursday blushed. 'They don't mean anything, you know they don't. Well . . .' she hesitated and Elsie raised her eyebrows, 'they do at the time because I feel so sorry for the poor chaps. But they don't mean I'm in *love* with them.'

'So what about the NCO? Are you in love with him?'

'No!' Thursday looked down at the writing-pad again. 'Well, I don't know. When I'm with him – with any of them – I feel as if I might be. It's a nice feeling. I *want* to feel in love with someone, I want to kiss and cuddle and all that, but I don't think it's any special man, and I don't think it's serious. It's just – well, fun. You know.'

'Yeah, I know,' Elsie said quietly. 'We all want a bit of loving, the whole lot of us. And whether we've got someone waiting for us at home, or thousands of miles away like your Connor, we still want it. We want it *now* – not in God knows how many years' time, or perhaps never.'

Thursday sighed. 'Oh, Elsie, I don't know what I feel, half the time. I really do love Connor, I'm sure I do, but he's so far away, and we don't know how we'll really feel when we meet again. If we ever do meet again,' she added soberly. 'And meanwhile, here we are, and here are all those men, all of them going back to the fighting after their hospitalisation or their leave, and we'll probably never see them again. By this time next week, they could be dead. It doesn't seem wrong to love them just for a little while – when they're here and alive. It doesn't seem wrong to have fun and enjoy ourselves, just for a little while.'

'It's not wrong,' Elsie said robustly. 'It's natural. And I don't see as it does any harm. In fact, I reckon it does us all good.' She glanced at Thursday. 'So why don't you have some fun with Dr Sangster? Because I'm darned sure you like him, Thurs. I've seen you looking at him.' She waited a moment, watching her friend, and then said quietly, 'I'm right, aren't I? You do like him.'

Thursday looked up and met her eyes. Her face flooded with scarlet. She took in a breath, opened her mouth to speak – and then, quite unexpectedly, flung down the writing-pad and jumped to her feet.

'For heaven's sake, Elsie, leave me alone!' she cried, and stalked towards the door. 'Just don't keep *on* at me, all right?'

Several other girls, also engaged in writing letters or mending stockings or lying on their beds reading, glanced up in surprise. Elsie rolled her eyes at them, then inclined her head towards the wire screen door that Thursday had let swing violently behind her.

'Seems to me someone's getting a bit touchy,' she remarked. 'I wonder why.' She bent and retrieved the pad, placing it face down on the bed. 'Never mind, Connor,' she murmured. 'It won't be long now before she gives way and gets it out of her system. She'll be back then – don't you worry.'

Thursday walked out into the grounds, breathing quickly. Her heart was thumping uncomfortably and she could feel the ache of tears in her throat and the sting of them in her eyes. In all the time they'd known each other, she had never quarrelled with Elsie before. I don't know what's got into me lately, she thought miserably. I snap people's heads off for no reason at all, I feel like crying over the slightest thing and now I've rowed with Elsie. Over nothing.

No. Not over nothing. Over Mark Sangster.

But why should she quarrel with Elsie over him, of all people? Why was he so different from all the others – Johnny on board ship, Geoff the NCO who'd taken her to the pictures, Bob the Sergeant who'd taken her dancing, James the young Lieutenant who'd taken her to dinner in Cairo? She'd enjoyed herself with them, flirting and fluttering her eyelashes, she'd kissed them and let them hold her in their arms, knowing all the time that it would go no further than that, that this delicious feeling of being just slightly in love was doing no one any harm. Knowing too that the tiny undercurrent of danger – that they might really fall in love – added spice to the affair, yet could be kept under control. So why couldn't she let herself fall just slightly, deliciously, in love with Mark Sangster? Why couldn't she enjoy a similar, quite innocent, romance with him?

Because you might not be able to keep it under control, she thought suddenly, and her heart sank as she realised the truth. The attraction was too strong. The danger was more than a tiny undercurrent – it was a tide that could sweep her away. And he knew it too.

She leaned against the wall and stared up at the night sky. Here, close to the desert, the stars were clustered so thickly that you could scarcely have put a pin between them. The tall, fronded palm trees were silhouetted against their brilliance, swaying gently with the soft breeze, whispering a shush-shush; shush-shush. From somewhere beyond the hospital walls she could hear the sound of horses' hooves and the rattle of a gharry's wheels, or the softer plod of a camel. Now and then an Arab would call or the wail of Egyptian music drift across. From the Italian sector came the sweet, liquid sound of singing. A ripple of laughter sounded through the open, wire-screened windows of the building behind her, and she felt suddenly very lonely.

Elsie's right, she thought. We just want to be loved. And, perhaps even more, to *love*. It all seems to be passing us by. Here I am, almost twenty-four and I don't even know what it's like to love a man properly. And Connor might not even *want* me by the time we meet again.

A soft movement nearby made her turn. A tall, dark figure was standing close to the wall and she started in sudden panic. The man moved again and spoke in a quiet voice.

'You're looking very sad, Nurse Tilford. Care to tell me about it?'

'Dr Sangster!' she gasped. 'What – what are you doing out here?'

'The same as you, I imagine. Came out for a breath of air and a look at the stars.' He came to stand close beside her and stared up at the sky. 'Beautiful, aren't they? Millions of them. So magnificent. And so hard to believe there's a war going on down here. It makes me wonder why we do it – all this pitiful struggling and killing – when the universe is so vast and we're so very, very small.'

Thursday said nothing. She could feel the warmth of his arm, almost touching her through the thin cotton of her sleeve. Her heart was thudding and she felt almost sick. She moved away abruptly and said, 'I must go in. And so should you. You – you ought to be in bed.'

He turned his head and looked down at her, and for a moment she was afraid he was going to make one of his wicked remarks, designed to bring a blush to her face. Instead, he reached one hand up and touched her cheek with his fingertip. He let it trail gently down the line of her jaw until it rested beneath her chin, and then he tilted her downcast face up towards him.

'They say your name is Thursday,' he said. 'Is that true?'

'Yes. I was named for Armistice Day – it was the day I was born.'

He nodded. 'You must have interesting parents.'

Nobody had ever said that before. Thursday considered. 'They seem quite ordinary to me.'

'Well, so they would – you're an interesting person too. But it takes quite a lot of imagination and courage to give a baby an unusual name like Thursday.'

'My father was in the First War,' Thursday said. 'He saw a lot of things he never talks about. I think it meant a lot to him that I was born just then.'

'And do you mind if I call you Thursday?'

She felt herself blush. 'We're not supposed to—'

'Fraternise. I know. But I'm a doctor, so perhaps it makes a difference.' It didn't, so far as Thursday could see, but she knew Dr Sangster well enough by now to know that he liked to get his own way. That was one of the things that alarmed her about him.

'And you can call me Mark,' he said.

'Oh no, I—'

'Not on the ward, I know. But when we're off it. When we're together, on our own.'

Thursday stared at him. 'When are we ever going to be off the ward together, on our own?'

'Whenever I can manage it,' he said, and lowered his head to hers and kissed her lips.

Thursday stood very still. She felt his good arm around her shoulders. The damaged one was almost better, the plaster due to come off in a day or so, and then . . . She shivered suddenly and he drew back a little and looked at her. She could see the shine of the starlight in his eyes.

'Cold?'

'No,' she whispered, and laid her head against his chest.

'Thursday,' he murmured against her hair. 'Thursday, Thursday, Thursday . . . It's a beautiful name. A beautiful name for a beautiful girl.'

'No. You mustn't say that.' She lifted her head and stepped away, staring at him with fear in her eyes. 'You mustn't do this. Please.'

'Mustn't?'

'No. Please. I – I ought to go in now. You'd better go back to the ward, they'll be missing you.'

'Just a moment or two longer,' he said quietly, and drew her against his side again. 'Just let's stand here together for a minute or two and look at the stars.'

Thursday stood close, her head lifted. He felt warm and firm against her side, his breathing steady. The kicking of her heart slowed to a more peaceful rhythm and she sighed.

'Better now?' he murmured. 'I don't want to frighten you, Thursday.'

She nodded without speaking, knowing he could feel the movement against his shoulder. After a moment, still gazing at the stars, she said, 'They look so close, don't they? As if you could reach up and touch them.'

Mark released his hold on her shoulders and reached up, his hand open and fingers outstretched as if he were grasping for the brilliant pinpricks of light. Then he closed his fist and lowered it, opening it into Thursday's palm as if depositing something of immense value.

'There,' he said. 'A handful of stardust for you to keep, to remind you of the night of a million stars. Better than diamonds.'

'Yes,' Thursday said, staring down at her palm and imagining the glitter now cradled there. 'Better than diamonds . . .'

Chapter Fourteen

'There were two more poliomyelitis patients today,' Elsie said, sitting down to supper with the others. Having already had experience of infectious diseases in Haslar's Zymotics wards, she had been quickly moved to the same work in the 64th, but she was encountering diseases here that they'd barely heard of at home and sometimes found herself unable to mix with the other girls because of some infectious or contagious illness she was in contact with. She'd already nursed several men through diphtheria, which was a constant scourge, and she'd seen others die from it. Smallpox occurred from time to time, and those patients were removed immediately to isolation – a small hut or tent situated as far away as possible from the main hospital. Elsie had been told the story of one case, kept a mile away, which still managed to spread the infection back to the main buildings.

'Nobody knew how it was getting there. They knew it was coming from this poor bloke, because the new cases were all happening in the nearest ward – even though it was all that distance away. They thought of birds and rats, and set traps and everything, but it still kept coming out – and then the CO went over one day and noticed a trail of ants marching away from the tent. They were carrying bits of scab and stuff off the bloke's skin, and they were taking it all the way back to their nest, right under the hospital walls! Would you believe it? A *mile*. They had to move the isolation tent five miles away to get out of the pesky things' range!'

'Poliomyelitis? Isn't that what they call infantile paralysis?' Thursday asked. 'I thought only children got that.'

'No, older people can get it too. It can leave them paralysed and if it gets into their chest they just can't breathe.' Elsie helped herself to some rice and lowered her voice. 'And listen – don't spread it around – but someone told me today there's a case that might be *plague*.'

'*Plague*? You mean like in London?' Thursday asked, horrified. 'We did it at school. It's terrible—'

'I thought it didn't happen any more,' Priscilla said. 'Wasn't it rats that carried it?' She remembered the rats the QARMN had told them about and gasped, her hand to her mouth. 'But what will they do if it's true? We might all get it!'

'They've put him in isolation,' Elsie said. 'They're giving him M&B. He'll be nursed by volunteers – there's a vaccination, so they should be all right.'

A few days later there were more cases, when some Basutos arrived at the hospital in various stages of the disease. Some of the Zymotics nurses disappeared into isolation with them and Elsie said, 'I reckon they're going to be asking for more volunteers. If they do, I'll go.'

'Elsie! Won't you be scared?'

'Listen, I could get dip, or typhus, or smallpox – anything. Half the time they're in the ward for days before we even know what they've got. And I've had the vaccination.' She rolled up her sleeve to show them. 'Someone's got to go and help the poor blighters.'

Elsie's offer was refused, the Sister saying she was too valuable with the polio patients, but word of the epidemic was spreading around the rest of the hospital. Thursday, going on duty, found the men beginning to panic. Everyone had heard of the Great Plague of London and their injuries seemed like nothing beside this new threat. A young boy, no more than nineteen, reached out to Thursday as she passed and implored her to tell him it wasn't true. 'I learned about it at school. You come up in huge black lumps everywhere and just rot away inside. I'd rather go back to the front lines than that, I'd rather *anything*—'

'It's all right. You won't get it in here.' Thursday smiled at him, praying that it was true. She'd seen a rat outside only the night before. 'They're all in isolation. It's safe here.'

The men weren't convinced. The ward buzzed all morning with increasingly anxious voices, and in the end the Wardmaster himself came in and shouted for quiet. They fell silent at once, eyes fixed on him, but one man whispered to his mate that this was it, they were going to be told it was all over the hospital, it was curtains for the lot of them . . .

'I said, *quiet*!' The Wardmaster's brows came down in a heavy scowl. 'Next man to utter a sound gets put on a charge! Now listen, all of you. This panic about the plague has got to stop. You're acting like a pack of bloody babes in arms. Soldiers? I wouldn't give tuppence for any one of you. Strikes me you've been laying about in bed too long, getting soft. I've a good mind to tell the doctor to discharge the lot of you and send you back, bandages and all.' He paused and glowered at each man in turn. 'I've never seen such a disgraceful shower. And there's young girls like these VADs and QARMNs, not too scared to volunteer to go into the plague wards and nurse the poor blighters who've got it. Put you all to shame, they do.'

The men hung their heads. Thursday, glancing at their downcast faces, felt sorry for them. They'd been through a lot already, fighting in the desert with all its discomforts and then being wounded and brought back to a hospital which was scarcely luxurious. Some of them had lost families at home in the bombing too, or were afraid that their wives and sweethearts would grow tired of waiting for them. The threat of something as terrifying as bubonic plague had been just too much. It was almost too much for her too – like all the nurses, she was just as afraid but knew she mustn't show it.

'It's all right,' she murmured as she went round with lime juice after the wardmaster had gone to harangue another roomful of frightened men. 'They'll get it under control. You won't catch it here.'

That evening they heard that two of the Basutos had died and one of the nurses had caught the disease. They stared at each other in dismay.

'But wasn't she vaccinated?'

'It doesn't always work,' Louisa said grimly. 'Does anyone know who it is?'

'It's one of the QARMNs,' Priscilla said. She hesitated, glanced at Elsie, then added, 'I've volunteered as well. I went to Sister and asked for the vaccination this afternoon.'

'*You*, Priss? But you've always said you hated infectious diseases.'

'Well, so do we all.' She shrugged. 'I just feel I ought to do something – something more. I've been so lucky all my life.' She glanced down at the ring she always wore off duty. 'Quentin's out there risking his life, and I feel I ought to be doing the same. Not to be a heroine, or anything,' she added hastily, 'but to be – well, more worthy of him, if you know what I mean.'

'You're worthy of him already,' Thursday said at last. 'You don't have to put yourself at risk.'

'No, but it's what Elsie said the other day – someone's got to nurse the poor blighters. Anyway, there it is. I've volunteered – can't take it back now.' She gave them all a somewhat tremulous smile and brushed back her pale, spun-gold hair. 'So I shan't be here for breakfast tomorrow, I'm afraid. You can have my sausages between you.'

Thursday looked at her. She hadn't known Priscilla long, and would never have expected to be friendly with a girl from her background. But these days, she thought, you got to know people so quickly and class didn't seem to make any difference any more. Priscilla, Elsie and Louisa were almost like sisters – closer, in some ways, than real sisters. She bit her lip.

'You just be careful,' she said gruffly. 'Don't go taking any daft risks, and come back here the minute you can, see? We can't manage without you, Priss.'

'I'll be all right,' Priscilla said, giving a little nod. 'You don't have to worry about me, Thursday.'

'Worry?' Elsie said in her normal robust tones. 'Who said anything about worrying? I'm just looking forward to all those sausages!'

Once back on the wards, there was no time for worrying about anyone other than the patients.

'Captain Roberts has collapsed – dehydration. Ice!'

The order caught Thursday on her way to the sluice. Immediately, she wheeled round and set off at a fast walk for the other door. Dehydration was always a risk in the heat of the desert: no matter how hard you tried to keep the men's fluid levels up, every now and then someone would succumb to heat stroke and, if not dealt with at once, it could kill.

By the time she ran back, lugging buckets filled with ice and followed by an Indian orderly carrying more, the patient was stretched out on a bed, naked apart from a cotton sheet, with a fan whirring overhead. Sister snatched one of the buckets and tipped it out on to the bed. Thursday did the same with the other and, working swiftly, they began to pack the ice around his body, into his armpits and groin, and along his backbone. Another VAD arrived with the jugs and tubes necessary for a cold enema, and Sister began to set up saline and glucose drips.

'Keep dousing him with cold water,' she instructed Thursday, 'and don't move from his side. His temperature was up to a hundred and ten, so keep taking it. He'll have to be monitored until it comes right down, and then very gradually and gently rewarmed. It's a critical task.' She looked down at the shuddering body. 'I'll be back in ten minutes but if there are any symptoms, anything at all, call me at once, and *don't take your eyes off him for a second*, understand?'

Thursday nodded. She pulled up a chair and sat beside the patient, watching him closely. She knew that he could go into convulsions or even into a coma, and if that happened he would almost certainly die. A young Private had died of heat stroke only a fortnight earlier – he'd been brought in already in a state of collapse, and treatment had simply come too late. The whole ward had been upset by this needless death, not even caused by wounds, and the Wardmaster had decreed that there must be no more such deaths on his ward. Thursday, sitting beside the Captain, replenishing the rapidly melting ice and cooling his overheated body with more cold water, hoped desperately that this would not be the next.

Captain Roberts was beginning to show signs of recovery. His temperature was down a degree or two and Thursday signalled her relief to the Sister the next time she approached. 'That's excellent, Nurse. Now, he'll need very careful monitoring to get him back to normal. We're not out of the wood yet – but at least we can see the edge of the trees.' She felt the patient's pulse and nodded. 'You're doing very well, Tilford. You're an excellent worker.'

She departed again, promising once more to return within ten minutes, and Thursday continued to sponge her patient with cool water. He moved and moaned a little and she bent hastily, laying her palm on his forehead and praying that he wasn't going into a convulsion. With her free hand, she gestured for more cold water and the orderly poured it over the naked skin. Captain Roberts opened his eyes.

'What the hell?' His voice was no more than a mutter.

'You've got heat stroke,' Thursday told him, relief washing over her. 'You'll be all right but I'm going to stay here with you for a while. I'll get them to bring more ice.'

'Ice? If I'd known gin was part of the treatment . . .' His voice faded and Thursday smiled.

'It's not. And you'll be off alcohol for a while anyway. Just lie quietly and go to sleep.' She touched his forehead again and was relieved to find it less burningly hot.

The next time Sister came back, she decreed that he was out of the wood and Thursday was sent off for a brief tea break. She took her cup outside and sat in the shade, half her mind with Priscilla in the plague ward, and half wondering where Mark Sangster was now.

She had not seen him since the evening he had plucked the stardust from the sky. Overcome by a welter of emotion, so tangled that she barely knew what she felt, she had turned and scurried back into the building then and hidden in the washrooms. When she finally crept into the dormitory Elsie was in bed, and Thursday had slipped into her own bunk without disturbing her. The next morning they had been slightly awkward with each other, until Elsie suddenly threw her arms about Thursday and said, 'This is daft! We're not going to let a little thing like a man come between us, are we? I'm sorry I upset you, Thurs.'

'I'm sorry too,' Thursday said, wiping her eyes and grinning shakily. 'I was stupid, going off at half-cock like that.'

She didn't tell Elsie what had happened outside, however, and when she went on duty it was to find his bed already occupied by another patient. She looked at him in some surprise and Sister said, 'Oh, that's Major Lewis. He's a trauma – broken ribs, collar-bone, several shell splinters. He was admitted during the night.'

'What happened to Lieutenant Colonel Sangster?'

'He's gone. Doctor saw him this morning and decided he was fit to leave. He'll be back in, of course, to have his plaster removed and his final check-up, but there was really no need for him to be taking up a bed. I believe he's found a room at one of the local hotels.'

Thursday had gone back to her duties, feeling oddly perturbed. She had lain awake most of the night, her senses awakened by the encounter, reliving his touch and his kiss, hearing his words in her mind again and again. She'd thought of Connor, and her longing for him, for his warm presence, for the love that had grown between them and never been fulfilled, had brought an ache to her heart. I want so much to be loved, she thought, I want so much to love. But it's Connor I want. It is. It *is*.

It's a good thing Dr Sangster's gone, she thought now, as she leaned against the hospital wall and gazed out over the gardens. It's for the best. I shan't have to worry any more, I shan't have to feel guilty because I think about him. If he's not here, I'll be able to forget . . .

But she was wrong. She hadn't been able to forget.

The Battle of El Alamein had lasted for eleven days – eleven days in which the distant roar of gunfire could be heard, eleven days of horror in the desert, eleven days of the steady stream of wounded men being brought back to the hospitals. It had ended on 7 November with Rommel on the run and Lieutenant-General Montgomery – 'Monty' – victorious. His face and name were on the front pages of all the English newspapers and he was the hero of the hour. On 10 November, the day before Thursday's twenty-fourth birthday, he was both knighted and promoted, becoming officially General Sir Bernard Montgomery – but nobody took any notice of that. He was Monty to everyone now, and Monty he would remain.

'It just shows how important it is out here,' Thursday said. 'And Monty – he looks a funny little man when you see him, yet they obviously think he's the bee's knees at home. Fancy making him a knight, just like that. It's really romantic.'

'And we're a part of it,' Louisa agreed. 'It's something we'll always remember – being here during the Battle of El Alamein.'

'Let's celebrate,' Elsie suggested. 'It's your birthday tomorrow, Thurs – let's go out somewhere, somewhere posh. I've saved up a bit of money, we'll treat you. What d'you say, Louie?'

'Good idea. We'll go to the Cecil. Best bibs and tuckers. OK?'

They laughed, knowing they had only their white uniform dresses to wear. However, Louisa had found a local dressmaker not far from the hospital and got a new frock made, still white as per regulation but in sharkskin instead of cotton, and much more smartly cut. Sister had given it a look when Louisa had first worn it on the ward, but said nothing, and now all the girls had been there, marvelling at the cheapness and delighting in their new elegance.

Thursday never counted herself as being a year older until eleven in the morning, knowing that this was the precise minute at which she had been born on 11 November 1918. From early childhood, she had been taught to stay still and quiet during the two minutes' silence of remembrance, and only then allowed to celebrate. On this day, the ward fell silent, each man sombre as he thought of his fallen comrades, and then, as the hands of the ward clock passed the hour, she was startled by an enormous cheer.

'What on earth?'

'Happy Birthday!' shouted the Lance-Corporal in the nearest bed. 'Happy birthday to you!' And with both his arms, one still in plaster, he began to conduct the song, all the others joining in. 'Happy Birthday, dear Tilford, happy birthday to you!'

Thursday stood in the middle, her hands to her face, feeling the blush run up her neck and over her cheeks. 'Who told you?' she demanded, and then caught sight of Louisa grinning in the doorway. 'Oh, you wretch! It was supposed to be a secret.'

'Don't be daft,' the Lance-Corporal said. 'Birthdays shouldn't be secret. Not when it's a pretty young nurse like you, anyway. And not when it's on a day like today. That makes you special.' He foraged with his good arm under his pillow and brought out a box, wrapped in white paper and tied with ribbon. 'Here. This is from all of us.'

Thursday stared at him, then slowly took it. She looked doubtfully at the box and then around the ward.

'From all of you?'

'Thass right. Open it!'

She gave them a suspicious look and they laughed. 'It's all right, nursey! It ain't full of bed-bugs or nothing. You can open it up.'

Thursday untied the knot carefully. The ribbon was blue, and would do to tie in her hair later. She took off the sheet of white paper and smoothed it out. It was good enough to use again, for another present. The box inside was of chocolates – the best sort you could buy in town, and needing to be eaten quickly before the heat melted them. Thursday, beaming from ear to ear although there were also tears in her eyes, went round the entire ward offering the box to the patients.

'Here, no, love, we got them for you. You 'ave 'em tonight when yer off duty. Share 'em with yer pals.'

'I *am* sharing them with my pals,' Thursday said, offering the box again. 'This is my party, see, and you're all invited.'

'Well, all right, then,' said a Sergeant, taking one. 'I was always brought up that it was rude to say no. Thanks, nursey, and a happy birthday to you.' He leaned closer and whispered loudly, 'And we won't split on how old you are. We won't tell a soul you're fifty-two!'

The ward erupted into laughter and Sister appeared in the doorway, her face stern. 'Now what's all this noise? I could hear you all the way from B Ground. Tilford, shouldn't you be blanket-bathing now?'

'Yes, Sister. I'll start right away.' Her cheeks burning, Thursday hurriedly pushed the empty box under the nearest pillow. 'Now see what you've done!' she hissed at the occupant, but the soldier just grinned.

''S all right, love. She knows what was goin' on – I spotted her outside, hanging about waiting for us to give it yer.' He winked. 'Thanks for the party, ducks. Now let's get on with winning the war, eh?'

The newspaper stands in town were blazing their headlines in half a dozen languages. The girls, on their way for their evening out, stopped and grabbed all the English ones they could find, reading them eagerly.

'Look at this!' Louisa waved a copy of the *Egyptian Mail*. ' "ALLIES CAPTURE ORAN NAVAL BASE. *Us Tanks Close on Casablanca. Calm in Algiers after Surrender*." ' Her face was alight. 'They've invaded Algeria! Listen – it says that American troops have been landed all along the North African coast. They've lost a lot of men and some ships – British ones as well – and the French are putting up a terrific resistance, but they're winning and—'

'The *French*?' Elsie broke in. 'But they're supposed to be on our side!'

'Well, this is Algeria. I suppose it's different – they don't want to be invaded. And it's like Vichy France, isn't it? They've gone over to the Germans. I don't really understand it either, Elsie, but that's what it says here. And listen to what Mr Churchill has said about Alamein.' She cleared her throat and read aloud, her voice dropping almost involuntarily into the grave, sonorous tones of the Prime Minister:

' "This is not the end. It is not even the beginning of the end. But it is, perhaps, the end of the beginning." '

'I love the way he talks,' Elsie said after a moment. 'It's so clever – almost like poetry.'

'Anyway, the Allies are winning, that's the main thing.' Louisa folded the paper and grinned triumphantly. 'I'm going to send these papers home to my father. He'll be tickled pink.'

'He'll have heard all about it long before they get there.'

'Doesn't matter. He won't have seen *these* papers.' Louisa gave a little squirm of delight. 'Well, what a celebration for your birthday, Thursday! I think we'll have a bottle of wine, don't you? And something really, really scrumptious to eat.'

'It's a shame Priscilla can't be here,' Thursday said, looking up at the hotel façade. 'She'd have loved this.'

The Cecil Hotel was, as always, crowded with military, RAF and Naval officers, with plenty of their American counterparts. Tonight, the talk was all of the Algerian invasion and excitement was running high. The girls found a table and sat down, fending off a few attempts to occupy the fourth chair. 'Later on, maybe,' Louisa said with a smile at an undeniably good-looking American Lieutenant. 'This is a private celebration.'

'Say, ain't we all got sumpin to celebrate tonight?' he drawled, but he drifted away and the girls were left in peace to order their meal and their bottle of wine.

'It still seems strange to be able to eat like this, while the people at home are on rations for everything,' Thursday said, eyeing the mountain of couscous that had been placed before her. 'I'd never even heard of this before we came to Egypt. I suppose rice is the nearest to it, but we only ever had that as a pudding!'

'I reckon we'll all have some new ideas when we go home,' Elsie said, tucking in. 'And I bet we'll never use any of them. Too glad to get back to good old steak and kidney pie and roast beef! That's if you can still get 'em by then.'

'No, it'll be Spam and corned beef, and sardines on toast. So make the most of it,' Louisa said, giving Thursday a severe look. 'And no feeling guilty – this is your birthday party, remember!'

They were just finishing their ice cream – another thing the family back home wouldn't have seen for years, Thursday thought – and had ordered coffee when a shadow fell across the table. They looked up, expecting to see the American Lieutenant, and Thursday drew in a sharp breath.

'Mark – Dr Sangster!'

'Mark will do,' he said, smiling. 'May I join you?' He glanced at the vacant chair and laid his hand on the back.

'We're just going—' Thursday began, but Louisa smiled and nodded, and Elsie put her own hand on the chair to draw it out, her voice drowning Thursday's confused protests. 'Course you can, sir. We've got hours yet. Have some coffee.'

'I will, and perhaps you'll join me in a brandy to go with it.' He flicked his fingers at a hurrying waiter, then leaned his elbows on the table and smiled round at them. 'And how are you all getting along? What d'you think of the news about Torch?'

'Torch?'

'The invasion of Algeria – Operation Torch.' He grinned. 'I'd love to know how they choose the names for all these different operations – just open a dictionary at random and stick in a pin, I should think.' He glanced at Thursday. 'What do you think, Thursday?'

'Yes, I expect so,' she stammered. 'I don't know . . .' She glanced imploringly at Elsie, who leaped obligingly to the rescue.

'It's Thursday's birthday today, did you know? She was twenty-four at exactly eleven o'clock this morning – the eleventh hour of the eleventh day of the eleventh month. Here, I bet they pushed the boat out on your *eleventh* birthday, didn't they, Thurs? And you should've seen the blokes in the ward this morning, sir. Singing and dancing they were, practically – gave her a big box of chocolates and all. I wasn't there myself, of course, because I'm over in Infectious Diseases, but Louie here'll tell you, won't you, Lou?'

Louisa nodded, smiling. Thursday, looking from one to the other, caught a small conspiratorial grin pass between them, but before she could speak Mark was pulling something out of his pocket. He laid it on the table and she saw that it was a small box, wrapped in delicate silver gauze and tied with the thinnest of silver ribbons.

'I did know it was your birthday, Thursday,' he said quietly. 'You told me, remember? And I wanted to give you a little present.' He lifted her hand from the table and turned it over, placing the box in her cupped palm. 'Happy Birthday.'

Thursday stared at it. She looked up and met his eyes, then looked accusingly at the other two. 'You told him we'd be here! You laid a trap!'

They were both laughing. She felt her cheeks grow hot and bit her lip, not knowing whether to laugh with them or to cry. In her heart was a mixture of anger and a strange, burgeoning delight. In her hand, the little box felt both light and heavy.

'I—'

'Open it,' he said softly, and the other two joined in. 'Go on, Thursday, open it!'

Still scarlet, Thursday fumbled with the wrappings, trying not to tear the fragile gauze. It fell away and she opened the box, her fingers trembling.

'Oh,' she said, and then again, '*Oh* . . .'

'What is it? Let's see.' Elsie was craning over the table. Louisa, next to Thursday, leaned over for a better view. 'Oh, how lovely!'

'It's a star,' Thursday said shakily. 'A little silver star. Oh, *Mark*.'

'I wanted something for you to remember me by,' he said quietly. 'I'll be going back in a day or two. I wanted you to remember the night of the million stars.'

There was a moment of silence. The other two girls had drawn away, and it was as if Mark and Thursday were the only two people in the restaurant. She stared into his eyes, and felt the full force of the attraction he had for her, the passion that could so easily flare between them. Desperately, she tried to think of Connor, but he seemed very small and very far away. Mark was here – and he loved her. She could see it in the darkness of his eyes. And she – did she love him?

'May I take you back tonight, Thursday?' he asked. 'Elsie and Louisa can take a gharry. I want to ride with you under the desert stars and the rising moon, just this once. So that I too have something to remember.'

She was helpless, caught in a spell. She nodded, and the other two girls got up.

'We're going now, Thursday,' Louisa said gently. 'We'll see you back at the hospital.' She glanced at Mark Sangster. 'Look after her, Doctor. She means quite a lot to us, too.'

Then they were gone, their white dresses gleaming in the darkness outside the window. Mark and Thursday looked at each other. She felt a sudden flurry of panic and half rose to her feet. 'I ought to go too.'

'No,' he said, his hand burning on her arm, 'no, don't. Just give me this one evening, Thursday – this one last evening to be with you. It's all I'm asking.'

Thursday sank back into her chair. It was all he was asking. Yet, if he could only see into her heart, he would know that she was ready to give him the world.

'There are terrible things happening out there,' Mark said as the gharry clopped along the desert road. They had left Alexandria behind and, apart from their Arab driver, were alone under the million stars. Thursday was wearing her new brooch, pinned to the right shoulder of her white dress. On the left, she wore the marcasite Naval crown brooch that Connor had given her before he too had gone away to war.

'I know,' she said. 'This war goes on and on, and more and more people being killed all the time.' She looked up at the velvet sky with its studding of diamonds. 'There must have been almost as many killed as there are stars.'

'I hope not,' he said. 'I hope there'll never be that many.' They were silent for a few moments, then he said, 'It's not just the soldiers, though, and the sailors and airmen – the fighters. It's all the civilians. And worse still, the people who were being ground under Hitler's heel when it all started and still are.'

'The Czechoslovakians, you mean, and the Polish?'

'And the Jews,' he said, 'forced to live in ghettoes, walled away from the rest of the cities, made to wear yellow stars so that they could be recognised in the streets and beaten and kicked. And the little villages where people have dared to resist. An American I met was telling me about a poster that's been going up, showing some poor fellow with a sack over his head, waiting to be shot. It's about a village called Lidice, where all the men were shot, and the women sent to concentration camps and the children to what they called "appropriate centres". And there've been places in France too where old men and women have been shot down in their own homes just because they were working in their gardens when the Germans passed by and didn't stand to attention. That's not war, Thursday, not honest fighting between trained men. It's hideous brutality.'

Thursday tried to find words, but there were none that were adequate. She sat close to him, seeking reassurance in the warmth of his body, and after a moment he slipped his arm around her and held her tightly.

'I'm sorry, sweetheart. I shouldn't be talking like this, not on your birthday and when I've got you to myself for the first time. But it's just because of that – because it's the first time, and it may be the last – that I have to tell you what I feel about it all.' His voice was more serious than she had ever known it. 'I expect you think I'm just a fool, clowning about in the ward, making ridiculous jokes – but there's more to me than that, Thursday. I care very much about what happens in this war. I care about what happens to the people – and I've never forgotten the people we started out fighting for. The ordinary people of those little countries that Hitler overran, the ones who didn't want any part of his regime but had no choice.' He paused, and she sensed that he was fighting down the passion in his heart. 'I just wanted you to hear that, Thursday, so that you know what makes me tick.'

'I think I do know,' she said softly. 'It's the reason I'm here too – why I became a VAD. I wanted to help. We all want to help.'

'And with all of us fighting on the same side,' he said, 'we're bound to win. We're *bound* to.' He turned his face towards her and she lifted hers. The kiss was as natural as breathing, and as soft as a sigh. Yet in the tension of his lips she could feel the desire that simmered in his heart, the longing of his body for hers.

'Oh, Mark,' she said, feeling a rush of all the yearning she had felt in the past months, the yearning that had touched her whenever a man took her in his arms for a dance, and most of all when she had thought of Connor, yet was now, here in Mark's arms with the warmth and hardness of his body against hers, more powerful than she had ever known it. 'Mark, I want you to love me properly. And I want to love *you*.'

He held her very close, his lips moving in her hair, drifting down her cheek and neck and into the softness of the cleft between her breasts. Her blood surged at his touch and a weakness invaded her body, so that her arms loosened about him and she lay back against the leather seat. Her fingers found his hair and she played with it, feeling its softness like tendrils catching at her heart.

He raised his head and kissed her again, then drew back a little. 'This is all there is,' he said quietly. 'I'm not going to ask you to go any further than this, Thursday. Believe me, it wouldn't be fair. But at least I have this to remember – we both have this to remember.'

'You'll come back,' she whispered. 'I know you'll come back.'

'I hope so.' He touched the silver star. 'And until I do, wear this for me. But,' his fingers strayed across her breasts and she shivered, 'you're wearing another man's brooch as well. I don't doubt your feelings for him, and I don't hold it against you. But one day you may have to decide which you'll wear for good, Thursday. One day – if we both come back.'

She stared at him, then hid her face against his shoulder. 'What sort of a girl am I? Connor—'

'He didn't want you to promise. He knew the future was uncertain. And I'm the same, Thursday. I know I may never come back. I just want to stake a claim, so that if I do, you'll give me a chance. Same as him. And if we both come back . . .'

'I don't know what I'll do.'

'You'll know,' he said, smiling down at her, and she could see the stars reflected in his eyes. 'You'll know.'

The gharry turned and made its way back to Alexandria. The two passengers sat very close, their arms wrapped tightly about each other. Thursday, her head resting against Mark's shoulder, felt a strange, poignant sense of loss, mingled with the headiness of passionate love. Of all the men she had known, kissed, flirted with and loved, only these two had really caught her heart. I love them both, she thought with dizzy bewilderment, and then, as if an icy finger had touched, her: *and I may lose them both.*

The gharry stopped at the hospital gates. In sudden anguish, she turned and lifted her face again, and Mark caught her lips with his. In the midst of their passion, she dimly heard the sound of the gate opening and closing, and then to her astonishment, Elsie's voice from close by.

'Thursday! *Thursday*! Come in, quick – we've had some patients brought in, bad burn cases off a ship that's been hit. One of them's asking for you, he wants you. Sister said to come out and find you – please, come quick!'

Thursday lifted her face away from Mark's. Elsie was standing beside the gharry, her eyes wide with anxiety. She held up her hands, begging Thursday to come.

'Someone who knows me? Off a ship? Oh, my God, Elsie – it's not –?'

'Just *come*!' Elsie urged. 'I can tell you as we go, but for God's sake, come quick. He – he –' she gasped and swallowed. 'Sister says he may not last the night.'

Chapter Fifteen

Mark refused to leave her. 'I'm a doctor,' he said. 'And still almost a patient – I don't get full clearance till tomorrow. Of course I'm coming.'

Thursday cast him an agonised glance. He understood immediately. 'It's all right, I'll stay outside. I want to make things easier for you, not more difficult.'

They can't be more difficult, Thursday thought as she raced through the corridors. If it's Connor – and who else could it be? – *nothing* could make things more difficult. Nor any easier. But she was thankful, all the same, for Mark's hand firm around hers.

Elsie paused at the door of the ward. 'He's here. Right by the office.' It was the bed where they put the most gravely ill patients, the ones who needed to be under Sister's eye, with special nursing; the ones who weren't expected to live past the next few hours. Thursday brushed the tears from her eyes, giving Elsie a brief, twisted smile of thanks, took a deep breath and went in.

Sister was by the bed. She rose as Thursday hurried in. 'He came in an hour ago. His ship was set on fire and sunk by an air attack. We've had a number of casualties, mostly burns. They're very extensive, I'm afraid, but he knew you were here and he's been asking for you. He's a member of your family, I believe.'

'My *family*?' Thursday began, and moved towards the bed, her eyes on the swathed figure lying there so still beneath the mosquito net. She stared for a moment, bewildered, then her hand flew to her mouth and she gave a gasp that was almost a tiny scream. 'Oh! Oh!' And then she fell silent, the tears falling thick and fast down her ashen cheeks as she dropped to her knees beside the iron bed.

Elsie's head came round the ward door. 'Thursday? You all

right?' She too looked at the injured man. 'Who is it? Can you recognise him?'

Thursday nodded, her hands covering her face, the tears seeping between her fingers. 'Yes, I can.'

Elsie tiptoed in. She cast another brief glance at the still figure and slid her arms around Thursday's shoulders. 'Who it is? It's not Dr Kirkpatrick, is it?'

'No,' Thursday said, taking her hands away from her face. She felt for a handkerchief and held it against her streaming eyes. 'No, it's not Connor.' She felt a huge wave of relief, followed almost at once by a surge of guilt. She looked up into Elsie's face. 'It's my young cousin's husband, Vic. I didn't even know he was in the Med. I don't suppose Dizzy did either. Oh, Elsie, it's *Vic* . . .'

She stayed by his bed all that night. Mark sat with her, his hand in hers as they watched over the young man who lay there, covered in dressings, a saline drip in his arm to replace the vital fluids he had lost. Thursday gazed at him, her heart filled with pity. Even if he lived, she thought, he would be badly scarred. And she thought of her young cousin, Denise, only just turned eighteen years old, who had defied her parents to marry him two short years ago. Eighteen years old, with a baby of eighteen months, and perhaps before the dawning of her second wedding anniversary, in only a few days' time, she would be a widow.

'It isn't fair,' she said, breaking into tears again. 'It isn't *fair*.'

The figure on the bed stirred, turning its head with difficulty. The burned lips parted and a cracked, almost unintelligible voice whispered her name. 'Thursday? Thursday, is that you?'

She leaned closer, controlling her tears. 'Yes, it's me, Vic. Thursday. Can you hear me?'

'Thursday,' he breathed again. 'Thursday . . .'

She glanced at Mark. 'I don't know if he can hear me.'

'Thursday,' the whisper came again, more insistently. 'I – can hear – Thursday.'

'Oh, Vic. Vic.' She touched his hand, the only unblistered part of him that she could find. 'Vic, you're going to be all right. You are. You're safe now, in hospital, and we'll look after you. *I'll* look after you. We'll patch you up and send you back to Denise as soon as we can. You're going to be all right, I promise, and you're going home to Denise.'

'Dizzy,' he whispered. 'Home to Dizzy.' There was a pause. 'And Leslie. Our Leslie. God, Thursday, don't let me die. Promise you won't let me die.'

'I won't,' she said, and felt the strength of her determination, willing it to flow through her fingers to his. 'I *won't* let you die.'

On that same day, Thursday's twenty-fourth birthday, the Germans marched into Vichy France 'to protect it from Allied invasion' and in the space of twenty-four hours had taken control of almost the entire territory. In Russia, they launched another offensive against the bombed and ruined city of Stalingrad. But in Libya, the Eighth Army, which had sent Rommel on the run, took Bardia without firing a single shot; in the Indian Ocean two Japanese ships were sunk by an Indian minesweeper, and in Papua, New Guinea, the Australian forces killed six hundred Japanese and took the town of Oivi.

The war surged back and forth, sometimes one side winning, sometimes the other. As Mr Churchill had said, it was not the end, nor anywhere close to it.

Sister came in just before the morning duty was due to come on. She laid her hand on Thursday's shoulder. 'You'd better go and get some sleep now, Tilford. You've done wonders to get him through the night. I never thought he'd make it.'

Thursday turned her head stiffly and looked up at her. 'I can't leave him.'

'You must. You've got to rest. I'll stay with him now, until the day staff come on. I'll make sure he has a good special.'

'Louisa,' Thursday said, turning back to Vic. 'Can he have Louisa? Wetherby,' she added in case Sister didn't know Louisa's Christian name.

'Yes, that'll be all right.' Sister looked at Mark. 'And you ought to be going too, Dr Sangster. You're looking as white as a sheet.'

'I know.' He hesitated, glancing at Thursday, who was whispering to Vic that her friend would be here shortly to take care of him, that she'd be back as soon as she could, that he was to stay alive until she did so. 'Thursday, I have to go now. I'm on duty at noon.'

'Yes.' Together, reluctantly, they left the ward. Outside, Mark paused and laid his hands on her shoulders. 'You know what this means?'

'You're going away.'

He nodded. 'This is the last time I'll see you, Thursday. Unless . . .'

She nodded. Neither of them wanted to finish his sentence. It was like asking for bad luck, tempting Fate. She felt her tired eyes fill with tears. 'Oh, Mark.'

'I'm not asking for any promises, Thursday,' he whispered against her hair. 'You've already made one, I know. And last night, when Elsie told you there was someone asking for you, I knew what you thought. It's him you love. Really love. I know that now.' He paused again, 'but keep the little star for me, won't you, and remember me, just once in a while. And if we're meant to be together, we will be.' He kissed her. 'Goodbye, Thursday, my love. Goodbye.'

'Goodbye, Mark,' she whispered and, dazed with tears and tiredness, returned his kiss and then pushed him gently away. Through a blur of tears, she watched him walk along the corridor, and then he turned a corner and was gone.

As she walked back to the dormitory she felt light-headed with fatigue, yet tingling with a strange, febrile energy that she was sure wouldn't let her sleep. I ought to have stayed with him, she thought. I ought to have stayed beside him, holding his hand, willing him to live. Oh, Vic. Poor Vic. And Denise, and little Leslie, who wouldn't even remember his father. I can't let him die.

The other girls were hurrying to get ready for duty. They stopped as she came in, and Elsie and Louisa ran across to her, searching her face. 'How is he?'

'He's still alive. Just.' She sank on to Elsie's bed and looked at Louisa. 'You're to special him. You will keep him going, won't you? He's in a dreadful state, but Sister says that now he's got through the night there's a chance. A – a very small chance.' She buried her face in her hands and her two friends sat down one on each side of her, their arms about her shoulders. 'Oh, Louie, Elsie, it's so awful when it's someone you know. Someone in your own family . . .'

'Ssh, ssh,' they murmured, rocking her gently.

'He looks so pitiful, all wrapped up in dressings. There's hardly a bit of him that hasn't been burned. It must have been so awful on that ship. I know we've seen men just as bad before, but somehow, seeing someone you know, it all comes home to you.' She was crying now, great harsh sobs forcing their way up from deep inside. 'I mean, I *know* him. I've sat and had Christmas dinner with him, my cousin's his wife, they've got a baby . . . I can't let him die, I can't. I'd never be able to face them again.'

'Thursday, Thursday,' Louisa said, holding her close. 'You mustn't upset yourself like this. It won't be your fault. How could it be? All you can do is be with him, like you've been with all those others you sat with. And if he does die—'

'He mustn't! He can't! I can't let him!'

'He won't, of course he won't,' Louisa said soothingly. 'But if he did, at least you'd know you'd given him comfort at the last. And you could tell your cousin that.'

'I can't let him die,' Thursday moaned, shaking her head. 'I *can't* let him die.'

Elsie took charge. 'Now listen to me, Thurs. You're getting yourself all worked up, and that ain't going to help no one, least of all young Vic. Me and Louie have got to go on duty now and what *you've* got to do is get some rest. You won't be no good to man nor beast else. Lou's going to look after him, and when you wake up and go back he'll be on the mend, you see if he's not. Now let's get you into bed.' She forced Thursday gently back against the pillows and began to unbutton her dress. 'Blimey, you've been in this frock all night. And look at this pretty brooch what Dr Sangster give you. I'll put it over here, see, with the other one. No, don't worry about getting up on your own bunk, you can doss down in mine. Why, you're worn out, and no wonder. Look, Lou, she's practically asleep already. Help me get her into bed, there's a pal.'

Thursday lay back, suddenly overwhelmed with fatigue, and felt thankfulness wash over her as the two girls slipped off her petticoat and stockings and spread the cool sheet over her. She felt Elsie sponge her face with water – just as if I were a patient myself, she thought dizzily – and heard a whispered goodbye. The other girls had already left the dormitory, and when the door closed there was silence.

Eyes shut, she lay waiting for sleep, drifting in and out of a tumble of fleeting dreams and memories. Denise as a toddler who won everyone's hearts, Denise growing up, a pretty but wilful schoolgirl, Denise out at work, painting her nails with red varnish, buying lipstick, making herself look older. Denise, meeting Vic Pearce from the Post Office in secret, telling him she was eighteen, letting him make love to her. Denise, pregnant, confessing to her parents, facing her father's wrath, insisting she wanted to get married . . .

Poor Uncle Percy, Thursday thought, half conscious, half dreaming. He hadn't liked it, but that was what had happened, and they'd got married in November – 15 November, the great raid on Coventry overshadowing what muted celebrations there had been. Two years ago next Sunday, Thursday thought, jerking awake. Their second anniversary. He *mustn't* die.

She slept at last, worn out by anxiety and a day that seemed to have gone on for ever. And when she finally woke, it was to find Elsie and Louisa beside her bed, gazing down at her.

Thursday blinked at them. For a moment or two, she couldn't understand what they were doing there, nor why she was in Elsie's bunk instead of her own. Then memory flooded back and she started up.

'What is it? Why are you here? How's Vic? He's not dead?' She stared accusingly at Louisa. 'You haven't let him die – and me not there!'

'Ssh. It's all right.' Louisa reached out to touch her shoulder. 'He's not dead, Thursday. He's very, very ill, and Sister still doesn't know if he'll make it, but he's still alive and he's asking for you. We're here because we're off duty now – you've slept all day – and as soon as you're ready, you can go back on the ward. But,' the pressure of her hand increased, 'Sister says you must have something to eat first. We aren't to let you even think about going back without a good meal inside you.'

Thursday stared at her. Then she nodded and swung her legs out of the bed.

'I will. I'll have a shower, and then I'll get a meal. Then I'll go back.' She stood up and gave them both a hug. 'Thanks, Louie. Thanks, Else. You've been marvellous.'

She hurried off to the washrooms, feeling suddenly hungry and ready for something to eat. It seemed a long time since supper last night. Since the meal at the Cecil.

The Cecil! She stood beneath the cool spray, shocked by the realisation. Was it only yesterday that it had been her birthday, only last night that they had gone out together, the three of them, to celebrate? Only last night that Mark had found them there – by arrangement, she strongly suspected – and given her the star brooch? Only last night that they had driven out to the desert together and kissed under the million stars?

It seems a lifetime away, she thought, reaching for the sponge and squeezing it over her shoulders. And now he's gone. He was leaving at noon. And I may never see him again.

She closed her eyes and felt a tear trickle slowly out between her lids and down her cheek, mingling with the soapy water. At least he didn't ask me for another promise, she thought. And I didn't break the one I had already made.

Not quite.

Thursday stayed beside Vic for seven nights without taking a break, until the Army doctor was as sure as he could be that the young man would survive. 'There can never be absolute certainty,' he told Thursday just outside the ward. 'There could still be complications – heart, kidneys, further shock – but I'd say he's out of the worst of the wood. There are just a few bushes to squeeze through now.' He smiled at her. 'He's a relative of yours, I understand.'

'Yes, sir. My cousin's husband.'

'Well, he and your cousin have a great deal to thank you for, er . . .'

'Tilford, sir.'

'Tilford. Yes. Sister's told me you've nursed him devotedly. She says he would certainly not have come this far without your dedication. We didn't expect him to come through the first night, you know.'

'No, sir, I know.'

'It makes a lot of difference,' he said, 'if a patient has someone beside him, someone who cares. Even if the patient dies, the death itself seems to be easier in some way. I suppose that's why a priest can be so helpful, even if the man isn't religious. But to have someone like you – someone who seems able to give strength as well as comfort,' he patted her shoulder, 'well, it's a great gift, Tilford. A very valuable gift.'

Thursday bit her lip and looked down. She felt suddenly close to tears, and desperately tired. For a week she had spent every spare off-duty moment, as well as all her duty hours, beside Vic's bed, holding his hand, talking to him, telling him everything she could think of about Denise – how she'd been like a fairy child, so small and delicate, how she'd enchanted everyone she met, how she'd grown up able to twist the whole family round her finger – even her father. Until . . . but Thursday had veered away hastily from what had happened after she met Vic. Instead, she'd begun to tell him about her own family, about Steve and Jenny, about her own days as a tailor's apprentice, about her little dog Patch and Auntie Maudie's Jack Russell, Nipper, and Snowy the stately white Persian cat.

On and on she talked, her voice no more than a soft murmur, repeating the same stories over and over again as the nights wore on. She believed and hoped that they kept Vic's brain alive, that as long as she could hold his attention he wouldn't die. He wouldn't want to die. And the longer she kept him alive, the better chance his body had of healing itself, of mending the ravaged flesh.

Sometimes he slept, and she sat quietly, still holding his hand, watching his face for any sign of a change. Gradually, his sleep became more peaceful, more healing, and she knew that her strategy was working. He was staying alive. He was getting better.

On the first morning, she had asked Elsie to go into town to send a telegram to Denise to tell her that Vic was here. After that, she wrote letters every day, telling her cousin of his progress, constantly assuring her of her determination that he would get better, that he would come home again. She didn't tell her how badly burned he was, nor that if he did recover his face and body would be badly scarred. That could come later. For now, it would be enough for Denise to know that he was here and being cared for.

The plague epidemic was almost over. Two Basutos had died and one nurse, but everyone else seemed to be recovering. And then another patient went down with the disease, and the VADs were shocked to learn that it was Priscilla.

'*Prissy!*' Elsie said, running into the mess one suppertime to tell the others. 'We heard this morning. It's awful. I mean, she was vaccinated and everything. I can't believe it.' Tears ran down her cheeks and she sat suddenly on the nearest chair. 'Poor, *poor* Prissy.'

'She'll get better,' Thursday said, wishing she felt sure of it. She'd been eating her supper as quickly as possible so as to go on duty with Vic. 'The others have, haven't they?'

'Not all of them. There was that QARMN, she died.' Elsie stared up at them, her mouth working. 'I can't bear to think about it. Our Prissy, all covered in black lumps. They bleed and ooze pus and—'

'Don't!' Thursday cried, covering her ears. 'It's horrible, *horrible*. She's so pretty. Elsie, she's got to get better, she's got to.'

'Of course she'll get better,' Louisa said. 'Of course she will.'

They stared at each other. Bubonic plague. It was one of the most frightening diseases they had ever heard of. It could kill within days, and not everyone did get better, even if they'd been vaccinated.

'She's engaged too,' Elsie said miserably. 'Quentin.' For once, she spoke the name without trying to sound funny. 'Shouldn't we inform him? I don't even know what ship he's on.'

'I expect Sister knows,' Louisa said. 'They took all our family details when we arrived, didn't they? I told her about Andrew, so she'll know about Quentin.'

Thursday stood up. 'I've got to go on duty. Vic'll be waiting for me. Elsie, you'll let me know if anything happens, won't you?'

'Course I will,' Elsie said. 'She'll be OK in a day or two, Thurs, don't you fret.' But her normally cheerful voice was subdued and she brushed her hand across her eyes again.

Thursday hurried back to the ward, praying that she was right. The thought of that pretty face with its cloud of spun-gold hair, blackened by the plague, the image of those slender arms and legs swollen by buboes, were too horrible to contemplate, yet she couldn't dismiss them from her mind. I've got to though, she thought. I've got to stop thinking about Priscilla and concentrate on Vic. Like the doctor said, he's not completely out of the wood yet. And it's up to me to get him better, for Denise and Leslie.

Vic was sitting up in bed when she came through the door, his dark curls falling over his eyes. His blisters were healing and new skin beginning to form; it seemed that the burns hadn't been so deep as was first thought, although he would certainly be scarred and would not be sent back to the fighting. Instead, once recovered, he would be given support work behind the lines.

As soon as she came in, he began to make his presence felt.

'Time you washed out some of these bandages, Thursday. I've

had this one on since yesterday. Where's that other nice girl, the one who looked after me during the day? Louie, that's the one I mean. She didn't bully me like you do. Always making me wash when I don't want to and sleep when I'm wide awake, and waking me up to give me that horrible medicine. I don't know why I had to fetch up in a ward with my cousin-in-law, I really don't.'

'It's a judgement on you,' Thursday told him briskly, sweeping under his bed. They had developed an easy, bantering relationship, far removed from the deep, anxious bond that had been formed during the early days and which was still there, hidden beneath their teasing. 'And if you don't behave yourself I'll write and tell Denise. She'll have something to say, I can tell you!'

'Go on, she worships the ground I walk on,' he said lightly, and Thursday stopped what she was doing and looked at him.

'Yes,' she said slowly, 'I believe she does.'

There was a moment's silence. Then Vic said quietly, 'And I think the same of her too, you know. I wasn't sure to begin with – I mean, I knew I fancied her a lot, I didn't want any other girl while we were going out together – but when she told me about the baby I was proper shaken. I didn't know what to do. I'd never thought of getting married, not then. And later, when I found out how old she was and thought I might get the police after me, might even get sent to prison – well, I was in a muck sweat. I nearly cut and run, only there was nowhere to run to. And there didn't seem to be anything else to do but get married. It was a proper mess, I don't mind telling you.'

'Yes,' Thursday said, 'it was.'

'And then, when we did get married, living with her mum and dad – it wasn't easy. Not until the day we heard Leslie had been killed.' He paused. 'I was the first one home that day – found her mum in a proper state. After that, it seems awful to say it, but things were a bit better. And then when little Les was born and Dizzy's dad come round to him – well, it all seemed different. And I never thought no more about being trapped or anything like that. Dizzy was my wife and we had a kid, and everything seemed all right after all.' He paused. 'And then I got me papers and got put in the Army, and that was it. Basic training, and then off. I haven't seen her or the kiddy since.' He bit his lips, healed now but pulled a little to one side by the puckering scar that crinkled the whole of one cheek. 'It's all I want,' he said in a low voice, 'just to get home to my wife and kiddy and be a proper family. Get our own place – couple of rooms somewhere, maybe a little house later on – and be a family. Because that's what it's all about, isn't it?' He waved a hand. 'All this fighting and suchlike – it's all about people living ordinary lives, with their families. Isn't it?'

'Yes,' Thursday said, staring at him. 'Yes, that's what it's all about.'

She went on with her sweeping. Families. That was what it was all about – freeing the world so that ordinary people could live peaceful lives with their families.

A simple enough wish. Or so you might think.

Priscilla died the next day. The disease had rampaged through her body, and she had had no chance. The girls clung to each other, weeping, and the entire unit was stunned with grief.

'It's so unfair,' Thursday said. 'She was young and pretty – she had everything to live for. I just don't see why it had to happen.'

'Life isn't fair,' Elsie said bitterly. 'Didn't no one ever tell you that?'

'But Priscilla . . .'

'Listen, we all think that, don't we? What about your Mike? And your Cousin Leslie, shot down in the Battle of Britain? And our Dave?' she added in a lower tone. 'They had everything to live for too, and they were young even if they weren't pretty.'

'I know,' Thursday said, 'but they all died because of the war. That could happen to any of us. But Prissy – getting that horrible disease. Well, it seems different, somehow.'

They were silent. Then Louisa said, 'What about the funeral, Elsie?'

'It's tomorrow. We can't even go – it's got to be in a special place, out in the desert.' Elsie shook her head. 'But there's going to be a service for her next week, in the English church. We can all go, and Sister says we can choose one of the hymns.' Her voice trembled. 'I thought – I thought perhaps "All Things Bright And Beautiful".'

'Bright and beautiful,' Thursday said quietly. 'That's exactly what she was. Yes, Elsie. Let's have that at her service.'

Priscilla was the last person to catch the plague and the service in her memory was the last to be held for its victims. Every nurse, VAD and doctor who could be spared attended, and when they sang the hymn that the girls had chosen, every eye brimmed with tears. Afterwards, the wards were subdued for a day or two and then gradually returned to normal. As the priest who had officiated quoted, 'In the midst of life, we are in death' – but life must, nevertheless, go on.

'Poor Prissy,' Elsie said as they walked in the hospital grounds. 'We didn't know her long, and we laughed at her a bit but she was a smashing girl. It's awful that she should die like that.'

Louisa nodded. 'I'm writing to her people. And Quentin. I'll go and see them when we go home, too. Tell them about some of the times we had together.' She sighed. 'Well, at least it's over for her. She doesn't have to suffer any more.'

It was a poor comfort, Thursday thought, but all they had. And it had been quick, too. But she could not forget the cruelty of it – the cruelty of such a death, come needlessly, a death that Priscilla herself could have avoided by simply not volunteering. 'She was a heroine,' she said quietly. 'Just as much as if she'd been fighting. She deserves a medal.'

Vic's improvement continued. Sooner than Thursday had dared to hope, he was being discharged and returning to his regiment. His left arm was damaged and nothing could be done about his scars, but he was in better shape than many who left the hospital and when he said goodbye to Thursday he held her tightly.

'We never knew each other all that well back home,' he muttered. 'Never had much time, did we? But I reckon we know each other pretty well now. Know things none of the rest of the family do, eh?' He tried to grin, but his mouth twisted and Thursday felt tears sting her eyes. 'I reckon you've been more than an in-law to me, Thurs. More than a cousin, too. More like a sister – a real, good sister.'

'I'm just glad I was here, Vic,' she said, hugging him in return. 'I'm glad I was able to be with you, especially in that first week or two.'

'I tell you what, if you hadn't been I don't reckon I'd be here now. It was you kept me going, Thursday. All that talking you did, about Dizzy and the family and all that – I couldn't slip away, even if I'd wanted to.' He thought for a moment. 'I did want to, you know, when they first brought me in. I didn't think I could take it, you see.

And then I found out where I was, and somehow or other I remembered you were here in the 64th, and I asked if you were around. I wanted to give you a message for Dizzy, tell her I loved her, and then I was going to just hand in my dinner-pail, as they say. Close my eyes and say bye-bye. But you wouldn't let me. Kept on and on at me – "you're not going to die, you're going to be all right, I won't let you die" – and making me want to stay alive so I could go home again, and be with Diz and the kiddy.' He looked into Thursday's wet eyes. 'That's all I want now – to be back home with my family – and it's all because of you, Thursday. You're a heroine, that's what you are.'

'For God's sake, stop blathering and go!' Elsie's voice broke in from behind them. 'You're making her even more big-headed than she is already! We've got to live with her, remember.' She gave Vic an affectionate wallop on his backside. 'Go on, get out of here before we find something else wrong with you.'

Thursday laughed, and Vic grinned and gave Elsie a smacking kiss. 'If I wasn't already spoken for, I might have tried my luck with you,' he told her. 'I always did like the brassy blonde ones.' He shouldered his kitbag and gave them both a salute. 'And remember me to Louie too. I said goodbye to her last night, but she said she might nip out for a minute if she could. I expect she's busy.'

'Yes,' Thursday said. 'I expect she is.' She stood with Elsie and watched him march off down the drive, between its avenue of date palms, and sighed. 'Well, there he goes. At least he won't be fighting any more, but – well, I wonder if he will survive to go back home, Elsie. Nobody knows for certain, do they? Even we don't know what's around the corner for us.'

'And that's probably just as well,' Elsie said bracingly. 'Come on, Thurs – back to work. I'm only over here because I managed to wangle a message to the labs. If I'm not back in two ticks, I'll be jankered!'

Thursday smiled at her. 'And so will I. But the first thing I'm going to do when I come off duty is write to Denise and tell her that Vic's been discharged. You know, I don't think she's ever realised how near to dying he was.' She paused, then added quietly, 'I don't think she ever will.'

Chapter Sixteen

When *it's the right one.* The words had come back into Thursday's mind over and over again as she settled back into Haslar during the tumultuous summer of 1944. Connor was the right one, she was certain of it, she *knew* it – and yet . . . And yet there was that other face in her mind, that dark, thin face with the teasing eyes that seemed to see and to know so much. No, she thought, no. I've put Mark Sangster out of my mind. We've said goodbye. He's not coming back for me, and I'll never see him again.

And now, almost two years after they had said goodbye, here he was at Haslar, where she had never dreamed he might come, lying on a trolley and waiting to go into the operating theatre – a casualty of Market Garden, looking to her for comfort.

And still able, with one glance from those dark eyes, to turn her heart over in her breast.

Mark's wounds had looked worse than they were. The gash on his cheek would leave a scar for life – not the ugly puckering that Vic and so many others had been left with, but a thin white line that would probably even enhance his looks. The kind of romantic scar that a Regency buck might have received in a duel, Thursday thought, gazing at him as Surgeon Commander Sharp sewed up the final stitches and straightened himself. There were other cuts and some deep grazes, and he'd broken his arm again – the same one as before – and a couple of ribs, but in a few weeks he would be healed and ready to go back into action. Like a cat, he seemed to have nine lives.

'I can't believe he's here,' Elsie said when she told them. 'I'd have thought he'd be in Italy. What on earth was he doing in France?'

'Wasn't he in the Parachute Regiment?' Louisa asked. 'Perhaps he went over to help bring people back from Arnhem.'

'I suppose he must have done.' Thursday thought of the stories she had heard, of paratroopers shot down as they descended, hanging in trees, impaled on wire fences. She put her hands over her face, fighting the sudden sickness. 'Oh, *Mark* . . .'

The others glanced at each other. Louisa reached out and laid her hand on Thursday's arm and Elsie put her arm around her. Their concern brought tears flooding from her eyes and dripping between her fingers. She drew in a long, shuddering sob. 'Sorry.'

'It's reaction,' Elsie said. 'Reaction' was what they always said when someone broke down unexpectedly. It didn't have to be a reaction to something that had only just happened – everyone knew that it could be delayed, especially if there were a lot of other things going on. But when it was all over and there was time to breathe again, people often did break down. 'We've all been working flat out ever since we got back. And it must've been a shock, seeing him like that with no warning.'

'It was just *thinking* of him, parachuting down and being shot or caught on barbed wire,' Thursday said shakily. 'We've heard such awful things – I just couldn't bear it.'

Elsie and Louisa glanced at each other again. 'He's here now,' Louisa said gently. 'You don't have to worry, Thursday. He's safe.'

'I know. I know. And he isn't even very badly injured.' She took her hands away from her face and gazed at them through still streaming eyes. 'I don't know why I'm behaving like this. I haven't heard from him for nearly two years. I haven't even *thought* of him. Well,' she added honestly, 'I've tried not to. And I never expected to see him again. So why am I crying because he's here? When he's not even badly wounded? Why?'

Elsie looked as if she could have answered that but chose not to. She bit her lip and glanced at Louisa again. Louisa shook her head very slightly. 'It's just because it was so unexpected, Thursday. And you were fond of him, you know. There's nothing wrong in that.'

'Isn't there?' Thursday asked. 'Even when it makes me cry like this – when I can't bear to think of him out there, hanging on some barbed-wire fence, being machine-gunned by German soldiers, bleeding to death and *me not there?*' She stared at them, white-faced. 'I haven't seen him for two years – we said goodbye – I never expected to see him again, and yet when I do, I break down like a lovesick schoolgirl! Because that's what I am – *lovesick*. And I shouldn't be. I've got Connor. Why should I be crying like this over someone else? I've no right to!'

'We can't help who we cry for,' Louisa began, but Thursday shook her head violently.

'We can! We *can*! I wouldn't be like this over Mark if I really loved Connor, I couldn't be.' She waved her hands in despair, then ran them through her brown hair. 'But I do love him, I *do*! I don't understand it!'

Louisa touched her arm again. 'Don't try, Thursday. You've had a shock and it's brought it all back to you. And you've been working hard all day, for weeks now. Elsie's right – we all need a break. You'll feel better when you've had a bit of time off; it'll help you get things back into perspective.'

Thursday stared at her. Then she wiped her eyes with the back of her hand and shook her head again, more slowly. 'I don't think it's going to make any difference. I'm in a muddle now and I'm going to stay in a muddle.' She heaved a sigh and rubbed her hand over her forehead. 'Oh, I'm such a selfish person! Thinking about myself and my own feelings, when all the time Mark – when *all* these poor men— Oh, Elsie!' She broke off and covered her face again, her shoulders shaking. 'Oh, Lou!'

The two friends sat close to her, their arms about her. Over her head, they exchanged silent messages. It was natural, Elsie's eyes said. Thursday was worn out and seeing Dr Sangster had been just the last straw. It didn't really mean anything. She needed a rest, a bit of time at home with her family. Once she'd had that, she'd be herself again, loyal and strong, keeping her promise to Connor Kirkpatrick and looking forward only to his return.

Louisa read the message and sighed. She'd seen the look on Thursday's face after she'd said goodbye to Mark in the desert; she'd seen the longing there and the shadows in her eyes over the past two years, and she'd known that they weren't always for Connor.

It would have been better, she reflected, if Mark Sangster had never come to Haslar.

Thursday dithered for almost a whole day before going to see Mark in his ward. He'd been weaker than expected from his injuries and took some time to recover from the anaesthetic. Ellen Bridges, who was specialling him, told Thursday that he was thought to have been out in the open for some time before being found.

'Has he asked about me at all?' Thursday enquired, trying to appear casual. 'Only he was conscious when he came into theatre and I think he recognised me. I just wondered if he remembered it.'

'Oh, is that what he's been on about?' Ellen said with a grin. 'We thought he'd got a date next Thursday! Keeps on and on, he does. You'd better go and see him, he's driving us all mad.'

Thursday gave her a suspicious look, not sure whether the other girls had told Ellen about her relationship with Mark, but Ellen met her eyes with total guilelessness. The trouble with Ellen was, you never knew when that straight face was real and when it wasn't. But she didn't think Elsie or Louisa would have gossiped.

'He seems a real nice bloke,' Ellen said innocently. 'Ever so good-looking, too. If it was me he was asking for I'd be there like a shot.'

'Well, I'm afraid he'll have to wait,' Thursday said aloofly. 'I can't visit him yet, I've promised to go with Elsie this afternoon to see her mum. I might pop in tonight before I go on duty.'

Ellen sighed. 'I'll tell him. Maybe he'll give me a chance instead.' She rolled her eyes. 'He was saying something about dinner at the Savoy. Not over in Southsea – there's one in London, he says, proper posh.'

Thursday gave her a look of exasperation. 'You're having me on, I know you are! He hasn't said any such thing, and if he does you might as well accept the invitation, because I'm not going to!'

Ellen laughed, and Thursday gave her another look and marched away. Ellen Bridges knew a good deal more than she was letting on, she thought, and if Elsie and Louisa hadn't told her, there was only one other person who could have done. She wondered just what he'd been saying, either when he was still under the anaesthetic and rambling a bit, or when he'd come round.

Elsie's mother was staying with her own mother in Gosport. The old lady lived close to the railway line in a maze of tiny streets. Thursday had often gone to visit the family when they lived in Portsmouth, before the house was bombed and Elsie's brother Dave killed, and had been to her grandmother's house for Christmas dinner soon after, but she'd only managed one visit since returning from Egypt. She cycled beside Elsie along the Avenue and then past the cemetery, turning off just before the slope of the railway arch.

'The only hill in Gosport, that is,' Elsie remarked. 'Dunno why it's called Ann's Hill, or who Ann was. Not much of a hill anyway, but then what d'you expect of Turktown?'

Thursday grinned. As a 'Pompey' girl, Elsie never missed an opportunity to disparage Gosport. Portsmouth people, she'd found, had no time for the smaller town on the other side of the harbour and knew very little about it. Most of them had been across on the ferry at some time and walked up the High Street and, finding no bigger shops than a rather small Woolworths and Littlewoods, had turned and walked back, wondering why they'd wasted their time. Few had ventured as far as Stokes Bay or even Lee-on-the-Solent – why should they, when they had Southsea on their doorstep? – and parts like Rowner, Brockhurst and even Alverstoke might as well have been in a foreign land.

'Doesn't bother us,' Gosport people said, shrugging. 'We can go over to Pompey any time.' And they did, to work, shop, go to the cinema – even though Gosport had three of its own – or to dance. Gosport, with all its fortifications and moats, was left mostly to the Army, the Navy and the Marines – a garrison town.

Thursday rather liked it. When she had first come here she'd been fascinated by the redbrick forts and moats that surrounded the town and enraptured by the sea which turned up in unexpected places, reaching creeks like long fingers right into what looked like ordinary little backstreets far from the shore. You could walk past a row of plain little workman's houses and find yourself suddenly faced with the bobbing masts of a cluster of sailing boats and dinghies. The harbour too was always bustling with ships, with a spectacular view of Portsmouth from the ferry approach: the masts and black rigging of HMS *Victory*, Nelson's flagship, just visible in its dry dock in Portsmouth dockyard, and the square tower of the cathedral tucked behind the rounded bastion of the sallyport, to remind everyone of a glorious past.

'How's Eddy?' she asked as they turned the corner into the little cul de sac where Elsie's grandmother lived. 'Are your mum and dad going to let him come home soon?'

Elsie made a face. 'Not just yet. You can't blame them – not after losing Dave the way they did. He's safer out in the country, Mum says, and I reckon she's right. It might look as if we're winning, but I reckon Hitler's still got a trick or two up his sleeve.'

They propped their bikes against the garden wall and went into the cottage. It was tiny inside, with two small rooms downstairs, two bedrooms above and a scullery tacked on to the back. The lavatory was outside, beyond the scullery, but at least it was a flushing one – at the bottom of the garden was a small wooden hut that had once housed a bucket under a plank of wood with a hole cut in it. Thursday shuddered at the thought of creeping down there at night with a candle. No wonder they'd all kept chamber pots under their beds.

Old Mrs Jenkins was in a chair beside the fireplace, and Mrs Jackson was out in the scullery mixing up a cake. She popped out as soon as she heard the door, her face lighting up. She looked thinner than Thursday remembered her, her cheeks drawn and her eyes shadowed. She still hadn't got over losing her elder son Dave, who had been killed in an air raid as he went up to the house to make cocoa for the family in the Anderson shelter at the bottom of the garden. And she'd been separated from her younger son since then too, sent out to safety in the country. No wonder she looked so unhappy.

However, she was obviously delighted to see her daughter, and pleased to see Thursday as well. She hugged her and then held her away, examining her face. 'You're looking well, Thursday, but you've got thin. Are they feeding you right?'

Thursday laughed. 'I eat like a horse! We all do. It's the hard work that keeps us slim.'

'Well, it don't seem to have done much for our Elsie,' Mrs Jackson said, looking at her daughter's ample figure. 'Perhaps she doesn't work like you do.'

'I flipping well do!' Elsie exclaimed, dipping her finger in the bowl of cake mixture. 'It's just the way I am and always will be. Pleasantly plump.'

'Yes, and you'll be a lot plumper if you eat all that cake mixture before it's even baked,' her mother said, snatching the bowl away. 'There's half our egg ration in that bowl, I'll have you know. Sit down and talk to your gran while I make a cup of tea and I *might* find a couple of broken biscuits in the tin.'

Elsie grinned and plonked herself down in a kitchen chair beside her grandmother, while Thursday lifted the old tabby cat out of the second armchair on the other side of the small fireplace and sat down with him on her lap. Elsie took the shrunken old hand in hers and stroked it gently. 'How are you, Gran? Is our Mum looking after you properly?'

The faded eyes, once cornflower blue like Elsie's, were weak and rheumy and had lost most of their sight, and the old lady's face was a mass of deep wrinkles but her smile lit her whole face. 'Is that our Else? Marge told me you were coming. Brought that nice friend of yours with you, have you? Monday, or whatever her name is?'

'Thursday,' Elsie said with a grin. 'Yes, she's here, sitting right opposite you with old Tibby on her knee. We came over on our bikes.'

'On your bikes? I'd have liked a bike when I was a girl, but all you could get then was either penny-farthings or side-saddle, like horses, and my dad said they were too dangerous for ladies. Your ma had a bike though, went all over the place on it, she did. Dad said they were an abomination. He didn't reckon it was right, young girls being able to go out like that and their parents never knowing where they was.'

'And where d'you reckon she did go, then?' Elsie asked, winking at Thursday. 'Off after the boys, was she?'

'Elsie Jackson! What a thing to say about your own mother.' The cracked old voice tightened with glee. 'Mind you, she was one for the lads, I can't say she wasn't. Gave your grandad and me a few worries, I don't mind telling you.'

'I hope you're not telling those girls any of your daft stories,' Mrs Jackson called from the scullery. 'Don't you believe a word she says, you two. She's wandering.'

'Not as much as you used to, by all accounts,' Elsie retorted. 'I've heard all about it – off on your bike down by St. George's, sparking with soldiers.'

'*Elsie*! How dare you talk like that! I don't know what's got into you since you joined the VADs, you've lost all respect.' Thursday heard the oven door open and close. 'There, that's the sponge in the oven, and now we'll have a cup of tea and I'll see if I can get some better sense out of Thursday here. Honestly, Thursday, I thought when our Elsie brought you home that you might be able to have a bit of influence on her, but it don't seem as if you have. I only hope she's not leading you into her bad ways.' She came through the door, wiping floury hands on her apron. 'Get the biscuit tin out, Else, will you.'

'Thursday doesn't need leading into bad ways,' Elsie said, getting up to open the door of the cupboard by the fireplace. 'She's got enough of her own. One of her old flames turned up at Haslar a day or two ago.'

'Elsie!' Thursday protested, blushing.

'Well, it's true. You had quite a thing going with Dr Sangster out in Egypt. Remember your birthday? You never did tell me and Lou just what went on after we made ourselves scarce.'

'No, and I'm not going to either,' Thursday retorted. 'Not till you spill the beans about that sailor you were dancing with at the Pier the other week. *I've* seen the letters arriving.'

'I can't help it if he writes to me,' Elsie said with some dignity, her blush almost as deep as Thursday's.

'You can help writing back though!' Thursday turned to Mrs Jackson who was setting teacups out on the little table. 'How's Eddy? He must be getting on for twelve now, isn't he?'

'Twelve in November, and shooting up. I'm hoping he'll be home for Christmas, though it'll be a bit of a squeeze. Not that I'll mind that – I miss him something chronic, I don't mind telling you. Elsie's told you we're living over here permanent now, hasn't she? That place they gave us in Pompey after we were bombed wasn't up to much and what with Mum being on her own here and not getting any younger it seemed the sensible thing to do.' She glanced around the tiny room and made a rueful face. 'Never thought I'd end up back here, not after what we had in Copnor. Here's your tea, Thursday.'

'Thanks. Is this where you lived when you were a child, then? I never realised.'

'Oh yes, Gosport girl born and bred, went to Brockhurst School as a kiddy. I worked down Lipton's in the High Street when I left school, and then I met my Bert at a dance and when we got engaged we started looking for a place in Pompey. Couple of rooms in Fratton, that's where we started, till we decided to go in for a house of our own.' She shook her head. 'Not many people bought their own place in those days. Millstone round your neck, that's what

Bert's mates told him, but he wouldn't take any notice, and I was so proud when we moved in, even though money was tight. And now it's gone, smashed to bits, not a thing left. It makes you wonder if it was all worth it.'

'But you'll get some sort of compensation, won't you?' Thursday asked, taking a broken biscuit from the tin Elsie was holding out. 'Insurance or something?'

'Oh yes, but is it going to buy us another place once the war's over? Nobody can tell us that. There's been so many places lost, see, and thousands needing new homes. I don't know how they're going to get them all built in time.' She shook her head again. 'No, I reckon we'll be here for a few years yet. Now look, Mum, I'm putting your tea here on the shelf beside you. Don't try to drink it yet, it's hot.'

'Any apples on the tree?' Elsie asked, her mouth full of biscuit. She turned to Thursday, grinning. 'I brought one of my friends over here for tea with Gran once when I was about nine. Grandad said we could pick up the windfalls to take home, and there were so many we didn't know how to carry them. We wanted to take as many as we could, but we didn't want Grandad telling us off for being greedy, so guess what we did.'

'What?' Thursday asked obediently.

'Stuffed 'em into our knickers! It's surprising how many pounds of apples you could get into those navy-blue bloomers – so long as the elastic holds! We got so many in we could hardly walk, and when we went indoors with half a dozen each in our hands Grandad could hardly keep a straight face. He knew very well what we'd done – not that we realised that, of course. We really thought we'd got away with it as we waddled off up the road. I reckon he and Gran must've split their sides laughing as soon as we got outside the door.'

'I remember that,' old Mrs Jenkins piped up. 'I never saw my Alf laugh so much in all my life. I thought he'd choke himself, I really did.'

Mrs Jackson stared at them. 'You mean you came all the way back on the ferry and the bus like that?'

'No, we fetched 'em out when we got round the corner and carried them in our pinnies. And we ate some on the way, of course.'

'And then you brought them home and put them in the bowl? Without even washing them? And we ate them – after they'd been in your *knickers*?' Mrs Jackson looked so appalled that Thursday burst out laughing, and Elsie grinned.

'It doesn't seem to have done you any harm,' she pointed out. 'Anyway, I promise not to do it again, if you let me and Thursday take some back with us.'

'Well, I should hope not indeed! And of course you can take some with you. I'm sure Thursday knows better than to stuff them into her knickers.' She turned to Thursday. 'And when are you going to be able to go home again? I suppose you haven't had any leave since you got back from Egypt.'

'Well, only the first few days. What with D-Day and then Market Garden the hospital's been at full stretch. But I'm hoping to have some time off in a week or two.'

'You could take Mark with you,' Elsie suggested slyly. 'Introduce him to the folks.'

Thursday turned on her. 'Don't be ridiculous! You know perfectly well I won't do any such thing. All that's over – he doesn't mean a thing to me any more. He never did, not really. We were just friends, you *know* we were. And I haven't even seen him, not since he came into the theatre . . .' She floundered to a stop, her face pink, and Mrs Jackson glanced at her shrewdly and picked up the teapot.

'I'll just freshen this up a bit. You'd like another cup, wouldn't you, love? And another biscuit, if our Elsie hasn't wolfed them all.'

Thursday took a breath and subsided. She gave Elsie an apologetic grin.

'Sorry, Else. I didn't mean to blow up like that.'

'That's all right,' Elsie said. 'It was a daft thing to say.' But the look in her eyes said something different, and Thursday saw it and knew.

She'd flared up like that before when Mark's name was mentioned. His return had brought it all back to her – the nights in the ward, the gharry ride through the darkness of the desert night. And the burning in her heart as his lips touched hers.

Chapter Seventeen

It was late in the evening and the ward was quiet. Thursday trod softly so as not to disturb the patients, some of whom were already asleep; all were recovering from operations. She passed three beds and then stopped.

'Mark?'

The figure in the bed stirred and half sat up, then lay back with a grunt. Thursday was at his side at once, pressing him gently back against his pillows. 'Don't try to sit up – you're not ready for it. Oh, Mark . . .'

He lay gazing up at her. Involuntarily, she reached out one hand and touched his cheek with her forefinger. 'I couldn't believe it when I saw you on the trolley. Do you remember seeing me?'

'Remember?' he whispered huskily. 'It got me through the op. And when I came round, all I wanted was to see you.' To her horror, a tear crept from the corner of his eye and spread into a small, damp patch on the pillow. 'Oh God, this infernal weakness!'

'It's the shock,' Thursday said quietly. 'It doesn't mean anything.'

'My God, d'you think I don't know about shock? I'm a doctor, remember! And it does mean something. It means I was damned glad to see you and damned disappointed not to find you beside me when I surfaced again. Thursday, where the hell have you been?'

Thursday gazed at him. There were tears in her own eyes and she knew that when she spoke her voice would shake. 'I – I've been on duty. And then I went to see Elsie's mum.'

'You went to see Elsie's mum? When I was lying here needing you?' His voice was hoarse and she couldn't tell if he were joking or not. It was the sort of joke he would have made, back in Egypt. She realised that her hand was still on his cheek and removed it hastily, but he reached out with his good hand and snatched it back. 'Don't stop, Thursday. Please don't stop touching me. If you knew how I've longed . . .' He turned his head aside and she saw the tears again, flowing down his cheeks. 'God, it's been so long, so bloody long.'

Thursday sat very still. Her heart was jumping and her skin was hot. She gazed down at his face, noting the small changes – the crow's feet splaying out from the corners of his eyes, where he had been so long in the hot African sun, the few strands of white in his black hair. He was thinner too, his cheeks drawn into deep hollows, one sliced across by the thin, silvery scar he had acquired at El Alamein. His recent injuries had left him with his arm in plaster, just as when she'd first known him, his ribs strapped up and one ear bandaged. There were other wounds too, less serious but probably painful and uncomfortable. She stroked his cheek, her fingers tracing the scar, then slipped her hand over his, and he turned his head back and looked up at her.

'I thought I'd never see you again,' he whispered. 'That night, when your brother-in-law came in . . .'

'Cousin. My cousin's husband.'

'Right, well, when he came in and you thought it was Connor Kirkpatrick, I could see then which way you'd go when he came home.' He paused. 'Is – is he still alive?'

Thursday nodded. 'He hasn't been home yet though. I don't think he will, until the war ends.'

'Well, that may not be so long now. We're on our way, Thursday.' He paused again and Thursday glanced around, fearful that Sister might come in and tell her she must go. She'd been given permission to visit Mark, but he was tiring and she knew that she could easily be forbidden a second visit. She opened her mouth to quieten him, but he was already going on. 'That night, I told you that if we were meant to be together, we would be. And so we are. So we are.'

'Mark—'

'Don't say any more now,' he whispered, and she saw that he was drifting into sleep. 'Don't talk. Just – just stay with me and hold me. Just be here . . .'

His voice faded and she saw that his eyes were closed and he was asleep. Her tears falling fast, she lifted his hand to her mouth and laid her lips on the dry skin.

'Mark,' she whispered in the silence of the ward. 'Oh, Mark.'

As September entered its third week most of the paratroopers who had been trapped in Arnhem managed to escape across the Rhine. Over a thousand had been killed, and nearly six and a half thousand taken prisoner. After the triumph of D-Day it was a dreadful blow, yet in other parts of Europe the Allies were still pushing ahead. In Italy, the Eighth Army, whose fortunes the girls had followed at El Alamein, was thrusting its way north, liberating towns and villages as it went. In Greece, authority had been ceded to the British, and the Germans were being forced out. And on the last day of the month, the news came that the Canadians had taken Calais.

Calais! It was a sign of hope, a cause for celebration. Calais had been the closest the Germans had ever come to invading England; a mere twenty miles or so from Dover, it had been the site for the most massive mortars which had fired their shells across the narrow neck of sea. The girls hugged each other and jumped for joy, and when Thursday went to see Mark she found him sitting up, bright-eyed, waiting for her.

'You've heard the news? Calais! We're on the home straight now, my sweet.'

'Don't call me that!' she whispered, casting an anxious glance around the ward. 'You'll get me into trouble.'

He winked. 'Don't tempt me – we might frighten Sister. All right, all right,' he held up his hand, 'sorry I said that. Put it down to excitement. There are only two things I want now, and d'you know what they are?'

'No,' Thursday said cautiously.

'One,' he held up a finger, 'to get out of here and give you a thorough kissing. And two,' another finger, 'to get back over there for a final crack at those bastards. Sorry about the language, Thursday, but I'm too fired up to watch my words. My God, if I could only get out of this straitjacket,' he indicated the plaster on his arm and the strapping around his chest, 'I'd show 'em what for, I would!'

Thursday gazed at him. 'Haven't you been through enough? I'd have thought you'd be glad of a rest, somewhere safe.'

'Rest? *Safe*? Thursday, I'm a soldier! I didn't join the Army to rest and be safe. For heaven's sake, girl!'

She looked down at her lap, feeling abashed. 'Well, I know that, but surely you must wish sometimes that it was all over. The war, I mean. Don't you want peace, Mark? Do you actually *like* war?'

There was a short silence. She looked up, meeting his eyes, and after a moment he said, 'Of course I want peace. That's what we're fighting for, isn't it?'

'Is it?' she asked quietly.

Mark shifted irritably in his bed. 'Well, of course it is! For God's sake, Thursday, what do you think I am? I don't kill people – I'm a doctor, I go to save their lives. But I'm a soldier too. I can handle a gun, I can kill if I have to, and if I'm in a situation where it's me or an enemy, I kill him, because that's what I'm trained to do. But I don't go looking for people to kill. I don't *enjoy* it.'

'Not the killing, no. But you enjoy being in the thick of it all, don't you? You enjoy the excitement of it.' She frowned. 'I can see it must be exciting, in a way. I remember the air raids – they were terrifying but I felt sort of lifted up, if you know what I mean. As if I'd suddenly got more energy from somewhere, as if I could do anything.'

'That's right,' Mark said, looking at her intently. 'That's exactly what I feel. As if I could do anything.' He paused. 'And then you see what's happening all around you. The poor blighters shot down, trampled by their mates, the paratroopers machine-gunned out of the sky, the kids barely out of nappies killed before they've had time to fire a single shot. And *that's* why I want to get back, Thursday,' he said with sudden force. 'To help bring an end to it all. Yes, it's exciting, yes, more people are going to be killed – but we've got to end it, and this is the only way. What's more, we're doing it. We're *winning*. We've had some setbacks but we're overcoming them. We're ploughing up through Italy and France, we've got them on the run, we're going to win this bloody war, and the sooner the better.' He lay back against his pillows, his breathing ragged. 'And once we've done that,' he said more quietly, 'we can get back to our normal lives and I can ask you to marry me.'

Thursday stared at him. The shock seemed to hit her full in the breast. She put a shaking hand to her cheek. 'What – what did you say?' she whispered.

He met her eyes. His were very dark, the pupils wide. 'I think you heard me, Thursday.'

'No,' she gasped. 'No, you can't say that. You mustn't.' She began to rise to her feet. 'I've got to go.'

His hand shot out and gripped her wrist. 'No, you haven't. You've only been here a few minutes.' He waited while she hesitated, then slowly sat down again. 'I'm sorry, Thursday, I didn't mean to blurt it out like that. Put it down to the excitement of today's news, together with the sheer damned frustration of being trapped in this bed. And we seemed to be getting into quite a deep conversation anyway. But – well, you must have known the way I was thinking.'

She shook her head. 'No. No, I never dreamed ... Mark, you know I can't even think of it. You know I've already promised ... We're just friends, no more than that. You mustn't say such things to me.'

'Mustn't I? Why not?' His mouth tightened, like that of a child being denied a new toy. 'Don't I have the right to fall in love, Thursday? Don't I have the right to ask a girl to be my wife? *I* haven't made any promises.' He glinted a look at her. 'Nor, as I understand it, have you.'

Thursday gazed at him, wishing she'd never told him how Connor had said he didn't want to tie her down. 'I did,' she said. 'I made a promise to myself, and I want to keep it. You know that, Mark.'

'It's one of the things I love about you,' he said quietly, and she sighed and covered her face with both hands.

'Mark, please. I can't talk like this. I can't let Connor down. He's thousands of miles away. I can't tell him I don't love him any more, that I'm not going to wait for him. I can't.'

'Plenty of girls do.'

'Yes – they send a *Dear John* and break a poor man's heart when he's miles from home and can't even talk to her about it. I won't do that, Mark, I just won't.'

'But if it were true?' he asked. 'If you'd realised you didn't love him after all – if you realised you loved another man – wouldn't you *have* to do it? How could you go on writing to him, telling him lies? What does a girl like you do in that sort of situation, Thursday?'

'I don't know,' she wailed, her voice muffled.

'Perhaps,' he said, 'it's time for you to start thinking about it.'

There was a small silence. Then she lifted her hands away from her face and looked at him. 'No. No, it's not. Because I *do* love him. I love him very much, and I mean to wait for him.' She stood up, and this time he did not try to detain her. 'I don't think I'd better come to see you again, Mark. I'm sorry.' And she turned and walked away, out of the ward.

Outside, in the unexpected warmth of some mild November sunshine, she felt sick and shaky. She pressed her hand against the red bricks and felt the heat radiate into her cold palm. She leaned her head against the back of her hand, and let the tears run from her eyes and down her bare arm. Deliberately, she tried to conjure up Connor's face, his smiling blue eyes, but to her horror she couldn't put the picture together. It was as if he were swimming away from her.

'What's happening to me?' she whispered to herself. 'What's happening to our love?'

Keeping away from Mark's ward was the hardest thing Thursday had ever done. She longed to be able to go to him, but dreaded what he might say to her. He seemed so certain that they'd been meant to meet again, that they were meant to be together. Suppose he's right, she thought. Suppose there is something – someone – driving us together. But each time she found her thoughts veering in this direction, she remembered Connor and the promise she had made. I meant that promise, she thought, and I'll keep it.

She lay awake at night, trying to stop the thoughts going round and round in her head. They were there all the time, as she ate, as she washed, as she walked or talked with her friends. It was only while she was working, totally absorbed in the operations the surgeon was performing, totally concerned with the patient before her, that she was able to push them aside. Once she came off duty, they all rushed back.

'You're not eating, Thursday,' Louisa said. 'And you're looking as white as a sheet. You're not sickening for something, are you?'

Thursday shook her head. 'There's nothing the matter. I'm all right.'

Elsie and Louisa glanced at each other. 'You're letting it get you down,' Elsie said. 'Go and see him again, Thurs.'

But Thursday shook her head.

Thankful for her work in the underground theatre, she tried not to go near the block where he was, afraid that her steps would take her along that corridor and into the long room with its rows of beds. Instead, she would come up the stairs into the arched stone arcade and walk down the smooth marbled way with its iron tracks, taking the long way round to the dormitories and mess in D Block. Once, she strolled down to the jetty and stood there, gazing across the neck of the harbour towards Portsmouth Cathedral and the sallyport. There was a pinnace there, waiting to ferry people across, and the sailor standing by the wheel looked up and caught her eye.

'Waiting to go ashore, love?'

Thursday shook her head. 'Just going off duty.' It was on a pinnace from Portsmouth that she had first spoken to Connor. 'I wanted a breath of fresh air – I've been down below all night. It's a lovely morning, isn't it?'

He nodded. 'Better make the most of it, the winter'll be setting in any day. Another Christmas with Hitler breathing down our necks. Blimey, you wonder how long it can go on, don't you.'

Thursday shrugged. 'I've almost given up thinking about it. What's the point? We won't know what to do with peace when we do get it. Five years of war. Nobody ever thought it would go on this long, did they?'

He took a packet of Player's Weights from his pocket, offering it to Thursday. She shook her head. 'You seem a bit down, love,' he said kindly. 'Had a row with the boyfriend?'

Thursday gave him a wry look. 'I wish it was that easy. No, I'm all right. Just a bit chokker.'

'We all get like that now and then,' he nodded, striking a match. 'Dare say you're tired. You'll be OK after a bit of grub and a kip.'

'Yes.' She looked again at the skyline of Portsmouth. From here, you couldn't see any of the bomb damage that she knew had laid the centre of the city to waste. The ships moored in the harbour or against the jetty were quiet. Even the sky was empty of aircraft. This is what peace will be like, she thought. Quiet. And with no dread always in your mind about what's going to happen next. We'll be able to go to dances at Southsea without wondering if there'll be a raid before we get home. We'll be able to be as sure as you ever can be that our families are safe and will be there when we go on leave.

Hang on, we won't be going on leave! We'll be home with them, if we want to be, living our own lives. Going where we please, living where we please, loving whomever we like . . .

She was swept by a sudden wave of loneliness. I've had enough of all this, she thought. I've had *enough*.

The matelot was watching her. He took the cigarette from his mouth and tapped the ash into the water.

'You know what you need, love?' he said. 'You need a spot of leave.'

'Yes,' Thursday said, and she nodded. 'You're right. That's exactly what I need.'

Madam had agreed. 'You should have had some before, but when Market Garden happened all that was put aside. However, I think we can spare you now.' Her brown eyes smiled kindly. 'Go home and have a few days' rest, Tilford. You deserve it. You've worked hard. And you're looking pale and tired. Get some good country air.'

Thursday packed her bag and caught the train from Portsmouth to Waterloo. Crossing London was another reminder of how badly the war had struck; despite the efforts of the authorities, there was still bomb damage to be seen everywhere, and now there was the threat of the V2 rockets. They'd been coming for several weeks, apparently, and the resulting explosions were blamed on the gas mains, but now the Government had admitted that they were really another form of air raid, even worse than the doodlebugs. You never knew where or when they would come.

She was thankful to be on the Worcester train at last, heading west through the Cotswolds. The signboards hadn't been replaced yet but as the train rumbled closer to Worcester she began to recognise many of the stations – Oxford, Evesham, where Patsy had come from, then Pershore – and the dull misery she had been feeling during the past week began slowly to dissipate.

Her sister Jenny was waiting on the platform. She jumped with excitement and hugged Thursday as she hauled her suitcase out of the carriage. 'Gosh, it's good to see you. How are you? You should see the dinner Mum's getting ready – I don't know where she's got half the food from. And we've got a surprise for you.'

'A surprise? What's that?'

'Well, it won't be a surprise if I tell you, will it? But you'll never guess, not in a million years.'

Thursday grinned and rose to the challenge. 'You've got engaged.'

'Oh.' Jenny looked disappointed. 'Well – yes, I have, as a matter of fact. I was going to tell you that next. But that isn't *the* surprise.'

'You mean there's something more?'

'Something *else*,' Jenny amended. 'I wouldn't say it was more, exactly.' Her grin broke out again, almost splitting her face, and she bit her lips in an attempt to control it. 'Well – yes, I suppose it is, really. I mean, it's something . . .' She closed her mouth again firmly and her eyes glinted with secrets. 'I'm not saying another word. I mustn't give it away.'

Thursday gave her an exasperated look. 'All right then, tell me about this engagement. Who is he? I didn't even know you were going steady with anyone. Have you got a ring?'

'Of course I have!' Jenny waved her left hand and they both stopped just before the barrier for Thursday to examine it. A woman behind them clicked her tongue and they moved hastily out of the way. 'Solitaire diamond, see.'

Thursday gazed at it enviously. Connor had given her the little silver crown brooch when he'd gone away, saying he wished it could have been a ring. At that moment, Thursday wished it too, with all her heart. If I had a ring on my finger, she thought, Mark would have respected it and we'd never have got into this situation. But Connor didn't want to tie me down . . .

'It's lovely,' she said wistfully as they walked out of the station. 'And what about the lucky man, then? Who is he?'

Jenny gave a little wriggle of joy. 'Well, you know him actually, quite well, in fact. You used to—'

Thursday stared at her. 'You're not going to tell me you're engaged to *Sidney*?' Not Sidney, the rather dull young man Thursday had gone around with before she'd joined the VAD. 'Jenny, you *couldn't*!'

'No, of course it's not Sidney. What on earth d'you take me for? Honestly, Thurs.'

'Well, who is it, then?' They came to the bus stop and Thursday put down her suitcase. 'Come on, Jen, don't keep me in suspense.'

'It's Charlie Harris, next door.' She looked self-conscious. 'I know it sounds daft, marrying the boy next door, but—'

'*Charlie*? But you always hated each other!'

'Well, we don't now. That was when we were kids, anyway.' Charlie had been the sort of boy who ran after girls, pulling their pigtails, and Jenny's had been particularly long and tempting. 'He's different now, honestly, Thurs.'

'So how long's this been going on? You never said a word when I came home in May.' The bus came along and they climbed aboard, squeezing Thursday's case into the little cubby-hole under the stairs and climbing up to the top deck. Jenny lit a cigarette.

'Well, we'd only just started going out then. He's in the RAF, came home on leave at Easter and asked me to go to the pictures with him, for company. We hit it off and went to a dance, and that was when it all started. Then he was in the D–Day landings – giving air cover, you know – and I was so scared he'd get killed that when it was all over and he wangled a forty-eight hour pass I told him we'd got to get married. So he bought me a ring and—'

'You mean you proposed to him?' Thursday stared at her sister, then looked up as the conductor came to collect their fares. She scrabbled in her purse for the money and waited impatiently while he punched out their tickets, then turned back to Jenny and hissed again, 'You *asked* him to marry you?'

'Well, actually I *told* him.' Jenny grinned. 'I said I wanted to know just where I stood. I wanted a ring on my finger, and I wanted to be Mrs Charles Harris. Well, we couldn't get married straight away, obviously, so we went out and got an engagement ring and we're getting married as soon as he can get leave.'

'What do Mum and Dad say about all this? And Mr and Mrs Harris?'

Jenny tossed her head. 'Doesn't matter what they say. I'll be twenty-one in December so there's not much point Dad putting his foot down now. Anyway, they're all pleased so that's OK.' She grinned. 'Mum was scared I'd meet a GI at some dance and go off to America! Lots of girls are doing that, you know.'

Thursday looked at her. Jenny had always been one to go her own way, and she'd always been able to twist her father round her little finger, too. As the eldest child, Thursday had felt that she had responsibilities – it had always been her job to look after her brother and sister. 'Take the baby with you,' her mother would say when Thursday was going out to play with her friends in the street. And Jenny or Steve would toddle out, clinging to her skirts, and be either a nuisance or an asset depending on what games the crowd wanted to play. It was always Thursday's fault if they came back dirty or with their clothes torn, as they invariably did. So Thursday had grown up burdened with a sense of responsibility which Jenny, dancing through life, didn't seem to feel.

'And if you had met a GI, I suppose that's what you'd have done,' she said. 'Swanned off to America without a backward glance. No wonder Mum's pleased you've chosen the boy next door.'

Jenny made a face at her. 'That's not a very nice thing to say, Thursday. Anyone would think I didn't care about my family.'

'Well, of course you do – I didn't mean that. But you would have, wouldn't you? You wouldn't have let anything or anyone stop you, if that's what you wanted to do.'

Jenny took a draw at her cigarette. 'No, of course not. We've got to live our own lives, Thurs, not let other people live them for us. Mum and Dad have had their lives and now we've got ours. Anyway, who's to say me and Charlie are going to stay in Worcester? We might do anything, once the war's over. Go and live in Canada or Australia – anything.'

Thursday looked out of the window. The bus was just crossing the bridge over the River Severn and she could see the great tower of the cathedral on her left. Its reflection shimmered in the smooth water and she thought of the cities that had lost similar beautiful buildings in the so-called 'Baedeker' raids in 1942, when the Germans had deliberately attacked towns that had no military significance, but were famous for their history. She thought of Coventry, not so far away from Worcester, almost razed to the ground in one night, its own cathedral no more than a shell, and thinking of Coventry reminded her of her cousin Denise, who had been married the day after that raid.

'How's Dizzy? And my godson?' she asked.

Jenny's face twitched, almost as though she were trying to suppress a sudden storm of giggles. 'Oh, they're all right. They'll be home when we get there. Everyone's coming to see you, Thursday.'

Thursday stared at her. '*Are* they? Why? I was going to go round to Auntie Flo's tomorrow – I wouldn't have thought they'd all want to trail down specially tonight.' She gave her sister another suspicious look. 'Something's going on, isn't it? This surprise you were on about – it's to do with them. It's not Vic, is it? Is he home? Surely he's in Italy with the Eighth?'

Jenny shook her head. She closed her lips firmly, but her eyes were sparkling and Thursday was sure she was right. 'I promised I wouldn't tell. You'll have to wait. Oh, *Thurs*.' She wrapped her arms around her body, hugging herself tightly. 'I can't wait to see your face!'

They were almost there. The bus trundled to a stop and the girls ran down the stairs. The conductor dragged out Thursday's suitcase and handed it down to her, and they set off for the last few hundred yards to Waterloo Street. They turned the corner and Thursday stared.

'What are all those flags doing, draped over the front of the house? They're not for me, surely! Jenny, what's going on? *Tell* me.' But once again Jenny shook her head, and Thursday quickened her steps. It must be Vic, she thought, but why was he home now, and why had Mum and Dad put all these flags up? Denise and Vic didn't live here.

'Have you got a key yet?' she asked Jenny. Thursday had had to wait for her twenty-first birthday for hers, but she couldn't believe that Jenny would have been satisfied with that, especially as her work at the Royal Infirmary would have meant coming home at all sorts of odd hours. But Jenny shook her head and she saw that the front door was standing ajar, as it always used to and, feeling her heart suddenly kick with excitement, she pushed it open and went inside.

'Here she is!' A great shout went up, and she found herself in a sea of faces and then enveloped by hugs as her family rushed forward to greet her. Laughing, kissing whoever happened to be nearest, she hugged them back and then, with her mother's arms still around her, found herself staring into a face she had thought never to see again.

It was her cousin Mike. Mike, missing believed killed at Dunkirk.

Chapter Eighteen

'*Mike!*' she whispered, and put both hands to her face. He looked very different from the way he'd been when she last saw him, four long years ago. He was thinner, older, and he'd grown a beard. But she still knew him. His eyes were the same, and when they looked into hers she found disbelief washed away by a sudden rush of incredulous joy.

'*Mike!* But you're dead!' She stared wildly round at the rest of the family. They were all watching her, both tears and smiles twisting the faces of her mother and aunt, and even her father's and uncle's eyes moist. 'Is – is it really Mike? I'm not dreaming?'

'It's me all right,' he said, giving her a hug. 'Hullo, Thursday. Good to see you again.'

'But – but they *said* you were dead!' she stammered again. 'We had a telegram. I don't understand.'

'It's a long story,' he said. 'But I'm alive and I'm here in Worcester, as you can see. And not half glad to be home, I can tell you! Anyway, haven't you got a kiss for your long-lost cousin?'

Thursday, her face streaming with tears, laid her cheek against his, feeling the roughness of his beard, the warmth of his skin. Mike, home again. It seemed impossible. She looked around at the rest of them again. They were all beaming at her, although there were still tears on her mother's face and her Aunt Flo was sobbing. Denise, with little Leslie in her arms, was wiping her eyes on the back of one hand. Jenny, who had managed to keep the secret all the way from the station, was half crying, half giggling.

'Mike,' she said wonderingly. 'It's like a miracle. But – how long – when did you come back? Why didn't anyone let me know?'

'We didn't know ourselves till yesterday,' her mother said. 'It all happened so quick, we've hardly had a chance to get used to it ourselves. Anyway, Thursday love, you sit down and I'll fetch you a cup of tea. You must be tired out after that journey.'

'Me, tired out!' she exclaimed, allowing herself to be pushed into a chair. 'What about the journey Mike's had? Where have you been?' she asked him. 'How did you manage to get home?' She put her hand to her forehead. 'I just can't seem to take it in.'

He grinned. 'I told you, it's a long story. I was left just outside Dunkirk – never even got back to the beach. Got caught in the blast from a bomb, you see, and it blew all my clothes away. Mother-naked, I was, when they picked me up. Most embarrassing moment of my life.' He grinned cheerfully and drank half his own cup of tea with one swallow.

'That's four years ago – where've you been all this time? Were you caught by the Germans? Did you escape?'

'I told you – it's a long story. I was found by a French farmer, lying in one of his fields. God knows how I got there. I was knocked about the head and dazed by the blast. Didn't even know who I was for a few days. He took me home and they put me up in the attic and looked after me until I was fit to move on. By then, they had some idea what had happened.'

'But they must have known about Dunkirk and the Germans occupying France.'

'You'd be surprised how little they did know,' he said. The family had gathered round to listen and Mary handed Thursday a cup of tea. 'Don't forget, they weren't allowed to use their wirelesses, and when the newspapers did start coming out again they were only allowed to publish what the Germans wanted them to publish. And when they realised the British had gone, they felt as if they'd been abandoned.'

'But we had no choice!' Thursday exclaimed, sitting up straight. 'What were we supposed to do, leave our boys there to be slaughtered?'

'They didn't know that,' he pointed out. 'All they knew was that the British had gone, leaving them to the Germans. A lot of French people were really upset about that.'

'I'm surprised they didn't hand you over,' Jenny said. She was sitting in her favourite spot, on the hearthrug, her legs folded under her. 'They were taking quite a risk, looking after you, weren't they?'

He nodded. 'They were risking their lives. And they weren't the only ones. But as some of them began to use their wirelesses again, secretly, and heard the BBC news, they started to see what had happened – and by then they'd come to realise what life was like under the Germans too, and – well, they began to be more keen to help us. And there were British agents getting in as well – men who were there to help us.'

'Us?' Walter asked. 'There were more of you?'

'Yes, quite a lot. Blokes who hadn't been able to get on the boats or were left in the countryside, injured or just lost. We were milling about all over the place.' He grinned. 'It was worse for those who still had their uniforms – they stood out like sore thumbs! At least my family had to give me a few bits and bobs, for decency's sake!'

'And you really were suffering from amnesia?' Jenny asked professionally. 'I mean, you didn't know who you were?'

'Not at first. Combination of shock from the blast and the bang on the head, I suppose. What I did know was that I was English – well, it was the only language I could speak, for a start! – and must be a Tommy. It didn't last long, and they didn't really want to know too much. Anyway, it was more important to get me somewhere safe and back to England.'

'But you were near the coast. Couldn't you just get a boat?' Denise frowned. 'There must have been fishing boats or things that would have brought you over.'

Mike shook his head. 'Look, the beaches were being watched day and night. Don't forget, the French had surrendered by then. They had to co-operate with the Germans. They weren't allowed to use their boats, and if they'd tried they'd have been shot. The Germans weren't going to take any chances of people coming in or out. We just might have invaded again, you know. And the Vichy Government was going along with them. It wasn't safe for the French families.' He shook his head. 'We had to go south, away from occupied France. It was our only chance of getting back home.'

'But that's an enormously long way!' Thursday exclaimed.

He nodded. 'I know. And we had to take it slowly. Me and three other blokes, we made our own way, getting lifts where we could and hiding up during the day. We used to make for the local *abbé* – the priest – when we came to a village. They were usually sympathetic and a lot of them were in touch with the local

Resistance. They could contact people who would help. We worked on farms to get food or money. I got ill the first winter – flu to start with, then pneumonia.'

'Pneumonia!' Flo exclaimed, horrified. 'I always knew you'd have chest trouble!'

'Oh, I was all right. The family I was with then kept me for three months, looking after me. I'd learned a bit of French by then, but by the time I left I could speak it like a native – local accent and all. So then I was useful, see, because I could help other blokes who were trying to get away as well. There were a lot of us left over from Dunkirk, but as time went on there were others too – airmen, shot down, who'd got away, and secret agents who were brought in to find out what was going on and help organise the Resistance movement. I stayed quite a while, working with them.'

The family was silent, listening in fascination. Thursday noticed that her Aunt Flo, sitting close beside her son, was crying quietly. What a shock this must have been for her, having her son come back from the dead. And yet, joyful though it must be, there must be pain as well in knowing that her other son, Leslie, shot down in his Spitfire, couldn't possibly come back as well.

'So what happened then, after you got better?'

Mike looked at her. 'I just kept on going south. We were making for Marseilles. There were safe houses there, and an escape line that would take us over the Pyrenees and into Spain. From there, we'd be able to get a ship to England, or maybe America. So that's what we did, in the end. It just took a hell of a long time.'

And a lot of dangerous adventures along the way, Thursday thought, gazing at him. She tried to imagine the life Mike had been leading during the past few years. Trudging through the endless, unfamiliar countryside, never really sure it was safe to accept lifts; sleeping under hedges or in barns, sometimes in the home of some brave family who were prepared to take a risk. Making cautious contact with those who worked in the Resistance, staying for months, even a year or so, to help other escaping servicemen, when all he really wanted to do was get home himself.

'Couldn't they have let us know?' Flo asked suddenly. 'I mean, just let us know you were alive? It's cruel, letting us go on thinking you were dead.'

Mike looked uncomfortable. 'I know. It upset me a lot, that did.

But they couldn't afford to let anything leak out about the safe houses, see. The people there – they were risking their lives, helping chaps like me escape. They kept them in their own homes, secretly, and if they were found out they'd be arrested. Some of them were,' he added soberly. 'They ended up in places like Buchenwald – concentration camps. They still don't know what goes on in those places, but not many people come out, I can tell you that. There was one man I knew – he and his wife sheltered hundreds of blokes before someone gave him away. He died . . . ' He bit his lip. 'Just one word in the wrong place and hundreds of others could have gone the same way, and I'd have been one of them. It had to be kept secret.'

'I don't see what difference it would have made us knowing, all the same,' Flo said resentfully. 'I've been through years of misery—'

Mike put his arm round her. 'I know, Mum. It's cruel. But war *is* cruel, see, and you know what they say – walls have ears. If someone *had* found out . . . It wasn't just soldiers – I told you, it was airmen as well, chaps who'd been shot down. They had to be got back to England; they were too valuable to lose. What we were doing – what the people who let their houses be used were doing – was really important. We just couldn't risk it being found out. And I *am* alive, and I'm back now, that's the main thing.'

Flo blew her nose and wiped her eyes. 'I suppose so. Well, of course it is.' She gave him a tremulous smile.

Mike kept his arm around her. 'And I was pretty useful by then too, because I could pass for a Frenchman with my country accent. The *abbé* got me some papers and I had a job, working as a handyman, so I could go round meeting people and taking messages between the houses, and I could keep my eyes and ears open for any problems too. There was one bloke they suspected of being a traitor. An Englishman, he was,' he added, looking angry, 'and they reckoned it was him got the poor old codger arrested. I'd like a few minutes on my own with him, I can tell you! I'd show him a thing or two.'

'These safe houses,' Walter said. 'What were they, exactly?'

'I told you – just people's homes. They'd keep blokes in a back room or an attic, somewhere that the neighbours wouldn't notice. They had to be dead quiet and never go near the window or do anything that might make people wonder. You never knew who might give you away, see. And there were all sorts of things you'd never think of that might make someone suspicious – getting enough rations was one, and getting rid of rubbish. Even flushing the lavatories too much. It was even worse once the Germans took over the south as well – the Gestapo were everywhere. They were watching all the time – they knew it was going on, see.'

'Is all this secret?' Thursday asked suddenly. 'Are you allowed to talk about it?'

Mike looked rueful. 'I've probably said more than I should. But I'm not going back – I've had trouble with my chest ever since the pneumonia.' He gave his mother a reassuring grin. 'It's not serious, Mum, you don't have to worry. But I've been a bit off-colour lately so they decided I'd better make tracks. It was tough enough coming across into Spain as it was. I had to report back to barracks of course,' he added. 'I'm still a soldier! I've got to go back to hospital next week to see what they can make of it. But they gave me a couple of days' leave first.'

Thursday turned on her sister. 'How on earth did you manage to keep all this quiet? She never breathed a word, Mum.'

'Well, we only let her go to meet you on condition she promised not to let on. We didn't want to spoil the surprise. You didn't guess, did you?'

'How could I?' Thursday glanced at her cousin. 'I thought it must be Vic, to tell you the truth. Though I couldn't see how he could be home either.'

'Wish he was,' Denise said wistfully. 'Here's our little Les nearly four years old and never seen his daddy, not to know him. And Vic hasn't seen him since he was a tiny baby. He'll be at school before Vic comes home.'

'Oh no,' Thursday said. 'The war's going to be over soon, I'm sure it is. Look at the way we're going through France. *And* Italy. The Germans must give in soon.'

'Don't forget these V2s they're sending over, though,' her father warned. 'That Hitler's still got a few surprises for us, mark my words. And then there's the Japs, too. We've still got them to deal with.'

'I know.' Thursday fell silent, thinking as she always did of Jeanie Brown, possibly in Japanese hands. She felt a light touch on her own knee and turned to see her four-year-old godson looking up at her.

With an exclamation, she scooped him up in her arms and cuddled him against her. 'Leslie! I haven't even said hello to you yet. I was so surprised to see your Uncle Mike, I forgot all about you.' She nuzzled her face against him. 'Give your Auntie Thursday a big kiss now, and tell me what you've been doing.'

'Getting ready for my daddy to come home,' Leslie said importantly. 'He's coming home soon, Mummy says.'

'Is he? Well, won't that be lovely. And have you got a nice photo of your daddy, so that you'll know what he looks like?' Thursday asked, knowing that beside Denise's bed at her parents' house stood a framed photograph of Vic in his Private's uniform. Leslie nodded.

'My daddy's a soldier. Like Uncle Mike,' he added, glancing shyly at the newcomer.

'He thought Mike was Vic when he first saw him,' Denise said in a low voice to Thursday. 'It's the uniform, see. He thinks any soldier in uniform must be his daddy, poor little mite.'

Thursday smiled. '*I've* seen your daddy,' she told Leslie. 'I saw him when I was in Egypt. D'you know where Egypt is?'

'Grandpa showed me on the map. It's over the sea.'

'Yes, a long way over the sea. There's lots and lots of sand there, and your daddy had been out in the middle of all the sand—'

'Was he building sandcastles? I saw a picture of a boy building sandcastles.'

'No, he wasn't building sandcastles. He was – he was doing some work. Soldier work.'

'Killing Germans,' he said, nodding matter-of-factly, and Thursday felt a small shock at hearing a four-year-old boy speaking so casually. He raised his arms, miming the action of holding a rifle to his shoulder. 'Bang-bang, you're dead. My daddy's killed lots of Germans.'

Thursday looked over his head at Denise. Her cousin shrugged. 'It's true, isn't it? He hears about it all the time, on the wireless and people talking. And he's got ears like a hare, he hears everything. You can't help him knowing.'

'That's right,' Mike said unexpectedly. 'Kids like him, they've got to know, Thursday. They've got to know what the world's like. It's no good keeping it from them, like it was kept from us. Pretending it didn't happen. I tell you, if it hadn't been for Dad taking me down the pub one night and giving it to me straight what happened the first time, same as Uncle Walter did with Steve, I'd have gone off without any idea of what war was like. And I'd have felt proper let down. Betrayed. Because someone ought to have told us, someone ought to have said what it was like in the First War, and if we'd all known what it was like maybe there wouldn't have been a second one. Maybe we wouldn't have had to fight and kill, and see our mates ripped to bits by bullets and us not able to do a thing to help them, maybe our Les would still be alive and all the other poor bastards who—' His voice had been rising almost to a shout and he stopped abruptly, his thin cheeks reddening. He glanced around at the ring of startled faces and mumbled, 'Sorry. Didn't mean to go off at half-cock like that. Sorry, Mum. Sorry, Auntie Mary.'

Flo, her hand at her throat, sat down on the only vacant chair. She was breathing quickly, her face pale, and Thursday began to lift Leslie from her lap to go to her. But Denise was already there, holding a cup of tea under her mother's nose.

'Have a sip of this, Mum. You'll be all right in a minute. Mike didn't mean to upset you.'

Percy cleared his throat and glared at his son. 'Now look what you done. I told you, I didn't want her upset. It's always upset her, all that sort of talk.'

'Yes, but Mike's right, you know,' Denise said, still helping her mother to sip the tea. 'People ought to know. *We* ought to have known. And youngsters like Leslie, they ought to know too, so that when all this is over there are no more wars at all, ever. How can we expect them to stop when nobody ever says what it's like?'

'Now look—'

'All right,' Flo said, lifting her face, 'that's enough. I'm all right, Perce. It was just a bit of a shock, that's all, hearing Mike raise his voice like that. But he's right. They all are. I know I got upset whenever you talked about the First War, but for goodness sake, haven't we been through enough in this one for me to be able to take a bit of truth? All the bombing and killing, and all those boys lost, God rest their souls, and us thinking Mike was dead same as Leslie, and not knowing if we'd ever see Steve again. And I've come to think that maybe I *should* have been upset. Why should I be saved from hearing about it when other people have had to go through it and suffer? And Mike's right about children. They've got to know. They've got to be told.'

'But not at four years old,' Mary said, her voice trembling. 'He's too little, too innocent. He doesn't have to know these things just yet.'

'I don't think he understands yet anyway,' Denise said. 'But he will, when he's old enough. And like I said, he hears everything. There's nothing we can do about that.'

Flo got up again. Her colour had returned and she looked around at the family gathering.

'Don't let's argue about it,' she said. 'Don't let's argue about anything. Not now, when our Mike's come back to us and Thursday's here too. Let's just have a lovely time together, like we used to before the war.'

There was a brief silence. Thursday bit her lip and glanced under her lashes at her aunt and uncle. But we're not all together, she thought. Steve and Leslie aren't here, even though Mike is, and Les never will be again. And Denise is missing Vic too, and she doesn't really know if her Leslie will ever see his daddy.

Percy cleared his throat. He laid his hand on his wife's shoulder and spoke a little loudly.

'That's right, Flo, love. It's not often we get together like this and we ought to make the most of it. Let's have a slap-up tea – or as slap-up as tea can ever be, these days – and then a game of cards or something. Something to make us laugh.' He was silent for a moment, and then said more quietly. 'Nobody can change what's already happened, and nobody can bring back those that have gone. But the news is pretty good, for all that, and we've got something to celebrate, so let's make a proper job of it – all right?'

The family, relieved to have the tension of the past few minutes dissipated, broke into a spontaneous cheer. And Thursday, her face once again wet with tears, turned to her cousin and laid her face against his sleeve.

'Oh, Mike,' she said. 'It's *so* good to have you back home.'

Mary had, as promised, put on a good spread for tea and the game of cards had them all laughing, forgetting the war for an hour or two. Thursday had learned a few new games, and they played these, together with the old favourites like Chase the Ace and Where's the Lady? Leslie sat on his grandfather's knee and caused more hilarity with his attempts to help, and it really began to seem like old times.

They finished up with a cup of cocoa all round, and then Flo and Percy said they must go, it was past that young man's bedtime, and they wrapped themselves up in their old winter coats and departed.

'Mind you come round and see us before you go back, Thursday,' her aunt said, kissing her cheek as they stood by the front door. It was dark by now and although the blackout had now become a 'dim-out' you still had to be careful about showing lights. 'And you come too, Mary, before our Mike gets taken off to that Army hospital.'

Thursday gave him an anxious glance. Mike hadn't said much yet about the reason why he had to go to hospital but she didn't like the sound of it. She didn't like the look of him either. He was too thin, too bright-eyed and there were spots of bright red on his gaunt cheeks.

'What's the matter with him?' she asked Jenny when they were in their own room. 'He ought to have got over that pneumonia by now. Has it left him with a weakness?'

'Something more than weakness, I'm afraid.' Jenny was smoothing Ponds cold cream into her face to take off her make-up. 'It looks to me a bit like TB.'

'TB? Oh no!' Thursday was already undressed and in bed, sitting up against her pillows. 'You don't really think so, do you? Does Auntie Flo have any idea?'

'No, and I'm not going to mention it until we know for certain. I could be wrong. Anyway, he's home now and he'll be looked after properly. It could just be because he's had such a hard life these past few years. They'll probably use penicillin – I can't imagine how we got on without that now, can you? It's made such a difference.' Jenny removed the cream with a scrap of cotton wool. She took off her engagement ring and laid it tenderly on the dressing-table. 'What about you, Thursday? There's been so much excitement here I don't think anyone's even asked you about Connor. Have you heard from him lately?'

'Yes, of course. I get letters all the time.' Her defensive tone brought a lift to Jenny's eyebrows. 'He won't be coming home though, not till it's all over.'

'And then you'll get married.' Jenny, peeling off her stockings and examining them for holes or ladders, spoke as though it was taken for granted. Thursday said nothing and after a moment she turned her head. 'Won't you?'

'I don't know. We'll have to wait and see, won't we.'

Jenny laid the stockings on her bed and stared at her. 'What d'you mean? I thought it was all decided.'

'No, it wasn't. It never has been. We're not engaged – I know Connor gave me my brooch and said he wished it was a ring, but it isn't one, is it? And he said he didn't want to tie me down. He *said* that.' Her voice rose a little and she stopped and bit her lip, aware of her sister's curious glance. 'I'm only saying we'll need to see how we feel when we meet each other again. Things might be different. *We* might be different.'

There was a long silence. Jenny put her stockings aside to be washed in the morning and took off her dressing-gown. She climbed into bed beside Thursday and then said quietly, 'Is there someone else, Thurs?'

'No! Of course there's not. Why should you think that?'

'Well, you've never said anything like this before. You've always been so sure . . . Look, I wouldn't blame you. You must be meeting men all the time. It'd be a funny thing if you didn't fancy any of them.'

Thursday said nothing. She slid down in the bed and lay there, her arms behind her head, staring at the ceiling. Jenny sat quietly beside her, filing her nails. At last she said, 'There is someone. An Army doctor. I met him in Alex two years ago and he's just come to Haslar.'

'An *Army* doctor? But what's he doing in Haslar? I thought it was all Navy.'

'He's a patient. Haslar's a clearing hospital – they bring them there first and we do emergency operations and then, when they're fit to be moved, they go on. Mark came in a week or so ago—'

'Mark?'

'Mark Sangster.' Thursday drew in a deep, troubled sigh. 'Oh, Jenny, I don't know what to do! When we were in Alex – well, it was so different there, everything was different, we were so far from home and I hardly knew where Connor was – I almost fell in love with him then. We used to do it all the time – almost fall in love, I mean – with lots of men. You know, go out dancing or driving in a gharry. It was so romantic and we needed it after being in the wards, and they needed it too. It never meant anything. It was just flirting, and it never went any further than that. Except . . .'

'Except with Mark,' Jenny finished for her.

'We never did anything we shouldn't,' Thursday said quickly. 'Not a thing. I didn't want to – well, I *did*, but I never forgot Connor, I couldn't let him down. And Mark understood that. When he went back to the desert, we said goodbye. We didn't think we'd ever see each other again. And I tried to forget him. I *did* forget him – almost. And then he turned up in Haslar and it all came back.'

'And what does he feel about it?'

'He thinks it was meant,' Thursday said miserably. 'He thinks we're meant to be together, and he says he wants to marry me.'

'Oh, lor,' Jenny said after another brief silence. She looked down at Thursday's face. 'You've got yourself into a bit of a muddle, haven't you?'

'I never meant to,' Thursday protested. 'It all just happened. I've always wanted to be true to Connor. I still want to.'

'So why are you bothered about this Mark? Why don't you just tell him to take a running jump?'

'Because I can't,' Thursday said. 'He doesn't deserve it. He's nice, Jenny, really nice. We get along together. And he says he loves me. How can I be nasty to him?'

'You could if you didn't like him so much,' Jenny observed, still filing her nails. She spread her fingers out in front of her, nodded with satisfaction, then put the nail file on the small bedside table. 'You could if you were absolutely sure about Connor.'

'I *am* sure!' Thursday rolled over and punched her pillow. 'Look, I've done all I can. I've told Mark I won't see him any more. I haven't been back to his ward for days. What else can I do?'

'It's not what you do that's important,' Jenny said shrewdly. 'It's what you think. And what you feel.' She waited a moment, then pointed out, 'You don't actually have to marry either of them, you know.'

'Oh, don't make it all more complicated than it is already,' Thursday groaned. 'Honestly, I do want to marry Connor – I've always wanted to. I just think – well, it's been a long time and things have changed so much, and we might be different. We shouldn't rush into anything. And then – I don't know *what* I feel about Mark. I can't seem to sort it out.'

'Don't do anything, then,' Jenny advised. 'Let things sort themselves out. Wait till Connor comes home, and when you see him again you'll know. And tell Mark if he won't wait till then it's just too bad.' She looked down again. 'The other thing to do is what a lot of people are doing – go where the wind blows you. Take what happiness you can get while it's on offer. You might not get the chance again.'

She put out the light and a few minutes later Thursday heard her steady breathing. She lay still, staring at the pale square of the window, her thoughts reeling with the events of the day and the problem that was ever present in her mind.

Keep the promise that Connor hadn't asked her to make – or let her relationship with Mark go ahead, and go where the wind blew?

Chapter Nineteen

Her brief leave over, Thursday returned to Haslar. She spent the train journey deep in thought. The shock of Mike's return still hadn't quite sunk in. All that first evening, she'd kept looking at him, wanting to touch him to make sure he was real. But one look at the faces of her aunt and uncle told her that it was true. They looked dazed with happiness and relief, and Auntie Flo didn't seem able to bear him out of her sight. She sat beside him all the time, and tears trickled out of her eyes every time she turned her head and looked at him.

'It gives us all a bit of hope,' Mary had said as she kissed Thursday goodbye that morning. 'If Mike can come home from the dead like that, anyone can. Well, maybe not *anyone*,' she added, her face shadowing as they both remembered Leslie. 'But it makes you realise good things *can* happen. It helps you to look forward.' She held Thursday close for a moment. 'It'll be Steve next, and Vic, and your chap too. They'll all be coming home.'

Yes, Thursday thought, watching the countryside flash past. They'd all be coming home. Steve, from prison camp. Vic, from Italy. And Connor . . .

She and Jenny hadn't talked any more about Thursday's dilemma. Jenny had gone back to the Royal Infirmary early next morning. She had only one more year to go before finishing her training and would then be a Registered Nurse. 'You could have done this too, you know,' she told Thursday, pinning up her curly hair. 'Didn't you think about it?'

'Not at the time. I've thought about it since, but – I don't know, Jen. I've enjoyed being a VAD but I don't know if I want to go on being a nurse. I don't know *what* I want to do, to tell you the truth.'

Jenny paused and looked at her, sitting up in the bed. Then she laid a hand on Thursday's leg. 'It'll all come out right, Thursday. You'll see. Just stop worrying so much, and enjoy life. That's what I do, and look where it's got me!'

She danced out of the room and down the stairs and a few moments later Thursday heard her calling a cheerful goodbye to Mary. She smiled to herself and snuggled down under the quilt. Jenny was right. She should enjoy life, and she'd start now by having a long, lazy lie-in.

The rest of the time had been taken up with visiting. She went to see all her old friends who were still around, and spent a good deal of time with her Aunt Flo and cousin Mike. Denise was at work at the glove factory, so she played with Leslie and one afternoon took him on the train across the Malvern Hills to Ledbury to visit her Aunt Maudie. Maudie was still nursing at the cottage hospital but hurried home across the road and welcomed them both with tea and fresh scones, while the white Persian cat, Snowy, looked more majestic than ever on the rag rug by the fire.

'You heard Nipper died, I suppose,' Maudie said. 'He was a good age – nearly sixteen. I miss him a lot, but I don't suppose I'll have another, not at my age.'

'Go on, Auntie,' Thursday said, her mouth full of scone, 'you're not old.'

'No, but I would be by the time a new puppy got to the age Nipper was. Anyway, there'll never be another dog like him. Have you still got that little watch I gave you?'

Thursday nodded. She wore the little silver fob watch whenever she was on duty and it had become a talisman, bringing her safely through the war. She would give it back to her aunt when the war was over. Thursday knew that Maudie treasured it.

When the war was over . . . Talk was of peace now, all the time. The Germans had been driven back even further through France and were now defending their positions from the Moselle to the Low Countries. They had been chased out of Finland by the Finns and Soviets, and were retreating across their own borders. At the same time, the war in the Pacific and Far East was being fought ever more vigorously, with the Japanese army on the defensive all over Burma. The Red Army had launched a massive assault on the Baltic coast, prior to their attack on East Prussia. On all fronts, the enemy were caught in pincer movements and fighting, as Jenny remarked with satisfaction, like rats in a corner.

It wasn't all good news, though. On the day before Thursday left to go back to Haslar they heard that a V2 rocket had struck a Woolworth's store in London, killing a hundred and sixty people and injuring at least two hundred more. Poor souls, Mary said, her eyes filling with tears. Just gone out for an afternoon's shopping, the kiddies with them as likely as not, and smashed to rubble without any warning. Not even time to get to a shelter. It wasn't *fair*.

'It's awful,' Mary had said, reading the newspaper out loud. 'There's a young girl here saying what it was like. Things falling out of the sky, she says, bits of things and bits of people. She saw a horse's head lying in the gutter – just its *head*. And a pram all smashed and twisted and a little baby's hand, still in its sleeve.' She laid the paper in her lap, her face twisted with horror. 'Poor little soul. And there was a bus with people still sitting in it in rows, all of them stone dead. And nothing left of Woolworth's at all – just a huge pile of rubble, and people screaming underneath.'

The image had haunted Thursday all night and still over-shadowed her mind as she sat in the train. Suppose a V2 hit the train now . . . Well, there was nothing you could do to guard against it, so it was no use worrying. Determinedly, she turned her thoughts back to her own life.

I'm not going to make up my mind about anything at the moment, she thought. I can't, and nobody can force me to. I'll go and see Mark again, but I won't agree to marry him, I won't even think about it until the war's over. But I won't think about marrying Connor either – not until I've seen him, and until we've had time to get to know each other again.

At the back of her mind was the thought planted there by Jenny. She didn't have to marry either of them. She didn't *have* to marry anyone at all.

By the time she crossed the harbour, night had fallen and the wind was whipping the tops off the choppy waves. In spite of the 'dim-out' both towns were in darkness, with barely a glow from the few street-lights that were now permitted. Thursday sat in the pinnace, watching the shadowy bulk of the hospital block out the occasional glitter of stars behind the flying tatters of cloud. How many more times am I going to do this, she wondered.

The other girls had already gone to the mess for supper when she arrived. Tired and suddenly despondent, she dropped her case on the floor beside the bunks, went to the washroom to sluice water over her face and hands, and then walked along to join them. Haslar shepherd's pie was rather a comedown after her mother's cooking, but she'd got to eat. She found the others in their usual places and slipped into her seat.

'Hello, Thursday,' Elsie said, her mouth full of mince and potato. 'You're back, then.'

'I think so,' Thursday said, picking up her knife and fork. 'I think it's me, anyway. What does everyone else think?'

'All right, ask a silly question! Did you have a good time? How're the family?'

Thursday looked around the table. They all appeared much as usual, cheerfully eating their shepherd's pie and sipping their water. There was, after all, no reason why they should look any different. She'd only been away for five days. Yet she felt as if she'd been away for months. As if far more had happened than could possibly have been packed into only five days.

'My cousin's home,' she said baldly. 'Mike. The one we thought was killed at Dunkirk.'

They stopped eating to stare at her. 'The one you thought was killed at Dunkirk? He's *home*? But—'

'You mean you haven't heard from him in all that time? And he's just come home? Out of the blue? But how?'

'You're joking. You're having us on. He *can't* have just turned up, just like that.'

'I don't *understand*.'

'Here, have a bite to eat, Thurs,' Elsie said, watching her. 'You're looking all in. Get some grub inside you and then tell us all about it. I reckon she's had a real shock,' she said to the others, 'and it's only just begun to hit her. Leave her be for a bit while she gets herself together.'

Thursday nodded. She felt suddenly close to tears. It's daft, she thought, trying to hold them back, it's daft to feel like this. It's good news – wonderful news – and I was so pleased, so excited about it. I still am. So why should I break down now, the minute I get back to

Haslar? And I feel so *tired* . . . She leaned her head on one hand and used the other to fork up the meat and potato. Its warmth and solidity gradually penetrated the numb coldness of her body and she began to feel better. After a few more mouthfuls she looked up and grinned shakily.

'All right. I'm OK now. Just felt a bit woozy, that's all.'

'I'm not surprised, after that journey,' Patsy said. 'I remember the first time we came, in all that snow – I thought it was going to take for ever. Now, tell us about your cousin. Has he really come home?'

Thursday nodded and recounted as much of the story as she thought she ought to. 'He's been in France all that time, just dodging the Germans, but he managed to get to Spain and find a ship. He's been ill, too. Jenny, my sister, thinks it may be TB. He's going to the nearest Army hospital.'

'They'll soon sort him out, then,' Elsie said bracingly. 'My goodness, what a story! Imagine being on the run all that time in France! I bet your auntie's over the moon.'

'She is. She thought she'd lost both her boys. She knows Leslie won't come back, of course, but it does give you hope, doesn't it?' She glanced around and caught Patsy's eye and a wave of sorrow struck her. 'Oh, Pats, if only it could happen to Roy.'

'I know it won't, though,' Patsy said sadly. 'They found his body. It was buried somewhere over in Normandy – they say there's huge graveyards stretching for miles with little wooden crosses by each grave. My Roy's in one of them and one day I'll go and see him.' She gave Thursday a wobbly smile. 'But I'm glad about your cousin. Really glad.'

'So am I,' said Elsie, and then Louisa, and then each girl at the table. 'So am I. So am I. So am I.' Even Vera Hapgood, who rarely joined in any congratulations, smiled and nodded, and Thursday felt a warm, all encompassing glow as she looked at them. My friends, she thought, all these girls are my friends.

As she rose from the table, however, she knew that there was another friend to whom she had not yet told the news. Not Connor – she'd written to him twice during her leave, telling him about Mike and all the rest of the family news. No, this friend was here in Haslar, but in order to tell him she would have to walk across to the wards and ask Sister to let her in to see him.

Mark, she thought. I want to tell Mark.

It was too late to go that evening, and she was exhausted anyway. The emotion of the past few days had suddenly caught up with her and she felt almost sick with fatigue. She went back to the dormitory and sat round the big iron stove with the others, sipping cocoa and listening to their chatter. As usual, it was mostly about the hospital and the social life they managed to squeeze into their off-duty hours, and Elsie was coming in for a good deal of attention. Thursday looked at her curiously.

'This sailor – is it serious, then?'

Elsie blushed and nodded her fair head. 'I think it might be, Thurs. Well, you know we've been out a few times since that dance at South Parade Pier. We get on really well. He's a local boy too, comes from Fareham, so he's not going to go disappearing up north or anything like that.'

'And you can check he hasn't already got a wife,' Patsy said wickedly. 'Not round here, anyway.'

Elsie gave her a withering look. 'He hasn't got a wife *anywhere*. Anyway,' her fair skin was suddenly tinged with pink, 'we're thinking of getting engaged at Christmas. Might be going over to Pompey to look at a few rings on Saturday.'

'A *few* rings?' Patsy echoed. 'Crikey, how many d'you want, Elsie? One for every finger? Most people are satisfied with just the one.'

'Oh, shut up, you fool.' Elsie gave her friend a push and Patsy almost spilled her cocoa. She turned to Thursday. 'Honestly, Thurs, I'm glad you're back, at least there's a chance of a bit of sensible conversation.' Ignoring the derisive howl from Patsy, she went on, 'I can't make up me mind between three diamonds or a solitaire, what d'you think?'

'Not a solitaire,' Patsy said, suddenly sober. 'It's unlucky. Everyone I know who had a solitaire got left on her own. Have three diamonds.'

There was a short silence. Nobody could help glancing towards Patsy's hand, where her own tiny solitaire engagement ring winked in the harsh light from the overhead lamp. In a sense it wasn't really an engagement ring, since Roy had bought it for her on their honeymoon – their wedding had been arranged so quickly there hadn't been time for an engagement – but that was what it was meant to be.

'Well, maybe that's what I'll do then,' Elsie said after a moment.

'I think I like them better anyway. Not but what yours isn't really pretty, Pats,' she added hastily, 'but my hands are bigger than yours and one stone will just look lost.'

'I can't believe it,' Thursday said. 'I've only been away a few days. You weren't talking about getting engaged when I went.'

'Not to you lot, no. But we've been thinking about it. I wasn't going to say anything tonight either – it just slipped out. So keep it under your hats.'

'Fat chance of that,' Ellen Bridges said. 'Now we all know it'll be all round the hospital, even if none of us says a word. You know what it's like here – talk about walls having ears! I bet the whole of the ward will hear of it by tomorrow.'

'Well, if they do I'll know who to blame,' Elsie said, fixing Ellen with a stern look.

'So when's the wedding going to be?' Thursday asked quickly. 'I mean, won't Pete be going away soon?'

'No, he's got a desk job in Cambridge Barracks,' Elsie said. 'He copped some shrapnel in his shoulder when his ship was sunk in the spring and he was in the water for seven hours so it did it a bit of no good. They don't reckon it'll ever be properly right again. He'll be there for a while, anyway, so we can take our time. We thought we might make it February the fourteenth.'

'St Valentine's Day!' Joy said. 'Oh, that's so romantic. Are we all invited? I'll need to save up my coupons for a new frock.'

'For cripes' sake!' Elsie exclaimed in exasperation. 'We haven't even got engaged yet! I'm not supposed to have told you any of this. Look, it's almost ten o'clock, I'm going to bed, and Thursday here's almost dropping. Whose turn is it to wash up?'

'Yours!' said several voices, and she groaned and collected up the mugs. Thursday followed her out to the washroom and began to clean her teeth while Elsie swished the mugs under the tap.

'I'm really pleased, Else. I liked Pete the first time I met him. I think you'll be very happy together.'

Elsie rested her hands in the water and looked at her. Her face was unusually serious. 'I hope so, Thurs. I really hope so. You know, there've been a lot of blokes I've fancied before I met Pete, and I've had a bit of a fling with a few of them – well, you know that – but I've never felt the way I do now. I know it's awful to say it when so many other chaps are out there in danger, but I'm just so thankful he's got that bad shoulder and they've put him in the barracks. I don't think I could stand it if he went away and I lost him. I couldn't be as brave as Patsy. I know I couldn't.'

Thursday heard the wobble of tears in her voice. She dried her hands and put her arm around Elsie's shoulders. 'Yes, you could. But you're not going to have to. This is one story that's going to end happily ever after – I know it is.' She laid her cheek against her friend's for a moment. 'Congratulations, Elsie. And mind you do invite us all to the wedding, see? Or you'll have me to reckon with!'

Climbing into her bunk, she thought how good it was to be back amongst her friends, and a wave of sadness washed over her as she realised that in some ways she felt more at home here than she did back in Worcester. It had been lovely to be with her family again – especially with the added joy of Mike's miraculous return – but it hadn't always been easy. There was so much about her life that her family, especially her parents, didn't understand. So much of what in Haslar would have been casual comment or banter, immediately understood by the others, seemed to need explanation that she had begun to find herself weighing her words before uttering them. Even Jenny seemed to have grown away from her. Her training as a Registered Nurse had taken her beyond Thursday's medical knowledge, yet still remained far short of her experience. Jenny had attended numerous lectures, studied piles of books and passed detailed examinations in a number of areas of which Thursday knew very little, but she had never encountered a flood of wounded soldiers, encrusted in blood and sand, nor sat beside a dying sailor as he moaned and wept for his sweetheart. She hadn't helped unload a man with a torn and mutilated face from a small ferry boat after Dunkirk and realised it was her own sweetheart. It was as if they inhabited different worlds. And the rest of the family seemed even further apart, concerned with the difficulties of civilian life and the Home Front.

I've been away too long, Thursday thought. It's nearly five years now since I left home, and two of those years I spent in Egypt. I've changed, and I don't think I'll ever be able to change back. I'm a different person.

She felt the tears seep from her eyes and spread into a damp patch on her pillow. I don't *want* to be different, she mourned. I don't *want* to be the kind of person who can only feel comfortable in a crowd, in a dormitory, in a hospital or some other sort of institution. I want to be ordinary again, to be able to go back to ordinary life after the war and be a wife and mother, just as Mum always meant me to be.

Ordinary life. She didn't even know what that was, any more. And as for being a wife – another whole world of confusion must be settled before that could come about.

She went to see Mark the next morning, before going on duty. Her heart beating fast, she crossed the quad and entered the door of the medical block. Almost running, she joined the throng of nurses going up the stairs and paused at the door of the ward. The QARNN Sister came out and looked at her.

'I'd like to see Lieutenant Colonel Sangster,' Thursday said. 'I've been on leave for a few days. I won't stay long but I'd just like to see him before I go on duty. Just to – to say hello.'

The QARNN looked at her curiously. 'Lieutenant Colonel Sangster? He's not here any more. He's gone.'

Thursday stared at her. Her heart, which had been beating so fast, seemed to give an extra kick and then drop right through her body. 'Gone? But – but where? When? He—' Fear gripped her. 'He's not worse, is he? He was doing so well.'

'No, of course he's not worse. He was fit enough to be moved, that's all. He's gone to the Army hospital.' The Sister paused for a moment. 'I'm surprised he didn't let you know. Since you're such good friends.'

Thursday felt the colour burn her cheeks. 'I've been away, otherwise . . .' She looked at the Sister. 'Do you have an address for him?'

'Sorry,' the QARNN said. 'All I know is that he's gone to the Army hospital, but I'm sure he'll be in touch, if he wants you to know it. Now if you'll excuse me— She was already turning away, anxious to get on with the business of the ward.

'Yes,' Thursday said dully, not missing the sardonic note in the senior nurse's voice. She moved away along the corridor, feeling suddenly bereft. 'Yes, I'm sure he will.'

Chapter Twenty

'**G**one?' Elsie echoed. 'You mean he's just buggered off without even telling you?'

'*Elsie!*' Thursday was used to hearing people swear now, but she still didn't like hearing it from her friend. 'Well, yes, I suppose that's about it.' She twisted her mouth wryly. 'I shouldn't be surprised, I suppose. I made it pretty clear I wasn't going to see him again. But I didn't really expect him to *believe* it!' she ended on a wail.

Elsie couldn't help grinning. 'You shouldn't say such things if you don't mean them.'

'I thought I did at the time,' Thursday said despondently. 'Oh, Elsie, I'm in such a muddle! Why couldn't I fall in love with a nice uncomplicated sailor like Pete? Why does it all have to be so *difficult?*'

Elsie watched her. 'Is it? Isn't it just that you've realised there can be more than one Mr Right in the world, and you happen to have come across two of them? Strikes me it doesn't really matter which one you choose, Thurs, you'll have a pretty good life with either.'

Thursday stared at her. 'That's an awful thing to say.'

'I don't see why. I bet it's true. Look, if there's only one man for any of us, out of all the millions of men there are in the world, it's a pretty big coincidence that so many of us happen to meet him, isn't it? Stands to reason there's got to be lots. And what about all the widows who get married again? *They've* met more than one, haven't they? So—'

'Stop it, Elsie, you're making my head ache.' Thursday put the heel of her hand to her forehead. 'Look, I can't think about millions. I can only think about two. And I *don't* know which one's Mr Right, as you call him – or even if *either* of them is. I just don't know what to do, that's all. And I wish Mark hadn't gone off like that without even leaving me his address.'

'Maybe you've convinced him you do know, and thinking he's out of the picture, he's done the decent thing.' Elsie paused. 'Anyway, it wouldn't be that difficult to find him. You know he's gone to an Army hospital. You could easily find out which one.'

Thursday looked at her. 'You think I ought to try to contact him again? Go and see him – wherever he is?'

'Good Lord, *I'm* not saying what you ought to do!' Elsie exclaimed, flapping her hands. 'I'm just saying what you could do. You've got to make up your own mind over this, Thursday.'

Thursday sighed and the two girls parted, Elsie to go to Zymotics and Thursday to the operating theatre. They were still using the underground theatres even though the risk of raids had diminished – apart from the threat of V2 rockets – and she ran down the wide stairs, conscious that she was only just in time. The theatre sister gave her a severe look as she pushed open the big double doors.

'You're almost adrift, Tilford.'

'I know, I'm sorry. I – I wanted to see someone in the wards first and I cut it rather fine.'

'Well, keep your visiting time for off-duty hours. We've got a lot of ops this morning and the boss wants to get started as soon as possible.' The QARNN detailed the morning's work briskly, allocating jobs to the nurses and VADs. Thursday accepted her tasks meekly and set to work, determined to thrust her own problems out of her mind for the next few hours. Wherever Mark was, and wherever Connor was, they would have to stay there without her thoughts. For the time being, while she was on duty, the only men who mattered to her were the patients lying on the table, their lives and their recovery held in the hands of every person in the theatre.

It was almost Christmas. People were beginning to discuss what they were going to do and whether they'd be able to go home. A few people who were due for leave managed to organise it for the two or three days of the holiday, but Thursday, who had already taken her leave, was to stay at Haslar. Since they would both be on duty on Christmas Day itself, Elsie invited her to go to her grandmother's for Boxing Day to help celebrate her engagement to Pete.

'I don't mind being here for Christmas anyway,' she declared as they sat darning their stockings. 'We've had some good times in hospital at Christmas, haven't we? Remember those we had out in Egypt?'

'Do I! It was almost like pre-war with all those coloured paper chains and funny hats. And the *food*! I've never seen such a spread.'

'Mm. It was good, though it seemed funny not to be having turkey or chicken. And sweet potatoes, too – not like our spuds, are they! Still, it was a smashing spread. And couldn't the men just put it away! Got through a few gallons of beer too, if I remember right.'

'I'm surprised you can remember at all,' Thursday said with a grin. 'I know by the time we'd gone carol singing round all the wards we weren't singing the usual words to half of them! But I couldn't help a little weep now and then when I looked at them all. Poor souls, all so far away from home with nobody of their own to come and hold their hands. I'll tell you now, I went back to bed and cried myself to sleep that night.'

'You weren't the only one,' Elsie said quietly. 'And here we are, back where we started, getting ready for yet another Christmas. D'you reckon this really will be the last one, Thurs – the last one of the war, I mean?'

'I hope so,' Thursday said. She rolled her stockings into a ball. 'I've had enough of wartime Christmases. I want to be able to have the whole three days doing just what I like, with a huge spread of turkey and Christmas pudding, and cakes and trifles, and lots of sweets and chocolates, and oranges and bananas, and figs and dates and—'

'Blimey O'Riley,' Elsie said, 'I thought it was me that was the greedy one! You'll burst.'

'I don't care,' Thursday said. 'I want to burst!'

Elsie laughed. 'You're in a good mood today. Had a letter from Connor?'

'No.' Thursday gave her a sideways glance. 'Actually, I've decided to go out somewhere on my next day off. I'm going to Rochester.'

'*Rochester*? But why on earth . . . ?'

Then light dawned in Elsie's eyes. 'Ohhh. There wouldn't be an Army hospital there, by any chance?'

'As a matter of fact,' Thursday said, 'there would.'

'Mark?'

'Yes. I've decided to go and see him. I've got to, Elsie,' she added rather defensively. 'I can't just leave things as they were. I've got to give him his chance. I'm not going to *agree* to anything, mind. I shan't get engaged, or anything like that – I still want to wait till I see Connor again before I make up my mind. But I can't simply walk away from Mark.' She glanced down at the rolled stockings in her lap. 'I just can't.'

'No, you can't,' Elsie said after a moment. 'But – be careful, won't you Thurs? He's got a dangerous look about him, Mark Sangster has. Just watch yourself, all right?'

'Yes,' Thursday said. 'I will.'

She didn't ask Elsie what she meant by the word *dangerous*. She knew only too well. She'd seen it herself in the glint of Mark's dark brown eyes, in the narrow lines of his face; she'd heard it in his voice. He *was* dangerous – dangerous to her heart.

On the day Thursday went to Rochester, news began to come through of the 'Battle of the Bulge'. The US Army, now in the Ardennes, had been attacked by a massive German force and left in disarray. It looked like another step backwards.

On the same day she read in her newspaper of the disappearance of the bandleader Glenn Miller somewhere over the Channel. He'd been flying to Paris to perform for General Eisenhower and somewhere over the freezing sea his plane had vanished. His band had gone in a different plane and were all safe – but what would they do without him, Thursday wondered. With his famous tunes 'String of Pearls', 'Moonlight Serenade', 'American Patrol', and 'In the Mood' he had come to represent the very sound of America at war.

The crowded train rumbled through the countryside. Thursday had never been to Kent before but the scenes outside did little to hold her attention. She tried to read the paper again but the words danced before her eyes and she laid it back in her lap. I wish I knew if I were doing the right thing, she thought restlessly. I wish I knew if Mark really wanted to see me again . . .

Elsie had advised her to let him know she was coming, but Thursday had shaken her head. 'I just want to surprise him – to see what he does. I'll know then if he really loves me.'

'And will you know if *you* love *him*?' Elsie had asked shrewdly, and Thursday had sighed and shaken her head.

'I don't know when I'm going to know that.'

She reached into her bag and reached for an envelope. It was yellow and crumpled with much folding and unfolding. She drew out the sheet of paper inside and stared at it.

My Darling Thursday,

I seem to feel you with me with every step I take. I miss you every moment, more than I can say, more than I can ever show you – but oh, how I long to show you and to love you, and when all this is over I swear we'll never be parted again, never. I love you, my darling.

Her eyes blurred and she bit her lips hard and stared out of the window, determined not to let the tears fall. I wasn't the only one to make a promise, she thought. Connor did too, in this letter. We promised each other.

What was she doing here, with Connor's letter in her bag, going to see another man?

Perhaps Elsie was right. Perhaps there were many men in the world that she could love. It was just bad luck that she'd happened to meet two of them.

The soldier sitting opposite her gave her a sympathetic look. 'Letter from your sweetheart, love?'

'Yes.' She wondered what he would say if he knew the truth. She'd known so many men in Egypt, worrying themselves sick about what their wives and sweethearts might be doing back at home, and she felt a lurch of shame. 'It's an old one, though.'

'Been away a long time?' He nodded. 'Feels like it'll never come to an end, don't it. But don't fret, ducks, it'll all be over soon.' He glanced out of the window. 'One or two more big pushes, that's all it'll take, and we'll smash old Hitler into the dust. They say he's dying on his feet anyway.'

'Do they?'

'Yeah, mate of mine says he's heard he's in a bad way. Get rid of him and the others'll fall to bits. Good riddance to bad rubbish, that'll be. You wouldn't credit one man could make such a mess of the world, would you? Pity old Chamberlain never saw what he was up to – him and his "piece of paper"!' The man snorted with derision. 'Blooming politicians. There's only one thing a devil like that understands, and it ain't appeasement!'

'But so many people have been killed,' Thursday said, and he shrugged.

'That's war, innit. That's what it's all about. Mind you, it's all right for me to talk like that – I'm a Regular, went into it in thirty-six with me eyes open, got proper training. I can see it's rough on the poor sods that got called up straight out of school and didn't even know one end of a gun from the other. Cannon-fodder, that's what they were right enough. But you gotta have it, ain't you? You got to waste the Jerry's ammo on something.' He glanced out of the window and started to get to his feet. 'We're just coming into the station now. Be seeing you, love.' He winked. 'Hope the boyfriend gets back soon.'

'Yes,' Thursday said faintly. 'Yes, so do I.'

She folded Connor's letter – the first real love letter he had written to her, just before Patsy's wedding – and put it carefully away in her bag. For a moment or two she sat staring out of the window, thinking over what the soldier had said.

Cannon-fodder. The lives of young boys, barely trained, used to 'waste' the Germans' ammunition. Was that really how the Army saw war? Was it how the politicians who ran the war – Mr Churchill, Mr Atlee and the others – saw it? Was that all her brother Steve and her Cousin Mike and all those others who had never wanted to be soldiers, meant to those in power?

I hate it, she thought with sudden force. War, and all it means – I *hate* it.

The hospital reminded her of the 64th in Alexandria, with the influence of the Army apparent from the entrance, guarded by Privates instead of matelots, to the ward where eventually Thursday managed to find her way. Almost exhausted by her efforts to persuade the guards and nursing staff that she was a friend of one of the patients – what do they think I am, she wondered crossly, a spy? – she approached the QARMN sister and made her request yet again.

'Lieutenant Colonel Sangster?' The military nurse frowned. 'Yes, he's here. Who are you?'

'I'm a VAD at Haslar Naval Hospital, near Portsmouth. I was

nursing him there, and we knew each other in Egypt too. I'd like to see him.'

The Sister gave her a sharp glance and to Thursday's horror her eyes moved down to inspect her waist. 'It's not that!' she exclaimed in dismay. 'We've never – I've never – I just want to *see* him, that's all. I've come a long way.'

'Did he know you were coming?'

'No – I wanted it to be a surprise. Please,' she begged, 'please let me see him, just for a minute or two. There's something important I have to tell him.'

Suspicion returned to the Sister's eyes. 'I think I ought to ask him if he wants to see you, first. In any case, he already has a visitor.'

'I'll wait,' Thursday said. 'I don't mind waiting. If you could just let him know . . .'

'I'll see. You'd better wait out here. I don't want my patients upset.' She rustled away, leaving Thursday standing in the corridor, at a loss.

There were no chairs to sit on. She stood with her back against the wall, trying to look as if she belonged there. Nurses, doctors, patients and visitors brushed past her, some giving her curious looks, some not even appearing to notice her. I wish I hadn't come, she thought miserably. Elsie was right. I ought to have let him know. It was a crazy thing to do.

The door swung open. She looked up eagerly and saw a woman emerge. She was tall, with a pale, oval face and huge violet eyes. Her hair was set in immaculate Marcel waves and she was swathed in a lush, deep brown fur coat. Her shoes had the highest heels Thursday had ever seen.

She took no notice of Thursday. Instead, her attention was on the man behind her, the man holding the door open for her to pass through. She turned as she came out and lifted her hand to his cheek, and her voice carried clearly to Thursday, standing only a yard or two away.

'Goodbye for now, darling, and take care of yourself. I'll be here to fetch you first thing in the morning, and we'll have our own special Christmas together. Till then . . .' She reached up and kissed the man on the cheek, and then turned and tapped away along the corridor, leaving him looking after her.

Then he turned. His dark brown eyes met Thursday's and she

saw them widen with surprise. For a moment they stared at each other, then he said uncertainly, as if not quite believing what he saw, '*Thursday?*'

Thursday felt as if she had been nailed to the brown linoleum floor. She stared at him, unable to speak, unable to move. Then she pressed the back of her hand to her mouth and shook her head. She turned and began to run along the corridor. Behind her, she heard his voice. 'Thursday, wait! *Thursday!*'

But Thursday couldn't wait. Her whole body burning with shame and humiliation, deeply aware of her old coat and scuffed flat-heeled shoes, her brown hair with only natural waves and the Pond's lipstick that was all she could afford, she wanted nothing but to get away. Away from the hospital, away from Mark and, most of all, away from the rich, beautiful woman with whom he was going to spend Christmas.

You're a fool, Thursday Tilford, she told herself angrily as she made her way back to the station and climbed on board the next train returning to Portsmouth. A stupid, gullible fool. And it serves you right. It serves you *bloody* well right.

Chapter Twenty-One

'S he looked like a film star,' she told Elsie when at last she was back at Haslar, shivering by the stove with her hands wrapped round a mug of cocoa. 'All expensive make-up and furs. Honestly, I felt such a fool. Such an *idiot*. Standing there in that old overcoat, looking like a *ragbag*!'

'You don't look like a ragbag. It's a very nice coat.'

'I did, beside her. Honestly, Else. I mean, I'd been travelling all day, I was all covered in smuts from the train, my hair was a mess – I could see what that snooty QARMN Sister thought. This little naval VAD chasing after him all the way from Portsmouth, not even letting him know I was coming. It was as plain as the nose on your face, she thought we'd had a fling and I was after him to marry me. She thought I was expecting a *baby*!' Her voice broke and she leaned her head on her hands and sobbed. 'I have never felt so humiliated in my life, never. It was *awful*.'

Elsie stroked her back sympathetically. 'It must have been. You poor thing. But didn't Mark say anything when he saw you?'

'I didn't give him a chance. I just got out as fast as I could.' Thursday raised a woebegone, tear-streaked face. 'Anyway, what could he have said, Elsie? It was obvious what was going on. They were going to spend *Christmas* together. She called him *darling*. She's his girlfriend, probably his fiancée. Maybe even his *wife*, for all I know. He was just stringing me along, that's what, having a bit of fun, and I was stupid enough to fall for it. Oh, *Elsie*!'

Elsie didn't know what to say. Thursday was probably right, yet she would never have thought Mark was the sort to string a girl along like that. 'He always struck me as a really nice bloke,' she said.

'When we were in Egypt he seemed as straight as a die. I'd have put money on him being really sweet on you.'

'Well, maybe he was,' Thursday agreed. 'And maybe he wasn't.' She remembered the starry nights in the desert, the ride in the gharry, the handful of stardust, and began to cry again. 'Oh, Elsie, I've been such a fool. And I've let Connor down too. I'll have to write and tell him—'

'No!' Elsie was alarmed. 'Don't do that, Thursday! What's the point of upsetting him now? It's all over anyway, he needn't ever know a thing about it. And you haven't done anything wrong. You and Mark – it never went further than a kiss or two. Did it?' she added, a little doubtfully.

'Of course it didn't! But I've let him down all the same. I *wanted* it to,' she confessed miserably. 'And there were times when I – I would have. I don't deserve a decent man like Connor, Elsie. I'll have to tell him.'

'Well, wait till he comes home then. Don't send him a *Dear John* and break his heart while he's thousands of miles away and can't do a thing about it. And if you'll take my advice you won't tell him at all.' Elsie took the mug gently from her hands. 'Look, this has gone cold. I'll make you some more.'

'That's wasteful. I'll drink it.'

'No, you won't. You need something hot inside you. Thursday, promise me you won't write to Connor about this. I bet we've all done some daft things in the past few years. Blimey, look at all the dances we've been to, all the blokes we've met. Look at all those little romances we had on the way out to Egypt. That chap you used to go out and spoon with – what was his name? – Eddy. And the others – you're not going to tell Connor about them, are you?'

'That's different.'

'It seems different now,' Elsie said, mixing cocoa with sugar and a spoonful of milk, 'but it might not in a few months' time. I'm only saying you shouldn't do anything in a rush, not while you're all upset. Once you've got over this, you'll see that it isn't so important after all. I mean, what you have to think about is what you're upset *about*. Is it because you know now you don't have a chance with Mark, or is it because you just feel you've made a fool of yourself?' She took the kettle from the top of the stove and poured it into the mug, stirring briskly.

Thursday took the mug and held it in her hands. She still felt cold, chilled right through to the bone. The journey back had seemed endless, with the train stopping at every tiny station plus a few times, without explanation, in the middle of the countryside with not a light showing anywhere. It had been cold and draughty, and the compartment had been filled with smoke. She'd been unable to stop the tears trickling down her cheeks and a sergeant sitting next to her had tried to offer comfort, but she'd brushed him away.

'I don't know, Elsie,' she said at last. 'I'm in such a muddle. And it was awful – I feel hot and cold every time I think about it. That Sister's face, and that woman, calling him *darling* and kissing him. And me in my old coat. But I wouldn't have gone if I hadn't wanted to see him again, would I? I mean, I wouldn't have gone all that way to see Eddy or the others.' She shook her head. 'I can't sort it out now. I'm just too tired, and I feel all muzzy.'

Elsie gave her a concerned look. 'You'd better get yourself into bed. Look, go and have a quick bath, that'll warm you up a bit, and I'll put a hot water bottle in your bed. I wouldn't be surprised if you hadn't caught a chill. And don't lay there going over it again all night. It's sleep you need. Things'll look better in the morning – they always do.'

Not always, Thursday thought as she rose obediently. Not when your life has been ruined, and you did it yourself.

Thursday had caught more than a chill – she developed a nasty dose of 'flu which kept her in bed for a week. She was moved into the Wrens' ward and became a patient for a while, nursed by – of all people – Vera Hapgood. If that wasn't an incentive to get better fast, she said to Elsie who popped in to see her, bringing a copy of *Woman's Own* and a small bar of chocolate, she didn't know what was.

'Actually, she's not a bad nurse,' she admitted, wiping streaming eyes. 'Not exactly the motherly type, but she does all the right things. Though she did keep me hanging on a long time for my tea this morning.'

'Probably goes against the grain, bringing one of us tea in bed!' Elsie grinned. 'Can't say I'd be in a hurry to do for her, to be honest. Anyway, the main thing is, will you be out in time for Christmas?'

'Oh yes, just about, though Sister says I'll need a few days to get my strength back. 'Flu knocks you right back. She says I might be a bit low for a while too.'

'Well, just remember that and don't start worrying about Connor again. Oh, that reminds me – a letter came for you.' Elsie fished in her pocket and brought out an envelope. 'Dunno who it's from.'

'You mean you haven't read it?' Thursday asked sarcastically, and caught her breath in a coughing fit which lasted a good three minutes. Vera Hapgood came bustling over and bossily dragged her into an upright position, pushing her pillows behind her. She took the letter away from Elsie and put it on Thursday's locker under the magazine.

'You'd better go now. She isn't really fit for visitors.'

'Yes, nurse. No, nurse. Three bags full, nurse,' Elsie said mockingly, but she got up and gave Thursday a grin. 'Got to be moving anyway, me and Pete are going to the pictures. We're going to see *The Way Ahead*. It's got David Niven in it – Pete says he's smarmy but *I* think he's gorgeous.'

Thursday leaned back against her pillows and gave her a faint smile. 'Thanks for coming, Else.'

'That's OK. Had to make sure you weren't being murdered.' Elsie gave a dark glance in the direction of Vera Hapgood, now attending to another patient. 'Anyway, you get better soon, we're missing you. And Gran says you've got to be sure and be better for Boxing Day, or she'll come in herself and drag you out.'

Thursday chuckled a little painfully. 'She would, too. Even Vera Hapgood wouldn't scare your gran when she'd made up her mind.'

Elsie departed and Thursday slid down in the bed and closed her eyes. Sitting up had eased the cough but made her feel faint, and she wanted nothing more than to sleep. She dozed off into an uneasy world of dreams, where she was on an endless train journey trying to reach a destination that grew further and further away and, as she dreamed, tears of weakness trickled from her eyes and soaked into her pillow.

The letter lay beneath the magazine, and when the ward orderly came to tidy up it slipped into her waste bucket and was thrown away.

The fighting continued. For some days there had been a news blackout on the Battle of the Bulge but there was plenty to be heard about the other areas of the war. All over Christmas and into the New Year, the battles in Italy, the Pacific and the South China Sea continued remorselessly, and thousands more people died. Thousands of families torn apart, Thursday thought, thousands of fathers, husbands, brothers killed, thousands of wives made widows and children left fatherless. It was cruel.

On Christmas Day she went round the wards with the others, singing carols in a rather cracked, husky voice, and being kissed under the mistletoe that one of the doctors had brought in from his garden at Hillhead. She had received a telegram from Connor, assuring her yet again of his love, and she carried it in her breast pocket, close to her heart, feeling a mixture of love and guilt. Since being ill, she had managed only to scribble a few short notes, but she was uneasily aware that she'd used her illness as an excuse. I don't know what to say to him any more, she thought. I feel as if everything I say could be a lie.

Boxing Day was a relief. She cycled with Elsie past Alverstoke church, where Patsy and Roy had got married, and down the Avenue to the War Memorial Hospital. The sight of the verandahs where the TB patients sat to get fresh air reminded her of her cousin Mike who had, as Jenny had predicted, been diagnosed with the disease and was in a sanatorium near Worcester. Luckily, the illness wasn't far progressed and he was expected to recover but his war was over, and Auntie Flo had said it was a blessing. At least she knew where he was and could visit him and see that he was being properly looked after.

Thursday was looking forward to seeing him again. She would have her own Christmas leave soon, and would be going home to see the family. Mary had dropped a hint or two in her letters about Jenny and Charlie planning a wedding, and she wanted to see Leslie again – he seemed to change every time she saw him, and Denise had written to say he was talking nineteen to the dozen and kept asking for his Auntie Thirsty.

Thinking of weddings reminded her of Elsie's plans. 'So is it the big day today, then? Is Pete giving you a ring?' Ever since she had told them the news in the dormitory, Elsie had refused to say any more about her engagement. 'Come on, Else, you've been just teasing us all this time. You've got to come clean now.'

'No, I haven't. You just wait and see.' Elsie turned her head to grin at her. Her face was alive with excitement, and Thursday laughed.

'I can see it in your face! Honestly, Elsie, you're like an open book.'

'Well, you just read quietly then. Me and Pete want to announce it properly, all right?' They crossed the road for the final lap along Ann's Hill Road, and she gave Thursday a concerned look. 'You OK?'

Thursday nodded. 'My legs are a bit shaky but I'll make it. I'll be glad to get in by the fire, though.'

Within another ten minutes they were being welcomed into the cottage. Mrs Jackson fussed around them, taking Thursday's coat and exclaiming over her thin, pale face. Mr Jackson pushed her into the second best chair by the fire, opposite old Mrs Jenkins, and she found a cup of tea thrust into her hand and a plate of biscuits – whole ones, not broken – set on the little table beside her. Elsie, who was still in the passage renewing acquaintance with Pete, whom she had not seen for almost forty-eight hours, came in after a few minutes, flushed and smiling, her hair somewhat tousled. Pete followed, his brown hair flopping over his beaming round face.

'Happy Christmas, Mum and Dad. Happy Christmas, Gran. Did you have a nice day yesterday?'

'Well, it wasn't like before the war,' began old Mrs Jenkins, rehearsing a well-worn theme, and then, catching her daughter's eye, 'but it wasn't so bad. Your mum cooked a nice dinner. I done the sprouts – straight out of the garden they were – and the pudding was all right, though she only let me have a bit, said it was bad for me.' The old lady snorted. 'Bad for me, I ask you! Christmas pudding! It's not even as if it was *rich*, not like before—'

'Before the war!' Elsie joined in. 'Never mind, Gran, we've got a nice box of chocolates for you, all soft centres, and you're to have them all to yourself. Here's a box for you too, Mum – Black Magic, your favourite. And some baccy for Dad, that Pete got with his issue. So no more complaints about the war, all right? It's Christmas and we're going to forget all that.'

'Oh, Elsie, you shouldn't have. These must have taken up all your ration for the past two months.'

Elsie patted her tummy. 'Do me good to go without. I need to lose a bit of fat for me wedding.'

There was a tiny silence. Marge and Alf Jackson stared at their daughter and then at Pete, standing self-consciously beside her, while old Mrs Jenkins gave a cackle of laughter and exclaimed that she knew it all along, she'd seen it coming, blest if she hadn't.

'Wedding!' Marge threw her arms round her daughter. 'Oh, Elsie, you naughty girl, you never gave us a clue! And you Pete, you're just as bad, coming in here and not saying a word. It's a good job we've got some sherry and port in for Christmas or we wouldn't even be able to drink your health.'

'And I dunno what happened to asking the father's permission,' Alf added, gripping the young sailor's hand and shaking it hard. 'But we'll say no more about that. Too glad to have someone take her off our hands.'

'Dad! What a thing to say!' But Elsie was laughing, and Thursday caught the sparkle in her eyes. She came forward and gave Elsie a kiss.

'Hey, shouldn't we be congratulating you? Where's the ring?'

Elsie held out her left hand. 'I thought you'd never ask. Well? What d'you think?'

Thursday gazed at it. Three small diamonds, just as Elsie had said she would have, glittered on her third finger. They were no more than tiny specks, but they were real enough and she felt a sudden lump in her throat. 'It's lovely, Elsie.'

Mrs Jackson took Elsie's fingers in hers and inspected the ring. 'It is. I'm really pleased. Congratulations, Pete.'

'Though I'm not sure you know what you're letting yourself in for,' her husband added, giving Elsie a smacking kiss. 'Better not be in too much of a hurry to tie the knot. You know what they say.'

'No, we don't, Dad,' Elsie said cheekily, bending to show her grandmother the ring. 'What do they say?'

'Marry in haste, repent at leisure,' piped up old Mrs Jenkins. 'That's what he means, ain't it? Not that he practised what he preaches, mind. He and our Marge were only engaged six months before they had—'

'Yes, and that's not all they say,' Mrs Jackson interrupted, her cheeks suddenly pink. 'Change your name and not the letter, marry for worse and not for better! Jenkins to Jackson, that's what I did, and look at me now.'

'Go on, love, you haven't done so bad,' her husband said, putting his arm round her plump waist. 'We haven't had a bad life, have we, all things considered.'

Marge Jackson gave him a glance that mixed fondness with mild exasperation. 'No, we haven't, as a matter of fact. If these two youngsters do half as well, they'll be all right.'

'That's true,' Mrs Jenkins agreed, 'but I hope they won't take too long getting round to the wedding. I want to see me granddaughter wed before I die.'

'Don't talk daft, Gran, you're going to live for years yet. But we're not going to hang about, are we, Pete? We've set the date already – St Valentine's Day, ain't that right?'

'Blimey, that don't give us long,' her father said. 'Still, I can see your point, Else, grab him while he's keen. And now what about something to celebrate? Didn't I see you put a bottle of sherry in the cupboard the other day, Marge? I'll get it out now, if young Thursday'll excuse me.' He leaned past her to open the door of the alcove cupboard and brought out the bottle. He poured a measure into each of the glasses that his wife brought in on a little tray, and lifted one into the air. 'Congratulations to the happy couple, and may all your troubles be little ones.'

'Alf! Honestly,' Marge said to Thursday, 'I don't know what to do with him sometimes. I'm already dreading his wedding speech.'

Alf Jackson grinned and then lifted his glass again. This time, his grin faded and his voice was solemn as he said, 'And here's a toast to absent friends.'

'Absent friends,' they echoed, and Thursday saw the moisture in their eyes and felt the tears pricking at her own.

Absent from the family today were Elsie's brothers Dave and Eddy. Dave, who hadn't been able to go into the Forces because of his leg which had never grown properly since he had infantile paralysis, had been killed by the bomb that had flattened their home in Portsmouth during the Blitz. Eddy, who was nearly twelve now, had been sent to the countryside soon after that and stayed there. Thursday knew that his mother had begged for him to come home for Christmas, but Alf had shaken his head. 'Not as things are now, love. Next year – it'll all be over by then. He'll be back for good. It won't be long now.'

Was he right, she wondered, lifting her glass in a private toast to her own 'absent friends' – her family in Worcester, her Cousin Mike in the sanatorium, her brother Steve in a German prisoner-of-war camp and her other cousin, Leslie, lost in his Spitfire. And Connor, somewhere off the coast of Africa.

And there was another absent friend too. Mark, who was no doubt enjoying Christmas with his rich, beautiful lady friend. His fiancée, perhaps. Possibly even, by now, his wife.

The sherry burned her throat and she blinked away the tears.

'That was a smashing day,' Elsie said dreamily as they cycled back through the darkened streets, their lights showing only the faintest glow to reveal the way. 'I think I'll get engaged more often.'

Thursday laughed. 'You're a dope. You just be satisfied with the one you've got. He's a nice chap.'

'Course he is. I only meant I'd get engaged to *him* more often. Anyway, we've got the wedding to think about now, I reckon that'll keep me busy. It's only two months, you know.'

'As you've pointed out at least a dozen times already.' Thursday was beginning to feel tired. It had been a good day but underneath all the celebrations she'd been conscious of a sense of loneliness. I'm missing Connor, she thought. I ought to be used to it by now but it seems to get worse as time goes on. It's been so long.

And she knew too that it wasn't just Connor she was missing. Try as she might, she couldn't push Mark's image out of her mind. His dark, narrow face and deep brown eyes wouldn't be pushed away. It was as if he were trying to force himself into her thoughts, refusing to be forgotten, refusing to be put into the past. It's because we never said a proper goodbye, she thought. And whose fault was that?

'What did that letter say?' Elsie asked suddenly, and Thursday turned her head to stare at her in the darkness.

'What letter?'

'You know – the one I brought you when you had 'flu. Postmarked Rochester. Don't tell me it wasn't from him. I've been waiting all this time for you to tell me,' Elsie added a little reproachfully.

'I don't know what you're talking about. I didn't have a letter.'

'Yes, you did. I brought it to you. I brought you a *Woman's Own* and a Mars bar. Cost me sixpence ha'penny, that lot did, and you say you never had them?'

'No, I'm not. I had them all right, but I never had a letter. Honestly, Elsie.'

'So what happened to it?' Elsie asked after a minute. They passed under the wall of St Mary's Church and cycled past Anglesey creek. 'What on earth happened to it?'

'I don't know. I must have gone to sleep or something. The *Woman's Own* and the Mars were inside my locker when I found them next day. But there wasn't any letter. Why – do you think it came from Mark?'

'Certain it did. Told you, the postmark was Rochester.' Elsie came to a halt and put one foot on the ground. 'Oh, *Thurs*. And I've been waiting all this time, wondering what it said.'

Thursday stopped too and put her head down on her handlebars. She felt a great flood of loneliness and misery engulf her. A letter from Mark. A letter, unread and unanswered. And now she would never know what he had said.

'I don't suppose it would have helped anyway,' she said, as much to herself as to Elsie. 'I expect it was just to tell me he was getting engaged. Or married. I expect it was to say goodbye.'

Chapter Twenty-Two

The battle for the Ardennes continued. In the Pacific, the Japanese began to launch kamikaze raids on American ships, their pilots screaming abuse as they plunged their aircraft into the helpless vessels below. In Italy, the Allies were slowed down by bad weather. In Burma, the British made a continual and steady advance. Back in Europe, Hungary declared war on Germany.

'Blimey,' Elsie said, 'talk about better late than never. Haven't they noticed the war's been going on over five years?'

'They couldn't do it before,' Louisa explained. 'They've only just—' But Elsie flapped her hands at her.

'It's all right, Lou, don't bother. I've given up trying to understand what's going on. All I know is they say we're winning, yet there's all these things happening all over the world and we're still getting the poor blokes here day after day. It don't make any sense to me.'

The Germans were still making raids over Britain. The V2s were inflicting terrible damage wherever they fell and V1s were still coming over too, fired now by Heinkel He-111 aircraft. At the same time, the authorities were, as Elsie said, behaving as though the end of the war must be in sight. The Home Guard had been disbanded before Christmas and paraded in Guildhall Square for their stand-down ceremony, and Portsmouth City Council was already planning the rebuilding of the city. There was talk of people being allowed to sail and boat off the local beaches by spring.

Thursday went home to see in the New Year with the family. As usual, everyone crowded into her parents' front room and Walter handed round glasses of sherry. He and Percy had dropped in at the pub earlier in the evening, but were home by ten, ready for the sandwiches and leftover Christmas cake that Mary and Flo had laid out on the table in the back room.

'Well, here's to another year,' he said, lifting his glass. 'Maybe this is the one that'll see the end of the war at last.'

'Oh, please God, I hope so,' Mary said feelingly. 'We've all had enough of it. Too much. Whoever would have thought, when we had our Thursday's twenty-first birthday party, that it'd still be going on over five years later?'

'It's probably just as well we didn't know,' Flo said. 'If I'd known then all the things that were going to happen – well, I don't know as I could've stood it.' She turned to Denise. 'Mind you, it's not been all bad. At least we've got our little Leslie to bring a bit of sunshine into our lives.'

'And we've done a lot of things we might not have done,' Thursday added. 'I have, anyway. If it hadn't been for the war I'd still be stuck in the tailor's workroom, setting sleeves! Being a VAD's been more interesting than that, specially going to Egypt.'

They sat quietly for a while. Thursday glanced around at the familiar faces, imagining the thoughts that were going on in each head. Her mother would be thinking of Steve, still in the POW camp, robbed of years of his youth but still alive. Auntie Flo would be grieving for Leslie but thankful that Mike had so miraculously returned to them. Denise would be missing Vic while Jenny, curled up on the settee with Charlie's arm around her, was looking forward to her own wedding, set for June.

The clock on the mantelpiece gave the whirring sound that meant it was about to strike. They all turned to look at it and saw the minute hand almost on the figure twelve. Midnight. The threshold of a new year.

'I'd like to propose a toast,' Walter said, clearing his throat. 'To all of us here. To absent friends. And to the end of the war.'

'The end of the war,' they echoed, and raised their glasses to their lips.

The room was quiet. And then Thursday lifted her head and took a little breath. 'Listen! Listen, everybody. They're ringing the bells!'

Denise, who was nearest the front door, scrambled to open it and they rushed outside, closing the door from the habit of five long years so that no light should escape. All along the street, other doors were opening and people coming out, calling greetings to each other and then falling silent to gaze at the stars and listen to the sound that had once been so familiar and was now so rare.

The bells of St John's Church, just around the corner, were ringing out into the frosty air. And over the river, in the city itself, they could hear the deeper tones of the cathedral bells, pealing with joy and hope and promise. Thursday felt the tears spring to her eyes and spill over her cheeks, while a hand groped for hers and gripped it hard.

'Is it really going to finish this year?' Denise whispered in her ear. 'Will Vic and Steve and all the others really be home this time next year, and everything be like it was again?'

'I hope so.' But Thursday didn't really believe that anything could be just as it had been before – not after all that had happened. They were going to have to start from scratch, building a new and different world. There was going to be so much to do . . .

But we'll be part of it, she thought with a sudden thrill of excitement. We're the ones that are going to do it. And as the bells sounded their message of hope, she thought of Connor and sent him a little prayer of love. *Perhaps we'll be part of it, together.*

Would 1945 really be the last year of the war?

It was bitterly cold all through January, and halfway through the month there was a tremendous thunderstorm accompanied by a powerful gale. Thursday and Louisa, deep in the underground theatre, knew little of it until the electricity failed and the hospital's own generators came into hasty operation, but Elsie reported later that it had been the best firework show she'd seen since before the war. 'You'd have thought it was another Blitz, except there were no bombs. There must have been some places struck, though. Honestly, the lightning was all over the sky, great jagged forks just like huge rips in a blackout curtain.'

A week later they woke to find the ground blanketed in snow. It was ankle-deep and all the matelots available were marshalled to clear the footpaths and roads through the hospital grounds. Some of the younger VADs built a snowman on the Quarter Deck and garnished it with a Petty Officer's cap. Thursday stared at it.

'Gosh, remember how we got hauled over the coals just for cycling along there? Do they realise they're dicing with death?'

'I think it's a case of catch 'em first,' Louisa said, looking amused.

'Doesn't it make you feel old, though. Once upon a time it would have been us getting up to tricks like that.'

'Yes, Thurs and me and Patsy, and the SBAs,' Elsie agreed. 'It all seems like a lifetime ago.'

'It was, for the boys.' Of the three of them – Tony West, Doug Brighton and Roy Greenaway – only Doug was still alive. He'd sent Elsie a Christmas card from somewhere in the Far East and asked her to remember him to the others. *Especially Thursday*, he'd scribbled. *'Tell her she's got to wait for me – like she promised!*

'I never did anything of the sort,' Thursday had protested when Elsie showed it to her. 'He's just taking the mickey – he knows we never got on.'

'Maybe he fancied you after all,' Elsie said wickedly. 'Maybe when the war's over he'll come marching back expecting you to fall into his arms and marry him. Then what will you do?'

'Well, that's one thing I *won't* have to worry about!' she retorted. 'I'll tell him to take a running jump, that's what. Anyway, he never will, and you know it. It's you he'll be coming back for, and what are *you* going to do when he asks you why you're a married woman?'

'A married woman,' Elsie sighed. 'Sounds lovely, doesn't it? Oh, I wish we'd decided to do it sooner – February seems ages away.'

But January, with is storms and blizzards, gave them too much to think about to bewail the slowness of time passing. All too soon, the month had drawn to a close and Elsie was beginning to panic.

'I'll never be ready in time! Mum's gone down with 'flu, and she's only got my frock half-made. She'll never get it finished now, and I'm useless with a needle.'

'Well, I'm not,' Thursday said. 'I was apprenticed for five years to a tailor, remember? I'll finish it.'

'Oh, Thurs, would you? Would you really?'

'Course I will. I'll go round every time I'm off duty. It'll be lovely to sew.' Thursday had seen the material for Elsie's wedding dress. It was actually a pair of cream satin curtains donated by a friend of Miss Makepeace, with some net for a veil. It had to be given back afterwards, but not many young women were able to have such a sumptuous wedding dress these days and Elsie knew how lucky she was. She had almost fallen to her knees in gratitude when Madam had given it to her, and had to have the swathe of silky fabric snatched away before her tears fell on it and stained it.

'Don't be silly, Jackson,' Madam had said sharply. 'Get up at once. My friend just happened to have this in a cupboard – no use during the blackout, of course – and she says once the war's over she'll refurbish right through. Naturally, I thought of you.'

'I don't know why, Madam,' Elsie said through her tears. 'I never thought you had that much time for me.'

Madam gazed at her for a moment, her bright brown eyes warm. 'Of course I have a great deal of time for you, Jackson,' she said. 'You're one of my best girls. You deserve something special for your wedding.'

'You can borrow it if you want to, for your wedding,' Elsie said to Thursday as they inspected the half-made dress at her grandmother's cottage. 'Madam says she's going to lend it out to anyone that wants one. She reckons there'll be a lot of Haslar weddings once the war's over.'

'I don't even know if I'm going to have a wedding,' Thursday said. 'I'm not making any decisions. I'm just going to wait and see.'

She had heard no more from Mark. Whatever the missing letter had said, he made no other effort to contact her, and she knew that it must have been goodbye. Even if it hadn't, she thought, he would have taken her silence for one. And she couldn't bring herself to write and tell him that she had never received his letter. The humiliation of another rejection would be too much to bear.

St Valentine's Day was on a Wednesday. Funny day to get married, Elsie said, but never mind. If people couldn't come to the wedding itself at St Mary's Church, they could pop round to the village hall in the evening where everyone was invited. Now that Thursday had taken over the frock, her mum would be able to do a bit of baking, helped by various neighbours and relatives in both Gosport and Portsmouth. Marge still wasn't a hundred per cent, she said, but she could manage a few cakes and sausage rolls, and she'd saved the Christmas cake for the wedding cake. No icing, of course, but icing hadn't been seen for years now and they'd almost forgotten what it looked like. Instead, she covered it in white paper and stood a figure of a sailor and his bride on top. She had shown Thursday the two lead soldiers, rescued from Eddy's old toybox, and while Alf found some dark blue paint to turn one into a matelot Thursday sewed a tiny satin frock on the other and covered its head with a scrap of net.

'It's not the sort of send-off we'd have given her before the war,' old Mrs Jenkins said in her reedy voice, 'but there you are, it's the best we can do, and I do want to see her settled before I die. At least she's getting married in white. And entitled to be, too, I hope,' she added, fixing her daughter with a stern look. 'Not like some I could mention.'

'Isn't it time for your medicine, Mum?' Marge interrupted. 'You know the doctor said every four hours prompt. She wanders a bit,' she added to Thursday in a low voice. 'And she's not been herself at all since Christmas. Keeps going off in a sort of dream, as if she's not quite with us, you know what I mean? I asked our Elsie to have a look at her when she was over yesterday and she said we ought to get the doctor in. But Mum's getting on, when all's said and done – eighty in March. It's a good age.'

Thursday glanced at the old woman. She lay back in her armchair, her eyes closed, and Thursday was alarmed to see how papery and yellow her skin had become, and how it seemed to have shrunk against the bones of her face. Her eyes too had a yellow tinge when she opened them for a moment, and her breathing seemed shallow and difficult.

'Has she had 'flu as well? Elsie didn't say.'

'No, not 'flu. Just going downhill, you know.' Mrs Jackson mouthed the words so that the old woman wouldn't hear them. 'It's old age. The doctor can't do anything.'

'I think you ought to call him, all the same. I mean, I don't know anything about old people but she really doesn't look well. It would be a shame if anything happened before the wedding.'

Marge looked alarmed. 'You think it could be that bad?'

'I don't know. I don't know anything about it. But . . .' Thursday left her sentence unfinished, afraid that the old woman's hearing might be sharper than they supposed. She might not be asleep at all, but listening to every word. Marge frowned anxiously.

'I suppose you and Else see more than we do, not being here all the time. You know, we get used to how she is, we don't see the changes. Oh dear, I don't know what to do for the best.'

'Get the doctor,' Thursday advised. 'I know it costs money, but Elsie would rather have her granny at the wedding than another dozen sausage rolls.' She snapped off her thread of Sylko and began to put away her sewing things. 'I'll have to be going now, Mrs

Jackson. With all this snow and ice still about, I couldn't ride my bike and you can't be sure when the buses will run. I want to get back while it's still light – I don't like walking down Clayhall Road by myself in the dark. It feels haunted.'

'I expect it is,' Mrs Jackson said. 'All those poor sailors who've been along there and through those gates. And ending up in the cemetery,' she added ghoulishly. 'And then never knowing if one of those awful rockets will come down on top of you.'

'Yes, well, I'll be going, then,' Thursday said hastily. Elsie's mother was remarkably like her daughter at times. She bent over the recumbent figure of old Mrs Jenkins and laid her hand on the thin, bony wrist. The pulse felt light and jumpy. 'And you will get the doctor, won't you?'

'Yes, if you think I should.' Marge Jackson stared at her mother, her mouth working a little. 'I can see what you mean. I've been able to see it for days really, only I felt so poorly meself. And I didn't want to think about it, somehow. I mean, she's me mum. She's always been there. I know she's old but – well, you never want to lose your mum, do you?'

'No,' Thursday said, thinking of how terrible it would be to lose her own mother. 'No, you don't.'

She went out of the house and began the walk back to Haslar. It was hardly even worth waiting for a bus, and she would have had to walk the last half mile anyway. The worst half mile, she thought, between those high, haunted walls.

I wish I'd never said that to Mrs Jackson, she thought ruefully. It was bad enough before, just being in the dark and wondering if a rocket was on its way, but now I've got all those dead sailors to think about as well. And those poor young Wrens who were killed in that big raid and buried in the cemetery here. Plus all the others who have died at Haslar over the last two hundred years and whose ghosts may be out on a night like this . . .

It was stupid to think like that, letting her imagination run away with her. But death seemed very much in the air, somehow, and as she half-ran that last half mile she shivered with sudden premonition. Something was going to happen. She was sure of it.

Daylight next morning dispelled Thursday's fears and she scolded herself for being silly. After five years of war, she ought to be used to fear and death – it had become so much a part of daily living that you just pushed it out of your mind – but there had been something particularly eerie about the idea of the dead sailors. Thousands of people were buried at Haslar – it was one of the first things Madam told new arrivals during her welcoming lecture, when she related a little of its history. Even before the hospital had been built, it was a common burial ground, and then most of the sailors who arrived were already dying. In one year alone, nearly two thousand men had died there, and then there were thousands more who came back from Corunna already too far gone with typhus to be saved, and nearly four thousand others in the paddock – and then the Turkish colony which had settled in Gosport ... No wonder I got the shivers, Thursday thought. You could drive yourself right round the bend, thinking about them all!

Firmly, she thrust her fears away, yet a few shreds still remained, hanging like cobwebs at the edge of her mind, and she couldn't quite rid herself of the sense of dread that had attacked her as she scurried between those high, redbrick walls.

As February came, the fighting continued as bitterly as the winds that scoured the frozen rutted slush still lining the roads. Yet it did seem that the tide was turning the Allies' way. The Red Army had crossed into Germany and were less than a hundred miles from Berlin. The United States, led by General MacArthur, were advancing through the Philippines to Manila, preparing to attack Japan, and the British had raided Japanese-controlled oil refineries in Sumatra. And there were *still* countries joining in – in South America, Ecuador declared war on Germany and Japan, Venezuela was reported to be considering the same action, and it seemed likely that Chile would follow suit before long. As Elsie said, it was better late than never, and if they all joined this new United Nations that was being talked about it would be all to the good.

Not that Elsie had much time to bother about the news these days. When she wasn't in the ward she was entirely wrapped up in wedding preparations. You wouldn't think there'd be so much to do, Thursday thought, when there was so little in the shops and the happy couple weren't even going to set up a proper home together. But they both seemed to have endless numbers of relatives in Portsmouth, Gosport and Fareham, and all would expect to be invited, even if they had to bring their own sandwiches. 'And that wouldn't be a bad idea,' Elsie observed. 'Be easier all round. But you can't ask people to do that, can you, even in wartime. And I don't want to look back in fifty years' time and just remember spam sandwiches!'

In the event, a number of relatives got together and organised a wedding feast, collecting contributions from the rest and spending the final week in a frenzy of baking. They descended on the Memorial Hall the night before the wedding and set up trestle tables, covering them with sheets and an assortment of crockery, and refused to let Elsie in when she and the other girls arrived begging to see how they were getting on. 'Go away,' said a middle-aged lady who seemed to be one of the aunts, although Thursday never made out whether she was Elsie's or Pete's and wasn't convinced that they knew, either. 'Go away. You can't come in. It's to be a surprise.'

'Blimey, what the flipping heck are they up to in there?' Elsie muttered as the two girls turned away. 'All they're supposed to be doing is a few sausage rolls.'

Thursday giggled. 'Maybe the sausages are trying to escape. Come on, let's go to the village inn and have a drink to celebrate your last night of freedom. I don't see why it should be just the man who gets a stag night.'

'And Pete had better not enjoy *his* last night of freedom too much,' Elsie said darkly. 'I've told him, if he turns up with a thick head it's all off.'

They strolled on to the village inn, passing the church where Elsie would be married next day. Thursday felt Patsy close beside her, and squeezed her arm, knowing she must be thinking of her own wedding day. Elsie had been afraid that Patsy wouldn't want to come but Patsy had told her not to be so silly. 'Of course I'm coming to your wedding. I can't moon around here while all the rest of you are having fun. And I don't expect people to stop living just because – because –' It was obviously not going to be easy for her, but Patsy had surprised them all with her courage and Thursday knew that nobody seeing her next day would guess that she nursed a broken heart.

'Looking forward to being a bridesmaid, Thursday?' Louisa enquired as Elsie went to the bar for their drinks. 'It's your second time, isn't it?'

'Yes.' Thursday had been Patsy's bridesmaid too. 'Once more, and that's my chances of ever getting married gone right out of the window. You know what they say – three times a bridesmaid, never a bride!'

'That's a pity,' Louisa said. 'I was going to ask you to be mine too.'

They stared at her. 'When are you getting married? Is Andrew coming back?'

Louisa laughed. 'Not as far as I know. I'm just thinking ahead to the end of the war. There'll be hundreds of weddings then, and I want to be ready for mine – I don't want to wait. How about you, Thursday?'

Thursday flushed. 'I don't know. We've got to see if we still feel the same. And there's his family too – they're so different from mine.'

'What does that matter? They're not marrying each other.'

'No, but it means *we're* different. He's more like you, Lou – in ordinary life, you could have met and gone out together and nobody would have batted an eyelid. But me and Connor, we'd never have come across each other. My family are just working class, and his father's a doctor like him.'

'I don't think that sort of thing'll matter after the war,' Louisa said. 'Class, and all that – it doesn't mean a thing these days. Look at you three, you're as good VADs as the rest of us who come from privileged backgrounds. Better than some. And look at all the working-class girls and men who've gone on to get commissions in the Services. And done good things in civvy life, too. We'll never be able to go back to a class system, with people firmly put back in their boxes.'

Thursday shook her head. 'I don't know. There'll still be a huge amount of working-class people who'll stay there. People in factories and things. How can they ever get out, once things go back to the way they were?'

'But they won't, that's the point. The Government's talking about making education better for everyone, so that you can go to a grammar school just through passing a scholarship exam, and not have to pay. Anyone bright enough will be able to go. *You* three could have gone.'

'Gone where?' Elsie asked, bringing the drinks over.

'To grammar school,' Thursday said. 'Lou says we'll all be posh when the war's over.'

Elsie gave a hoot of laughter. 'That'll be the day! Common as muck I am, always have been and always will be. What are we going to do, take elocution lessons? "How now, brown cow" and all that?'

'No, but your children might,' Louisa said. 'Honestly, this war is going to make a difference. Look at the last one – women did so much then, they just *had* to give them the vote. Well, this time they'll see that it's intelligence and hard work that matter more than inheriting a lot of money.'

'And that's just as well,' Elsie said cheerfully, 'because I'm never likely to inherit money, and neither are my kids. Now look, you've all got a drink in front of you – isn't anyone going to drink my health? It's my wedding day tomorrow, just in case you've forgotten!'

They laughed and raised their glasses. 'To Elsie,' Thursday declared. 'Elsie and Pete. A long life and a happy one.'

Patsy and Louisa echoed her words. They drank, and then set down their glasses. But as the other three began to laugh and chatter, Thursday felt once again that tiny chill of premonition, as if something were about to happen.

Don't be daft, she scolded herself. Of course something's going to happen. Elsie's getting married. That's all. And everything's going to be all right.

Chapter Twenty-Three

Elsie's wedding day dawned bright and sunny, one of those February days when spring seems suddenly to have woken up and rushed to action stations. Thursday, waking early, stretched in her bunk and rolled over to peer down at Elsie on the lower bed. 'Come on, slug-abed. You're getting married, remember?'

Elsie yawned and pulled the blanket over her head. 'I'm getting my sleep in. Don't expect I'll get much tonight.'

'Oh, *Elsie*.' Thursday grinned and slid down to the floor. She took hold of the corner of Elsie's blankets and tugged, leaving her curled up in her pyjamas. 'Hope you've got something a bit daintier than those to wear. Talk about passion-killers!'

'As a matter of fact,' Elsie said, sitting up reluctantly and trying to drag the blankets out of Thursday's grasp, 'I've got a smashing new nightie. Gran gave it to me yesterday. She said she didn't need the coupons so she'd saved them up and they had it in that shop in Stoke Road, kept since before the war. Only found it a few days before, apparently. I meant to show it you.' She gave up trying to get the blankets back and reached under her bunk for her suitcase. 'Look.'

'It's lovely.' Thursday gazed at the shimmering white fabric. 'It's Swiss cotton, isn't it? You mean to say they'd got this hidden away all these years?'

'Yes, you can tell because there are still yellow marks where it's been folded so long, see? Mum gave it a good wash but she couldn't get them all out.' Elsie held the nightgown against herself and swayed dreamily. 'I never thought I'd have anything like this for my wedding night.'

'You'll knock him out,' Thursday declared. 'Show it to the others and then put it away again. There's a lot to do and *you* might be on leave as of now, but me and the others have still got duties to go to. Now look, me and Patsy'll be off at twelve and we'll have our baths then and come straight over to your gran's, all right? Right – you can have your blankets back,' she added, piling them on Elsie's bunk, 'and have your lie-in.'

'Go on, I'll never get back to sleep now. I'll come over to breakfast with you. Got to keep up my strength.' She glanced out of the window. 'It's going to be a nice day! Maybe I'll have a walk along the sea wall first to pass the time. Just you make sure you and Patsy are there by one o'clock. Mum wants us all to have dinner together before we start to get ready.'

Thursday ran down the steps to the operating theatre with a lighter heart. It was just the bad weather that had made her feel a bit down lately, she thought, that and the 'flu she'd had before Christmas. Today, the sun was out and everything seemed brighter. Elsie was getting married, and even though there was still a long way to go, the war really did seem to be coming to an end. Mike was doing well in the sanatorium, Steve was OK in prison camp, Connor was now on his way to Australia as part of the South Pacific Fleet, and Vic was in Italy. She turned her mind away from the things that might yet go wrong. Today wasn't a day for being miserable.

By lunchtime, all those going to Elsie's wedding were in a frenzy. Everyone who could get the afternoon off duty was going, even Vera Hapgood who had apologised (rather ungraciously, but then as Elsie remarked she probably didn't know any other way) for her remarks about Elsie when they'd first returned from Egypt. 'She's not really so bad,' Thursday had said, urging Elsie to include her in the guest list. 'I feel rather sorry for her. She just finds it difficult to make friends, that's all.'

'She could try being nice to people for a start,' Elsie said, but she wrote her name on the list and Vera had responded by giving her a toasting fork as a wedding present and got out her best civvy clothes for the occasion. Being Vera, however, even that hadn't gone right.

'Oh *no*, there's a moth-hole in my green jumper! Look, right in the front.' She held up the garment and they crowded round to look.

'It's not very big,' Ellen said uncertainly, and Vera snorted.

'It'll show, just the same. I'll have to darn it – anyone got any wool that might match?'

Nobody had, and Vera had to darn it with a scrap of navy-blue wool which was all that they could find. 'It'll show even more now,' she moaned. 'I'll have to wear my waistcoat to hide it, and Elsie wore that herself, when Patsy got married!'

Thursday bit her lip and glanced swiftly at Patsy. It was inevitable that there would be reminders of that other wedding day four years ago, but Patsy gave no sign. It was as if she had determined that Elsie's day was to be a happy one, with no sad memories.

'You'll look OK,' Thursday told Vera. 'I think a waistcoat looks smart anyway, and it just picks up the colour of your jumper. Nobody'll notice that darn if you keep it buttoned up.'

She and Patsy, as bridesmaids, were going to the cottage near Ann's Hill, to help Elsie get ready and dress in their own finery. Carried away by her success in finishing Elsie's wedding dress, Thursday had altered two old dance dresses, sent for by Louisa from her own pre-war wardrobe, and when the three girls were all arrayed in the tiny bedroom they looked at each other in amazement.

'Blimey,' Elsie said in an awed tone, 'is this really us? We look proper glamorous.'

'It's this gorgeous material,' Patsy said, touching the satin of Elsie's dress with her fingertips. 'It's like something in a film. And these lovely frocks of Louie's. That colour looks really smashing on you, Thursday.'

'Well, I've always liked green but I was afraid Elsie might not like it for her wedding,' Thursday admitted. 'I mean, you might have thought it was unlucky.'

'Not that colour – it's more of a turquoise, isn't it? Sea-green, anyway. And that rose pink's lovely on you, Pats, with your dark hair.' Elsie turned slowly, trying to glimpse more of her own dress in the dressing-table mirror. 'Mum thought it was a bit funny not having matching bridesmaids but I reckon it's going to look smashing. A rainbow wedding.'

'Yes,' Thursday said slowly. 'A rainbow wedding. Bringing hope – that's what rainbows are supposed to do, aren't they? Hope for the world.'

'Coo, we are getting deep!' Elsie giggled. 'Come on, Thurs, stop going all poetic and come downstairs. You're supposed to be going on ahead with Mum, remember, and then Dad and me in the second taxi, and I don't want to be late, even if it is the bride's privilege. Pete might decide to call it all off while he's still got the chance!'

They went downstairs carefully, trying not to catch their dresses against the walls of the narrow staircase. The Jacksons were waiting in the front room, all arrayed in their Sunday best and with Eddy, home for the occasion, in a jacket handed down from one of his cousins. It was the first time Thursday had seen Eddy since she'd returned from Egypt and she could scarcely believe that this tall, lanky youth was the same noisy little boy she'd first met over in Copnor. He grinned at her self-consciously but there was no time to talk, for the rest of the family were exclaiming over the girls' appearance.

'Oh Elsie, you look beautiful,' Marge Jackson said, her eyes filling with tears. 'Doesn't she, Alf?'

'Looks a proper picture,' he agreed a bit huskily. 'So do you other two, for that matter. If I was young Pete, I'd be hard put to it to know which one to marry, and that's the truth! Now look, the taxi's at the door and you'd all better get in, though it's going to be a bit of a squash with five of you.'

'Let Gran come with us,' Elsie said. 'It's daft having that lot in one car and only you and me in the other one. You can sit in the front, Gran, with the driver.'

'I don't know as I want to come after all,' the old lady said, and Thursday noticed with alarm that her colour seemed bad again, despite the new medicine that the doctor had prescribed. Following her advice, Marge had called the doctor but he'd shaken his head and said there wasn't much he could do, it was old age and nature must take its course. All he could do was prescribe something to help her but all it seemed to do, Marge said, was make her sleep more. Though maybe that wasn't a bad thing; sleep was always good for you.

One of these days, Thursday thought, she's going to go to sleep and not wake up again, and the doctor knows that.

'Not come?' Elsie echoed in dismay. 'Gran, you've got to come. You know you've been wanting to see me married. And you've got all dressed up, too.'

'Perhaps it was too much for her,' Marge said in a low voice. 'All the fuss and bother – she's had enough.'

Elsie went down on her knees beside the old lady. 'Please come, Gran. It won't be the same without you.' She laid her plump hand over the skinny claw and looked into the rheumy, yellowing eyes. 'Please.'

There was a little silence, then the old lady sighed. 'Oh, all right then, seeing as it's you. Get me into the car. But I'm not doing any dancing, mind. Nor any washing up or any of that.'

Elsie laughed. 'You won't have to! Just see me get married and enjoy yourself, that's all I ask. And you won't have to stay late, we'll get a taxi specially to bring you home, whenever you want it.'

Marge looked at the clock on the mantelpiece. 'Come on, you girls, it's time we went!' She kissed her daughter. 'Have a happy life, Elsie,' she said softly. 'If you do half as well as your dad and me you'll be all right. Now, I'll see you in church, and mind out for that dress in the car door!'

The wedding went smoothly from start to finish, not counting the small cousin who cried through the entire service, the row over a piece of wedding cake between two of Elsie's aunts who hadn't spoken for years and ought (Alf Jackson said caustically) to have stayed that way, and the local stray dog which somehow got in and made off with a whole plate of sausage rolls. But everyone agreed that the bride looked lovely, the groom not too hung over and quite overwhelmed when he saw her walk up the aisle, the bridesmaids were pretty and the reception every bit as good as a really posh do. (Better, said Louisa, who'd been to more posh do's than most of them.) And there was plenty to eat and drink, thanks to all the contributions that had been made, and all that was left at the end of the meal were six Spam sandwiches.

'I knew someone'd bring some,' Elsie remarked, helping to clear up for the dancing. 'Even the flaming dog turned its nose up at them.'

'Go away,' Thursday said, giving her a push. 'You're not supposed to be doing this. You're the bride.'

'Once a skivvy, always a skivvy,' Elsie said cheerfully, but went off to find her new husband. 'Come on, Pete, let's get the gramophone going and have a dance.'

'You're not supposed to be doing it either, Thursday,' one of

Elsie's cousins said. 'You're a bridesmaid. Go and find a partner and enjoy yourself. There are plenty of us here to do this.'

Thursday hesitated, then went to join Patsy beside the dance floor. One of Pete's mates was looking after the gramophone and plenty of people had brought records. There seemed to be a bit of everything, from Victor Silvester to Ambrose, and just at the moment he was playing Glenn Miller's 'Little Brown Jug', with everyone singing the words.

'They never found him, did they?' Thursday said sadly. 'He must have been shot down, I suppose.'

'Like that film star Leslie Howard a couple of years ago,' Patsy agreed. 'I liked him, didn't you? He was lovely in *Gone with the Wind*. And *Pimpernel Smith*, and *The First of the Few*. It seems an awful shame when people like that get killed, when all they're trying to do is entertain people.'

They watched the dancers for a few minutes. The record changed to an old Tommy Dorsey, with Frank Sinatra singing. Else and Pete were jitterbugging, to applause from their friends and the amazement of their families. Alf Jackson, his mouth open, blinked as Pete swung his bride over his shoulder, and called out, 'Is that what you get up to at those dance halls? I'd have put my foot down if I'd known!'

'And a fat lot of good it would have done you,' Elsie shouted back. 'Come on, Dad. Have a go!' She dragged him out on to the floor and nodded at Pete's sailor friend to play the record again.

Thursday giggled. She turned to Patsy to say something and then, over Patsy's shoulder, her eye caught the movement of the door opening and she felt her voice die in her throat.

A man had come quietly in. He was tall, with broad shoulders and a dark, narrow face. His glance moved intently around the room, noting first the dancers and then the people who stood or sat around the fringe. As Thursday watched, frozen, he saw her and for a moment of icy, unreal silence, she felt as if the world had stopped.

'Patsy,' she whispered, 'tell me I'm dreaming. Please, for God's sake, tell me I'm dreaming.'

'How did you know where to find me?' she asked as they moved around the dance floor in a slow foxtrot.

Mark smiled down at her. 'I went to Miss Makepeace. She told me you were all here at Elsie's wedding reception.'

'Oh yes, she was at the service, but she went back after that. But – I still don't know why . . .'

'Why I'm here? I came to find you, of course, Thursday.'

She was silent. It was obvious that was what he had come for, but *why* was another question. And it was just one of the tumult of questions flooding her brain, now that the first shock of seeing him was over. The girl at Rochester. The unread letter. Why – why – *why*?

'Why now, after all this time?' she asked, half to herself. 'Why today?'

'Surely you know what day it is,' he said, whirling her round the corner.

'It's Elsie's wedding day. But you didn't know that, did you? And I still don't see—'

'Thursday,' he said gently, 'it's St Valentine's Day. The day for sweethearts to find each other. What better day could there be for me to come and find you?'

St Valentine's Day! She stared at him, shocked. 'It's my godson's birthday,' she said stupidly, her mind veering away from his words. 'Leslie, my cousin Denise's little boy. He's four.'

'It's the day for sweethearts,' he insisted, swirling her around again. 'Thursday, for God's sake let's get out of here. I can't hear myself think with all this racket going on, and I want you to myself, somewhere quiet.'

'But I'm a bridesmaid!'

'The wedding's over. Look, Elsie and her man are getting ready to leave. The party'll be breaking up soon anyway. Come *on*.'

'I've got to be in by ten-thirty.'

'You haven't,' he said. 'I squared it with Miss Makepeace. She says you can have till midnight. Come on, Thursday, we've got things to talk about.'

She stopped in the middle of the floor and stared at him. 'You squared it with Madam? You asked her if I could stop out late, without even knowing if I'd want to? Just who do you think you are, Mark Sangster? Who do you think *I* am?' Only vaguely aware of the other dancers trying to pass them, of people stopping to look, she went on, her voice rising, '*I* decide when I want a late pass, right? *I* decide when I'll stay out late, and who with! And why on earth do you think I should want to stay out late with you anyway? What's all this about? Your glamorous fiancée left you, has she, so you thought you'd slip back to Haslar and see if that little VAD was still in love with you? Well, take it from me she's not! I don't know why you came here, and I don't know why you've gatecrashed Elsie's wedding, and I *don't care*! I never want to see you again – *never*!'

There was a moment of complete silence. Thursday stood glaring at him, panting slightly, her eyes snapping with fury. Mark stared back at her, his lazy eyes open wide. And then the little ring of onlookers who had formed about them broke into spontaneous applause.

'That's it, Thurs! You tell him!' 'Tell him where he gets off!' 'Crikey – don't she look a smasher when she's in a bate!' 'Tell you what, *I* wouldn't like to cross her, matey, straight I wouldn't.' 'Bet she's a right tartar on the wards.'

Thursday glanced around and flushed scarlet. With a little sob, she put both hands up to her burning face and ran towards the door. It opened as if by magic and she ran straight through and out into moonlight. The night air struck like ice against her bare arms and she hesitated, then turned left for the hospital. I don't care if I do catch cold, she thought, I'm not going back in there again. *Nothing* would make me go back in there again.

'Thursday! *Thursday!* Wait a minute!'

The voice only made her run faster. Go away, she thought frantically, stumbling along the slippery pavement, go away. Leave me alone. But as she heard the footsteps behind her draw nearer, she knew it was useless and she stopped and leaned against the cemetery wall, panting and half sobbing. In another moment Mark was beside her, wrapping her coat – the same old blue overcoat that she'd worn to visit him in Rochester – around her shoulders. Gently, he took her in his arms and with one hand pressed her head to his chest, and she gave in and rested there while the sobs turned into real weeping and she trembled against his body.

'There,' he said softly. 'There. It's all right. My sweet, sweet Thursday, everything's all right.'

'It's not all right,' she wept. 'It's not all right at all. I was getting over you. I was *sure* I was getting over you. And now you've come back and – and I don't – I don't know – oh, Mark, what am I to do? What *am* I to do?'

He said nothing for a while. He continued to hold her, his hand stroking her hair. At last her sobs began to diminish and she lifted her tear-streaked face to look at him. He cupped her chin in his hand and bent to kiss her lips.

'I don't know what's going to happen, or what you're going to do,' he said. 'All I know is, I couldn't go away again without seeing you just once more. Without trying to find out,' he paused, 'without trying to find out once and for all just what we mean to each other – even if we mean anything at all. At least,' he laughed a little shakily, 'I know what you mean to me, Thursday. What I don't know, is what I mean to you.'

She stared at him. 'But you do. Why else would I have come all the way to Rochester to see you?'

'So why,' he asked, looking at her very seriously, 'didn't you answer my letter?'

The letter! Thursday had almost forgotten it. With the excitement of Mike's return, followed by the anxiety over his illness, and then Christmas and the hustle of preparing for Elsie's wedding, together with the worry over old Mrs Jenkins's health, she had completely forgotten the letter. In any case, she had made up her mind that it was no more than a formal goodbye, written perhaps from a guilty conscience. It had never occurred to her that Mark might be waiting for an answer.

'I never got your letter,' she said. 'At least, I did – Elsie says I did – but I was ill with 'flu and never saw it. It got lost. I only knew about it when Elsie asked me about it after I came out of the ward.'

'You were ill?' he broke in. 'Badly enough to be in hospital?'

'It was only 'flu,' she said, brushing it aside. 'I'm all right now. But I never saw your letter, Mark. I don't know what it said. And after I saw you with your – your fiancée that day – well, I knew it was all over anyway.' She looked up at him. 'Is that what you've come to tell me? That you're getting married?'

'Getting *married*?' He stared at her, then broke into laughter. 'Thursday, you've got it all wrong. That wasn't my fiancée. That was my . . .' He laughed again. 'This is beginning to sound like an old music-hall joke! Thursday, that wasn't my fiancée, that was my—'

His voice was drowned by a sudden clamour from the direction of the Memorial Hall. They both turned, startled, and saw in the silvery light a little crowd of people spill out on to the pavement, and then heard another voice – Elsie's voice. 'There they are!'

'They're coming after us,' she said, bewildered.

'Thursday!' Elsie's voice sounded again, and she recognised the note of panic in it. 'Thursday – is Mark there with you?'

'Yes,' she called. 'Why? What's happened?'

'We need him! We need a doctor.' Elsie was running towards them, a pale, shimmering ghost in her satin wedding dress. 'It's Gran, she's been took poorly. Louie and Patsy are with her now, but I'm scared. Oh, Thursday, I'm scared she's—'

Thursday gave him a push, but he was already running. The crowd seemed to gather him up, Elsie clinging to his arm as they raced towards the hall, and Thursday followed as quickly as she could, her overcoat still clutched around her shoulders. By the time she reached the door there was a crowd around it, everyone trying to scramble in at once. She thrust her way through, and they recognised her and let her pass. But when she stood at last looking down at the crumpled little figure on the floor, covered now by the coats that had been draped over her to try to keep her warm, she knew the truth. Old Mrs Jenkins had seen her granddaughter married, and then died.

Chapter Twenty-Four

'So why *did* you come?' Thursday asked. She was sitting opposite Mark in the British Restaurant that had been opened in the grammar school premises in Walpole Road. He'd wanted to take her somewhere smarter but, exhausted by the events of the day before and upset by Mrs Jenkins's death, she'd begged to go somewhere simple, close by. And British Restaurant food wasn't bad, after all. Meat and two veg and a pudding to follow, for just one and sixpence.

'I meant to spend more than one and sixpence on taking you out,' Mark said, looking ruefully at the menu. 'Woolton Pie and apple and custard. It's not much of a celebration.'

'I don't know what we're supposed to be celebrating,' Thursday said. She propped one elbow on the table and leaned her aching head on her hand. 'I wouldn't feel like it even if I did know.'

'Oh, come on, Thursday. The old lady was a good age and she had a nice easy death. Think of all the people you've seen die in pain and agony. The young men you've sat beside in hospitals. Look, if anyone asked me how I'd like to die, that's just the way I'd choose – at a party with all my family and friends around me, having just been to the wedding of my favourite grandchild! What more could anyone ask?'

'You've got some then, have you? Grandchildren?' Thursday said with a weak attempt at a joke. 'Oh, I suppose you're right, but well, for the past fortnight I've had this feeling something sad was going to happen, and I've been worried about Mrs Jenkins too. I knew she was poorly. It seems such a shame that it should happen on Elsie's wedding night.'

'Well, that's the way things go,' Mark said. 'It could have been a lot worse. I knew a fellow whose wedding reception was ruined by a bomb falling on it.'

'Oh, no!' Thursday stared at him, horrified. 'Was anyone killed?'

'Most of them. Thursday, you know we can't keep mourning, and Mrs Jenkins had had her life. It's not as if it was a baby or a young person dying.'

'No, you're right.' She took her elbow off the table and leaned back in her chair. 'So why *did* you come, Mark? And what about the letter you sent me? And the person you say isn't your fiancée?'

'Well, she isn't.' He looked at her and shook his head slowly. 'Oh Thursday, Thursday. If only you hadn't rushed off like that it could have been all cleared up there and then. Saved us both a lot of heartache.'

'Who says my heart's been aching?' she demanded at once, sitting up straight, then drooped again as he smiled at her.

'There must have been *some* reason why you came all that way, and it wasn't to bring me a Christmas card! Thursday, let's stop playing games with each other. One of the things I've always liked about you is that you're so straight, so direct. Anyway, I don't mind admitting *my* heart's been aching. Especially when you never replied to my letter.'

'I really didn't get it, Mark. I don't know what happened to it. Elsie said she put it on the locker, and I can only think it got tidied away and lost. Are you going to tell me what it said?'

'Yes,' he said, and reached across the table for her hand. 'But let's start at the beginning, shall we? First of all, let me tell you about Phoebe.'

'Phoebe? Is that the girl I saw you with?'

'Yes. Phoebe, my sister.' He looked at her and Thursday felt a blush run up her neck to cover her cheeks.

'Your *sister*?'

'Yes.'

Thursday bit her lips hard. She looked down at the table with its covering of slippery American cloth and its gravy stains and saw the pattern swim before her eyes. 'Oh, *Mark*.'

'She'd come to take me home,' he said, 'to our parents'. To have our own special Christmas as a family. The first we'd had together since the war began.'

'I've been such a fool,' Thursday said after a moment.

'It was understandable. She's certainly very glamorous – she's married to someone with a country estate – and I can see that it would never occur to you that an ugly devil like me might have a sister like that.'

Thursday's head snapped up. 'You're laughing at me!'

'Well, it *is* quite funny really, isn't it? Now that we're getting things sorted out, anyway – I must admit I hadn't seen the funny side before.' He smiled at her. 'Look, it doesn't matter now – we're together again. Let's enjoy ourselves.'

Thursday shook her head. 'But I feel such an idiot. The way I ran off and wouldn't even listen to you, and then didn't answer your letter. I can't see why you bothered with me after all that. I can't see why you came all this way.'

'I came to say goodbye,' he said quietly.

'*Goodbye*?'

The waitress arrived with their pie and vegetables. She was about fifty, a plain woman with a long, sour face, flat brown eyes and grey hair. She dumped the plates in front of them and went away again.

Mark looked after her ruefully. 'They're not like those girls in the Lyons Corner Houses, are they, these British Restaurant waitresses! Nothing Nippy about them.'

'They're doing their best. All the young women have been called up now. Mark, tell me what you mean. Why have you come just to say goodbye? If you thought I didn't want to hear from you again . . .'

'Not that sort of goodbye,' he said seriously. 'This is the sort of goodbye people say at railway stations. I'm going back on service, Thursday.' He glanced around him and picked up his knife and fork. 'Look, we can't discuss it here. Let's eat and then get out – go for a walk somewhere.'

Thursday ate in silence, her thoughts whirling. Mark had come to see her, still believing she wanted nothing more to do with him. He had written to explain, presumably, and she hadn't replied, yet he'd still come to say goodbye before he went away. He wouldn't have done that if it hadn't meant a lot to him. She looked up at last and found him watching her gravely.

'Tell me about the letter.'

He shrugged. 'It just said what I feel. That I love you and want you for my wife. And hell's teeth, I never meant to say that *here*! He glanced around him again at the bustling, noisy restaurant with its smell of boiled cabbage and custard. 'Honestly, couldn't we have found somewhere a bit more romantic for me to propose to you? Last time I did it, I was in bed and now here we are in the middle of a lot of saucepans!' He sighed with exasperation and Thursday giggled, feeling suddenly light-hearted. This was more like the old Mark, the one who made a joke of everything. He looked back at her and smiled. 'That's better. That's my girl.'

Thursday looked at him helplessly. 'But I'm not your girl, Mark. I never was. And it was because of – of what you said that I stopped coming to visit you. I *can't* promise to marry you.'

'I understand that. You've got this other fellow. But that won't stop me asking you, Thursday. I've got the right to do that. And that was what I said in my letter.' He put down his knife and fork and leaned forward. 'Look, if you're not making any decision about him until after the war, I've got a chance, haven't I? I can at least stand in the queue. And *you've* got the right to think about it,' he added. 'It's your life, Thursday. You've got to be sure you're sharing it with the right person. You need to know who's applying for the position.'

She stared at him, then laughed. 'I'm not offering you a job, Mark!'

'It was a figure of speech,' he said impatiently. 'You know that.'

'Yes.' She looked down again. The Woolton pie, basically just a mixture of oatmeal and vegetables – you never knew quite which ones would be used – was stodgy and unappetising. She sighed and laid down her own knife and fork. 'I'm sorry, I can't eat any more.'

'I'm not surprised,' he said grimly. 'It's bloody awful! Sorry, Thursday, but it is. Look, let's go. I'll get the bill.'

The waitress came over and looked at their plates. 'Didn't you like it?'

'Not much,' Mark said. 'Does anyone? Oh, it's all right, I know you're doing your best, and it filled a hole. But we'd like to pay now, please.'

'Pay? But you 'aven't 'ad your apple and custard.'

'We don't want them, thanks. We're in rather a hurry.'

'But it's all in. You got to 'ave them.'

'No, we haven't. Look, I'm quite happy to pay for them but we're not going to eat them, so . . .' Mark stopped as the waitress turned on her heel and marched away. He looked at Thursday and raised his eyebrows comically. 'And you say they're only calling up the younger ones? She's wasted in Civvy Street – she'd make a first-class Sergeant Major. Oh lor', she's bringing the flipping apple and custard anyway.' He looked up as the woman held the plates out to them, a challenging look in her flat eyes. 'I told you, we don't want them. They'll just be wasted.'

'I got to serve you with them. The dinner's all in – Woolton pie, and apple an' custard to follow, one and six the lot. I can't take the pudding off that.'

'I'm not asking you to. I just don't want to eat the ruddy stuff!' Mark dragged a few coins out of his pocket and slapped them down on the table. 'Look, that's enough to cover the bill *and* give you a tip you don't deserve! Short of strapping us to our chairs and force-feeding us, that's as far as you can go. Give the apple and custard to someone else with my compliments – say it's seconds.' He rose to his feet and pulled Thursday up beside him.

'But we don't *do* seconds!' The waitress's cry of outrage brought looks from everyone around them. Thursday bit her lip hard to repress her laughter and began to sidle towards the door, half expecting to be hauled back to finish her dinner. She glanced around and saw the grins on the faces of other diners.

Mark drew in a deep sigh of exasperation, picked up the bowls and slammed them down in front of a couple at the next table, who were just finishing their own pudding.

'You do now,' he said loudly and, catching Thursday's wrist, marched her towards the door.

Outside, they leaned against the wall, giggling helplessly. 'The look on her face! I thought she was going to explode!' Mark chuckled.

'I'll never be able to go in there again, never!' Thursday said.

'Would you want to?' he asked, pulling himself upright at last. 'I mean to say, Thursday – that pie! It was terrible.'

'It wasn't very good,' she acknowledged. 'But it's all right usually. They just have to use what they can get, and at least it's cheap.'

'Yes, and there's good reason for that!' He tucked her hand into his arm. 'Come on, let's go for a walk. I've got to go back this evening. We've only got a few hours together – don't let's waste them.'

They crossed the street and walked into Walpole Park. The little boating pool still had a few dinghies on it, that you could hire for sixpence an hour, and they walked past these and headed across the grass towards the creek. A thin, chilly wind scoured across the water but Thursday's hand, pressed between Mark's arm and his side, felt warm and secure. Her doubts had vanished, for the moment at least, and she felt a deep contentment wash over her. She leaned her head against his shoulder, and he stopped under a tall tree and took her in his arms.

'Mark, not here!'

'Sorry, I can't wait any longer.' He gathered her against him and pressed his lips against hers. For a moment, she felt a resistance; no man had kissed her like this since Connor had left. And then the firmness of his body against hers, the tenderness of his lips, spread their warmth through her and she felt a flare of desire and let herself soften against him.

'*Thursday* . . .'

'Mark.' She was shivering. Shakily, she tried to pull away. 'Mark, no. Not here.' She glanced around. There were a few people wandering across the grass and a couple of men fishing off the low wall. 'Please, Mark.'

He stared at her. His eyes were almost black, with only the narrowest of brown rims. He was breathing a little quickly and there was a flush on his cheeks. 'Thursday, I love you.'

Thursday bent her head. 'Please don't say that. Please.'

'But why not?' His voice was urgent. 'Look, I have the right to say it. It's what I feel. You can't stop me saying what I feel.' He waited a moment and then said, 'You feel it too. I know you do.'

She faced him, then put one hand to her forehead. 'Look, I can't make up my mind just like that. I can't. Please don't try to force me.'

'I'm not forcing you to do anything,' he said after a moment.

'You are. It feels as though you are.' She sighed and pulled herself from his arms. 'Please, let's just walk. Let's just be together. Tell me about your draft.'

'We don't call it a draft in the Army,' he said a little stiffly, walking beside her.

'Posting, then, or whatever it is. Where are you going?'

'You know I can't tell you that. Europe, somewhere, that's all.' He closed his mouth.

Thursday sighed. She stopped and faced him again. 'Don't let's quarrel. I'm sorry I can't say what you want me to say, but I have to have time to think about it. I have to think about Connor too.' She looked up at him pleadingly. 'Imagine if you were the one who'd gone away years ago, wouldn't you expect me to at least *try*?'

He looked away, his lips still closed, then took a breath and shrugged. 'I suppose so. Well, all right then, I would. In fact, if I were Connor and came home and found you'd gone off with another bloke, I'd probably want to kill him.' He glowered at her.

'Well, then,' Thursday said gently, 'you must see that that's what I've got to do. I am not going to let him come home and find I've gone off with someone else.'

'But I love you, Thursday!'

'Yes,' she said, 'and so does he. At least, I think he does.'

He pounced. 'You only *think* so? You don't know for sure?'

Thursday lost patience. 'How can I know for sure? He's been away for four years! I can't know anything for sure – all I can do is *remember*. I don't know if we'll be the same people when he comes back. I know I've changed – I'm older, I've been abroad, I've seen and done things I'd never dreamed about when we were here together, but I don't really know *how* I've changed, and I don't know how *he's* changed. I don't know if we'll have changed towards each other. And I can't know that until he comes home. I've got to wait!'

'So what you're saying,' Mark said after a long pause, 'is that you loved him then more than you love me now, and you want to see if you still do. And meanwhile, what am I to do? Hang around in the hope that you'll take me as second best?'

Thursday looked at him sadly. 'I didn't say that, Mark.'

'You didn't have to.' He stared moodily across the creek. The big blue gasometer rose on their right, the high slope of Pneumonia Bridge to their left. Across the strip of water lay the clutter of houses, the cemetery and the pig farm of Clayhall, and the high walls of Haslar Hospital and the prison. A few shabby boats bobbed on the chilly water.

He turned suddenly and gripped her arms. 'Thursday, I didn't want to leave without saying goodbye, without making things right between us. When you walked out of the ward that day, after I'd asked you to marry me, I felt as if my world had come to an end. You didn't come back, and when I asked that other nurse where you were, she told me you'd gone on leave. I was transferred to Rochester the next day and I never had a chance even to write you a note. I asked her to give you a message – didn't she tell you?'

Thursday stared at him. 'No, she didn't.'

'Well, maybe she forgot. Anyway, when I didn't hear, I thought you really meant what you said, that you didn't want to see me again. I tried to forget you, but I couldn't,' he said, his eyes burning. 'I couldn't forget. And then, when I came out of the ward that day with Phoebe and saw you standing there, it was like a dream. I couldn't believe it was you. By the time I realised it, you were gone, running as if the hounds of hell were after you. Why did you come, Thursday? Why, if you didn't love me?'

She looked down. 'I don't know. I just felt I had to. I couldn't leave it like that either.' She lifted her eyes to look at him. 'It all seems such a *muddle*.'

'I thought about it so much,' he said in a low voice. 'In the end I decided I had to write to you. I had to try just once more. But you never got my letter.' He met her eyes. 'I poured out my heart to you in that letter, Thursday. I told you all I felt about you, all you meant to me. I asked you again to marry me, or at least to give me a chance. And when you never answered, I thought it was hopeless. I tried to make myself forget you.'

Tears slipped from Thursday's eyes and trickled down her cheeks. She looked down at her hands. Would it have made any difference now if she had been wearing Connor's ring? Would it ever have got beyond an innocent flirtation, out there under the desert stars?

'I couldn't do it,' Mark went on. 'I couldn't forget you, Thursday. And then, when I got my posting, I knew I had to make one more attempt. I had to see you again, if only to say goodbye.'

'Oh, Mark,' she whispered.

He shrugged. 'Well, I know now, don't I? I know where your heart really is. You've made it very clear.'

Thursday shook her head and the tears flew in the wind. 'I haven't. I don't *know* any more. Mark, I was feeling so happy just now – just being with you. Surely that must mean something too. But I don't know what I'm going to feel when – when . . .'

'When Connor comes home,' he said. 'But the very fact that you're saying that tells me the truth, Thursday, can't you see that? If you really loved me, you wouldn't have these doubts. You'd know.'

Thursday was silent for a moment. Then she lifted her head again.

'I'm not going to be rushed into this, Mark,' she said quietly. 'It isn't just a matter of what I feel or who I feel it for. I made a promise. It might have been only to myself, but it's still important to me. I want to wait until Connor comes home. I'm going to see how I feel then. When I see him again, I think I'll know.'

'And suppose I don't wait? Suppose when you finally realise it was me, I've gone for good?'

'Then that'll be just my bad luck, won't it,' Thursday said. She looked him in the eye. 'Things are going to be different after the war, Mark. Women have learned what they can do. We've had freedom and independence and we know we can do a lot of different things. We aren't going to be dependent on men, not in the same way as before. We're not going to just accept that we've got to get married and have a man to look after us. We've learned that we can look after ourselves.'

He stared at her. Then he moved his head slightly in acknowledgement. 'Well, we'll see. Maybe you're right, or maybe you'll find that once the men come home things will go back to the way they were, quicker than you expect. But since you're so keen to keep your promises, Thursday, will you make one to me as well?'

'What is it?' she asked doubtfully, and he gave her a crooked smile.

'It's all right, I'm not going to propose to you again! Three times is quite enough, I think. But promise me that you'll see me just once more when all this is over, will you? Promise me you'll give me an equal chance with Connor.'

She thought for a moment, then nodded. 'Yes, Mark. I'll do that. I promise.'

He looked down at her, his expression a mixture of regret and resignation. 'Well, if that's the best I can have, I'll take it. And one more kiss? Just to seal a bargain?'

She smiled and lifted her face. Once again, Mark gathered her close and bent his head so that his lips met hers. Once again, they clung closely together and swung giddily into their own reeling, leaping world, oblivious of the gulls that wheeled about their heads and the wind that cut through their bodies. Thursday, her eyes closed, felt his hands move on her shoulders, and cup the back of her head; she dug her fingers into the thick fabric of his jacket and leaned her body into his, sinking herself into the experience of the moment, trying to store it in her memory to be cherished and treasured in the lonely months to come.

The kiss ended. Mark lifted his head and looked down into her eyes. They gazed at each other and then he broke away.

'I'm going to say goodbye now,' he murmured. 'If I don't, I'll never be able to go. Oh, *Thursday*!'

'Mark!' She clung to him in sudden desperation. Shakily, he reached up his hands and unhooked hers from his shoulders. He bent his head and gave her one last, firm kiss, and then stepped back.

'Just keep that promise, Thursday,' he said huskily. 'That's all I ask. See me one last time before you make up your mind.' And then he turned and began to walk away towards the town.

Thursday watched him. She wanted to run after him, to call him back, to hold him once more and tell him that she'd promise anything, anything he wanted, if he would only stay with her. But once again Connor's face rose in her mind and his voice sounded in her ears. *I love you, Thursday . . . I wish it could have been a ring . . .*

He knew this might happen, she thought, her throat aching with tears. He knew I'd meet other people, he knew I might fall in love. That's why he wouldn't tie me down. But I wanted to be tied down. I tied *myself* down.

And now she had another promise to keep.

Chapter Twenty-Five

By the end of February 1945 almost every country in the world was at war. The plan to form a 'United Nations' amongst all those countries which had declared war by 1 March had resulted in a rush to sign up, from South America to the Middle East. In the last week of the month, Egypt, Uruguay, Syria, Lebanon and Saudi Arabia all declared war on Germany, and some on Japan as well. It was clear that the world wanted peace, and saw that only a concerted and co-operative effort would achieve and maintain such an ideal.

Elsie and Pete enjoyed a brief honeymoon of just two nights out in the country, with Eddy's foster-parents. They came back with their happiness muted by Mrs Jenkins's funeral, and Elsie told Thursday that she'd be back in Haslar by the end of the week. 'Not to sleep, mind,' she said with a wink. 'I'll be going back to Pete's place every night – his mum and dad have given us the front room. Of course, I'll have to move back into the dormitory if there's another emergency, but I'm afraid you won't be seeing so much of me now I'm a married woman.'

'Whereas Pete will see a lot more,' Ellen Bridges said with a grin, and Elsie blushed.

'You've got a dirty mind, Ellen Bridges. Mind you, it's true!' And she laughed her old, raucous laugh.

The news these days was full of the Allied bombings over Germany. On the day of Elsie's wedding, Dresden had been almost destroyed by such heavy bombing that a firestorm had been created, the flames causing their own wind that tore through the streets and fanned them into even greater heat. Over fifty thousand people died in one night, many more times those who had been killed in even the worst of the Blitz on London; even more died in the follow-up raids of the next two days. Berlin was raided over and over again, with the city set ablaze at the end of February by firebombs dropped by over a thousand aircraft.

In Japan, Tokyo too was bombed by American B-29 Superfortresses, with over eighty thousand killed in one attack; fifteen thousand more were killed when the city of Kobe was set alight, and in yet another attack Osaka was completely wiped out. It was almost impossible to count the number of people dead.

'It's getting worse and worse,' Thursday said in dismay, but the others shook their heads.

'We're winning. It's *good* news, Thursday.' But she could only think of those who had died. The old people like Mrs Jenkins, who had no part in the war, the women and children who had no voice. Too many people were being killed. Too many.

Mark had written to her three times since he'd been away. He had rejoined his unit somewhere in Europe. He wasn't required to parachute any more, but to work somewhere behind the lines, setting up hospitals and looking after the wounded. He had only enough time to scribble a few lines, but he always ended with love and a kiss. She read his letters again and again, and put them in her drawer beside Connor's. Then she took them out and put them into another drawer. It didn't seem right to have them there together.

The fighting in Europe was bitter, with the Allies flooding across the borders into Austria and Germany. Russia's Red Army was marching on Berlin, and Montgomery's forces had crossed the Rhine only a day behind those of the American General Patton's. The three major powers were now massing, ready for their final assault. It really did seem as if the Germans were about to lose.

'They won't go down easily, all the same,' Louisa said, studying the newspaper at lunch one day. 'They're still sending those doodlebugs and V2s over.' One had destroyed an entire block of flats in London, and another was shot down over Suffolk. 'Of course, these might be the last ones they send, but we won't know that till it's all over, will we?'

By the beginning of April, it was beginning to look as if the war might be almost over. Five million leaflets had been dropped over the Ruhr, telling the German forces there of the advances being made into the country, and over three hundred thousand were expected to join the mass surrender. Vienna itself was liberated, leaving Berlin as the next and greatest target. In Italy, the Allies had pushed the front line as far as Ravenna, and in Japan too the bombing had intensified. It was said that over a ten-mile square area of Tokyo, not a building had been left standing.

'Guess what!' Elsie came running into the mess waving a newspaper, and the others looked up with a mixture of excitement and anxiety. 'Mr Roosevelt's died!'

'The American President?' Patsy exclaimed, and Elsie threw her a withering look.

'How many Mr Roosevelts d'you know, goof? It says here he just collapsed while he was having his portrait painted. You wouldn't think he'd have time to worry about things like that, would you? Why not just take a photo?' She rushed on without waiting for Thursday's comment that it seemed he hadn't had time after all. 'Mr Truman's been sworn in as the new President and the Germans are jumping for joy. Why d'you suppose they're doing that? It isn't going to make any difference, is it?'

'They probably think the Americans and Russians will start squabbling,' Louisa remarked, stirring a saccharin into her tea. 'They won't, though – not while we've still got Hitler to deal with. Anyway, it's General Eisenhower who's really in charge now. We're still going to win.'

A few days later Thursday heard that the great German prisoner-of-war camp, Colditz, had been liberated by the Americans.

'Colditz!' She raced into the dining mess, shouting and waving the newspaper just as Elsie had done a few days earlier. 'They've opened Colditz! Our Steve'll be home. Louie – Patsy – Joy – Steve's coming home!'

The others leaped up from the table and rushed to hug her. All over the big hall, people were looking up and staring and then, as word went round, calling out and laughing with excitement. Some of them also had relatives in the same camp; they came running to see the newspaper for themselves, and the hall erupted into tumult. It was another real indication that the war was almost over.

'How soon d'you think he'll be home?' Thursday asked, spreading the paper out on the table. 'And look, the Russians are almost in Berlin. They're bombarding it every day, people are having to hide in cellars and creep out at night to get food and water – oh, that sounds terrible – and look at *this*! Hitler's hiding in his bunker and won't come out. He must be just about to give up, he *must*!'

More disturbing reports were coming through too. Colditz was not the only camp to have been opened. The troops had opened the gates of other wired-off settlements and found horrors there that they had never dreamed of. Buchenwald. Belsen. Auschwitz. The names were burned into the minds of all those who read or heard them. The girls looked at the newspapers in appalled silence and Elsie, who had been to the pictures with Pete one night, came in next morning looking pale and sick.

'We saw this newsreel. Honestly, you wouldn't believe it. People as thin as skeletons, you could see their bones sticking through their skin. Laying there in piles, some of them still just alive, just chucked there with the corpses. And the guards, they'd been burying them like it, throwing them into great big pits, and you could tell that some of them weren't properly dead. I've never seen anything so horrible in my life.'

'It's got to be over soon,' Louisa said, shaken. 'They can't let Hitler get away with it any more.'

The last nine days of April saw the greatest battle of all – the battle for Berlin that would finally end the war. Day by day, the Allies advanced, shelling, bombing, sending in tanks and troops to fight their way, street by street, to the very heart of the city. On the last day of all, the Russians took the Reichstag itself, fighting through the rooms and corridors until they possessed every inch. And to signal their victory to all who still stood in the ruined streets, to the country of Germany itself, and to the entire war-torn world, two Red Army Sergeants climbed to a pinnacle of the shattered roof and waved the Red Flag high in bitter triumph.

'It's over,' Thursday said in awe, as they listened to the news on the wireless. 'It really is over.'

'Not quite,' Louisa corrected her. 'There's still Japan.'

But they knew that the victory over Japan must be no more now than a matter of time. The greater part of this long conflict, which had taken up so much of their lives – which had brought them grief and pain, joy and laughter, new experiences, new friends and bitter losses that could never be regained – was over. The Second World War was drawing to an end.

*

The news was coming so fast now, and so mingled with rumour that it was almost impossible to keep track of it all or to sort out fact from fiction. Some of it was so sickening that Thursday felt she would rather not know – yet she was drawn by a horrible fascination to the newspapers and the wireless. She shuddered at the fate of Mussolini, the Italian leader, and his mistress, both shot and mutilated, dangling upside down over a garage forecourt and spat upon or riddled by more bullets from those who had come to jeer. It was such a squalid end. But even she could not feel pity for the suicide of Hitler himself, nor for those who died with him in his bunker. Too many millions had died because of his madness and greed. Too many lives had been wasted.

'It's going to be tomorrow.' The buzz ran round the hospital like wildfire. Mr Churchill was going to broadcast at three in the afternoon, and everyone knew what he was going to say. It seemed impossible to believe. They'd been waiting for this very day for five and a half years yet it seemed, in a way, to have come upon them almost without warning. The past few months had seen such bitter fighting – fighting that was still going on in the Far East – that it was difficult to comprehend a world without it, a world in which people would once more be able to travel safely, to go to bed at night in the knowledge that they would not be woken by air-raid sirens or killed by a rocket. The fear they had learned to live with had been taken away, yet it left a strange vacuum and they didn't know quite what to put in its place.

'No more blackout,' Elsie said gleefully as they walked along the sea wall after their duty. 'Not even a dimout. We'll be able to have lights on without drawing the curtains. Put proper lights on our bikes again. Use torches. Have parties and late dances. They'll be able to ring the church bells whenever they like – remember that time the ones at Alverstoke got rung years ago, because someone thought we were being invaded? Everything's going to be just like it used to be.'

'Andrew will come home,' Louisa said. 'I've started thinking about the wedding already, and you're all invited. How about you, Thursday? When d'you think Connor will be back?'

'I don't know. It'll be quite a while yet. Not till after the Japanese war's over, I suppose.' Now that the time was drawing near Thursday was beginning to experience something very like panic.

'To be honest, I'm not sure I want him to just yet – I don't feel ready. I don't feel ready for anyone.'

Louisa gave her a sympathetic look. 'You're not really over Mark, are you? Still not made up your mind?'

'I'm not even trying to. I decided to stop thinking about it and just wait till I see them both again.' Thursday turned away and stared out over the Solent. As usual, it was full of ships, and she could see men moving about the decks. 'What d'you think they're doing?'

Elsie craned her neck. 'They're putting up flags! Dressing overall. Oh, how gorgeous – d'you think all the ships are doing it?'

'Bound to.' Louisa stood still and lifted both arms above her head, her face glowing with excitement. 'You know what, tomorrow's going to be one huge party! I bet there's people everywhere putting up flags and getting ready for parties. What are we going to do? We can't just go tamely to bed!'

'We could go over to Pompey,' Elsie suggested. 'There's bound to be plenty going on over there. We'll walk up Queen Street and go to the Guildhall Square, that's where all the people will go.'

'I've heard there are going to be street-parties,' Thursday put in, beginning to feel excited herself. 'Will there be one where your mum and dad are, Elsie?'

'Might be. We could go round there first, then get the bus back down to the ferry and go over then. They might want to come with us anyway – we're Pompey folk really, after all.' Elsie gave a little skip and gripped her friends' arms. 'You know, I reckon this is going to be the biggest party any of us has ever seen!'

The other two nodded, and then Thursday said more soberly, 'What about Patsy?'

'Oh.' Elsie stopped jogging up and down. 'Oh, poor Pats. She's bound to feel a bit low, isn't she. What d'you think? We can't leave her moping all by herself, but if she comes, she's going to be thinking about Roy all the time. It'll be miserable for her either way.'

'Well, I think we should make her come,' Louisa decided. 'It's history, isn't it. We're never going to see a day like this again. Nobody ought to stop at home and pretend it's not happening – whatever the circumstances.'

The entire hospital was waiting next day for the moment at 3 p.m.

when Mr Churchill was going to broadcast and make the news official. There were wireless sets in most of the wards and as the hour drew near they were all tuned in and patients and nurses alike gathered round them. Down in the basement, there were no operations and the theatre staff came up and crowded into the rooms just off the arcade to listen. Thursday and Louisa stood together, just behind Surgeon Commander Sharp, holding each other's hands tightly.

It seems only five minutes since we were waiting for Mr Chamberlain to announce that the war was starting, Thursday thought, looking back down the years. And yet at the same time, it seems an eternity. So much has happened since. So many people have been killed, or had their lives changed for ever.

The hour struck. The familiar, sombre voice of the announcer John Snagge said, 'This is London.' And then they heard that other voice which had become so familiar over the years, which had become the voice of wartime Britain itself.

'The German war is over,' Winston Churchill proclaimed, his rolling tones booming over the entire country, and Thursday felt Louisa's fingers tighten. And then, lifting his voice in exhortation: 'Advance Britannia! Long live the cause of freedom! *God Save the King!*'

Immediately, the National Anthem itself was broadcast and everyone stood to attention and saluted. As the last strains died away, all those crowded into the room broke into cheers. Thursday and Louisa hugged each other and then found themselves in the arms of Surgeon Commander Sharp himself. He planted smacking kisses on their cheeks, then let them go and went round the whole room, hugging every person in it, and they all began to do the same. I just want to hug everyone in the whole world, Thursday thought, tears streaming down her face. Well, everyone on our side, of course! 'Oh, Louie! Patsy! Joy! It's over – it's really over!'

'I can't believe it,' Patsy declared, her face alight, and Thursday felt a swift delight that her friend was able to share in the excitement without having it marred by her own sorrow. 'It's finished at last – and we've won! We've *won the war!* Oh, *Thursday*!'

Thursday held her tightly. Patsy had been her first friend at Haslar and even though they had been separated when Thursday was sent to Egypt, there had always been a special bond between them. What would Patsy do now, she wondered. As a widow, she could hardly go back to her parents and live with them as a young daughter. I won't even be able to do that myself, she thought suddenly. I want to make my own life now – but how? Which direction should I go in? Marry, like Louisa, or stay single and enjoy my freedom?

Marriage seemed suddenly to be no more than exchanging one form of service for another. Wives were expected to stay at home, look after their husbands, have children. But for single women, the world was opening up. There would be opportunities – of what kind, she didn't know, but that there would be opportunities she was certain. I don't want to let them pass me by, she thought. Whatever they are, I want to be able to take them.

'Wake up, Thursday!' Louisa was shaking her arm. 'We're going to go round the wards, just like at Christmas. And then we're leaving with Elsie, remember? There'll be parties everywhere and we don't want to miss a minute!'

The party had started in Portsmouth that morning. There'd been a service in the Guildhall Square, led by the Bishop of Portsmouth, with parades of all the Services and, someone told them on seeing their VAD uniforms, a row of nurses along the front of the steps, their red capes, blue dresses and white aprons looking like a bit of the Union Jack itself. Some sailors had climbed up on top of the tower of the Guildhall, burned to a shell in the Blitz of 1941, and hoisted up the White Ensign, which had been flown from the same place on Armistice Day in 1918. The day I was born, Thursday thought. At the very minute I was born, they were flying that flag. She looked up at it and felt a lump in her throat.

The girls had gone over on the ferry. The afternoon had been an endless cacophony of ships' sirens and hooters, church bells and brass bands, and as they went through the streets after their tour of the hospital, they saw that bunting and flags were festooned across almost every house. The ferry boats were dressed overall, just as were the bigger ships, and the harbour was so alive with dancing colour that the steady drizzle didn't matter at all. What was a bit of damp, when you had the end of the war to celebrate!

In the Guildhall Square, the solemnity of the morning's service had abated and there was, as Elsie had predicted, a huge party in full swing. The square was thronged with sailors, marines, soldiers and airmen who were all cheered incessantly, while impromptu bands had been started up and vied with wind-up gramophones to play dance music. Long lines of conga dancers threaded their way through the crowds, breaking and joining up again, and there was a constant hubbub of song, laughter and calls from one to the other. Portsmouth had, it seemed, gone wild with joy.

The girls stayed until long after dark. Finally, with the party still going on behind them, they turned and made their way back down Queen Street to the harbour. The last ferry boat was waiting on one side of the pontoon, and on the other bobbed a pinnace with a lone sailor at the wheel. He grinned at them as they climbed wearily aboard.

'Had a good time, ducks? What a night, eh? All over bar the shouting, as they say. Now all we got to do is clear up the mess, eh!'

Thursday sank down on a thwart between Patsy and Elsie. She looked up at the sky, still lit with spears of light from the searchlights which had been so familiar a sight during the air raids.

She felt suddenly flat. After the joy of the past few hours, there seemed to be nothing ahead but drudgery and toil. The years of emotions, ranging from fear to excitement, had come suddenly to an end and, as the sailor had said, there was nothing left to do but clear up the mess. And what a mess it was.

I've had enough, she thought. I just want it to be properly over, so that I can get on with my own life.

Chapter Twenty-Six

The war might have ended in Europe, but there was still bitter fighting in the Far East, and still patients to be looked after at Haslar. Now that the flow of emergencies had eased, the operating theatres were taking on more commonplace work such as tonsillectomies or hernias, to ease the burden on the little War Memorial hospital in Gosport. After the terrible injuries that had been arriving almost daily for so long, it was both a relief and a comedown to find these filling the lists, and along with many of the VADs Thursday was feeling more and more restless. The urgency that had driven her to volunteer five years ago and kept her ready and willing to work all the hours she was needed, had now faded, and three haemorrhoid cases in a row seemed an anti-climax.

On top of this was the terrible news now coming from the concentration camps in Germany. The girls were appalled by the reports of thousands of prisoners starved down to skin and bone, their limbs like sticks and their bodies hollowed out as if they were already dead. As Elsie had told them after seeing that newsreel, guards had been seen callously tossing live people into deep pits, while those who were still able to walk were forced to crawl to the few standpipes or wells to collect water for themselves and their friends.

'This must be the worst war there's ever been,' Thursday said to her parents when she went home for a few days' leave. 'Even worse than the one you were in, Dad.'

Walter shook his head. 'I don't know that you can say any war's worse than another – there's always cruelty and death involved. We just keep thinking of new ways of killing each other – and more all the time. You know, they said the last one had got to be the war to end all wars, but it wasn't, was it? Now they're saying the same about this one, but they'll forget it soon enough. Seems to me they always do.'

'Well, I'm just thankful it's over,' Mary said. 'Our Steve'll be home any day, and so will Vic. Mike seems to be getting along all right too; they say he'll have to stay in the sanatorium for a few months yet, but he's going to get better. I know it'll take a lot of work to get things back to normal, but at least we can start to do it in peace. Then kiddies like little Leslie will have a better world to look forward to.'

'What are your plans, Thursday?' her father asked. 'I dare say you'll be getting demobbed soon. You'll be coming home, I suppose, until that man of yours comes back?'

Thursday glanced uncomfortably at her mother. 'I'm not exactly sure what I'm going to be doing, Dad. We're not all being demobbed straight away. The married women, and those who're getting married, are going first. And then some girls have decided to stay on and take training to be State Registered Nurses, like our Jenny.'

'You won't be doing that, though,' Mary observed. 'Not much point, is there, if you're getting married.'

'I don't know that I am getting married,' Thursday began, and they both stared at her.

'Not getting married!' Mary exclaimed. 'Don't tell me you've quarrelled! Or have you thrown him over? I must say—'

'No, it's nothing like that. I just don't want to rush into anything.' She looked at them appealingly. 'We haven't seen each other for more than four years. It's a long time . . .'

Her mother gave her a shrewd glance. 'You haven't found someone else, have you? Is that it?'

'No. I don't know.' Thursday got up restlessly and looked out of the window. 'I've just got to take time, that's all. Look, I think I'll walk round and see Denise and Leslie. And Auntie Flo and Uncle Percy,' she added, pulling open the door.

Mary and Walter watched her go and then glanced at each other.

'She's changed,' Mary said sadly. 'She's not the same girl as she was, Walter.'

'None of us is the same as we were. She's right, Mary, four years *is* a long time. It's not as if they knew each other very long before he went away. And there's the different backgrounds to take into consideration as well.'

'It's more than that,' Mary said. 'She couldn't look me in the eye when I asked her if there was someone else. She had that guilty look on her face, the one she used to have when she was a kiddy, remember?' She got up and went out to the kitchen. 'I just hope she's not gone through all those years just to make a fool of herself at the end of it.'

Thursday took her time walking round to her aunt's house. She walked down to the bridge and leaned on the parapet, staring across the shimmering water at the tower of the cathedral. From here, you'd never know there'd been a war at all, she thought. Not like in Portsmouth, where the heart of the city had been blasted away, nor in Plymouth which had been almost flattened, nor in Coventry or all those other places that had been pounded into the ground. Almost no city had escaped damage; almost no part of the country been left untouched in some way. And now it all had to be put right, repaired, rebuilt. After all they'd been through, people still couldn't say it was finished. They had to pick themselves up, weary and bruised, and start all over again.

She strolled slowly through the streets to her aunt's house. Denise was home from her job at the glove factory and welcomed her in, with Leslie jumping up and down behind her. Flo was out visiting her friend in the next street, she explained, leading the way through to the back room.

'I'll make a cup of tea. How are you, Thursday? Glad it's all over?'

'Well, of course.' Thursday followed her cousin out to the kitchen. 'It seems queer, though. I feel sort of flat.'

'I know.' Denise filled the kettle and lit the gas. 'I do, too. And a bit scared. I mean, I'm looking forward to Vic coming home, of course I am, but I feel nervous too. Suppose he doesn't fancy me any more? Suppose he's sorry he's got to come back to me? I mean, it was all such a rush – and I know I was daft, doing what I did. Not that I'm sorry we had Les, never for a minute,' she added quickly, 'but I just worry about how we're all going to settle down together. I mean, Leslie's never even seen him, not to remember.'

The kettle boiled and she swished a drop of hot water in the teapot and tipped it into the sink before spooning in the tea.

Thursday took the cups down from their hooks and went outside to the meatsafe to fetch the milk. She looked at her cousin. 'How d'you feel yourself, Diz? I mean, you're not sorry you got married, are you?'

'No, of course not.' She wrinkled her mouth. 'I think as much of Vic as I ever did – but it's as if everything's been frozen for the past four years, isn't it? We've been through so much – and Vic's had such a different life. He's been wounded and in hospital, he's done all sorts of things, he must be different from what he was. I hope he'll be the same Vic underneath it all, but I can't know that till I see him, can I? I *want* to feel the same,' she continued, pouring the tea, 'but how can I be sure I will? How can I be sure *he* will? And whatever are we going to do if we don't?'

'I think you've got to give yourselves time.' Thursday carried the cups into the back room and sat down in her uncle's chair while Denise took the one on the other side of the fireplace. 'It's bound to seem strange at first. And he's been away for so long, he'll need time to get used to being at home again and in civvies. Will he go back into the Post Office?'

'I don't know. I suppose so – civil servants will get their jobs back, won't they? But that's going to be queer, isn't it, stamping out parcels when he's been fighting in Italy.' Denise shook her head. 'It's going to be queer for everyone. You know, I don't think it will be any easier being at peace than it was being at war! At least there was some excitement then – it just all seems so flat now. And so much hard work to put it all to rights.'

Thursday looked at her thoughtfully. Denise had changed, she thought. A few years ago, when she'd had nothing more in her mind than the latest shade of nail varnish or which boy was going to take her to the pictures, her nickname Dizzy had suited her perfectly. Now, the mother of a small boy, she looked older and more serious. I hope she hasn't lost all her sense of fun though, Thursday thought. That was one of the things Vic loved about her.

'I don't think you need worry that he won't want you any more,' she said. 'I told you before, you were all he thought about when I nursed him in Egypt. He told me that all he wanted was to get home to you and Leslie and find a little home of your own and be together. And I expect he'll be feeling nervous too.'

'*Him* nervous?' Denise repeated, as if it was a new idea. 'But he's got nothing to be nervous about!'

'Well, he thinks he has.' Thursday hesitated. 'Don't forget, he's been burned. He's worried you won't fancy him—'

'Oh, I know all that,' Denise broke in. 'I wrote and told him after you first came home, it doesn't matter *what* he looks like, I'll love him just the same. More, because every time I look at him I'll see what he's been through. But it's the time I'm worried about. The time we've been apart. We're going to be different, Thursday – everyone is. We're *all* going to find it strange, settling down to Civvy Street again.'

'I know,' Thursday said. 'I've been thinking exactly the same myself. It's going to be really strange, and it's going to be hardest of all for the youngest ones, the ones who never really had much ordinary life before it all started. People like you and me, who'd hardly begun our lives – we've got to find out how to live without a war. I don't think it's going to be easy, Diz – I don't think it's going to be easy at all.'

The few days passed quickly, with visits to relatives and old friends. Slowly, Thursday began to feel that it might be possible to settle into civilian life again. But many of her friends seemed to feel the same way as she did: there was a restlessness, combined with a feeling of depression. And there was the knowledge that despite all the celebrating, the war wasn't totally over. There was still Japan.

'They won't give in, you know,' Walter said, spreading the *Daily Express* out on the table after tea. 'It's not in their nature. They think if you give in you might as well be dead. We're going to have to go on and on, hammering at them until there's hardly any left. There's no other way.'

'If we do that, there'll be hardly any of us left either,' Thursday objected. 'There's been thousands and thousands of Allied men killed out there, not to mention the ones in prison camps. They've got to give in.' But her father shook his head. There was no 'got to' about it where the Japs were concerned.

After tea, Mary and Walter liked to settle down to listen to the wireless or have a game of cards. For the first two evenings Thursday and Jenny settled down with them, but on the third, Thursday glanced at her sister. 'Fancy a walk? It's a lovely evening.'

Mary looked up, disappointed. 'I thought we might play crib.'

'Maybe later on, Mum. I just can't settle indoors when it's as nice as this outside.' Thursday gave her mother an apologetic smile. 'I've spent so much time underground since I came back from Egypt, I'm just starving for some sunshine! We won't be late.'

The two girls strolled out and walked down to the river. They crossed the bridge and wandered through the park, looking across at the racecourse. 'I suppose it'll all start again this summer,' Jenny observed. 'All the racing and the pleasure boats and everything. People just want to get back to normal now, don't they?'

'I suppose so.'

Thursday's tone was despondent and Jenny gave her a sharp glance. 'What's up?'

'Oh, I don't know – everything and nothing. I'm being daft, I know I am, but I can't seem to get used to it, somehow – not being at war any more, I mean. Except that we still are at war, aren't we, and there are still men being killed, but nobody's taking much notice. Because it's so far away and we're not in any danger ourselves, it's all been shoved under the carpet. People don't seem to *care* – unless they've got a man out there, and then of course they don't think the war's over at all.'

Jenny gave her a shrewd glance. 'You're worrying about Connor.'

'Well, yes, of course I am – but it's not just that. It's all of it. All the men coming home, expecting to find things the same as when they went away – and they can't be. I mean, some of them haven't even got a home any more, or a wife or family or *anything*. They've been through all that, and they've got to come home to nothing. How are they going to feel? They'll wonder what it was all about. And then there's the ones who come home and find they can't get along with their wives any more. Or their children don't want them. And even if they do, it's all so hard to get going again.' Thursday glanced around at the peaceful scene. 'You don't see much of it here, Jen, but back in Pompey you can see just what the war's done. All those buildings, smashed. All those houses and shops, gone. Everything needing to be put back together again. It's going to take years.'

Jenny looked at her again. 'You're sounding really miserable, Thursday. What's happened?'

The other girl shook her head. 'Nothing, not really. I just feel so flat, and I can't seem to pull myself out of it. I don't know what to *do* with my life, Jenny, not any more. When it all started, we were all so keen to get involved, to do something to help. There were so many opportunities. You could join the women's Services or the VAD or go and work on the land – all sorts of things. Now, suddenly, it's all gone. We're being demobbed and we don't know what else to do.' She stopped and faced her sister. 'Jen, I don't want to just get married and be a housewife like Mum for the rest of my life. I want to *do* something. But I don't know what!'

'You don't want to go on with nursing?'

'It won't be the same. Anyway, I think I've had enough. I want a change.'

They walked slowly on. After a few minutes, Jenny asked tentatively, 'But what about Connor, Thurs? Won't he want to get married? What will he say about all this?'

'It's not really up to him, is it!' Thursday stopped and bit her lip. 'Oh, there I go, flying off the handle when the poor man hasn't even said anything. I don't know what he'll want, Jen. I don't know what *I'll* want, until I see him again. And then there's . . .'

'Someone else,' Jenny said. 'You might as well tell me, Thurs.'

Thursday heaved a sigh. 'All right, then. Yes, there is someone else – an Army doctor. I do seem to go for the medical blokes, don't I! Or they go for me . . . Anyway, his name's Mark and I met him in Egypt. I didn't want it to lead to anything so we broke it off and I didn't see him again till a few months ago when he turned up at Haslar. He'd been at Arnhem. I tried not to let anything happen, but he said it must have been meant and he wouldn't take no for an answer.' She stared at Jenny, her eyes suddenly filled with tears. 'He's gone away again, back to Germany, but he keeps writing to me. He made me promise to give him a chance. Oh, Jenny, I don't know what to do. I think such a lot of them both, and yet sometimes I wish I'd never met either of them!'

They stood quite still staring at one another. Tears had begun to trickle down Thursday's cheeks. Jenny opened her mouth to speak, but before she could say a word a voice hailed them and they both turned in amazement.

'Hello, Thursday. Hello – Jenny, is it? Gosh, you've grown up!' The tall young soldier stood, legs straddled, beaming at them. 'Well, haven't you got anything to say? Haven't you got a kiss for your old sweetheart, Thursday?'

'*Sidney!*' Thursday gasped. 'Sidney – but what are you doing here?'

'I live here, remember? Not all that far from you.' He gave her a cocky look and winked. 'Don't tell me you've forgotten all those nights I walked you home from the pictures.'

Thursday flushed. 'No, I haven't,' she said a little sharply. 'And as far as I remember, nothing ever happened. Anyway, how are you, Sidney? You're looking well.'

'Fit as a flea.' He flexed one arm. 'Shame you can't see the muscles. Being in the Army suits me.'

'I can see that. So where have you been?'

He grinned. 'That'd take a bit of telling. Seen a good bit of action, been around a bit, made some good mates.' He winked again. 'Never thought it was going to last that long, did we? How about you, had a good war? Went for a nurse, didn't you?'

'That's right,' Thursday said shortly, wondering how he could have forgotten. It was the reason they'd split up, when she'd told him she was volunteering as a VAD. 'I've been at Haslar Hospital, near Portsmouth, but I was in Egypt for two years—'

'Egypt! I was out there for a bit, and in Algiers. Talk about sand! And flies, and God knows what else. Then we went on to Italy. The girls are better-looking there!' He winked for a third time.

Thursday looked at him. He had filled out and was no longer the rather weedy Sidney she remembered, and it certainly suited him. I suppose a lot of girls would think he was really good-looking now, she thought, but there was something she didn't like about him. He was too cocky.

'Suppose you've had a few boyfriends since those days, Thurs?' he went on. 'Not the little innocent you were, eh? Didn't know what it was all about, did we! Learned a few tricks since then, I can tell you – bet you have too, eh?'

'Sorry, Sidney,' Thursday said abruptly. 'It's been nice seeing you, but we've got to go now. Mum's waiting for us to go home and play cards.'

He stared at her and gave a short laugh. 'Well, you'd better go then! Mustn't keep Mummy waiting, must you. Shame, I was going to ask you to come round to the Swan With Two Nicks for a drink –

or maybe you're not allowed into pubs yet, eh?' He gave her a rather nasty smile.

'Goodbye, Sidney,' Thursday said and took Jenny's arm. They walked away quickly, and when Thursday turned her head at the corner of the road Sidney had gone.

'Whew!' Jenny said. 'He's even worse than I remember him. What on earth did you ever see in him, Thursday?'

'I don't know. I never did like him all that much anyway – we just got into the habit of going to the pictures together.' Thursday giggled. 'I remember the night we broke up – he took umbrage because I'd volunteered for the VADs without asking him first! I told him he didn't own me and he said he'd just been going to ask me to get engaged. We'd never even kissed properly!'

'I remember Mum being upset that you weren't going to marry him. She liked Sidney.'

'She didn't really know him. She just wanted me to settle down and have a husband.' Thursday looked seriously at her sister. 'I tell you what, Jen – girls aren't going to need to get married any more, not like they used to. We've found out we can do all sorts of different things – we don't need men to look after us any more.'

'I don't know,' Jenny said. 'I don't think it's going to be that easy. We don't get paid as much, do we? How can a girl afford to live on the sort of pay we get? That's why men get so much more – because they'll have a wife and family to keep. Women aren't supposed to need so much.'

'Well, that'll change, surely.'

'I don't know,' Jenny said again. 'Once they're all back, they'll want to take over again. You saw what Sidney was like. Thinks he's God's gift to women. I don't suppose they'll all be like that – my Charlie isn't, for a start – but they're going to want their jobs back, aren't they?' A bus went past and she waved a hand towards the woman driving it. 'I bet *she* won't be driving a bus in six months' time. She'll be back in the kitchen, washing clothes. And so will a lot of other women.'

'It's like I was saying just now,' Thursday said. 'It's not going to be easy, sorting it all out, is it? Nearly six years of war, and not over yet – it leaves a lot of mess behind.'

They walked back slowly. There were other people out walking too, couples strolling arm in arm along the riverbank, children running in front of them. It was a peaceful scene, a scene of contentment, yet all those couples and all those families would be facing their own problems. Peace didn't come easily.

'Do you really not know what you're going to do?' Jenny asked, breaking the silence.

'I've almost given up trying to make up my mind,' Thursday said. 'I think the best thing I can do is just wait and see. Maybe neither of them will want me. Maybe I won't get married at all – ever.'

'Don't be daft!' Jenny said robustly. 'You're just feeling a bit low, that's all. It's what Mum calls "reaction" – you've been working with wounded men for years and you've been in Blitzes and you've been abroad, and now it's all suddenly stopped and you don't know what's going to happen next. And you're worn out. That's all it is.' She squeezed Thursday's arm. 'You'll feel better in a little while. Honestly.'

Thursday gave her a smile. 'I hope so,' she said. 'I really hope so.'

They turned the corner of their own street. The front door stood open and there was a little knot of people gathered round, chattering excitedly. The two girls looked at each other and began to walk faster and as they came to the edge of the crowd a man came to the door and looked out.

'Thursday! Jen!'

Thursday stopped dead. Her heart rose within her breast and she caught her hand to her throat, staring in disbelief. He looked taller than she remembered – but perhaps that was because he was thinner. And he had a beard. He'd always wanted to grow a beard, she thought in bewilderment, and then her brain and her emotions caught up with each other and a huge surge of joy swelled to her lips.

'*Steve!* It's our *Steve!*' She gripped Jenny's arm and they pushed through the little crowd and flung themselves into their brother's arms. 'Oh, Steve, you're back, you're back at last!'

Behind him, her mother was crying with relief and joy, and her father was beaming, his mouth a little twisted with his own emotion and his eyes moist. The neighbours were laughing and chattering, and as Thursday felt his body, so much thinner than she remembered, but whole and alive as they had once thought he would never be again, she felt her depression slip away and a new optimism warm her heart.

Peace wasn't going to be easy. But it was *peace*, and if there was work to be done it could be done with a high heart. The world *could* be rebuilt, and people could learn to live their lives again in safety.

Chapter Twenty-Seven

The results of the General Election, which were announced the day after Steve's return and three weeks after election day itself, surprised everyone and shocked many. Mr Churchill, voted out and forced to resign after all he had done! Labour in power with an overall majority of a hundred and forty-six! Clement Attlee the new Prime Minister, and 'The Red Flag' sung in Parliament at the election of the new Speaker! It was as if the country had been turned upside down.

'I can't make it out,' Walter Tilford said, shaking his head. 'Mr Churchill was good enough in wartime, he ought to be good enough in peacetime. It's an insult to the man.'

'I think people want something different now though,' Thursday said. 'They want things to be better than they were before the war. We had a Depression then, remember. A lot of people were having a really bad time – no jobs, no money, couldn't afford the doctor, couldn't get a proper education. Labour want to change all that. They want children to be able to go to grammar schools if they're bright enough, without their parents having to pay, and they want you to be able to go to the doctor when you're ill and not have to be put on the panel before you get free treatment. They don't think the Conservatives will do that.'

Her father stared at her. 'Don't say you're going over to Labour! We've always been Conservative in this family, always. Never had any truck with trade unions – oh, they were needed in their day, I'll admit that, but once they'd done their job they ought to have closed down, not gone on asking for more and more. I tell you what, now that Labour's in again we'll have nothing but strikes. And where's the money going to come from for all this free education and doctor's visits? From the workers, that's where. It's all very fine to talk big, but who's going to have to put their hands in their pockets, eh? Tell me that.'

Thursday opened her mouth to reply, but caught her mother's eye and closed it again. There was no point in arguing with her father, who was a dyed in the wool Conservative and wouldn't ever change his opinions. Most working-class people favoured Labour, but when you found one who was a Conservative he was usually fixed that way for good.

'Well, let's forget it for now,' she said instead. 'It's my last night and Steve's home again and we just want to enjoy it. Mum and I've been busy all day getting a party ready for tonight, and the others are coming round so let's forget politics. There's nothing we can do about it now, anyway.'

That last evening had been almost like before the war, she thought next day as she boarded the train to return to Haslar. All the family together, except for Mike who was still in hospital, and Leslie who would never be with them again. But little Leslie had been there to win everyone's hearts with his beaming smile and comical remarks, and soon his father would be home again. They'd eaten the tea that Thursday and her mother had prepared, and played games and finished up with a sing-song. Leslie had been almost asleep before the others left, cradled in his grandfather's arms, and Mary had smiled as she closed the door and came back inside.

'What a little love he is. And Percy thinks the world of him, too. Funny, when you think how upset he was when Denise had to get married but like I said, they bring their love with them.' She glanced at her son and daughters. 'I'm looking forward to some grandchildren of my own now.'

'Crikey,' Steve said, 'give us a chance, Mum. I've only just got back from Colditz. I haven't seen a girl in five years, I can hardly remember what it's all about.'

Thursday and Jenny glanced at each other and grinned, but Thursday had felt a pang in her heart as she watched her cousin tending the little boy. I would like children of my own, she thought, I can't deny it. But I'm not getting married just for a family. It's got to be someone I truly love – and he's got to understand that I want my own life as well. I don't want to be just a wife and mother.

Mary and Steve had come to the station to see her off, and she waved until she could no longer see the platform. Then she sat back in her seat and watched the countryside flash by. I wonder if this will be the last time I go back to Haslar, she thought. I wonder if the next time I come home it will be for good. Or if I'll ever come home to live again.

July ran into August and still the war was continuing in Japan. It didn't seem to matter how much the Allies bombed them, the Japanese wouldn't give in. A bit like the British, Thursday thought but didn't say so. Nobody would have liked to be compared with the Japanese.

'How's it ever going to end?' Elsie asked. She was the first of the girls to be demobbed and they watched enviously as she packed her suitcase for the last time. Pete had found a couple of rooms in Gosport and would go to Portsmouth on the ferry every day, and was looking forward to being demobbed himself soon. Then he'd go back to work in the garage where he'd been a mechanic before the war and the pair would settle down in domestic bliss for the rest of their lives. 'Apart from the odd tiff, I dare say,' Elsie grinned, 'but we've found a good way to make up!'

Thursday grinned back, but she felt that little pang of loneliness which had struck her so often just lately as more and more girls announced their engagements and began to prepare for weddings. I'm not surprised people are rushing into marriage, she thought. If it hadn't been for the war, a lot of us would have been married and have children by now. We're fed up with waiting. *I'm* fed up with waiting. I want someone to love and someone to love me, but I'm still not sure about marriage. I'm still not sure about giving up my freedom.

She went with the others to wave goodbye to Elsie and then turned to go for a walk along the sea wall. Haslar would be a different place without Elsie's cheery presence and raucous laugh. I want it to be my turn, she thought. I want to move on: I'm ready to go.

Patsy fell into step beside her. 'It's going to seem queer without Elsie, isn't it?'

'It seems queer anyway. I feel as if we're all in limbo, waiting for something to happen.' They came to the edge of the sea wall and stared out over the Solent towards the Spithead Forts. 'What will you do when you leave here, Patsy?' she asked. 'Will you go back to Evesham?'

'I suppose so. I don't really know what else to do. I'll have to get a job, of course – maybe in a shop or something. I'll just have to see what there is.'

Thursday glanced at her. 'Wouldn't you rather do something else? Something more interesting?'

'Like what?' Patsy asked. 'All the interesting jobs are going to be taken back by the men, aren't they? It stands to reason. And women aren't going to want them anyway. They'll be wanting to start their families.' She sighed and gazed out across the silvery-blue water.

Thursday bit her lip and berated herself once again for her tactlessness and selfishness. There must be thousands of young women like Patsy, widowed before they'd had a chance really to begin their marriages and have a family. Thousands who would like nothing more than to do just what Elsie was doing – set up home in a couple of rooms with a few utility cups and saucers and a toasting fork, knowing that their lives could now take the course they'd dreamed of. Marriage, a modest home and children. Why can't I feel the same, she wondered. Why doesn't it seem to be enough for me?

They turned and walked slowly back to the hospital. The Quarter Deck, that long avenue leading to the little church, was peaceful, its cherry trees in full leaf. They had grown there ever since before the war started, coming into a foam of blossom every spring and turning a burnished bronze each autumn, quite unaffected by the war. Thursday thought of all the times she had gazed at them, drinking in the beauty of the froth of flowers or the coppery leaves against a clear blue sky, and felt a peace enter her soul. Whoever built this hospital, she thought, whoever decided there ought to be trees here and gardens and big open spaces, knew what would heal people as well as medicine. Whoever it was, knew about healing minds and hearts and souls, as well as bodies.

'I hope this place lasts for ever,' she said. 'I'm ready to go now, Pats, but I'm glad we came here. It's a lovely hospital. I'll never forget it.'

They stood for a moment, gazing along the avenue and remembering the time they'd been told off by an officer for running along it, the time they'd been upbraided by Madam for daring to ride their bikes. And then they heard a shout, and turned to see Ellen Bridges and Joy running towards them.

'What? What's the matter?' Thursday and Patsy began to run as well. It was obviously something momentous. Fear clutched at Thursday's heart and she tried angrily to push it away. We've done with that, she thought. We've done with feeling frightened. 'What's happened?'

'They've dropped a huge bomb on Japan.' Ellen stopped and put her hand over her heart, panting out the words. 'It's an atom bomb. It's the biggest bomb there's ever been. They're saying it's destroyed a whole city, and there are thousands of people killed. *Thousands.* They're saying it's going to end the war.'

The first atom bomb, dropped on Hiroshima, didn't end the war, but the second one dropped on Nagasaki three days later did. By then, there was some idea as to the damage done by the first – an entire city obliterated, miles of streets and buildings flattened, the inhabitants killed even more dreadfully than those who had died in Hitler's Blitzes. People whose clothes had been blasted from their bodies, their skin peeled away like an onion's, their brains bursting through their shattered skulls, people simply incinerated where they stood. There had been no chance for them to escape the inferno; even underground shelters offered no protection and of those who had survived, many, many more would die of their terrible injuries.

The girls were shaken by the news. Accustomed as they were to the wounds inflicted by war, these seemed worse than anything they had ever encountered. Thursday, reading an account in the newspaper, felt sickened. If this was the way war was going, what hope could there be for the world? In six years, it had gone from being able to destroy a few houses or a street, to a way of destroying civilisation itself. And now Russia, which had helped to conquer Germany, had joined in to declare war on Japan along with the other Allies. How many more cities would be flattened, how many more innocent civilians burned to death?

But it seemed that two bombs were enough. At midnight on 14 August, the Prime Minister announced that Japan had surrendered. For the first time ever, Emperor Hirohito spoke to his people and explained that they were laying down their arms. '*Should we continue to fight, it would not only result in the ultimate collapse and obliteration of the Japanese nation, but also it would lead to the total extinction of human civilisation.'* He asked his people to *'respond loyally'* to his command to surrender.

The Second World War was finally at an end.

To Thursday, the celebrations had a bittersweet quality. Just as had happened on VE Day, the whole Allied world seemed to go mad with joy. People flooded into the streets, lighting bonfires, setting up parties, bringing out their gramophones and singing and dancing late into the night. In the harbour, every ship sounded its siren madly for an entire hour. Rockets and fireworks soared into the sky, church bells rang, and as people answered their call and thronged to offer prayers of thanksgiving, impromptu church services were held. The little bell of Haslar's own church of St Luke was ringing, a small, pure sound against the cacophony of the sirens and hooters, and Thursday and the others found themselves joining a vast crowd of staff and up-patients in making their way along the footpaths and Quarter Deck towards its glowing windows.

Inside, the church was almost bursting at the seams. The chaplain stood before them and offered prayers of thanks, and the organist played the most rousing hymns, ending with 'O God, Our Help in Ages Past, Our Hope for Years to Come' and then the National Anthem. The tears burned hot in Thursday's eyes and then brimmed over, but she made no attempt to wipe them away, and as the sailors and the officers stood to attention she saw that every other face in the church was wet with similar tears, and nobody felt any shame.

Making their way out, Thursday became separated from the other girls and, thankful for the moment of solitude, lingered until everyone had gone. Then she walked alone down the length of the Quarter Deck and let the memories crowd about her.

Tony West, who had kissed her and then returned from Dunkirk too mutilated ever to kiss again. Doug Brighton, who had never failed to put her back up, and Roy Greenaway who had married Patsy and then left her a widow. Stoker Davis and his enema. The young German, Heinz Schmidt, who had listened to her chatter without revealing until the last day that he understood every word. The men who had flooded back from Dunkirk, wounded and burned and half-drowned. The young Wrens who had been killed in the air raid and buried in the little cemetery.

So many of them, she thought, looking up at the sky, its darkness brightened still by flashes of light and the glow of bonfires. Not so long ago, that glow would have been from burning buildings and there would have been searchlights looking for enemy aircraft. She remembered the night of the Blitz, when she had been up on Portsdown Hill with Connor in a borrowed car, and they'd rushed back and found themselves caught up in the devastation. She remembered Susie, the little girl whose leg Connor had amputated, and wondered where she was now.

And there were all the others as well. The constant flow of wounded sailors who had come through Haslar's gates or been brought to the jetty. And those who had never even made it that far; the Canadians killed at Dieppe, the soldiers who had died at El Alamein and in all the other desert battles. Those in Italy, in France, in Sicily, in Russia, in the Far East . . . The list was too long, and the countries too many.

Thank God it's all over, she thought. And that's all I want to do tonight – thank God. The others can dance in the streets and light fires and sound sirens and hooters, but all I want to do is feel thankful that it's over and do the job I came here to do, until I'm not needed any more.

She came to the main hospital block and turned to go down the basement steps to the operating theatre. There was work to be done still, and Thursday was glad of it.

Chapter Twenty-Eight

'What are you going to do when you get out?'

As summer wore into autumn and then into early winter, the question was being asked every day. Most of the VADs, like so many conscripted servicemen and women, were looking forward eagerly to demobilisation. Some would be returning to their pre-war occupation, others were starting a new life. Some were more reluctant to leave, recognising that the past six years had brought them experiences they didn't want to leave behind. Many, having joined up almost straight from school, had known nothing other than war during their entire working lives and felt strangely nervous about the free-for-all of Civvy Street.

'Let's face it,' Ellen Bridges said as they sat round the iron stove in the mess, 'we've been pretty well looked after all this time. We haven't been paid much but we've had everything found for us – food, clothes, a bed for the night. And plenty of company too. You've got to admit, we've had a pretty good time, by and large.'

'It's been rather like being back at boarding school,' Louisa remarked, glancing up from her writing-pad. 'Plenty of rules, but as long as you either obey them or don't get caught, you can have a lot of fun. More, actually,' she added with a wicked grin. 'There were plenty of boys' schools in Malvern as well as the girls' but we weren't allowed to have anything to do with them!'

'What are you writing?' Thursday asked curiously, and Louisa showed her. 'It's an advertisement for a job, see? *Ex-VAD seeks position requiring initiative. Driving licence, nursing and travel experience.* I thought I might do something while I'm waiting for Andrew to come back.'

'I didn't know you had a driving licence.'

'Well, I haven't yet, but I will have by the time I need it. That nice young Lieutenant's teaching me. It's all right,' she added defensively when they raised their eyebrows, 'that's all he's doing. Anyway, our mothers knew each other at school.'

The others hooted with laughter. 'And that makes him all right?' Patsy chortled. 'I don't think it'd be much recommendation to my mum. You ought to hear her on the subject of some of the girls *she* went to school with!'

'Well, she didn't go to a posh school like Louisa's mum,' Thursday told her. 'I think I might put an advert like that in one of the papers. What d'you think I should say? *Initiative and drive? Camel-riding a speciality? Sandcastles built to order?*'

'If you're thinking of advertising in the *Egyptian Mail*, yes,' Ellen scoffed. 'But seriously, Lou, what sort of job d'you think you'll get from an advert like that? Being a nanny, or something.'

'I don't know. I thought more of a personal secretary. Lots of people have them.' The other girls' blank looks told her that this was a new idea to them. In places like Worcester and Evesham, nobody had personal secretaries and, if they had, wouldn't have known what to do with them. She shrugged. 'Well, some people do, anyway. It's worth a try.'

'I think some of these training schemes sound interesting.' Patsy fished in her bag and pulled out a handful of leaflets. 'Look, I got these from the mess. The Government's fixing up all these classes for training people to do all sorts of things. You can learn shorthand and typing, or cookery, or teaching . . .'

'Teaching?' Thursday said. 'But don't you have to go to college to be a teacher?'

Patsy shook her head. 'Not for infants. Or for the older children at primary schools. It says here there'll be lots of teachers needed because so many of the men were called up and – and won't come back.' Her voice trembled a little but she went on determinedly. 'There are other things too. You can be a District Nurse. Or work in one of the homes and clinics they're setting up for servicemen who've been badly wounded and won't ever get properly better. There's a leaflet here about them – there's one near Portsmouth, and another one in Bristol, and they're looking for girls with experience. Or you can be a midwife – there are going to be a lot of babies born when the men come home!' She looked at the leaflet again, more thoughtfully. 'Actually, that might be a nice thing to do, bringing new babies into the world. Not exactly a nurse, but doing something like it – something *happier*.'

The door opened and Joy came in. She spotted Thursday and called across to her. 'Phone call for you, Thursday. Madam asked me to let you know.'

'Phone? Who is it?' But Joy shook her head and Thursday got up and hurried out. It was probably her mother, with some piece of family news – Vic come home, perhaps. She hoped it wasn't bad news about Mike. She ran up the stairs to Miss Makepeace's office and knocked breathlessly on the door.

'Oh, there you are, Tilford.' The Commandant indicated the receiver lying on her desk. 'You'd better hurry, the gentleman sounds a little impatient. I think he's just about to run out of money.' She smiled and got up to go out of the office. 'I'll leave you to it for a moment.'

The gentleman? Her heart suddenly quickening, Thursday picked up the instrument and put it to her lips. 'Hello?' she said uncertainly. 'Thursday Tilford here.'

There was brief pause, as though the person at the other end was unable to speak at once. Then a deep voice said, 'Thursday? Is that really you?' And then, when she too was unable to answer: 'Don't tell me you don't recognise my voice. It's Connor . . .'

She met him the next evening on Portsmouth Harbour railway station. She stood at the barrier waiting for the train to arrive, trembling with nerves, a chilly wind from the sea whipping her hair around her face. Four years had passed since she saw him last. What would he be like? What would he think of her? Suppose they didn't even like each other any more . . .

It was nonsense, she knew. In many ways, they had grown closer through their letters. You could spend hours with a person and still know nothing about them if you didn't talk to each other, but you couldn't be silent in a letter. You couldn't send sheets of blank paper.

But knowing and liking weren't necessarily the same as loving. And then there had been Mark . . .

The train was arriving now. Her knees weak, Thursday rested her hand on the barrier and stretched her neck to try to catch a glimpse of him in the crowd of people who were now jumping down from the carriages. He would be in uniform, she knew, one Naval officer amongst many. She might not even recognise him. She stared, trying to pick out his familiar face, the face that had smiled at her every day from the photograph beside her bed. She couldn't see him. He wasn't there. The crowd had thinned out, almost passed her by, and he hadn't come. She turned away, her disappointment almost too great to bear.

'*Thursday* . . .'

Unbelievingly, she turned again. And there he was. Tall, his face deeply tanned, a little thinner and more lined than she remembered, but his eyes still the same warm hazel. And as she gazed into them she had the most extraordinary feeling that four years were rolling away from her, like a burden she had been carrying on her back, and that nothing had changed. Nothing.

'Oh, *Connor*,' she said, and put both hands to her cheeks. It was as if she had, at last, truly come home.

There was so much to talk about, so much to tell and so much to hear. Yet on that first evening, they agreed that it could wait. Tonight they would just be together, revelling in the delight of being able to reach out and touch each other, in the sense that this must be just another of the vivid dreams they had each dreamed over the past four years and the swift, joyful realisation that this time it was real, that the waiting was over.

'You haven't changed at all,' he said as they sat on a bench on Southsea sea front, gazing out towards the twinkling lights of Ryde. He turned towards her, tracing the lines of her face with one finger. 'You're exactly the same as you were when I went away.'

'I'm not really. Four years is a long time, Connor. A lot's happened since then.'

'I know. But it hasn't changed us, has it? Not really. It hasn't changed the way things are between us.'

Thursday hesitated. She felt that she should tell him about Mark, that he deserved the truth – but how could she spoil this moment, this precious first evening, by raising doubts? Yet even as the thought slid through her mind, she knew that she had hesitated too long, and saw his brows come together in a frown.

'It *hasn't* changed us, has it? Things are the same?'

'Oh, Connor,' she said, 'I don't think anything's changed at all. Not while I'm here with you. But I've got to get used to it all again – to the war being over and getting demobbed soon, and you being back, and – and everything. I don't want to do anything too quickly. I've got to have time.'

There was a short silence. Then he nodded. 'I can understand that. And don't look so sad, my darling. So long as you give *me* time too – time to be with you, time to tell you I love you. Because that's what kept me going all these years – knowing that you were here. I know I said I didn't want to tie you down, but when you said you'd wait for me it meant the whole world. To know that, meant everything to me, through all the dark nights and the battles and the horror of it all. And look,' he felt in his breast pocket and brought out something small and flat, 'I kept this by my heart every minute of those four years, as a reminder.'

Thursday looked down and saw, held in his palm, her old fabric VAD badge, the one she had taken from her sleeve and given to him in exchange for the little silver crown brooch. It looked worn and rubbed, as if it had had much handling during that time, and she felt her throat ache and the tears come hot to her eyes.

'Oh, Connor,' she said softly.

He kissed her and she clung to him, letting her tears run down her cheeks. 'I'll make your uniform wet,' she said with a tiny laugh, and felt him smile.

'It doesn't matter. A sailor's uniform is used to salt water. Cry all you want to, Thursday, I don't mind. So long as I can hold you against me and comfort you and kiss you, you can cry all you want to. God knows we've both got a lot of crying to make up for – but we've got laughter too, and smiles, and loving. And when the crying's finished, that's what we'll share. Our loving, and our lives.'

Our loving and our lives.

For the next few weeks, Thursday held those words close to her heart. She was sure now that Connor would never willingly leave her life, yet she was still held back from her own final commitment. Whether it was the result of four years' separation, the restlessness that she'd been feeling for some months now or the feeling that she still had one more promise to keep – the one she had made to Mark – she didn't know; but although she felt herself to be as deeply in love as ever with Connor, although she had felt from that first moment of meeting again that they belonged together, she still could not bring herself to take that final step.

Connor was away again, spending his disembarkation leave with his family, and as she continued with her duties at Haslar Thursday felt the restlessness invade her even more strongly. The other girls were beginning to make decisions about their lives, yet she still seemed to be drifting in a strange limbo. It was as if she found herself tangled in invisible cobwebs, unable to free herself.

Patsy had made up her mind to train as a midwife. If she couldn't have babies of her own, she said, she wanted to help other women have theirs. The other girls were sure that Patsy would marry again, but knew that it would take her some time yet to get over Roy's death, and so they encouraged her decision. Louisa had got a job as a secretary to a doctor who was setting up a practice in London, and Ellen Bridges was going back to her old job as a hairdresser. Joy surprised them all by getting engaged to one of the sailors on the gate, and Elsie came in one day and told them she was expecting a baby.

The best news of all came when Miss Makepeace entered the mess one day while they were all off duty and, with her thin face wreathed in smiles and her bright brown eyes alight, announced that Jeanie Brown was coming back from the Japanese prison camp where she had been ever since the fall of Singapore.

'Jeanie!' The girls leaped from their chairs and hugged each other. 'Jeanie's alive! Oh, what wonderful news, what wonderful, wonderful news!'

'She's had a very bad time, poor girl,' Madam said, looking more serious. 'She's in hospital now, being brought back to health, and they say she'll make a complete recovery. They were treated terribly . . . But I understand that she did wonderful work in the camp, helping to nurse the others. I'm very proud of her.' She looked around and her eyes were brighter than ever. 'I'm proud of you all. *All* my girls.'

The news about Jeanie lifted Thursday's spirits, but she still felt as if she were strangely adrift. When Christmas came, with its round of parties and dances, she felt even more lost. She had a few days' leave before the festival itself to spend at home, and then returned to the hospital to join in the usual tour of the wards, with the officers, doctors and surgeons wearing paper hats and singing carols; however, the jollity seemed forced, at least on her part. I've had enough, she thought. The war emergency was over now and although she could still immerse herself in her work in the theatre or nursing the patients, she wanted to get on with her own life.

If only she knew what it was!

New Year's Eve came, with yet another party to go to. Thursday sat on her bed in the cabin she'd been recently allocated – the first time in her life she had ever had a bedroom to herself! – and gazed at Connor's photograph, wishing he could be here to celebrate with her. I don't want to go on my own, she thought. I want you here with me. But Connor was still with his family after his own demobilisation, and although she knew he was planning to come to Haslar the following weekend, it seemed an age away. It's now I want you, she thought, touching the little crown brooch she wore pinned to her dress. *Now*.

Patsy poked her head round the door. 'Come on, Thursday, aren't you ready? We're all going over together.' She looked better than she had for a long time, Thursday thought. A career lay ahead of her and although she was still grieving for Roy she was also looking ahead. Thursday felt ashamed of her own indecision.

As on so many previous occasions, they were going to Kimball's in Southsea. There was a particularly good band performing and the celebrations of the first New Year after the war promised to be hectic. They had decided to splash out and get a taxi from the harbour. 'Can't ride our bikes in our posh frocks,' Patsy said with a grin. 'Don't want them getting caught up in the chains.'

'It seems funny going out in civvies at last.' Thursday said. She had altered one of Louisa's old dresses from a bundle that the other girl had sent for from home and distributed around the mess. 'I feel quite odd – as if no one'll know who I am without my uniform!' She stood up and twirled round so that the skirt, a shimmering gold shot with olive green, flared out in a bronze cloud. 'Lou's a brick, letting us have all these things. I suppose she'll be getting a whole new wardrobe for her trousseau, though I don't know where she's going to get all the coupons from.'

'She's got a cousin in America who's sending her some material.'

Patsy twisted round to view her own dress in Thursday's small mirror. 'Does this look all right at the back?'

'It looks lovely. You'll be the belle of the ball.' Thursday hooked her arm through Patsy's and switched off the light as they went out together. 'D'you realise, this will be the last Christmas and New Year we'll spend here? By this time next year we'll all be living quite different lives. I wonder where we'll be.'

'Wherever it is,' Patsy said, 'we'll always keep in touch. We've made some good friends, haven't we, Thursday? We mustn't forget.'

'We won't,' Thursday said as they went down the stairs and out into the cold night air. 'We'll never forget.'

The dance was almost over. They'd waltzed, tangoed, foxtrotted and jitterbugged. Although many people had gone with partners, there were still plenty of young men anxious to dance with the girls and when they'd all linked hands and sung 'Old Lang Syne' Thursday was glad to slip outside for a few moments of fresh air. She wandered across the road to look at the sea, then caught her breath as someone spoke her name.

'Thursday.'

She turned slowly. The voice was instantly recognisable. Her heart seemed to stop and her blood turn to water. She stared into the darkness and saw him move into the light that spilled from the windows all along the front. When she tried to speak, her voice caught in her throat.

'Mark . . .'

He came closer. 'I've been looking for you everywhere. That Commandant of yours who never seems to sleep told me you'd come out with the other girls, but she didn't know which dance you were coming to. I think I've been to every one in Portsmouth!' He looked down into her face and put his hands on her shoulders. 'You're here with the other girls. Does that mean what I think it means?'

She stared up at him. 'I don't know. I don't know what you think.'

He shook her gently. 'Thursday, you're here on your own. With no partner. What does that mean? Tell me.'

'It doesn't mean anything,' she said, regaining her control. 'If you're asking about Connor, he's in Plymouth. He came home a few weeks ago and he'll be coming to see me again soon. He's expecting

to be demobbed soon and go into general practice with his father.'
She met his eyes.

'And?' he said quietly.

'And nothing. I kept my promise to him, and I'm keeping the one
I made to you too. I haven't decided anything.'

'So I still have a chance!'

'Mark.' She put her hand to her forehead and tried to turn away,
but he held her facing him. 'Mark, I don't *know*. I have to have time.
Connor understands that.'

'Does he? Well, I don't.' His tone was suddenly harsh. 'Thursday,
I don't *have* time! I'm only back for a few days and I've got a lot to
do. I have to know soon.'

'Know what? Don't shout at me, Mark.'

'I'm sorry,' he said more quietly, 'I didn't mean to shout. But I
have to know whether you'll go back with me. Not at once, I'm not
asking that, but—'

'Go back with you?' she broke in. 'Mark, what are you talking
about? Go back where?'

'To Germany, of course.' He took a breath, then said, 'Thursday,
there's work to do there. I went into the concentration camps when
they were first opened. You have no idea what it was like. People
like skeletons, barely able to crawl, left to starve. People with terrible
diseases coming from malnutrition, ill-treatment and total lack of
hygiene. People who will never properly recover but need care and
help. We can give it to them. We *have* to give it to them!' He was
speaking rapidly, his voice passionate. 'The Army's going to be in
Germany for a long time, helping to protect the people there who
had no part in the atrocities that went on, the people who suffered so
much. I want to be part of that, Thursday, and I want my wife to be
part of it with me. I want *you*.'

She stared at him. 'You want me to go to Germany with you? To
live? To work as a – a nurse?'

'Yes! Yes, that's what I want. You must come, Thursday. You
can't say no. You can't stay here and waste your life as a country
GP's wife.'

'Would it be such a waste? They're all human beings.'

'But they can manage, Thursday! They can manage without you.
I can't. I want you as my wife, you've known that for years, and I'm
not prepared to wait any longer.' He stared at her and she felt a

sudden spasm of dismay at the look in his eyes. It was the look of a passionate man, a man whose passion could turn to fanaticism. She thought of Connor and his more restrained understanding. 'If that won't convince you,' he was saying in a low, intense tone, 'let me try this.'

He caught her against him, his arms hard around her body in the thin dress. His lips touched and then crushed hers in a kiss of searing frenzy. Thursday struggled against him, pushing at his chest with both hands.

'Mark! Please! How dare you do that? How dare you!'

'Thursday, I love you!'

'No,' she said, and she was trembling all over with anger. 'You *don't* love me, not as I want to be loved. You just *want* me, that's all. You want a wife who'll want what *you* want, and *do* what you want. Look, what you're going to do sounds wonderful and good and worthwhile, and maybe it's the kind of thing I've been looking for – but there are other good things to do too. I can't make a decision like this all in a moment. I've got to have time to think. And pushing yourself on me like that won't help.'

'Time to *think*?' he broke in. 'For God's sake, haven't you had months – *years* – to think? It's what you always say, Thursday, whenever you're asked to give a definite answer. I'll tell you what *I* think, shall I?' He stepped back a little and glowered into her eyes. 'I think you've already made up your mind, and you just can't face up to telling me. It's *him*, isn't it? You've seen him again, and he's won.'

'There was never any competition,' she said. 'And I *do* need time to think. I'm *entitled* to it! Look, you've been to Germany, you've seen these things with your own eyes – you've had time to think about them. I haven't. I had no idea you were planning to do this.' She lifted her chin and met his angry stare. 'I'm not your possession, to be told what to do and where to go,' she said quietly. 'I'm my own person. *I* decide how much time I need to think about this, and if you can't accept that you'd better take no for my answer.'

She saw his eyes flicker and for a moment she thought that he was about to turn on his heel and walk away. Then his mouth moved a little and she saw his shoulders lift.

'All right. You assert your independence, if you must. Take your time think, Thursday, but bear in mind that it isn't just me who's setting deadlines. I'm a soldier – not a free person as you're so proud of being. I have to go where I'm sent, and when I'm sent there. I've got ten more days, and I need to have your answer within two. There'll be a lot to arrange.'

'Two *days*?'

'I'm not asking you to pack your bags and come with me,' he said impatiently. 'Wives won't be allowed out there yet. But if you're going to be my wife, Thursday, I want us safely married before I go. There'll be just time. I don't want any more of this dithering!' He stopped and looked at her again. 'Two days.'

'Mark—'

'I'll ring you at Haslar,' he told her and then, as the doors of the dance hall opened and people began to spill out on to the pavement, he turned away. 'I'll leave you to go back with your friends. Happy New Year, Thursday. And if you choose *not* to spend it with me, have a happy life as well.'

'You too,' she whispered, and watched as he marched away into the darkness. 'You too, Mark.'

Connor was demobbed a month later. He had found a position as surgeon in a hospital in Bristol, and was due to start work only a day or two after Thursday's own release from the Voluntary Aid Detachment. It was the middle of February 1946, already a year since Elsie's wedding. The war had been over for six months.

She had refused to be forced into a decision. Mark had telephoned as promised, and she'd told him that he must go to Germany without her. It hurt her to hear his voice, knowing that it was for the last time, but she'd swallowed her sorrow. 'I do love you, Mark,' she'd said, 'in a way. But it's not the way I need. It wouldn't be right for either of us.' And when he'd begun to argue, she'd said a quiet goodbye and then put down the phone. She'd stood very still for a few minutes, taking deep breaths to control herself, and then walked out of Madam's office and down the stairs, knowing that this time it really was over and that the pain was going to be sharper than she had imagined.

I'd have liked to go to Germany, she thought regretfully. I'd have liked to work with those people, knowing I was doing something really worthwhile. But I couldn't marry Mark just for that. It had to be because I loved *him* – not just the life he was offering me. And I don't think I did, not really. He excited me, he made my head swim and my knees go weak, but I don't believe we belonged together. I don't believe it would have lasted us all our lives.

And Connor? She shook her head, unable to think of him just yet. The feeling of belonging she had experienced when they had first met again still warmed her heart – but she had to get over Mark before she could go to him. She had to be able to offer him a whole and honest heart and, as she suffered the pain of having sent Mark away, she began to wonder if she would ever be able to do it.

As the day of their demobilisation drew nearer the girls still remaining at Haslar threw themselves into a frenzy of packing and goodbyes. There were so many 'last times' – the last time cycling over Pneumonia Bridge, the last time at the Swiss Café or the Dive, the last time on the ferry, the last time walking along Stokes Bay. Thursday and Patsy went to see Elsie, now in the throes of early pregnancy and bemoaning her state – 'sick all morning and starving the rest of the day!' – but obviously thrilled about the coming baby. They clung together, eyes swimming with tears, promising to keep in touch. Louisa, who had already left to prepare for her own wedding, sent them a telegram to wish them good luck, and even Vera Hapgood asked for their home addresses, to send Christmas cards.

'I know we've never liked her all that much,' Thursday said, 'but she's not bad really. Just got a funny manner, that's all.'

The dormitory was cluttered with possessions and suitcases. Madam marched up and down the corridor, ready to give a hand where needed and told them over and over again that they must keep in touch. 'I shall want to know what all of you do. I want to be able to go on feeling just as proud of you all.'

'She's going to miss Haslar even more than we are,' Patsy whispered to Thursday. 'I wonder what she'll do in Civvy Street.'

'Stay in the Red Cross, I suppose. There's still plenty of work to do.' Thursday was beginning to feel excited. A letter had come for her that morning that she hadn't yet told anyone about, and she could feel it in her pocket. She went to stand at the window, gazing out over the hospital grounds and past the sea wall to the green bulk of the Isle of Wight across the Solent. This is the last time I'll stand here, she thought. The very last time . . .

Patsy came quietly to stand behind her.

'Well, Thursday, this is it. It's funny – in one way, it seems so long since we first came here, and in another it seems like yesterday. Remember, Thurs? The snow and the ice, and the matelot telling us about port and starboard. We didn't know a thing, did we! We've learned a lot since then. Lived through a lot, too.' Her face was sober.

'Yes.' Thursday slipped her arm round Patsy's shoulders. 'Some of it good, some not so good. But I'm glad we came, aren't you, Patsy?'

Patsy nodded, and then turned her head as someone shouted from the corridor. 'Come on, Thursday. It's time to go.'

They walked down the stairs with their worn brown linoleum and brass strips. At the door to the block, Madam was surrounded by a crowd of girls, some in tears, all vying to shake her hand. She pressed her lips together and gave them all a sharp nod, then said in a voice only slightly less firm than usual, 'Well, off you go then. The pinnace is waiting. Remember, Naval time –'

'Is five minutes early,' they chorused, remembering one of the first lessons they had learned here, and then the crowd broke up and they turned to hurry through the arcade and down the smoothly paved tramway to the quay where the pinnaces were waiting to take them on their last trip across the harbour, to the railway station where they would begin their journey into civilian life.

Their luggage was piled on the quayside. Thursday looked for hers and then, to her surprise, found that it had been detached from the others and set at a little distance. She looked at it uncertainly and then a voice behind her spoke her name.

'Thursday.'

She spun round, staring in disbelief. The voices of the other girls faded from her ears. The quay, the pinnace, the harbour with all its ships, seemed to rock and swing around her and the sky itself tipped on edge. She put both hands to her face and felt the tears spring to her eyes, even as the relief of familiarity and belonging flooded her body and filled her heart with warmth.

In that brief moment, all her doubts, all her indecision, swooped away like a receding tide, and she knew exactly how she wanted to spend the rest of her life, and with whom she wanted to spend it.

'*Connor*,' she breathed, and stepped into his arms.

'And you really will marry me?' he asked for the twentieth time as they sat in a restaurant that evening. He had already arranged rooms for them in one of Portsmouth's hotels, in the hope that she would stay, and Thursday had telegraphed her mother to say she wouldn't be coming home until tomorrow. 'You'll come to Bristol and be my wife? You've made up your mind?'

Thursday smiled and nodded. 'I'm sorry I kept you waiting so long. I had to be sure.'

'I know. I had to be sure too – it just didn't take me so long. I knew the first moment I saw you.' He took her hand. 'I hoped you'd know too, but I've had to be very patient!'

'I did know,' she said. 'It felt so right, being with you again. But I'd promised Mark he should have his chance and I had to keep to it.'

Connor nodded. Thursday had told him about Mark. There could be no secrets between them, she'd said, not if they were to make their lives together. Secrets cast shadows, and they couldn't start a new life with shadows overhanging them.

'And you needed to find something to do for yourself too,' he said. 'You're not the sort of person to sit at home and wait for babies to come along. Are you quite sure that what you've found is right for you?'

Thursday nodded. She took the letter out of her pocket and smoothed it out on the table. It was from the matron of the home for wounded servicemen in Bristol, and it offered her a position working with those who were being rehabilitated. Men who were paralysed or had lost limbs, who needed to be taught to live again. The kind of work Thursday knew, from her experiences at both Haslar and in Egypt, that she would be able to do well.

It's not so very different from the work I might have done in Germany, she thought. But I'll be with Connor – and that makes all the difference in the world.

She looked up and met his eyes. 'We're going to make a good life together,' she said. 'We've waited a long time, but we can start now.' She tightened her fingers around his. 'I love you, Connor. I always will. That's a promise.'

Another promise, she thought, and one made willingly and happily, with a whole and loving heart.

A promise to keep.